recei...
becoming grown-ups, we lose that ability.
But it's never gone forever....

Come meet three heroes who think they know all
they need to know...until each one discovers a very
special woman who gives him some much-needed
private tutoring...in love!

LESSONS
IN
Love

WORLD'S GREATEST DAD
by Marie Ferrarella

HOUSE CALLS
by Terry Essig

A KNIGHT IN TARNISHED ARMOR
by Ann Major

by Request™

Flynn watched her skirt ride up high on her leg again. He

ABOUT THE AUTHORS

MARIE FERRARELLA

lives in California. She describes herself as the tired mother of two overenergetic children and the contented wife of one wonderful man. This RITA Award-winning author is thrilled to be following her dream of writing full-time.

TERRY ESSIG

says that her writing is her escape valve from a life that leaves very little time for recreation or hobbies. With a husband and six young children, Terry works on her stories a little at a time, between seeing to her children's piano, sax and trombone lessons, their gymnastics, ice skating and swim team practices, and her own activities of leading a Brownie troop, participating in a car pool and attending organic chemistry classes. Her ideas, she says, come from her imagination and her life–neither one of which is lacking!

ANN MAJOR

loves writing romance novels as much as she loves reading them. She is the proud mother of three children who are now in high school and college. She lists hiking in the Colorado mountains with her husband, playing tennis, sailing, enjoying her cats and playing the piano among her favorite activities.

MARIE FERRARELLA
TERRY ESSIG • ANN MAJOR

Published by Silhouette Books

America's Publisher of Contemporary Romance

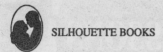 SILHOUETTE BOOKS

by Request

LESSONS IN LOVE

Copyright © 1997 by Harlequin Books S.A.

ISBN 0-373-20139-7

The publisher acknowledges the copyright holders of the individual works as follows:

WORLD'S GREATEST DAD
Copyright © 1992 by Marie Rydzynski-Ferrarella

HOUSE CALLS
Copyright © 1988 by Mary Therese Essig

A KNIGHT IN TARNISHED ARMOR
Copyright © 1992 by Ann Major

Printed in U.S.A.

CONTENTS

Dear Reader,

I am married to the second person who ever kissed me, so I'm not sure if that exactly qualifies me to offer any lessons in love. But, seeing as how we've been together for what my kids think is an eternity, maybe I am doing something right. So here are my thoughts, for better or worse. And while they're not profound, they do seem to work.

One: Treat your partner the way you wish he'd treat you. With understanding, compassion and caring. And back off once in a while and give him some space. Maybe he'll return the favor and give some to you (or at least pick up his socks once in a while).

And two: Remember, love is an ongoing, living, breathing thing that needs to be worked on constantly. It's a work in progress, if you will, not a prize you get to keep just because you both survived a wedding whose cost rivaled the national debt (or so your father will tell you any time you're willing to listen). I suppose the best analogy I can give you is that love is like a muscle. Muscles have to be exercised in order to be kept in shape and limber. You don't exercise that muscle and eventually it atrophies. In other words, use it or lose it. The same goes for love. You use it to guide you through the maze of everyday life. And when things get too much for you, when you're ready to throw up your hands and surrender, remember how important it was to win this person's love in the first place. Remember how excited you were getting ready for a date with him. How when you were together, it was special. The place didn't matter, just the company.

Try to remember that the next time you're collecting every pair of shoes your husband owns, which are now scattered everywhere in the house but the closet. (Personally, I think my husband is training to be a centipede.)

Just love each other. A lot. That should do it.

My very best,

Marie Ferrarella

WORLD'S GREATEST DAD

Marie Ferrarella

To Daddy, who got a late start, too.
Love,
Marysia

Chapter One

"What are we going to do without a housekeeper?" Michael stuck out his toes in front of him and wiggled them as he sat in the sports car, waiting for an answer.

Flynn O'Roarke looked down at the six-year-old on his right and smiled. "We'll manage."

Manage. He'd gotten good at that, managing, even when he was certain that he couldn't. He had managed because he had to. But God, it had been hard, hard to face life when Kelly wasn't in it anymore, smoothing the way, taking care of a hundred details he hadn't even known existed until now. His wife's sudden death after twenty-five years of marriage had made him as disoriented, as lost as a child. But Stephanie and Julia had still been living at home then, needing him. So, somehow, he had groped his way through the maze of pain and everyday living and he had managed.

And then the second blow had come, cutting him off at the knees, less than three months after Kelly's death. He had managed then, too, though he wasn't certain how he had faced the tragedy without Kelly beside him.

Six years earlier, Kelly had been there to hold his hand, to tranquilize his anger when his oldest daughter, Aimee, had come to him, tears in her eyes, and told him that she wanted to get married. The resounding no he'd uttered had softened to a yes when she told him she was pregnant. Pregnant. His brilliant, seventeen-year-old daughter, little more than a child herself, was with child. So, he'd said yes and he and Kelly had helped Aimee and Doug move up to San Francisco. Doug had been a likeable young man, full of ambition for their future. They'd all stuck together and made wonderful plans.

Flynn looked down at Michael as the boy pounded his brand-new mitt. Michael looked a lot like Aimee, so much so that at times it made Flynn's heart ache to see a familiar smile cross the boy's lips and know that he would never see it on Aimee's face again.

But he had managed. Somehow, when that call had come in the middle of the night from the highway patrolman at the hospital, he had managed to hold himself together, without Kelly to rely on. A prayer on his lips, he'd left his two younger daughters and gotten the earliest flight out to the hospital outside of Oakland. It had been just after the semester end. Doug, Aimee and Michael were driving down to Bedford to be with Flynn and the girls. A panel truck had changed their plans. Aimee and Doug were both gone by the time he had arrived at the hospital. He had allowed himself tears as he kept vigil at Michael's bedside.

Michael had managed to survive and Flynn had managed to go on, bringing the boy back to Bedford with him. Now he and Michael were struggling to find their proper roles in this new family structure they found themselves in.

But, at the moment, Flynn wasn't managing very well at all. Something had happened yesterday. Flynn had turned forty-five. Five years away from fifty. From half a century. Though the mirror before him reflected the image of a man who had never believed in overindulgence, who had exercised regularly, Flynn suddenly felt ancient.

Forty he had accepted, had laughed at when Kelly had given him a gag gift of a hot water bottle and a box of prunes. He had laughed because Kelly was with him and she made him feel young.

Without realizing it, he had depended on Kelly for too many things. After she died, he had sworn never to be that dependent again. But that decision didn't stop the feeling of floundering, of being emotionally adrift.

Fifteen months ago, he had been continuing a long-established pattern. He and Kelly were going to grow old together. He was going to watch his daughters mature and Michael grow up. As the boy's grandfather, not as his guardian. Then the pattern had blown up in front of him.

But somehow, he had managed. He supposed. One thing was certain. He promised himself never to be that emotionally dependent on another human being again. It was far too painful, being left behind.

Michael's voice brought him back to the present. "Are we going to get another housekeeper now that Mrs. Henderson had to move?"

Flynn picked his way through the tidy, serpentine streets of the residential development. "Do you want one?"

Discussing things with Michael made the boy feel more important. With Stephanie and Julia both away at college, that left just the two of them at home. The two of them to muddle through the maze of being thrown together and helping each other cope with the business of living each day. Flynn was still taking it one shaky step at a time, but Michael seemed none the worse for it.

Michael frowned as he tried to answer Flynn's question. "She was nice," he began with a sense of diplomacy beyond his years. "But she treated me like a baby."

"Can't have that." Flynn had sensed Michael's feelings and so had looked into alternatives. "I thought we'd get you into an after-school day-care center until we worked things out."

Michael looked up at him hopefully. "The one with the neat sportsman bus that picks Greg up?"

Flynn grinned. He wished everything was this simple. "That's the one."

"Great!" Michael almost bounced up and down. "Thanks."

He ruffled Michael's dark hair. "Hey, no problem. You're my favorite six-year-old grandson."

Up ahead, he saw the sign indicating Jeffrey Elementary School. He slowed down as a grassy lot behind the school came into view. There were several cars parked there already even though the game wasn't scheduled to begin for another twenty minutes. Flynn maneuvered his sports car into a space between two station wagons. The convertible looked out of place there, kind of the way he felt about himself and life right now.

With childish importance, Michael pounded the new mitt twice, then looked up as a thought struck him. "I'm your *only* six-year-old grandson."

Flynn pulled up the hand brake. "There's that, too." He stretched as he got out of the low-slung silver car. It had been a long day. They had all been long days lately. He thought of his own grandfather, the way he had looked when Flynn was six. Gnarled and hopeless, spending hours just looking off into space. He'd died when Flynn was ten.

With effort, Flynn shook himself free of the melancholy mood that had hung over him like a shroud since yesterday.

Flynn placed a hand on Michael's shoulder and guided him away from the curb, onto the field. There were several little boys dressed in blue shirts and white pants, running around, throwing and missing. God, he wished life could be that simple again.

He looked down and saw another frown on Michael's face. "What?"

Flynn didn't normally bring him to his practice sessions. For the past two weeks since practice had started, Mrs. Henderson had been the one who'd dropped him off. "I don't play all that great."

It was clear to Flynn that Michael was worried about disappointing him. The fact humbled him. Emotion stirred, but he banked it down. He'd had just about all the emotional stirrings he could handle right now. He probably would have sold his soul for some peace and tranquility.

Flynn touched the corners of the boy's sad little mouth, raising them up slightly with two fingers. "You'll get better. Before you know it, you'll be the star of the team."

Michael clearly hadn't explored that prospect. The smile that came to his lips was of his own making now. "Yeah?"

"Yeah," Flynn echoed solemnly.

Michael's expression turned eager. "Maybe you've got something there."

Flynn laughed. Being with Michael was always a joy. He hung on to that, even as he warned himself not to. He glanced around the field again, trying to locate someone who looked like a coach. Instead he saw a petite blonde, her hair hanging in her eyes, a look of deep concentration on her face. She was chewing her lower lip. She was also holding a hammer sideways and doing a rather inept job of pounding in a stake. A blue-and-white banner, proclaiming the team logo as well as all the players' names, was at her feet. The upper part of her body was encased in a light blue T-shirt that hung on her like a tent, but nonetheless did an interesting job of accentuating her body when the wind shifted. The words World's Greatest Dad were embossed across it in shiny, hot-pink letters.

Flynn shook his head as he watched her work doggedly at the stake. "Another woman going through her husband's closet and wearing his clothes."

Michael, having spotted one of his friends, began to dash off. He stopped for a moment longer. "Is that bad?"

Flynn hadn't realized he had said the words aloud. "Only if he doesn't want her to."

The six-year-old shrugged philosophically, his attention already directed somewhere else. "Maybe he does."

Flynn nodded, still watching. Hadn't anyone ever told her how to hold a hammer? "Yeah, maybe." He pointed toward a tall, genial-looking man with the word Coach on his sweatshirt. "Get some practice in, champ."

Michael eyed him hopefully. "And you'll stay for the whole game?"

"Absolutely. From start to finish," Flynn promised the retreating boy.

Flynn's attention was drawn back to the woman. There was no reason, he thought, for him to offer his help. After all, there were a couple of other men around, although they were involved with the boys. Besides, he didn't even know the woman. And if she wasn't smart enough to figure out how to hold a hammer, he really didn't want to. What would he have to say to a woman who hit a stake with the broad side of a hammer?

Still, he found himself drifting toward her, something male and protective and beyond his control getting the best of him. It was probably, he thought dourly, his Southern upbringing rearing its head.

The best part of Susanna Troy's days always revolved around Billie. When she was doing something with her seven-year-old son or for him, life seemed to have a certain warm glow around it, like a Christmas gift that went on forever. That was why, at the end of a long day filled with meetings and unresolved projections about the new ratebook calculations at Palisades Mutual, she had willingly come out to cheer him on to victory. More than that, she had come to do her bit as dugout Mom.

Since the age of four, baseball had been Billie's prime passion. Totally ignorant about the fundamentals of the game, Susanna had quickly educated herself about positions and players' names. She had become familiar with things like ERAs and vital stats, all of which had meant nothing to her a short while ago. She had sewn the banner and toted it to and from the games, baked brownies, bought bandages and gen-

erally helped out where she could, even when she'd rather
have been curled up on the sofa at home, watching a movie
on the VCR or reading a good mystery.

Billie came first. He always did.

Having finally gotten the first stake into the hard ground,
Susanna picked up the banner and measured off where the
second stake had to go. She hoped it wouldn't be windy, like
the last time. The banner had filled like a sail and then leaned
completely over, taking the stakes with it.

With a sigh, she picked up the second stake, wishing the
earth would soften up. Bedford had to have the hardest soil in
Southern California, she mused.

"Here, give me that."

The impatient voice startled her. She hadn't heard anyone
coming up. But then, the noise from the field was getting so
loud, it probably would have drowned out a herd of stampeding elephants.

Susanna raised her head, unconsciously chewing her lower
lip. The first thing she saw as a muscular upper torso straining
against a washed-out blue T-shirt. She wondered if she would
feel flesh or steel beneath her hand if she touched it. For a
moment, she was almost tempted to find out. Lifting her eyes,
she looked up into a rather somber, gaunt face with planes
and angles that instantly made her think of a soulful poet, one
who wrote testimonials to sorrow and pain. Because he lived
it. She felt a funny little ache dance through her as well as
something that was akin to anticipation.

And then she looked up into the greenest pair of eyes she
had ever seen. Her thoughts evaporated completely, as did her
breath. Susanna blinked, forcing herself back to the Jeffrey
School playing field, Tuesday and a dozen eager little boys.

"Give you what?" she finally managed to ask.

She was prettier close up, more delicate-looking. Not that
it mattered. Flynn nodded to the tool that hung suspended from
her fingers. "The hammer." Though it was none of his business, he couldn't help asking, "Do you realize that you're
holding it sideways?"

Susanna grinned. She felt rather than saw the fleeting look of appreciation that quickly flashed through his eyes and then disappeared as if it had never existed. She jiggled the hammer. It wasn't the first time someone had pointed that out to her. "It keeps me from smashing my thumb and it gives me a much broader surface to hit with."

In its own strange way, that made sense, but she still looked as if she was expending too much energy, seeing the results of her efforts. He made a movement to take the hammer from her and finish the job.

There were few things in life that Susanna hated, but one of them was being thought of as a "helpless little thing." She was used to doing things on her own, and had been doing just that for almost seven years, but at five foot two and a hundred pounds, frailty was a difficult image to shake.

She pulled the hammer back. "I'm perfectly capable of driving in the stakes myself."

His hand, surprisingly delicate and agile considering how muscular his body was, covered the handle just above her fingers. Warmth seared through her at the casual contact. Though it wasn't meant to be, there was something possessive about the gesture. She wondered if he blustered through life, used to getting his own way. It was easy to see how he could, with dark, good looks like his.

For some reason, he had a sudden flash of Kelly, of the way she had always forged through things. Of the way he had let her. Amusement highlighted his eyes for just a moment. "Most women are."

For a moment, Susanna considered using the hammer on his head, but with twelve little boys and two coaches nearby, there were too many witnesses. She surrendered the hammer to this overbearing chauvinist. If he wanted to flex his muscles, literally and figuratively, so be it.

Flynn took the hammer from her and swung hard. The stake sank into the ground at least four inches. Susanna suppressed a shiver. "Bad day?"

He hadn't realized quite how angry he really was at life

until just this moment. He took a breath, struggling to get things under control. "The worst."

Probably his own doing, given his sunny disposition. "Your wife?"

He looked at her and noted that her eyes were a mixture of blue and gray and right now looked amused. He didn't care for being someone's source of entertainment. "Anyone ever tell you you ask a lot of questions?"

Susanna had had too much experience with hurt children to let a carelessly voiced sentiment bother her. "It's called conversation and you started it."

Yes, he supposed he had and he had no idea why he was even talking to this woman. He had come to be with Michael, to watch him play and offer encouragement. "I'm a widower," he told her, though he didn't know why he had offered this information.

She wondered if he'd been widowed recently. The wounds were still raw. She remembered what it had been like. It *was* incredibly hard. Obviously, his heart was not. Otherwise, it wouldn't have been hurt so much. Without thinking, she placed a hand on his forearm. "I'm sorry."

The concern he heard surprised him. Why should she care? They didn't even know each other's names. Her sympathy made him uncomfortable.

"Thanks."

He thrust her hammer back to her. He watched as she bent over and dropped it into something cavernous that he assumed was a purse. If he was honest with himself, he'd have to admit that the length of her legs, which seemed to elongate before his eyes as she stretched, had captured all his attention. The contrast between her white shorts and tanned legs made her look exceedingly sexy. When she straightened up again, the long T-shirt came down and just covered her shorts, creating the impression that she had nothing on underneath. The thought and his warm response to it caught him unaware.

She looked inquisitively at the expression on his face. Flynn was stumped for something to say. He nodded at her apparel. "Interesting shirt. Your husband's?"

She looked down, having forgotten for a moment what she had on. Then she smiled. "No, it's mine." She picked up one end of the banner and fitted it over the stake. "I don't have a husband."

Flynn picked up the other end and followed her example. He raised one eyebrow. "Managed to get the shirt off his back, did you?"

"I'm not divorced. I'm a widow."

He had just naturally assumed that she was divorced. She looked too young to be a widow. The bitter taste in his mouth was like shoe leather. Awkwardly Flynn withdrew his foot from his mouth. "Oh, hey, I'm sorry. I didn't mean—"

He looked so genuinely contrite, she was surprised. And touched. Flashing a dismissive grin, Susanna came to his rescue. It was second nature to her. She absolutely hated seeing anyone or anything in distress. "I'm sure you didn't. The shirt's from Billie."

"Billie?"

She pointed to a tow-headed boy out in the field. As she did so, a ball went between Billie's legs. The boy scowled before he gave chase. "My son."

Flynn looked back at the bright pink lettering across her chest. "A little nearsighted, is he? World's Greatest *Dad?*"

She laughed. Flynn was struck by the depth of the delight he heard ringing in her voice. "No, the shirt was a gift for Father's Day last year." She saw his brows draw together in confusion. "Billie said he thought I had earned it."

She reminded him of someone who needed to be taken care of, not someone who had another life depending on her. He thought of his own experiences with Michael in the past year. There were times he hadn't thought he'd make it with his sanity intact. It must have even been harder for her. "Isn't it a little rough, being a single parent?"

"At times," she agreed. She took a clipboard from her bag. The batting schedule and playing positions were attached to it. She glanced at them before elaborating. "It's never easy balancing a child and a career."

Someone yelled, "Heads up," and Flynn's hand flew out automatically. He caught the misdirected ball and tossed it back onto the field. Warm-up, he noticed, was almost over.

When he looked at Billie's mother again, she was busy making notes. The wind was ruffling her blond hair, teasing the ends and brushing them against his bare forearm. Something tightened within him. Unconsciously, he took a step back. "So, you're not a housewife, or homemaker or whatever the popular term is these days for a mom who keeps the home fires burning. What is it that you do?"

She thought of her desk at work, overflowing with papers. "Mostly tread water."

Flynn tried to interpret the comment. "You give swimming lessons?"

Susanna shook her head, sliding the pencil into place on the side of the clipboard. "I'm an actuary."

Actuaries made him think of stuffy old men in three piece suits who had offices located on the top floor of insurance companies. Occasionally they recalculated mortality projections that told people when they were expected to die. Very cut-and-dried stuff. She looked more like someone who, if she got a haircut, could try out for the stage role of Peter Pan. "You're kidding, right?"

She saw the way his eyes measured her. "Do actuaries have a height requirement?"

He wondered if she was laughing at him and why that even mattered. "No, it's just that, when I think of an actuary, I think of someone old, someone—"

"Male?" she supplied, amused, when he hesitated. Her dad had been an actuary and she remembered his surprise when she had announced her intentions. It wasn't exactly a run-of-the-mill choice for a girl, even one who loved math.

Flynn shrugged as he shoved both hands into his pockets. "Yes."

Her eyes danced and he could have sworn a dimple was struggling to form in one cheek. "I'm neither."

His eyes swept over her again. Despite the baggy shirt, he could discern very firm, very high breasts beneath. An urge, warm and demanding, filtered through him, stunning him. It was a strange sensation for someone who had felt physically dead inside. "I noticed."

The man had the sexiest scowl she had ever seen and it was making her lose her train of thought. Again. She reminded herself that she had duties to see to. Looking over her shoulder one last time to make sure the banner was secure, she moved away from him. "Well, thanks for the help, but I've got dugout duty."

He didn't move, although he knew that it would be wise to return to the sidelines. "You've got what?"

"I have to keep them in line." She gestured at the field. There were now about twenty boys running around, vainly attempting to execute successful throws and catches.

Flynn looked around the field slowly. Activity seemed to hum out there. It always amazed him to see how much energy a little boy could generate. He looked back at Susanna. "All of them?"

"No, that would take a superwoman. Just the ones in Cub uniforms."

He eyed her quietly. "Did you bring a whip and a chair?"

"They're not as bad as all that." Although at times, it was close, she added silently.

This he had to see. Maybe he could even pick up a few pointers. Fatherhood at this stage of his life mystified him. He hadn't had that much practice the first time around. Kelly had always been there, to see to everything. All he'd had to do was look proud and say the right words. "Mind if I hang around and watch?"

She shrugged, though something small and faraway was pleased that he wanted to. "Suit yourself."

"I generally do."

If this had been a hundred years ago, she would have said

the tone was well suited to a legendary gunfighter riding through a small town. There was almost a warning note in the words. She wondered why.

She didn't have time to wonder for long. As she watched, the coaches from both teams, a total of five affable men who enjoyed reliving times when they ran faster and things like mortgages and insurance premiums had no meaning, got together to decide which team of eager, if slightly inept players went first. A red-headed boy with three times his share of freckles dusting his face and arms called the toss. The Pirates batted first.

Flynn stepped back as a flurry of boys in blue-and-white uniforms charged past him. Twelve little boys, all talking at once, crowded around the blonde and shouted questions.

Clipboard in hand, Susanna did her best to match each boy to his position. "Adam, first base. Billie, second. Nikky, left center," she read from the list that the head coach had handed her when she'd first arrived.

Having sent eleven boys onto the field, she was confronted with Drew. Drew was barely five and small for his age, but because his dad was one of the coaches, he had managed to get on the team comprised mainly of six- and seven-year-olds. He clutched a pair of red shin guards against his chest as he dropped an oversized helmet and mask to the ground. Despair was evident in his eyes.

"I'm the catcher."

Susanna bent down. "Yes, I know. And you'll be a very good one, too."

A smile began to form on the small face. Drew held up the guards. "You have to dress me."

Dropping down on one knee, Susanna grabbed the shin guards, either one of which looked to be about half as high as Drew, and took action. She had her doubts that he could move in the outfit, but refrained from saying so. "I thought you'd never ask."

Drew turned awkwardly as she struggled with the fasteners on the guard. "Huh?"

"Just a little humor, Drew. Best way to get through things that leave you confused." She tugged, but the last fastener refused to live up to its name.

She certainly did a lot of struggling. He wondered if she thought it was worth it. With a sigh, Flynn moved closer. "Need help with that?"

Susanna looked up. From this vantage point, the man looked twice as tall. Before she could answer, he was beside her, tackling the other shin guard. "Is riding to the rescue a sideline with you?"

He didn't have to look at her face to know she was grinning. A sudden image of Kelly flashed through his mind. The first time he had met her in high school, she had walked into him and dropped all her books on the ground. He had helped her pick them up. They were married a year later. "I minored in it at college," he answered flatly. "C'mere, sport, let's get you fitted properly." He realized how that had to sound and glanced in the woman's direction. If she took offense at his words, she didn't show it. That set her apart from a lot of other people he knew.

It was a little like watching twin copies of the Bad News Bears, Flynn thought. Two innings had stretched by and the game was tied ten to ten, not because of any phenomenal playing, but because the rules were mercifully different for six-year-olds involved in coach pitch. An inning ended with five runs or three tagged outs. In deference to coordination that hadn't yet developed, there was no such thing as a strikeout.

A red-headed little boy with the number three on his back swung hard and sent the ball sailing backward through the air. It landed at Susanna's feet. Flynn curbed the urge to retrieve it.

Scooping the ball up, Susanna threw it to the pitcher. Or at least she tried. It fell to the pitcher's left, about a yard short of its target.

Flynn laughed. So much for Supermom. "You throw like a girl."

She turned to look at him, unruffled. "There's a reason for that."

"Oh?" Flynn expected to hear some sort of involved explanation.

"I *am* a girl." She sighed. No, it had been a long time since she could have rightfully laid claim to that title. Brett had been part of her life then. She shrugged. "Or pretty close to one."

Flynn crossed his arms before him, curious about her response. Woman wanted to be considered equal, if not superior. His daughters had taught him that. "Haven't you heard that women are supposed to be able to do everything a man can—only better?"

She bit back the temptation to say that she could. He looked too eager for an argument. "I don't have to know how to throw a ball to feel secure, Mr.—" She cocked her head waiting for him to fill in.

"O'Roarke. Flynn."

"O'Roarke?" The name rang no bells. She glanced at her roster. "Which one's your boy?"

"Michael." He was about to tell her that Michael was his grandson but then the batter hit a double and Flynn's words were lost in the noise as she yelled encouragement to the right fielder who dropped the ball. She turned to look at Flynn.

"I'm glad you came to the game. Kids need to have their families show an interest."

The smile she gave him nudged away some of the darkness in his soul. He didn't know why the idea that she thought well of him appealed to him. It shouldn't. He didn't care what this woman thought of him. In all likelihood, he probably wouldn't see her again. Or if he did bump into her, he wouldn't recognize her.

She suddenly came to life, cheering an accidental catch on Michael's part. A small Pirate dropped his bat and shuffled off to the end of the lineup. "Way to go, Michael!"

Well, maybe he would recognize her again, Flynn amended

as he clapped for his grandson. But that was as far as it was going to go, or as far as he would let anything go for a long, long time.

"That's three outs!" Susanna called to the fair-haired man in the center of the playing field. Nodding, he took off his glove and signaled the team in.

"You keep score, too?" Flynn asked. He moved as the team filed enthusiastically back into the area designated as the dug-out.

Susanna shrugged as Drew presented himself to her to be unharnessed. She was better at removing things, Flynn noted absently, than she was at putting them on. Interesting.

"Someone has to." Carefully Susanna pulled the protective pad from Drew's chest. The catcher's mask plopped down at her feet with a thud and she jumped back, colliding with Flynn who hadn't been quick enough to get out of her way. He was beginning to doubt that anyone was quick enough for that. She seemed to be all over, as energized as the boys she was involved with. Instinctively, Flynn reached out to keep her from losing her balance.

His hands felt steady, capable. Sure. He was a man you could trust, Susanna thought. But one who didn't give his own trust easily. She could see that in his eyes as he regarded her.

"This 'job' could be hazardous to your health," he commented dryly, releasing her. Her skin felt incredibly soft to the touch. He had an urge to discover if it was like that all over.

It was obviously not a good day for celibacy.

Susanna began waving the boys into batting order. "Only if I forgot the brownies."

"Excuse me?"

She looked over her shoulder. "I have to organize them, then I have to feed them after the game."

He glanced back at the various mothers and fathers who had straggled in to cheer on their sons. Why was she the only one doing things on the sidelines? "Who made up the rules?"

She laughed again. Flynn felt his body responding to the

warmth of the sound even as something within him warned him not to. "No one. I'm an overachiever."

He could believe that.

Suddenly she swung around, looking down at a boy with a number seven on his shirt and mischief all over his face. He sat wedged in between two other players and was dusting them with dirt. Any minute, there was going to be a fight. "No, Chris, put the dirt down."

Eyes in the back of her head, Flynn thought, but then that went with the territory when you were a mother. His own had always known what he was up to, even when she wasn't anywhere in sight.

Number seven held up a fistful of dirt and seemed to be weighing his options. He put his hand down, but as Susanna turned away, he opened his fist and threw the dirt at her. Susanna swung around again, a reprimand on her lips.

Flynn beat her to it. Two strides and he was looming in front of the boy. "I wouldn't do that again." His voice was low, but stern. "Unless you'd like to be benched for the next three years."

The boy's eyes grew wide as he regarded Flynn, clearly buying into the warning. "Okay." He swallowed hard.

Susanna tried not to laugh as she listened to the exchange.

Michael beamed at Chris's retreat. "He lifts weights and works with space stuff. He knows astronauts," he added proudly.

Obedience came instantly with Flynn's references and the boys immediately settled down. "You guys better listen to—" His mind drew a blank as he turned to Susanna. "Say, what is your name, anyway?"

She plopped a batting helmet on number five's head. "Knock 'em dead, Jason." Turning, she extended her hand to Flynn. "Susanna Troy."

She smiled encouragingly at him when she saw that there was just the slightest hesitation in his eyes before he took her hand in his. It was almost as if he was afraid of making contact with her.

For the first time in a long while, Susanna found herself more than a little intrigued.

And very attracted.

Chapter Two

He had come strictly to watch Michael play baseball and to offer him a little one-on-one male bonding. Those had been his only intentions.

Instead, Flynn found himself watching both Michael and the exuberant woman to his left. Parents, he knew through first-hand experience, had a tendency to be prejudiced. Their own offspring was always the best. He'd been guilty of it himself. It was a normal reaction. Susanna, he concluded after watching her in action, was *not* normal. She cheered loudly for each and every boy on the team as soon as their bats connected with the ball, urging them to run. It was, Flynn thought, as if she regarded each boy as her own.

If she hadn't pointed him out, the only way Flynn would have known which boy was her son was by the way she tensed every time Billie came up to bat. But Flynn had a distinct feeling that she probably would have tensed even if Billie hadn't been her son. Flynn had noticed that she had a way of empathizing with each player and Billie had his own special problem. Billie swung in slow motion.

The first time he saw Billie swing at the ball, Flynn was certain he just hadn't been playing close enough attention. Little boys with bats in their hands swung energetically at everything. And so did Billie. At the empty air when he was taking practice swings. But whenever the coach who acted as pitcher threw a ball to him, Billie's swing inexplicably decreased until he swung the bat slowly past the space the baseball had just vacated.

Eight pitches and no contact. The coach's encouragement wasn't helping. Billie gripped the bat harder, his small shoulders rigid.

Susanna pressed her lips together, feeling Billie's growing agitation. She really wished he wouldn't put himself through this, but he desperately wanted to be on a baseball team. She couldn't forbid him to play. All she could do was just hope and pray his bat would make contact with the ball.

Some of the boys sitting on the ground, waiting their turn at bat, began chanting, "C'mon Billie, you can do it. Put a little power into it."

Billie missed again. The coach yelled another instruction to him.

"Let him concentrate, boys," Susanna murmured to the squadron of little boys at her feet. Her eyes remained fixed on the sweating Cub poised over home plate.

Twelve pitches whizzed by, each followed belatedly by Billie's bat. The coach pushed back his cap. "Someone want to help him bat?" he called out.

It was standard procedure after twelve misses. Otherwise, they would be there all night. Still, Susanna knew how much it had to hurt Billie's pride to have someone bat with him when the other little boys did it on their own. She turned to see which father was closest to the batting cage.

Flynn stepped in.

There was just so much agony he could tolerate watching. Flynn got into the batter's cage behind Billie. The catcher from the opposing team shuffled back to make room. Flynn hardly noticed him. He smiled down encouragingly at the slightly moist eyes as he positioned himself. Playing ball had been second nature to him when he was Billie's age.

"Let's show 'em how it's done, sport."

Billie sucked in air and nodded his head.

With his hands over Billie's, Flynn directed Billie's swing at the first pitched ball. And missed.

Billie craned his neck to look up at Flynn. "That's what I do."

Flynn heard the hitch of frustration bordering on tears in the boy's voice. With a slight movement, Flynn rotated his back muscles. "Just getting warmed up, sport. We'll do better next time."

Flynn crouched a little lower as the ball came toward them and guided Billie's aim. Contact. The ball went flying into deep left. Billie stared at the ball in open-mouthed wonder, the bat slipping from his fingers to the dirt.

"Run!" Susanna yelled.

Flynn turned and took a step toward first base, carried away by the enthusiasm in her voice before he realized she was shouting the directive at her son and not him. A small, self-depreciating smile touched the corners of his mouth as Flynn turned away. The look on Billie's face had made him feel good.

Hands shoved deep into his back pockets, he dropped to the sidelines. "You carry a lot of authority in that voice of yours," he commented as he watched a dark-haired boy dash in from third.

The runner reached home plate and Susanna scooped off his batting helmet, handing it to the next batter in line. Bases were loaded. Quickly, she noted the run on her pad.

"It's a gift," she answered Flynn belatedly.

She looked up at him and her expression softened. Flynn found he wasn't quite prepared for the look of gratitude that he saw in her eyes. It had a totally different effect on him than what he had seen in Billie's face. Why in heavens name should he feel aroused by the sight of gray-blue eyes and a face that could fit neatly between the palms of his hands? Grandfathers, he thought, weren't supposed to be aroused, only amused.

"Thank you."

She might have been thanking him for presenting her with an emerald necklace for all the feeling he heard in her voice. "For what?"

This was a man who didn't take gratitude easily or without suspicion, she thought and felt a twinge of sorrow. "For helping Billie."

Flynn shrugged noncommittally. "Someone had to."

"True, but it didn't have to be you." He didn't look as if he fit into this late-afternoon get-together of fathers and offspring. There was something that set him apart, a barrier he seemed to be keeping between himself and everyone else.

"I was closest." The look on his face warned her to drop the subject.

Susanna wondered why gratitude made him look so uncomfortable. "I'm glad you were." She was aware of his eyes on her as she turned her attention to the next batter. A hot flush stirred within her and she smiled. It was a nice feeling.

Susanna gave Billie the high sign. Her son beamed back, crouching, ready to run to second base on the next hit.

After what seemed like five incredibly long innings, the Cubs finally won. The score was twenty-five to twenty-four. That made them two for one for the season, Susanna told Flynn as he helped her pull up the stakes for the banner. He told her he was surprised she knew the terminology.

"Self-defense," she quipped, handing Billie her hammer to hold.

Without thinking, Flynn began rolling up the banner. "Excuse me?"

Susanna bent to pick up a piece of discarded plastic that had been wrapped around a giant brownie not ten minutes ago. She threw it into a large garbage bag.

"Billie eats, sleeps and breathes baseball." She looked at

her son fondly. The boy was engrossed in a conversation with Michael. "I had to learn the lingo in order to communicate with him." She went to take the banner from him, but Flynn had already picked it up and had it balanced against his shoulder. Lord, he looked powerful, she thought. "It's a little like mastering a foreign language." Picking up her knapsack and purse, she began to walk toward the parked cars.

The sun was going down. It would be cool soon. Cool and dark. Flynn watched the wind play with her hair and wondered what she would be like in the dark, against cool sheets—

Abruptly, he refocused his thoughts, wondering if his mind was going. "Is every game like this?"

"Like what?"

"Long. Chaotic. Disoriented."

She pointed out her car in the lot. "Yes."

Flynn shifted the weight of the stakes slightly, wondering how she managed to carry them back and forth each week. The load wasn't heavy so much as awkward, especially for someone as small as she was.

"You enjoy this." It was more than obvious.

"I enjoy children." She glanced over her shoulder at the field. Michael and Billie were straggling behind, throwing the ball to each other as they walked.

There was love in her eyes, love that suddenly had Flynn yearning to be touched by something like it, to feel the warmth of that kind of all-encompassing feeling. He reminded himself that that kind of love carried stiff penalties with it, penalties he no longer wanted to face. You love, you hurt, it was as simple and as complicated as that.

"How do you feel about adults?" And where the hell had that come from? He sounded as if he was making a pitch when it was the last damn thing on earth he wanted to do. Flynn turned his face away, looking toward her car, hoping she wouldn't say anything.

He might have known better. Susanna was the type, he realized, who could *always* say something.

"I enjoy them, too. Especially brooding poets who grudgingly do good deeds. Right here." She nodded needlessly at her white car.

He realized after a beat that she meant him. He rested the stakes and banner against the side of the car. "I'm not a poet."

"A pity." She couldn't think of an occupation he looked more suited for. "You've got the face for it."

Dropping her knapsack to the ground, she rooted through her purse for the car keys. She liked the slight flush that had come over his face at her comment. She wasn't sure if it was annoyance or embarrassment, but it did become him. Opening her door, she turned to face Flynn. Billie had reached her side and she placed an arm around his shoulders in easy camaraderie.

"Well, thanks again for your help and the conversation." She couldn't help grinning at the last part. "Most people prefer to sit on the sidelines."

And so did he. More than most. He still didn't fully understand why he hadn't gone with his first instincts. "Yeah."

A man of few words, she thought, wishing she knew how to set free what was bottled up inside of him. That it needed to be set free was something she wholeheartedly believed. It didn't matter that she had only known him for an hour and a half. Susanna made up her mind about people quickly. "I enjoyed the company."

She sounded sincere, Flynn thought. She was flirting—and yet, it didn't really seem like it, not if he were honest about his appraisal. There was a kind of innocence to her words. He wondered if that was possible, then shrugged off the thought. Women with seven-year-old boys weren't innocent.

The words, "See you at the game," were on the tip of his tongue, but then Flynn decided he had already said far too much. If he said that, it would sound as if he hoped to see her again. And he didn't. He distinctly hoped that he *wouldn't* see her again. He had more than just a small nagging feeling that for all her good intentions and supposed openness, Susanna Troy spelled trouble. With a capital *T*. And right now, his world was in enough turmoil.

With a curt nod born of a strong sense of self-preservation, Flynn took Michael's hand in his and turned away.

"Bye, Michael!" Billie called after them.

Michael craned his neck as he looked back over his shoulder. "See you at the game, Billie!"

Flynn purposely kept his back to Susanna as he walked toward his own car. And escape.

He would have kept on walking without so much as a backward glance, had the whining not begun. A very persistent, tinny whining. The kind an engine made when it refused to perform, like a petulant child throwing a tantrum. Without wanting to, he listened. She was going to flood the carburetor.

Michael dug his heels into the pavement and tugged Flynn's hand. It was obvious that he wanted to ride to the rescue, even if Flynn didn't. "Their car won't start."

"Yeah." There seemed to be no escaping this. Squaring his shoulders, Flynn turned around and slowly walked over to Susanna's car. He saw her frowning as she turned the key again. "Sounds like engine trouble."

That's what it was, all right, she thought, trying not to let an exasperated sigh escape her lips. "Nothing a good mechanic and three hundred dollars probably can't fix, I'm sure." She gave up trying to turn over the engine and pulled her key out of the ignition.

Flynn marveled at the nonchalant way she had mentioned that amount of money. "You have that kind of money to waste?"

She shook her head, dragging her hand through her hair. "No one has that kind of money to waste." She got out. Billie bounced out of the other side, joining her. "But I need a car. I'm a little old to ride a bike to work." Although, if worse came to worst, she thought, she could make the ten-mile trip.

Susanna leaned into the back seat and dragged her paraphernalia onto the pavement. This wasn't exactly shaping up as one of her better days.

Flynn watched her shorts ride up high on her leg again. He

grinned despite himself. "Oh, I don't know. It might be interesting to watch at that."

Susanna turned and he saw the surprised look on her face. Damn, she probably thought he was making a pass at her again. Well, he wasn't. The words had just leaked out. His voice became gruff again.

"Can I give you and Billie a lift home?" He couldn't see her walking home with all that stuff in her arms. Besides, it would be dark soon.

Her sigh of relief was audible. "If you don't mind." She looked down at the banner, stakes and knapsack, not to mention a purse that probably weighed in at slightly less than fifteen pounds. "My arms would be kind of full."

Flynn merely shook his head. The woman needed a keeper. Positioning the banner and stakes against his left shoulder, he picked up her knapsack. "I noticed. The car's right over here." He gestured toward it with the tip of the stakes.

The silver convertible was not the last word in roomy comfort. Flynn deposited her things next to it and unlocked the door. "Hop in."

She eyed it dubiously. The car was small and low-slung. Susanna looked at the boys and then at the car. "Is there room enough in that for all of us?"

Seating four would be a challenge. The car had been an impulse, bought last year, he supposed, by the twenty-six-year-old who was trapped inside him. His daughters had fairly drooled over it, each begging to be allowed to take it for a spin. It was an impractical purchase, to say the least. Still he had to admit that he liked it.

"The boys are small. They can scrunch up in the back." Even as he said it, the two scrambled into the rather crammed space behind the two front seats.

"How about these?" She indicated the banner and stakes.

"They can go in the trunk." He unlocked it and loaded the things in. That was a tight fit, too, even though there was nothing else in there except a jack.

"Good enough." She got in on the passenger side. After

almost two hours of cheering the team on, it felt good to sit down again. She watched as Flynn got behind the steering wheel, and then gave him her address. "It's just on the edge of the development," she added.

Flynn started up the engine. They passed her disabled car on their way out. He saw the accusing look she give it. "What about your car?"

"I'll call my mechanic in the morning. He'll send over his tow truck." She closed her eyes, not relishing the bill that this was going to generate.

Flynn glanced at her as he took a corner. The sight of her with her eyes shut like that stirred him. He pictured her head on a pillow next to his, sleeping after a night of—

Damn, what had gotten into him?

"What about work tomorrow?" His voice felt tight in his throat, even as he cursed himself for it.

She shrugged, wondering why his voice had gotten so gruff again. "I'll call someone for a ride."

Was there a special someone she turned to? A man in her life?

All the better for him, Flynn thought quickly. He didn't need to get his life entangled with an overzealous blonde. He knew that. Which was why he was surprised to hear himself asking, "You don't happen to work at Palisades Mutual, do you?" with a strange sense of forboding.

She leaned forward to look at him. "Why don't I? Take that turn there." She pointed to the left.

Too late. He missed it. Muttering under his breath, Flynn did a U-turn. "Then you do?" he asked impatiently.

He was the most reluctant do-gooder she had ever run into. Listening to his tone, one would have thought she had held a gun to his head, ordering him to bring her home. "The payroll department thinks I do. Why?"

Just his luck. "I'm an engineer at Worth Aerospace up the road from Palisades Mutual."

She was familiar with the company. She passed it twice a day, on her way to and from work. "Small world."

Flynn paused. He had expected her to ask for a lift. That would have taken it all out of his hands. *Was* there a man in her life? He wished he'd stop wondering about that. "I suppose I could drop you off tomorrow morning."

The reluctance in his voice had reached a new high. Why was he offering to do it if he didn't want to? Was this some sort of bet he had going? Or one he had lost? She felt confused.

Susanna held her hands up. "You'll notice that I am not twisting your arm here, Flynn." She said his name, although she had a hunch he would have preferred she call him Mr. O'Roarke. She was getting very mixed signals, his wanting to maintain a distance and yet not wanting to at the same time. He couldn't have it both ways. And she knew which way she would have preferred it. She enjoyed getting along with everyone.

"Besides, you don't know what time I have to be in," she pointed out, feeling obligated to give him a way out if he wanted it.

She was saving him from possibly making a mistake and he was grateful. "It was just a thought."

When he saw her smile, he knew that he wasn't saved after all. On the contrary. Somehow he had managed to voluntarily step into a mine field.

Susanna didn't want him to think that she was being ungrateful. Maybe she had only imagined his reluctance. Maybe that was just his way. She realized that she was making a rather hasty judgment about the man, but she had seen the way he was with Billie as well as the way he was with his own son. It was enough to convince her that though Flynn O'Roarke might scowl like an ogre, a warmhearted man lived beneath the brooding exterior.

Besides, she did rather like the brooding exterior.

And a very nice thought it was, too. "I'll make arrangements. For work, I mean," she added quickly when she saw the scowl threaten to return to his face. "You know, for a Good Samaritan, you do an awful lot of scowling."

"I'm not a Good Samaritan," he fairly snapped, his hands tightening on the wheel.

He might be into denial, but she wasn't. "Then what do you call offering your services?"

That was an easy one. "Temporary insanity."

She laughed, tickled. "I don't think so."

She had to be set straight right here and now. There were no hidden messages to his offer and he didn't want her to misunderstand. She'd been nice to Michael and this was just payback, nothing more. "Mrs.—Troy is it?"

His exasperation had taken on a formal tone. "That way," she said, pointing just as he began to head down the wrong street. She leaned back in her seat. "It is, but Susanna is easier."

He threw the car into reverse to regain the turn as the boys cheered on, enjoying the ride. "I wouldn't know about that."

Susanna decided that for the moment, it was better to back off. There would be other times to try to dig at the underlayer Flynn O'Roarke was trying to hide. Tomorrow morning if nothing else. And she had a very strong feeling that it would not be just tomorrow morning. There would be more times than that.

Some things a woman just felt. And she had a feeling about Flynn.

"Well, whatever you want to call your acts of gallantry, I think you've more than earned your merit badge this evening, starting with helping me put up the banner for the game."

"Yeah, well..." His voice trailed off as he shrugged away her thanks, not knowing how to respond. "What time do you need a pick-up tomorrow?"

His voice was harsh, but by now she had decided that keeping her at a distance was one of his defense mechanisms. "What time do you have to be at work?" He pulled up her street. "Last house on the left."

"Seven-thirty." Reaching her house, he turned off the engine.

That was a good half hour before she had to make an appearance at the office. Still, she didn't want to put him out. "What direction will you be coming from?"

"Never mind that." Flynn wasn't about to tell her where he lived. He had already talked too much to her as it was. He wanted to keep his life private. The less she knew about him, the better.

"Okay, you're coming out of thin air, then." The boys giggled at the solemn way she seemed to accept that. "All right." She smiled at Flynn. "Could you drop out of the sky at about seven?"

She was laughing at him. But that was better than her getting under his skin. As long as he remembered that. "That could be arranged."

Billie leaned forward, holding onto the back of his mother's seat. His eyes were large. "Can I watch?"

Flynn turned in his seat to look at the boy. "Watch what?"

"You drop out of the sky."

"You might have noticed that they take everything literally at this age." Susanna fought to keep a straight face. She turned to look at Billie. "It was just a figure of speech, Billie."

Wheat-colored eyebrows knitted together as Billie tried to puzzled that one out. "What's a 'figure of speech'?"

Susanna kept her eyes on Flynn's face as she answered. "Something someone says when they don't want to tell the truth."

"Union Street," Flynn said, damning her, not for this, but for what might come. What would come. "I live on Union Street. Look, I don't see what the fuss is over an address—"

Hardly hearing him, Susanna did some quick mental calculations. "Then you'll have to backtrack." She shook her head. She really didn't want to put him out. "I don't want—"

"I wouldn't have made the offer if I wasn't willing to go through with it," he snapped as he stomped out of the car and opened the trunk. Why in God's name had he ever even opened his mouth?

With a heave that was mightier than warranted, he removed

her things from his trunk, as if he was symbolically removing her from his life.

"I have a feeling, Flynn," Susanna said softly as she got out of the car, "that you wouldn't do anything you weren't willing to do. Thank you." She accepted the banner and the rest of her belongings as Flynn all but shoved them toward her.

The stakes clattered to the ground and Billie scooped them up, one in each hand.

Eyes the color of the sky over a stormy sea, Flynn thought suddenly, looking down into her face. It was an omen. One he was damn well going to heed.

Right after he picked her up in the morning.

Flynn slammed the trunk shut and got into the car as Michael crawled out of the rear and tumbled into the passenger seat. Susanna managed a wave as he drove away. Flynn didn't wave back.

Willingly. He was doing this willingly. He needed his head x-rayed. And fast.

Maybe, he pondered as he drove home, Michael chattering at his side, there was a twenty-four-hour lunatic asylum he could check into, preferably before tomorrow morning at seven.

Chapter Three

Swimming in a sea of euphoria created by winning the game, Billie burst through the front door just ahead of Susanna. Without looking, he pitched his glove and hat in the general vicinity of the sofa. The articles bounced once against the sofa and tumbled down under the coffee table.

Obviously remembering his mother's oft-repeated instructions Billie turned to see her struggling to open the hall closet door while balancing the banner and stakes and yanked the door open for Susanna. He hung on the doorknob, pivoting on his toes as he leaned back, swaying. "Did you like Michael's dad, Mom?" He watched her face, waiting for an answer.

Susanna knew that tone. She stood the banner and stakes upright in the recesses of the hall closet, securing them with the side of the ironing board. Satisfied that they wouldn't pitch forward the next time she opened the door, she closed the closet and turned to look at her precocious seven-year-old.

Billie had been playing matchmaker for a little more than

a year now, fancifully pairing her up with everyone from hockey immortal Wayne Gretzky, who she tactfully pointed out was married, to matching her up with the muscle-bound star of an eight o'clock action-packed series on Saturday nights, who wasn't. At least, not to her knowledge. It appeared that Billie was bringing his efforts closer to home now. Susanna wasn't at all certain that that was an improvement, and it might make for embarrassing situations.

"Yes, I like Michael's dad." Hope sprang into her son's eyes. She went on quickly. "I also like Drew's dad and Chris's dad—"

"Wow."

She could see the possibilities hatching in his very fertile little brain. The boy was seven, going on twenty. And at times she had to hustle to keep up.

Susanna placed her hand on the small shoulder, bending down to be eye to eye with her son. "Put your eyes back in your head, young man. I like everyone, remember?" Or at least she tried, she amended silently. Some people were harder to like than others. Some people, Flynn O'Roarke for instance, didn't seem as if they really wanted to be liked at all.

She looked over Billie's head into the living room. The boy was a positive whirlwind. Two seconds in a room and he turned it into a mess. "What I don't like is seeing things lying all over the place." Straightening, she pointed to the fallen objects.

With a frustrated huff, Billie marched to the sofa and picked up his glove and hat. Billie placed the two items on the first step of the stairs, an indication that he would take them up to his room later.

"If you like everybody so much," Billie said as he followed Susanna into the kitchen, "how come you're not married again?"

He was like a dog trying to get at a bone that was just out of reach, she thought with a sigh. She supposed she really couldn't blame him. It was rough being a boy without a father.

Susanna pulled open the refrigerator door and reached for a carton of milk. "Really cut to the chase, don't you?"

His eyes narrowed as he watched his mother take out a glass from the cupboard overhead and hand it to him. He held the glass in both hands as she poured. "Huh?"

Susanna popped the spout on the container closed again. "I'm not married, my love," she told him patiently as she slipped the carton back on the shelf, "because I've never met anyone who's made that something 'special' happen." No bells, no banjos, she thought fondly. Brett had made all that happen for her.

Billie knew the procedure. He placed his glass on the table and took out a small plate from the dishwasher rack. He held it in his hands as he waited for his mother. "Special?"

Susanna opened the cookie tin and counted out three chocolate chip cookies before she pushed the lid closed again. Taking out a spoon, she reopened the refrigerator and retrieved her own evening snack. Non-fat cherry yogurt. She had to admit that the cookies looked a great deal more tempting.

She smiled as she sat down next to Billie at the small kitchen table. Without its leaf, the table was just big enough for the two of them and Aunt Jane whenever she felt the urge to pop by for breakfast. And that was just the way Susanna liked it. Just the three of them.

She leaned forward in the chair, elbows on the table as she absently stirred the yogurt and let her mind wander back through the years. Her lips curved wistfully as she pulled up Brett's image. "When I first met your father, something very special happened."

A milk-drenched cookie stuffed in his mouth, Billie cocked his head. He chewed furiously, in a hurry to get the next word out. "Like fireworks?"

Susanna thought of the way she had felt when Brett had looked into her eyes that first day they had bumped into each other in the hall at the university. Brett's sky-blue eyes had rippled directly into her soul. She had known, right from the start, that he was the one. It had been as simple as that.

"Exactly like fireworks."

Billie sank his last cookie in the glass, counting to ten under his breath. He looked at his mother incredulously. "And is that what you're waiting for now? Fireworks?"

Susanna swallowed two spoonfuls of yogurt before answering. She wasn't waiting for anything. She'd had her perfect love and that was enough. She couldn't hope for anything more. Lightning rarely struck twice. "What I am waiting for, young man, is for you to get cleaned up and ready for bed."

"Aw, Mom. It's too early to go to bed." Billie purposely ignored the clock that hung on the wall.

Susanna used the end of her spoon to point to it. Her voice became formal. "It's almost eight. Your game lasted a lot longer tonight than it usually does, William, and you know what time curfew is."

Billie frowned deeply as he bit into the last of his cookies. When she called him William it meant she was serious.

His face brightened suddenly and Susanna eyed his expression cautiously. What was he up to now? She knew Billie could be devious. His next words were predictable. "Can I stay up another half hour, Mom, please?"

This was well-traveled territory. She knew what he was angling for. She was torn between doing what she knew was right and giving him everything he wanted. There were times when being a parent was no picnic.

"If you get all ready," she said slowly, not wanting him to feel that the battle had been won so easily, "there might be an extra fifteen minutes in it for you."

Billie got up and dutifully rinsed out his glass and washed off his plate. "The Angels are playing the Mets." He gave her his most dazzling smile.

She was raising a con artist. She should have named him Artful Dodger instead of William Brett, she mused. Susanna nodded approvingly at the dish and glass drying on the rack. "You can watch one inning."

He hung his head while raising his eyes. It gave him a hangdog expression. "Just one?"

Susanna had to struggle to keep from laughing. If Billie put this much effort into a future career, the boy was going to make president by the time he turned thirty. "Just one."

He stuck out his chin. "Aw, Mom."

She shook her head, holding firm for his sake, but having a sneaking suspicion that she would give in down the line. But at least she could put up a good front. "And if you whine, it might be just half an inning."

There wasn't another word out of Billie as he dashed up the stairs to get ready.

Susanna sighed and laughed. Looking at the bottom of her container, she scraped the last bit of yogurt out of the corners. This wasn't the easiest job in the world, being both mother and father to Billie, even though it had tremendous rewards. She knew he craved male companionship and she ached for him. She did the best she could to fill in on all those father-son things that kept coming up, but it just wasn't enough. He needed a father.

Still, she couldn't get married just to give him one. That wouldn't be fair to any of them, not to Billie, or to herself and certainly not to the man who would be pulled into the vortex of this bargain. It was hard, very hard being a single mother and raising a son.

She thought about the man who had given her a ride home and smiled to herself. Flynn O'Roarke had no idea how easy he had it, having a child of his own gender to raise. And although she wouldn't have traded Billie for the world, things might have gone a lot easier for her if Billie had been born a girl.

Flynn wished passionately that his daughter had given birth to a girl instead of a boy. At least then he would have had a vague memory as to how to go about things. Being put in charge of a boy was a whole different ball game, one in which he wasn't sure of any of the rules. Things were different with boys than with girls.

He shook his head as he peeked in on Michael in the family

room. The boy had made a beeline for the television set as soon as they had walked into the house.

Michael saw Flynn looking in. With nachos clutched in his stubby little fingers, he gestured for his grandfather to come in. "Wanna watch the game, Granddad?" he asked hopefully, in between crunching.

Flynn shook his head, not in answer to the boy's question, but at the way Michael had so effortlessly settled in. Michael was inviting him into the room as if Flynn was the late arrival to the household and not the other way around. Michael was certainly having a lot less trouble adjusting to this situation than he was, Flynn thought.

He took a seat next to his grandson. Michael repositioned the bag of nachos so that they could share them.

Michael was trying very hard to make things easier on him, Flynn thought. He was trying hard to be thought of as an integral part of Flynn's life. Poor little guy, Flynn mused as he looked at the boy's face. Michael needed to be part of a family, needed so many things that Flynn felt ill-equipped to give him.

Still, he had to admire his grandson's courageous approach to the curves life had thrown him so far. Flynn had yet to see Michael cry, even when he had woken up in the hospital to find that he no longer had parents. He had been silent for a long time, so long that Flynn had grown concerned. And then he had asked in a small, still voice, if he could come home with him. It had almost broken Flynn's heart.

The green numbers on the VCR announced the hour. It was after nine. "Shouldn't you be going to bed?" Flynn prompted.

"Not sleepy." Michael stifled a huge yawn that belied his words.

"Oh. I see." Flynn dropped the subject.

Kelly, he remembered, had always been a stickler about bedtime, even when the girls had begged to stay up. Flynn had always thought that was rather a silly rule, making someone go to bed when they weren't tired. But he had never opposed Kelly. She usually knew what was best in the long run.

On his own now, Flynn thought he'd wait Michael out. When the boy was tired, he'd be ready to go to bed.

"So," Flynn said, taking a handful of chips, and eating them one at a time. "Who's winning?"

Michael pointed with his chin, a look of pure disgust on his normally sunny face. "They are."

By Michael's tone, Flynn surmised that "they" were the Mets. He crossed his arms before him and settled back to watch the game. There was no work to catch up on tonight and he could think of nothing else he'd rather do than stay in the company of this complex little being who required so little of him to exist. It was only everything he had to give, Flynn thought with an amused shake of his head.

The whole situation still baffled him.

Rules, structure, things like that belonged on blueprints and designs for space station satellites. He was having trouble finding his way around rules and structure as they applied to everyday life. He had always been a believer in live and let live. It had been Kelly who had administered the rules, Kelly who had seen to the punishments on the rare occasions that they were needed. During all that child rearing, all those years of marriage, Flynn had been, by and large, an innocent bystander.

The roles they had taken on had evolved naturally. He hadn't cared to get bogged down in the details of day-to-day living. He had enough of that to contend with at work. Flynn hadn't wanted to run into it in his home life as well. So Kelly had taken over the budget, the bills, the children, and the myriad minutiae that went along with running a home. Flynn's capacity had been that of a silent backup.

When she died, leaving him so abruptly, everything had come crashing in all at once. The late payment notice from the mortgage company had been his first indication that every nook and cranny of his life was going to have to be overhauled. It had been a tough struggle, but he had managed somehow.

He had just been getting to the point where he could handle the day-to-day annoying details, blessing the powers that be that at least his daughters were full-grown and didn't need constant care, when that midnight call had come about Aimee and Doug.

Suddenly he was not only mired in life, but was instantly thrown into fatherhood all over again. Or perhaps, more accurately, for the first time.

So far, Michael seemed unharmed by his grandfather's inexperience. Michael had proven to be a rather resilient little boy. But still, Flynn felt he was on shaky ground.

He rolled the metaphor around in his head. The ground had really felt shaky under his feet this evening at the field. What had possessed him to offer to take that overly effervescent woman to work tomorrow? He didn't have time to play Good Samaritan. And God knows he certainly didn't have time to—to—

To what?

To feel something? Flynn sighed as the side was retired. Michael flashed him a conspiratorial, albeit sleepy, grin.

Flynn thought of Susanna. Hormones, that's what it was, pure and simple. He had felt a physical reaction to her company. He was certainly old enough to know all about hormones. His had been in suspended animation for the last fifteen months.

He could honestly say that he had been in love with only one woman in his life and he had married her. Sure, he had looked, but he had never wanted, never even fantasized. He'd been too happy, too content. Too busy counting his blessings. When Kelly died, he was so devastated, he was certain that all of him had died from the neck down.

To find that it hadn't was a shock all its own. A shock that didn't really please him. There were far too many complications that went along with this revelation. And too many people to consider. He just had to put the whole thing, the whole evening from his mind.

Yet there was something about Susanna. Something. That was the only way he could describe it. He couldn't put his finger on it, or maybe he just didn't want to give it a name.

What he knew was that he didn't want to want to voluntarily see her again.

But he did.

He wondered if senility hit some men at forty-five.

Michael suddenly slumped against Flynn's shoulder, the nachos bag falling to the floor. Flynn leaned slightly to peer into the boy's face. "Hey, Michael, what inning is it?"

Michael didn't even stir.

"Well, that was easy enough," Flynn murmured to himself. Shifting Michael over onto his lap, Flynn rose with the boy in his arms. Funny how something that felt so light could be such a heavy burden, he thought as he headed toward the stairs.

Michael's room was next to his own. The boy had asked for it. It had once been Aimee's. Somehow, it was fitting that Michael should have it.

Flynn tucked Michael into bed, removing just enough from the boy to make sleeping comfortable. He didn't bother with the boy's jeans or shirt. Flynn had long ago discovered that donning pajamas was somehow a signal to his system to stay awake. So when Michael asked to emulate him, Flynn saw no harm in it. Flynn slept in cutoff shorts. Michael usually did, too. But not tonight.

"You played a great game, sport," Flynn whispered to the sleeping boy as he closed the door behind him.

An image of Susanna, her T-shirt flapping in the wind, licking the tops of her thighs rose in Flynn's mind, immediately followed by a spontaneous tightening of his stomach. "But your grandfather is totally out of the game," Flynn added firmly, shaking off the grip of what he was afraid he felt.

He went downstairs to call Susanna and cancel tomorrow's pickup. He was sure someone as resourceful as she would find another way to get to work.

She was unlisted.

It seemed, Flynn thought as he shoved the telephone book back to its place under the phone stand in the hall, that the fates were conspiring against him, obviously determined to throw his life into even further havoc.

He turned toward the stairs again. Still, he absently mused, havoc had never looked quite as attractive as this before.

But attractive or not, Susanna Troy had absolutely no place in his life beyond a passing, friendly gesture. He'd pick her up, drop her off at work and be done with it.

She was standing in front of her house, Billie in tow, waiting for him.

Flynn saw her in the distance as he turned a corner. The mist had burned off early and a breeze was rifling through the newly minted foliage on the trees. The leaves fairly glistened in the morning sun. The daisies on the lawn next door to her house were nodding their white-and-yellow heads in rhythm to the wind. It teased the edges of her flared skirt, sending the navy blue material up way past her knees. For some reason, that seemed even more enticing than the sight of her in shorts.

It was as if he had been given a glimpse of somewhere he wasn't supposed to be.

And he wasn't. What was the matter with him? Was he having a midlife crisis, like Jake Emersol in stats? On Jake's forty-fifth birthday, the portly man had handed in a letter of resignation, left his wife of twenty years and bought himself a one-way ticket to Madrid, Spain.

But he wasn't Jake. He was a grandfather. He had no business feeling blood stir in him like a teenage boy. He had left that part of himself behind years ago, when he had married Kelly.

And Kelly was gone.

He blew out an impatient breath. When he pulled up beside Susanna, his frown was in direct contrast to the sunny expression on her face. He remembered his initial instinct this morning as he had climbed into the car. He had wanted to head the car toward Michael's school and then go to work, completely forgetting about Susanna and his rash offer. Not that Michael would have let him, he thought, glancing at the beaming boy next to him.

"What if I hadn't shown up?" Flynn asked Susanna.

"But you did," she said cheerfully. Her words were almost lost as Billie shouted a loud greeting to Michael. The latter was already scrambling out of his seat in the front and wiggling his way into the cramped, almost nonexistent back seat, dragging his lime-green backpack with him.

Billie clambered in beside him. As before, it was a tight fit. "Do you have another car?" Billie asked Flynn, clutching at the edge of the driver's seat.

Flynn waited, trying not to notice Susanna's legs as she pulled them in and shut the door. This morning, she looked light years away from the woman he had heard shouting encouragement on the field last night. That was a mom. The woman next to him was a very competent-looking professional. While he admired the latter, he found that he rather liked the former better.

He had no business liking either, he reminded himself.

Flynn addressed Billie's question. It was a lot easier than sorting out the cauldron of swirling thoughts and feelings that confused and mystified him even as they caused him concern. "As a matter of fact, I do. Why?"

Billie raised and dropped his shoulders in an exaggerated motion, striving to look innocent to the roots of his hair. "I just thought it'd be more comfortable for all of us."

I don't plan to make a habit of this, Flynn thought and very nearly said aloud.

"I'm afraid you're out of luck." He eased the car out of the development and onto the main street that cut through Bedford. "My daughters are sharing that one."

"You have daughters, too?" Susanna asked, interested.

He glanced at Susanna. She looked much too comfortable next to him. Didn't she feel awkward around strangers? He knew *he* did.

Flynn nodded as he looked back at the road. "Stephanie

and Julia. They're away at school. U.C. Santa Barbara,'' he
added.

He looked entirely too young to have college-aged daughters. Susanna looked at him, trying to guess his age. She settled for asking about his daughters. For now. "How old are
they?"

"Julia's nineteen, Stephanie's twenty." *And Aimee would
have been twenty-four,* he added silently.

Susanna wanted to explore this further, to ask him more
questions about his family, but she had the definite impression
that a curtain had just gone down around the subject. Maybe
his daughters reminded him too much of his wife. Some people, she knew, locked up their grief inside and wouldn't let it
out. She had worked through hers by talking, by remembering
all the good times. But everyone was different.

"Well, you've certainly spaced out your family," she
smiled. "Michael can't be more than seven."

"Six," Michael corrected her. "But I'm going to be
seven."

"You sure are," Susanna agreed, aware of the fragility of
the masculine ego, no matter how young it was.

"I didn't space out my family," Flynn told her after a beat.
He didn't want to talk about it, but it was best to get this all
out in the open now, before this woman got any ideas. She
was a nester if he ever saw one and he had no intentions of
being in a nest, no matter how inviting the plumage.

There were probably several ways to interpret his words,
but for the life of her, Susanna couldn't come up with even
one. "I'm afraid I don't understand."

"Michael's not my son, he's my grandson."

"Oh." The information threw her for a loop. If ever a man
had seemed virile and in top condition, it was Flynn O'Roarke.
There was nothing about him that would suggest he was even
remotely up for the role of grandfather.

Susanna recovered quickly, hoping Flynn hadn't noticed her
initial confusion. One look at his face as they stopped at a

light told her he had. "I'm sorry if I sound flustered, but you're not exactly the way I picture a grandfather."

He couldn't help the amusement that quirked his lips. "And exactly what do you picture?"

"A cane," Billie piped up before she could say anything. "My grandpa's got a cane."

"My father broke his hip last year and he's had to use a cane ever since," Susanna explained.

"Both my hips are fine." He addressed the remark to Billie, but his eyes strayed toward Susanna.

Yes, Susanna thought, they certainly were that. It was one of the first things she had noticed about him yesterday. The jeans he had worn had fit him like a glove. If he was a grandfather, he certainly was the youngest-looking one she had ever met. At least in appearance.

There was something about his manner, though, that contradicted the youth she saw in both his face and his body. His manner was intended, she had a feeling, to be off-putting.

But then, Susanna found that she was never put off by very much.

Chapter Four

The trip to the school that Michael and Billie attended took only five minutes. All too soon for Flynn, the boys were deposited at the front doors. The two dashed off to join their friends, determined to get in some serious playtime before the line-up bell rang.

And then it was just the two of them within the confines of the small car. The two of them and a pervading aura of awkward silence. At least, the silence felt awkward to Flynn.

As he fumbled with the radio dial, the same sensations he'd experienced last night returned. He couldn't help wondering why. This was just an acquaintance he was helping. Yet he couldn't shake the total awareness that this acquaintance was a single, attractive woman.

Which was what bothered him. Among other nameless things that pricked his conscience and played havoc with his nervous system.

A country-and-western song about unrequited love filled the car as he made his way into the stream of traffic heading south.

He glanced at her, wondering what she thought of the music. Flynn noticed that Susanna was moving her shoulders ever so slightly, in time to the beat. She seemed to be enjoying it, he thought.

Susanna could spot a case of nerves a mile away, even though this man was doing his damnedest to hide it. When she caught his eye, she flashed a smile, hoping for one in return. She was out of luck. Maybe next time.

She smoothed down her skirt beneath the briefcase she held in her lap. "I really do appreciate the ride, Flynn, but I hope I'm not taking you out of your way."

For a moment, he lost his train of thought. His name, when she uttered it, sounded like music. He told himself it was just the mood created by Eddie Rabbit and his mournful song, nothing more.

"You are," Flynn said, looking at the road again. He shrugged a little too carelessly, as if the mistake was his. "But I volunteered." He took the next turn a bit too sharply.

Susanna caught her briefcase as it began to slide off her lap. What was he running from, she wondered. It couldn't possibly be her. Or could it? "Why?"

Flynn thought he hadn't heard her correctly above the music. "Excuse me?"

She studied his profile. It was a rugged masculine face with just enough lines about his mouth and eyes to make him interesting. He was too young and too good-looking to lock himself away. And some part of him was trying to break out. But not all. "You're obviously uncomfortable about all this." She gestured around the car to indicate the ride he was giving her. "*Why* did you volunteer?"

He shrugged again, wishing she wouldn't press him on this. "It seemed like the thing to do at the time."

It was a lame excuse, but it was all he had. Saying that he had wanted to give her a ride didn't seem right. He couldn't reconcile the desire to be around her with Kelly's memory. Somehow, it made him feel disloyal.

"I see." Susanna paused for a moment, rolling over her

next words in her mind, testing them out. She knew that some might say that the next question was none of her business, but Susanna took a keen interest in everyone who crossed her path. And this man merited a stronger interest, a stronger response than most. She leaned toward him, her voice lowering, her tone gentle. "How long has your wife been gone?"

The question surprised him. He felt himself tense, as if his body was fighting off the image that was generated by the word "gone." The long vigil at the hospital. The clergyman droning on at Kelly's grave site. The way the air had felt that day, oppressive and stifling because she wasn't breathing it with him anymore.

"Too long," Flynn snapped without hesitation. His conscience caught up to him after a beat. He hadn't meant to bark at her that way. He sighed, taking the edge from his voice. It was as close as he was going to come to offering an apology. "She died fifteen months ago."

Rather than take affront, Susanna felt for him as empathy flooded her body. She remembered what it was like. Susanna wasn't even aware of the hand she placed on his shoulder. "It gets easier, you know."

There was immense comfort in the small gesture. But he didn't want comfort. He was doing just fine on his own. He had to hang on to that. "Does it?"

His voice had an uncertain tone. It was a mixture of bitter anger and sadness. She withdrew her hand. But not her offer of friendship. That he definitely needed, if she was any judge of things.

"Never easy, but easier." She thought back just enough for the words, but not the pain the memory generated. The pain came anyway. It always did. "Brett died when Billie was a baby. I was sure I was going to fold completely."

"But you didn't." It wasn't a question. Somehow he could have guessed that about her. Knowing her a total of two hours, he would have guessed. Delicate-looking, she still wasn't the collapsing type. The woman had survivor written all over her small appearance. Unless you looked at her eyes, or the set of her mouth. He realized that he had been looking at her mouth a lot.

"No," she said quietly, looking off into space. "You surprise yourself. You have to." She was talking more to herself than to him. Susanna looked at Flynn and smiled. "There are people depending on you, so you go on. One step at a time until you've forged a path. And then a pattern that you can live with."

It was a deceptively simple philosophy that required so much, he thought. He pressed down on the gas pedal as the road stretched upward before him, heading toward the Coast. Time to change the subject. "You have just one son?"

Susanna grinned. There was nothing she liked better than to talk about Billie. "There is no 'just' in front of Billie's name. He's a handful and a half."

The boy seemed to be well behaved from what Flynn had seen of him. "You seem to be bearing up to the job pretty well."

"I love him."

And that, Flynn could tell, said it all for Susanna. She loved and so she coped. Love was obviously the deciding factor for her, the great equalizer. He wondered if that was why he had managed to get as far as he had in this maze he had found himself wandering through in the last fifteen months. He knew it had to be. It was hard for him to show love and far harder to express it verbally. When he came right down to it, Flynn couldn't remember ever saying the words. But he did love his daughters. And Michael.

Flynn glanced at Susanna as the line of cars before him slowed at the next light at the top of the hill. "Your son's a lucky kid."

"It goes both ways," she said mildly.

What would she have ever done without Billie? She wasn't certain she could have managed nearly half as well if she had been on her own when Brett died. For the longest time, until she got her bearings, Billie had been her reason for living. Her only reason.

She wondered about the little boy Flynn had taken into his home. Was it just for a visit? Where were his parents? Questions popped up, seeing answers. She began cautiously, testing the waters. "Michael seems to be a very well mannered little boy."

Flynn thought of the way the boy had looked up at him from his hospital bed, his arm in a cast, a large bandage slanted over his left eyebrow. He'd been the picture of bravery.

"He's a resilient little guy, considering what he's been through." Flynn pressed his lips together. The words that followed were spoken harshly to hide the emotion that they evoked. "His parents died in a car crash a year ago. His mother was my daughter."

"Oh, Flynn, I'm so sorry." She had just assumed that he was taking care of Michael for a limited time while the boy's parents were elsewhere. She stared at him, compassion in her eyes. He had endured so much in such a short period of time. "It must have been hell for you."

"That's the word for it. Hell," he echoed. Sheer hell.

Flynn stopped, suddenly aware that he was sharing private matters, private pain with a veritable stranger. Someone he had felt awkward with only ten minutes ago. Flynn shifted gears mentally. It wouldn't do to get too comfortable here. He wasn't one of those men who needed to talk, to get his feelings out in the open. That was for others, not him. He didn't need it. He was never going to "need" anything from anyone again.

Searching for something to get her mind off the topic, Flynn glanced at Susanna and took in the flat gray briefcase on her lap. A tiny purse hung suspended by a thin black leather strap from her shoulder. Unless her lunch was very flat, she hadn't brought any with her. "You don't brown-bag it?"

Susanna shook her head, aware of his diversionary tactic. Maybe she had delved too much. She had a habit of overdoing. But only because she always became so caught up. Part of her problem was that she always cared.

"Making Billie's lunch is about all I can stand. I usually eat in the cafeteria. Or send out."

Flynn brought the car to a stop at the light right before the spacious mall that spread out to within a quarter of a mile of the edge of the harbor. He had already driven past his place of work. Palisades Mutual was just ahead. "Ever tried the restaurant in the mall?"

The mall was where Susanna did most of her last-minute shopping, flying from one store to another during her lunch hour. Except for the rare farewell luncheon thrown by people where she worked, Susanna didn't frequent the restaurants in the mall. "Which one?"

"Robert Burns." Deeper and deeper, he thought, unable to curb his tongue. Was he actually asking this woman out? No, it couldn't be that. He didn't ask women out. He wouldn't have the slightest idea how to go about that. The last date he had had was twenty-six years ago, with Kelly.

Susanna tried to match the name he had given her with a place and failed. "No."

Drop it here, now. Say something inane about the food and let it go. The words came out anyway. "Would you like to?" Damn, how had that happened?

A slow, intrigued smile curved her mouth as Susanna shifted in her seat, facing him. "Are you asking me out to lunch?"

Flynn cleared his throat. He felt as if his nerves were doing deep knee bends in his stomach. He kept his gaze glued to the road, grateful for the sparse flow of traffic. He wasn't completely sure of his reflexes at this moment. "In a roundabout way, yes, I suppose so."

Was she the first woman he had socialized with since his wife's death? Susanna had a feeling that she might be. The thought warmed her more than she thought possible. "I thought engineers were supposed to be rather direct and abrupt."

"We are." He knew he sounded gruff but he was having trouble justifying his own behavior to himself.

Susanna lifted an eyebrow. "Well, you have the abrupt part down pat, but I'd work on the direct bit if I were you."

She was turning him down. Thank God. It had been an impulsive thought that had absolutely no business even occurring to him. What the hell was going on with him, anyway? "Then it's no?"

She couldn't tell if he was relieved or disappointed. "Whatever gave you that idea?"

Confusion had taken over completely. Confusion at his own actions, and his reactions to this woman. He wanted her to say yes and yet he didn't. In either case, he wasn't sure what her answer was. "Aren't actuaries supposed to be direct, too?"

She grinned. He looked absolutely adorable when he was flustered. She wondered how he would respond to that assessment. Probably frown some more. "I was a changeling."

If that meant that she wasn't the garden-variety type of woman one usually met, she was a changeling all right. "Somehow, I think I can buy that."

She leaned slightly toward the right as he turned down the road that led to the outdoor mall. The surrounding blocks along the mall's outer perimeter were lined with office buildings. Hers was on the far end, closest to the ocean. "Speaking of buying, I am."

He was going to need a road map with this conversation. "You are what?"

"Buying." When his frown didn't dissipate, she took it to mean he had again lost the thread of what they were discussing. "Lunch."

Did she think he was going to ask her to lunch and then not pay for it? He didn't care what the nineties dictated, some things a man just did. "Now hold on a minute—"

His stern voice left her unfazed. She had been on her own far too long to cringe before authority. "I insist. After all, you've gone out of your way for me. It's the least I can do."

No, not really, he thought. The least she could do was to leave him alone.

God knew Flynn didn't want to be attracted to her. He

didn't want to take her to lunch. And he certainly didn't want to open up to her. He didn't feel right about any of it. Flynn had been married to Kelly all his adult life, he was too set in his ways, too out of practice to be having lunch with an attractive, unattached woman. And try as he might, he couldn't make himself think of Susanna as just Billie's mother. She was far too female for that title alone. He wondered how it was that she hadn't become involved with someone yet. And why the powers that be had made their paths cross.

"You're passing it," she prompted, pointing toward the circular, four-story building that stood with the ocean at its back. "That's where I work."

Flynn realized that his thoughts were drifting into a fog. Murmuring an unintelligible oath under his breath, he did an abrupt U-turn at the corner. Among other things, Susanna was having a bad effect on his driving skills. Going a little faster than he normally would, he made his way through the parking lot of a thriving department store on the edge of the mall. The wide, squat three-story structure faced the front of Susanna's office.

Flynn stopped the convertible at the curb in front of steps that spread out like a lady's fan, leading up to the glass front doors of Palisades Mutual.

Susanna unbuckled her seat belt, but made no further move to get out. She waited a moment for him to say something else. When he didn't, she took the initiative. Again. It was quickly becoming a habit. "So what time would you like to meet?"

Sunlight bathed the entire area with golden hues. The rays caught in her hair, making it appear even blonder and softer-looking than it was. Like silk, he thought, then struggled to bring his mind back to what she was saying. "For what?"

Susanna shook her head in mild disbelief. He certainly had trouble keeping his mind on the conversation. "Are they all as absent-minded as you in the space program?" she teased.

He liked the smile that flashed across her lips, the dimple that winked at him just above the corner of her mouth. He didn't want to notice it, much less like it. Was determined not to like it. And yet, he knew he did.

"No, I mean—" He dragged an impatient hand through his hair, wondering how the hell he had gotten himself into this mess. "It's been a rather difficult morning."

She glanced at her watch, amused. For a second, she pretended to play along. "It's just started." She raised her eyes to his, compassion highlighting the blue-and-gray irises. She didn't want him to feel that there was no way out. "If you'd rather skip lunch, I understand."

He stared at her, surprised. "Do you?" Flynn could almost believe that she did. That put her one up on him. He wasn't sure that he understood or even knew what was going on inside him. Right now, he felt as if his own thoughts and feelings were jumbled up in a massive hodgepodge that he couldn't begin to make heads or tails of.

"Sure. Maybe another time." Susanna opened the car door and slipped out, three-inch navy heels lightly striking the concrete. "Well, thank you again." With a little shove, she closed the door behind her, and began to hurry away.

He watched her back for a moment, his conscience taking him to task. She was pushy, but she knew just when to strategically retreat. "Wait," he called after her.

Susanna turned around and returned to the car. Someone called out to her as he passed and she waved, but her attention was on Flynn. She leaned into the car.

He caught another heavy whiff of her perfume as he inclined his head toward her.

He had never felt so unsure of himself in his life. "Um, do you have a ride home?" Even his voice sounded hopelessly stilted. It was the same booming voice that had made complex presentations before a roomful of NASA executives and had never once wavered. What had caused the uncertainty in it now?

"No." She glided her fingers slowly along her purse strap. "I thought I'd just call a cab."

"Those are expensive," he lectured. "You shouldn't go throwing your money around."

The gruff voice didn't fool her. He was going to offer to take her home. She wondered if he ever made offers willingly. She shrugged innocently, just the way Billie had last night. Her son came by it naturally, she realized. "Well, my car is out of commission."

He was doing it again, he thought. He was volunteering to help. But he couldn't very well leave her stranded, he reasoned. Sure she could call a cab, but what with the mechanic's bill she was probably facing, she would need all the ready cash that she could gather at her disposal. Flynn refused to look any further into his own motives. "What time do you get off?" He nodded toward the wide, imposing building.

"Four-thirty." She made it a practice never to work overtime. If a project needed extra time put in, she found a way to bring the work home with her. The hours she spent with Billie were precious to her.

Flynn left his second-floor office at four. That gave him a half hour to kill. He supposed there was some extra work he could do to kill time.

He nodded his head, sealing the bargain. "I'll meet you here." He threw the transmission into drive and began to pull away from the curb.

"All right," she called to him. "But on one condition."

His foot slid onto the brake. Flynn turned, looking at her in surprise. "You're setting up conditions?" he asked incredulously.

Susanna nodded as she shifted her briefcase into her other hand and approached the car again. "I want you to smile."

It sounded like a completely off-the-wall request. "When?" he asked archly.

"I'd say anytime the mood hit you, but I'm afraid if I said that, I'd never see one. How about when you pick me up?"

He turned to face the road, shaking his head. She was a strange one, all right. "I'll work on it."

"Please."

The word hung in the air, echoing in his head and mingling with the scent of her perfume in the car as he drove to work.

Several times during the course of the day, Flynn caught himself inexplicably whistling. Each time he would abruptly stop, mentally chastising himself for acting like an idiot. He was garnering strange looks from the people he worked with. Of late Flynn hadn't exactly been known for his cheerful demeanor.

Lunch came and went and he breathed a sigh of relief, remembering the rash invitation he had extended. Half of him fully expected to get a call from the guard at the front gate, telling him that a blond-haired woman was trying to crash the compound, a picnic basket in her hands. It probably would have been like her.

Like her.

It was hard, he realized, not to like her. But he really didn't have a place in his life for where this could lead. In all probability *would* lead. He had finally gotten to the point where he was independent and he liked it that way. If independence carried the weight of loneliness with it at times, so be it. He had had love in his life. Had treasured it, reveled in it. But it had been snatched away from him and he had found a way to go on living. He had no intention of getting back on the merry-go-round.

That's why his behavior struck him as so illogical. He had no idea why his step felt a little lighter today. Or why he kept whistling. Nothing had changed in his life, except that he was picking up a loquacious woman after work, one who somehow seemed to tap into a hidden vein within him and made him want to talk, as well.

Maybe his talking was just a self-defense mechanism. If he talked, he wouldn't find himself buried under her rhetoric.

But even as he formed the excuse, he knew it rang hollow. He talked because she seemed to draw the words out of him. She made him *want* to talk.

Sitting in front of his computer terminal, he tapped on the

keyboard slowly, bringing a three-dimensional design on the monitor around to face another angle.

All in all, Susanna Troy was a very dangerous lady.

He paused, his fingers hovering over the keys, his mind wandering. If she was such an unwanted threat, why was he looking forward to seeing her again?

Flynn had no answers handy, so he blocked the whole thing from his mind. He'd get to it, the way he intended to get to the bills that were piling up on his desk in the study.

Later.

"You're very punctual." Susanna slid into the silver sports car. She had been waiting on the corner of the building's steps for ten minutes, afraid that Flynn might arrive early and, not seeing her, leave without her. There were a lot of people at the office who would have willingly given her a ride, but Susanna wanted to go home with Flynn. Somehow, though she couldn't fully put it into words yet, it was important.

The flow of traffic home was heavier than it had been this morning. Flynn picked his way carefully through the serpentine roads of the mall. "I hate people who are late. It's rude."

He sounded unbending. But she already knew better. "Sometimes, it's unavoidable."

He shrugged. Kelly had never been on time, he recalled, marching to some inner clock all her own. It was one of the few things they had words over. "They have phones for that."

"You won't get an argument out of me." Susanna raised her hands, her palms facing upward. "Even if you do want one," she added quietly. Perhaps, she thought, he might be enjoying her company a little more than he thought he should and that bothered him. That, too, she could understand. She'd been through that herself once, in the beginning.

Flynn looked at her quizzically. The woman was crazy. "Why should I want an argument? I hate arguing."

She saw that he was having trouble with all this. It was easy to see the signs. "Maybe the fact that you're talking to me bothers you."

He let out an annoyed huff. "I think your analyzing mode is in overdrive."

Susanna backed off. Perhaps it was too soon for him to face the truth. "Maybe. Maybe I was wrong."

"Damn straight you were wrong." He glanced at her impassive face. Though she was admitting defeat, he couldn't shake the impression that she had somehow won. "But you don't have to be that agreeable about it."

She could only grin. He sounded like a wounded bear. Had she been like that at first, snapping at everyone because the one she loved was gone? She wasn't sure that had been the case, but that period of her life was a haze, as if she had been sleepwalking through life.

"Sorry, it's in the genes. Agreeableness," Susanna clarified as he raised his eyebrow in silent query. "Will you be at the game on Saturday?"

He shrugged. He hadn't planned on it, but without a housekeeper, he'd have to take Michael there himself. "I suppose so. What time does it begin?"

"Ten-thirty." Now that she thought back, Michael had been attending the games since the season started. "That woman who used to bring Michael—"

He saw the question coming. This one was easy. "She was my housekeeper. Mrs. Henderson."

"Was?"

"She quit."

She tried to picture working for Flynn. It almost made her shiver. "Your sunny disposition got to her?"

"Her husband's promotion and transfer got to her." The last thing he needed was sarcasm, he thought, then looked at Susanna. She was smiling. The woman's facial muscles really got a workout. "What do you mean, my sunny disposition?"

"You haven't smiled yet," she pointed out.

He took a breath, annoyed. "Mrs. Troy—"

Susanna shook her head. "Susanna," she corrected. "If you say it, your lips will curve and you don't even have to say it's a smile. You can call it an involuntary spasm if you like."

The laugh that came was automatic. He couldn't have stopped it if he tried. He had to admit it felt good to laugh. There'd been so little reason to lately. "Always get your way?" He glided the car onto the main thoroughfarè that would eventually lead to her house.

"Yes," she said simply. "But then, I don't usually ask for much. Toys to be picked up, a smile, a good mystery to read. Things I know I can attain."

He wondered if she was on the level. She sounded much too idealistic to have suffered through a death and its subsequent upheaval. If she was genuine, he had to admire her.

Another dangerous sentiment, his warning system informed him.

"I want to thank you again for coming to Billie's rescue yesterday."

He shrugged off her words. Gratitude embarrassed him. "I've never seen anyone hit like that before—in slow motion."

"It's something he has to work on. The coaches try but they don't seem to be getting through to him." She thought of the hours they had put in. The tears. She was at her wit's end, really. "I wish I could help him, give him some advice on how to improve his batting style, but I can't hit the broadside of a barn myself."

"I kind of figured that, after watching you throw yesterday." He chuckled, then gave the matter some serious though. "Maybe I could give Billie a few pointers the next time I'm in the neighborhood." The words slipped out before he could stop them.

"How about this Friday, after work?"

He was a man, he thought, determined to orchestrate his own funeral.

Chapter Five

"Friday?" Flynn repeated, as if saying the word would buy him some time.

He searched his mind for an excuse. It produced absolutely nothing he could use. His brain seemed to have suddenly gone completely numb. His job required that he brief management on a regular basis. That meant sharp, probing questions aimed his way, and he had always done well fielding them. Thinking on his feet was second nature to him. Why then, when a slip of a woman, who came up to his shoulder, tendered an invitation that he knew he should refuse, did his mind go utterly blank?

Was it because he wanted to accept? Flynn wasn't about to try to analyze his actions for a baser motive. He had never felt the need for introspection. Life had always been simple. Wife, family, work, in that order. Now that his world had been turned inside out, it seemed that nothing was straightforward anymore.

Susanna got the impression that everything triggered an internal war with him. The man was a great deal more complex than he seemed on the surface. She couldn't help being intrigued.

"You know, the day in the week everyone likes best," she prodded, her eyes bright, amused. "Friday. Tomorrow."

He cleared his throat, trying one more halfhearted attempt at dodging the invitation. "Well, I—"

Maybe he just needed a push. Otherwise, he would have said no immediately. Susanna played her ace card. The only one in her hand that counted to her. "It would really mean a great deal to Billie. I think his inability to bat in front of the others is destroying his confidence."

Flynn could remember what that was like, having your self-esteem blown to smithereens in front of a bunch of superior, smirking seven-year-olds. For Flynn, it had all come to a head with a bully named Seth who, at the time, seemed to be twice Flynn's size and had shown him up in every sport in school. The humiliation had grown to unbearable proportions. And then his Uncle Frank had given him a set of weights for his birthday.

Every morning before school, Flynn would exercise religiously, the image of Seth's sneering face shimmering before him, egging him on, making him work that much harder. Eventually, the skinny little boy disappeared and a teenager emerged, a teenager with a physique that made others treat him with respect before he ever opened his mouth.

With all that in his past, how could he say no to Susanna's request? "All right."

He made it sound as if he had just agreed to visit the dentist for a root canal. "I'll make it worth your while," Susanna promised.

Just how forward had women become while he had been safely bound up in matrimony all those years? Flynn leveled a look at her. "I beg your pardon?"

"Dinner." By the expression on his face, Susanna gathered that the prospect of a meal in exchange for his good deed hadn't crossed his mind. "I make a mean Yankee Pot Roast."

He blew out a breath, relieved. Maybe he was making mountains out of molehills, after all. Maybe Susanna was as genuine as she seemed and was offering him nothing more than friendship in return for a few favors on his part. He mulled over her offer. A home-cooked meal for a change sounded terrific. With Mrs. Henderson gone, dinners lately had consisted of sandwiches and things that he could readily boil in a pouch. Cooking was never something he had had to do for himself before. Michael didn't complain about the make-shift meals, but he knew the boy would have preferred something a little more flavorful to eat once in a while.

Either that, or frequenting a fast-food restaurant every night. He grinned. "I guess you're on."

Score one for the home team, she thought, noting his smile. It made him appear less forbidding. Maybe that was why he didn't smile too often.

Susanna thought of her son. He'd enjoy the company of a man helping him. She knew Billie loved her and Aunt Jane, but he needed a male influence in his life. She looked at Flynn, gratitude in her eyes. "Thank you. Billie will be very excited."

Flynn turned to comment and saw the look in her eyes. Something within him responded. Melted. He searched madly for his resolve and found it raining through his fingers. No, this wasn't going to be a woman he could easily cast off from his mind without a massive effort on his part. He was going to have to start gearing up now.

His grip tightened on the steering wheel. "Hope it's worth it, for him," Flynn muttered in reply, more to himself than to her. It had better be. God knew the effort might cost him more than he was willing to pay.

His thoughts playing bumper pool in his head, Flynn completely forgot about stopping at the day-care center for Michael. It was Susanna who brought the slip to his attention.

Mumbling his thanks, annoyed that he had had to be reminded, Flynn backtracked half a mile. Luckily, the center was closer to her house than he remembered.

Once Michael bounced into the rear seat of the car, Flynn found that the tight feeling in his chest had dissipated. It was a sad state of affairs. Flynn O'Roarke, forty-five-year-old senior design engineer for the space program was using a six-year-old boy as a buffer. He shook his head.

Susanna noticed the distracted look on Flynn's face as he resumed driving. "What's the matter?"

"Nothing." The denial came too quickly to be true, in Susanna's opinion. "Don't we have to pick up your son from someplace?"

He kept changing the subject, she thought. By her count, he had fumbled his way out of three so far today. "No, Aunt Jane picks him up at school for me in the afternoon."

Aunt Jane. Was that the name of her housekeeper? "She lives with you?"

Susanna grinned. She loved the woman dearly, but if ever a person needed her own space, it was Aunt Jane. Jane Carter Hall Caldwell was a financially independent, headstrong woman who could be loved and taken in small doses only. "No, Aunt Jane lives across the street from me. She's really a character, but I don't know what I would have done without her. After Brett died, she took it upon herself to sell her house in San Juan Capistrano and moved up here to help me out. She was a godsend."

"No parents?" He didn't know what made him tactlessly blurt out the question. He didn't want to know all the personal things he already knew about her. So, why was he asking more questions?

She thought of her parents and smiled fondly. "They live in Florida. They wanted me to come live with them, but I just couldn't leave my home. There were too many memories I wasn't ready to give up yet. So Aunt Jane humored me and moved up here."

They pulled up to the cul-de-sac. Billie was attempting to shoot baskets in the driveway of their trim, gray-and-blue two-story house. "That's her house over there." Susanna pointed to a one-story structure with a tall, white fountain in the front yard.

Flynn brought the car to a stop in Susanna's driveway. Billie ran to meet them, hugging the basketball to his chest. His eyes shone. "Hi!" he called out to them. "Wanna play?" he asked Michael eagerly.

Susanna turned toward Flynn. "Would you like to come in for a few minutes?"

That was the last thing he thought he should do. He'd made enough mistakes today. "No, I think we'd better be getting home." He nodded toward the rear. "Michael has homework to do."

"No I don't," Michael piped up, utterly destroying Flynn's one excuse. "Old Miss Fischer was out today. The sub was neat. She didn't give us any work and let us have an extra-long recess."

The exasperated look on Flynn's face had Susanna struggling not to laugh. He looked endearingly flustered. She gathered her briefcase to her, one hand on the door handle. "How about some coffee? I've been fantasizing about real coffee all day."

Flynn had a weakness for home-brewed coffee himself. But he was afraid that another weakness might crop up if he was alone with her. He wanted to get a better rein on himself, one he felt he didn't have at the moment, before he faced that test.

"No, I..." His voice trailed off as he watched a cat streak down the block, then up a tree. That's how he felt. Up a tree.

Susanna saw that Michael was on the edge of his seat, ready to shoot out of the car at a moment's notice. "Flynn."

He turned his head toward her, the lights that played in her eyes surprising him. "What?"

She smiled guilelessly. More melting went on inside him. If he wasn't careful, he was going to turn into a damn puddle soon.

"I don't bite," Susanna assured him.

"Why would you bite?" Michael looked at her, confused,

his thin eyebrows knitted together over the bridge of his nose. "People shouldn't bite other people."

"She doesn't," Flynn said gruffly as he tried to ignore Susanna's laughter. With a sigh of resignation, he got out of the car, slamming the door shut. Michael was out of the car ahead of him, dashing up the driveway with Billie. "All right, ten minutes."

The time limit was for both Michael and Susanna. It seemed safe enough. After all, what could happen in ten minutes?

Too late he remembered as he followed her through the front door, that championship games could be lost in less time than that.

The house wasn't what he had expected.

For some reason, he had been prepared to see a lot of clutter, photographs, knickknacks, mementos on every available surface, all vying for attention. She struck him as a saver. Instead, there was space, a feeling of vast space. The vaulted ceiling evident upon entry doubled the illusion of openness.

He liked that.

There was room here, room for a man to stretch out, to get comfortable. To breathe. Susanna's living room, with its green and dusty pink floral sofa and dark rose recliner surrounding a small white marble coffee table seemed almost Spartan in comparison to the clutter of his house. He wondered who had designed this room.

Susanna opened the front window and turned around to look at Flynn's reaction to her home. His face was an open book when he wasn't trying so hard to guard his thoughts. Susanna liked watching his emotions pass over it. "You look a little bemused."

He spread his hands out to either side, encompassing the room with this gesture. "Just taking in the decor."

"Do you like it?"

He rocked back slightly on his heels as he shoved his hands into his pockets. Expressing enthusiasm for things had never been easy for him. "It's all right."

She laughed, delighted. The man didn't give an inch. "Heady praise indeed."

He ignored the teasing comment. "Your husband pick out the furniture?"

"No, I did." Susanna led the way through the dining room to the country kitchen. She could tell her answer surprised him. "I like room when I move around."

That made sense, considering the fact that she seemed to always be moving. "That would keep you from bumping into the furniture as you streak through."

Crossing his arms before him, he leaned against the pale blue wall. The family room that was just beyond the kitchen was an echo of the living room. Except for the small plastic baseball figures that were spread out all over the floor in front of the television set, a testimony to an early game before school this morning.

She glanced at him as she poured water into the glass coffeepot. The corners of her mouth quirked in amusement. "You make me sound like the roadrunner in the Saturday-morning cartoons."

Yes, he supposed he did. But he thought it an apt description of her. "That was the impression I got, watching you on the field yesterday."

She opened the tin of chocolate chip cookies she had made earlier in the week for Billie and placed them on the kitchen table. "You have to move fast to be both mother and father." She nudged the tin toward Flynn, urging him to take one. "You should know that."

There was still a lot of things that he should know, things that he didn't know. He picked up a cookie and bit into it. The deep chocolate flavor exploded on his tongue. "I haven't got the hang of it yet."

She turned from the coffeemaker, a black, intimidating appliance with tubes and switches running over the length of it. One would need a degree in engineering just to turn it on, Flynn thought. He'd used an old dented metal drip pot for the last fifteen years. When he had tried to replace it recently, he found that there were none available in the stores. Not about to try anything new, Flynn contented himself with cleaning out the holes on the strainer with a toothpick when it warranted maintenance.

"Why would it be so difficult to raise a boy?" She had just envied him that last night. "You were one once," she reminded him. Empathy should make the job easier.

He reached for a second cookie. She had laced them with mint and he had a fondness for mint. "Yeah." Flynn nodded. "A hundred years ago."

The man was ridiculously determined to stick to this image of himself as old. "Oh, right." She pulled a dish towel from the rack and dried her hands. "I keep forgetting your advanced age."

She was laughing at him. He didn't appreciate that. "You don't even know how old I am."

She leaned her hip against the gray, tiled counter, studying him. He was, as Aunt Jane might say, very easy on the eyes. "You don't look old."

He shrugged, finishing what he realized was his third cookie. He pushed the tin farther back on the table. "Well, I feel old."

Susanna reached into the cupboard for a paper filter. Securing one, she glanced at him over her shoulder. "We all do at times."

"*And* I am a grandfather." The very word made him feel old.

It wasn't enough of a case for Susanna. "That doesn't automatically make you ready for a rocking chair." She frowned, hand on her hip. "Just how old are you?"

The woman was far too personal for his liking. Flynn almost caught himself about to tell her to mind her own business. But what was the harm in admitting it? "Forty-five."

Susanna dropped the filter on the tile, clutched at her heart and swayed, leaning against the counter. "And you still get around without a cane?" She straightened again, laughter punctuating her words.

He looked at her indignantly. She didn't seem to understand the natural progression of things. Of people. "You think it's a joke?"

"No." She sobered, but only slightly. The man was crying out for help, even if he didn't know it. He needed to lighten up. "But I think forty-five is young. It's all in your perspective, Flynn. Daisy Mae thought she was past her prime at seventeen."

Susanna opened the refrigerator door. Three coffee cans stood lined up one behind the other on the bottom shelf. She bent over to get them. "What's your pleasure?"

He blinked, watching the way her skirt hiked up on her thigh. No doubt about it. They were the best pair of legs he had ever seen. "What?"

Susanna looked over her shoulder. The impish grin on her face told him she had read the unguarded thought that had raced across his mind. "Coffee. I have regular, espresso and cappuccino."

He nodded at the ominous black object on her counter. "That gizmo can make all three?"

"And hum 'Amore Scusami' while it's doing it." Heaven knew it had cost enough. By all rights, it should tap-dance as well.

Strange. The woman was definitely strange. He'd have one cup of coffee and go. Quickly. "What do you normally have?"

"Well, I had espresso this morning. If I have another, I'll be up all night. Regular," she decided.

Because she felt warm, Susanna peeled off her jacket. The thin white cotton shell beneath it did an excellent job of re-affirming the initial impression Flynn had had yesterday. She was exceptionally well built. He had always admired a good figure. It spoke of health and discipline.

But right now, it spoke of other things that he didn't want to hear.

He turned his attention to her question, though it wasn't easy. "Make it two."

Flynn sat down at the table, his large frame making her kitchen appear small. He watched her as she moved about, measuring out the coffee, fishing out two cups and saucers from the cupboard. She moved quickly, fluidly, like the tempo of a fast song. He opened the top button on his shirt, suddenly needing air.

The sound of the boys shouting and laughing came in through the open window. In between the shouts was the jarring thud of the basketball as it missed the hoop and bounced against the garage door.

"Takes the paint off," he observed. When she raised her eyes quizzically to his face, he elaborated. "The basketball against the house."

She shrugged. It didn't faze her. "So does the sun. This way, he's having fun. The house can be repainted," she added philosophically. "He'll only be seven once."

Unable to help himself, Flynn toyed with another cookie. "Seems to me you've got this parenting thing pretty much down pat."

"Thanks. I just try to remember what it was like from the other end." She handed him a napkin and slid the cookie onto it with a grin. He might protest that he was old, but there was still a little of the small boy in him. "That was when I thought my parents knew everything."

The coffee was ready. She poured two cups and set them down on the table. Dragging the chair closer, she sat down next to him. Crowding him somehow. Or maybe it was just the scent of her perfume. Rather than dissipate during the course of the day, it seemed to have grown stronger, more intense. It was filling his head, weakening the resolve that should have remained strong.

She broke off a corner of a cookie, popped the morsel into her mouth and savored it. "Now I lie awake at night, worrying if I did this wrong, or that wrong."

She didn't strike him as the type to worry about anything. Parenting was just something she would instinctively know how to do. All women did. It was part of their genetic makeup. Or so watching Kelly and his daughters had made him feel.

"I'd say you were doing just fine." She took a sip of coffee and he absently followed suit. His eyes opened wider as the hot liquid lodged in his throat like a solid entity.

Susanna bit her lower lip. She had overdone it again. "Too strong?"

He managed to get it down, then coughed. "Depends on what you use it for." He cleared his throat again. "Asphalt comes to mind at the moment."

She flashed him an apologetic grin. "Sorry, Brett got me used to strong coffee." She rose and turned toward the pantry. "I'll get you some sugar."

"Milk." The single word struggled out like a plea and he had to clear his throat again.

She grabbed the half-filled carton of milk from the refrigerator and yanked it out. In her hurry to make amends, Susanna swung around and rammed her hip against Flynn as she placed the milk carton in front of him. The length of her thigh jarred his arm.

Something hot opened, then tightened within him as the outline of her body registered with every nerve ending he had, making anticipation spring to life. The pull was sudden and demanding, almost taking his breath away. It had been a long time since he had physically reacted to a woman. A long time since he had thought of women at all.

He was thinking of one now.

And he wasn't comfortable about it. Not in any way, shape or form.

Susanna looked down at Flynn, another apology on her lips. She wanted to apologize for the coffee, for her clumsiness. Both apologies evaporated on her lips as she saw the look of desire, dark and dangerous, in his eyes. Her mouth went dry, even as the center of her palms began to itch. She took a step back, away from him, rubbing her moist hands against the sides of her skirt.

"Sorry," Susanna mumbled. "I'm not usually this clumsy."

Flynn shook his head, dismissing her words. He didn't like what he was feeling, didn't like feeling at all. It opened up things, wounds, memories. Needs. He wanted none of that. None of them. His life was finally in order and he was finding his way again. What he was feeling now would throw everything back into chaos. He didn't want to redefine himself again. As it was, life was too complicated, too overwhelming just getting through each day.

Why the hell did this have to happen?

He rose quickly, as if backing away from his feelings. The chair tipped behind him as he sprang to his feet. He turned, trying to catch it before it crashed. Susanna reached out quickly, grabbing for the chair. Their hands touched, their bodies collided.

The chair fell, forgotten.

Hiding was something that had never sat well with Flynn. Neither had running away. Flynn had approached everything in his life head on. It was the only way to overcome things, to clear his path. He would have to face this situation that threatened to come into being if he was going to vanquish it. If he frightened her away now, he wouldn't have to deal with the situation, with his feelings any further. It would be out of his hands. He wouldn't be to blame.

Susanna saw it coming, saw the war going on inside of him. She watched first desire, then surprise and finally anger wash over him. She wasn't certain who Flynn was angriest with, her or himself. But right now, she didn't care.

Right now, all she wanted was for Flynn to hold her. To make her feel again. To touch that part of her that had been held in reserve for so very long.

Where had this devastating need come from? Flynn felt his knees almost give out beneath him. An ocean of feelings, all tugging from different directions advanced on him at once, tearing at him, trying to claim him. Guilt, desire, confusion.

And need. Need frightened him most of all. He never wanted to need again. And yet, at this moment, he did.

He sank his fingers into her hair, dislodging pins, taking hold of the silkiness, trying to anchor himself to something tangible.

His mouth touched hers even as an oath formed in his head, damning his own weakness, damning her for being here, for being accessible. And for being so incredibly desirable when he had no defenses. He closed his arms around her, pulled her against him, wishing her somewhere else.

Wanting her to be exactly where she was.

Open-mouthed, hungry, needy. It wasn't a gentle kiss. It wasn't meant to be. It was hot and passionate and was intended to make her afraid.

He wasn't expecting passion from her, wasn't expecting the devastating need he discovered within her, within himself.

Most of all, he wasn't expecting to be blown away.

Chapter Six

My God, what had he just done?

Flynn was stunned at his behavior. He had come in, against his better judgement, for a cup of coffee and had wound up holding a strange woman in his arms and kissing her. Worse, he wanted to do it again. He wanted to take that kiss further, to its logical conclusion. If his intentions in kissing her had purely been to frighten her, he had done the job royally on himself instead.

Speechless, confused, Flynn pulled away. He stared down at Susanna's face, bewildered at the incredibly small degree of control he seemed to possess when he was around her. He had never been impulsive before, never. And in the last year, he had prided himself on becoming emotionally independent.

So why had he felt this great need to kiss her? And why was he still feeling it?

He took a step away from her and backed up into the cap-sized chair that had triggered his downfall. Grateful for something to do, he bent down to pick it up. "I'm sorry," he mumbled to her.

Yes, he would say that. What else could she expect? But even though she had expected it, there still was that small prick of pain that nettled her.

"There's no need to be." Susanna's voice sounded oddly husky to her own ear. She cleared her throat, trying madly to steady herself internally. For a man who now looked as if he hadn't wanted to kiss her, he had certainly done a fantastic job of it. She couldn't remember ever feeling every part of her body vibrate this way, not over a kiss.

Flynn set the chair upright, shoving it under the table so hard it spilled the coffee. Avoiding her eyes, he nodded at the cup that had sloshed dark liquid over its sides. "Must have been your coffee."

Liar. You wanted to kiss me. Why can't you admit it? I can. She forced a smile. "I've got to remember the exact proportions I used."

Flynn dragged a hand through his hair, feeling totally out of place. He should have gone with his instincts and never set foot inside the house.

"I think it was a pound of coffee to six ounces of water." He made himself look at her. He was surprised to see hurt in her eyes. Why? What had he said? "Look, this wasn't supposed to have happened."

Next he'd be putting on a hair shirt to atone for having touched her. "I had no idea we were following a script." She curbed her hurt feelings. The man was stumbling. Sympathy budded. Maybe it was hard for him to accept the fact that he hadn't died along with his wife. That his needs hadn't, either.

Susanna placed a hand on his shoulder. "Flynn," she said softly. "It's all right."

"No, it's not." He lowered his voice. It would do no good to shout at her. It was himself he was angry with, not her. He sighed, shoving his hands into his pockets, wanting to shove himself into some small hole somewhere, far from everything. "I'm sorry. I shouldn't be yelling." He tried to make her

understand. He felt he owed it to her. "I haven't touched another woman since Kelly—" The right words wouldn't come.
After all, this wasn't about equations or launch patterns. He
was out of his element. "Well, since Kelly," he repeated helplessly. "That's over twenty-seven years if you count the time
we went together before we were married."

Flynn searched her face to see if she understood and wound
up wanting to bury his hands in her hair and drag her back to
him. God, he was a mess.

She smiled, wishing there was some guideline she could
follow, some way to make him not feel that he had committed
a cardinal sin. "I'm honored."

She wasn't supposed to be honored. She was supposed to
retreat, to forget about the whole thing. One of them had to.

He began to pace around the kitchen, a bull in a china shop
of emotions. "What I'm trying to say is that it's a matter of
hormones." And nothing else. He swore that to himself. It
was only his hormones overreacting.

Was he trying to insult her? To give her a polite brush-off?
No, she didn't think so. His struggle was too obvious for that.
Besides, there was something in his kiss, something warm,
needy. He had enjoyed kissing her. She was certain she hadn't
imagined it. "I'm not a child, Flynn. I know that's the way it
usually starts."

He turned to her, anger in his eyes. "There is no start because there's not going to be anything further." There couldn't
be. He wouldn't let himself get tangled up inside again. It
wasn't fair.

"Flynn. Flynn," she repeated a bit more loudly when he
didn't look at her, his expression a mixture of annoyance and
disorientation. Did he think she was some desperate female,
trying to lay a trap for him? She felt her own anger rise and
forced herself to push it aside. Two people arguing wasn't
going to solve anything. Especially since she wasn't sure what
the problem was. He wasn't the only one who had been
knocked for a loop here. "I'm not trying to do anything. *You*

kissed *me,* remember?'' If ever there was a mule-headed man—

She bit back her temper. ''Why don't we just...see?''

''See what?'' he asked, confused.

She smiled. ''What'' was the operative word here. ''Exactly.''

Flynn shook his head. What was she trying to say? ''Did I miss a turn here somewhere?''

He would be almost sweet in his confusion, if he wasn't being so difficult. ''Probably, but it'll come to you by and by.'' She thought of his resistance to what they had both experienced. ''Have you ever heard the old saying, life is what happens while you're making plans?''

He shrugged absently. Why was she spouting trite sayings at a time like this? ''No.''

''Don't get around much, do you?'' Susanna's eyes shone with amusement.

''My work and Michael keep me pretty busy.'' Why was he bothering to explain anything to her? He moved toward the living room. ''Look, I'd better go.''

She gestured toward the front door. Her amusement warred with annoyance because he was trying to make her feel that this was all her fault. That might make their encounter easier for him to accept, but it didn't make it right. Or true. ''The door's not locked.''

Flynn frowned. She was making it hard for him to blame anyone but himself for what had happened just now. But if she hadn't been there, if she hadn't been so damn desirable, if she had been Billie's father instead of his mother, it wouldn't have happened. So she was partially to blame.

He sighed. He was grasping at straws. It was his fault, and it wouldn't happen again. There was no reason for it to. He turned to leave when he remembered. ''You'll need a ride tomorrow?''

Susanna crossed her arms before her as she followed him. She felt suddenly cold, bereft. ''The car will be fixed Saturday.'' She was about to say that she would find a ride, but curiosity got the better of her.

Flynn realized there was no way out, not in good conscience at any rate. He couldn't just abandon her now. It would seem as if he was running. And though he wanted to, it wasn't his way. ''I'll be here at seven.''

She was about to ask if he was sure, but decided that would just get them into another round of conversation she didn't want to start. Besides, she did want to see him again. She wasn't certain what was happening between them or where it would go from here, but there *was* definitely something.

''I'll be ready,'' she promised. ''Oh, wait.'' She hurried to the kitchen and wrapped up six cookies in a rose-colored napkin. She returned and thrust them at Flynn. ''Here.'' Their hands touched as she gave him the bundle. This time, she couldn't help noticing the shiver of electricity that danced through her. Yes, definitely something. ''Why don't you take these for Michael? They're homemade.''

Flynn stared down almost dumbly at the cookies. ''Thanks.''

''Anytime.''

Her tone made him look down at her. He knew she wasn't talking about the cookies.

As far as he was concerned, he had no idea what he was talking about, what he was thinking, or even feeling. Later, he told himself as he shut the last few minutes out of his mind. He'd sort it out later.

With his free hand, Flynn yanked open the front door. ''Michael, we're leaving,'' he announced, stalking out of the house as quickly as he feasibly could.

Susanna followed, keeping a few feet between them. She figured he needed the space.

Michael jumped to attention at Flynn's tone of voice. He passed the basketball to Billie with one bounce and turned toward the sports car.

''Yes, Granddad.'' He hurried after Flynn and jumped into the front seat just as Flynn turned the ignition on.

Billie ran over to the passenger side, the basketball rakishly carried over to one side, under his arm. He'd seen the big boys do it this way at the schoolyard. His arm was straining to keep the ball in place. "Bye!"

"See you tomorrow," Michael called out over his shoulder as they sped away. The back tires squealed. Michael shifted in his seat to look straight ahead. He sat quietly for a moment, waiting for Flynn to say something.

When Flynn said nothing, Michael shifted restlessly in his seat. He peered at Flynn's face. Flynn saw an almost anxious look on Michael's face as the boy asked, "Why are you mad?"

"Dogs get mad. People get angry." Flynn knew he was nit-picking, but he didn't want to talk about it. He didn't even want to think about it. Which was why there seemed to be nothing else on his mind.

Michael's expression was puzzled but he was willing to agree. "Okay, why are you angry?"

Now he was taking his mood out on Michael. What the hell was wrong with him? "I'm not angry."

"Your face is," Michael pointed out.

And so was the rest of him. Angry at himself for giving in to what he took to be a purely physical reaction. Angry at Kelly for leaving him. Angry at the world at large. Forty-five and he was having an internal tantrum, he thought in disgust.

Michael's wistful voice interrupted his thoughts. "Is it Billie's mom?"

"Is what Billie's mom?" Flynn asked evasively. Did all kids ask this many questions at the wrong time?

"Is she the one who got you mad—angry?" Michael repeated patiently.

He couldn't begin to find the right way to explain this to Michael. He hadn't a clue himself. "It's been a long day, Michael."

"We only stayed there ten minutes, like you said."

That showed him how wrong he could be about how much damage could be done in under a quarter of an hour. The light before Flynn was turning yellow. Flynn stepped on the gas, getting through the intersection before the light turned red. "Sometimes, things happen fast."

Michael looked off, his small face growing solemn. "Yeah, I know."

Flynn heard the pain in the small voice. Guilt built on top of guilt. It had been a hell of an afternoon, all right. Damn, how had he managed to mess up so many things in such a short space of time? He searched for a way to make amends, at least with Michael.

He saw a mini-mall on the next corner. "Say, since you don't have any homework, what d'you say to going out for some pizza?"

Michael turned toward his grandfather. The solemn look dissolved. "At the arcade?"

"Sure, we'll shoot the works."

"Yeah!"

Flynn smiled at the bright, happy face, and felt a little better.

Susanna watched as the sports car sped down the block and turned, disappearing down the next street.

Coward, she thought.

With a sigh, she turned around. "I want you to start your homework, Billie. Dinner will be ready in half an hour." She passed Billie and echoed, "Aw, Mom," along with him as she ruffled his hair. They both laughed.

Billie followed her inside. She heard the sound of his sneaker-shod feet pounding up the stairs to his room. For a boy who only weighed forty-eight pounds, he sounded like a miniature elephant.

Walking into the kitchen, Susanna began to tick off numbers in her head in a mental countdown. She had gone from ten to three when the front door flew open again.

"Hi, Susie, where are you?"

Susanna smiled. Right on time. She braced herself, waiting for what she knew was going to come. "I'm in the kitchen, Aunt Jane."

On first glance, Jane Carter Hall Caldwell looked like a carbon copy of Susanna, except that she was an inch taller. It was only on closer examination that the small, fine lines about her bright gray-blue eyes and wide, inviting mouth could be detected. Susanna smiled as she thought about her aunt. Laugh lines Jane liked to call them, and then she would laugh to prove that they had been honestly earned. And Jane's laugh was loud and lusty, as was her approach to life. She believed that everyone should have a good time whenever possible. The fact that her niece seemed satisfied to live hers out quietly, closeted with ratebooks, data and dust greatly disturbed her and she didn't hesitate to speak her mind.

Wearing a pink pullover and white short-shorts that did a magnificent job of showing off the legs that she was still very proud of, Jane entered the kitchen.

Susanna was standing next to the stove, distracted, staring into the frying pan in her hand.

Jane joined her, looking over her shoulder. There appeared to be nothing wrong with the pan. "What's the matter?"

Susanna looked up, startled at the sound of her aunt's voice. Just for a moment, her mind had wandered. The sensation of Flynn's mouth pressed hotly against hers had suddenly washed over her. The image had come out of nowhere, and her breath had been snatched away, just as it had when it had actually happened. And then his apology had played itself back in her head.

Susanna roused herself. "Nothing. Why?" She placed the frying pan on the stove and slowly turned toward the refrigerator. She took out a package of skinless chicken breasts. She felt like making something special tonight.

Knowing the procedure, Jane handed her the bread crumbs and oil from the pantry. "You were frowning into your frying pan."

Susanna shrugged, accepting the bottle of oil in one hand, the container of bread crumbs in the other. "Sorry."

"Don't apologize to me." Jane took out an egg from the refrigerator and placed it on the counter next to the bowl Susanna had retrieved from the cupboard. "It's the frying pan's feelings you've hurt." Jane reached up from behind and placed her hands on Susanna's shoulders. Slowly, she massaged the twin knots. "So, is it about a man?"

Susanna almost purred. Jane's fingers kneaded just the right spots. Her aunt probably did it to get her mind off the fact that she was indulging in her favorite habit—prying into Susanna's affairs. But there was no use lying. From her window across the street her aunt missed nothing that went on in the neighborhood, and certainly nothing that transpired in her niece's life. "Yes."

Jane stopped massaging. Moving around to face Susanna, she clapped her hands together, rolled her eyes heavenward and exclaimed, "Finally," much the way Columbus must have when he first sighted the New World.

Jane, Susanna knew, would have liked nothing better than to see her married off. Susanna aimed the frying pan at Jane's midsection as if it were an extension of her hand. "You follow that up with 'hallelujah' and I'm cutting you out of the will."

Jane laughed, then nodded. Disposing of the empty plastic wrapper for her niece, she turned toward Susanna, curiosity flowing from every pore.

"So, what's he like?"

Jane's eagerness made Susanna smile. She had seen Jane peeking out the window and had seen the look she'd given Flynn. If she had been about ten years younger, Jane would have considered Flynn worth any effort.

Susanna thought of Flynn's grunted apology, of the annoyed look on his face. The frying pan went down on the burner a little too forcefully. "Impossible."

Jane's expression grew hopeful. "The most fascinating ones usually are."

Susanna looked at her aunt, swirling the first piece of chicken in the bread crumb mixture. "Is that why you've married so many of them?"

Jane shrugged as she picked up the chicken and placed it in the pan. She waited for the second piece as Susanna worked.

"Hey, once the mystery's gone, so am I. But enough about me." She plopped the next piece in. "Tell me about Mr. Johnny-Come-Lately."

Susanna knew that Jane's feelings regarding her marriages ran far deeper than she let on. There had been three. The first had ended when her husband died. The other two had ended in divorces that seemed amicable enough on the surface, but Susanna knew Jane had grieved privately, even though she had been the one to initiate the proceedings. She still got together with her ex-husbands occasionally. Susanna had met both of them and they were a lot friendlier to Jane than Flynn had been to her as he had hurried out.

Flynn. His reluctance, the fact that he seemed to be pushing her away with both hands, as if she were throwing herself at him, irritated Susanna. "Johnny doesn't want to come at all."

Jane moved the chicken around to make room for the last two pieces. "And that's stopping you?"

Susanna looked at her aunt oddly. "Shouldn't it?"

Jane shook her head. "Oh, Susie, Susie, where have I gone wrong?"

Susanna found she wasn't quite in the mood for jokes as she started on the next part of the meal. "I don't want to force him into anything, Aunt Jane. I just wouldn't feel—"

But Jane didn't let her finish. As she cleared away the remainder of the bread crumb mixture, she kept her eyes on her niece. "Hasn't anyone read you the rules of the game? This is for his own good."

Carrots tumbled out of their plastic bag onto the tiled counter. Susanna counted out six. "What is?"

"You." Jane turned and stroked her niece's cheek fondly as she smiled at her. She had no children of her own. Susanna was her older sister's daughter. Susanna knew that Jane had directed all her maternal instincts that had gone begging toward Susanna and Billie.

She took Susanna's hand in her own and held them. "Listen to me, Susie. If anyone was for a man's own good, you are."

It was much too soon to even be thinking of things like that.

Susanna drew her hands away and got back to preparing dinner.

"You don't know anything about the situation." She placed the first peeled carrot on the chopping block and diced it quickly. "Or the man. For that matter, I don't know that much."

Jane obviously saw no problems in the future. She scraped another carrot for Susanna. "Facts only get in the way."

"You would say that."

"Yeah, I would." Jane grinned, finished with the carrots. Everyone who knew Jane knew that facts and figures were things she left to her accountant. Jane went for the highlights, the grand picture. She wiped her hands on a nearby towel. "So, what can I do to help?"

Susanna thought for a moment. Everything was almost done. "You can make the salad."

"I mean with Mr. Shoulders-Out-To-Here." Jane spread her hands out wide as she rolled her eyes again.

"Stay out of the way. That's an order." One Susanna had little hope would be obeyed.

Jean read between the lines. "That means he's coming back, doesn't it?"

The woman was hopeless. "Not if you put bear traps out for him."

Jane washed off the chopping block. She looked over her shoulder at Susanna. "A snare?"

"Aunt Jane!" Susanna wouldn't put it past her aunt.

"Only kidding." She wiped dry the chopping block and put it away. "Loosen up, Susie. Life's too short to be serious."

That wasn't anything that Flynn would ever buy into, Susanna thought. "Well, he is. Very." She remembered what he had told her. "And with good reason."

Jane took out three dinner plates from the cupboard and placed them on the table. "Such as?"

"In the last year, his wife died and then his daughter was killed in an accident." Even as Susanna said the words, empathy flooded over her. How must he have felt, getting one blow on top of another? She was surprised he had managed as well as he had. She didn't know what she would do if anything ever happened to Billie.

Jane had heard all that she needed to hear. "He's going to need a lot of comforting."

Flynn would have disagreed. "What he seems to want is a lot of space."

Jane waved her hand at her niece's comment. "Men don't know what they want."

Susanna couldn't help grinning. She turned the heat down as the oil snapped at her, spitting hot trajectories through the air. It reminded her of his kiss. "But you do."

"Absolutely." Jane nodded her head firmly. She reached for the napkins, folding them mechanically and placing them at each setting. "I've had three husbands. And none of them left me," she reminded Susanna proudly. Her voice softened. "Except Kyle, and he didn't have any choice, poor lamb." It was thanks to his fortune that Jane was financially independent, but she owed Kyle a great deal more than that. It was Kyle, with his gentle, caring ways that had Jane firmly hooked on the concept of love and romance.

Susanna eyed the table. "You staying for dinner?"

"Am I invited?" Jane asked innocently, taking out three glasses.

Susanna laughed. "Always." She wavered. She didn't want the conversation at the table to center on Flynn's eligibility. She didn't want Billie getting his hopes up for no reason. "Just don't push this, okay?"

Jane held her hands up in mute surrender. "Okay. Fine. Oh, can I ask just one more question?"

Susanna sighed. She should have known better. "Just one more."

"What's my future nephew-in-law's name?"

Susanna stifled a frustrated scream. "Aunt Jane—" she began warningly.

"No, that's too confusing. We'll have to call him something else." Jane took out the bottle of diet soda and placed it in the center of the table, her hooded eyes dancing mischievously.

Susanna gave up. "His name's Flynn O'Roarke, he's a senior design engineer at Worth Aerospace—"

Jane's head bobbed up and down approvingly at each bit of information. "Sounds good."

"And he's a grandfather."

Jane's eyes narrowed. "A grandfather?"

Susanna nodded, turning the chicken pieces for the last time. "That little boy you saw him with was Michael, his grandson."

"A grandfather?" Jane echoed again incredulously. She eyed Susanna. "Well, if you don't want him—"

"I didn't say that."

Susanna stopped. Had she just said what she thought she had? Up until this very moment, she hadn't really thought about actually wanting the man, wanting him to be in her life.

Susanna raised her eyes to her aunt's face. The older woman was positively glowing.

"I believe the term," Jane said as she began draining the carrots for Susanna, "is 'gotcha!'" She looked very pleased with herself.

Susanna turned off the heat beneath the frying pan, feeling her own rise. "The term is justifiable homicide, Aunt Jane, if you don't drop this subject here and now."

Another innocent look crossed Jane's face. She was well versed in them. It was her, not Susanna, that Billie took after. "Consider it dropped.

"For now," she added softly as she turned away.

Chapter Seven

Flynn couldn't fall asleep that night. He tossed and turned until his sheets were a tangled mess at the foot of the bed. Giving up, he angrily kicked them off onto the floor. For what seemed like hours, he'd been staring at the moving shadow on his wall, cast there by the tree branches outside his window.

Restless, wired and utterly exhausted, Flynn sat up in bed. Frustration fueled his edginess as he stared into the darkness. It was hopeless. He was wide awake.

Normally, he could always sleep, anyplace, anytime. Kelly used to kid him that he could fall asleep standing up in the closet.

But not tonight.

Tonight the vision of blue-gray eyes, wide with surprise and desire, kept him from finding the solace he so desperately sought in sleep. He couldn't sleep because, among other things, his conscience was bothering him. How could he have let his impulses get the better of him; how could he have let himself kiss Susanna? After a lifetime with Kelly, how could he kiss someone else? It seemed wrong, disloyal. His weakness had thrown him into turbulent waters.

And yet—

Flynn rose, hiking up the waistband of his cutoffs that had sunk low on his lean hips. He crossed to the window and opened it. The night air was cool, damp, still. It didn't help to calm him.

There was something that was calling to him, whispering to his senses, stirring him. Something that was within Susanna's power to give him.

He sighed. His mind was wandering. And keeping him awake.

The entire night was a patchwork quilt of insomnia broken only intermittently by small squares of sleep. Rising at six, Flynn felt like hell.

A great way to face Friday, he thought darkly, finding his way into the kitchen. Michael was already up and at the table. Three different boxes of cereal surrounded his bowl. He was making his first decision of the day. When Flynn groped toward his own chair, Michael looked at him for a long moment, then asked Flynn if he was sick.

"No, I couldn't sleep last night."

"Oh," Michael murmured thoughtfully, settling on the box in the middle. "Billie's mom again?"

When Michael had come to live with him, Flynn had promised himself to answer each of the boy's questions truthfully. Honesty was to be the cornerstone of their relationship. "Eat your breakfast. You don't want to be late."

Michael dutifully filled his bowl with multicolored little balls of cereal, then poured an ocean of milk over them until the round balls bobbed precariously close to the top. There was enough sugar there, Flynn mused, to charge up three children for a week.

Flynn sought his own source of energy. Coffee. Hot and potent. One sip had him thinking that his own was like brown water compared with the coffee Susanna had served him yesterday afternoon.

Coffee, he thought ruefully, taking another long swallow, wasn't the only thing she had served up hot and potent yesterday. If he closed his eyes, he could still feel her mouth, her lips parting beneath his, inviting him to take, offering him what he needed so badly.

Damn, he didn't need anything at all.

Flynn finished his coffee in another two gulps, instructed Michael to hurry along and went upstairs to prepare for his morning ordeal. They had to pick up Susanna at seven.

Susanna and Billie were waiting for him, just as they had been the day before. She wore red today. A two-piece red suit that bespoke power and femininity all in one statement.

As if she needed the color to be noticed, he thought.

It wasn't until after they had dropped off the boys at school that Susanna said anything other than hello to Flynn. Once they were alone, Susanna felt obligated to fill the silence between them. She was relentlessly cheerful. Susanna was determined to act innocently oblivious to the fact that life as they both knew it had been irrevocably changed in her kitchen yesterday.

As tired as she was cheerful, Flynn attempted to ignore her and merely answer in monosyllables whenever she required a response. He found that it was probably easier to ignore a flash flood as it engulfed you than it was to ignore Susanna.

He glared at her as they stopped for a red light. "Are you always this annoyingly cheerful in the morning?"

She was stubbornly determined not to let him ruin anything. Just because he was afraid of being open didn't mean that she was. "It's a beautiful day, it's Friday, and my son is going to get some helpful tips about his batting, which should make him very happy. Why shouldn't I be cheerful?"

The light changed and they were moving again. "Because it's morning."

She had already guessed that he wasn't a morning person

after seeing him yesterday. But that didn't seem enough of a reason for him to behave like a bear that had been stung by a bee. "And?"

And you kept me up over half the night. But he knew he couldn't say that.

She leaned forward and saw the dark smudges beneath his eyes. Though there could have been a dozen reasons for their presence there this morning, still Susanna felt heartened. She hadn't slept all that well herself. "Didn't you get any sleep last night?"

"Minimal," he bit off.

"Noisy neighbors?"

Was it his imagination, or was her tone just a little too innocent? Flynn glanced at her, then looked back at the road. "Disruptive neighbors," he amended. It was as far as he would go in admitting the effect she had had on him. He didn't know how to lie believably.

"Oh." Susanna smiled to herself as she rolled his words over in her mind and savored them. She felt vindicated. No matter how much this young grandfather with the age complex protested, yesterday's incident was not something he was going to casually wipe clean from his mind.

Which was good, because neither could she.

Faced with her unmitigating cheerfulness and optimistic viewpoint, Flynn finally began to relax a little by the time they approached her office building.

"See you this afternoon." She made it sound as if they had been doing this everyday for the past month instead of just twice this week. Worse, she had him almost believing it.

"Right," he murmured.

Susanna picked up her briefcase and began to climb out of the car. Impulse seized her. She turned around and surprised both of them by leaning over and kissing Flynn's cheek.

The imprint of her lips was so light, the kiss so fleeting, so unexpected that he hardly felt it at all. And yet it burned itself into his skin.

He splayed his fingers over the spot almost immediately and stared at her back as she slid out. A bittersweet feeling filtered through him no matter how hard he tried to shut it out. "What was that for?"

She wasn't even certain why she had done it. Maybe because she felt so happy. Maybe because she just wanted to share the feeling. She shrugged. "You looked like you needed it."

His eyes darkened. "I don't need anything." And the sooner Susanna realized that, the better off they would both be.

Susanna looked at him. *That's what you think.*

Aunt Jane's words replayed themselves in her head. Men didn't know what they wanted. Aunt Jane, Susanna decided, was a very wise woman.

"Okay, have it your way." She winked at Flynn. "*I* needed it."

He didn't know what to say to that, but then he didn't have to make a comment. Susanna had turned away and was already hurrying up the steps to the building's entrance.

Faster than the speed of light, he thought.

That served to describe both Susanna and the unsettled feeling she seemed to transfer into his veins. The ocean gently lapped at the shore less than a mile away. The breeze that drifted from it flirted with the hem of her flared skirt as she went up the steps. Flynn caught himself looking longer than he was supposed to.

It wasn't that he was afraid of intimacy, he told himself as he backtracked to Worth Aerospace. He just didn't want it in his life. Not the kind she represented. The kind of intimacy that had you looking forward to seeing someone, to letting them slowly infiltrate your life and make you depend on them.

He was determined to depend on nothing and no one but himself.

Parking at the compound was difficult. He knew it would be. Dropping Susanna off had cost him precious minutes, minutes that meant the difference between getting a good parking space by the main building and getting one by the rear gate. For ten minutes he cruised up and down the aisles, looking for an opening. His mood was close to foul by the time he entered his office.

It didn't improve during the course of the day.

The problem, he thought as he got into his car eight hours later, was that part of him was actually looking forward to this. He was looking forward not just to playing with his grandson and helping Susanna's son learn how to bat properly, but to Susanna's company. He muttered under his breath as he jammed his key into the ignition and turned on the engine. It was as if he were at war with himself. Flynn didn't know which made him more uncomfortable: being drawn to the similarities or the differences between Susanna and his late wife.

He had no business, he told himself sternly, being drawn to either. Romance was for the young. He thought of Susanna's assessment of his appearance. The chronologically young, he amended with a slight twist of his lips. He had had his good fortune.

Besides, getting involved with someone meant depending on someone else for his happiness. And that was a trap Flynn was completely committed not to fall into again. Once had almost been fatal. There would be no hope for him the next time around.

She was, Susanna thought as she stood before the tall, imposing glass doors of Palisades Mutual Insurance Company waiting for him, too much of a Good Samaritan. Her mother had always scolded her about that, warning her that she would be hurt more times than not, giving her heart so unconditionally. But Susanna couldn't stand seeing anyone suffer, not even a disgruntled bear of a man.

A disgruntled bear whose one kiss, she thought with a smile, had almost melted every single one of the bones in her body.

"Hi, Susanna, need a lift?"

She turned to see Dave Ackerly walking out. At six-two, with just a hint of gray touching his temples and wearing an expensive suit that would set most people back two weeks' salary, David Ackerly looked as if he belonged between the pages of a fashion magazine. And had the two-dimensional personality to match. Over the last three years, he had tried, unsuccessfully, to ask her out several times. Susanna had found herself totally unmoved and uninterested. She saw no light in his eyes, no spark. Smooth, intelligent, mannerly, with never a hair out of place, he held about as much attraction for her as wax fruit.

Her taste, she thought with a smile, ran to frowns and grudgingly offered good deeds.

"No, I'm waiting for one, thanks."

He took a step closer, as if that would make her change her mind. "Sure I can't take you home?" His smile broadened invitingly. "Your ride doesn't seem to be here."

She found the smell of his cologne stifling. With an inward sigh of relief, she saw Flynn approaching. To the rescue again, she thought.

"No, there's my ride now." She pointed toward the silver convertible. "See you." Gratefully, she ran off as David stood, shaking his head and watching her go.

She all but bounced into his car the way Michael had the day before.

"Friend of yours?" Flynn nodded toward David. He had imagined David trying to put the move on Susanna as he had approached and something possessive had reared its head as temper licked at his insides. If he didn't know any better, he would have said he was jealous. Except that he had never been jealous, not in all the years he could remember. Why would he be jealous now, about a woman he hardly knew?

"David?" This time, she rather liked the way he had growled his question. "No, not really. We work on the same floor. He's an underwriter."

Flynn disliked David on sight. He looked like a mannequin. It was eighty degrees and the man was wearing a jacket. And looked comfortable. Flynn's was slung over the rear seat, with his tie stuffed into the pocket. "Am I supposed to be impressed?"

"No, just informed." She'd caught the note in his voice and smiled to herself. His scowl would break his face if he didn't stop soon. "Hard day?"

"No, nothing out of the ordinary," he answered, careful to look at the road and not her. No, that wasn't true. *She* was out of the ordinary for him.

Susanna settled into the seat, shifting so that she could put her seat belt on. She bit her lower lip as she regarded his expression. It hadn't changed that much from this morning. Maybe he hadn't been jealous just now. Maybe he just growled about everything. "Billie is really looking forward to this afternoon, but if you'd rather not—"

He jerked his head toward her. "Why wouldn't I?"

She shrugged helplessly. The man was impossible to figure out. "Well, for one thing, you're grimacing. I don't want to be accused of forcing you into anything. If there's something else you and Michael would rather be doing, I don't want to stand in your way."

She was offering him a way out. Faced with it, he realized he didn't want one. Not when it meant disappointing a little boy. At least, that was the excuse he gave himself. Digging deep, he tried to sound properly apologetic. "Look, if I'm biting your head off, I'm sorry. It's just been a long day tacked on to a long night."

Apologies always had the same effect on her. Any annoyance Susanna might have been harboring immediately vanished. "Then you're coming over?"

"Yes." A singsong voice in his head chanted, *You'll be sorry, Flynn.*

Susanna let out a relieved sigh. "Good. Otherwise, Billie and I will be eating pot roast sandwiches for at least a week."

He took the turnoff that led toward Michael's day-care center. "Doesn't it take a long time to cook a pot roast?" Flynn vaguely remembered Kelly mentioning something about pot roast taking hours to prepare. He certainly didn't want to stay at Susanna's house for hours. Ten minutes had nearly proven fatal the last time.

This was a mistake.

She glanced at her watch. Dinner should be done within half an hour of their arrival. "Oh, I started it this morning." She saw the quizzical look enter his eyes. "I'm making it in my crock pot."

"Crock pot?" he parroted. What the hell was a crock pot?

She grinned. Flynn said the name as if the appliance was some ancient form of torture. She wondered if he knew what to do with a microwave and what mealtimes must be like at his house. "Never mind. I'll show you when we get home. Dinner'll be ready by the time you feel like taking a break."

Home. She made it seem so natural, Flynn thought. Almost—he quickly stopped that thought and promised to keep a closer guard on his mind.

Michael ran out to meet them, leaving his teacher waving in the background. Conversation immediately switched from pot roasts and crock pots to baseball and the endless weekend that loomed ahead.

Billie was running alongside the car before Flynn could bring it to a full stop in Susanna's driveway. "Hi! I thought you'd never get here!" His greeting was for Flynn. "Oh, hi, Mom."

"I live for these warm, enthusiastic welcomes," she told Flynn with a laugh as she got out of the car. "Hi yourself."

On the far side of the driveway Billie had dragged out every single piece of baseball-related equipment Susanna had bought for him in the last year. Flynn looked at the impressive pile and let out a low whistle. "You've got enough here to outfit a minor-league team."

"He said he needed it all." Susanna kissed the top of Billie's head. He wiggled out of her grasp, embarrassed.

"It's okay," Flynn confided to the boy. "She kissed me, too."

"Yeah?" Billie's eyes grew large and hopeful.

Flynn knew he had made a tactical mistake in his efforts to relieve Billie's discomfort.

"Well, I'll leave you men to your game. Dinner will be ready in a little while," she promised.

Flynn watched her disappear into the house, swinging her briefcase at her side. He could have sworn he heard her humming.

"You gonna stare, or play?" Michael asked impatiently.

Flynn swung around and tossed the ball he had been holding to Michael. "Play!"

Michael jumped and caught the ball. The boys laughed gleefully as they fell upon the mass of gloves, bats and extraneous paraphernalia that went into making up a game. Flynn felt himself beginning to relax as he applied himself to tackling Billie's problem and forgetting about his own.

With Michael serving as catcher, Flynn went back and forth between pitching and showing Billie how to swing. The method was cumbersome at best. But when he attempted to use Michael as a pitcher, things went from bad to worse. As a pitcher, Flynn observed, Michael made a great bowler.

"I think you need a fourth to even things out."

Flynn turned toward the woman who had made the offer. For a moment, he thought Susanna had abandoned her crock pot, whatever that was, and had come out to join them. Though it annoyed him to react this way, a shaft of tension immediately splintered through the lower part of his abdomen.

But if it was Susanna, she was approaching from the wrong direction. This woman was crossing the street, coming from the tidy one-story building Susanna had told him yesterday belonged to her aunt.

As the woman walked toward him, Flynn realized that she was at least several years older than Susanna and a little more shapely. She carried herself well and with pride, as if the years that had advanced on her didn't trouble her one bit.

"Hi, I'm Jane, Susanna's aunt." Jane extended her hand, waiting for Flynn to take it. When he did, she gave him a firm, no-nonsense grip that had him liking her immediately. Hands on her hips, Jane regarded the three men thoughtfully. "Seems to me that you could do with a pitcher."

"Can you pitch?" Flynn asked, amused. He remembered the way Susanna had thrown the ball.

"Can I pitch?" Jane laughed as she picked up a glove from the driveway. Her hands were small, like Susanna's. Still, the glove was a tight fit. She pounded it expertly, making a serviceable indentation in the palm. "Does the sun set in the west?" She grinned at Flynn. "My second husband played in the majors for two years." She positioned herself opposite Billie. "Let's play some ball, handsome."

Flynn got up behind the boy and wrapped his hands around the bat over Billie's. He watched as Jane wound up. If Susanna had an aunt so obviously versed in the game, then why hadn't *she* given Billie the appropriate pointers? He began to smell a rat. Then he realized Jane was holding the ball in her left hand. He supposed it might be difficult for a lefty to correct a problem for a righty.

The ball sailed past him, into Michael's glove.

"Gotta think fast, handsome," Jane said laughing.

The noise from the street had Susanna pushing aside the white nylon curtain and looking out the living-room window. What she saw made her smile as a contented warmth spread all through her. Her aunt, Michael and Flynn were all involved in helping her son attain his heart's desire—a healthy swing. Behind her, on the kitchen counter, the crock pot was coming to the end of its day-long preparation. It wouldn't go anywhere, she thought, opening the front door to watch the practice for a few minutes.

She folded her arms across her chest and stood in the doorway, quietly observing. Billie seemed to be in his element, lapping all this up. A bittersweet feeling shot through her. Her son needed this, needed this kind of male contact. She wished with all her heart that there had been someone for her after Brett, someone she could have loved enough to give Billie the sort of life that a lot of little boys took for granted.

Her eyes strayed to Flynn as he hunched over the boy's small frame, his arms wrapped around the bat, his body poised to stay as clear of Jane's ball as possible. He looked as if he was having fun, as well. Relaxed, the wary, guarded look gone from his face, he looked more like a boy than a senior design engineer with the weight of the world on his broad shoulders. He was handsome, she observed. Very handsome. She wondered if he knew. Probably not. He seemed oblivious to a lot of things.

And stubborn as hell.

Susanna sighed. Just her luck. The first man who made her feel absolutely anything since Brett had left her life and he was hung up on age and probably a whole lot of things she couldn't begin to unscramble.

Leave well enough alone. She eased the front door closed and returned to the kitchen.

She knew it was good, sound advice. And she knew that she wouldn't pay attention to a word of it. It just wasn't in her nature.

Dinner was dynamic. Michael had heartily told her so at least three times, each time he took another helping. He, Billie and Jane had dominated the conversation at the dining table, leaving little leeway for Flynn to say much of anything. He hardly seemed like the same man who had played so energetically with the boys only half an hour ago.

Susanna wondered if it was her, if she made him this uncomfortable. And if that was a good sign.

"Well, who's for dessert?" Aunt Jane asked, pushing her plate back. Two small hands shot up in reply.

The pot roast was gone, as were most of the string beans and baked potatoes. Susanna wondered where any of them would find the room for dessert. "I have some ice cream in the refrigerator," she began, rising.

Jane leaned over and placed her hand over her niece's, stopping her. "That's not any fun." She turned toward the two boys. "We want choices, don't we, boys?"

Two sets of small eyes looked at Jane questioningly.

"How about a ride to the ice-cream parlor?" she suggested, already on her feet. "Over two dozen flavors to choose from."

"Okay," Susanna agreed. The dishes could wait.

"Who invited you?" Jane asked innocently. Susanna looked at her as the boys giggled. Jane winked at them. "I want the exclusive company of two very interesting ball players."

"What's 'clusive?" Billie asked.

"*Ex*clusive," Jane repeated. "You and Michael." She nodded to Susanna. "You and handsome here can have the ice cream in the refrigerator," she instructed cheerfully. "C'mon, boys—" she waved them on to the door "—I have to get my purse."

They began to follow her like mice scampering after the Pied Piper. But Michael stopped at the doorway, one foot over the sill, hesitating. "Is it okay?" he asked Flynn hopefully.

Flynn wanted to say no, it wasn't okay to leave him alone with Susanna. That he needed Michael's small frame as a buffer against his own feelings. But he couldn't very well put any of that into words.

Flynn waved him on. "Go ahead. Just don't get sick." He dug into his pocket to give Jane money, but she shook her head.

"My treat, handsome." She gave a wave to Susanna and left.

Flynn felt like the last one left on the deck of the *Titanic* just before it went under. He told himself he was being foolish. He looked over to see Susanna gathering dishes together. He needed to have something to do, something to talk about. "Need help with that?"

"Sure." She mustered her best encouraging smile. Children and wild, skittish animals responded best to gentleness. "You can help me take these out to the kitchen and stack them in the dishwasher if you like."

He didn't want to say what he'd like. They both knew.

Bland topics were safest. "Dinner was very good." He

picked up the remaining dishes she had stacked and followed her to the kitchen.

"Thank you." She nodded toward the counter. He set the pile down next to hers and started scraping them. "I like to cook." She opened the door of the dishwasher and began to place the plates in the rack. "I don't paint or write and I'm not very good with my hands. Cooking is the only creative outlet I have. I don't get to do it nearly often enough though. Most nights it's spaghetti and meat sauce."

He remembered the feel of her hands, soft and light on his shoulders, creating swirls of sensations within him. No, he wouldn't say that she wasn't good with her hands. She was *too* good.

He moved out of the way as she took out the dishwashing detergent from beneath the sink and measured out just enough. Yellow crystals rained into the tiny compartment. "I'm sure Michael welcomed the change from sandwiches." Watching her, Flynn made a mental note to give his dishwasher a try the next time the dishes piled up.

"Is that what you've been living on?"

He nodded. "That, fast food and those little self-contained dinners that you boil."

"Well, you can come by any time you want." She slammed the dishwasher door, turned around and came face-to-face with Flynn. Pulses began to hammer to a new, faster beat. "For dinner," she added haltingly, her breath catching in her throat as she looked at his eyes. They had grown dark again. And pulled her toward him like a magnet. She felt herself losing ground fast. "And someone to talk to, if you'd like." The words dripped from her lips. Why was coherent thought suddenly such a lost art? "I've been through all this, you know. I know what it's like." Her voice lowered to a whisper that feathered along his skin. "I know what you're thinking."

"I don't think you have any idea what I'm thinking," he murmured, threading his arms around her waist, finally surrendering to the craving that had awakened yesterday.

Her mouth felt dry. "Then why don't you tell me?"

Chapter Eight

He brought his mouth down to hers and completely lost his bearings, his way home again.

The sweet taste of her lips, the enticing scent of her breath, the feel of her body as it curved against his heightened Flynn's excitement and magnified his pleasure. It was as if he had terminated a year-long fast and was finally getting his first real taste of food.

He plunged his hands into her hair, cupping the back of her neck as he slanted his mouth over hers again. He needed to feel her, his fingertips sending messages to his brain that she was real, that she was here.

Needs ravaged him, remaining unsatisfied. The more he got, the more he wanted. At each plateau, he went begging, and she was there to meet his demands, which continued to mushroom until he ached.

His head spun.

There were no words to describe how he felt at this moment, no way to relate it to anything that had come before. She was all things to him, shy, eager, giving, taking. Her body felt soft and supple and so sublimely wonderful against his lean, hard frame. Every shred of his being was aware of her, only her. Nothing else existed in the universe beyond this one small woman who had cast him to the depths of agony one moment, the pinnacles of ecstasy the very next.

His hands roamed her back, eagerly pressing her closer, committing each subtle curve to memory. How could someone feel so frail, so delicate and still make such cataclysmic sensations erupt within him?

He held her tighter, closer, afraid that if he loosened his grip those wonderful feelings would fly away, escape, leaving him to return to his world, empty, lonely.

Hunger. Flynn had never known such hunger. He wanted to carry her upstairs to her bedroom and make love to her lyrically, passionately, endlessly. Only the fact that the others would be returning soon stopped him from acting on the overwhelming impulse.

Impulse. Flynn felt like some misguided youth, stumbling into his first romance.

But he wasn't some misguided youth. He was a mature man with an entire life already behind him. How could this be happening now? How could he be at these crossroads again? He wasn't up to it anymore. He didn't want the responsibility of a relationship. Or the pain that inevitably went with it.

And yet, holding Susanna, wanting her, made him feel alive again.

She made him feel alive again.

But this wasn't just happening in a vacuum. If he let go, if he let himself feel, then a whole host of other things would follow as a result. He couldn't divorce himself from that. He couldn't just take and then walk away. He wasn't that kind of man.

Flynn drew away and framed her face in his hands, his eyes searching hers for an answer to his dilemma. All he saw was desire mixed with wonder, anticipation. It was the sort of look small children had on Christmas morning as they stood in front of a tree with a mountain of gifts bursting under it. She was beautiful, and just looking at her made something quicken inside him. He refused to think of it as his heart.

His breathing was far from steady. He heard his own blood roaring in his ears, his own needs hammering through his body, demanding release. It had been so long since he had felt like more than half a man. Too long.

As he trailed his lips along the hollow of her throat, he felt her pulse jump. Her response made him ache to take her, knowing he couldn't. The words seemed to flow out of him on their own, against all reason. "I want to make love to you."

She gripped his forearms, pleased, touched. And filled with the bittersweet ache of desire. She longed to be made to feel totally alive again, to have that special pleasure exploding within her. "With me."

He blinked, confused at her response. "What?"

She smiled, her cheeks brushing against his palms as her smile spread. "These days, you don't make love *to* a woman, you make love *with* her." She placed her hands on top of his as they still framed her face. Her own hands hardly began to cover his. He had large hands, powerful hands. But they felt so gentle against her face, as if he was afraid he'd hurt her. "We share the process. Together."

Something else that had changed, he thought, while he had been safely, comfortably married to Kelly. He was beginning to feel as if the whole world had changed and he was out of step. He didn't belong in this part of life anymore. His path was somewhere farther down the road.

So what was he doing, wandering around like Alice in Wonderland, going from one unique sensation to another, looking for the way home, yet tarrying too long?

"It'd be pretty lonely, doing it by yourself," Susanna murmured when he made no response. She turned her head slightly and brushed a light kiss against his palm.

Fire licked at his loins.

She looked up and saw the war raging within him. "You're going to say you're sorry again, aren't you?" She thought, this time, that her heart would be badly bruised if he did. She didn't want him to be sorry. She wanted him to be glad.

He started to agree, but hesitated. It wasn't the truth and she deserved that at least. He couldn't give her anything else.

"No, I'm not sorry." He moved aside the wisp of hair from her face. "I'm only sorry that this is happening now, instead of at the right time."

Was he trying to say that he wished he had met her first instead of Kelly? She didn't know. But it wasn't an excuse she would accept. Nor let him hide behind, either. "Anytime is the right time when two people care about each other."

He let her assumption go without comment. To deny that he cared would be to lie. It seemed to be a given at this point, however she wanted to define the word "care." Flynn knew he liked her, he knew what he had here had gone a step beyond mere physical attraction, though the pull of that was slowly undoing him. "It isn't as simple as that."

She drew his hands from her face and then linked her fingers with his. "Nothing is completely simple, but it only gets complicated if you let it."

No, she was wrong; it was far too complicated already. "I'm not single."

The words jolted her. Was there someone else, after all? Had he lied when he'd told her yesterday that he hadn't been with anyone else since his wife? No, she didn't really believe that.

Silently she led him into the living room, to the sofa. She sat, urging him down beside her. And waited for him to explain.

He stared at the white marble coffee table and saw a small fissure at one corner. He curbed the urge to trace it, to feel something cool that would smother the burning ardor he felt gripping him. "I have Michael, and Stephanie and Julia to consider."

Susanna let out the breath she had been holding. She could understand commitment. Admire it. It was just one more thing she liked about him. "And I have Billie. It makes for a fuller life."

Why didn't she understand? He had fallen in love with Kelly when there had been nothing else in his life. She had been the beginning of his life. With her, he had faced college, parenthood and the challenges of his career. That was all in its place now. He couldn't begin to reshuffle his life and start over. "It makes for trouble. My plate's already too full."

She took his analogy one step further. "Life is a feast, not a diet."

He turned to her, a rebuttal on his lips. He made the mistake of looking at hers. A feast. Yes, that would be the word to describe what it was that he had found on her lips. A feast. And he had been starving.

"Oh, God, Susanna. What are you doing to me?" His fingers tangled in her hair and he pulled her to him, against his will, against everything that he held as logical. He couldn't operate on two levels this way. Right now, the only level that counted was that he wanted her, that his body vibrated from wanting her.

It was the first time she had heard him say her name. Sunshine spread within her.

Susanna gave her friendship readily, her affection when it was needed and her understanding without reservation. But her body was something that she had given to only one man before. She had given her love and her body freely to only Brett. She had gone to him without hesitation. It had been right. She had known it, felt it.

Just like she knew it now.

She caught her breath as she felt Flynn's hand edge toward her chest. Large hands, striving so hard to be gentle as he cupped her breasts through the silk of her blouse. Trembling, she felt herself shiver at his very touch. Oh, God, it had been so long.

Tears formed in her eyes as she clung to him.

His kisses grew deeper, more demanding, his need almost savage as he tried to harness it, to hold himself back for both their sakes. He felt as if he were free-falling. There was no control, no restraint.

Flynn knew that he could very easily become addicted to this, to her. A veritable prisoner of his own desires, of what she held out to him with both hands. He had never felt this sort of rush before.

Dependent.

The thought ricocheted through his head. His body snapped to rigid attention, as if he had suddenly been thrown headfirst into ice-cold water. One step before the plunge, he slowly, cautiously backed away. That had been close. Too close. He'd have to be very, very careful not to let it happen again. But at what price? The loss that would be his suddenly filled him with a melancholy yearning that left him bereft. God, he hated common sense.

Dazed, on the brink of falling over into a wild, endless abyss whose boundaries were comprised of walls of sheer emotion, Susanna could only stare at Flynn as he pulled away. "What's the matter?"

He held her by her shoulders, held her in place. Held her away from him. "I can't."

She tried to piece together an explanation and ignore the hurt she felt welling up inside. How could he cast her aside so easily? A spark of temper flared.

"Can't what? Kiss me? Hold me? You're already doing all of that. Can't care for me?" Her voice cracked. She struggled for control. This thing between them had happened fast, so fast. Like lightning flashing across a sky that had been bright and peaceful only a moment before. "I think that's out of your hands, too."

He couldn't look at her. If he did, he'd falter. Again. "This is wrong."

"Why?" she demanded. Why couldn't he unlock what was inside? He wanted to. She could feel it. Taste it. Couldn't he?

"Because."

She rose, surprised that her limbs could actually manage to hold her up. Everything felt shaky from her neck down. Well, that certainly explains everything, she thought, but swallowed her sarcastic retort. You learn something about yourself all the time, she thought. She had just learned that she could be hurt, badly. Susanna had believed herself beyond that by now. "Flynn, it's not wrong to open up, to need."

"Yes, it is." He slapped his hands against his thighs as he rose, angry with himself for having let things go too far. He hadn't been fair to her. "And I don't—"

"—Need anything, yes, you already told me." Susanna sighed as she heard a car pull up across the street. That would probably be Jane and the boys. Just as well. She didn't know how much more of an emotional roller coaster ride she could handle tonight. "Well, right now it's a moot point what either one of us needs. Your marines have landed."

"What?"

She nodded toward the front door as she tucked her blouse into place. "Unless I miss my guess, Aunt Jane has brought Michael and Billie back."

The words were no sooner out of her mouth than the door flew open. Jane shepherded the two lively boys before her. Each was wearing globs of several different shades of ice cream on his shirt like badges of combat. The older woman took one look at Susanna and Flynn and her pleased smile widened. Though they had frantically smoothed and patted in an effort to make themselves look presentable, there was no mistaking their slightly mussed appearance, or what it implied.

"I could take them out to the arcade," Jane offered, half turning toward the door again.

Susanna shook her head, grabbing Jane's arm before her aunt could be off and running again. "It's been a long evening, Aunt Jane. I think Flynn would like to go home now."

"Oh." Jane looked from Susanna's face to Flynn's.

Susanna made it sound as if he were running. And he was, Flynn thought. Running to preserve the safe little slice of life that he had managed to carve out in the last fifteen months. But he didn't have to like the way that sounded. "Let's go, Michael."

"Aw, do we have to?" the boy said, pouting, then abruptly stopped, withdrawing.

Susanna saw and wondered at the sudden change.

"It's getting late, Michael," Flynn said, placing his hand firmly on the boy's shoulder. Michael turned and walked obediently out of the room in front of his grandfather.

Billie bracketed Flynn's other side. "Will you be back?" he asked Flynn hopefully.

It was the look in Billie's eyes and not the demands of his own body, Flynn told himself, that had him agreeing. "I'll be back," he told him.

Billie followed them to the door. Susanna trailed behind. If Flynn wanted space, she'd give the insensitive lout space.

"There's a game tomorrow," Billie reminded Flynn as they reached the door. "If you come early, you could maybe coach me some more. I really learned a lot tonight."

Flynn almost laughed. So had he, he thought ruefully. And then he thought of tomorrow, and of seeing Susanna again. It was too soon. Who could he get to take Michael to the game tomorrow? Perhaps if he—

No, damn it, he had never been a coward before. He wasn't about to start being one now. He had enough fortitude to resist what he knew was bad for him. "We'll see," he told Billie.

Flynn knew he couldn't leave without saying something. Steeling himself, he looked over his shoulder at Susanna. Her chin was raised, but he could see the look in her eyes, the hurt she was trying to hide. "Thanks for the meal and everything." Lord, that sounded so lame.

"At least the meal turned out well," she said with a purposely studied shrug. "The 'everything' we'll just have to work on."

A small, sad smile played on her lips. He felt a twinge of conscience that he was responsible for that. On impulse, Flynn cupped Susanna's chin in one hand and brushed a kiss over her mouth. The smile, he could feel beneath his lips, widened. And grew genuine. He thought he heard something like a little cheer coming from Billie, but he wasn't certain. It was hard to hear anything with that buzzing going on in his ears.

"It all turned out well. It's not you, it's me," Flynn told her quietly, and walked out with Michael.

Susanna watched him go, then closed the door. "No," she whispered to herself. "It's going to be us. Somehow, in some capacity, it's going to be 'us.' You just don't know it yet."

She turned around to see her aunt and her son grinning at each other. For them, it seemed simple. But as Flynn had said earlier, it was a lot more complicated than what it seemed. "I wouldn't break out the champagne just yet, you two."

Billie made a face. "I don't like champagne. How about grape juice?"

Susanna laughed and hugged him to her, grateful that he was in her life.

"Grape juice it is."

Flynn's plan was a simple one. He intended to bring Michael to the playing field, make some sort of excuse about catching up on work he had brought home with him and then leave. He grudgingly conceded that it might be the coward's way out, but in this case, it was the more prudent approach. Besides, lots of parents dropped off their children on the field and then went to run errands. The game would be over by noon and he'd come back in time to pick up Michael.

Michael hadn't protested when he had outlined his plan to the boy in the car. At least, not in words. But it was there in his eyes, in the way he sat rigidly. Michael was disappointed, but resigned.

His six-year-old grandson was acting more of a man then he was, Flynn thought. The plan began to disintegrate. Flynn couldn't make life more difficult for Michael just because he was trying to hang on to his own sanity, on to the frail niche in the world he had carved out in the last year.

He'd just have to find another way to do it, that's all.

Flynn turned down the street behind the playing field. There were a lot more cars parked here today than there had been on Wednesday. Searching for an available space, Flynn eyed Michael's solemn profile. "Well, I guess that maybe I can do the work later."

"You sure?" Michael turned toward Flynn, looking at him warily with eyes that were far older than any six-year-old should possess.

"Yeah," he said grinning at Michael, tugging the boy's cap down over his eyes. "I'm sure."

"All right!" Michael drew the last word out as if it had four syllables.

If you say so, Flynn thought stoically, carefully squeezing his car into a small space between two full-sized vans.

She was already there, her team banner firmly planted in the ground, clipboard in her hand. Flynn walked toward her slowly, his hands shoved deep into his pockets. Why he had nurtured the small hope that she wouldn't be here was beyond him. She'd probably be here even it she were on crutches. She had that kind of dedication, that kind of spirit. Which was admirable, but it also bespoke a stubbornness that wouldn't give way. It indicated a person who was used to doing whatever she felt like doing. Independent. Like him. There was no hope that a relationship between them would work. He knew that. In his head. It was just going to take the rest of him a little while longer to catch up, that's all.

Flynn felt his gut tightening, a small spasm shooting through his right side. The sensation had him catching his breath and holding it a minute before the unpleasant feeling passed. This, he thought, was going to a little too far. Could anticipation, nerves, whatever, create such pain? he wondered.

If so, this attraction between men and women, he told himself, was highly overrated. There was a great deal more pain involved than anything else, both physical and emotional.

He realized that Michael was holding back, matching his steps to Flynn's. The boy was afraid he'd renege, Flynn thought with a pang. A year together and they were still politely skirting each other. When did unconditional acceptance take place? *Did* it take place at all? He didn't know.

He placed his hand on his grandson's shoulder, giving it a squeeze. "C'mon, let's go."

Michael's smile lit up his face. Maybe, Flynn mused, it would take place soon after all.

Billie raced up to them before they got very far onto the field. He hopped from one foot to the other as he looked up at Flynn. As he tilted his head back, his cap tumbled off.

"You came!" Billie scooped up the cap and plopped it back on his head, where it sat slightly off to one side.

Flynn straightened it. "Didn't you think I would?"

This time, Billie held onto his cap as he looked up. It was a long way to Flynn's face. "Mom thought you might have other plans."

Mom, Flynn thought, looking into the distance and catching Susanna's glance, seemed to be able to read his mind. A very dangerous talent.

"Is it okay if we practice?" Billie asked, waving the bat in front of Flynn.

Flynn took hold of it, his eyes on Susanna as she walked toward them, her gait unhurried, the unconscious sway of her hips making him yearn for her. Flynn forced himself to look down at Billie instead of at his mother. "That's why I'm here."

Susanna was within earshot. She was sure that Flynn's assertion was meant more for her than for Billie. He meant to tell her that he wanted to close the door on what had happened between them the last two days. This was his way of saying that he was starting out fresh, with a clean slate.

Susanna only smiled, as if she knew something he didn't.

She probably did, he thought as he went out onto the field with the two boys. And it annoyed the hell out of him.

The baseball game between the Cubs and their challengers of the day, the Giants, got underway within the half hour as the rest of the teams straggled onto the field, their parents hauling blankets and beach chairs behind them.

Flynn found himself falling back to the sidelines near Susanna. With a lot more parents spread out over the field than there had been on Wednesday, Flynn reasoned that it was the only logical place to stand. And he had always been a great believer in logic.

Like Lancelot girding himself for battle, Flynn reached for a shield as he came closer to his doom. "Did I tell you I was applying for a transfer?"

Susanna looked up from the latest batting-order sheet the coach had handed her. "From what?" She half expected Flynn to say, "From life."

"My job." He tried to look casual. "There's an opening in the San Francisco branch."

Though he had been interviewed for the position before he had ever met her, he felt as if he was stuttering some flimsy fabrication. What was it about this woman that reduced him to an errant little boy, even as she made his blood run hot?

Susanna looked at him, her pencil hovering over the third child's name. Was Flynn just making up an excuse to create space between them, or was he really looking into a transfer?

In either case, Susanna felt a pang take hold. Well, true or not, she was determined to look unaffected and pleased. "Will it mean a promotion for you?"

She sounded almost happy. Had he misread all the signals? And if he had, why was he feeling this strange prick of desolation? Wasn't that what he wanted? He was beginning to think he didn't know what he wanted. And it was all her fault.

"Not really." He thought of the job description that had initially caught his eye. He had been restless to try something new, something different in his life. He looked at Susanna, as the sun streaked through her hair. But not this different, he assured himself. "It's a lateral transfer. But the work will be more interesting."

She avoided his eyes. She had never been much of an actress and could only keep up her cheerful front for so long. "When will you leave?"

"Well, it hasn't come through yet and then again—" He began to falter as he looked into her eyes, finding himself getting lost again, just as he had last night. "I'm not sure I'll take it if it does. There are a lot of things to consider."

"I see." Susanna fervently hoped that she might be one of those things. But she made no further comment as she turned her attention to the game.

Chapter Nine

Since Susanna's car was once more among the functioning, and was parked in her driveway, there was no reason for Flynn to see her on a daily basis. No reason, except for one that he tried to ignore. He wanted to.

As Monday's lunchtime approached, he struggled with an intense desire to get into his car and drive to the mall, specifically to the department store that stood facing the Palisades Mutual building. If she had errands to run, he might catch a glimpse of her.

Stop it, he admonished himself. He was acting like a lovestruck teenager, when he was neither a teenager nor lovestruck.

With all the projects he was responsible for at Worth Aerospace, there was more than enough to keep his mind occupied. The week ahead promised to be a hectic one. There were briefing charts to prepare and data to gather for a meeting set up by NASA officials. An entire team of experts was flying in from Houston tomorrow. Their plans were to stay for the remainder of the week. And today, meetings were scheduled from morning until late afternoon.

Flynn hardly had time to draw two breaths in succession, much less think about Susanna. But his mind did wander at noon. Fortunately, he mused, his body was too busy to go with it.

What little time he had to himself was spent at home, being with Michael, trying to restore some order into a life that was post-housekeeper and chaotic to say the least. There hadn't even been time to interview anyone for the position.

At eleven-thirty Tuesday night, down to his last briefs and a pair of mismatched socks, Flynn was forced to have his first meeting with the washing machine that resided in his garage. Muttering under his breath as he tried to unscramble the mysteries of cold and warm loads as detailed on the back of the box of detergent, he sorely missed his daughters.

Flynn embraced the concept of independence when they had returned to college in the fall. He dug himself out from beneath myriad details that threatened to overwhelm him. One of the girls would come down once a month to help out, and of course there had been the housekeeper. Now, with no housekeeper and on an off-weekend with no daughter to help, Flynn felt like Atlas with the entire world on his shoulders.

The washing machine made threatening noises as it went into spin. He eyed it warily and elected to spend the duration of the cycle in the garage, on guard against a possible fire. Past experience with household appliances had taught him anything was possible.

It was after twelve when he threw everything into the dryer and went to bed, wondering why most of his shirts had a pink hue to them and if Michael's red baseball T-shirt had anything to do with it.

By Wednesday, Flynn had nearly talked himself into believing that his reaction to Susanna the previous week had been the results of stress combined with feelings of loneliness. The detailed reasons he cited in his mind were far more complex than the charts he had prepared for the visiting brass from NASA. They all seemed airtight and completely convincing.

And then he saw her.

Her hair was bound up in a ponytail that bounced from side to side as she moved quickly about, rounding up all the little boys into their respective batting order for the day. Wisps of blond hair were escaping at either side of the clasp, making Susanna look like a young girl instead of the thirty-odd-year-old actuary that she was.

He knew he had been lying to himself.

"Hi, stranger!" Susanna waved to Flynn, the effervescent feeling within her rising another notch as she watched him approach. She could feel a smile spreading through her. She'd been afraid he wouldn't come.

Billie broke formation, running to Flynn before Susanna had a chance to say anything further, but she understood. After all, Billie had missed him, as well.

Susanna smiled to herself. Funny how quickly children formed attachments to people. The smile became rueful as she looked away. In some cases, she mused, stopping to tie long, flowing shoelaces for one of the younger boys, that held true for adults, as well.

Look at her, she mused.

She rose, brushing her palms against the seat of her denim shorts, feeling a combination of shyness mixed with elated anticipation as Flynn came up to her. Billie dutifully returned to the line, wedging in between two boys and Michael followed. She nodded her approval, then turned to Flynn.

"How have you been?" Now there was an exciting question. She was becoming as scintillating a conversationalist as he was.

"Fine." No, not fine, he thought, allowing himself a moment of truth. He had missed seeing her. Missed her more than he should have missed someone he had known for such a short period of time.

Absently, he rubbed the dull ache in his side. He had come to the conclusion that she wasn't the source of his momentary light jabs of pain. Considering all the factors that were taking place in his life, he was probably working his way toward an ulcer.

The man was never going to be accused of dominating a conversation. She distributed the four batting helmets and stepped back as the first player took his position in the batting cage. Stubbornly, he hefted a wooden bat. Susanna frowned, picked up the lightest one the coach had packed and walked up to the little boy. "This one'll get you a hit, Drew," she promised.

He looked doubtful as he took it from her and stiffly struck a position, bat raised high, his little rear end sticking up just as rigidly in the opposite direction.

Returning to Flynn, Susanna leaned the bat against the back of the batting cage. "Billie asked about you. He wanted me to take the car back to the mechanic so that he'd have an excuse to see you."

The sound of a ball making contact with the bat echoed for a minute and Susanna turned to cheer Drew on to first base. With a nod from her, Michael went up to take his turn.

Flynn cleared his throat, uncomfortable in his omission, though he hadn't a clue why. It wasn't as if time had exactly hung heavily on his hands. "Billie doesn't need an excuse to see me."

"He's rather small to drive over himself," she pointed out. "His foot doesn't reach the gas pedal."

He shrugged, annoyed with himself for feeling guilty. "I've been busy." He raked a hand through his hair. Why did that sound so lame? It was true.

In one glance, she had looked him over from head to toe. "I can tell." He must have come directly from the office. He was the only man on the field in dress pants and a button-down shirt. Her eyes narrowed as she took a closer look. The shirt was wrinkled, not to mention that in the late-afternoon light, it appeared a little pinkish. He didn't strike her as the kind of man who would be comfortable wearing the color pink.

"Who does your ironing?" she asked.

He looked over his shoulder, trying to see what it was that she was looking at so intently. "I do."

"I see."

The woman would have made one hell of a lawyer. She had the most defensive-creating "I see" Flynn had ever heard. "What?"

"You missed a spot." Why not tell him the whole truth. "Actually, you missed a whole side."

He turned so that his back was away from her. "I'll get the hang of it."

She hadn't meant to make him go on the defensive. "Still no housekeeper?" she asked sympathetically. Another little boy marched up to bat, his cap pulled low over his eyes. He'd left his batting helmet on the ground behind him. Seeing it, Susanna grabbed the helmet and dashed out to him before he had a chance to swing.

She seemed to worry about each of the boys as if they were her own. How did she find the energy? And where could he get some? Susanna half turned toward him as she kept one eye on the field, waiting for him to continue. "I don't even have the time to interview one. I've been in meetings all day and swamped with preparations every evening."

He sounded as if he needed to kick back a little. Overwork had been Brett's main failing, as well, she thought fondly. "Up to a home-cooked meal?" She slanted a casual look his way.

Michael ran toward them, tossing his batting helmet to the ground. He had been tagged out at second. He had walked right into the invitation. The frown turned into a broad grin. "Boy, are we ever."

Susanna picked up the helmet and handed it to the next child in line. She grinned at Michael. "You were robbed," she said of the play that had cost him the base. Michael's face was shining with love and excitement. His adoration embarrassed her. She turned to Flynn and flushed slightly. He was studying her in that way he had that made her feel as if she had just walked three feet off a cliff and hadn't noticed that there was nothing under her feet yet. "What's your pleasure?"

The answer was on the tip of his tongue, but he let it go. A Little League baseball field was not the place to tell a woman she was slowly driving him crazy with desire, utterly against his will. "You keep asking me that."

And I'll keep doing it until you get it right. "Maybe I just haven't heard the right answer yet." Susanna's eyes twinkled just before she turned them toward the batting cage.

Twinkled, for heaven's sake. Eyes didn't twinkle. Lights on Christmas trees, *they* twinkled. Eyes didn't twinkle, Flynn silently insisted, annoyed with his own foolishness.

Yet he would have sworn on a stack of bibles that hers seemed to.

Michael had been waiting for his grandfather to answer Susanna. When he didn't, Michael took it upon himself to answer for him. He tugged on the hem of her T-shirt until she looked at him. "Lasagna."

Had she missed something? She looked down at the small, intent face. "What?"

A small tongue darted over his lips nervously, hope shining in his deep-brown eyes. "Can you make lasagna? My mom used to, for special times."

The sad note that entered his voice created a tightness in Susanna's throat. She dropped to one knee so that she and Michael were at eye level. "Lasagna it is, Michael. If you can't get the big guy to drive you—" she nodded at Flynn "—I'll come for you myself."

Michael's broad smile was all she needed.

It would have been all Flynn needed, as well, except for one thing. She was taking charge and he didn't like that. Didn't want that. He gave Susanna his hand as she rose to her feet. The tug was less than gentle. "Take right over, don't you?"

"Sorry, single parents get used to doing that." She picked up her clipboard again, trying to ignore the annoyed note in his voice. Now what was wrong? "Comes with the territory. There's never anyone else to consult with."

And that, he thought, summarized their problem in a nutshell. They were both too independent to ever make a go of it. There was no need to worry about complications arising again, as long as he kept that in mind. He and Michael would come over for a simple meal and nothing would go any further than he wanted it to go.

Which meant it wasn't going to go anywhere because Michael, he promised himself, wasn't going to go on any icecream runs no matter what Susanna's pushy aunt had in mind.

Feeling a little more in control, he turned toward Susanna as the Cubs got their third out. A mad scramble for caps and gloves and they were flooding back onto the field. "What time?" he asked Susanna.

The catcher was having a hard time with his getup. Susanna sighed as she beckoned the small boy over. "What time is convenient for you?"

The twelfth of never. "One o'clock?"

She was back on her knees, adjusting knee pads for a little boy who was having a hard time standing still. Dressing a moving target was a skill that was hard to master. "Perfect," she murmured to Flynn.

He had his doubts about that.

The sound of the doorbell caught Susanna off guard. Hurrying to the door, an open box of lasagna noodles in her hand, she was surprised to see Flynn and Michael standing on her doorstep. She glanced at her watch. Twelve o'clock. Had she gotten the time confused? She opened the door wider. "You're early."

"Blame it on your son." Confident, Flynn could afford to be cheerful. He had the rest of the afternoon mapped out and it didn't include one unattended moment spent with Susanna. He'd play with Michael and Billie, eat and then take the boys out for dessert. Perhaps he'd even take Susanna along. But today was definitely going to be a group affair. Flynn was feeling rather cocky about the whole thing and not a little relieved.

"Billie?" Susanna turned to look at her son as he flew down the stairs in answer to the doorbell, baseball equipment dripping from his arms and littering the stairs in his wake. "What does he have to do with it?"

"Are they here? Are they here?" Billie cried before he got to the bottom.

Flynn stepped into the house, moving past Susanna to give Billie a hand. Michael silently picked up two of the fallen articles. "He called me," Flynn told Susanna.

Susanna's eyes narrowed as she regarded Billie. Where did he get Flynn's phone number? "How did you—?"

Billie was too excited to let his mother finish. He was fairly hopping from foot to foot. "The team roster, Mom, remember? It's got everyone's phone number on it. Michael's, Nikky's, even the coach's."

And she had posted it on the bulletin board in his room. Well, that cleared up one mystery. Still, she had to make Billie accountable for his actions. "Why did you call Mr. O'Roarke?"

Billie shifted and a glove fell at his mother's feet. Susanna scooped it up and plopped it on the pile that Flynn already had in his hands. She noticed that he winced slightly and wondered why. The load certainly wasn't very heavy, just cumbersome.

"So we could have more time to play." It all seemed very logical to Billie. "He said okay," Billie pointed out, forestalling any lecture his mother might feel obligated to deliver. Billie turned his eyes toward Flynn. "Ready?" he asked eagerly.

He found the adulation in the boy's face hard to resist. "Let's play some ball, champ."

"Is your aunt going to play, too?" Michael asked Susanna. She was surprised to hear the hopeful note in his voice. *He's hungry for a family,* she thought with a pang.

"If I know Aunt Jane, nothing could keep her away." She

looked down at the box of noodles in her hand. "Take your time, you guys, dinner won't be ready for another hour or so."

An hour was probably all he could handle today, Flynn thought. The dull ache in his side had been progressively growing stronger. He had actually been debating calling this afternoon off but then Billie had telephoned. Between Billie's eager request and the look on Michael's face, he had found himself being roped in.

"I should be good and tired by then."

She let her eyes skim down Flynn's hard, muscular frame. You didn't get that physique by being an armchair athlete. "I'll see if I can't have the easy chair ready," she promised with a grin.

She wasn't taking this age thing seriously, he thought grudgingly. The woman had a Peter Pan complex. He rubbed the ache in his side, wishing it would just go away. It seemed to him that it had begun on the afternoon he first met her.

Susanna stopped. There was a great deal of discomfort evident on his face. "Anything wrong?"

He shook his head. The last thing he wanted was her concern. "I think I'm probably working on an ulcer." Given the nature of his work, it was understandable.

She knew when she was being dismissed. She turned toward the kitchen. The water would be boiling by now. "Well then, stop working on it."

"Easy for you to say," he muttered at her back. *You're part of the reason the ache is there.*

He had no more time to debate the matter any further. Billie and Michael were pulling him, one on each side, urging him outside.

Just as Susanna had predicted, it wasn't long before Jane joined their ranks. Less than five minutes. Flynn had vowed to maintain his distance from the older woman. He didn't want to give her any false impression as to why he was here. He had come only in the capacity of Michael's grandfather and a coach for Billie. Nothing more. He didn't want to encourage any fantasies she might be harboring about Susanna and him. People like Jane, he believed, were born encouraged. Just like her niece.

By the time Susanna walked outside and announced that dinner was ready, Flynn was exhausted. Far more exhausted than he believed he should be.

Susanna noted his gray pallor, but made no comment about it. He'd probably bite her head off if she did, she thought, following him inside.

Dinner was being served in the dining room. He realized that he was taking the same seat he had taken last week. Flynn promised himself that this would be the last time he'd come over for dinner for a while. He didn't want to establish a pattern. That would undoubtedly make Susanna believe that they were having a relationship. And they weren't.

He didn't lower himself into the chair, he collapsed into it. An uncomfortable, ill feeling beginning to take a firm grip on him. He attributed it to the game. Just a stitch in his side. "I'm getting too old for this."

Susanna raised her eyes toward him as she cut the first piece of lasagna for Michael. "Got your plot all picked out at Forest Lawn and everything, do you?" Lifting the piece, she placed it on Michael's plate.

Flynn failed to see the humor in the situation. "Age is not something you can ignore."

Susanna nodded to Billie to move his plate closer to the pan. "It's not something you give in to, either." She gave Billie his portion and began to cut a third. "And you agree with me."

"I can cut my own," he told her, taking the knife from her.

She lifted her shoulders and let them fall, wondering why it was that she should happen to care for such a pigheaded man.

"Mind reading a hobby with you, or a sideline?" he asked, referring to her comment.

"Neither." She turned the pan toward her aunt and offered her a choice of ends. "You wouldn't work out if you believed that you should just throw up your hands and let time ravage you.''

The small piece he had sampled was excellent, but his appetite had suddenly vanished. The ill feeling was becoming insistent. What the hell was wrong? He tried to divorce his mind from the way he felt and concentrate on what she was saying. "How do you know I work out?"

He was fishing for compliments, she thought, taking her own slice. "That would be your male ego asking, wouldn't it?" She leaned over and tapped his biceps with her fingertip. It was like tapping a rock. "As far as I know, this isn't regulation issue at birth." Her smile faded as she saw a line of perspiration along his forehead. The room wasn't warm. Glancing at the boys, she saw that they were perfectly comfortable. Something was wrong.

Another hot poker of pain had jabbed at his side. Flynn tried his best not to let it show, but his eyes gave him away.

Susanna dropped the debate, concerned. "How long has that been going on?"

"What?" Flynn looked down at his plate, pretending to eat. But the very idea made him want to gag. He was beginning to feel sick to his stomach. He shifted in his seat, trying to get comfortable. It was like trying to find a cool spot on top of a layer of hot coals.

She placed a hand on his. "Pain," she clarified. "How long have you been in pain?"

He pulled his hand away, aware that all conversation at the table had stopped. Michael was looking at him with large, frightened eyes. "I'm not in pain."

Enough of this macho nonsense. "Flynn, you scowl at me and I'm getting used to that, but you don't usually look as if I were trying to skin you with a dull knife."

He bit his lip. It would pass. Any second now, it would pass. Just like all the other times. "Colorful."

"Observant," she corrected. He had her so frustrated, she wanted to scram. "Mothers learn to look for telltale signs from uncooperative children."

"I'm not your child, Susanna." He threw his napkin onto the plate. It would have been more forceful if he hadn't suddenly grabbed at his side.

Out of the corner of her eye, she saw her aunt rising. Susanna waved her back. "Then don't act like one. Where's the pain?"

He mustered the darkest look he could. "Sitting opposite me."

She gritted her teeth together. "The one in your body," she said clearly and slowly. "Lower right quadrant?"

Maybe she did read minds. He hoped she hadn't been at it for too long. "How did you know?"

The situation was really serious, if he had to ask. "That's where your hand is." Only one thing came to mind. "Do you still have your appendix?"

"And my tonsils," he put in stubbornly. He wasn't about to let her start playing doctor, although that might have some merit when he was feeling more up to it. He realized that his mind was beginning to drift.

He was wasting time. "Your throat doesn't seem to be giving you any trouble."

"No, but you are." The sick feeling continued, but the pain subsided somewhat. Enough to have him rallying against her. "Look, maybe we'd better make this some other time."

Flynn began to rise. Perspiration drenched him. He sank back onto the chair, amazed at how weak he felt.

It was all she had to see. "Billie, bring me my purse." She looked sternly at Flynn. "You're going to see a doctor."

He gripped the sides of the table, as if that would help him stave off the weakness. She wasn't going to order him around. "Not unless there's one on television."

Susanna completely ignored him as Billie ran up with her purse. She slung it onto one shoulder. "Aunt Jane, can you look after the boys?"

She nodded, looking at Flynn. "Don't give it another thought."

Susanna positioned herself on one side of Flynn's chair. "Help me with him, will you?"

She was acting as if he couldn't hear or speak for himself. Worse, as she and Jane each took an arm and slung it over their shoulders, they were acting as if he was completely incompetent. "What do you think you're doing?" he demanded weakly. Flynn tried to pull away, but he felt too sick to make the effort. In only a matter of minutes, he had turned into a bowl of mush.

As Billie opened the front door, Susanna and Jane walked slowly outside with Flynn between them. "I'm going to take you to the emergency room."

"The hell you are. It's probably just something I ate."

Susanna nodded toward the car. Jane maneuvered down the walk as best she could. Leaning Flynn against the car, Susanna tugged open the passenger door with her free hand. "I may not be the world's greatest cook, but I've never lost a dinner guest yet. This is something more serious. You were grimacing when you got here."

He shook his head. The effort made him dizzy. He struggled to keep the world in focus. "I'll just go home and—"'

"Crawl under a table and die? No, I don't think so." Too late, she realized her choice of words.

Michael stood before them, tears shining in his eyes. "You're not going to die, are you?" he asked Flynn, his voice quaking.

Her heart ached for the boy. "He's going to be fine, Michael, as long as he listens to me." She turned to Flynn. "Now, you're going to the hospital if I have to tie you to the roof of the car, is that clear?"

He was too weak to fight, but he wasn't going to be agreeable about it. "Like giving orders, don't you?"

"I live for it. Now shut up and get into the car."

"But—"

"That's the part that goes into the seat, yes. Now put yours into it." She pulled the seat belt back to give him room. "That's a direct order."

The stricken look on Michael's face had him doing as Susanna directed. The effort completely drained him. "If I wasn't feeling so lousy, you wouldn't be getting away with this, you know."

"If you weren't feeling so lousy," she snapped, buckling his belt, then closing the door on him, "we wouldn't have to be doing this." She stopped only long enough to offer Michael a reassuring smile and pat his shoulder. "I'll call you as soon as I know anything, Michael." She got behind the wheel, Jane and the boys closing ranks around her. "In the meantime, why don't the three of you finish eating and then watch some television? Billie's got three thousand videotapes for you to choose from." She turned the key and the engine started.

"Always given to exaggeration?" Flynn wanted to know, his voice growing farther and farther away as he strained to hear it.

"I find it keeps people guessing. Now hang on, Flynn. You're in for the ride of your life."

His mind was beginning to grow fuzzy as he leaned back against the seat. The pain almost seemed inviting as it surrounded him on all sides. Flynn felt as if he were sinking into a dark abyss. "I had a feeling about that the minute I met you."

Susanna covered his hand with her own and tore out of the driveway, steering with one hand.

Chapter Ten

Impatience clawed at Susanna as she pressed hard on the gas pedal. Switching from lane to lane, she bypassed slower-moving vehicles on the freeway. She was filled with a sense of urgency.

"Trying to set a new record?" Flynn asked as she swerved to the right, narrowly missing the nose of the car behind them. They wouldn't need the hospital by the time she was finished, he thought. They'd need the morgue.

"Trying to get you to the hospital before something horrible happens. I have a feeling about this." She glanced in her rear-view mirror. Where were the police when you needed them? she wondered, frustrated. They could be making much better time with a policeman leading them in.

She looked at Flynn. His complexion had turned completely gray, despite the shot of bravado he was stubbornly clinging to.

"'Feeling.'" She could hear him trying to raise a sneer. "Nothing's going to go wrong."

He wished he could put some sort of strong conviction into his words. The dull, sick feeling that was gnawing away at him was sapping not only his strength, but his breath, as well. "I hate hospitals," he told her vehemently. After the last time, he had vowed never to set foot in one again.

"Fine," she agreed. "I'll tell them you won't be moving in."

Seeing an opening, she swung into the right lane. For some reason, Susanna couldn't shake the feeling that she was trying to outrace time. It was a premonition. Superstition was something she normally scoffed at. That was for people who believed in reading tea leaves, or for those who trusted the prophecies of fortune tellers. But she couldn't deny that she felt something urging her on, something she couldn't shut her eyes to. It was a matter of preferring to be proven wrong later, with a speeding ticket in her hand, than to ignore it now and be eternally sorry.

As the freeway came to an end on a surface street, Flynn debated getting out of the car. It got no further than a nebulous wish. He hadn't the strength for it. "I'm not sick," he insisted, though he felt just that. Right up to the roots of his hair.

She wondered if he thought he *had* to go through this elaborate protest. "I've seen less pained looks in the movies, on the faces of Freddie Kreuger's victims."

He had no idea what she was talking about, but that was becoming par for the course. "Susanna, I want to go home."

She set her mouth hard. He certainly wasn't making this easy. Part of her felt that she should just turn around and go home. After all, he was a grown man, up to making his own decisions. But one look at him overruled objectivity. The man needed a doctor. "Too bad, O'Roarke. I'm driving."

He tried to sit up straighter. It was hard to sound forceful slumped in his seat. The effort was too great. "I'm serious."

She didn't even bother looking at him. "You're weak and in pain and we're going to find out why." Her voice softened. Maybe he was afraid to find out that something really was wrong. "I'm doing this for your own good."

He shook his head, trying to muster annoyance. "You sound like a mother."

Susanna smiled as she raced through a yellow light. The hospital became visible in the distance. One more light to go. "I've had practice."

He gave intimidation one last shot, though he was feeling less than up to it. "I'm forty-five years old. I have two degrees from UCLA. I am a senior design engineer in the aerospace program. Don't you think I know whether or not I need a doctor?"

She made a right, into the side street that fed into the emergency room parking lot. A security guard eyed the car curiously as she drove in. "In a word, no."

Another pain speared through his side and he paused to keep from gasping out loud. Okay, maybe there was something wrong. But he hated admitting it. "And you do know?"

She stopped the car in the space closest to the entrance and ran around to his side. Opening the door, she unfastened his seat belt. "I'm psychic that way."

Sweat trickled down his back as he contemplated the walk into the building. He resigned himself to her managing ways. "You know, you're getting to be very annoying." But there was a slight smile on his lips as he said it.

Bracing herself, Susanna helped him out. With his arm over her shoulder, she guided him toward the entrance. Flynn tried to take his weight himself to make it easy as he could for her. The automatic doors leaped open as they approached. She caught the attention of a passing orderly and the man hurried over to help.

Susanna let out a sigh as the load lightened considerably. "You can tell me all about it once the doctor gives you a clean bill of health."

The emergency room was mercifully empty. All the chairs before the registration desks were unoccupied. The orderly helped Flynn into the one closest to the door.

She all but sank into the chair next to Flynn's. The man might be all muscle, but muscle weighed a lot. "Looks like they've had a spate of good health around here. The doctor will probably see you right away."

He hated hospitals. They smelled of death. Kelly had succumbed to pancreatic cancer in a hospital. He wanted to go home. But his legs wouldn't obey. He turned toward Susanna, trying to keep the world from tilting as he did so. "Don't count on it."

"You know, you're positively surly." She saw a young woman approaching the desks from the rear of the room, coffee cup in hand. The woman nodded toward them and began walking quickly. "How does Michael put up with you?"

"Why are you putting up with me?" He'd tried everything possible, he realized, to drive her away in the last half hour. Why was she still here? He wouldn't have been.

"I enjoy being kind to dumb animals," she answered. The administrative assistant sat down behind the computer terminal, ready to take the pertinent insurance information. Susanna looked at Flynn. She could see the beads of perspiration on his forehead. "Want me to register you?"

A wave of pain was beginning to suck him in. "No." Flynn gritted his teeth. "I can handle it." He leaned forward, trying to grasp his wallet in his back pocket. Even that took too much effort.

The room grew hotter and smaller.

When Flynn opened his eyes again, he realized that he was horizontal. The surface he was lying on felt too soft to be the floor. There were curtains around him and the smell of antiseptic mixing with the scent of wildflowers. Someone was holding his hand, gently rubbing his knuckles. Struggling against another wave of pain, he focused on the shape in front of him. Susanna. Her delicate face was no longer sunny. It was outlined in solemn concern.

She saw confusion in his eyes. He tried to rise and she lightly touched his shoulder, pushing him back down. It wasn't difficult. "Hi, welcome back."

His head hurt. He probed it gingerly. There was a small bump over his temple. "What happened?"

"You hit your head when you passed out." Her fingers feathered along the bump. "Lucky thing you've got such a hard head."

He frowned. "I didn't pass out."

She shrugged, biting back her impatience. He was far and away the most difficult man she had ever known. For some reason, maintaining this strong, invulnerable image was important to him. The big idiot. "Have it your way—you decided to do an intensified study of the hospital floor and got a little carried away." Susanna's frown softened as her annoyance gave way to concern. "How do you feel?"

"Like hell," he admitted. And being here wasn't helping any. He felt agitated, and frustrated that he was too weak to do anything about it.

She tried to remember the other symptoms that went along with appendicitis. Her cousin Jennifer had had an attack when they were sixteen. It had happened during a slumber party. The party had ended up in the emergency room for Jennifer, while her older brother Kurt had driven everyone else home at one in the morning. "Do you have a burning sensation?"

Flynn nodded. Stubborn, he still refused to concede the round. "It's just an ulcer."

Maybe it was. She looked around, wishing someone would come. The doctor and nurse had taken all of Flynn's vital signs while he was unconscious. The nurse had also drawn some blood to run standard tests. Then they had left, promising to return "soon." She supposed everyone had their own definition of the word. "They'll tell us if it is."

For a moment, the pain abated. Savoring the reprieve, Flynn looked at Susanna. She looked tired. "You don't have to stay here."

Her hand tightened on his. "Like hell I don't." The look she gave him told Flynn she was in for the duration. He didn't say it, *couldn't* say it, but he was grateful.

His eyes widened as he remembered. "Michael—"

This much she could do for him. She could assure him that his grandson was being taken care of. "—Is going to spend the night at my house. Aunt Jane is with the boys now." She glanced at her watch. Michael was probably frantic by now. "Since you're conscious, I'm going to call and tell them it's going to be a while longer."

There was no clock on the wall. He'd lost track of time. "How long was I out?"

She made her voice sound casual. "Hardly any time at all."

He glanced down. Obviously long enough for someone to have undressed him. Instead of the pullover and jeans he had worn to Susanna's house, he had on a thin blue-and-white floral hospital gown. He felt beneath the blanket that was thrown over him and found that the gown was incredibly short. Whoever manufactured these things believed in economy. "What happened to my clothes?"

The look in his eyes made her think he was contemplating leaping off the bed in search of his things. "I decided to see if those muscles of yours were real. Then I had my way with you." She raised her brows so high, they disappeared into her bangs. "Was it good for you?"

He couldn't help it. He laughed, then clutched at his side. "You're crazy."

"Yes, but at least you're smiling." Susanna moved toward the foot of his bed. "Where there's a smile, there's hope."

Despite the pain, he felt a fondness slip over him. She really was rather unique. Having seen what she had of life, she still managed to be optimistic. "Learn that from Mr. Rogers?"

"I was a permanent resident of his neighborhood for the longest time. I'll go phone Michael. And as for you, you stay put," she warned. "Or I swear I'll hunt you down."

She was just persistent enough to do it, too, he thought, watching her walk away.

Susanna hurried to the nearest pay phone she could find. She fed the phone some change, then dialed her own number.

It barely had a chance to ring before the receiver was snatched up.

"How is he?" Jane asked without preamble.

"Demanding to go home." She leaned against the wall, suddenly feeling very tired. "The doctor should be with him any minute. I just wanted to tell Michael that everything was under control. Put him on, will you?"

Using her brightest, most positive voice, Susanna told Michael that his grandfather was with the doctor and everything was going to be fine. The doctor would make him feel better.

Michael listened quietly and thanked her. Even over the telephone, she could tell he was trying very hard to be brave. Promising to call again very soon, she hung up.

Susanna shook hear head and hurried back to the emergency room only to find that the cubicle where she had left Flynn was curtained off. Taking a deep breath, she stood off to the side and waited.

She heard a deep male voice asking Flynn if "this" hurt. "This" obviously did as she heard Flynn emit a hiss of air before answering affirmatively.

Probably biting on a bullet, she thought. The doctor's next words had her snapping to attention.

"We're going to have to operate, Mr. O'Roarke. I would recommend immediately. I'll send someone in with the proper papers and I'll have the nurse start your IV."

The air backed up in Susanna's throat. She told herself that she was panicking needlessly. After all, lots of people were operated on everyday. Operations were routine. Still, she felt her heart hammering in her chest.

This was childish. She had to get herself under control. There was nothing to worry about, she told herself fiercely. Nothing.

By the time the curtain was drawn back, she had a smile fixed into place. It only felt tight around the edges. She nodded at the doctor as he passed her. "So, they're going to operate," she said to Flynn. She couldn't think of anything else to say.

"He looks too young to know what he's doing," Flynn

muttered as Susanna moved to his side. He made up his mind. The doctor was wrong. He'd get better on his own. "Get me my pants." He would have pointed if only he knew where they were.

Susanna glanced at the dark green plastic shopping bag the orderly had stuffed all his belongings into. It was tucked under the wheels of the bed. "If I do, it'll be to tear them into strips and tie you to the bed." Didn't he know this was past the time for games? If the doctor wanted to operate, that meant Flynn's condition was serious, very serious. When would he get it through his thick skull?

He saw her concern and tried not to let it affect him. Flynn tried to smile. "You really get kinky when you get angry."

She let her anger go. It served no purpose. "Remember that. Now be a good boy and let them do what they have to do in order to save your hide." Flynn merely nodded, finally accepting the inevitable.

The same administrative assistant who had registered Flynn came by with release forms for him to sign. He had just finished when the nurse arrived with his starting IV.

It was all happening fast, too fast. Flynn felt himself losing what little control he thought he had. Something potent and warm began to fill his system. He began to drift, float. Each time he tried to hold on, his grasp weakened a little more.

She was still standing there. Susanna. Looking small and lost and worried. She refused to leave him. He wondered why.

Affection washed over Flynn. He was too tired to be on guard, too tired to try to reach for the control that had, up until a few moments ago, been so very important to him. He tried to keep her in focus, but that was getting more difficult with each passing moment. "Have I told you thanks?"

"No." She smiled, surprised and touched. "But it'll come to you."

She stepped out of the way as two husky orderlies arrived with a gurney. The small cubicle was getting very crowded. The nurse moved the IV bottle and its stand aside, waiting for the two men to shift Flynn from his bed to the gurney in order to transport him to the operating room.

The shorter of the two men looked Flynn over and shook his head. "You're sure a big guy." Positioning himself at Flynn's knees, the man let the other orderly handle Flynn's upper torso.

"Yeah," Flynn muttered disparagingly as he was rolled from one bed to the other. "The bigger they are, the harder they fall."

Susanna grabbed at Flynn's blanket as it began to slide off. She moved it over him, trying her best to leave him his dignity. "You're not falling, Flynn, you're just leaning a little." Taking the plastic bag with his clothes, she moved to the side opposite the IV stand.

Leaning. It was just what he didn't want to do, but he couldn't remember why. He felt the rolling motion and began to feel sick. Except it didn't really seem to matter. The drug was blotting it all out. Instinctively, he fought for consciousness and realized that they were wheeling toward the door. He wasn't moving, the bed was.

"Susanna?" His fingers groped along the bedclothes, though he felt as if he were searching for her everywhere. He didn't want to lose her.

"Right here." She gripped his hand as the orderlies guided the gurney quickly from the emergency room to the long corridor.

Flynn opened his eyes, his mind feeling full of cotton. And swirling colors. She was still there. "Thanks."

He probably wouldn't remember any of this later. Susanna savored it anyway. "See, I told you you'd get around to saying it."

The distracted, vacant smile on Flynn's face told her that he was no longer hearing anything she said. The sedative had done its work. At least he wasn't feeling any pain, she thought.

"You'll have to wait out here, ma'am," the taller of the two orderlies informed her gently. "The doctor'll be out to tell you when it's all over."

She nodded slowly and loosened her fingers from Flynn's lax hand. Susanna suddenly felt cold. She moved her hands up and down her arms and stepped back. The doors swung closed behind Flynn, shutting her out, leaving her alone to wait.

"You're not the only one who hates hospitals, Flynn," she murmured, wishing the fear wouldn't come.

But it did.

Six years ago, she had been standing in this very corridor, as she was now. Except that six years ago, she had watched the doors close on Brett. They'd never opened again. The hernia he had refused to pay attention to had become strangulated. By the time he had reached the operating table, it had been too late.

Oh God, don't let it be too late now.

Susanna passed her hands over her face and shuddered. The memory of that night was one she tried very hard to keep at bay, far away from her conscious mind, but being here brought it all back.

It was going to be all right, she told herself.

She walked slowly to the cheerfully decorated room just a few feet down the hall. It was set aside for the friends and relatives of the people being operated on. There was no one there now. The room was as empty as she felt inside. Susanna sat stiffly. The light coffee-colored vinyl whooshed quietly around her. There was nothing left to do except to mark the passing of incredibly slow minutes. And wait.

It was taking too long, she thought, twisting her fingers together. Much too long. Her cousin's appendectomy had only taken forty-five minutes. The doctor had told the family that an hour was standard. Flynn had been in the operating room for almost two hours. Terrible thoughts were crowding Susanna's mind.

What if something went wrong? What if—?

How would she ever face Michael if something happened to his grandfather?

And how could a man be taken away from her just when she had finally found one she could care about?

It wasn't fair.

Restless, worried, Susanna rose and began to pace. Life, she knew, wasn't fair. It didn't work that way. There were no checks and balances to adhere to. It hadn't been fair that Brett had died before he could see Billie grow up, not fair that Michael had had to deal with pain so early in life.

She turned and looked accusingly down the hall. It wasn't fair that the big lummox should suffer any consequences because she hadn't bullied him into coming here sooner. She should have, she told herself. She had noticed his discomfort earlier. Hell, she had noticed it on Wednesday, when he had talked to her. He had been massaging his side then. She had thought it was because she was making him nervous.

She smiled ruefully. And now she was paying for her vanity.

"Mrs. O'Roarke?"

Susanna jumped as she swung around. The surgeon Flynn had claimed was too young to operate was standing behind her, still dressed in his green gown, his surgical mask dangling about his neck.

Dear heavens. He looked so solemn, so drained. Was he going to tell her—

Susanna's heart began to throb in her throat, nearly cutting off her air. "Yes?"

The doctor paused for a moment before he spoke. "It was touch and go for a while, but he's one lucky man. If you hadn't brought him in when you did, quite possibly you'd be making funeral arrangements by now."

No drama, right? she thought, her bones instantly turning to water. She collapsed onto the sofa. He was all right, she thought, almost giddy. He was going to be all right.

The doctor sat down next to her, obviously quite proud of the work he had just done. "His appendix burst as soon as I touched it, but we managed to drain the area. We got all the poison out. Dr. Moyres assisted."

Susanna stared at him, trying to gather her wits together into some semblance of order. The name of the assistant surgeon was familiar. But something didn't make sense. There had to be two of them.

"Carla Moyres?" When he nodded, her surprise dissolved into a relieved giggle. Dr. Carla Moyres was her gynecologist.

The doctor looked a tad uncomfortable about the revelation. "Yes, she's a very competent doctor."

"I know. She's mine." Susanna couldn't help the smile that emerged. "You had a gynecologist assisting?" Wait until Flynn heard this one. This certainly put the cap on a very long, difficult day.

The doctor shrugged a little helplessly. "It's Sunday. We're not overstocked with doctors at the hospital on Sundays. It was a slow day until your husband arrived."

She had to correct him before things got any more complicated. "I'm not Mrs. O'Roarke."

The surgeon nodded as he rose to his feet. "Well, even if you're not, according to some ancient cultures, his life is yours, since you were instrumental in saving it."

And wouldn't Flynn just love to hear that one? she thought, feeling suddenly buoyant. She rose with the doctor, picking up Flynn's belongings. "When can I see him?"

"He'll be in his room in about an hour." He nodded at the bag. "You can bring those up there then. Admissions can tell you which room. In the meantime, I suggest you get something to eat. You look as if you need it." He grinned. "No charge for the advice."

Susanna could only nod. Relief was a wonderful thing. You never appreciated it fully until you didn't have it. "Thank you, Doctor."

Humming, Susanna went to call Michael.

An hour later, fortified with a bacon, lettuce and tomato sandwich from the hospital cafeteria, Susanna slipped into Flynn's individual care unit. She found him asleep. There was an IV in either arm and he was still very pale. But for a man who had been on the brink of death, he looked damn good, she thought. Even in a blue-and-white floral hospital gown.

She closed the door behind her and put away his clothes in the small closet on the side. Then she stood at the foot of his bed, content to just look at him. Content to know he was alive. Michael had asked her twice if she was certain that Flynn was all right. It felt wonderful to assure the small boy that he was.

There was someone in the room. He could feel it. Flynn fought his way to the surface, struggling with heavy blankets that threatened to smother him. His eyelids felt as if they weighed ten pounds apiece. And there was pain, oceans of pain, radiating from his side, washing over him each time he tried to take a deep breath.

Somehow he managed to open his eyes.

The images before him swam until the three women merged into one. Susanna. He might have known. He tried to say something but the words wouldn't get past his throat. He tried again. "Where are my pants?" he rasped.

His pants again. Didn't this man ever give up? Susanna found herself smiling. Right now, even his bad mood was encouraging. "The nurses had a raffle."

Flynn tried to swallow. His Adam's apple felt stuck. He coughed, then narrowed his eyes as he looked at her. "Is that humor?"

"A very poor attempt." She moved closer. "I brought all your clothes up." She nodded toward her right. "They're in the closet."

He turned his head. The room shimmered. The closet looked a hundred miles away. The effort in turning his head cost him. He felt weak. He hated feeling weak. "What's all this?" He tried to raise his tethered arms and couldn't manage it.

"That one's whiskey," Susanna pointed to the left one, "That one's Scotch, take your pick." She blinked, suddenly realizing that there were tears in her eyes. Now that it was all over, now that he was conscious, there were tears threatening to fall. Talk about timing, she thought, annoyed as she brushed one away. "One's to feed you," she said seriously. "The other's in case of infection. The nurses told me."

He had to know. "Was it my appendix?"

She nodded. "According to the doctor, it exploded like an overblown balloon."

He didn't like the image, or the fact that he was in debt to her. "I guess I should thank you."

She wondered what it had cost him to say those words. "You already did."

He couldn't remember. "When?"

Susanna perched on the arm of the lone chair that was next to his bed. "When they wheeled you in to the operating room."

He searched for the memory. It eluded him. "I don't remember."

"I know."

He felt so tired, as if he could sleep forever. He struggled to stay awake. "Michael—"

She was one step ahead of him. "—Is all taken care of."

What else was there? Oh, now he remembered. "My daughters should be informed."

She had made a list while sitting in the cafeteria. "I already made note of that. I'll talk to them tonight."

He looked at her, puzzled. "How?"

She smiled, wishing he would stop talking and get some rest. "By telephone."

"You don't have their number."

"They're at the campus at Santa Barbara right? Information will do the rest. Now go to sleep."

He wanted to, yet fought it because it was what she wanted him to do. Couldn't have her winning every round. "Thought of everything, haven't you?"

"I try."

He should be grateful. She was just being helpful. And he was grateful, dammit, but in the midst of all that, he felt hemmed in. And too damn tired and weak to do anything about it.

"Susanna?" he whispered as he felt himself drifting back to sleep.

She lowered her head next to Flynn's mouth in order to hear him. "Yes?"

"Don't try too hard."

She knew that it was wrong to want to hit a man just out of surgery, but she was sorely tempted.

Chapter Eleven

By nine-thirty the next morning, Susanna felt as if she had packed three days of living into one. After leaving her telephone number at the nurses' station with the nurse who was taking care of Flynn, Susanna had gone home to comfort Michael and let him know in person that everything was fine.

Because she thought that familiar surroundings might help, she took Michael with her to Flynn's house. It took almost an hour to gather together the essentials for Flynn's stay at the hospital and Michael's stay at her house. Once that was accomplished, she asked Michael to help her find his grandfather's telephone book so that she could copy down the personal and business numbers she needed.

She returned home and put both boys to bed. Fighting off exhaustion, Susanna sat down and braced herself for the task of calling Flynn's daughters.

There was no easy way to break the news to two girls who had already had their share of emergency phone calls. After introducing herself, Susanna prefaced her information with

"Your father's fine now" and then in a quick and straightforward manner, raced into an explanation of what had happened.

It went a lot easier than she thought it would. It took only a few minutes of conversation to discover that the girls' personalities seemed to be light years away from their father's. Stephanie and Julia were grateful to her for calling and for having taken it upon herself to handle the details. When they began to make plans to drive down immediately, Susanna assured them that at this point speed was no longer the essence. The morning would do just fine.

By the time Susanna finally crawled into bed, it was close to two a.m.

Four hours later, she was up, making sandwiches for Billie and Michael and mentally listing the calls she had to make and things she had to do before she went to see Flynn at the hospital.

The first order of business was calling in to work and informing her superior that she was taking a few days off. She had amassed more than her share of vacation days, but James Harper, the senior actuary who was collaborating with her on the ratebook revisions for the whole life policies saw her leave as nothing short of desertion. The new ratebook figures were due by the end of the month. This was no time, he told her, to take off on a whim. Susanna made her apologies, but remained firm. Some things, she thought as she dialed the next number, took precedence over ratebook figures.

Flynn's boss, she discovered to her relief, was a great deal more compassionate than Harper had been. He told her to inform Flynn that if there was anything he needed, he shouldn't hesitate to call and that he himself would initiate the paperwork for a six-week medical leave of absence for Flynn.

Some people, Susanna thought, hanging up the phone, were just basically nice. She wondered if Flynn knew that.

Stopping only for toast and an extra-strong cup of coffee to keep her going, Susanna packed up the items she had selected for Flynn last night and drove to the hospital. On an impulse, she stopped at a florist and landscaping shop, which specialized in the unusual. She thought that summed up Flynn quite neatly.

Susanna had no trouble selecting a gift for Flynn. She knew the plant was meant for him the second she saw it. If sweets were for the sweet, she mused as she paid for the gift, then the same could be applied to the term prickly.

She grinned at her own analogy as she hefted the unwieldy plant into the car.

Her grin had faded slightly around the edges by the time she walked to the bank of elevators in the rear of the hospital. The plant was growing steadily heavier. Still, it would be worth it to see the expression on Flynn's face.

She hoped he was still doing all right and that nothing unforeseen had happened during the night. No, she thought, drawing on her overabundant supply of optimism, they would have called if anything had gone wrong. Everything, consequently, was fine.

The elevator doors opened and she did her best to hurry to Flynn's room. With the plant before her, Susanna nearly crashed into Flynn's attending physician as he left Flynn's room.

The man grabbed the tottering plant by the only accessible place, the base, as he eyed it with the healthy respect it deserved.

"Sorry." Susanna took a moment to get her bearings. "Thank you, Doctor." She nodded toward the closed door behind him. "How is he?"

The young physician was clearly pleased. "The man has the most marvelous constitution I've ever come across. Better than a man half his age. Most men are lying in bed and calling for painkillers this soon after surgery. Your Mr. O'Roarke is asking for solid foods and the nearest escape route."

She laughed, shifting the plant slightly. That would be Flynn all right. Except that he wasn't *her* Mr. O'Roarke, not if he had anything to say about it. But now at least they would have time to work on that prospect.

Susanna asked the question that she knew Flynn would confront her with as soon as she walked through the door. "When *can* he go home?"

The doctor checked the chart he had under his arm and shook his head again in amazement. He flipped the metal cover back over the pages and looked at Susanna. "If no complications set in, I see no reason to keep him here longer than Thursday."

By then Flynn would probably be tying sheets together and planning to lower himself out the window on them, but not before alienating every nurse within a forty-mile radius. Good looks and an incredible body went only so far. "Believe me, you won't."

The doctor looked at her a little oddly. Perhaps the two did deserve each other. "Here, let me get that for you," he offered as she began to struggle with the door handle.

Balancing the plant before her, Susanna tottered in. If she didn't set it down soon, her arms were going to break. It hadn't been heavy at first, but after ten minutes, it felt like it weighed a ton.

Flynn was sitting up in bed, frowning at the IV that was still attached to his arm. He was down to one but it was still one too many as far as he was concerned. He wanted to get up and test his legs. How was he going to get around with this thing tethered to his arm?

He turned when he heard her enter and stared at the large flat dished plant she set down on his windowsill. "What's that?"

Susanna let out a sigh of relief. It felt wonderful to get rid of the plant. Her arms felt so light, she momentarily forgot about the shopping bag she had dangling from her wrist.

"I brought you a little gift." She turned the plant so that the bright yellow bow faced Flynn instead of the pigeons on the ledge outside. "I thought a cactus was more appropriate than flowers." She smiled at the tall, single dark green column, spines as sharp as needles covering every available inch.

"It seemed to suit your personality a lot better than carnations."

Flynn eyed the cactus. It had to be just about the ugliest thing he had ever seen. And yet somehow it was oddly pleasing in its ugliness.

"Very funny." He picked at the bedclothes, uncomfortable. She was doing entirely too much for him. It made him remember things. And yearn for a life that he had shut the door on. "Aren't you going to say it?"

"Say what?" She moved closer to him. The room was small, but airy. Flynn probably thought of it as a cage. "How are you?"

"No." She was playing games. "That you were right and I was wrong."

He hated being wrong, she thought. Probably hated it more than anything, except being confined. Susanna shrugged casually. "I think that part went without saying." She looked at him innocently. "And I'm not the type to gloat."

She didn't have to. It was there, in her eyes. She was smug about all this. About saving his life. He owed his life to an over-efficient woman who looked like a Barbie Doll come to life, he thought grudgingly. He nodded at the shopping bag she had brought. "What do you have there?"

Susanna glanced down at it. "Oh." She set the bag on the bed next to his leg. "I stopped at your house and got some things I thought you might want." She left it for him to open. "Michael helped me."

He left the bag where it was. He wanted something explained first. "How did you get in?"

How did he think she got in? Actuaries didn't learn how to pick locks as a sideline. "With your keys."

"My keys?" he repeated. He hadn't given her his keys.

Oh-h, she had undoubtedly trespassed. She smiled soothingly, knowing it did no good. "I picked your pocket," she explained simply. "You didn't look as if you'd be driving anywhere last night."

Regardless of that fact, she hadn't asked if she could go

through his pockets. He didn't like being treated as if he had no say in anything, no wishes of his own to be observed. "Aren't you taking a little too much upon yourself?"

She wasn't going to get angry at him, she wasn't. Susanna fisted her hands at her sides. "No, I don't think so. After all, your life is mine."

Now what was she talking about? "What?"

She laughed at his confused expression. "Just a little custom the surgeon told me about." She leaned toward him, patting his hand the way she would a child's. "Now behave yourself or I'll tell everyone the assistant surgeon was a gynecologist."

He stared at her as if she had lost her mind.

"That's right," she said mildly. "They needed another surgeon right away and it just so happened that the doctor who delivered Billie was on call at the hospital."

"And he came?" That sounded a little unorthodox to Flynn.

"No." Susanna had to admit she was enjoying this. "*She* came."

Flynn blanched, then recovered. The woman had a weird sense of humor. "You're making this up." His eyes dared her to contradict him.

Susanna sat on the edge of the bed, her arms folded before her. "I don't need to. You'll believe me when you get her bill." She'd tortured him enough, she decided, changing the subject. "So, how are you feeling?"

"Lousy." He fairly growled the word.

"Ah, nothing's changed."

She didn't deserve to have him take his frustration out on her. It wasn't her fault his appendix had decided to give up the ghost. "I'm sorry I snapped at you. I don't like not having control over things."

She could identify with that. Still, she couldn't help teasing him. "You could have fooled me." Idly, she toyed with the side of the shopping bag, dropping the wordplay. "Everyone needs to be taken care of sometime, Flynn. Sometimes, you can't help it."

Perhaps it was the near meeting with death that had him wanting her to understand. "I spent most of my life being taken care of, Susanna. I didn't know it until it wasn't happening anymore. I *don't* want to be dependent again."

She waved her hand around the room. "This is only temporary."

"Yes, I know." His tone made her feel that he wasn't referring to the operation or his subsequent hospital stay. Lord, he made her angry. "How's Michael taking this?"

Nice safe ground, she thought. For the moment, she'd retreat. "I calmed him down and assured him you were all right. He's staying with me. By the way, I called Mr. Ecklund. He's a nice man."

His supervisor? What was she doing calling him? "Why did you call him?"

"To let him know what happened and that you weren't playing hooky. He's putting you down for a six-week medical leave and says to call if you need anything."

Was there any part of his life she hadn't invaded? he wondered. It was bad enough that she had haunted him all through the operation. It had taken him several hours, after the drugs began to wear off, to realize that he had dreamed of fairies and mermaids and all sorts of creatures he had never believed in as a child. And they had all had her face. It bothered him that he had tried to capture every one of them. But then, a man couldn't be held accountable for what he did in his sleep.

He swallowed his ill temper. She was just trying to help. It wasn't her fault that it made him feel threatened. "I guess I should thank you."

She rose. Being close to him this way was affecting her. She kept remembering that she had almost lost him. The realization made her emotions raw. "Not unless you want to."

He looked at her, wishing she could understand. Wishing he knew why it was so hard for him to say. "I do. It's just that—"

"You don't want to be in the position to have to, yes, I figured that part out. You don't have to." *Yes, you do*, she thought, *but I'm not going to drag it out of you. Maybe I can wait you out.* "In the meantime…" She upended the shopping bag and a black bathrobe along with various toiletries came tumbling out onto the off-white blanket. "I believe that this is what the well-dressed patient is wearing and using these days." She folded the robe in half and slung it over the foot of his bed. "I couldn't find any pajamas."

"That's because I don't own any."

She nodded, pretending that the image of him that generated hadn't made her palms suddenly grow damp.

"That's what Michael said. He pointed out these." She drew his cutoffs out of the pile and held them up. Looking them over, she shook her head. "You wear this and the nurses are going to think you're going surfing." *Not to mention the fact that their bones will probably turn to mush.*

He took the shorts from her. "It's a lot better than what they have me in now."

"Oh, I don't know." She stood back and cocked her head, pretending to study him. "Blue's your color."

He glanced down at the lightly starched, washed-out gown. A network of daisies covered the entire field. "Flowers aren't."

She placed the other items, his razor, toothbrush, comb, one by one on the small table. "Maybe they can scrounge up a hospital gown with a cactus on it." Moving the table within his reach, she turned to brush back the lock of hair that had fallen into his eyes. He caught her hand, stopping her. She was surprised at how much strength he had. He certainly did recover quickly.

"I'm a toucher, Flynn," she said softly. "You're going to have to get used to that."

"Why?" It wasn't a challenge. Maybe he wanted to hear something that would force him to change his mind. Maybe he was still a little groggy from the medication. He wasn't sure of anything anymore.

"Because."

"If you can't do any better than that—" he muttered, echoing words she had said to him.

"Oh, I can." She leaned over his bed, bracing her hands on either side of him. "I can." She lightly brushed her lips over his. The flash of fire came. It didn't take much. She leaned her forehead against his. "God, you scared me, Flynn."

He sifted her hair through his fingers, then framed her face. Just this once, he'd allow himself to savor, to feel, knowing that once he was on his feet again, back in control, things would return to what they had been. As they should. "It wasn't exactly a picnic on this end, either," he admitted.

Despite his weakened state, he felt the strong pull of desire course through his veins, demanding one more taste, just one more. Flynn brought her lips to his.

Was it his imagination, or did her mouth taste sweeter than it had before? Lost in the heady sensations she always generated with him, Flynn wasn't aware of the door to his room opening until he heard Stephanie's amused voice. "Pop?"

Surprised, embarrassed, Flynn dropped his hands from Susanna's face.

Slightly dazed, Susanna took a step back. The operation hadn't affected his ability to scramble all her pulses, that was for damn sure.

Flynn looked at the two young women who, looking clearly confused and somewhat amazed, were standing behind Susanna. "Stephanie, Julia, what are you doing here?"

Stephanie, the older of the two by eleven months, assessed the situation quickly and grinned. "Coming to see if you were all right." Her eyes flicked over Susanna and apparently liked what she saw. "Obviously, you are."

"Hi. You must be Stephanie." Michael had pointed out pictures to her when they had stopped over at his house last night. There was no confusing the two sisters. Pleased at their arrival, Susanna shook the tall, vibrant brunette's hand. She looked like Flynn, the coloring, the mouth, everything. Except that she was smiling. "I'm Susanna. We spoke on the phone last night."

Julia was always quick to forge a place for herself. The youngest of three very out-going girls, Julia had always had to nudge her sisters aside to be noticed. It had become second nature to her. She grasped Susanna's hand as soon as Stephanie released it. "And I'm Julia."

Julia, Susanna decided, took after Kelly. There was hardly a trace of Flynn about her, except in the slight slant of her eyes. She was as fair as Stephanie was dark, with long blond hair that fell in deep curls almost to her waist. Night and day, Susanna thought, as she appraised Flynn's handiwork.

"I'm very pleased to meet you both." Time to withdraw, Susanna thought, sliding her purse from the bed. The reunion would be more relaxed for Flynn without her here. "Well, I'd better leave the three of you alone."

Stephanie was quick to take hold of her elbow. Flynn realized with an inward groan that now that there was someone in her father's life, his daughter didn't want to take the chance on the woman slipping away. "Oh, please don't leave on our account."

It wasn't on their account that she was leaving. She didn't want to crowd Flynn. "No, in this case, four's a crowd. Besides," she nodded toward Flynn, "let him snap your head off for a while. I've had my quota for the morning." She grinned at him, relief still fresh in her veins. "I'll be back later tonight, Flynn, whether you like it or not."

Stephanie claimed the chair by right of seniority, making herself comfortable. She glanced toward the door as it closed, then at her father. "I like your lady, Pop."

It was a hard thing to deny, after what they had seen as they'd walked in, but he tried. "She's not my lady."

Stephanie laughed and shook her head. "Oh, that's right, it was your appendix, not your stubborn streak they removed."

His eyes narrowed. When under siege, man an offensive. "Why aren't you two in school?"

Julia, sitting at his feet, reached over and placed her hand on top of his. "School can wait. We can make up assignments."

He didn't like the fact that they had come down all this way. It was a one hundred fifty mile trip from Santa Barbara. They'd probably driven half the night. "Did she tell you to come?"

Neither daughter missed the tone of voice he'd used. They knew him well enough to know that he was trying to hide his feelings. Fat chance.

"*She* gave us a very detailed report and let us know how well you were doing," Stephanie told him. She smiled with relief. "But you know us, we have to see for ourselves. We also wanted to check her out."

It was a conspiracy. There was no other term for it. "There's no need."

"I think," Julia told him, "there's more of a need than you think." She exchanged looks with her older sister. "Personally, we're very relieved."

Flynn raised his eyebrow. "Relieved about what?"

"That Susanna's here to look after you," Stephanie said, completing her sister's thought. "We felt pretty guilty, leaving you like that in September."

Why did everyone think he couldn't manage? He was a man. Men always manage. Besides, he was their father. "I'm not a toddler," he reminded them impatiently.

"No, you're a pop." Julia leaned over and kissed his cheek. "And you're ours and we love you. We want you to be happy."

"I am happy."

Stephanie crossed her arms before her chest and eyed Flynn. "Maybe it's the scowl that fooled us."

Julia joined ranks with her sister. They stood on either side of him, twin smiles of approval on their faces. "Definitely," she said to Stephanie.

Flynn suppressed a laugh. "Stop talking over me as if I were dead."

Stephanie sprawled boneless in the chair. She took his hand and held it in both of hers, her young face serious. "That's just it, Pop, you're not dead. And we want you to enjoy life, like you used to. With someone at your side.''

He didn't want to risk the hurt that was out there. Didn't want to ever be bereft again. Not like that. "I have Michael."

Stephanie gave his hand a tug. "Somebody a little taller and closer to your own age," she amended.

Flynn sighed. "You women are in cahoots, you know that?"

Laughter met his ears from both sides. Stephanie and Julia each kissed a cheek as they prepared to leave. "We have to be, you men are so hopelessly stubborn," Julia said. Stephanie nodded in agreement. "We're going to check in on Michael and then come back. Need anything?"

He said the first thing that came to mind. "Freedom."

Stephanie was undaunted. "Prisons are created in your mind, Pop."

He tried to look stern but the effort was getting to him. He loved each of his daughters equally, but there was a special bond between Stephanie and him that went back to the time she had lamented about being the middle child and neglected. He had told her that the middle of a sandwich was the best part. "Is that what I'm paying for? Philosophy?"

"No, that's a freebie," she said fondly.

A nurse walked into the room with a plastic basin in her hands. Towels were slung casually over her forearm. Stephanie and Julia took the opportunity to withdraw. "See you, Pop."

"Bye." The girls grinned as they pointed to the basin.

The small, heavyset nurse gave Flynn a no-nonsense nod. "It's time for your sponge bath, Mr. O'Roarke."

He drew himself up as tall as he could, given the fact that he was sitting. It was enough. Flynn O'Roarke cast an intimidating shadow. "Not on your life. Leave the bowl. I can do it myself."

"I'd listen to him if I were you, Nurse," Julia told the older woman solemnly. "He bites."

Stephanie pointed toward the windowsill. "I like the cactus, Pop."

Flynn glanced at the specimen. It was growing on him. "Susanna brought it. It's her idea of a joke."

Stephanie nodded her approval. "I think it suits you."

Flynn frowned. The nurse left the basin and towels, then shuffled out, wisely following the girls' advice. "That's what she said."

Stephanie was the last to leave. She smiled fondly at her father. "Just remember, even a cactus needs a little water once in a while."

When she returned to the hospital that evening, Susanna brought Michael and Billie with her. She thought that Michael needed to see Flynn for himself. He had seemed satisfied, but there was a wary look in his eyes when she had told him that Flynn was recovering quickly and would be home soon. Even the sight of his aunts hadn't settled him completely. Obviously, he needed visual proof. Billie had wanted to tag along. She saw no reason to make him stay home with Jane.

Flynn's room was empty.

Nothing short of panic entered Michael's eyes as he looked around. He grabbed hold of Susanna's arm. "They took him!"

Though her own heart lurched, she managed to calm herself down. Doing the same for Michael was another matter. "I'm sure there's an explanation, honey." She searched her brain for one. They didn't do tests at this hour unless something was wrong. But he had seemed so healthy this morning.

Desperate for a way to reassure Michael, she opened the closet. "Look." She pointed to the jeans that were neatly hung. "His things are still here. He couldn't have gone very far." She closed the metal door, then looked down at Michael. "Maybe he escaped."

The dark brows knitted together in confusion. "Escaped?"

She nodded solemnly. "He told me this morning he wanted to break out of here. He doesn't like being in the hospital."

Michael struggled manfully with his feelings. "Maybe."

She took the small hand firmly in hers. "Let's go ask the nurse."

They didn't have to.

As Susanna turned the corner to the nurses' station with Billie and Michael in tow, she heard an odd clanging noise. It was the sound of glass tapping against metal. And then she saw Flynn, his robe draped around his body, one hand on the IV stand as he pushed it before him.

Susanna didn't know whether to laugh or cry. The man put a new spin on the word *stubborn*. She hurried over to him, wanting to punch him for frightening her and Michael so much. Wanting to hug him because he was all right.

She looked Flynn over. He looked winded, but there was no missing the stubborn set of his chin. "Is it alms for the poor you're collecting, or trying out for the part of the Hunchback of Notre Dame?"

"Hi, Michael, Billie," he murmured to the boys. Susanna merited a nod. He gritted his teeth. When he had started this walk down the corridor, it had seemed a good idea. It didn't any longer, but he was too proud to say so. "I'm trying to get some exercise."

"You're trying to open your stitches," she contradicted. Two could play at this stubborn game.

He took another step, focusing on the handle of the last room down the hall. If he didn't, he'd fall over. "You're not a doctor."

She wanted to hold him, but fought back the desire. She knew he wouldn't let her. *Please don't let the big jerk fall.* "And neither are you. Aren't you supposed to be in bed?"

How had the damn hall become so long? It hadn't been this long when he had walked in the opposite direction. All he had wanted to do was to make it once around the corridor by himself. Just once. Was that asking too much? "I'm supposed to be where I am."

"Are you okay, Granddad?"

Michael's small, awestruck voice brought Flynn around. He felt chagrined at his show of temper in front of the boys. "I'm fine, Michael.'' He looked at Susanna. ''A hospital's no place for them. Why did you bring them?''

''To show them how well you looked. And how stubborn you could be.'' Pride or no pride, she couldn't just stand here and watch him struggle. ''C'mon, Jesse Owens, let's get you back into bed so these little guys can talk to you.''

''We'll help with this,'' Billie offered, wrapping his hands around the slim metal column before them. Michael placed his hands below Billie's and they pushed together, each eager to help.

Susanna watched the IV bottle sway. She steadied it quickly. ''Not too fast, boys, Mr. O'Roarke's racing days are temporarily on hold for now.''

Flynn would have protested both her assumption and her help if he had had the strength. ''So how was school today, Michael?'' he asked.

The sound of Michael's voice soothed him as Flynn made his way back to his room.

Chapter Twelve

Flynn stretched his legs out gingerly before him in the car as it sped down Jeffrey Road. It felt wonderful to be out of the hospital. It had annoyed him that he had had to make the trip from his room to the hospital's entrance in a wheelchair, as per hospital policy. What annoyed him more was that just being in the open air seemed to sap his strength.

He wanted to be well now, this instant. It frustrated him that he had to wait.

But he was on his way home, which was what counted. He glanced to his left at Susanna. She had arrived on the heels of the discharging physician, informing him that she was taking him home.

Flynn had already made arrangements. "I have a cab coming."

He would, she thought, rather than ask her to pick him up. When would he learn to accept the smallest favors? "That's all right, we'll cancel." She was already picking up the phone, waiting for him to supply the number.

Since he was anxious to leave as soon as possible, he didn't argue with her.

Still, he thought as they drove home, he didn't want to give up too much ground. After all, she hadn't bothered to consult him about this, either. "You didn't have to come to the hospital to pick me up."

It was too much to hope for a simple thank you, she supposed. She passed a large open field. In the distance, there were cows grazing. It was a sharp contrast to the shopping center to her left. Soon all the fields would be gone. It made her feel sad. "No trouble. Besides, I didn't like picturing you rattling around in the back seat of a cab in your condition."

He wished she'd stop making him sound like an invalid. He'd had appendicitis not a fatal heart attack. "My condition is fine."

"So you keep telling me." She was going to stay cheerful if it killed her. Mentally counting to ten, she calmed herself down. "The doctor is absolutely amazed at your speedy recovery. Said he wouldn't have expected it of a man half your age."

She had an incredible collection of euphemisms, he thought. "You mean a young man."

She blew out a breath, losing her temper, forgetting her vow. "Nice to see that some things don't change." She passed a row of towering eucalyptus trees, straggly branches raking the sky, their bark peeling in the sun. "Everyone's got someone around who's half their age, Flynn, even newborns." She looked at him as she slowed, then stopped at a four-way stop sign. "I wish you'd rid yourself of this attitude that your life is on the decline. You've just been given a new chance to live." She took her foot off the brake and pressed too hard on the gas. The car jerked forward. "Use it."

There was truth in what she said, at least the last part. He had been given a second chance. He just didn't want to get carried away with it. There were penalties for recklessness.

Flynn stared at the road, seeing it for the first time. "This isn't the way to my house."

"No," she said slowly. "If you recall, it's the way to mine." She waited for the explosion, knowing it would come even though this was the only sensible option open to him.

He looked at Susanna suspiciously. "Are we picking up Michael?"

"No, we're setting *you* down." She took a breath, then plunged ahead. "The girls and I decided you're staying at my house for a few days until you're stronger." She hadn't said anything earlier because she knew he'd argue with her. But it *was* the only sensible way to proceed. She slanted him a look when the explosion didn't come. He really *was* weak.

"I am stronger," he insisted. She had no right to keep making decisions for him. He hadn't abdicated control over his life. Just who did she think she was?

Susanna licked her lips. Why couldn't he just accept things instead of always making them difficult? Why wasn't he just grateful that she cared? "Let me rephrase that." She slowed the car so that she could look at him. "Until you can bench press your own body weight."

It didn't make any sense to him. Why was she putting herself out like this? She hardly knew him. "Why are you taking me in? I'm basically a stranger."

Yes, you would think that, even after what they had gone through together. Even after the kiss they had shared. She felt as if she were hitting her head against a stone wall. But two could be stubborn.

"Maybe, but a weak one." She reached for humor. It had seen her through a lot before. She regarded the tall, strapping man next to her. "I could probably throw you to the ground before you had a chance to try anything funny."

Though he had meant that when he'd asked, he didn't like her thinking that he actually was someone she should fear. "I wouldn't try anything funny."

Yes, she knew that, too. "A woman can dream, can't she?"

She had lost him completely now. "Really, I don't think—"

It was the lead-in she needed. "Fine, don't think. Do us

both a favor and just heal, okay?'' She took on the same tone as she used with Billie when he was being stubborn. ''You're in no condition to take care of yourself and Michael.'' Her voice softened as she approached her street. ''Let me live out a fantasy. I'll make you chicken soup, you'll get well, then fold up your tent and slip into the night.'' When he made no answer, she looked at him.

He was studying her, a look of pure amazement on his face. ''Are you always like this?''

She grinned. ''Only when I get mad.''

''Angry,'' he corrected out of habit, then wondered if she would be annoyed. He might have known better. That kind of thing didn't seem to bother her.

''That, too. Settled?''

Right, as if he had a chance to debate this. Besides, he supposed it did make sense. If only she had asked instead of told. ''Do I have a choice?''

''No.''

He shrugged. He'd concede this one time. For Michael's sake. ''Then it's settled.''

Michael had sat, waiting, in the driveway since Jane had brought the boys home from school. When Susanna had turned the corner onto the block he jumped to his feet, his expression changing from pensive to excited.

He dashed toward the car as Susanna pulled up, then ran next to the passenger side until she cut off the engine. Flynn's window was down and Michael reached in to put his hand on his grandfather's shoulder, touching him for reassurance. His chocolate eyes danced as a grin threatened to split his face. ''Hi!''

''Hi, yourself.'' Emotions ran through Flynn, surprising him. He hadn't realized how much he had missed seeing Michael everyday. Susanna came around the hood to his side of the car. ''Mrs. Troy taking good care of you?''

Michael's head bobbed up and down, his eyes never leaving

Flynn's face. "Real good. She lets me call her Susanna. Are you gonna stay?" Michael asked hopefully.

Flynn eyed Susanna as she opened the door. "So my warden tells me."

Susanna paused, one hand on the door. "Tell me something, Michael." She leaned over to the boy, then asked in an audible whisper. "Is he always this cranky?"

Michael shook his head.

Susanna sighed dramatically, her mouth curving. "Then it must be me."

"Must be," Michael agreed solemnly, responding to the laughter in Susanna's voice.

Susanna leaned in to help Flynn out.

Flynn moved her hand aside with his own and swung out his legs, albeit a lot slower than he would have liked. Where had this wave of weakness come from? And when would he finally feel like himself again? "I can do it myself."

She was tempted to let him try, but he was just stubborn enough to do it. As annoying as he could be, she didn't want him falling. It would hurt his pride, not to mention everything else. "I'm sure you can."

As he rose on shaky legs, Susanna took his arm and forcibly rested it across her shoulders. She was a lot stronger, he thought, than she looked.

She smiled up at him. "Humor me. I like having big strong men pretend to lean on me. It feeds my ego."

He had a comment about her and her ego, but he kept it to himself. Michael pulled out Flynn's belongings from the back seat.

"Leave the plant," she warned. "I'll take it in later." The last thing she needed was for eager, helpful little hands to wrap themselves around a cactus.

Michael struggled to the front door with the bag, three steps ahead of them. "He's here!" he announced, yelling to Billie. Seconds later, Billie met them in the foyer, his eyes as vibrant as Susanna's as he greeted Flynn.

It almost felt as if he was actually home. Almost. He told himself not to let his emotions get the best of him.

He tried to support his own weight, but it was getting difficult. He looked at Susanna, embarrassed that he would have to lean on her, impatient with the frail state of his own body. He could feel her other hand along his back, holding him, her fingers pressing along his spine. He could probably be dead and still aware of everything about her, the smell of her hair, the feel of her hip against his. This wasn't a good sign, he told himself.

Susanna nodded to the left as she directed him. "Your daughters will be here on the weekend to see how you're doing."

Here. She meant her house. "I'll be home by then."

He made it sound like a mandate. "We'll see," she answered, annoying the hell out of him.

How could someone who filled him with desire one moment make him want to commit justifiable homicide the next? Flynn had no answer for that. He chalked it up to her just being Susanna.

"I've given you the downstairs bedroom," she told him as she turned right. "It's close to the refrigerator in case you get hungry and want to forage for food." Walking into the small bedroom, she nodded for Michael to place the suitcase next to the table.

He wanted to sink down on the bed, but forced himself to take the chair instead. It was a matter of pride. "Is that some kind of crack?"

"You figure it out." She turned her attention to more important things than sparring with him. "C'mon boys, let's get the man settled."

Billie and Michael scrambled to obey.

It was, Flynn thought, watching her put his things away, what she was used to. Giving orders and being obeyed. Independent. And stubborn as all get out.

Flynn had meant to be gone by Saturday, he really did. He was mending quickly, just as the physician had foreseen. Just as he himself willed.

But something made him linger at Susanna's house a little longer. He told himself it was for Michael's sake. The boy had changed during their forced encampment at Susanna's. For one thing, he laughed a lot more. And he played. He and Billie pounded up and down the stairs, playing space invaders, just being little boys. It made Flynn's heart glad to hear the ruckus.

When he had collected Michael from the hospital in San Francisco and brought him home to live with him, there had been something almost too adult about the child. Having lived through a tragedy, Michael acted far older than his years. Now Flynn was seeing the small boy in Michael emerge.

Because of Susanna.

Flynn was fair enough to give credit where it was due and human enough to wish that he could have done more for his grandson himself.

True to Susanna's prediction, Stephanie and Julia swept in midafternoon on Saturday, bringing their exuberance with them. The house rang with noise, laughter and the opening and closing of a refrigerator that never seemed to get empty. The whole thing left him feeling slightly in awe, slightly out of step.

It would have been so easy, he thought, to get swept away himself, but he hung on, determined that what was happening now wouldn't undermine his basic resolve to handle things for himself, to keep his life untangled. Separate from hers.

When the girls began to leave for home, Susanna talked them out of it. They stayed up and watched an old movie on TV. Susanna made popcorn for everyone, then found places to put them up. No matter what she confronted, Susanna found a way to manage. She seemed to thrive on the challenge. She gave new meaning to the word *independence*.

And she was, he thought late that night as he got ready for bed, impinging on his.

When he heard the noise at his door, Flynn thought that one of the girls had come down to have a late-night talk with him.

The subject probably revolved around his needing a wife. He had his answers prepared, pat.

"Come in."

He was surprised to see Michael standing in the shadows of the doorway, looking at him uncertainly. The hour was far too late for the boy to still be up. Maybe he had had a nightmare. Flynn could remember sitting up with his daughters when they were small, assuring them that there were no monsters lurking in their closet.

"Hi, champ." He beckoned the boy forward. "What's on your mind?"

Looking small and frail in a pair of faded cutoffs he loved, Michael hesitated, then walked slowly in. "I was just checking on you."

Flynn patted the space next to him on the bed and Michael scrambled up, then sat very straight, his legs jutting out, parallel to the floor.

"Checking?" Flynn asked. It seemed an odd thing to do.

Michael looked down at his folded hands. "To see if you were okay."

"I appreciate that." Flynn placed his arm around the small shoulders and pulled his grandson closer. "Michael, I'm going to be okay for a long time to come."

Aimee's eyes looked up at him as Michael tilted his head back. "Promise?"

Flynn thought of all the honest things he could say, things all grounded in reality. But Michael had had too much reality, far more than a six-year-old should have. Flynn squeezed the narrow shoulders. "Promise."

Michael nodded, as if digesting the word. Suddenly, he turned and threw his arms around Flynn's neck, his small body shaking with sobs. All the tears that had been stored up, all the tears that hadn't been shed when he had discovered he was orphaned, poured out now. He clung to his grandfather and cried.

Flynn sat for a moment, stunned in the face of so much emotion, so much grief. He didn't know what to do, what to say. Michael had always seemed confident and amazingly in control. Flynn thought of his own feelings, of the emptiness that lived outside the perimeter of his life. He gathered the boy to him, then held him tightly. He felt his own eyes sting.

With his cheek against Michael's head, he murmured, "Hey, it's okay, champ. It's okay."

Michael hiccuped, his face buried in Flynn's chest. "I was so scared that you'd go away, too, and leave me. Then I'd be all alone."

Flynn thought of how frightening that thought would have been for a boy. How frightened he had been when Kelly died. He drew Michael back, holding him by the shoulders. "You'd never be alone, Michael." He enunciated each word clearly to make the boy understand. To make him feel more secure. "You have Stephanie and Julia."

Michael nodded, brushing his tears away, obviously embarrassed that he had been caught crying. "Um, can I ask you something?"

"Sure." Flynn wondered what was going on in that little head of his. He hadn't a clue. It occurred to Flynn that he didn't know what a lot of people were thinking. Maybe he hadn't been paying close enough attention.

Michael rocked nervously. "Could I maybe call you 'Pop' like they do? Stephanie and Julia, I mean. So that you could love me the same as them."

What kind of signals had he been giving off? Flynn wondered. How could Michael doubt the strength of his love? "You don't have to call me anything special for me to love you, Michael." He kissed the top of the boy's head, his heart brimming. "I always have."

Michael twisted in the circle of Flynn's arms, his face hopeful. "I'd kind of like it, though."

Flynn laughed. "Then you can call me 'Pop.'"

Michael wiggled off the bed, ready to resume his role as a fledgling man. He sauntered over to the door. Flynn couldn't help wondering if Michael was trying to imitate him and if he actually swaggered when he walked. "See you in the morning, Pop." He beamed as his tongue rolled around the name.

"You bet."

Mealtime the next day was a circus of sounds and voices competing for center stage. Flynn sat back and watched as his daughters and grandson merged with Susanna, her aunt and son, in a cacophony of syncopated movement.

He shook his head. It looked like the set of *The Brady Bunch Revisited*, he thought, but there was a contentment moving through him that he couldn't deny.

Removed, he had to stay removed, no matter what his feelings were to the contrary. Flynn knew he had to be careful not to slip and allow this contentment to sabotage his guard. This feeling was only temporary. Life could never again be allowed to fall into a pattern where he would just let it pull him along. If he did, it would dash him against the rocks of reality when he was least prepared. And this time, most probably, crush him.

But for a few days, at least, he could pretend that life was actually the wonderful thing that Susanna seemed to believe it was.

He caught her eye over the quiche lorraine she was slicing and for a moment, everything else faded. Desire, hot and demanding, suddenly pulsed through him, here, in the midst of all this. Perhaps because of it.

It appeared that he was getting a whole lot better than he thought, Flynn mused. Happiness, or some reasonable facsimile thereof, made for strong medicine.

The week that stretched ahead found him alone for the better part of each day. He mended and grumbled to himself, finding small odd jobs around the house with which to keep himself occupied. He owed it to her. Flynn O'Roarke stayed in no one's debt and though he knew it was but a small repayment, at least it was something. He fixed her broken screen in the bathroom, rewired the frayed cord on her iron and got a discarded tape recorder operational again.

Mostly, he spent the day thinking about her and trying not to think about her. At that, he was a miserable failure. But a man wasn't accountable, he reasoned, for his thoughts. As long as they went no further than that.

Susanna had returned to work and the boys were in school for six hours of the day. Jane looked in on him from time to time to see if he needed anything.

He never did.

"You know, handsome," Jane said, regarding him thoughtfully as she paused at the front door, "it doesn't hurt your stature as a man to need once in a while."

He shook his head. The woman meant well, she just didn't know. "You're wrong there, Jane. It does. It hurts a lot."

Jane pursed her lips. "It hurts more being alone. Trust me, I know." She began to leave, then turned around, remembering. "Oh, I'll be picking the boys up from school and taking them straight today."

The entire family talked in riddles. If he wasn't careful, he would, too. "Straight?"

"To the jamboree," she explained patiently. "The Cub Scouts are having a camp-out tonight, since tomorrow's a holiday." The smile she gave him as she closed the door spoke volumes.

It was time, Flynn decided, to go home.

He was still there when Susanna arrived home from work. Somehow, he couldn't make himself leave. Not yet. There was time enough, he thought, after dinner.

But after dinner, there was a movie she wanted to see. Somehow, with very little effort, he found himself talked into watching it with her.

"It's no fun watching a movie alone," she insisted.

He was inclined to agree with her. Except that he was watching her more than the movie, the way her face tilted slightly to the left when she laughed, the way the corners of her mouth always seemed to lift upward. The way she smelled, fresh and tempting at the same time. It amazed him how much pleasure he derived from just being near her, a bowl of popcorn between them.

Comfortable. He was getting too comfortable, dammit. Her mouth was far too enticing and his resistance was getting far too low. It seemed to be decreasing in direct proportion to his healing. He was overwhelmed with the desire to make love to her, here, on this small sofa.

He should have gone home. But it was too late for that. But it wasn't too late to retreat. Fast.

Stiffly he rose as the credits began to roll down the screen. "I'd better get to bed."

She nodded, staying where she was. She had felt the hum of electricity between them, the same as he had. She had refrained from acting on it for another reason. She didn't want to start something that he was too weak to finish.

But she was tempted.

He stopped for a moment by the bay window and glanced out. He thought of Michael. Such a little boy. Such a large wilderness. He glanced at Susanna. "Think they'll be all right?"

It was nice to know he was concerned. It reinforced her feelings about him. "Sure. They're with a whole camp full of Cub Scouts. What could go wrong?"

He would have said the same thing about coming over to her house for Sunday dinner two weeks ago and look what had happened.

His mind humming, his body restless, Flynn found himself unable to court sleep for the second time since he had met Susanna. With a huff, he threw off the covers and sat up. Maybe he'd feel better if he got up for a while. With all those cable stations, there had to be something on TV that would take his mind off Michael. And Susanna.

When he walked into the family room, he found her there,

standing by the same window he had passed on his way to bed. She was staring out, lost in thought.

Flynn's thoughts weren't lost to him. Moonlight was streaming in, casting beams of light into the room, bathing her body in a silvery hue. She had on a long robe with a matching nightgown beneath it. Both were made of a smoky blue gauze material that allowed him to see enough to make his palms itch, reminding him just how much he missed the intimacy between a man and woman.

He tried to ignore the fact that his blood pressure had gone up several numbers on the scale. She looked worried. "Can't sleep?"

She turned, startled. She hadn't heard him approach. Her nerves were jangled. The warm glass of milk had done nothing to help. Neither did the cutoffs he was wearing. He looked magnificently male in the dim light. She felt her mouth go dry.

"No, I can't." She smiled ruefully, caught. "I lied before."

He took a step toward her, a step toward his destiny. "Oh?"

"I am worried." She knew she was being silly, but she couldn't help it. "Sure he's with a bunch of other boys, but boys wander off. They take dares. They get lost." She sighed. Because she had no pockets to shove her hands into, she made do with folding them across her chest. "I suppose I'm just being overprotective, but if anything ever happened to Billie, I don't know what I'd do."

Moonlight wove its way through her hair, making him want to touch it, to see if it felt as silvery as it seemed. "Nothing's going to happen to him."

"Can I have that in writing?"

She made him think of Michael and the promise he had asked for. "Sure, I'll even have it notarized for you." *I'd even do it now, if I could only draw myself away.*

She turned, a smile on her lips. "When I was a little girl, if my father or mother promised that something would or wouldn't happen, I believed them. Even when I grew older, somehow it seemed to help to have the words to cling to."

She shrugged at her own foolishness. "Like a talisman, I guess. Pretty silly, huh?"

Her admission surprised him. It made her seem vulnerable. "I didn't think you needed that."

"Why? Because I do everything on my own? That's because I have to." She realized it probably sounded as if she was complaining. "Oh, I don't mind being needed. I *like* being needed, but once in a while—" her voice grew wistful "—I'd give anything just to lean."

It was a side of her he had never seen before, a side he knew he shouldn't have seen. It upset the balance of things the way he had arranged them in his mind. She had a habit of doing that, he thought, throwing him off balance.

He saw a pad and pencil one of the boys had left, forgotten, on the coffee table. Picking the pad up, Flynn scribbled something on the first sheet.

She tried to see what he was writing. "What are you doing?"

"Here." He tore off the sheet and handed it to her. "Here's your written guarantee. 'I promise nothing is going to happen to Billie.'"

She held it to her and laughed. Flynn probably hadn't a clue how sweet he had just been.

But then her laughter slowly faded as she saw the look that had entered his eyes. They had darkened ever so slightly. A flash of desire penetrated her. Without thinking, she took hold of his arm to steady herself.

Anticipation slammed through her as he lowered his mouth to hers.

Her body melted against his, seeking the warmth, seeking the heat. The note he had written fluttered to the coffee table as she slipped her hands into his hair, giving herself to him so completely in that one kiss that it staggered him.

"We're alone," he murmured against her mouth. He knew it was dangerous to think, yet he couldn't help thinking. It was dangerous to want, yet he couldn't help wanting.

"No," she whispered against his mouth. "We're together."
For tonight, they would be together, two souls reaching out to
one another. Tonight, they wouldn't be alone.

Chapter Thirteen

It had been so long since she had been touched like this, so long since she had felt the way a woman could with a man. She had almost forgotten what it was like to yearn for that special feeling. When he kissed her, when he held her this way, a hunger consumed her, devouring the morsels cast her way, wanting more, needing more.

As she clung to him, her head spinning, her points of orientation dissolving, as he took her to places she wanted so desperately to revisit, Susanna felt sunshine bursting through her veins.

Yes, oh God, yes.

He had tried so hard to avoid exactly this. And yet, it seemed that every step he had taken, every path he had followed somehow had led him to this point in time. Had led him to her. She felt so good in his arms, like quicksilver he had managed to capture for just a moment. Fingers glided along the soft gauzelike material of her robe, he felt Susanna's skin heat to his touch, heard her soft intake of breath as he brushed along the curve of her spine.

His desire threatened to overwhelm him.

In a fiery haze, Susanna felt his body mold itself against hers. She felt his desire, hard and demanding. Shivering from the thrill of knowing that he wanted her, a rush seized her. Susanna prayed the feeling would never leave.

And yet, she was afraid. Physically, this might be too soon for him. She felt she'd be ripped apart if he stopped now, but Susanna moved back, her hands braced on Flynn's bare chest.

"Flynn—" His name tumbled from her lips as her breath escaped her.

With effort, Flynn steadied his own breathing. She was completely destroying his equilibrium, not to mention scrambling his emotions. Had she had a change of heart at the last moment? He wouldn't force himself on her, but oh Lord, after he had allowed himself to come this far, it would cost him.

Unable to release her, he kept his arms around her, savoring her supple softness. "Woman, this isn't the time for conversation."

No, it was a time for loving. But at what price? She couldn't have that on her conscience. "Do you think you should?"

No, he thought he shouldn't, but it was past the time for warnings, past the time for common sense. His fingers grazed her face lightly, barely making contact. It was enough to make him want her again. "No, but it's happening anyway."

He didn't understand. She could see it in his eyes. She wouldn't forgive herself is something happened to him because of her. "You were just operated on."

"Two weeks ago." His fingers slowly slid along the planes of her cheeks, memorizing the curve there, the way her mouth lifted in a smile. Excitement thundered through his veins. "A lifetime ago. When I thought I had a life."

Now, he knew he hadn't. What he had had was an existence. Life, that vital, exciting force, was in the palm of her hand. And she was offering it to him. Though that wouldn't be acceptable in the light of day, for now, in the shadow of night, he could pretend that it was all right.

Pretend? Hell, right now he *needed* to be all right. He needed her. He *needed* her. The simple phrase held him prisoner, pinning him as surely as a butterfly was pinned against a mounting board.

Her eyes searched his face. She felt herself melting as his touch floated along her lips, her forehead. In another moment, she wouldn't be able to think straight at all. "Flynn, I don't think it's good for you."

He laughed softly. Even now, she was giving orders. She was incorrigible. In an odd way, he found that exciting. He found everything about her exciting. "You have no idea what's good for me." He brushed a kiss against her forehead and heard her sigh. "*I* have no idea what's good for me. I just know I want you."

Her eyes were beginning to flutter closed as she gave herself up to the drugging effect of his mouth. It was dissolving her senses, common and otherwise. "But—" The word slipped between lips that were barely moving.

"Susanna?"

She felt his breath feather along her face and it made her want to cry out, a mixture of anticipation and impatience tugging for equal attention. "Yes?"

"Shut up and let me make love to you—with you," he amended, remembering the words she had used. Things in the world had changed. And they were taking him with them. Not entirely against his will in this instance.

Susanna felt tears gather as she nodded her head in reply. She couldn't resist both him and herself any longer. She needed this as much as she had ever needed anything. More. She curved her fingers along his shoulders, the sensation of his bare, lightly haired chest sending incredible tremors through her.

Amusement quirked the corners of his mouth. She was giving permission. "No more arguments? You're sure?"

There was no amusement in her eyes when she looked up at him. Only desire. "I've been sure a lot longer than you."

She rose on her toes, slipping her hands to his face, bringing his mouth to hers. Words, concerns, everything evaporated.

He had never known it could be so intense, that desire could be this overpowering, this demanding. This sweet and gentle even as it raked through his soul with both hands. He wanted her. Sweet Lord, he wanted her more than he wanted life itself. Just kissing her, being kissed by her, was churning up his insides, making alarms go off in his head while the rest of him got ready for meltdown.

It was, he realized, as if he had just been apprenticing all those years, preparing for this moment. Preparing for her. He was in total awe. Always before, he had felt in control, the one who set the pace. This time, neither set it. It was more like a duet. Susanna not only received, she gave, gave back more than he thought it possible to give. Lovemaking had become a totally new experience for him.

Susanna splayed her hands over his chest. Hard ridges met her touch. The man was a veritable rock. Was his heart just as hard? What would it take to break through and touch him there, too? She knew she had his passion. For tonight, it was enough. But tomorrow, she would want more, so much more. Would he be able to give it to her?

She wanted his love. She wanted the part of his heart that was reserved for the woman in his life. Maybe she had wanted this from the very beginning, but it hadn't been clear to her until she had sat alone in the hospital, waiting to find out if he would live or die. She had wanted him to live for Michael, for his daughters. And for her.

That he was alive and well and desired her filled her with gratitude.

But she wanted more.

Susanna wanted him to want her long after the embers of desire died down to a peaceful glow on the hearth. Long after hunger had been sated. She wanted him to want her at his side.

She wanted, she knew, the moon. But he was offering her the stars and she was determined that in time, she'd have it all. She was just going to have to show him, she thought, that he couldn't live without her.

Flynn hadn't thought that the first time he made love to her would be here, in the middle of the family room. As the thought flashed through his mind, he realized that he had anticipated a first time, that he *had* thought about it. More than he would have even admitted to himself. The dream during the operation had shown him the way. He had thought of slipping her clothes from her body slowly and making love to her inch by agonizing inch, bathing her body in soft, moist kisses.

He had fantasized about taking her quickly, plunging himself into her and spiraling to the heights.

He had thought about it.

He felt her shiver as he pushed her robe from her shoulders, his lips teasing the hollow of her throat. Arousing her. Inflaming himself.

Trouble, he was asking for trouble. But he could handle it, he swore to himself. He could handle it.

Desire twisted, raw and biting, within his belly. He moved back, needing to see her, needing to watch the look in her eyes as he slowly slipped the straps of her nightgown from shoulders that gleamed alabaster white in the moonlight. He caught his breath as the blue cloud slipped to her breasts, the swollen tips clinging to the material for a heartbeat. He tugged just a little more, feeling his blood sizzle through his loins. The thin material whispered to the tiled floor, a pool of gauze and dreams about her small bare feet.

He felt clumsy, his hands feeling much too large to touch her. But he had to. He had to worship her with his hands. "You're beautiful," Flynn whispered.

Her eyes held him prisoner as she moved closer. She pressed her body, her flesh hot, demanding, against his as she fumbled with the catch on his cutoffs. She was going to break it in her eagerness, she admonished herself, feeling impatience surge through her.

He covered her fingers with his own and helped her. The very act made his breath back up in his lungs.

Her irises had grown huge as she watched his face, her cool, long fingers sliding the shorts from his hips until they fell to the floor, joining her discarded nightgown.

It was as if someone had put a torch to her body. Heat suffused her, surrounded her as Flynn pulled her to him.

Unable to hold back any longer, he cupped her face and brought his mouth to hers in one fierce movement, wanting to have her now, here. Wanting to make love all night.

Wanting. Needing. Needing when he had sworn not to. But he couldn't have walked away now even if his life had depended on it.

If that was the price for this one night of ecstasy, so be it.

Susanna arched against him, loving the way his hands roamed her body possessively, as if she had always been his. Loving the heat she felt from his. She moaned his name, then forced herself to move back before she had no will to do anything but be with him.

He looked at her, bewildered.

Almost shyly, Susanna took his hand and turned toward his room. Her own bed was larger, but that was upstairs and she couldn't wait that long. "We'll save the tile for the next time," she murmured.

Next time. He didn't know if he could survive a next time. But he knew there had to be a now. He curved his fingers around hers and followed, never once thinking that she was setting the terms again.

The small bedroom turned into a little piece of paradise as they tumbled onto the gray-and-pink comforter, delighting each other the way young lovers did on the brink of first love.

She made him feel like springtime. It was as if the life he had lived before had never happened, had only existed in a dream. Only this was real. Lost in the fragrance of her body, in the way she drugged his senses, he could almost believe that everything was good and pure, the way she painted it.

Because he was with her.

With practiced skill, he showed her his gratitude for the precious moments she had given him. He explored all the secret places of her body where pleasure hid, his for the taking. He memorized the soft curves with his hands, with his lips, leaving her trembling and nearly frenzied, gasping for him.

Susanna heard the hoarse, dazed gasp and only vaguely thought that it sounded like her voice as Flynn found another, far more volatile erotic area and teased it to explosion with his tongue, bringing her up and over the first crest. She shuddered, a powerful, delicious sensation ripping through her as she arched her back, clinging to him. Pleasure and exquisite agony filled her, exhausting her, making her want more.

When he did it again, she fought back to a level of consciousness, her heart pounding, her body vibrating. She needed to give him ecstasy in kind.

She took her pleasure by giving it to him.

In a movement more agile than she thought herself capable of right now, she reversed their positions until she was on top of him. When he tried to rise, she pushed against his chest with the flat of her hand, her thighs cradling his. She heard him groan.

"The doctor said to take it easy."

This was a hell of a time to bring that up, he thought. "The doctor didn't see you in a nightgown made out of blue cellophane." But he lay back, savoring the feeling of her body over his. "Just what is it you have in mind?"

She didn't answer. She showed him.

With movements that came instinctively, driven on by her desire to pleasure, and be pleasured, Susanna made love with him as he had never had it made before. Following the pattern he had set forth, she drove him crazy with desire as she darted her tongue along the length of his body, pausing at strategic places, making his pulse leap, bringing him to the very edge. Only sheer self-control had him hanging on and kept him from scaling upward and then plummeting without her.

When he had taken all that he could possibly bear, he

reached for her. "Come here, Susanna," he rasped, his throat hoarse, desire closing it.

She surprised him by rolling on top. When he tried to move her, she resisted. Taking him to her, she sheathed him and began to slowly rock, breaking through his resolve and old-fashioned notions.

The protest he would have uttered died, forgotten, burning in the flames she fanned. Without realizing what he was doing, he held onto her firm hips and began to move her in a primal rhythm that was as old as Time, as new as tomorrow's sunrise. Susanna gripped his shoulders and rode him.

When they reached the end of the journey, they arrived at the summit together. He groaned her name, pulling her down to him as his mouth covered hers.

A century later, he opened his eyes. She was still lying across him, her body limp, lazily curled like a well-fed kitten stretched out before a warm fire. He could feel the curve of her lips against his chest. She was smiling.

So was everything else, he thought, savoring the afterglow. His hand felt heavy as he raised it to stroke her hair. It was fanned out along his chest, a curtain of spun gold.

Susanna raised her head and looked at him. She loved him, but she bit back the declaration. No use frightening him. Yet. "Did I hurt you?" she asked. Now that the raw flame of passion had abated a little, common sense pricked her conscience. She should have had more self-control than this.

He sifted her hair through his fingers and watched in fascination as golden rain fell. No, there had been no physical pain. But there would be other wounds to reckon with, other scars that would be formed. "More than you could possibly guess."

She knew it. This was too much for him. She had tried to be careful. Obviously, she hadn't succeeded. She started to move from him, ready to investigate his scar, afraid of the damage she would find. His hands slid down to her hips in a fluid movement, igniting a flame that wasn't thoroughly banked.

"Not yet," he told her. "Not yet." Amazing as it seemed to him, he hadn't had his fill of her. If anything, he was even hungrier than before. It was an interesting thing to discover about himself at this point in his life. He grinned, shaking his head.

Susanna traced the outline of his mouth with the tip of her forefinger and watched his lips quirk. "What?"

"I've never had a woman on top before." In all the times he and Kelly had made love, it had always been a sweet, gentle expression of their feelings. This searing passion was something entirely new to him.

She bracketed his body with her hands, shifting her weight. "Am I too heavy?" She searched his face, concerned. He wouldn't tell her. She'd see her answer in his eyes.

"Depends on your perspective." Slowly, he began to massage her hips and she began to move rhythmically. He felt himself responding. "You don't weigh much in pounds." But what she wanted from him was heavy. Perhaps too heavy for him to offer.

Susanna didn't want him taking the thought any further. If he had regrets and voiced them, something was going to die within her. "You realize, of course, that if you say you're sorry you're going to die."

The laughter bubbled up in his chest. They could both feel it before he finally let it free. "No, I'm not sorry. Not for this."

But for other things, she thought. Things that would come. But those could be faced later. One step at a time, she promised herself, on step at a time. She wasn't looking for major miracles, just pieces of one.

"Not about anything," she promised, hoping that she could make good on it.

The feel of her breasts gently moving against him as she breathed distracted him. He struggled to focus on his thoughts. He didn't want her to believe, in the end, that he had just been using her to satisfy himself. He wanted her to know that there were reasons for what was to come. "Susanna, it's a little hard, after you've been cut off at the knees, to learn how to dance again.''

She couldn't accept that. She had to make him see that he shouldn't, either. ''You weren't cut off, you were wounded. We all are in one way or another.''

She had the right to say that. She had been through it too, he thought. And yet, he couldn't understand how she *could* say it. ''How do you manage?''

She shrugged, her hair falling over her shoulder. He pushed it back, his hand closing over her breast. It just filled his hand. The way her lovemaking had filled his soul.

''I just do. I don't think about it much.'' In the early stages, after Brett died, to think would have been her undoing. Now, it was easier. ''The way I see it, you have two choices. You let life run you over, or you run with it. Maybe even a step ahead of it at times.''

He wanted to lose himself in her philosophy. In her. But he couldn't. He was too much of a realist for that. ''You really believe that, don't you?''

She nodded solemnly. ''With all my heart.'' She only wished she could make him believe it, as well.

She didn't seem real. This whole evening didn't seem real. Yet she was here, her body still pressed against his, still one with him. He wished he could tap into her source, but wishes were for fools who didn't know about life. ''You really are incredible, you know.''

She smiled, sliding her fingers along his lips, willing a smile into place. She shivered, surprised, as he licked the tip of one finger. Desire came, hard and wanting. ''Tell me more. You're on a roll, Flynn.''

''No,'' he contradicted, shifting so that she could take him in farther. His need for her magic was growing again. ''I'm on a roller coaster and I'm about to plunge down.''

She grinned broadly, wickedly. ''Then hang on, I'm coming with you.''

She brought her mouth down to his.

* * *

When Susanna awoke the next morning, she found the bed empty. Her pulse quickened and she forced herself to take a breath, then let it out slowly. He had probably just woken up early. He wasn't gone. He wouldn't leave without telling her.

Was she so sure?

No, she wasn't sure about anything when it came to Flynn, except how she felt about him. The other side of the coin was a mystery to her. She only *thought* he had felt something last night, too. But she wasn't sure.

She pulled the sheet to her as she sat up. Where was he? Flynn's robe was lying bunched up on the floor. She slid out of bed and quickly yanked the robe on, pushing her arms through the large sleeves as she hurried into the hall.

The smell of burnt coffee had her running into the kitchen. The string of muttered, colorful oaths had her slowing down again. He was still here.

Flynn swore he could smell her as she entered the room. The fragrance of wildflowers mingling with the scent that lovemaking left on her skin. It drifted to him, teasing his senses, even as he stood, puzzling over an incomprehensible piece of machinery. She had got to him, he thought, not at all happy about the matter.

He turned and looked at her accusingly. "How do you get this damn thing to work?"

"Not by hurting its feelings." Pulling the sash of the robe tight, she headed toward the refrigerator. So this was how the morning after was going to go. In warfare. She braced herself. "Sit down, I'll make coffee," she offered. "Do you want breakfast?"

"No." He snapped out the word.

Susanna turned to look at him. Barefoot, wearing only his jeans, he appeared no different than he had the other day. Actually, he looked more annoyed if that was possible. Seeing him this way hurt. She had expected, oh, she didn't know, something. A mellowing perhaps. Just something to indicate that they had gone up another plateau. Instead, she had the sinking feeling that they had returned to square one.

Worse, they were back in the box, before the game had even begun. The lid was shut tight.

She wet her lips. Crying would be stupid. So would hitting him with the frying pan, but of the two options, it was the more tempting. "What do you want?"

To make love to you until I die. To have my life back in order. But I can't have it both ways. "I think Michael and I will be going home this afternoon." He couldn't look at her, couldn't bear to see the hurt. "I'm certainly well enough. I think last night proved it."

Her voice was low, even, when she spoke. Without a strong control it would have broke. "Last night wasn't about physical endurance, Flynn."

"Last night—" he helplessly searched for words, "—was very nice."

"Nice?" she echoed in disbelief, her temper flaring. She moved around the table and poked an accusing finger at his chest. "A passing report card is 'nice.' A hit at bat is 'nice.' A glass of soda is 'nice.'"

He grabbed her hand. She was making a hole in his chest. "What's your point?"

She yanked her hand away, furious. "The point isn't mine, it's at the top of your head."

He supposed he deserved her anger and a lot more. He shouldn't have let last night happen, for both their sakes. "Susanna, last night, things got out of hand."

"Yes, they did. You forgot to put the stopper on your feelings." He made her so mad, she wanted to scream. What did it take to make him open up? She hadn't expected last night to be a religious experience for him, but she had hoped that he would open up just a little. She had glimpsed his soul in that small bedroom. Why did he insist on burying it?

It was better to hurt her a little now than to hurt her more later. "There are no feelings. I'm a man. That sort of thing can happen without any feelings being involved at all."

She wasn't buying that. It was a stupid, mindless argument. Men felt. *He* felt, she knew he did. "Then act like a man and stop running." She brought her hand to her mouth, trying to calm down. What was she doing, tossing out insults like that? She had always been so reasonable. "I'm sorry."

"No, I deserve that." That, and more, he thought if I hurt you.

She strove for patience. It wasn't easy. "What you deserve is a frying pan across your head, but I'm too much of a lady to do that." *Maybe.* "Now sit down, I'll make you breakfast and then you can plan your escape. Like you said, you proved last night that you're certainly well enough to take care of yourself and Michael."

He was standing behind her. She saw his reflection in the upper oven. He moved to place his hands on her shoulders, then let them drop. *Mustn't have physical contact,* she thought bitterly.

"About last night—I didn't mean to hurt you." The words felt awkward in his mouth.

"You didn't. Last night." She blinked back her tears, keeping her face turned from his as she reached into the refrigerator. "Orange juice?"

"I can get it." He brushed her aside and took out the carton himself. Getting a glass from the dish rack, he poured without knowing why.

"Nobody ever said you couldn't," she muttered. Love, she thought as she filled the coffeemaker, certainly didn't account for taste. She closed the lid on the machine, then turned toward him. "I'll help you pack."

He set the glass of orange juice on the table untouched. He wasn't hungry. Not for food. But he couldn't allow himself to indulge. Not again. "I can do that."

Yes, he could do everything. Pour juice. Pack. Bend steel with his bare hands. He didn't need her for anything. She watched as he walked out. "Flynn?"

He stopped, but didn't turn around. Tension knotted at the back of his neck. "What?"

"There's a difference between being independent and being mule-headed. Maybe you should learn it."

He was going to answer, then thought better of it. He knew if he got into a debate with her, he'd lose.

Technically, he already had. He kept on walking, reminding himself that it was better to hurt her a little now than a lot later.

Chapter Fourteen

Damn that woman. Damn her for invading his life, invading his mind and throwing what limited order he had attained into complete chaos again.

Flynn tossed aside the newspaper he had been unsuccessfully trying to read for the last ten minutes and rose from the kitchen table. Steam rising from the small pot told him his water was boiling. He took the lid off the dented drip coffeepot and poured the water in.

When would the order return?

He'd been home for three days. Three days now and he felt more like a stranger here than he had at Susanna's house. He looked around and took a deep breath. There was no subliminal scent of flowers everywhere, no hint of her wafting to him.

Dust, actually, was what he detected. The musty smell reminded Flynn that he had yet to hire a housekeeper. Now would be the perfect time to interview one, when he had nothing else to do.

Except go stir-crazy. Thinking. Wishing his life was back to normal. Wishing she were here.

He returned to the newspaper and paged through the sections until he found the Classifieds. Somehow, he couldn't get himself organized. Even the other times, when life had struck him such a horrible low blow, he had found a way to rally. It had been slow-going, but his basic sense of order had come to his aid. It had all but deserted him now. He found himself wandering from room to room, flipping through books, staring at the TV screen without seeing for whole blocks of time.

It was all her fault, he thought grudgingly, pouring a cup of coffee. All he could think about was his desire for her, the way her body had felt against his, the soft murmuring sound she had made as they had found that timeless, special place that lovers inhabit and make their own.

He took a sip of his coffee and pushed it aside. Maybe he had had too much coffee and was just wired. He should cut down. On coffee, on thoughts of her. The coffee would be the easy part.

She had come by today. Susanna buzzed by each morning, picking Michael up and taking him to school. She did it to spare Flynn the trouble of making arrangements. Yet unintentionally, she caused him more difficulties.

Or maybe it wasn't so unintentional. He wouldn't put it past her. He saw just enough of her to make him remember how much he missed seeing her. How much he missed being with her. Touching her. She appeared just long enough to ruin him for anything else the rest of the day.

No, he thought as he absently took another sip of coffee, he sincerely doubted that it was unintentional. He had no doubt that she was the more resilient one. She seemed to be able to cheerfully bounce back from anything. It wasn't like that for him.

By the beginning of his fourth week on disability, Flynn had restored a little order into his life. He was using this time to get a new perspective and a stronger grasp on things. Applying himself to the task diligently, he had interviewed twelve housekeepers before he had found Mrs. Duffy. She came with glowing references. The maternal-looking woman had had to leave her last position because the family she worked for was being transferred to Puerto Rico. Though they had offered her twice her pay to come with them, Mrs. Duffy had remained regretful, but firm. Puerto Rico was much too far away from her grandchildren. She was very sorry, but she couldn't go. Family meant everything to Mrs. Duffy. She slipped into Flynn's scheme of things very easily. Michael liked her.

"But not," he told Flynn in confidence, making sure that the older woman didn't overhear, "as much as Susanna." They walked outside to the car. When Flynn made no comment, Michael prodded, "How about you?"

Flynn got into the sports car and waited until Michael had buckled up. "How about me what?"

Michael peered into Flynn's face intently. "Do you like Susanna more?"

The kid had the makings of a lawyer, Flynn thought. This came under the heading of badgering the witness. Flynn turned on the ignition, then pulled out of the driveway. "It's too soon to tell."

"Not for me."

No, not for him, either, Flynn thought. That was just the trouble. Flynn turned on the radio, searching for something to take his mind off the topic.

"Can she come with us?" Michael raised his voice hopefully over the music.

"Who?"

"Susanna." Michael let out a sigh. "Aren't you listening?"

Yes, but he wasn't hearing, Flynn thought ruefully. His mind was drifting, as it usually did these days. What he needed, he was convinced, was to get back to work, to occupy his mind with facts and figures—figures other than hers.

Flynn turned down Susanna's street, annoyed at the feeling of homecoming that washed over him.

"Where would you like her to come?" he asked Michael patiently.

That was easy. "To the space 'zibt." They were picking Billie up to take him along with them.

"Exhibit," Flynn corrected. He slowed the car. "She might be busy." At least, he fervently hoped so, knowing where this was leading.

"I'll ask her!" Michael volunteered, jumping out of the car as soon as Flynn pulled up the hand brake. He didn't even wait for Flynn to shut off the engine.

She wasn't too busy.

When Flynn had initially suggested taking Billie with him and Michael to the annual space exhibit Worth Aerospace was holding that weekend, Susanna had been disappointed that Flynn hadn't included her in his invitation. The omission had stung. He had been so reticent, so distant each time she saw him since the night they had made love, she had felt as if that had been the end of everything instead of just the beginning.

Michael's eagerly extended invitation had her hoping that perhaps Flynn had had something to do with it. But she was afraid to ask. If she was uncertain, she could hope, pretend that perhaps Flynn was just being shy. Thinking back to their evening together, she realized that she was stretching hope to its limits.

She walked out to the car. "Hi."

"Hi," Flynn answered stiffly.

Was it just her, or did he look uncomfortable again? Why? They had made love, not declared war. She pretended not to notice. "Thanks for the invitation. I'll be glad to come."

She wasn't wearing any makeup and she looked terrific. How was that possible? "Um, don't you have to change or something?"

Susanna looked down at what she was wearing, jeans and a bright red silky T-shirt that made him think of roses in the spring.

"Why? Something wrong with this?" she asked innocently.

She didn't see anything wrong, but it was hard to second-guess him.

"No, no." He shook his head quickly. Most women seemed to take a long time. Life with four girls in the house had taught him that. And even Kelly, who was marvelously organized about everything, had never been able to get ready at a moment's notice. She had required a half day's warning before they went anywhere. Spontaneity had never been a part of their lives even before the children were born. He wasn't used to the idea of a woman being ready so quickly.

Michael and Billie came up behind her, impatient to leave. "You look great," Michael told Susanna.

"Great," Flynn echoed.

A recycled compliment was better than none at all, Susanna thought. She would take what she could get. At least she knew he wasn't given to empty flattery. She cupped Michael's chin and smiled at him, then at Flynn.

"I'll take that as a four-star rating. Just let me grab my purse and I'm ready."

Flynn wished like hell that he was. But no preparation would ever make him ready for Susanna. Each time he saw her, he felt anticipation tingling along his skin, knotting his stomach. This time, there was no appendix to blame it on. She was the cause.

Susanna had taken over his life. Yet he hadn't surrendered it to her. It almost seemed like a dream, all of it leaving him confused. His feelings these last few weeks had gone through drastic changes. It was difficult to come to grips with all the emotions he was experiencing. Flynn sighed. He could understand complicated mathematical concepts, but human behavior, even his own, baffled him. It was almost as if he had no choice but to feel what he was feeling, go in the direction he was going.

No, dammit, Flynn thought as Susanna got into the car, the boys scrambling into the back seat. He *did* have a choice in this matter.

He'd just exercise it tomorrow. Today, the boys deserved an outing.

At least his motive sounded noble.

The compound had been turned into something akin to a fairground. There was even a booth where free hot dogs and sodas were being dispensed. The line for that, Flynn noted, was twice as long as the one snaking into the main building, where the space station mock-ups were being housed.

"We'll eat later," he promised the boys as he herded them toward the main building. As they passed the entrance, a man in a silver space suit handed the boys balloons.

"Now there's a way to lose weight," Susanna commented. "Standing out in the broiling sun wrapped in aluminum foil." She shook her head as she gave the man in the space suit a sympathetic smile.

For a minute, Flynn thought Susanna was going to double back and get the man something to drink. She had the capacity, he thought, to feel empathy for everything and everyone. It was hard to keep someone like that at arm's length, but he was going to have to try if he wanted to hang on to his identity. More than try, he was going to have to succeed. The odds, he was beginning to feel, were strongly against him.

To keep Susanna from acting on impulse, Flynn took her arm. "This way, Pearl Pureheart."

Susanna just flashed him a grin and came along quietly. It was a first, Flynn thought.

At the exhibit, Flynn ran into several people he knew. Hearty greetings came, coupled with words of concern about his health. He shrugged the concern off, saying he'd be back at work soon. More than a couple of people commented that he looked a lot haler than he had of late, then eyed Susanna as if she were the reason for the improvement.

"Just how long a leave are you taking?" Howard Black, a slight-built man with a fringe of red hair surrounding a perfectly shaped head, asked. He peered at Susanna over the tops of his rimless glasses.

"Until he's well," Susanna spoke up before Flynn could answer. He glared at her. Now she was taking it upon herself to speak for him, as well.

Susanna bit her tongue. She had a habit of talking for others when their words failed to materialize at the right speed. She flashed Flynn a look of apology.

Howard chuckled as he moved on, his children demanding his attention. "Just don't tire him out too much," he told Susanna. "We need him back in Design." He turned toward Flynn and said, "Lucky devil," over his shoulder before he was yanked away.

Flynn made no comment and shepherded the boys to the next station, where they could walk through the tiny quarters that were meant to house the astronauts for weeks at a time.

"That tiny space?" Billie marveled. "Are they using midgets?"

Flynn laughed and launched into an explanation. At least here he was on familiar ground, not the way he felt when he was with Susanna. There nothing was familiar, not anymore.

Working with the minute details that went into constructing such a huge project as the space shuttle had given Flynn tunnel vision. He had lost sight of the overall picture, the breathtaking creations that a marriage between science and technology could accomplish. Seeing it through the eyes of two little boys brought it all back to him, making him remember why he had gone into the space program to begin with.

"Wow, and what's this?" Billie grabbed Flynn's hand and dragged him toward an actual space module.

Moments later, Michael was pulling him toward the long bulletin board that had a series of photographs tacked to it, documenting the project's progress. Flynn laughed in protest, but let himself be dragged off. He began to feel like a giant wishbone. A giant, satisfied wishbone.

He looked over his shoulder to see if Susanna was keeping up. She was watching him, amused. She probably thought all

this was funny, he mused. Yet there was no denying that it
felt right. The whole day felt right. Just the way she had in
his arms.

He pushed the thought from his head.

It wasn't going to happen. He wasn't going to allow himself
to slip into it. He'd been through all this once, raised his family, moved on to the next level of life. He couldn't start all
over again. Because he knew exactly what there was at the
end of the exhilarating roller coaster ride. A solid wall of emptiness. He'd worked his way through it before, he wasn't going
to go through it again. *Couldn't* go through it again. A man
could only endure so much before he folded.

If he didn't depend on anything outside himself for his happiness, for *anything* at all, he would never again know the
devastation of suddenly not having it there.

Of suddenly not having *her* there.

Doggedly, Flynn cleared his mind and focused it on answering the boys' questions.

Susanna watched Flynn, watched the contentment take hold,
then watched another emotion fight for possession of him.
And, from the look in his eyes, she saw it temporarily win.

What sort of devils did he have, she wondered. She knew
him intimately, knew some of what he probably felt, had felt
it herself. And yet, there was a place he wouldn't let her into,
a space he wouldn't share at all. And she didn't know how
long she could put up with that. Above all, Susanna needed
to share. She needed trust, and while she wanted someone in
her life to do all those things with, she also needed to be
needed.

Flynn didn't want that, didn't want her help, her support,
didn't seem to want anything. He had made it clear that while
he might enjoy her company, he didn't need her, wouldn't let
himself need her. She couldn't go on like that forever.

For now, she would just enjoy the outing.

She laced her arms about Billie's shoulders, stood behind
him and listened to Flynn's explanation. A small rumbling

sound coming from Billie's stomach punctuated Flynn's final statement. The boys broke into giggles.

"Lunch?" she suggested pleasantly to Flynn.

He was about to suggest that himself. The fact that she had beat him to it irritated him even when he told himself he was being unreasonable. But the woman was always one step ahead of him.

"Sure." They had seen everything that there was to see at the exhibit. He pointed toward the exit. They made their way past another line leading to the space module. "How about that restaurant I mentioned the first day I took you to work?"

Susanna blinked as they walked out. The exhibit had been moderately lit. Outside, the sunlight seemed almost blinding for a moment. Getting accustomed to it, Susanna turned to make sure everyone was out.

Flynn's suggestion sounded divine. It would have sounded even better had she been wearing long, teardrop earrings, a simple, understated black dress and could look at him over candlelight. Two hungry, squirming little boys didn't seem to fit the picture.

"I'd love to," she told him wistfully. "But I think Hamburger Heaven might be more their style." She glanced at the two boys.

"Yeah!" Billie grinned from ear to ear.

Michael looked at Flynn, waiting. "Could we, Pop?"

"Sounds like a good idea to me," Flynn agreed, taking Susanna by the elbow. A woman who put children's pleasure before her own was not an easy woman to turn his back on. Flynn felt his resistance lowering another notch.

After lunch, Billie and Michael talked Flynn into allowing them to spend some time wandering around the sprawling outdoor mall. With the homing instincts little boys were born with, they zeroed in on the pet shop and dragged Flynn in their wake.

Susanna was just as enchanted as the boys were. To Flynn's

surprise, she didn't recoil at the snakes and even expressed a fondness for the mice.

"Aren't girls supposed to find those things icky or gross or whatever the popular term these days is?" Flynn asked her as they stood by a tank filled with straw-and-white rodents.

She laughed. "I don't know. I haven't been reading my girl handbook lately. I'm too busy trying to raise a boy."

And doing more than an adequate job of it, Flynn thought. Every which way he turned, her total competence assaulted him. He admired her for it, yet he would have been lying to himself if he pretended that he didn't wish she were just a little less capable. It would be nice, he mused, if she needed him once in a while.

"Hey, Pop, look at this!"

Michael and Billie were circling a topless, wire-rimmed cage that was placed out in the middle of the floor. The dalmatian puppy inside was madly shredding the paper on the floor. The dog barked and ran back and forth, trying to get at the little boys. He wanted to play.

"Oh, isn't he an adorable puppy?" Susanna reached over the barrier and let the dog sniff her hand, then petted it.

Flynn had never had a pet. He'd grown up in an apartment and dogs had not been allowed. His daughters had never wanted anything larger than a hamster. Warily he eyed the large dog with its over-sized paws. "That's a puppy?"

"It sure is!" Michael exclaimed, his eyes dancing. "Could we buy him, Pop?"

"No, I don't think so." Flynn placed a hand on the boy's shoulder. "Owning a dog is a big commitment, Michael. We're going to have to think about it carefully and discuss it."

Michael nodded, subdued. Disappointed.

Flynn felt bad. A boy needed a dog, he thought. But then, a boy needed a mother, as well, and he wasn't running out to get one of those, either. Each step in life needed to be carefully thought out; otherwise, the consequences could be overwhelming. He slanted a look at Susanna.

Billie turned pleading eyes on his mother. "Could we get him, Mom? Could we? Then Michael and I could share him."

How could she possibly squelch a burst of generosity? And, after all, she *had* promised him a dog for his next birthday. The dog licked her fingers and added his two cents worth. She was a goner. "Okay."

The boys let out a cheer.

Flynn stared at her as Susanna beckoned to a salesgirl. "You're buying a dog?"

"Yes." The pet shop attendant looked at Susanna questioningly. "We'd like this dog, please."

Flynn couldn't believe it. "Just like that?"

Susanna pulled her wallet out and flipped through the compartments for her charge card. "How would you like me to do it?"

Was she simpleminded? "With some thought."

Susanna flashed a smile as she approached the counter. The clerk behind the register was already writing up the paperwork. "I did think."

The woman was impossible. "I mean, more than half a minute." The clerk gave Flynn a curious look, but he ignored it.

Susanna didn't understand why he was getting so worked up. This was natural to her. "It doesn't take me very long to make up my mind, Flynn. Something is either right, or it's not." *And when will you get that through your thick head?*

It just didn't compute. You didn't make decisions that were binding on a whim. This was a pet they were talking about, not a stuffed animal. "What kind of an actuary are you?" Actuaries were supposed to be a logical, pragmatic breed, not whimsical.

She watched as the attendant brought the dog out. Billie and Michael fell upon it, one boy on either side, both trying to get their arms around the dalmatian. She turned to look at Flynn. "A very happy one."

With dog food, a squeaky toy and various other doggie paraphernalia, they left the pet shop with the newest member of

Susanna's family in tow. Getting into the car was a feat, but they managed.

The matter of a name was a little trickier. Billie wanted to name the dalmatian Manfred and Michael thought that Marmaduke would be a good name.

Susanna twisted around in her seat and cocked her head, studying the dog. "George," she pronounced, as if divinely inspired. "We'll call him George."

"George?" Both boys groaned at once.

Susanna nodded. "George. I like it."

"George," they chorused in a surrendering sigh.

Flynn was surprised at how quickly they retreated. But then, children had a remarkably keen sense of survival, he thought. They knew when the odds were against them. Sometimes adults lost the ability to see that when they grew older.

No sooner had they arrived at Susanna's house than the boys begged to show off their new acquisition to Aunt Jane. Flynn noticed that Michael referred to her as Aunt Jane, as well. The boy was doing his damnedest to fit in, Flynn thought. But they weren't meant to, not into this family.

Damn, she was making it hard to keep that in mind, he thought, watching Susanna putter around the kitchen.

Jane was in the house within moments. The dog bounded behind her, joyously laying claim to the entire house, leading the boys on a merry chase.

"Hi, handsome, nice to see you again," Jane tossed off to Flynn as she entered. "Susanna in the kitchen?" He nodded and she walked past him. Jane looked at her niece, shaking her head, hands on her hips. "I don't suppose you know what you're in for."

Flynn leaned against the doorjamb, his arms folded across his chest. "I tried to warn her."

Jane nodded. "Like talking to a wall, though. She has a mind of her own. Don't know where she gets it from," she told him with another shake of her head. The puppy rose up on his hind legs, his paws on Jane's legs. She petted him absently, looking at Susanna. "Lucky for you I know how to train dogs." She glanced at Flynn and saw his surprise. "Kyle trained animals for the movies."

"Kyle?" Flynn looked at Susanna for an explanation.

"Her first husband," Susanna said, getting the coffee cups from the cabinet.

Flynn shook his head, amused. First a baseball player, now an animal trainer. "You have a husband for all occasions?"

If she saw his amusement, Jane didn't show it. "Pretty nearly." Jane took a firm hold of the dog's leash and kept him from bounding off again. "Actually, I came over to borrow your boys."

"Borrow?" Susanna repeated.

"Overnight." Jane smiled at the boys who looked at her eagerly. Their expressions seemed to say that this was turning out to be a super day. "I've been waiting for you to get back. I just rented two great horror videos, but I'm too afraid to watch them on my own."

Flynn could have sworn a sly, satisfied look slid over the older woman's face, then disappeared.

Jane looked down at the small faces. "I'm going to need two brave men, one to hold each hand. What do you say, are you up to it, men? There's all the popcorn and ice cream you can eat in it for you if you agree."

As if they needed a bribe. "Aunt Jane..." Susanna said warningly.

"You can have some, too, if you want," the woman offered innocently.

Billie looked at George, who was trying to chew his leash. "Can George come, too?"

Jane nodded solemnly. "I'm counting on it." She looked over the boys' heads at Susanna. "Is it all right?"

"It is with me." Susanna glanced to her left. "Flynn?"

He had already vetoed buying a dog, he wasn't about to play the heavy twice in one day. "Sure, why not?"

They were gone before he finished the sentence.

Chapter Fifteen

Flynn watched the door close behind the boys. He shook his head, turning to look at Susanna. She had already retreated into herself and started taking out an assortment of different herbal teas. Undoubtedly for her "pleasure," he thought with a smile, remembering the way she had phrased it before.

Susanna felt him staring at her and looked up. Flynn nodded toward the front door. "Subtlety doesn't run in your family, does it?"

She plopped a packet of spiced cider into the midst of the teas. "No, but honesty does." She placed the assortment on the table before him.

"You want me to be honest?"

His voice was low. Anticipation crackled in the air. Susanna knew she was asking, almost demanding this confrontation, yet she was afraid of the results. She took a breath and held it. "Yes."

"Brutally honest?"

She flipped the kettle on and then turned. There was nothing else for her to do, no more busy-work to fidget with. "You're not the type to tiptoe around things."

No, he never had been. "You're driving me crazy."

She relaxed a little. "You've already told me that before." She shrugged and was surprised when he took hold of her shoulders. Tilting her head back, she saw that his eyes had grown dark.

"No, really crazy." He felt the slight tremor that pulsated through her body. God, he wanted her. It wasn't fair to himself, to her to let this happen. And yet, he couldn't stop it. "I can't get you out of my mind, out of my blood. I close my eyes and I see you."

"Sounds like a man who's haunted." But she was smiling when she said it. She couldn't help it. It felt wonderful to know that she wasn't alone in this, that his emotions were as churned up as hers.

"Haunted?" he repeated, rolling the word over in his mind. Yes, that was the best way to describe it. He was haunted and she was the haunter. "Yes, I'm haunted. Haunted by the way you felt against me. Haunted by that damn perfume you wore." He sniffed. She was wearing it now. "What is it?"

Susanna grinned. She didn't wear perfume. There was an assortment of bottles on her bureau, but they were almost all full. She could never remember to put any on in the morning. "Soap."

Flynn raised a lock of her hair. It was in his way. He pressed his lips to her throat and felt her quiver. Felt himself quiver.

"Soap and you. A heady combination." He trailed his lips along the side of her neck, touching just the tip of her ear. She gripped his forearms. His own knees felt weak. "This was all I could think about since Saturday. Having you like this."

Susanna fought her way to the surface. He was making her mind drift, fantasizing. "You could have fooled me."

"I doubt it." He took a step back before he couldn't. "The only one I was trying to fool was myself."

"And did you?" She searched his face for the answer.

"I'm here, aren't I?"

Not enough. It wasn't enough. She needed to have him say something more, to verbalize his feelings, his commitment. "Yes. So is the dog."

He pulled her toward him. The hell with safe. His arms didn't feel complete without her in them. "No one put a collar around my neck and dragged me." She had to know how much he wanted her, he thought.

"No," she agreed slowly, watching his eyes. Why was he torturing himself this way? Why couldn't he just accept things and take it one step at a time? No one was rushing him. "No one did."

Maybe she needed a declaration, but he couldn't give her one. It wouldn't come. He was afraid to let it come. "Susanna, if I make love to you—with you," he stumbled over the phraseology and she found it endearing, "what does that make us?"

She touched his cheek. "Happy."

He pressed her cool fingers to his face, then kissed them one by one. "But later—"

She covered his lips with her fingers, stopping him before he could say something to spoil the moment. "Later will work itself out later," she promised. Then, because she thought he wanted to hear it, she lied. "No twenty-year plans, Flynn. Just here and now. You and me."

He glanced toward the front door. If he didn't miss his guess, Jane wouldn't let the boys come back for anything. "Has anyone nominated your Aunt Jane for sainthood?"

"I'm thinking about it." The kettle went off, whistling insistently. Susanna reached behind her to shut off the burner. Flynn kept her within the circle of his arms. Susanna leaned back slightly, amused. "Can I get you anything?" She nodded at the tea packets on the table.

No thoughts, he promised himself. No consequences. Just here and now, as Susanna had said. "Yes."

"What?"

He brushed his hand along the outline of her T-shirt, his fingers just touching her breast. "Guess."

The laugh caught in her throat. "I need a hint. I'm kind of slow."

He pressed another soft, lingering kiss on her throat, losing himself in the feel, the taste of her skin. He skimmed his fingers along her spine and felt her arch against him. "Hardly."

The passion sizzled instantly, demanding tribute, leaving him in awe. Leaving him breathless. Flynn had sought an explanation for the last time. It had been over a year since he had made love to a woman, perhaps he had just been carried away physically, made more of it in his mind than it was. It was possible, he had argued. He was here to prove his theory. Dispelling the myth, he would get himself back under control.

This time, he assured himself, he was prepared for her. Prepared for what was about to happen between them.

There was no way to be prepared for plunging out of an airplane without a parachute.

She had missed him. Lord, she had missed him. Knowing he was only a few miles away had made it even worse. A few miles away and not here. Not with her. Of his own volition. She hadn't been ready for the kind of pain that had generated.

She shivered as he impatiently drew her clothes from her, first the T-shirt, then the jeans. He was trying not to tear them off. His fingers got tangled in the straps of her teddy. With a soft laugh, she moved his hand away and slid the straps from her shoulders, watching him watch her. Hot sensations poured through her, like lava spilling from a volcano. There was nothing but pure desire in his eyes.

When the delicate white lace had slipped to the swell of her hips Flynn stopped her. "I think I can take it from here." His voice was thick from wanting her.

She said nothing as she took his hands and placed them on her hips. Watching only her eyes, Flynn pulled away the teddy. He let out a small sound of appreciation as the material slipped off and he looked at her, his eyes touching her everywhere. She felt the touch as surely as if his hands had been there, instead.

"My turn," she murmured thickly, pushing his shirt from his shoulders, tossing it to the floor.

When he felt her long, tapering fingers slide against his hips, urging both his jeans and briefs down at the same time, he could feel his blood surge through him, pounding in his loins. He pulled himself free of the confining clothes, anxious to feel her against his naked body, to have her flesh warm his.

"My room still free?"

"No one's checked in yet." As an afterthought, she grabbed the clothing, taking it with her just in case the boys had to come back for something. But if she knew Jane, they wouldn't be back before morning.

"Keep it that way." He swooped her up in his arms. "I'm making a permanent reservation."

She thought of his operation. He shouldn't be carrying her like this. "Flynn, be careful."

"Too late for that."

And it was. Too late for caution, for thought. Too late for anything but getting lost in the taste, the feel, the lure of her.

Gently, he laid her down on the bed, then drew close to the haven that only she could create for him. The covers became tangled around their bodies as they sought the pleasure they knew was waiting, the pleasure each could give to the other.

She had lied, Susanna thought as she felt his moist, open-mouth kisses outlining the hollow of her abdomen, making it quiver. She had lied when she'd told him that tomorrow would take care of itself. She wanted him today, tomorrow, forever. And it grieved her that he didn't need her the way she did him, in every part of her life.

Coherent thoughts vanished, evaporated by the heat created by his lovemaking.

Flynn couldn't believe it. It was even more overwhelming than before. More satisfying even as it continued to be arousing. He plunged himself into her after holding back longer than he thought humanly possible. A half-dozen times she had almost pushed him over the ragged edge, but he had restrained, held back. Now, he couldn't. He had to have her, had to take

her. There was no more time. He drove himself up to the
pinnacle, taking her with him. She cried out his name as her
nails dug into his shoulders. They both tumbled from the cliff
together.

Exhausted, Flynn tried to keep from crushing Susanna by
balancing himself on his elbows. She shifted beneath him and
he wanted her. Again. Though he had no strength with which
to take her, he wanted her.

He'd never have enough of her.

Dependence. He was growing dependent again in a way he
never had before. Addicted to the way she made him feel:
happy, whole, eternally young. He was afraid. Hell, he was
scared out of his mind. How had it happened, when he swore
it wouldn't? When he was so sure that it wouldn't?

She saw the look, the doubt, enter into his eyes. *Too soon,*
she thought. *Too soon. Be mine for a little while longer.*

"What's the matter?" she asked.

He couldn't tell her, not now. He smiled, framing her face
in his hands as he drew himself up. "Were you ever a gym-
nast?"

It wasn't what she had expected to hear. She laughed with
relief. "No, why?"

He indulged himself and nipped at her lower lip, sucking
slightly. He felt her shift beneath him, his arousal growing.
Maybe he wasn't as exhausted as he thought. "I never knew
anyone who could bend that way."

It was on the tip of her tongue to say that love could make
her do incredible things, but she knew he wasn't ready to hear
the word, even though she ached to say it. Now that she knew,
she wanted to tell him. Instead, she shrugged. "I'm double-
jointed."

He shifted slightly so that their bodies remained touching,
but his weight was on the bed. His hand rested possessively
on her thigh. "Anything else I should know about you?"

"I have all my own teeth, I love children and sometimes, I
tend to take charge." She slanted him a look beneath hooded
lashes.

"Sometimes?" he echoed with a laugh. She was a soft general.

All right, maybe all the time, she thought. "Sometimes, I sleep."

He laughed. She was extraordinary. "Tell me, why aren't you married yet?"

Why? So I wouldn't pose a threat to you?

She wouldn't let him see how much his question bothered her. "You sound like Aunt Jane." Susanna turned her head away from him, hoping she wouldn't cry.

She was evading him. He wondered why. What had kept someone like her, someone with such optimism for life from marrying? He cupped her chin and made her look at him. "Seriously," he pressed.

"Seriously?" *All right,* she thought. *You asked for this.* "Because I never met anyone who made bells ring since Brett." She raised her eyes. "Until now."

Before he could shut it away, he felt a tenderness sprout within him in response to her words. Flynn sat up. This had to stop before she was hurt. Before they both were. "Susanna, I'm not going to get married again. I'm not going to have another relationship."

Susanna scrambled out of bed and grabbed the closest article of clothing. With a muffled oath, she struggled into the teddy. The man was impossible. "In case it escaped you, there's more happening here than washing socks."

"This isn't a relationship," he said quietly, damning himself for being so weak. For needing her.

T-shirt in her hands, she swung around to look at him. "It's not? Then what is it?" she demanded. If she cried now, she'd never forgive herself. Or him.

"An anomaly." He pulled on his jeans, then tried to take her by the shoulders. She hit his hands aside. "Susanna, it can't be a relationship."

She raised her chin pugnaciously. If she took a swipe at him, she knew it wouldn't hurt, not anywhere close to the way his words had hurt her. But still she wanted to. "Why?"

He wished she could understand, wished he wasn't the cause of the hurt in her eyes. He had never wanted to hurt her, just to save himself. "Because in a relationship, my guard will slip and I can't have that." He yanked on his shirt, then dragged a hand through his hair. "I can't be dependent on someone else for my happiness. Not again."

She stood before him in a T-shirt hanging down to her thighs, her eyes blazing. A delicate Fury.

How dare he run from this? How dare he push everything into her hand? "I think you have something twisted here. We don't depend on others for our happiness. Happiness comes from inside." She poked at his chest. "From you. Not me."

She lowered her voice, struggling to get her emotions under control. "I'd like to think I add to it, but I'm not the source. That's inside of you. I can't change you. I can't make you into something you're not." She wouldn't have wanted to try. What she was trying to do was reach the person she thought was buried inside. The person who made love with her and needed love in kind. "If I can't do that, how can I possibly make you dependent?"

It was so simple. Didn't she see? "Because a day without you is empty. Because I want to see you, hear you, touch you. If that's not dependency, I don't know what is."

Her anger melted. The look in his eyes had made it burn away. "So you're swearing off me?"

Her hair was still tousled from the wild, breathtaking ride they had been on. Her lips were slightly bruised from the imprint of his. He had her scent along his body. And she had his on hers. How was he supposed to resist that? How was he supposed to resist her? With a halfhearted effort, he tried.

He wasn't surprised when he lost.

Muttering an oath, Flynn pulled her to him roughly, a groan on his lips. "No, just swearing at you." He buried his face in her hair. Soft, silky. Tangling his common sense into knots. "Do you have to look so damn desirable all the time?"

She grinned. He had the oddest way of giving her a compliment. "No, I don't have to. But right now it helps."

"Only one of us, Susanna. Only one of us." He pulled off her T-shirt again, knowing he was plunging over the falls once more. Knowing, too, that sometime soon, the barrel was going to smash against the rocks.

He was going to handle it. There were no two ways about it. Flynn had made up his mind to handle it and he would. As long as he kept that in mind, kept a tight rein on his feelings and allowed himself only so much slack, everything would be all right. He could see her. Even make love with her and not get himself hopelessly lost. The trick was to do it in small doses.

The trick was remembering his plan.

It seemed that everything conspired against him. Stephanie and Julia surprised him the following Saturday, arriving before noon and announcing that they were taking Michael and Billie to Disneyland.

"I'm not included?" Flynn asked, amused. He watched Michael help Julia gather the necessary "supplies" that would make an outing to the Magic Kingdom complete. Michael had stopped eyeing him warily, as if Flynn were going to evaporate the next moment. He was no longer worried about Michael. The boy was going to be just fine.

"No, you're going to be busy," Julia told him, depositing several cans of soda into the backpack.

"Doing what?" Flynn asked suspiciously. "Your car acting up again?"

"The car's fine." Stephanie threw a light jacket for Michael to Julia. She looked at her father. "You're going to be busy taking Susanna out for a proper dinner." She shook her head.

Flynn followed Stephanie as she walked into the bathroom, where she rummaged through the medicine cabinet until she found a bottle of sunscreen. It amused Flynn that Stephanie managed to be so thorough while giving off this careless image. "Proper? What is that supposed to mean?"

Stephanie cocked her head, her dark hair spilling over her shoulder. "She's always cooked for you, the least you could do is pay for a meal.'' Finding everything she wanted, Stephanie crossed back to the family room.

Did this bossy streak come naturally to all women? he wondered. He was beginning to think so. "For your information, I already have."

"Terrific." Julia's eyes brightened as she accepted the half-empty bottle of sunscreen and tucked it into one of the myriad zippered compartments on the blue-and-red backpack. "Where?"

"Hamburger Heaven," Michael put in, coming to Flynn's defense. The smirk on Stephanie's face had him mystified. How had he struck out?

"Indigestion in record time," Stephanie proclaimed. She placed her hands on her father's arms, giving him a patient look. "I think Susanna would like to go somewhere where the meals don't come in individual containers on plastic trays, Pop.''

He could spend the afternoon arguing with them, but that would keep them from the amusement park and he didn't want to disappoint the two boys. Besides, he supposed that his daughters did have a point. Susanna had technically saved his life. He owed her a night out.

Moreover, if they were in a restaurant, he couldn't very well give in to temptation. "All right." He started to go call Susanna when he caught the girls giving each other a high five. Michael leaped up to add his small hand to the celebration.

Time to nip this in the bud. "Look, everyone, this is just dinner."

Stephanie crossed to him, an affectionate smile on her lips. She straightened his collar. "There's another *D* word that's applicable here." He raised an eyebrow quizzically. "Date, Pop. Date."

He removed her hands from his collar and held them firmly. His expression was very serious. "I don't date, Stephanie." Lord, he didn't even know how anymore. Up to now, there had been no need.

"Then you should, and it should be with Susanna."

She sounded so positive about it, the way only the very young could. It amused him despite himself. "Have the church picked out?"

"No," she said cheerfully. "That we'll leave up to you."

They were going to leave other matters up to him, too, he thought. This was his life, not theirs, to work out. "Come here." He moved farther out of the room. The subject was too serious to discuss in front of Michael. "I'm not about to get married again."

"Not with this attitude."

"Not with any attitude." He looked into her eyes and saw some of himself, saw the optimism that had once resided in his soul. Before he had learned. "Stephanie, I'm forty-five years old."

"You're the youngest forty-five I've ever known." To emphasize her point, she tapped his biceps. "If you weren't my father, I'd give Susanna a run for her money."

He was going to make her understand if it *did* take all afternoon. "Be that as it may, think logically for a minute. I'm ten years older than Susanna. If I did marry her now, in fifteen years, I'll be sixty."

Stephanie looked at him, her expression growing somber. "And how old will you be in fifteen years if you don't marry Susanna?"

The simplicity of her question confounded him. He had no answer for her. "Anyone ever tell you that you have a smart mouth?" he asked affectionately.

"I come by it naturally." Impishly, she patted his face. "I have a smart pop. Until now." She swung around. "Ready?" she called to Julia and Michael.

"No," Flynn murmured to himself. "But that doesn't seem to matter to anyone."

He didn't seem to have a say in any of this, Flynn thought as he drove to Susanna's house later that evening. Everyone was trying to take it out of his hands. Everyone was eager to propel his life down the track. Stephanie, Julia, Michael, Susanna's aunt, they were all behind him, pushing. But only he would come to the station at the end of the line. Only he would face the loneliness after all was said and done, the way he had once before. He had no desire to reach that destination again.

Flynn parked the convertible at the curb next to her mailbox and got out. He didn't care how beautiful Susanna was, how desirable she was and how much everyone else liked her. He simply wasn't going to be railroaded into doing anything he didn't want to do. And that was that.

The trouble, he thought when she opened the door, the porch light bathing her in an ethereal glow, was that he did want to. Desperately.

Damn, even he was fighting against himself.

Of course, it was hard not to want her when she was wearing minimal clothing disguised as an evening dress. Her shoulders were bare and tempting. Her hot-pink halter dress was completely backless with a straight skirt that emphasized every curve he had already memorized with his fingertips.

"What's this all about?" Susanna pulled the door closed behind her and went down the walk. When he had called earlier, asking her out in that noncommittal way of his, she had been pleased, but completely surprised. Seeing him in a suit and tie was even more surprising. He looked stunning.

Flynn opened the car door for her and waited until she got in. "It's about conspiring daughters and grandsons and aunts." He shut the door, then came around the hood to his own side.

She didn't understand. "Is this some kind of classified information you're giving me in code?"

He wove his way to the main drag in Bedford. The familiar path toward the mall seemed different in the dark. He had done it five days a week for eight years, half-asleep. Traveling down this road with Susanna, dusk painting the sky shades of muted pink and purple, made it seem unusual. Romantic.

He was going to have to steer clear of that kind of thinking if he was going to survive. "Everyone thinks we're good together."

He made it sound like a life sentence. "It doesn't matter what everyone else things. It matters what you think."

If he could blame his being here on someone else, it wouldn't be as difficult for him to accept. Knowing he was acquiescing of his own free will put another light on the matter. And she knew it, too, he thought, glancing at her. "You fight dirty, you know that?"

"I fight to win." She settled back. "So, where are we going?"

"That restaurant I keep talking about but never seem to take you to. Robert Burns."

"The one at the mall?" He nodded. She had the impression that this wasn't his idea. It wasn't any good unless he wanted to do it. "Sounds wonderful, but you don't have to."

There she went again. "I wish you'd stop telling me what I can or can't do."

Susanna could hear the shift in his tone. She was tired of always worrying if she was saying the right thing and second-guessing his reaction. She wasn't trying to lead his life for him; she was just making a suggestion.

"Sorry," she said tightly. "I thought this was a dialogue. I keep forgetting you want to be autonomous." She felt her temper flaring. Dammit, she wasn't throwing a lasso over him. She thought he *wanted* to be with her. "You know, for a fee, I read somewhere that you can declare yourself your own country and be as damn independent as you want." With a huff, she crossed her arms before her and stared out the window.

If he lived to be a thousand, he'd never understand the opposite sex. "What set you off?"

If he wanted to fight, he was going to get one. "You. The damn wall you keep rebuilding every time I find a chink to crawl through." She drew herself up as he slowed down at the light. "You know, you might call what you want independence, but I call it being lonely." Incensed, Susanna suddenly got out of the car and slammed the door behind her, making it vibrate. As Flynn stared, stunned, she started to walk away.

"Get back into the car," he ordered. Crazy. The woman was positively crazy.

Susanna just kept walking. It was probably two miles to her house and she was in three-inch heels, but she didn't care. Anything was preferable to being in the car with that heartless brute, even if he was the best-looking thing she had ever seen in a suit.

Flynn did a U-turn in the middle of the road, grateful that there were no cars behind him. When he called to her again, she just raised her chin higher. Her pace never slowed.

She wished she had taken a shawl with her. The wind was beginning to pick up. "I don't have to listen to you."

Any second now, a policeman was going to pop out of nowhere and give him a ticket. Is that what she wanted? "Susanna, I'm driving on the wrong side of the road."

She didn't even spare him a glance. "Shouldn't bother you. You're just showing off your independent streak."

Letting go of a string of choice words, Flynn jumped out of his car, abandoning it. Susanna began to walk faster, but he quickly caught up to her. Grabbing her arm, he jerked her around. "What is it you want?"

How could he ask her that? Shutting her out at every turn, how could he ask that? "To get in, Flynn."

He looked back at his car. He hadn't thrown her out. What was she talking about? "What?"

She didn't want to have to spell it out. "I don't want to be your mother, I don't want to baby you, I want to be there for you. There's a difference. It involves trust and caring and, oh yes, the *L* word." Her lips twisted in a mirthless smile. How could he be like this after they had made love? "The one that'll make you choke if you say it."

What he wanted to choke was her, but he kept his temper bridled. "What are you talking about?"

She shook her head, her eyes shining with tears. "You haven't a clue, do you, Flynn?" Pulling away, she began to walk again. "Tell your daughters and everyone else involved that I had a very—enlightening time."

Incredulously, he fell into step. "You're going home?"

"Watch me."

"It's two miles. In the dark." And she was hardly dressed for a stroll. That dress would stir the imagination of anyone with any kind of libido.

Susanna swallowed past the lump in her throat. "We independent people are very resilient. You ought to know that."

His patience at an end, he pointed behind him. "Get in the car." To his astonishment, she just kept walking. "I said, get in the car."

"Make me."

He wasn't about to let something happen to her because she was so damn pig-headed. For tonight, she was his responsibility. "Okay."

The next thing she knew, she was being lifted in the air and then slung over his shoulder. "What the hell do you think you're doing?"

Carrying her fireman style, he began to walk back to the car. "Taking you out to dinner."

"You idiot, you'll break your stitches. Put me down!" She tried to wiggle off, but he had a firm grip on her.

"They're my stitches to break."

Unceremoniously, he deposited her into the car. Coming around to his side, he got in and turned on the ignition. With effort, he let out a breath, trying to calm down. He'd never acted that rashly before and it left him as stunned as it probably did her. He glanced toward Susanna. "Still hungry?"

That he cared enough to *make* her come made her smile. Perhaps there was hope for him yet. "Why not? Playing cavewoman always makes me hungry."

He supposed he should apologize. He hadn't a clue what had come over him. "I didn't mean to do that."

She grinned. "Too bad. It was the most spontaneous thing you've done so far, other than have your appendicitis attack."

No, he wasn't going to understand women, Flynn decided. Not if he lived forever.

Chapter Sixteen

He had no idea that the restaurant had dancing on the weekend. The announcement was posted outside the building, which had been designed to resemble an old Scottish castle. Leaning his hand against the cool, smooth, gray stones, Flynn read the notice and was tempted to alter his plans. But the look on Susanna's face made the decision for him. They went in.

Flynn held up two fingers in answer to the maître d's unspoken question. The genial-looking man in the red-and-green plaid kilt turned wordlessly and led them to a table just off the dance floor.

"Will this do, ma'am?" A soft Scottish burr enveloped every syllable.

"It's lovely," Susanna answered as the man helped her with her chair.

Flynn saw the appreciative expression on the maître d's face as he took a long lingering survey of Susanna's bare back.

The man looked up at Flynn and there was a congratulatory note in his eyes as he waved him to his seat.

Flynn scanned the wine list. "I suppose you want to dance." He hadn't danced in years. Probably no longer knew how, he thought.

Resting her chin on her raised, linked fingers, Susanna looked at the dance floor. A lovely ballad echoed softly through the restaurant as a lone couple took advantage of the romantic atmosphere. They looked very much in love, she thought wistfully. "You're getting good at reading my mind."

"No, not really." Flynn selected a wine and indicated his choice to the young, slight waiter who had appeared at their table to take their order. Like the maître d', the waiter wore a kilt. "I don't think I have a clue about what goes on out there."

He made it sound like no-man's-land. "Nothing that complex," Susanna assured him. "It's all very simple, really."

Flynn uttered a short laugh. She clearly underestimated herself. "Any woman who can juggle as many things, as many roles as you do, can never lay claim to the word simple."

Susanna smiled at the waiter as he returned to serve her first, then pour a glass for Flynn. He left the bottle on the table. She waited until they were alone again. "That's your problem, you make things far too complicated. Like the dog."

He took a sip and let the light wine curl through his system. It hadn't anywhere near the kick that she had. But then, she was far more potent. He looked at Susanna over the rim of the glass.

"The dog," he echoed, not having the slightest idea what she was driving at.

"George." Absently, she sipped her wine, then smiled. "It's a simple matter, Flynn. Boy, dog. Dog, boy." She indicated each coupling with a wave of her hand. "They belong together."

He failed to see the simplicity she obviously thought was so evident. To him the purchase of the animal had a great many complications attached to it. He tossed one at her. "How about the vet bills?"

She shrugged. He watched the candlelight play along the slope of her shoulders. He remembered the way her skin felt there, delicate and silky. "Those will belong to me. It's a small price to pay for happiness."

"Whose?" Was she talking about herself now, or her son? Or both?

"Billie's. George's." She thought of the look on his grandson's face when the puppy licked him. "Michael's." All of which made her own heart glad. "Mine."

All this because of one dog. Only she could pull that off. And she had even included the dog in this group. "That about covers the whole bunch, doesn't it?"

She looked at him pointedly. "Almost."

There was some hidden message here that he didn't quite fathom. And he didn't want her to spell it out for him, either. "It would take more than just a dog to make me happy, Susanna."

"Tell me about it. Maybe we can come up with something." What was it? she wondered. What would bring the lights back into his eyes on a permanent basis?

She was digging and he didn't want her to. He didn't want to talk about the past, or the problem that gnawed away at him. The fear. He didn't want to burden her with it. "No."

He was closing the doors again. One step forward, two steps back. Susanna sighed, looking down into her wineglass. The crystal shimmered and sparkled, but gave off no warmth. An illusion. Was that what they had between them? Only an illusion? "Looks like the big guy pitched another shutout."

Now she was talking to wineglasses. Maybe he had jarred something loose before, carrying her over his shoulder the way he had. "What are you talking about?"

"Never mind." Her smile was tight, to keep herself from unraveling. "I don't think someone as complex as you would understand."

There was only one way out of this. He rose. "Care to dance?"

She took the hand he offered. "I'd love to." She smiled at him, striving to maintain her sense of humor. It was the only weapon she had. "This way we're both satisfied. You get to move and I get to stay with you."

He led her to the dance floor and took her in his arms. "Love Is A Many-Splendored Thing" was being played by the three-piece band. He pressed her closer to him and felt her sigh vibrate against his chest. Her bare skin made his fantasies take flight despite his resolutions to the contrary. Every minute with her was a struggle of some sort, he thought.

"Susanna, someday you're going to have to print a code book so the rest of us can understand what you're talking about."

"The one who really counts will understand. He won't need a code book."

Then it probably wouldn't be me, Flynn thought. And that was just as well. For both of them.

It was all right, Flynn assured himself. There was just a week left before the end of his leave of absence. It was all right to indulge a little, all right to let his guard slip. Once he was back at work, things would get back to normal. For now, he'd let them drift.

He thought he was safe.

For the next week, Flynn saw life, his and Michael's, fall into a pattern. Though Mrs. Duffy had turned out to be every bit as resourceful, every bit as competent as Mrs. Henderson had been before her, Flynn found himself eating dinner at Susanna's house. The fault was Michael's.

Susanna still came by each morning to pick him up for school. She insisted on it really, saying his house was on her way to the school. Since going with them made Michael happy, Flynn agreed.

Because George was there, Michael begged to be allowed to go over to Billie's house every day after school. Jane was more than willing to bring Michael along when she picked Billie up from school in the afternoon. Since the arrangement was only temporary until he went back to work, Flynn saw no reason to deny Michael this small pleasure, either.

Around five o'clock, Flynn would drive the short distance to Susanna's house to pick the boy up. Once there, Flynn found himself being subtly persuaded to stay for a while. He never refused.

George, Flynn noted, was coming along by leaps and bounds. The leaps were mostly aimed at Flynn. Though he didn't want to, Flynn found himself growing fond of the gregarious dalmatian. He became involved with Jane's short training sessions, acting as her less-than-willing assistant. Since his protests fell on deaf ears, he complied. Besides, watching the dog's progress was rewarding. The rest of the time, he spent coaching Billie on his batting technique. He found that to be rewarding, too.

On Saturday and Sunday, it seemed as if they spent the entire time with Susanna, Billie and Jane. And Jane was more than willing to take the boys and the dog off their hands for long stretches of the afternoon. Because he had the shelter of knowing it would all change soon, Flynn allowed himself to relax and enjoy Susanna.

He wasn't growing dependent on this feeling of contentment, he argued silently. It was just a vacation of the spirit, nothing more.

They sat on the sofa, watching *Wuthering Heights*. Susanna astonished Flynn by reciting whole blocks of dialogue along with the main characters. Watching old movies was one of her hobbies. He had no idea when she found the time.

Susanna nestled in the comfortable crook of his arm, her feet curled up under her. "Billie's really coming along with his hitting."

Flynn couldn't resist playing with a lock of her hair, winding the silken threads around his finger. "He has a lot of natural ability going for him. He was just a little afraid, I think.''

There was a lot of that going around, Susanna thought. She turned so that her mouth was just below his. "Still, thank you for taking the time to help.''

He didn't want her making too big a deal of it. Gratitude was something that still made him feel uncomfortable. "I had nothing else to do.''

She tugged on his shirt until their eyes met. Hers were impatient. "Can't you just say yes, I did a good deed and I'm proud of it?''

"Okay, yes, I did a good deed and I'm proud of it.'' He slid his tongue lightly over her lips and felt the shiver that had come so familiar so quickly. "Satisfied?''

Curling her fingers farther into his shirt, she kissed him with breathless feeling. "It's a start.''

It was an end.

As he drove away from Susanna's house that Sunday, he told himself that he had to make a break here and now. Tomorrow he would be returning to work. Perforce he would have to return to his old routine. The routine didn't include Susanna.

He'd have an excuse to stay away from her. There was no doubt in his mind that while he had been out, six weeks of work had piled up on his desk, waiting for him to plow through it. Mrs. Duffy could drop Michael off at his games and pick him up. There would be no opportunity for Flynn to do it himself. He'd see to that. He needed time away from Susanna to regain his senses, his bearing. He was getting to look forward to seeing her too much.

Getting?

All right, he thought, pressing the button for the automatic garage-door opener. It yawned open in front of him. He had *gotten* used to seeing her every day. And that was very, very dangerous to his survival. He had to draw the line here, before it was too late.

Before he was completely lost, completely emotionally dependent on her.

If he wasn't already.

"We're home, champ," he said, nudging the sleeping boy next to him. But if they were home, he thought, why didn't it feel that way?

Just further evidence, he assured himself as he took Michael by the hand and guided the sleepy boy inside, that he needed this break.

Flynn stared at the neatly printed letter in his hands. Linen. Top-grade linen, he mused. Nothing but the best for the corporation's vice-president. The letterhead proclaimed Worth Aerospace's logo. Neatly embossed beneath was the vice-president's name.

Flynn sighed, fingering the letter. His transfer was approved. The position he had asked for a hundred years ago, before his life had been upheaved, was his. The relocation expenses involved in moving to San Francisco were all going to be paid for by the company. The new position entailed a promotion and more money.

Added to that, he'd be near Michael's old neighborhood.

And away from Susanna and the chaos she represented. On that single sheet of paper was everything he wanted. Everything he *thought* he wanted.

So where was the relief? Where was the satisfaction?

Flynn stared out the window, one of the few on his side of the building. It had been a coup, getting this spot. So was getting this transfer.

Why didn't he want it?

He knew the answer to that.

Oh God, woman, what have you done to me?

When she saw him approaching the field at the end of the game, Susanna felt her heart begin to beat double time. There was a fleeting burst of joy before she recovered and took herself to task for it.

She was an idiot, she thought angrily, turning to take down the banner. A hopeless, romantic idiot. The man obviously could do very well without seeing her. He hadn't been around for over a week, hadn't called, hadn't attended either of the games. And he hadn't been to this one.

What he had been, she thought with the sting of angry hurt tormenting her, was avoiding her like the plague. She shouldn't be wasting her time on a man like that. And certainly not her heart.

So why was she doing it?

Easy. Stupidity, pure and simple.

To her far left, Billie and Michael were helping to hand out the after-game treats and all the little boys were forming a ring of outstretched hands around them. Normally, Susanna would hurry to try to get them into order. But she wasn't up to it right now.

The boys were resourceful, she thought. They could handle it. It would prepare them for later hurdles they would have to take. The kind presented by hard-hearted, hardheaded jerks.

The banner was giving her trouble. Billie had asked to help her put it up. Somehow, he had bent one of the stakes so that it now refused to budge out of the ground. She wiggled the slim iron rod to no avail.

She could feel him behind her, but didn't turn around. "Need help?" Flynn asked.

Susanna set her jaw rigidly. "No. I can handle it myself."

He was tired of her Tarzan approach. "Move aside, woman, and let someone help you for a change." Her head jerked up and he saw that her eyes were blazing.

"You could do with a dose of your own advice."

He began to answer her, then stopped. Holding on to the stake, he yanked hard, bringing it up and a plug of dirt, as well. He handed the iron rod to her. She looked as if she could spit nails, he thought.

"Could I come over?" he asked as she threw the stake on

top of the other one and then rolled up the banner. He jumped aside as she accidentally dropped the hammer near his foot. A sting like an asp, he thought. He'd have to keep that in mind. "I'd like to talk to you."

He was being formal. This wasn't good. For the first time, Susanna felt a clutch of panic, then forced it away. She had promised herself never to panic. Never. He was probably going to tell her: Thanks for the six weeks, but now I have to go back to my life as a design engineer, or something of that ilk. Well, if that was the way he wanted to play it, then fine. Who needed him? Who the hell needed him?

She did, that's who.

"Sure," she said tonelessly. "Door's always open."

She worked at fixing a smile on her face. Under no circumstances was she about to let him see how this was hurting her. She didn't want his pity, just his love. She waved to Billie and Michael, who had finished handing out treats and were eating themselves. They scrambled over, raising dust as they came.

"Why don't you two ride with me?" she suggested. "I could use the company."

Michael looked to Flynn for permission. "Okay with you, Pop?"

"I'll follow in my car," Flynn told him. He glanced at Susanna. Why was she insisting on taking the boys with her? And why was she acting as if he were an investigating IRS agent?

She arrived at her house first, but Flynn's car was only half a beat behind. Susanna had a sense of doom as she got out of the car. Flynn was already beckoning the boys over. He pointed across the street, to Jane's well-lit front porch.

"Why don't you ask Aunt Jane to take you two out for a nice ice-cream cone?" he suggested to Billie, handing him a ten dollar bill.

Billie's eyes grew large and he turned the bill around and around in his hands. "This is going to buy some big cone," he cried.

Flynn patted the boy's shoulder. "I know you guys are up to it. Tell her to take her time." The two were off and running, debating their first choices of flavors.

Susanna squared her shoulders as she opened the front door. The silence hung like a heavy curtain between them as they walked in. She heard him shut the door behind him. Busy, she needed to be busy. Susanna made for the kitchen. If her hands were busy, she couldn't beat on that hard head of his.

"So, what would you like to talk about?" Her voice sounded so stilted and she hated herself for not having better control. She should have waited until he started. Let him feel the pressure.

Upbraiding herself silently, she yanked out the box of herbal teas and slammed it on the table.

He saw the tension in her shoulders. Maybe she was afraid of what he was going to tell her. Maybe he shouldn't tell her yet. No, he'd come too far, thought about it too much. "My transfer came through."

She was right. Twelve points for the lady with the broken heart. She refused to turn around as she put the kettle on the burner. "To San Francisco, wasn't it?" She wasn't going to break down if it killed her.

"Yes."

She pressed her lips together. *You don't care, remember*, she ordered herself. "Well—" she turned around to face him, smile in place "—it's what you wanted. I'm very happy for you."

It wasn't what he expected. Her words felt like a slap in the face. "Really?"

Maybe he had been wrong about her feelings, after all. Maybe he had been wrong about everything. He could stand, he now knew, her independence, possibly even the fact that she didn't need him for anything. He had already resigned himself to the knowledge that he was as emotionally dependent, as tangled up inside as any man could ever get. He could handle all that.

But not the fact that she didn't care. Had he driven her away? he asked himself.

"Really." She put on the water. Susanna took a deep breath, trying to find the strength to go on with this charade. It didn't come.

She whirled on him, fire in her eyes. "No, dammit, not 'really.' I'm not happy for you. And I'm not happy for me, either."

Hope began to rear its head. "Why? You don't need me."

She felt the tears coming and damned herself for it. "A hell of a lot you know."

His eyes narrowed as he studied her. It was time to iron out the double-edged problems between them. "I've never met a woman who was so self-sufficient, so on top of everything. Every time I turned around, you were competently handling everything. Taking over."

Annoyed that her emotions showed, she angrily brushed a tear from her cheek with the back of her hand. "It seemed to me you had enough to handle without having a clinging vine on your hands."

She was crying, he realized. Crying. Over him? It didn't seem possible. Tenderness flooded over him. "Not a clinging vine," he said softly. "Just someone who needed me."

The big jerk! Didn't he understand what the word *need* meant?

"I *do* need you, you idiot. Not to pull up stakes for me or to help load the dishwasher. That's fine and dandy, but I don't *need* it. I just need you to be there for me, to let me lean a little if I want to. Because I do need to lean once in a while." She placed her hands on his chest, pressing her words in. "I need you to trust me with what's in your heart. And I need you to need me. You want to toss around the word *self-sufficient?* Mister, in the dictionary, the word has a picture of you."

A mental image of that flashed through his mind and he almost laughed. Maybe he had come on a little strong on that subject. Maybe they both had. "I just didn't want to grow dependent again, the way I had the last time."

"We all need each other sometimes, Flynn, that's what it's all about. Risks and needs. And loving." She sighed, her hands dropping to her sides. She was getting herself worked up and he was trying to say goodbye. "But you wouldn't know about that."

"Oh yes, I would." He pulled her to him. She wanted to resist, but couldn't. This could be the last time and pride had no place here. "Ever since I met you, I've done nothing but need you, no matter how hard I tried not to. I needed to see you, hear you, touch you. I still do. I need you inside of each day, or else it's empty. It scares the hell out of me, Susanna," he admitted. "Needing you."

"It shouldn't. I'm not going anywhere." She'd be here if he needed her. Always. "You are."

He shook his head. "No, I'm not."

He wasn't making any sense. "The transfer—"

Flynn began to think of undressing her slowly, inch by inch. Of making her skin heat, her body arch against his. Nothing else mattered. "I turned it down."

"You turned it down?" She laced her arms around his neck, hope flashing high. "Why?"

"I thought that four hundred miles would be a hell of a nightly commute."

Maybe her brain was getting foggy. "I don't follow you."

"That would be a first for you. You always seemed to know more about me than I did." His hands fitted about her hips easily. As if they had always meant to be there. "I discovered that I like this fathering business. So, while I'm at it, I might as well do it for two. Billie," he added when her eyes grew large with confusion. "I'm asking you to marry me."

"Marry—?" Her voice vanished in shock. "I don't understand."

It hadn't really come home to him until this afternoon, when he held the transfer in his hand. "When the transfer finally came through, when I realized that it meant not seeing you, *really* seeing you, I had to turn it down. I knew what this short separation had done to me. It didn't get you out of my system. The separation totally backfired. It just made me want you more.''

The tea kettle whistled, reminding Susanna of the herbal teas she had set out. She had banged it down so hard, the various packets had flown out of the box. She looked at them now. "What's your pleasure?"

He finally had the right answer, he thought. He had had it all along, he just hadn't known it. "You, Susanna. It's always been you since the first day I saw you. I love you, for now and for always."

Susanna grinned. "Bingo."

He pulled her closer. "I haven't held you in over a week."

"One week, two days, four hours and ten minutes, but who's counting?"

"I am." He lowered his head. "And the countdown starts now."

She stood on her toes, her lips brushing his teasingly. "Ready to blast off when you are, Flynn."

* * * * *

Dear Reader,

Fall has always been my favorite time of year. I love its colors, that special autumn smell in the air and, most of all, the much-anticipated moderating temperatures. I just can't get used to these Indiana summers!

Now, as an adult with six children, I find fall even more appetizing. After attempting to entertain a slew of increasingly bored kids for almost three months, I can pack some off for college and wave goodbye to the rest as the school bus whisks them away. On that late-August morning, I leave the bus stop, go home and have a good cry over how fast they're all growing, then settle in to enjoy nine months of nine-to-three peace with the knowledge they're all safely— and hopefully happily—involved in the educational process.

Even my oldest, with his college diploma safely in hand, is still taking part in the learning experience, but now from both sides of the desk. Working on his master's at night, he teaches in Chicago's inner city during the day, where he tries hard to give back all that he was given over the years. Marty finds it a two-way street, learning as much as he imparts and somehow falling in love all over again each September with a new batch of students.

Loving to learn; learning to love. Isn't that what life's all about?

May none of us ever stop either one. The loving or the learning.

Terry Essig

HOUSE CALLS

Terry Essig

For Ellen Parent Caputo. She never let me give up.
Not for three long years. Thanks, Ellen.

Chapter One

Returning the telephone to the phone company was one of the few things remaining to take care of before Greg Rennolds could leave the East Coast and long years of medical training behind forever. He was heading for the Midwest and a partnership in an ob-gyn practice in Chicago's northern suburb of Evanston.

The phone rang just as he was reaching for the plug. He jumped a good inch. "Lord," he muttered, "that just proves what bad shape I'm still in." He stared at it for a moment as its loud ring broke the silence once again. It couldn't be the hospital, he thought. His residency had ended two months ago. He had only come back to Baltimore to move his things after having spent the summer in Florida. It would be best to ignore it, he decided, telling himself it was probably just a wrong number. But in the next instant, his curiosity won out.

"Hello?"

"Oh, thank God I've caught you."

He should have ignored it. It was not an inconvenient wrong number. No, it was much more annoying than that; it was his sister Loretta. "Loretta, how are you? I was just on my way

out the door. Long drive ahead of me, you know," he began
heartily, hoping to head her off at the pass.

"And I'm so glad you haven't left yet, Greg. The most
terrible thing has happened." Greg winced. His ploy had failed
and his sister was off and running. His carefully planned time-
table for the day had more than met its match. Sometimes he
felt as if he were the elder sibling rather than the other way
around. It was hard to believe Loretta was actually fifteen
years his senior. She rarely acted it.

"Let me call you from Evanston. I want to get on the highway. Tomorrow afternoon, I promise."

"No, no. This won't take long." Famous last words, he
thought, stifling a sigh and squatting on the floor. All his furniture had already been sold two months ago. Loretta rambled
on, still skirting whatever point there was to her call. "You
must take care of things the minute you hit the city limits."

"What city?"

Loretta sounded confused, which was nothing compared to
what Greg felt. "Why, Evanston, of course. What else were
we talking about?"

"Sorry, I'm still not operating up to par. What about Evanston's city limits?"

Loretta was silent for a moment. Greg would've bet she'd
forgotten he'd just been released after a couple of weeks' en-
during the wrong end of the hospitalization process. She must
have felt guilty because she did pause long enough to inquire,
"That's right, you haven't been well, have you?" He didn't
need her to confirm it, he knew. "How are you feeling, dear?"

"Tired, too dragged out to go back to work. And yellow."

"Funny how hepatitis turns one yellow, isn't it?"

"'Funny' hardly describes it."

"You should never have donated your summer to that Cu-
ban refugee camp."

Had he known he was going to stick himself with a needle
he'd just used on a lady carrying the disease, he probably
wouldn't have, he thought, looking at his watch. He really

needed to get going. But Loretta evidently wasn't going to be swayed.

"Poor dear," she continued, evidently deciding that this was enough sympathy because she forged on, "But about Karen…"

Greg started getting that familiar ache over the bridge of his nose that Loretta seemed to bring on. "We were talking about Karen?" Karen was Loretta's only progeny and only a few years younger than Greg himself.

"Of course we were."

He sat back against the stained beige wall. He might as well get comfortable. "We talked about my being sick all summer in Florida and the fact that I'm getting a late start on a long drive halfway across the country to Illinois. When did we discuss Karen?"

His sister's tone was impatient. "You're moving to Evanston. Evanston, Illinois."

"Not if I don't get out of here and return the phone."

"And Karen is living in Evanston now."

"So?"

"I'd think you could show a little more concern for your niece's well-being, Gregory."

He thought about that for a moment. Karen's biggest problem was an independent streak a mile wide that usually put her in direct conflict with her overprotective mother. Other than that, she was as straight as an arrow. Maybe she was sick. Trust Loretta to call a doctor half a continent away. That must be it, he concluded.

But that wasn't it. "She's gone completely off the deep end. This pregnancy of hers has completely unglued her. I'm very worried, Greg."

Greg watched the shadows lengthening outside the apartment window. The phone store would be closing in an hour. "She and that boy she up and married have left that darling little apartment on Lee Street and moved in with a madwoman who has them slaving from dawn till dusk remodeling some hovel she calls a house."

It sounded rather like "Hansel and Gretel" to him. Only "that boy" was twenty-four years old and he couldn't see Karen as Gretel at all. She had a mind like a steel trap. Greg couldn't see her losing it over a few extra hormones.

"And you know how Karen insists on doing everything for herself. She won't discuss it with her father or me at all. You must go there first thing. Maybe she'll talk to you. The landlady probably needs to be taken to court. Whatever rent they pay, it's robbery. She must have some kind of hold on them. I just can't believe they haven't enough sense of their own to…"

Greg's headache was worsening by leaps and bounds. Right about now he'd promise his sister anything to get her off the phone. And he did.

The drive was even more grueling than he had anticipated. Coffee and cola only went so far in keeping him awake, and frequent rest stops were necessary. It was shortly after noon the following day when he finally pulled up in front of the address he had gotten from his sister as the scene of her concern. He turned off the engine, pulled his keys from the ignition, and stepped out of his car and into what seemed to him the twilight zone. He heard yelling and pounding and doors banging. With all the noise, the billowing puffs of white coming from the second-floor window could well have been the residue of cannon fire rather than the plaster dust he suspected it was.

Greg stood out on the curb, amazement showing in every line in his brow. Karen's voice was easy to identify. The only male rumbling had to be his niece's husband, Tim. That left two participating voices in the higher, feminine range to place.

The landlady had quite a rip-roaring scene going with these people. From the sound of it, Karen and Tim had their own battle going on as well. But even that didn't prevent the couple from horning in on the others by throwing in pithy observations when they deemed it necessary.

Reluctantly, disparaging this idea of his sister's every step of the way, Greg made his way to the front door, jumping as a piece of drywall sailed out the second-story window and into a Dumpster parked below. Didn't everyone park Dumpsters on their front lawn? Good heavens!

He began eavesdropping on the argument drifting down from the second floor and learned there was no working furnace in this Chicago bungalow. The landlady, addressed as Andrea, intended to warm the house with the living-room fireplace tonight when a cold front was predicted to come through. The voice of another woman they called Lisa argued with this Andrea person that she had to bite the bullet and get a new furnace. Andrea insisted throughout that they would all survive, just as the pioneers had.

Didn't the woman understand that pioneers had heated one-room cabins while she had an entire house with indoor plumbing and pipes that could burst? Greg knew Chicago. Ordinarily, Indian summer did not last into November, as it had this year. This lady's luck was running on overtime.

No one answered the doorbell's call, which gave Greg's ire a chance to rise another five notches. The third female voice, it became clear, was not a relative of Andrea's, but of Tim's. And when Tim refused to be drawn into their arguments concerning the furnace and his ability, or lack thereof, to do all the drywalling by himself, he ringingly advised his sister Lisa, to "Stop putting words in my mouth. I don't want Andrea changing her mind and throwing a woman five months pregnant out onto the streets. I can't support her yet. I'm only an *almost* lawyer, and *almost* only counts in horseshoes."

Greg saw red. And for probably the first time in his life, he decided that his sister's concerns were valid.

While he waited to see if a second doorbell ringing would break through the cacophony of sound inside, he was treated to a lecture from the heartless wench within telling Karen to "get away from all that plaster dust immediately." Not because it was bad for her in her condition but because "you're bothering Tim. Now go down to the kitchen and mix paint the way you're supposed to be doing."

Greg reached for the knocker, determined to make himself

heard. He would remove Karen from this loony bin personally, with force if necessary. But before he could put action to thought, the door swung open, almost crowning him with the storm door. First one, then another female barreled through, slapping it wide with each passage.

"Lisa, I swear, if you call my family, I will never spea... Oh, hello." Andrea Conrades halted and turned. She had been so upset that she'd practically passed right by the most magnificent male form she had ever seen. And he was perched right here on her own front stoop. He had the kind of body a phys-ed teacher, such as herself, could really appreciate. Tall, with nicely shaped broad athletic shoulders, minimal hips and rear, just enough to fill out his tailored navy slacks to perfection. He had thick mahogany-colored hair with a riot of curls that cried out for a woman's fingers to instill a little order. Who might this interesting specimen be? she wondered. "Can I help you?" she questioned politely, all the while wondering if he already belonged to anybody. She was quite taken aback by the look of out-and-out hostility she got in return.

She shivered. What had she done to deserve that? Was he a new neighbor upset by the remodeling noise? If she promised to be very good would he stop glaring at her?

What Greg saw was a little sprite a full foot shorter than his own six foot two. She was swamped in an oversize men's shirt that clearly had served as a painting smock many times in the past. Snug jeans completed the ensemble, which, coupled with her wide-open baby-blue eyes, gave the effect of diminutive vulnerability.

Greg became even more irritated as he had to stamp down an urge to protect. But was this little shrew innocent? Vulnerable? No way! Disgruntled, he straightened to his full height advantage and informed her, "I'm here to see Mrs. Nyland." Somewhat sarcastically he added, "That is, if she can take a few minutes from painting and scrubbing without being tossed out onto the street."

Andrea's eyes widened at what she considered an unprovoked attack. "Who the heck are you?" she riposted. She tried not to let her size allow people to think she was a pushover, but whatever tactics she used seldom worked. The rude giant stalked past her as though she were of no consequence, and entered the small foyer.

"Screen her visitors, do you? Very wise," he said. "Otherwise, someone might slip her a file hidden in a cake and spring her out of this place." Impatiently he looked at the various paths he could take. "Which way? Through to the left or up the stairs?" Grudgingly, he tacked on, "I'm her uncle."

Andrea merely tapped her foot impatiently and placed arms akimbo, staring at him. "Her uncle, huh? Poor thing," she said. "Go to the left, she's back in my kitchen."

He pushed the left inside door open and strode into her living room. "Ah, yes. I do recall hearing you order her to paint the kitchen. In case you haven't noticed, she's pregnant. She shouldn't be breathing all those fumes or doing such strenuous work. It's your building, and you look perfectly capable of doing your own painting. The very picture of health, in fact."

Somehow, it didn't seem a compliment. He seemed irritated by her looks, and she didn't have to listen to insults in her own home. She trailed him into the living room. If he would just hold still long enough, she'd set him straight. "You don't have the foggiest idea—"

"As a doctor," he interrupted smugly, "I'm trained in differentiating the healthy from the un."

The pompous jerk.

Greg looked around at the simple but well-appointed room. The focal point was the fireplace at the far end with its beautiful marble trim. The stained-glass windows on either side were true to the characteristic layout of a Chicago bungalow.

In anticipation of the approaching solstice, the noontime sun already hung low in the southern sky, its streams of light bringing to jeweled life the violet blue iris and orange day-lily motif of the windows. The delicate tones were echoed throughout the room in the pastel patterned sofa, iris throw pillows and cream draperies with their bits of nubby orange and blue thread. The walls were also cream, the woodwork was stained to match the highly polished floors, and a shiny ebony baby-grand piano stood at one end of the room.

"Well, at least your apartment is quite nice," he commented before proceeding to the next room. He stopped and blinked at the empty kelly-green dining room, the walls of which hadn't even been spackled and primed. "I'll amend that. You have a nice front room. How much do you charge them to live in this dump, and is there anything in writing?"

The nerve of the man! "They've promised me their firstborn child," she responded sweetly.

"I heard them calling you Andrea. It's your last name that's Rumpelstiltskin, then?"

"No, it is not," she retorted spiritedly, not bothering to fill in the blank. "And for future reference, not that I expect there to be any need, the name is *Ann*drea, not Ahn*drea*. This is the Midwest, sonny. More specifically, this is Chicago. Your high-brow, patrician accent is wasted here."

"I'm sure it is, most particularly on you. Ahn*drea* is a far softer and more feminine pronunciation of the name," he pointed out, pushing his way through the half-stripped double French doors to the back of the house. "Just spare me the Chicagoese 'dese' and 'dose.' I'm not up for those at the moment."

She was getting tired of trailing him through her own home so she pushed in front of him to enter the kitchen first. "Karen," she said. "Your charming, silver-tongued, devil of an uncle has come to pay a call. You neglected to mention him, dear. Is he actually your uncle? He seems rather young for the role and much too obnoxious to be related to you."

Karen looked up from her labors at the ramshackle gray Formica table. "My gosh, I don't believe it!" She jumped up from her seat to hurtle herself across the room. "Greg! How are you? What are you doing here? Can you stay?"

Clearly the girl had no taste in relatives, Andrea thought. She sniffed. "I'm going out to see how Tim's coming with the wood chopping."

It was the wrong thing to say. The accusatory brown eyes of Karen's "uncle Greg" were back to their glaring.

"You do know you are required by law to maintain a certain temperature in a rental unit?" he started. "I believe it's sixty-five by day and fifty-five at night."

Andrea didn't bother to respond. Instead, she rolled her eyes meaningfully at Karen and said, "I can't handle any more today. Get rid of him, will you? Maybe he'll take you for a ride in that fancy car I saw parked out front."

When Karen and her uncle stood side by side, as they were now, she could see the family resemblance. Obviously the same trace of Italian ancestry flowed in their blood if the dark crop of tight curls each sported and the large, soulful brown eyes were anything to go by. Only Karen's complexion differed—much lighter and pinker than her uncle's creamed-coffee color.

Karen's delighted expression had drooped considerably at Andrea's request to dump Greg. Andrea sighed in resignation. "Never mind. I was going out anyway. It's probably not the wisest thing to do, but I'll leave you to him."

As she slammed out the back door she overheard Greg inquire, "Why is she bothering to paint in here? This room needs to be torched. Paint isn't even going to touch the problem."

Let Karen explain it to him. Andrea was trying so hard to organize her life. She was sick and tired of circumstances grabbing away the reins of control from her. Now here she was, virtually forced out of her own house. Who else would it happen to? She found Tim and told him that Greg was visiting. Then she stalked off on a vigorous neighborhood tour in an effort to cool down.

Even after the brisk walk, she wasn't quite up to facing the duo in the kitchen. She sat on a fat log waiting to be split and talked to Tim instead. "How come you're not in visiting with good old 'Uncle Greg'?"

"I thought I'd wait a bit for Karen to soothe his ruffled feathers." He leaned on the ax while shooting her a rueful glance from under thick blond brows. "I'm still feeling a bit raw about the situation myself. I'm not ready to have my face rubbed in it."

"You're doing the best you can, so don't be so hard on yourself. You tried family planning but nothing is infallible. It's not as though you weren't married when it came about. It's not your fault Karen had such bad morning sickness that she had to quit her job so early in the pregnancy."

"I should leave school and work full-time for a while. Finish up when the baby's a few years old. With just a part-time job, everything I earn has to go for books and tuition. It's not fair to dump my burden on you. I'm taking advantage of a friend."

"That's what a friend is for. This will work out fine, you'll see. You can't afford to pay rent without Karen's salary, and I can't afford to pay a contractor to remodel. Every penny I had went for the title to this place, such as it is. It would have taken me forever by myself. It's a perfect symbiotic relationship. You'll see. You'll feel differently when you've got your law degree in your back pocket this June."

"I suppose," he muttered gloomily. Reaching for the flannel shirt hanging gaily from a fence post, he slipped it across wide shoulders that strained against his snug white T-shirt. He didn't bother to button it or to tuck in the tail end. Extending a hand to Andrea, he pulled her from her perch. While she dusted her bottom with her free hand, he spoke with all the enthusiasm of a man facing imminent execution. "We might as well go in and face the music. If we're lucky, he'll have left."

"Sorry, but he seemed a bit determined to stick around. Tell me, how is it possible for her uncle to be so young? He's not much older than I am. Five, six years is all. He's thirty, at most."

Tim thought for a minute. "Karen explained it to me once. I think her mother was supposed to have been one of a kind, but Greg surprised them all fifteen years later as a change-ofife baby. Karen's mother turned forty-five last August as I recall, so I suppose Greg is right around thirty."

In an effort to spot the enemy Andrea stuck her head through the back door before going in. To her relief, the kitchen population had been reduced by one-half. "By George, I believe he's gone," she muttered in relief. Bravely now, she entered the room and spoke to Karen, who was bent over the open oven door.

"Your uncle's left, has he?" she questioned in self-satisfied tones. She ventured to the stove and held a match to the old-fashioned burner, deciding to make some tea. "Much as I love you, Karen, I have to say your uncle rather reconfirms my belief in the Darwinian theory of evolution. Definitely a direct link to our cave-living forebears: overbearing and under-brained." She continued conversationally, "How are the cookies coming? Did the paint fumes from the condensed milk and food coloring knock you out? Your uncle took a rather dim view of someone in your delicate condition painting, I can tell you."

Karen laughed. "You know good and well he thought you were coercing me into painting walls and woodwork, not butterfly-shaped cookies for a dry run of a Brownie troop project." She flipped the cookies expertly off the baking sheet and onto the limited countertop space to join the others already cooling.

"He never asked or gave me any opportunity to insert anything into his running monologue." She came over to view the product of Karen's labors. "How did they come out? Will it make a good project for them?"

"They're fine. I think the Brownies should be able to handle this all right. The only tricky part comes when you cut the dough circles in half and invert them to make the wings. Make sure the girls overlap them sufficiently onto the rectangular body pieces. They seem to have a tendency to break off otherwise. Painting the wings wasn't tricky at all. They'll like that part."

"Thanks. You're a sweetheart," Andrea complimented as

she viewed the warm cookies. "These are really beautiful. I was worried the food coloring mixed with the condensed milk would turn brown as it baked, but these colors are still quite bright."

"Greg painted them while I cut them out."

"Your uncle? I wouldn't have thought he was the cookie-decorating type. More the 'me important doctor, you peon' sort."

"Umm. Well I think I should warn you that I put him to rest on your bed after he almost fell asleep in the cookie dough. I'm sure ninety percent of his being crabby was from exhaustion. He had a long drive here."

Andrea reached to absently brush flour from Karen's over-size shirt front. "My bed! What's wrong with a hotel? The Orrington isn't that far away. What's the matter with him, anyway? Why is he so tired?"

Karen tapped her spatula reflectively on the edge of the cookie sheet while turning off the flame under the whistling teakettle with the other hand. "I'm not actually sure. I was too busy trying to convince him you weren't an ogre to find out. But I will," she stated positively.

Andrea believed her. Karen never yelled, threw things or had tantrums. She was very low-key. Somehow, though, she always ended up with precisely what she had set out to achieve. Karen never lost control of the situation the way she herself did.

"Did you convince him?"

"What?" The other girl looked puzzled.

"That I'm not an ogre," she clarified.

"Oh, well, I sowed the seeds of doubt. Now it's up to you."

Andrea snorted her opinion of that suggestion in an unlady-like fashion. "He won't be around long enough to make it worth my while." Too bad, too. What a body on that man! After pouring the steaming water into the pot, she threw in the teabags that Karen had set on the countertop for her. "Why is he in my bed? What's wrong with yours?"

"You know perfectly well as soon as Tim is done stacking

logs on the porch, he's going to come in and insist I lie down for a while." Karen's eyes rolled skyward. "As though cookie baking is enough to physically exhaust me."

"Pregnant women need rest," Andrea stated empirically, gathering up a stack of cookies to have with their tea.

"I don't stand a chance against the two of you. But," Karen threatened with a jabbing forefinger, "I'm going to ask my doctor at my next appointment exactly how much sleep I need. Then look out!" She grabbed three cups and plopped down on the old stainless-steel kitchen chair.

Her husband entered to wash his hands at the sink. "Did you get a chance to nap yet, Karen?"

"Oh, yes," she lied sweetly to his back. "A good forty-five minutes at least."

"I haven't been gone forty-five minutes," he pointed out while Andrea laughed at Karen's caught-with-a-hand-in-the-cookie-jar expression. "As soon as you're done with your tea, go in and lie down. You're just now getting over that awful morning sickness, and I don't want it to come back."

"Yes, master," his spouse grumbled.

"And don't you forget it," he ordered, kissing the top of her head.

"I'm fine now, you know. Have been for two weeks. I just wish you'd both believe that. Maybe you should come talk to the doctor with me."

"Why? What do you want to know?"

All heads turned to the drooping male propped against the kitchen doorframe. He shrugged his shoulders at their questioning looks and padded shoeless into the kitchen, grabbing a cup on his way to the table. "I couldn't sleep with all the racket," he explained, as though his tiredness was all their fault. "I hope whatever that is has some caffeine in it. I'll need it if I'm to spend the afternoon apartment hunting. I had planned to take care of finding a place a few weeks ago, but I was too out of it to do it."

Why did she feel like apologizing for making noise in her own home, Andrea wondered. But she knew. For all his tiredness, this was a man used to taking charge. Wherever he stood, it became his turf. He exuded confidence and control, even when dead on his feet, and that charismatic aura was making her feel a trespasser in her own kitchen.

"Why are you so tired? What's wrong with you? You look in terrific physical shape, you should have plenty of energy." She sprawled back in her chair, letting her arms dangle as she studied him. "And why are you apartment hunting up here? If you're such a hotshot doctor, don't you have a medical practice somewhere?"

He returned her perusal while she poured the tea. They both ignored Karen wrangling with her spouse over her impending nap. "I am apartment hunting because I have just finished my specialization and passed my boards. I am now certified in ob-gyn as well as internal medicine and pharmacology. I bought into a practice here in Evanston. I was supposed to start six weeks ago, but I've had a run-in with a hepatitis B carrier. See how yellow the whites of my eyes are?" He leaned forward to give her a closer look.

She retreated.

At her reluctant nod, he continued, "I'm over the infectious part, but I'm still left with this jaundice and rotten sense of pervading fatigue, both of which should clear up in the next few weeks. I think I must have been rather run-down from the stress of years of medical training. It shouldn't be taking this long to get my strength back." He stopped talking to take a sip of tea, but the cup never reached his mouth. He stared into its confines instead.

"It's only tea, it won't hurt you." Even if she did make it on the weak side, surely his look of utter repugnance was overreaction.

"Uh, Andrea?" Tim too was studying his cup.

"Yes, Tim?"

"Is this some new kind of herbal tea we're trying?"

"No. Why do you ask?" She sat up straight in her chair to take a closer look in her cup. "My goodness. The tea is blue!" She looked up incredulously, trying to figure out what had happened to her normally brown brand. This brew wasn't even the light tan she generally achieved from her chintzy habit of using only one bag per pot. It was a biliously brilliant azure.

"Where'd you get the teabags?" Karen asked.

"It was sitting out on the counter. Didn't you put them out for me?" She blinked again at the oddly colored concoction.

"That explains it, then."

"It does?"

"Sure." Karen waved her hand in easy dismissal. "I had set them out to make a cup of tea while Greg and I talked, but I spilled some of the blue food dye there. I meant to throw them out, but I must have forgotten."

Andrea was tipping her cup in all directions, fascinated with the blue-tinted contents. "If you say so. Too bad it isn't Easter. This would make a wonderful color bath for eggs."

Tim rose to collect the cups and dump them into the sink. "Be that as it may, at the moment I have to go to work." He pointed at his wife. "You have to rest, and you two can start over with fresh bags."

"No, thanks." Greg rose slowly, noticing Andrea's orange-stained lips and Karen's green ones—proof of the painted cookies potency. The woman was probably harmless enough, as Karen insisted, but still crazy. He ought to get out while he could, his sister be hanged. "I think I've lost my yen for tea." He would like to talk to Karen, however. Looking at Tim, he asked, "Is it all right for Karen to come apartment hunting with me? We could do some visiting and she knows the neighborhoods where I should look. I won't let her overdo."

Tim looked doubtful, but at Karen's eager expression, relented. "Well, okay. Being a doctor, you should be able to tell if she looks strained."

Karen gave her husband a hug and a peck of a kiss. "Thanks. We'll be back for dinner so you won't have to eat alone, Andrea."

"Don't worry about me. It's an easy out for my turn at cooking," she said.

"Oh, no, you don't. We'll be here. You'll eat something awful if we don't show up," Karen insisted.

Greg let loose an exasperated growl. "I've never seen such an overprotective crew. Don't any of you believe in live and let live?"

"Andrea doesn't think it's worthwhile to cook for only one. You should see some of the stuff she came up with before we started eating together," Karen informed her uncle.

"So it's up to us to save her from herself, huh?"

The peace of an empty house was a soothing balm to Andrea's thoroughly irritated frame of mind. She seared a pot roast on both sides, threw in chunks of viciously chopped vegetables along with a can of cream of mushroom soup, and clunked the heavy cast-iron lid on the pot to let it simmer for the next three hours. The rest of the afternoon was spent chiseling nauseating pink-and-gray-swirled plastic tiles from the bathroom walls and muttering a great deal as she continually scraped her knuckles in the process.

Dinnertime came, marked only by a phone call reporting that Karen and Greg would eat out after all so they could keep looking for an apartment. Andrea warned them of Tim's ire, but they seemed unimpressed. She turned off the pot roast, ate an apple and a wedge of cheddar cheese instead and went back to the bathroom muttering.

The predicted cold front arrived. The temperature on the thermometer was dropping as though it had developed a leak. Hopefully the heat exchanger she had bought for the fireplace would live up to the claims of its flamboyant brochure. The fire was no problem for a former Girl Scout, and it was soon crackling cheerfully. After flicking the hearth insert's motor on, she left to ease her body into and out of a hot tub. She was snugly encased in a floor-length crimson velour robe, contentedly reading and toasting her toes in front of the roaring blaze when the various troops returned.

Karen plunked dispiritedly on the sofa, pulling Greg down

beside her. "I never realized how many tacky apartments there were in this town."

"Yeah. The only decent one we saw isn't available for sub-leasing for another month," Greg moaned in return. "I guess I'll have to take a room at the Orrington. I hate living out of a suitcase in a hotel room."

"You'll find something tomorrow," Andrea muttered encouragingly, knowing in her heart what was going to happen but refusing to face it. She watched as Greg lay his head back on the sofa to close his eyes disconsolately. The man was exhausted.

Tim, who had just wandered in from stocking grocery shelves at the Dominick's market, noticed it too. "You're too tired to go to a hotel tonight," Tim stated. "This sofa opens into a bed. Karen and I will sleep here, and you take ours."

Greg looked up. "What? Oh, no, it's all right. Don't worry about me." He smiled bravely and hoped they'd go for it. He wasn't about to stay in this loony bin even one night. Blue tea and painted cookies. Good Lord, he thought, what next?

Andrea sighed. Here it was again. Another stray washing up on her doorstep, and she was powerless to prevent it. She had led a relatively blameless life. Why did the gods continually torment her like this?

"The pull-out sofa is too small for Karen and her stomach, let alone the two of you. I'll stay here and feed the fire. Greg can sleep in my bed," she said resignedly.

There was no contradictory argument coming from the dark form slumped against the sofa back. When she looked closer, his even breathing told the story: he had drifted to sleep in the middle of the discussion. Waifism must run in Karen's family. "Karen, turn down the bed. Tim, help me get him in there. I'll get his suitcase from the car while you undress him."

By the time she struggled in with the suitcase, Tim had him under the blankets with barely a murmur of acknowledgement. Andrea's rummaging through his bag didn't reveal any pajamas, so she pulled a man's robe from the case and lay it across the bottom of the bed before closing the door behind her.

Throwing two more logs on the fire, she made herself as comfortable as possible on a bed that spent most of its time folded into thirds. With concentrated effort, she was soon asleep herself. Vague forms of dark-skinned, broad-shouldered men with tousled mahogany hair and bodies that Michelangelo could have chiseled flitted through her dreams. They smiled and beckoned her near only to freeze her out with accusing, icy stares when she drew close. She didn't feel particularly well rested when morning finally arrived. She blamed it on the permanent creases in the sofa-bed mattress, along with the necessity of rising twice during the night to toss more wood onto the fire.

Chapter Two

Andrea found a pale primrose thermal running suit neatly folded by the washing machine. Thank goodness she wasn't too efficient about putting clean clothes away immediately, as she had no idea when access to her room might be regained.

Force of long-standing habit got her up at six in the morning. Since company was hard to come by at that hour, Andrea generally breakfasted alone. She crept into the kitchen in her socks and reached on tiptoe for the blender. Then she mixed her breakfast. Someday she would get around to rearranging the cabinets. The glasses were up much too high for a person her height. The tumbler she managed to flick to the edge of the high shelf seemed to have a life of its own. It teetered precariously for a moment. Then, as her usually quick reactions failed her, it slipped over the edge and shattered. She stood there in her socks, not wanting to move for fear of picking up a shard the hard way—with her foot. As she debated the alternatives, her bedroom door opened and a rumpled head of hair appeared.

"What's going on?"

"Don't come out here without shoes," she warned. "I've just dropped a glass, and there are slivers all over the floor."

"Right. Don't move. I'll be there in a second." He disappeared, but only momentarily. When he came back, he was in the thick green terry robe Andrea had left on the bed for him. But that, paired with yesterday's perfectly polished wing tips made him look ridiculous.

As Greg picked her up and set her on the edge of the cabinet top, he noticed the way she was avoiding his eyes. Correctly surmising the cause, he threatened, "Laugh, and I'll leave you stranded there." He made a disgusted sound as he studied her averted face and dancing eyes. "Never mind. Where's the broom?"

She pointed and then watched as he efficiently disposed of the broken pieces. As he lifted her down once more to the floor, she asked, "Are you going back to bed or would you like some breakfast? There's enough here for two."

"I might as well stay up. I used to be quite an early riser."

"Until six weeks ago?"

"You've got it. It's all I can do to drag myself out of bed at all lately." He looked around at the empty range top. "Exactly what is it there's enough for two of?"

Andrea indicated the blender. "If you could just get down two glasses…"

"That's all you're having? A glass of juice?"

"It has everything you could possibly need," she primly informed him.

He snorted his opinion of that. "That shows how much you know about nutrition." He studied the odd-looking concoction. "This is damn peculiar-looking orange juice."

"Just drink it. It'll make hair grow on your chest."

"I already have hair on my chest, and you sure as hell don't need any." He questioned suspiciously, "You're a health-food nut, aren't you? What's in here?"

"Oh, a little of this and a little of that."

"How very scientific. Could you possibly be a little more specific?" He set the glass she had handed him back on the countertop. "On second thought, never mind. I don't think I want to know. I don't suppose I could talk you into some bacon and eggs?" He offered the suggestion hopefully. "I'll replace them for you as soon as the stores open."

"No point in getting a lot of pans dirty for just the two of us. Besides, bacon is bad for you—high in cholesterol and all of that—and there are eggs right in here." She handed his glass right back to him.

He was turning a little green. "This is a liquid. It would logically follow that any eggs in here would have to be raw." He hadn't gotten an A in logic for nothing.

"Umm," she agreed.

"What else?" he whispered hoarsely.

"Fresh banana, six ounces of concentrated orange juice, milk, wheat germ, lecithin and a little brewer's yeast." She drained her glass. "Drink up, it's good for you."

"Oh, no. You *are* a health-food nut. I have to get out of here while I'm still quasi-normal."

She tried not to laugh. She really did. Clearly he viewed sanity as some tangible commodity over which he maintained only tenuous control. "You can't waste it. At least give it a try."

"I can't believe I'm really doing this," he muttered before taking a tentative swallow of the loathsome mixture. She was surprised he didn't hold his nose. "This will probably raise my voice an octave."

"Be truthful, now," she warned while watching closely for his reaction. "And remember, Adele Davis will come and get you in the still of the night if you say anything too nasty about her recipes."

"You mean this stuff actually came out of a recipe book?" She noted the amazement in his voice. "Actually, it's not that bad. Drinkable. I'd still prefer bacon and eggs, though," he qualified, finishing the contents of the glass in one brave gesture before setting it down with a thump.

He watched in growing consternation when, after giving a warm giggle, Andrea began to search for something—first looking under the table, then behind the kitchen door, and finally in the bathroom.

Eyeing her cautiously, he asked, "Uh, is there anything wrong?"

"Hmm? Oh, I can't remember where I left my running shoes. I don't want to wake Tim and Karen with my banging about, so I thought I'd go jogging. By the time I get back, they should be up, and I can start working around here."

"Ah, I can help with that. They're right by your bed. Banged my skin when I tripped over them to come investigate the racket out here. Be right back."

He disappeared into the bedroom while Andrea rinsed out the blender.

"Can I come with you?" he questioned as he produced the shoes.

She looked shocked. "I wouldn't think a man who keeps falling asleep at the drop of a hat would be a very likely candidate for a five-mile run."

"That far, huh?" He seemed genuinely disappointed. "I was hoping to start building back up. I used to do ten miles, but I expect I shouldn't try more than two or three to start now."

From what she had seen, he shouldn't try more than a brisk walk around the block. On the other hand, as she eyed his physique in an appraising manner, Andrea was forced to admit, "With a body like that, I can well believe you used to be fairly physically active." Even an untrained eye would have to admire his perfect form, she thought before doing a double take. Her candid remark had disconcerted him to the point where he was actually blushing. His reentry into the real world after years of concentrated academia was going to hit him hard.

"Tell you what," she offered magnanimously. "We'll go to a track I know of nearby. Then we can both do what we want without leaving the other behind. You get dressed while I find my keys."

Greg was quick, and they left the house, closing the door

quietly behind them. As they drove to the track, Andrea noticed that the weather was crisp and clear, perfect for running. Soon Andrea was well into her third mile, but it was not going well. She was so interested in keeping an eye on Greg who, even recovering from a serious illness, was such a supple study in lithe symmetry as he alternated running and walking around the track, that she stumbled and ignominiously skidded on her stomach several feet along the gravelly path. It seemed Greg was instantly at her side, helping her up and checking with a practiced hand for injuries.

"Here, let me see."

Andrea, who had been peering down the neck of her sweatshirt to check for damage, snapped the yellow top back against her chest. "Fat chance."

He took her hands firmly in his and pulled her over to the car, opening the door and sitting her sideways on the seat. "Don't be childish. I'm a doctor, remember? I doubt your stomach is anything special."

Stomach? She had thought he'd wanted to check... Suddenly, her thoughts were cut short. For someone who had recently been so sick, he was amazingly strong. By now he had both her hands effortlessly under control in one of his and was reaching for her sweat top with the other. She wriggled uselessly.

"Hold still," he commanded.

"Greg," she said, looking him directly in the eye. "I'm telling you I'm fine. I don't want you to do this, okay?"

He stopped and searched her face for a long moment. Slowly, he nodded his head and released her. "Okay. Not if you're not willing. But you're passing up a golden opportunity to have the damages checked by an expert. And there would have been no charge for a good looker like you." He leered and winked uncharacteristically as he stepped back.

Andrea relaxed and figured she had it made when he continued, back in his doctor role, "You don't seem to be wearing a bra, though. A woman's breasts need to be supported during exercise, you know. Otherwise you can tear the underlying supporting muscles.''

Even though—as a physical education teacher—she knew he was right, she refused to discuss underwear with him or even look at him, studying instead the padded gray vinyl of the car's interior roofing. Not everyone practiced what they preached all the time.

"And how long has it been since your last checkup?" he badgered, on a favorite soapbox now. "You women let these things ride far too—"

"Six months. It's only been six months. Come back and yell at me some time next spring, all right?"

Greg was in the driver's seat now, reaching to switch on the ignition of his car. Andrea never had found her keys. He seemed determined to get in the last word. "At least get a good sports bra. Liberated women sag, especially liberated athletic women."

"I haven't got anything to sag," she informed him through gritted teeth, her face going red in spite of herself.

"I'm sure you have as much as ninety percent of the women I see. Women seem to be hypersensitive about breast size for some reason."

Andrea thought about the women Greg had seen and the one he had almost seen a moment ago. A warm flush crept over her, and she was very much afraid that Greg would not attribute her rise in color to her jogging. She leaned back against the navy fabric seat and directed all her mental powers to calming herself.

Noontime found Greg and Tim sitting at the kitchen table watching Andrea set a large cast-iron pot on top of the stove. She placed metal trivets inside and poured in a few inches of boiling water. Then she mixed cornmeal, whole-wheat and white flours, molasses, eggs, baking powder and raisins into a sticky mass and poured it all into two old metal cans she had washed and saved. Covering their tops with tinfoil, she carefully lowered them onto the trivets and adjusted the flame under the steaming bath.

"I'd ask her what she was doing," Greg remarked to no one in particular, "but after the breakfast she made, I'm afraid to find out."

Tim ignored him, instead fixing Andrea with a baleful glare. "I can't believe you're doing this to me. You know the smell of that stuff permeates the entire house, and it takes three damn hours for it to cook!"

"I knew it would be something awful," Greg moaned fatalistically.

Andrea was feeling decidedly picked on. "There was nothing wrong with that breakfast other than the fact your taste buds are all in your toes," she snapped in exasperation before turning on Tim in wounded tones. "I thought you liked this."

Apparently feeling rather persecuted himself, Tim reproached her, "You're going to tantalize me for the next three hours with the perfume of home-baked Boston brown bread..."

Greg perked up at that.

"And then you're going to tell me it's for somebody at work who needs a boost. I know you," Tim finished.

Greg sank back down in the chair with a disappointed air, his posture again echoing Tim's.

Andrea gave him a look of haughty disdain before yelling into the other room, "Karen! The pot roast I made for you ingrates for dinner last night is just about heated. Come on."

"Sure." Tim sniffed, his martyrdom evident. "We get reheated pot roast while some perfect stranger gets my Boston brown bread."

She took great pleasure in informing him, "It's for someone strange all right. You! It's a treat you'll get after you finish sealing the drywall in the upstairs apartment this afternoon."

"It is?" His posture straightened miraculously.

"A little bit of incentive. The sooner you two are up there living and out of my hair, the better I'll like it."

Tim got up and swung her into a Valentino-like dip. Then

he kissed her soundly, right in front of his wife. "You'll miss us when we're gone, you sweet thing," he predicted, cheerfully beginning to toss the plates with the atrociously gaudy pink and lavender floral design onto the table. Sniffing the air appreciatively as he passed the stove on his way to the silverware drawer, he rubbed his hands together and gleefully intoned, "It's mine, all mine. Look out, drywall, here I come."

"I don't suppose you'd consider sharing a piece with a poor sick relative who needs his strength built back up?"

"No way, buddy." Then Tim appeared to reconsider. "Unless, of course, you want to help me seal the walls so we can get to it sooner."

"Do you have cream cheese to go with it?" Greg questioned Andrea. Then at her nod he agreed, "Right. I'll do it."

Andrea was stunned. "What about your apartment hunting?" If Greg spent his limited energy reserves helping Tim, she'd never get rid of him. This was her home, not a motel, yet the guests seemed to keep multiplying.

"You and Karen go," Greg suggested offhandedly. "The Realtor knows my price range and specifications, and Karen knows my taste. It might be fun for you, but I'm finding it draining."

"Painting isn't draining? Besides, Karen needs to nap."

"Karen is as healthy as a horse." The recipient of that observation didn't look quite sure whether she should be pleased by that or not. "You two are killing her with kindness. She'll have a much easier delivery if she's in shape."

Andrea was doubtful of that, but agreed because her only option was helping Tim herself, and she hated sealing drywall. The sealant always dripped in her face and down her legs and arms. She said nothing further.

The roast and accompanying vegetables were piled on a platter and placed in the center of the rickety table along with a bowl of apple sauce and a basket of biscuits. Tim played head of the house, carving the meat into servable pieces. He directed his remarks to Andrea. "So, chief, what do we do about the furnace? The heat-exchange unit in the fireplace is working fine while the temperatures are above freezing, but we both know it's all downhill from here in the temperature department for at least three months.'' He took the platter back after Karen had served herself and spooned extra carrots onto her plate. "Eat those," he ordered.

Rolling her eyes skyward, Karen groaned, "I certainly hope you can learn to love Rubenesque women because that's what you're going to be left with when this is all over." He refused to be stared down, and she finally gave in, albeit ungraciously. "Okay, I'll eat them, but you'll be sorry."

"I'll take my chances," he said in a no-nonsense voice. "You lost too much weight with all that morning sickness."

"It isn't necessary to make it all up in one sitting."

He ignored her and turned expectantly to Andrea. "Well?"

Andrea sighed in reply. "I should have some money by the end of next week. It's the beginning of a new term for all my exercise classes. It was supposed to be a start on remodeling the kitchen, but it'll cover the cost of a new furnace." She gave a delicately rueful shrug. "I guess we can live with this excuse of a kitchen for a while longer."

Greg's dark eyes were intently studying her. "So you do plan to replace the furnace?"

Her puzzled eyes met his. "Of course. What did you expect?"

"I must say that's a relief. For a while there, I thought you had something against central heating. On a back-to-nature kick or some such thing. Why didn't you want Tim's sister to call your family for help?"

"Oh, my." Andrea cringed at the mere thought. "If they ever found out how bad this place was, they'd descend like the plague. The whole place would be redone in twenty-four hours or less—all very livable and all very tacky. None of it would be me. I'd rather do it myself, my own way, and wait until I can afford to buy what I want and not buy just to buy."

"I can understand that." He nodded in agreement. "My parents couldn't understand why I had to go into debt and go

to Johns Hopkins for medical school. But I wanted the best
education I could get.'' Suddenly disconcerted to find himself
agreeing with her on an issue, he made an obvious move to
change topics. He cut another bite of tender roast and had the
forkful almost to his mouth before complimenting her. ''This
is really good...especially after eight years of hospital-
cafeteria food. Is it hard to make? I'd like to learn to cook
now that I'll have more time.'' His mouth was open, ready to
accept the morsel coated in its rich brown broth.

''It's quite easy. Adding a can of cream of mushroom soup
at the beginning is the whole trick. As the roast simmers, it
makes a delicious gravy.''

His mouth snapped shut. ''You made the gravy with soup?''

''As long as it tastes good, who cares? You couldn't tell it
wasn't scratch gravy.'' She shrugged. ''Same with the biscuits.
If you can't tell the difference, why bother?''

''Oh God. What's wrong with the biscuits?''

''Nothing. But they're not scratch either. I made them from
a mix. I only care about the end product, not how I get there,''
she defended. ''Cream of mushroom soup makes a terrific
gravy. Better than I could do on my own, that's for sure.''

Greg's head shot up, and he looked as if he were about to
gag. ''Mushrooms? Did you say mushroom soup? I hate mushrooms!''

Three sets of eyes swung to his plate; its pink and purple
flowers previously covered with healthy servings of meat and
vegetables were once again visible. He'd made short work of
a large amount of food that he claimed to dislike.

''Did you bother to inform your stomach of that fact?''
Andrea inquired with acid sweetness. ''You certainly looked
as though you were enjoying it, mushrooms notwithstanding.''
Here was a classic example of an intelligent, well-educated
man allowing childish prejudices to ruin an adult enjoyment
of good food.

His attention turned to his openmouthed niece. ''Why didn't
you warn me she went in for poisoning her victims?''

''Hey,'' Karen protested. ''She's taught me everything I

know about cooking. I think it's terrific. You were enjoying it yourself until someone mentioned mushrooms and soup. It must be the hepatitis that's made you so intolerant and crabby. You never used to be like this."

"Living in this house has changed you. Your mother was right to worry," he informed her darkly before turning to Tim. "Get out while you can. You two would be better off on welfare. First thing you know she'll have the baby hooked on canned soups instead of formula."

"Right, that tears it." Andrea threw her napkin on her plate, glaring at Greg who was cautiously tasting a small amount of the potato he had been hungrily downing moments before.

"They must not use a whole lot of mushrooms in the soup," he judiciously decided. "You really can't taste them."

Andrea rose disgustedly from the table, pulling Karen with her. To think she had actually been softening toward him! "Where and at what time are we supposed to meet this Realtor?" She would move the heavens if necessary to find the turkey an apartment—one available immediately.

After receiving the necessary data, she grabbed her car keys from the kitchen windowsill and spitefully directed Tim, "I don't care how much he paints. He only gets one slice of bread, do you hear me?"

Tim saluted, "I hear and obey, O mistress of the house." Then he directed Greg, "Since I know where the supplies are, I'll get things lined up while you take my turn at the dishes."

But Tim's glee at escaping the sudsy water was quickly dashed by his earnest wife. "That's not fair," she interjected. "We'll just put him in the rotation, and you can delay your turn until dinner."

Her uncle's next remark illustrated how adulthood could serve to strip the rosy glow from a bad case of hero worship. "Dishes are women's work!" Greg protested, which caused Karen's mouth to gape in shock. "Tim, you've been brainwashed," he added. Then, seeing all three implacable expressions, he turned dejectedly to the pile by the sink. "Okay, I'll do them. You two just find me an apartment I can move into tonight, understand?''

Andrea was determined to do her best.

Five-and-a-half long hours later, Andrea pulled herself once more from the cramped confines of her little yellow car. She glanced absently at the sky as she and Karen trudged through the bungalow's backyard and reflected on the seasons. November was traditionally the most overcast month of the year in Chicago. This November appeared to be trying to outdo itself. The thick gray blanket hanging ominously overhead accurately reflected Andrea's bleak mood. Karen had found some insignificant flaw in each of the apartments they'd seen. Frankly, Andrea thought she had been nitpicking. But why? Surely she could sense the antipathy between Andrea and her uncle. And even Karen must be feeling the space crunch. Well, good old Uncle Greg could go to the hotel tonight and carry on his search himself. Tomorrow was Monday, and Andrea had to go back to work.

Her heart sank at the sight greeting their return. Tim and Greg were descending from the second story, painting supplies in hand. Spatters of white paint added to their pallor and general air of fatigue. Tim was dragging, but Greg had been absolutely done in. Andrea suspected that sheer contrariness was all that kept him still moving.

"I think I may have overdone it a bit today," he admitted. "All those weeks of forced inactivity have every muscle in my body aching from today's light workout. I can't see how I'm going to be able to put in full days at the medical center in just a week's time," he added disconsolately.

Clearly it would take a heartless shrew to send a man in his state of exhaustion to an impersonal hotel. The big baby, he would undoubtedly recover more quickly during the next few days with the placebo of Karen's hovering love and concern. Then he would have to go, Andrea decided. Positively by the end of the week. Karen and Tim would be occupying the upper apartment by then, and she wanted the first floor to herself again after two months of communal living.

She carried the brown grocery bag into the kitchen and emptied the supplies onto the countertop. "I'll make dinner while you two get cleaned up. The tile grouting in the upstairs bathroom has had over twenty-four hours to dry. Why don't you shower up there, Tim? Greg can soak his sore muscles in a hot tub down here."

She could hear the upstairs shower as she ushered her unwilling victim toward the steaming bath she had prepared. "Stop treating me like an invalid," he protested. "I'm just a little tired." As Andrea closed the door on his complaints, he raised his voice again. "I noticed this morning there's no lock on this door. If you want me to get in here, you'll have to keep everyone away. I'm not into exhibitionism."

"Not to worry," she called sweetly as she went to drag out the brandy bottle. Where had she stuck the brandy snifters? After giving him enough time to have taken off his clothes and gotten into the tub, she knocked on the bathroom door. Andrea could hear the water swish as Greg sat up suddenly. She could imagine the panic on his virile but inhibited features as he called in a slightly panicked voice.

"Yes?"

"I thought a little brandy might help you relax," she called through the door, having a hard time not giggling. The way he answered, she knew his teeth were clenched.

"No, thank you."

"Oh, well, want me to see if I can knead out some of the knots in your back?" She jiggled the doorknob and wondered if Italians ever went completely pale. It might be a genetic impossibility.

He was a lot of fun to tease right now, but even in his present condition there was a blatant masculine virility about him that told her getting the best of him was a crime she wouldn't get away with in more normal times. She was living dangerously, but some inner devil made her press on. Andrea pushed the door open a crack, just enough to see the bare beginnings of the bathroom's old-fashioned white octagonal floor tiles. Water splashed again. He must be reaching for something to cover himself with.

"Don't you dare come in here," Greg warned.

"Just relax. I seriously doubt you have anything I haven't seen before." That was true enough. Her college roommate had kept a hunk-of-the-month poster pinned to their dorm room bulletin board. She joked that it was to remind her why she was in school.

"I hope you're enjoying this," he called in dangerously soft tones, "because you're going to pay."

Andrea was starting to feel guilty for teasing him. After all, he had stopped when she'd asked him this morning when she'd fallen. So he was inhibited. We all had our little foibles, didn't we? She set the snifter on the floor outside the door and pulled it tightly shut again. "I'll leave the brandy out here for you. I'm afraid it took you too long to make up your mind about the massage," she bluffed. "I have to go now and check if the spaghetti water is boiling yet. But you just relax. I'll call you when dinner is ready."

Andrea's teasing hadn't worked out exactly to plan. She ended up back in the kitchen feeling rather small. She had made a guest in her home uncomfortable. She was shy, too, and could have been more understanding of Greg's conservatism. Maybe if she dressed up dinner a bit it would ease her conscience and take his mind off any immediate plans for retribution. Leaving her not-quite-boiling pot, she went into the living room. She put an extra log on the fire and flicked a hidden switch under the round coffee table, making the table magically rise to dining height. She found a pale blue linen cloth and went back to the kitchen to dig out her good china and crystal. Everyone needed a little spiritual uplift now and again, she rationalized. And this would be as good an occasion as any.

The heavy sterling silver her aunt had left her joined the table setting, and she stood back to admire the flash of fire reflected in her heavy cut-glass goblets. As she wandered back to begin the salad, she heard Tim whistling his way down the stairs. But as Andrea got out the lettuce, there was dead silence.

Suddenly Tim's resonant bass bellowed, "Karen! What have you done? Why am I being buttered up with a romantic dinner in the firelight? Did you put another dent in the car?"

Andrea tried hard to choke back her laughter while she stuffed lengths of stiff, straw-colored spaghetti into boiling water and went back to tearing lettuce. Tim had no idea how close to hitting the truth he was. But, he wasn't the one being buttered up. Karen's sounds of utter bewilderment as she came from their room to see what her spouse was yelling about were quickly followed by expressions of such indignation that Andrea had to stop and wipe tears of merriment from her eyes.

Tim and Karen converged on the kitchen together.

"What's going on?" they demanded in unison.

Andrea turned guileless eyes in their direction. "I merely thought the men deserved a little effort on our part in return for all their hard work. Do you realize, Karen, that between the two of them, they got the entire second story sealed? All it needs now is the final coat of paint. They deserve a little pampering, don't you agree?" And she reached to the radio and flicked on a classical station. A soothing violin concerto swirled through the first floor, adding, she hoped, to the general ambience she strove to create. Maybe she should dim the lights everywhere but the living room to disguise the remodeling mess. She could leave just enough light so that she wouldn't trip and land in the pot of spaghetti.

Karen eyed her lamblike expression suspiciously. Andrea knew she was doubting her own capability of pampering the male of the species. Coddling—at least the blatant type— wasn't her style. Tim reached to place the flat of his hand on Andrea's forehead and then his own, checking for fever. He shrugged his puzzlement. "Well, okay. If you're sure I'm not going to find a dent in the car or a new load of drywall that needs putting up, there's a bottle of wine I've been saving on the back porch. I'll get it."

"Andrea?" The single word was laden with inquisitive speculation.

"Hmm?"

"Is there anything I should know?"

"'Know'? Nothing that I can think of Karen. But if you're not too tired, you could slice the French bread and put the butter out to soften."

"There's more to this than meets the eye," Karen muttered, digging through a drawer to locate a bread knife. "I get the distinct impression I may be caught in a crossfire of some kind before the evening ends. Tim had better check that our life insurance is paid up."

"Coward," Andrea chided.

Twenty minutes later all was ready. Burgundy-hued wine had been poured into stemmed glasses. Pachelbel's Canon in D hung its moody presence over the room, and the fire cast a flickering light across the table, framing it and dropping the rest of the room into subdued shadow. Karen carried the food in while a cowardly Andrea sent Tim to roust Greg from the tub. Andrea, always going in two directions at once, decided to quarter some apples and sneak them on the burner to boil while they waited for Greg to make his appearance.

Chapter Three

"Sorry," Greg apologized as he emerged from the bathroom. "I actually fell asleep in the tub. I never realized how enervating a hot tub of water could be."

Andrea had never realized how enervating it could be to have a six-foot-two hunk of man come padding barefoot out of her bath in nothing but snugly fitting blue jeans. Wordlessly she measured the width of his strapping shoulders and analytically tried to gauge the amount of gently curling deep brown hair it took to cover the breadth of the chest in question with enough left over to taper down a flat stomach and disappear, still going strong, under the waistband of his faded jeans. Idly she wondered just exactly how far the band of hair went.

She turned red as the direction of her thoughts hit her conscious level. Turning back to her apples, she assured him, "It's all right, grab your shirt and come out to the living room. We're ready to eat."

He nodded his agreement and started to swing around to the bedroom when he noticed what she was doing. "Hey!

That's vinegar you're pouring into those apples. You must have picked up the wrong bottle."

Andrea snapped to. "What? Oh, no. It's all right. I've just developed a sudden craving for apple butter on toast for breakfast tomorrow. You need vinegar in apple butter."

"You make your own apple butter?" he questioned in astonishment.

"Yes."

He reiterated the facts, perhaps to make sure he had them right. "You bake Boston brown bread from scratch and make your own apple butter, but you can't add a little flour to meat drippings and come up with real gravy?" His whole body radiated disbelief.

How could one man be so hung up on her cooking methods? "Look, can you make a better gravy than what I turned out with that can of soup?"

"No," he admitted, then qualified, "But I've never really tried, either."

"Until you can, leave my culinary quirks out of any conversation we might have." Her lips clamped tightly on her pique. "If I ever find a good shortcut to apple butter or Boston brown bread, believe me, I'll use it." She turned back to stir the apples with more vigor than strictly necessary. Honestly, he might *look* good coming out of her bath, but educating this man back into the fun and joy of the real world would take someone with suicidal impulses.

He also seemed reluctant to fall under the spell she had so carefully staged. "My, my," he remarked on seeing the table. "From the ridiculous to the sublime. No one would ever guess from your taste in everyday crockery that you harbored a predilection toward Wedgwood and Waterford."

Karen and Tim eyed him warily as Tim held Karen's chair for her. Andrea was too resigned to hearing whatever came next to be surprised by a man's recognizing fine china and crystal on sight.

"How one person could embody so many diametrically opposed concepts is beyond me," Greg added.

Andrea dropped into her chair by herself before Tim could cover Greg's lack of social graces. She then explained rather shortly, "I used to work part-time at Marshal Field's. I collected one stem of Waterford per paycheck until I had service for eight. Then I started on china—piece by piece, month by month for three years before I had the whole set." She lovingly rubbed the rich cobalt-and-gold encrusted border on her plate. "I don't think I'll ever get tired of looking at it." The food was being ignored while Andrea warmed to one of her favorite topics. "Do you know what the difference is between fine and bone china?"

"She's going to get disgusting, and right before dinner, too," Greg warned.

Andrea ignored him and went blithely on. "The name does not refer simply to its color, but bone china has actual animal bone ground into its batter. When it's fired, it gets its characteristic white-white coloration. Fine china, on the other hand, is a batter made with white clays. It has a higher concentration of feldspar. When it's fired, it takes on a creamy hue."

"What about porcelain?" Karen asked, interested.

"Now, porcelain is—"

"Uh, ladies? Could we possibly come back to this fascinating discussion at a later time? I'm starving. If you could, perchance, start the food around? It smells great," Tim said.

Andrea grimaced in apology. "Sorry, I tend to get carried away. I always found it fascinating to work in that section. I learned a lot, that's for sure." She helped herself to an abundant amount of pasta then passed the bowl to Greg.

Greg suspiciously eyed the spaghetti he had just spooned onto his plate and questioned, "Does this sauce have any mushrooms in it?"

"You have a mushroom fixation. What the hell is wrong with mushrooms that makes you so totally irrational on the subject?"

"Mushrooms," he intoned darkly, "are a fungi."

"An *edible* fungi."

"A fungi, nonetheless."

"Oh, for heaven's sake. This is ridiculous. I don't know if there's mushrooms in there or not. If you can't live it up and take a chance, go out and read the label. The box is out in the garbage in the kitchen."

Greg's Italian heritage seemed to inspire an open rebellion. "The box? You mean you didn't make it? We're eating *store-bought* sauce? Candlelight can't camouflage taste, you know."

If the man didn't let up, he was going to be thrown out long before the week was out, sick or not. Sometime in the next ten minutes would be more like it, Andrea thought. He could just recover all by himself. "Spaghetti sauce takes hours of simmering to make properly," she informed him sweetly. "Did you happen to notice any simmering away while I was out looking for *your* apartment?"

Once again, his mind seemed to have stalled on what he saw as the only pertinent issue: "Store-bought sauce. That's revolting. Probably has mushrooms, too."

Andrea stared at him wide-eyed, her own food forgotten. How could anyone be so totally narrow-minded?

Karen, too, studied her uncle through slitted lids. From her expression it was clear she had never known her uncle to be so finicky before. It wasn't likely that medical school had changed him so radically, and years of cheap cafeteria eating were unlikely to develop such discerning taste buds. It was almost as though he were being difficult on purpose...trying to maintain an emotional distance.

"Try it, you may find you'll like it. This happens to be Fanny's Sauce, from an extremely popular Italian restaurant here in Evanston," Andrea explained as if to someone so dense that each word had to be spoken slowly and enunciated clearly. "They freeze it and sell it through the local groceries' freezer sections. I'm not sure if you can even get this anywhere else in the country. I bought it as a special treat. It's quite expensive."

Greg looked doubtful as he wound a single strand around

the tines of his fork and chewed it dubiously. "It's okay," he allowed after swallowing and taking a sip of his wine.

Andrea leaned back in her chair and watched him pass the bowl on. "Well, hallelujah! He's going to condescend to eat our food."

Andrea noticed Karen looking at Tim in silent communication, as if pleading him to offer a new conversational topic.

As he doused his salad in the ranch-style dressing, Tim casually asked, "I noticed an envelope stuck in the door from the heating place. How much?"

Andrea wasn't too thrilled with this line of conversation either. "Too much," she sighed. "Fifteen hundred dollars."

Tim whistled. "Wow!"

"My reaction was a little more explicit."

"You weren't kidding that the kitchen would have to wait."

"What's really annoying," she grumbled, "is that the Kitchen Store is practically giving away one of their floor displays that was made to order for our kitchen. Solid oak, too. It even had a pantry cabinet with shelves on the doors, swing-out racks on piano hinges and more shelves behind those. They were holding it all for me until tomorrow night so that I could measure the kitchen and be sure." She sounded as if she were going deeper into mourning over her potential loss with each word. "I was really looking forward to a decent work area out there."

Greg had eaten half his pile of spaghetti with no further complaints. He slathered butter on a piece of bakery-fresh French bread as he spoke. "Couldn't you take out a home improvement loan or increase your mortgage? It seems a shame to miss out on such a good deal."

"I haven't got a mortgage to increase."

"Of course you do. Everybody gets a mortgage when they buy a house. It's those monthly payments you make."

"Not me. I don't believe in credit buying."

"How did you pay for the house then? Nobody pays cash for a house."

Andrea was aware of Tim holding his breath. He knew Andrea's background, having grown up next door to her; Greg did not. And Greg was trespassing on dangerous ground.

Instead of snapping off his head the way Tim was probably anticipating, Andrea responded with an only slightly strained smile. "My mother's sister, a charming lady, had no heirs. When she died a year ago, she left everything to me and my two sisters. We each chose some of her furniture to remember her by, and I used my share of the estate to buy this place. I've been slowly fixing it up ever since."

Greg looked around with new understanding. "The piano?"

"And this two-position coffee table we're eating at." She nodded. "Also some pieces I've got stored in the basement for the loft apartment."

"If you took out a home improvement loan or a small mortgage, the monthly payments wouldn't amount to much and you could have both the new kitchen and the boiler with enough left over to furnish the dining room," he pointed out reasonably.

Andrea's "No" came out with such vehemence that Greg was momentarily taken aback. He looked ready to pursue the argument when Andrea grabbed his dinner plate and piled it with the others.

"Hey! I wasn't finished yet."

"Yes, you were. You've had two helpings of store-bought sauce. I'm saving you from compromising your high standards and principles. Anyway, there's still dessert to come. You don't want to be too full, do you?"

"But there's still a little bit of spaghetti left in the bowl; it would be a shame to waste it."

"Have it for breakfast," Andrea advised as she whisked the bowl out of the line of fire.

Greg blanched at the thought. "Spaghetti for breakfast?"

"You didn't like what I made this morning," Andrea pointed out.

Greg called to her receding back as she carried the stack of dishes off, "What's wrong with eggs? What have you got against French toast or pancakes for breakfast? Something normal, for goodness' sake.''

"Normality is a relative term," she called back. "If you'd break out of that rut you're in, widen your mental horizons, you could enjoy spaghetti for breakfast...or mushrooms at any time of day, for that matter.'' She was giving him a hard time for the heck of it. She wasn't all that sure she could face spaghetti at six o'clock in the morning, either. But it certainly was fun razzing him about it.

He was rising to follow her with another stack of dishes, but Tim detained him with a hand on his wrist while Karen took the dishes. "Don't pursue the loan bit, Greg. She's very sensitive about not buying on credit.''

"A small loan would hardly be getting in over one's head," he argued equitably. "Especially if it's her only outstanding debt. Hell, I've got school loans up to my eyeballs, but I never could have been an M.D. without them.''

"You know that and I know that. But her dad could probably fill out bankruptcy forms in his sleep. Her outlook has been colored by that for as long as I've known her, and we go back a way," he explained. "She's afraid it's like alcoholism or gambling—if she starts buying on credit, she won't be able to quit. Irrational, but there you are.''

Greg felt compelled to argue further, "She's missing all kinds of tax advantages by allowing herself to overreact to her father like that.'' He sighed before capitulating. "Fine. I won't press it. It really isn't any of my business.''

Tim's hand dropped away and Greg rose to follow Andrea out to the kitchen with the empty breadbasket in hand. "What's for dessert?'' he called.

"*Gâteau de Sara,*'' came the unhesitating reply.

"What's a gattoe, and who's Sara? Some relative of Fanny's?''

"*Gâteau* is the French word for cake, and Sara may or may not be related to Fanny, I really don't know. She's the one nobody doesn't like. Sara Lee?''

"Out of a box from the freezer section," he grumbled on a low rumble.

"That's right," she trilled sweetly, flicking on the flame under the teakettle. "So cheer up. She makes a better Black Forest torte than I could even contemplate."

"I thought it was a *gâteau*."

"Same difference. It's still good, and I checked the label. No mushrooms, no soup."

"Thank heaven for small favors," he grumbled in mock relief. Grabbing the last slice of Boston brown bread, he trailed her back into the living room. At least with the bread he'd have *something* for dessert. He watched while she sliced the cake into even wedges. Cherries on chocolate cake. What mental midget had thought up that one? He viewed it from all angles while the other three participants made short work of theirs.

He tried a tentative forkful. It was a strange combination, but edible. And he wouldn't want to appear rude. He ate the whole thing before turning to his piece of Boston brown bread. It really was amazing, considering some of the strange concoctions that had been served since his arrival, how his appetite had gone from nonexistent to ravenous.

Karen looked stuffed. Greg knew the baby was big enough to crowd her stomach and not leave much room for a meal. He grinned as Karen leaned back in her chair and crossed her ankles instead of her knees to allow the baby as much room as possible. Karen looked from her uncle's empty plate to his eyes. He didn't have to be psychic to read the ironic expression. Greg flushed when he thought of the production his mother used to make of counting the silverware after a family meal just to be sure he hadn't inhaled any.

He winced as Karen attacked. "I can remember when you used to eat like that all the time. Years of bland cafeteria grilled cheeses and instant vanilla pudding have warped your taste buds. It's no wonder you've gotten so thin. Who could thrive on that junk? With a frame as large as yours, you should put on at least ten to fifteen pounds, maybe more. What you

need—'' Karen paused to ensure his attention and to emphasize her next words ''—is a wife to take you in hand. Yep.''
She nodded in agreement with her own analysis while Tim
looked nervous and took a hurried sip of water. Greg eyed her
skeptically.

"A good woman," she continued, "would broaden your
horizons in more ways than just food. You've had a very narrowly focused life out of necessity for so long, you're going
to need help breaking loose and branching out. You know
what's wrong with you?"

Her uncle shook his head, taking a hearty bite out of his
brown bread.

"Being an M.D., I'm sure you've heard of babies who literally die for lack of love and touching."

Greg shook his head, positively this time.

Karen leaned forward to point at him in emphasis. "You're
in danger of that as an adult. That's why it's taking you so
long to recover from this bout of hepatitis. You need someone
to bond with before you waste away." And she leaned back
in the chair again, very pleased with her analysis of the situation.

Before Greg could swallow the lump of bread now uncomfortably lodged in his throat and begin to refute her claim,
Tim decided to join the cause. "I know a likely candidate who
could volunteer for the position. She suffers from the same
problem, only she doesn't know it yet."

Andrea stared at him wide-eyed. "How can you talk about
your own sister that way? Lisa would murder you in cold
blood if she knew you were putting her on the auction block
that way."

"I wasn't referring to Lisa." Tim looked at Andrea pointedly.

"Oh, no. Ooh, no." She reached forward to clatter her cup
down in its saucer before pounding a choking Greg on the
back. "Look what you've done! You're supposed to be helping him recover and now you're going to have to save him
from choking instead. Someone to bond with. How ridiculous!

It will be on your conscience if he dies,'' she said with a steely-eyed glare at Tim, her displeasure with him evident.

Greg was still sputtering but managed to draw in a struggling breath and wheeze, ''Stop hitting me. You've managed to dislodge the bread, there's no need to shake loose every organ in my body.''

''Rotten ingrate.'' She gave him one final healthy whack before crossing her arms indignantly and sitting back in her chair.

Between little residual coughs, Greg spoke. ''I admit it's probably time I found someone to carry on the family name. I'm aware that I'm the last male in a long succession of Rennolds.''

Andrea's glare let him know her opinion of his callous approach to love and marriage. All to be done in the line of familial genetic duty, she supposed. Pity the poor girl stuck with this clod. She hoped he and his little paragon of a wife produced nothing but girls. Then she determinedly stifled the warm chill that came over her at the thought of carrying Greg's babies.

''However, when I take a wife, it's not going to be some pseudoliberated woman who couldn't cook if soup manufacturers went out of business and who'd burned all her bras—''

''I've never burned a bra in my life,'' Andrea gasped in outrage, not even noticing how Tim and Karen perked up at the reference to her underwear. ''I just didn't choose to wear one this morning. There are at least three in my drawer. You were in my room when I got dressed and I couldn't—''

''Are you implying you would like to audition for the job?''

''Absolutely not. There isn't enough gold in Fort Knox to…''

Greg waved away her rantings with a negligent hand. ''The woman I marry, as I was saying, will be gentle and petite. Into baking bread.'' His gaze was caught by the slice of homemade Boston brown bread he was waving in the air to underline his words. Carefully, he placed it down on the edge of his saucer before continuing. ''The kids will be scrubbed and shiny, ready to be tucked in when I arrive home, and then I'll share a romantic candlelit dinner for two with my wife before we go to bed ourselves."

"Brother, talk about fantasy. That kind of 1950 paragon is hard to find nowadays. A lot of women either want to or have to work to help supplement their husband's income and are too tired to wait on anybody like that. Besides," Andrea concluded dismissingly, "you haven't got the personality to draw that side of a woman out. She'd hit you with her empty soup cans before putting dinner on the table."

"There won't *be* any empty soup cans in *my* wife's kitchen." Greg glared at Andrea, but further remarks were forestalled by the chiming doorbell.

Andrea declared the evening's attempt at creating a mellow atmosphere a failure by flicking a switch on her way to answer the door. The room was suddenly bathed in stark light and its occupants blinked in an effort to adjust to the glare.

Shivering on her doorstep, she discovered her next-door neighbor's son, eight-year-old Jimmy McKnight, who looked up soulfully, an entreating expression on his freckled countenance.

"Jimmy! You're not allowed out after supper. Is anything wrong?" She ushered him quickly into the warm living room, and in her momentary concern, did not notice the small yellow and blue rectangular box clutched to his chest.

The child shook his head mutely in response to her question. No, nothing was wrong. Andrea eyed him speculatively. He had only recently begun opening up to her when they were alone. Now, with so many people in the room, Jimmy's tongue was not about to loosen its grip from the roof of his mouth. He studied the polished golden oak planking beneath his feet for a full sixty seconds before silently proffering the small cardboard box.

"What have to got there, Jimbo?" Andrea inquired more softly as she read the label. "Official Cub Scout Pinewood Derby Kit. And your name on it, hmm? I didn't know you were a Cub Scout."

He nodded vigorously. "Just this year," he whispered in barely audible tones.

Andrea read further. "It says here this is supposed to be a father-son project. Can't your dad do this with you?" Warning bells were beginning to clang in her head. She didn't know anything about building cars, for heaven's sake, and once again, she knew what was coming.

She had to lean closer to hear the barely audible explanation. "He has to work the night shift all this month, so we're never home at the same time. Mom said she'd do it with me, but she's never sawed or hammered anything before," he confessed in a rush. "I've seen you hammerin', though." He looked up from his intent study of his scuffed and stained sneaker tips, glanced shyly at her and quickly reverted his gaze back to the red and blue striped canvas shoe. "I was hopin'... Mom said I could ask... Maybe you would, you know..."

Andrea's heart sank to her toes. Yeah, she knew all right. She knew she was trapped again, for one thing. She'd kill Maureen when she saw her in the morning. Any car she might make would be an unmitigated disaster. She knew that with a deadly certainty. She turned the box in her hands, pretending to study the label again and glanced surreptitiously at the anxious visage before her. Why did he have to have so many little freckles sprinkled across his nose? And how had he gotten so pale and orphanish looking already? Damn, it was happening again. She wouldn't be able to turn him down.

Karen had been clearing the table and Andrea now headed for the vacated area. "Let's dump the contents of the box out on the table and see what's here, okay?" Maybe it wouldn't be so bad and she could talk Tim into—

Her hopes were summarily dashed as Tim rose and stretched languidly. "I'll get the dishes and then I absolutely have to get some studying done. It won't have done you any good to have taken us in if I flunk the tortes exam." He was letting her know he didn't have time to help her out of this one. Her spirits sank further. Flipping open the top of the box, she tilted it down to the table and gave a gentle shake. Out came a block of pine, four nails, and four wheels—also a set of directions, which she gingerly unfolded, fingering it with all the distaste of a registered letter from the Internal Revenue Service.

"I'll help you," Jimmy was saying eagerly. "All you hafta do is tell me what to do. Dad says I'm a big help to him, handin' him nails and stuff. Oh, and Mom says she has some drapery weights we can use."

Andrea had been looking morosely back and forth from the directions to the chunk of unfinished wood, but his last words broke through her shell-shocked state. Drapery weights? What the heck was she supposed to do with those? Frantically, she went back to the directions. She had to cut the wood twice, and on an angle, no less. Weights…weights… There it was. The finished car was to weigh no more than four ounces, but should be weighted to come as close to the allowed weight as possible without exceeding it. The heavier the car, the faster it would travel down the track. Wonderful. Nowhere did it say how one was to attach these indispensable weights.

Closing her eyes, the backs of her lids provided the screen for a Technicolor nightmare. Jimmy's car was rolling in slow motion down the track, spitefully shucking off one wheel at a time in a disorderly progression, each one bouncing off with a defiant *ping* until all four had been heartlessly cast off. Now it came to a grinding halt halfway down the speedway while the other Cubs' cars flashed by, streaking onto the finish line in a blaze of sawdust.

The vision cleared, and Andrea gave her head an impatient shake to clear away the fading image. Painfully she turned to Jimmy. "Uh, let's go on down to the basement, okay? We can go through the toolbox and see what we'll need."

She turned to Karen and instructed in an aside, "If you still have any energy whatsoever, I think there's some of that cookie dough left from the other day in the back of the refrigerator. Don't let Tim see what you're doing until it's too late. He'll have a fit if he sees you greasing the cookie sheet before he's even finished cleaning the last batch of pans. Don't bother with the food coloring. A little sugar sprinkled on top will be fine.''

Karen nodded sympathetically while Andrea bent to gather the various nails and wheels, directions and wood. She squared her shoulders and motioned to the small boy in the patched jeans and cotton T-shirt emblazoned with a cartooned elf and the logo Cookie Elves Believe in the Cubs, to precede her.

Leaning over to whisper in Karen's ear, she curtly directed, ''I don't really care what that unfeeling hulk in the kitchen says, get me those cookies. I'm going to need them to raise my stock with Jimmy after he sees what kind of incompetent clod he's aligned himself with.'' She straightened up and fatalistically saluted Karen while rolling her eyes. ''We who are about to die...and all of that.''

Karen laughed. ''Never mind any last words. Go down and face the firing squad like the big brave girl we know you are. You'll do fine.''

''That only shows how little you really know me, even after living in the same house all this time,'' Andrea muttered in resignation.

Greg watched the delicate sway of Andrea's gray velour-clad hips as they receded into the rear of the house. He spoke contemplatively, almost as if he had forgotten Karen's presence. ''Interesting. The longer I'm here, the more of an enigma she becomes. I'm beginning to suspect that under that gruff exterior a heart beats after all. Maybe not twenty-four karat, but eighteen at any rate. She has no child, yet runs a Brownie troop. You and Tim pay no rent. She's said nothing to me about money, either. A blind man could see she's worried over disappointing that little kid. Interesting.''

Karen leaned forward to place her neatly tapered fingers flat against the blue linen cloth. Her own brown eyes met her uncle's in a direct, no-nonsense fashion. ''Don't make the mistake of letting Andrea's bark turn you off to the inner beauty of the person. She's sandpapery, but only on the outside. She didn't have to let Tim and me stay here. Plenty of other people commiserated with us on our bad luck, then figured their duty had been done with lip service. Not Andrea. She's given us a way to keep our pride. Tim is well aware that Mom didn't really approve of him, and we both hated to give her the chance to say 'I told you so.' Sure, Tim works around here when he can, but we don't begin to put in what we get out. And Andrea honestly doesn't care. Tim's been like a brother to her. They've been close since they were five years old. The moment she met me, she made it clear I could place any demands on her that a member of her family might.''

Much to her uncle's surprise, Karen's eyes glistened damply as she continued, although her gaze never wavered. ''I can't tell you what that meant to me, having lived most of my life as an overprotected only child. And as for kids, she loves them. She wasn't kidding when she said she had demanded our child in return for room and board. One of the only stipulations she made when we came here to live was that anytime we went out after the baby came, she would get to baby-sit. She is truly a caring, loving person.''

Greg was surprised by Karen's outburst—not only by the depth of emotion Andrea seemed to evoke in her friends, but also by the feeling of hurt he felt at the transfer of an allegiance that had always been his. Suddenly he was the outsider in Karen's life. It was food for thought.

''It was nice of you all to host me for the weekend,'' he attempted. ''But tomorrow I plan to get a room at the Orrington until I can find an apartment. I don't want to take advantage.''

Karen flicked her hand to show what she thought of that. ''You have to admit, three decent meals a day for the past two days haven't done you any harm. You're already looking better, although I like to think that's from being around your scintillating niece rather than Andrea's cooking.'' She dimpled easily at him, her former earnestness submerged. ''Tim and I will make it up to Andrea eventually, don't worry. Just be nice to her.''

Greg gave her a disparaging glance, letting her know that not only did he believe her to be a lost cause, but also that he could see right through her. "For your information, I am not quite the dirty so-and-so you seem to believe. I have been too busy studying to leave much of a trail of broken hearts behind me."

"With your looks?" Karen asked in a disbelieving tone.

"Looks don't get you grades, unfortunately." He rose majestically from the table, towering over Karen. "Be that as it may, *I* was a Cub Scout, and *my* cars always placed high in the Pinewood Derbies. If you will excuse me, I will go rescue Jimmy from the clutches of that *Brownie* leader before his car is irreparably damaged." "Brownie" came out as a dirty word, beneath the dignity of a Cub Scout's association.

Karen hummed a little tune as she followed Greg through to the kitchen. Greg was too preoccupied to remember that Karen had always hummed when scheming.

Chapter Four

By eight o'clock that evening, the block of natural pine had made remarkable progress. It had been carefully molded into its proper shape and then sanded with not one or two, but three progressively finer grades of sandpaper. Now it was clamped in a vise like a turtle sprawled on its back. Andrea watched Greg's large, blunt fingers make a delicate adjustment to the wide-bladed bit he had inserted into the drill. Then he began to exactly drill out the precise area he required on the car's understructure. Greg explained to Jimmy as he worked that this way, the weights could be hidden up in the underside, and not mar the lines of the finished racer.

Andrea had concluded that Greg had missed his calling, that his agile fingers might have been put to better use as a carpenter or sculptor, when Karen called down the stairs, "I'm bringing milk and cookies. You'll have to eat them fast, though. Jimmy's mother called, and she wants him home. It's a school night, she says."

"Don't do the stairs, Karen," Andrea called back. "We'll be right up."

"Not to worry. I have to give my seal of approval to the

product of the last few hours' labors anyway." With that, she started down the steep steps. It was an interesting challenge, as the stairs were narrow and her stomach large. Her oversize tummy kept her from holding the plastic tray with its plate of sugar-dusted cookies and half-filled Dixie cups of milk anywhere near her body. Instead, she had to hold it out where it interfered with her already diminished sense of balance.

Andrea was too busy admiring the ease with which Greg handled himself around the tool bench to notice Karen's struggling descent. Her first inkling of a problem came with Karen's smothered shriek as, right at the bottom, victory almost hers, she lost her balance and sat down hard on the second step. The cacophony of the clattering tray on the cement floor, the spreading puddle of milk, and the flying cookie chunks made it seem far worse a catastrophe than it really was.

Andrea turned, frozen in horror as she took in Karen's shocked expression. She heard herself calling as if from a distance, "Oh, my God! Peggy! You'll lose the baby. Oh, my God!"

Greg, on his way to help Karen up, looked at Andrea strangely: but more concerned with getting Karen out of the spilled milk, he let his curiosity over Andrea's scream of "Peggy" wait.

"Oh, my God! We'll have to call the doctor right away. The emergency room... No, she probably shouldn't be moved. An ambulance, that's it. They have radio connections now that go right to the hospital in them."

From his crouched position, Greg urged, "Relax, Andrea. All she did was sit down. I'm a doctor, remember? She's going to be fine."

"But the baby..."

"Pregnant women do stuff like this all the time," he assured her. "Their sense of gravity changes and babies sometimes put pressure on the nerve at the top of the leg, causing the leg to go out from under them. It's not a big deal. Those babies are so well cushioned, it would take a whole lot more than just sitting down hard to shake them loose. Really, she's okay.''

Just to be sure, he checked Karen's legs and arms before helping her up. "Let's go on up now. I've got my stethoscope upstairs. We'll listen to the fetal heart tones and put Miss Worrywart's mind to rest.''

Andrea escorted a tongue-tied Jimmy up the stairs where she found a small cache of unbroken cookies. Trying not to be too obvious, she breathed a sigh of relief as she pressed a handful on him and hustled the eight-year-old out the door, waving goodbye before hurrying to Karen's bedroom.

Breathlessly she took in the scene. Karen lay ensconced on her bed decked in a frilly white nightgown with lace up to her chin, a solicitous Tim paying court on one side while Greg tucked his blood-pressure cuff and stethoscope back into his traditional black doctor's bag on the other. The martyred expression on Karen's face would have done credit to a queen in a Victorian melodrama, and Andrea was immediately on her guard.

"The baby's okay?" she warily questioned.

Greg nodded. "Yep. Judging by the amount of activity going on down there right now, Karen had better put in a supply of track shoes just to keep up with this kid after he's born. She thinks she might have pulled a muscle, though.''

"Oh? Where?" Andrea's gut-wrenching fears were rapidly dissolving into frissons of suspicion. There was something peculiar about the current arrangement of Karen's facial features that might lead a less trusting sort to doubt the reality of the damage in question.

"Ooh, my wrist," Karen moaned piteously, hanging the offended limb out for inspection. "I think it's sprained.''

"Perhaps we ought to get it checked at the hospital," Tim said worriedly.

"Oh, I'm sure it'll be all right if I just don't use it for a few days. They can't X-ray it anyway. I'm pregnant, remember?" Karen quickly broke in before turning oddly complacent eyes on her uncle. "But you know how hard it is to do things one-handed, and I do have a lot to do this week."

She pretended not to hear Andrea's strangled "Like what?"

"I don't suppose, since you're free this week anyway, that you'd consider sticking around a few more days? Just to kind of be here, if you know what I mean. That fall has made me quite wary of being by myself. What if it happens while I'm alone?" she questioned in what sounded like smug satisfaction rather than real worry.

"Ah, Karen, my love. You forget I've known you for a long, long time. Sorry, but tomorrow I go to a hotel." He snapped his black bag shut, but was prevented from leaving.

Tim broke in sheepishly, "Actually, I'm a little shook-up by all this myself. If you're going to the hotel because you're worried about outstaying your welcome, I'd really appreciate it if you'd reconsider. This has got to be nicer than any cramped hotel room until you find an apartment. And Andrea doesn't mind, do you, Andrea?"

Andrea's arms were crossed in front of her body, and she rocked from heel to toe and back again as she eyed Karen speculatively. "Why do I get the distinct impression that I'm being had?"

"I'm sure I wouldn't know." Karen sniffed. "I would never sink to manipulation, even if it would be in the best interests of some other party."

"Hah. I'm only agreeing to this for Tim's peace of mind and because my own Red Cross certificate expired two months ago—although considering the shape the doctor in question is in, I ought to get it renewed. Who's going to doctor the doctor?"

"The doctor doesn't need doctoring," Greg retorted, "only rest, which would be a more likely possibility elsewhere. However, since my presence has been so graciously requested, how can I say no?" He turned to Andrea. "When you're done coddling the noninvalid here, come into the living room and we'll discuss the price of room and board."

Andrea waited until Greg had firmly closed the door behind

his departing back before threatening her friend on the bed. "If you've conjured up some crazy idea of propinquity and wedding bells, you can just forget it. He's not my type."

"He's awfully good-looking…" Karen tempted.

"Now you listen to me. I will dump you out the front door right on your sprained wrist if you start throwing him at me, or me at him, for that matter."

"I won't have to," Karen said in satisfied tones. "Things will happen all by themselves if I can just manage to keep you around each other long enough to give it time. I can feel it in my bones."

"That, no doubt, is the onset of rheumatism, and this is not going to work. We'll be at each other's throats again in no time."

Karen lay back against the pillow, placing the back of a languid wrist over her closed eyes. "Tim," she complained, "I'm getting a headache. Make her go into the living room and discuss rent with Greg, will you? But you stay here with me, in case I black out."

"Oh, for heaven's sake. I'm going. Just don't say I didn't warn you it wouldn't work. You'll really have a migraine with all of us living on top of each other the next week or two."

"Oh, it could be months before an apartment becomes available, you know. A really nice one in the proper area, that is," Karen advised.

Andrea could hear Tim's amused voice as she went down the small hallway. "I hope you know what you're doing. She looks ready to chew nails."

Darn right, Andrea thought, fuming. *I'm not so totally without saving graces that I have to resort to prospective husbands being hog-tied and held so I can grow on them like some darn piece of* lichen *on the side of a darn tree. Those two will soon realize they're beating a dead horse on this issue,* she decided. *I don't need a man, I don't want a man, and I'm certainly not going to allow them to force-feed me that…that emotionally backward…jerk!* The realization that she could quite easily come to love that particular jerk galled her, feeding her righ-

teous indignation with each step until by the time she reached
the living room, she was virtually stomping and the look on
her face would have quelled a lesser man.

"Women who smoke are terribly unattractive, you know."

"I don't smoke."

"You must. Furthermore, it looks as if you exhale through
your ears. There are big gray plumes of noxious smoke billowing out of them right now. Calm down and let's talk. We
need to get to know each other a little bit."

"Why?" Andrea demanded, viciously poking at the flag-
ging fire only to jump back from the maelstrom of bursting
sparks she had set loose.

Greg pulled her back from the spitting blaze and quickly
set the mesh curtain over the opening. He pushed her down
on the sofa, directing, "Sit down and listen to me."

Andrea struck out against that indefinable chemistry that
attracted her to him. "You don't have to stay here, you know.
There's no reason we have to coddle that crazy woman's
whims just because she's pregnant. Ice cream and pickles at
two in the morning, fine. But no way is she going to saddle
me with her idea of the perfect mate. The vagaries of expectant
motherhood will only take her so far. We don't even like each
other." She crossed her arms obstinately and glared at him.

She panicked at Greg's endearing grin, feeling the noose
tighten yet another notch. "I don't know," he said. "This
place and all you loonies that populate it are starting to grow
on me. It's what I feared, you know."

"*Us* loonies!" Andrea sniffed.

"Yeah, you loonies," Greg agreed. "And before you go
getting all indignant again, let's talk about this rationally."

Andrea's face was set in stubborn mutiny although she remained silent. Greg settled his tall frame next to hers on the
plumply pillowed sofa and threw a companionable arm along
the rise of the back, behind but not quite touching Andrea's
shoulders. She could feel the heat of his body jump the short
distance to her own and, oddly, it produced a shivery chill that

feathered its cold fingers down the length of her spine and back up again.

"Look at it this way," Greg urged. "This could work to both our advantages. I could use some decent meals, and I can't cook. Going out for every meal would be a pain while I'm still feeling so tired. You, on the other hand," Greg continued in his calming deep bass, "why, you get a bit of extra income at a time when you could use it, without that much extra effort. You cook anyway, and you could throw my laundry in with yours without a big deal. Karen and Tim will be moving upstairs by the end of the week, so I can just take their room. And while I'm well aware that Karen thinks she is being terribly cunning, I also think Tim might feel a little better if there was a doctor in the house, so to speak."

"You'd have to take your turns at the jobs around here; I don't feel like playing glorified maid," Andrea stipulated crossly.

Greg cajoled her teasingly. "It won't be so bad, and we might even have a little fun at Karen's expense," he whispered.

"How?"

"Watch this," he instructed before he gently pulled her into his arms and began lowering his mouth to hers.

"What do you think you're doing?" Andrea squeaked and then winced. Had that high-pitched squeal actually been her voice?

"Shh, relax." His mouth made firm contact with hers. She lay rigidly in his arms, too stunned by the suddenness of the maneuver to struggle. He lightly nibbled her generous lower lip while his arm adjusted her position in his lap to maximum advantage. Then his capable doctor's hands began drawing teasing, light circles along her upper arms and across her collarbone. The sensuous feel as he moved against her velvety velour jogging top added to the power and effect of his touch, making her shudder and relax.

"What are you doing?" she moaned in much different, lower tones.

"Just enjoy," he muttered against her lips as he continued marauding the treasures of her mouth. "I certainly am." His tongue questingly probed the tight line of her clenched lips, and she parted them, allowing him free access to the damply dark plunder beyond, and she was shocked by her own actions. Never in her twenty-four years had she ever experienced anything with the rampaging power of this kiss. She felt hot and then shivery cold in rapid succession and her arms, with a will all their own, moved to a spot low on his back.

Not that she was much of a judge, but it seemed that Greg was not exempt from the powerful current she felt flowing through their bodies. His breath had noticeably quickened. One hand had roamed to a position just under her breast, allowing its weight to rest against him. And Andrea, who had never before been interested enough in any man to allow intimacies past the mandatory good-night kiss, found her whole body tingling in anticipation of some unknown end. For the first time, she was fighting her bodily instincts. It was all she could do to prevent her own hand from moving his up the last few inches to its throbbing goal. There was the oddest, almost *compulsive* type of budding feeling building down deep in her very being. She could feel her pulse racing, her blood rushing to bring its flush to her normally delicate pearl skin tones and act as witness to the kiss's potent effect.

She leaned back in his arms to search his face in wonderment. It was a humbling experience to realize that she, who had always sworn never to be used to satisfy a man's baser instincts, had a few base instincts of her own. Much more of this, and *she'd* be pleading with *him* to finish what he'd started.

"My!" Andrea muttered in amazement. "I'd ask where you learned to do that, but my tender sensibilities would probably be shocked, so don't tell me. I'm sure I don't want to know."

"It was rather good, wasn't it?"

A door clicked shut in the background. Greg grinned roguishly and tipped his head to the side. "Hear that? That was

Karen going back to report to Tim on our progress as a loving duo.''

Andrea looked shocked. "She was listening?"

"Mmm."

"You devastated me like that because she was listening and you wanted to shock her?" Greg's expression grew warily rueful as he nodded again. "I hope she turns into a pillar of salt, just like the biblical people who turned back for a final look at Sodom and Gomorrah."

"It was pretty good as far as kisses go, but I'm not sure it would be in quite the same category as the fall of Sodom and Gomorrah."

A dazed Andrea was having a little trouble taking it all in. "I'm sitting here shattered, and it was all some kind of game. You did this to me to teach your niece some kind of lesson. I hope you both rot in—"

"Now hold on a minute. That was how it *started*. I admit I thought it would be fun to take her for a ride and let her think there was something between us for a while, but now I'm not so sure it would work. You're not the only one feeling a little shattered right now. I initiated that kiss to make Karen realize her error, but it seems to have backfired. I may have to credit her with more insight than I thought possible."

He sank back into the sofa's cushions and pulled Andrea down beside him, tucking her head onto his shoulder, his left arm comfortably resting along the wary, slightly trembling breadth of her shoulders while his free hand played with a tendril of lustrous ebony hair that curled across the swell of her firm breast.

Andrea was appalled to discover her own delicately-boned hand testing the texture of the silky brown hair protruding from the top of his hunter-plaid flannel shirt. As she watched in a detached manner, she spoke almost reverently. "It boggles the mind to think what might have happened here. I almost threw myself at you. I have never thrown myself at a man. Never." She took in a long breath before slowly expelling it. "I've just had a rather startling revelation into my character, and I'm not sure I ought to be alone in the same room with you for a while."

Her voice was so incredulous, as though she couldn't quite believe what had just happened, that Greg laughed and hugged her to him. "It was rather dynamic, wasn't it? We'll try to exercise more discretion in the future." It seemed to her that he did the exact opposite as he instituted a series of butterfly-light kisses along her hairline and down the slender length of her neck. Finally he snuggled closer to her body and lay his head next to hers on the sofa back. Brushing her hair away to expose the tender nape of her neck, he kissed her there, too. "I knew it would be fun teasing Karen, I just didn't realize how much fun. You all were right earlier; I do need to loosen up."

"I'm not sure jumping feetfirst into an inferno is exactly what we had in mind, especially since you seem intent on taking me with you. Couldn't you start off by learning to like mushrooms?"

"Uh-uh," Greg returned languidly, nibbling on her earlobe. "This particular portion of your anatomy is infinitely superior to any mushroom." His warm breath gusting down her neck made her shudder. Not realizing the cause of her chills, he pulled her closer to share his body heat. "Besides, any good Scout knows how to tend a flame without anyone getting burned."

"Yeah? Well I've got news for you. If you don't quit fanning the flames, the entire sofa is going to go up in smoke."

There was no response, but his tongue had stopped inflicting its slow torture on her suddenly erotic earlobe. She pulled her head back to bring him into focus. His eyes were closed, his generous lips slightly parted. His steady breathing gave it away. This was not a man trying to control his flaming passion, but rather a man who had fallen sound asleep, dousing the flames by rolling on them with his body, like a good Scout.

So much for her uncontrollably passionate appeal. Andrea grimaced as she pushed against his body, now heavily slumped upon her in its relaxed slumber. She would have been insulted by the turn of events had she not also been relieved. His body shifted enough to take off the heavy pressure, but not enough to gain her release. Even if she called to Karen and Tim, they probably wouldn't hear her through their closed door, and she rather thought the enjoyment they would display at her predicament would not be counterbalanced by the benefits of release. It would be better to suffer in silence than suffer under their knowing looks for the next few days. At least now she could honestly say she'd slept with a man.

Chuckling at her wayward thoughts, she leaned as far as she could, just managing to hook a finger into the gay profusion of multicolored woven yarns making up a granny-patch afghan that hung barely within reach across the back of the sofa. Awkwardly, she managed to spread it over them with her one free hand, hoping that, combined with his body warmth next to her, it would be enough to see them through the night.

She needn't have worried. Waking once during the night, she knew the house was cool but was amazed at how warm she was. She, who normally bundled for bed during the colder months with layers of wool socks and quilted robes, actually had to stick an arm and a foot out from under the crocheted blanket in an effort to lower her body temperature. At that moment, a large plus in marriage's favor made its way into her consciousness. Warmth in winter, what heaven! Greg's male heat in such close proximity was infinitely superior to any brand of electric blanket she'd tried—the problem being, of course, what did one do with a spouse during the summer months? You couldn't fold up a man and put him on the closet shelf with a mothball or two until fall. After giving the problem her due consideration, she decided thoughtfully that if things got too bad, one could try ceiling fans or twin beds. She wondered if many married couples traded beds with the seasons. She'd have to think about that some other time. There were more pressing problems at the moment—such as what to do about the top that had ridden up her back and the strange hand that had burrowed and trespassed onto forbidden territory.

It would have to be done without waking him up. She didn't want him to be aware of what had been allowed during her sleep. It was bad enough to live with his knowledge of her earlier wanton response. There was no point adding fuel to the fire. Gently, gently, she tried to ease his hand out so she could pull her top back down. But it was not to be. Annoyed in his sleep at losing his warm sanctuary, he grumbled, twisted and turned, then grabbed her with two hands before shaping her like a pillow underneath his head, cradling his tousled hair on her trembling breasts and jamming one hand back up her shirt, higher than before.

And she thought she was warm before. Darn! She was so hot now she felt his head as an almost suffocating weight clamping down on her lungs as they labored to bring in some air. Her breathing took the form of short gasps, and she watched as his head rose and fell against her.

Her imagination began to take flight, pulling her right along in its wake. She could see him slowly wakening, his inhibitions still suppressed in his half-slumberous state. She could literally *feel* the swelling in her breasts begin and grow at the thought of his hand, which now rested casually at the base of her breast, moving to take up a gentle, rhythmic cadence against the tender pink tip eagerly waiting for his warm, slightly roughened palm. She could see his languorous dark eyes studying her face before centering on her slightly parted lips. She imagined delicately licking her expectant, pouting lips with the tip of her tongue, inviting him to follow as it disappeared again from sight. His own mouth would slowly lower to claim hers, their heated breaths mixing and fusing into one. The feelings shooting through her were so intense, they could only be described, however incongruously, as *excruciatingly* pleasurable.

By now Andrea's entire leg was out from under the blanket in a fruitless attempt to control a bodily thermostat gone thoroughly haywire. This was awful. One kiss and she had turned shamelessly wanton. What was she to do? This was not the type of man she had foreseen for herself. Not at all. What woman could boast of falling for the original stick-in-the-mud? He viewed life with such narrow vision. How could she be happy with someone who had lost his joy of living and sense of humor while picking up his medical degree? The M.D. had cost him, but was she willing to pick up the tab? Heavens, she wanted to. She could possibly view it as a great work of mercy. Saving the world from another humorless doctor.

A sudden slight snore from the head resting on her chest brought Andrea back from her prurient flights of fancy. She listened to the dull sound of his slight grunt and watched his two fingers deal with the end of his twitching nose before he buried his face once more into her chest. Sometimes works of mercy had their own rewards.

Andrea pushed her other foot out from under the afghan, and giving in to a little whim, threaded slender fingers through the thick tangle of his cropped curls. In his sleep he would never notice the hand cradling him to her bosom.

She gave conscious attention to slowing her breathing rate, and it was a credit to her persevering willpower that she gradually drifted back into a deep slumber, not awakening again until her ever-faithful internal alarm went off at precisely five forty-five.

As she contemplated how to squirm her way out of the intimately enmeshed tangle of arms and legs, Greg's long lashes began to flicker. Andrea, who had never had the opportunity to watch a man awaken before, observed, fascinated as the lean body next to her gradually took on the more hardened muscle tones of alert awareness. "Hi." He grinned sleepily. "You make a great pillow. Soft and comfortable," he complimented. He was lying on his side next to her, having lifted his head from her breasts to watch her while he spoke.

"Thank you. The pleasure was all yours." She rubbed the sleep from her eyes and stretched, her arms high over her head. "You weigh—" She stopped in midsentence as Greg, who had successfully maintained his perch on the narrow couch all night, was knocked from its safe confines by her hyperextended elbows and fell with a yelp and accompanying dull thud to the floor below.

"Hey! If you wanted me to move, all you had to do was ask. I'm going to have to warn any boyfriends you bring around that you have all the earmarks of a potential husband-beater."

Andrea was too happy to point out the flaws in his reasoning. "First of all, I tried for a good twenty minutes last night to get you to move so that I could go to bed. You, sir, are dead to the world when you sleep and are an equally dead-weight to try to budge. Furthermore, if you think I'm stupid enough to bring any prospective mates home while I've got my own private loony tunes going on here, you have more than one screw loose up there." She tapped the top of his head to lend significance to her words. "What man would understand not only the general chaos around here, but a platonic rooming arrangement with a doctor type who my mother would refer to as having prospects?"

Greg thought about that while Andrea sat up, combing her tapered fingers through her hair. Somehow the thought of his being the cause of other prospective suitors taking a hike for a while didn't seem to upset him terribly.

"Yes," he said, "I can see that it might be hard to explain." He was speaking a little too brightly to convey any truly remorseful feelings on the matter, but he did make a generous offer. "However, I'd be more than willing to try to clarify it for you. Is there anyone special in your life to whom I should worry about defending your honor?" The question was put casually, but there was a certain underlying tension.

Andrea studied him disgustedly. Men could be so obvious at times. "No, there is no one special I would care to have you explain yourself to. But don't get your hopes up; this relationship stays platonic. Yesterday evening meant nothing. A pleasant little interlude." With all the lies she was spewing out this morning, it was fortunate there was no Uncle Geppetto in her life. She rose and turned toward the door. "Now, if you'll excuse me, I have to get ready for work."

Greg watched from his seat on the floor as she flounced from the room. He murmured into the slightly perfumed vacuum left behind, "'Pleasant interlude,' my foot. There is one hell of a responsive woman hiding behind that brave rhetoric, and I fully intend to uncover and claim her." Then he rose and absently brushed the lint from the back of his pants before heading for the kitchen with vague thoughts of preventing a repeat of yesterday morning's breakfast.

A dab of margarine was heating in the bottom of the skillet while Greg whipped several eggs with a fork. Andrea stepped from the bathroom, dressed for work. His eyes flared with a deeper, more brilliant mahogany, and his mouth dropped open in his surprise. He mutely studied her. Her shining blue-black hair was clipped in a loose knot at the back of her head with an oversize tortoiseshell barrette and she wore a jazzily striped white, charcoal and black form-fitting leotard with leg-hugging black tights that showed every curve of her gently muscled thighs and calves.

"Wow!" he muttered, respect evident in his tone. "I wondered what was hiding under all those loose sweats you've favored since I've been here. I had no idea it would be so...so..." He stopped, momentarily at a loss for an adequate descriptive term.

She looked disparagingly at him. "Considering where you and your hand spent last night it's a little hard to believe you don't know exactly what was under the sweats." She sounded piqued. "And don't expect me to believe I'm suddenly irresistible. I don't buy it."

"Obviously I missed out on something pretty spectacular while I slept. Can I have an instant replay?"

"Oh, for crying out loud, what a—"

"Besides," he went on bluntly, "you yourself intimated that your breasts were not your best feature." He glanced meaningfully at the flare of her hips and the well-defined curve of her calf. He poured the bowl of scrambled eggs into the pan, his gaze still firmly drawn to her shapely legs. Miraculously, none of the mixture missed. In a distracted manner, he threw pieces of sliced cheddar into the pan to melt with the eggs.

Andrea flipped open a pair of baggy gray sweats she'd had folded under her arm with a disbelieving defensive gesture. In an uncomfortable tone of voice, she muttered while stepping into the elastic-legged drawstring-waist pants, "Look fast, then, ye of little vision, because it's all going back under lock and key, even as we speak."

Chagrined, Greg turned back to the stove, watching while he stirred the eggs. So far, he had avoided slobbering over the stove top, but it had been more through blind luck than any skill on his part. "Where do you work, anyhow? I can't see anybody letting you show up in that outfit. Do you run and change when you get there? Is that why you leave so early in the morning?"

"Actually, I teach an early-morning aerobics class geared for working people from six-thirty until seven-thirty. It gives them time to exercise, shower, change and still get to work on time. I do shower and change myself, but only into clean sweats." Greg groaned at that and Andrea looked smug. "Then I head for Washburne Junior High where I teach physical education for the remainder of the day." She glanced at her wrist, to the slim gold watch with its utilitarian brown leather strap. "And I'm running late, what with all the unusually scintillating conversation this morning. I'll have a quick glass of juice and be off." She reached for one of the two glasses of orange juice he had set on the table.

"Absolutely not." Quickly he held the tumbler to the table with his own hand, countermanding her efforts. "You can't possibly do all that physical work without a decent breakfast. By the time you find your shoes and get them on, this will be ready." With a flick of his spatula he indicated the skillet of eggs already nicely thickening.

"Damn, I'm really running late, and I don't know where I left them. I spend half my life looking for my shoes. If it's not them, then it's my car keys. I don't suppose you know…"

"I believe I landed on them when you knocked me off the

couch this morning. You must have kicked them off before you fell asleep." He eyed her reflectively as she breathed a sigh of relief. "There's an old saying, something to the effect of 'a place for everything, and everything in its place' that might go a long way toward easing your frustrations."

"You must meet my mother sometime. She'd love you," Andrea muttered under her breath as she turned to retrieve the shoes from the living room.

"Sounds like a worthy woman of good taste and refinement," Greg returned blandly. "Too bad she's already spoken for."

Andrea gave him a meaningful glare over her shoulder, allowing it to speak for her.

Chapter Five

The ensuing week, however chaotically begun, went remarkably smoothly. The house's odd mixture of cramped occupants fell into a schedule of sorts, albeit not a totally smooth-running one. Andrea and Greg alternated nights between the bed in her room and the living-room couch. Somehow, even from the opposite end of the house, Greg was aware the second Andrea rose and would appear in the kitchen to breakfast with her, determined to add something edible to the morning fare. He would drink her health juice if she would at least sit with him if not join him in eating "normal" breakfast food. It was a quiet time in the house, a time of peace and tranquillity when they could get to know each other before the day's craziness had put them on edge. Andrea grew to look forward to it in an odd sort of way, even stooping to rummaging loudly through the cabinets the one morning he was late. And still she wouldn't admit that she was having an odd reaction to the absence of a person she professed not to like very much.

The boiler was replaced. Andrea paid for it with funds collected as tuition for the next semester's aerobics classes. Every time she walked into the kitchen, she thought about how that money could have bought new cabinets and hated the old ones even more.

Greg divided his days among apartment hunting with Karen, naps, and helping ready the upper apartment for its imminent occupancy. His naps grew shorter and further between. He accomplished a great deal on the second-floor flat, but he and Karen never did find an acceptable apartment. His jaundice faded noticeably, with each passing day and increasingly, Andrea found his presence more disturbing to her strangely off-balance mental state.

Andrea returned each evening around four-thirty after teaching school all day to shower and begin supper. Greg was oddly silent about some of the methods she used to achieve the end product—dinner on the table.

Monday night it was chicken tetrazzini. Greg gravely thanked her for using regular sliced mushrooms and not button as these were at least big enough to see easily and remove. She said she'd had him in mind when she'd bought them. Her thoughtfulness was reciprocated with a compliment on the high quality of the tetrazzini sauce the chicken resided in. She bit her lip and looked a little uncertainly in Karen's direction before responding that it was two cans of cream of chicken soup and a pint of sour cream and then bowed her head to examine an oddly shaped noddle on her plate.

She looked up again, surprised when nothing more than a noncommittal "Oh, well, it's very good" was forthcoming. Her look turned to shock when she saw the forkful of tetrazzini with a very large, very identifiable mushroom chunk halfway to his mouth. He noticed the look and in a slightly defensive tone informed her, "So maybe they'll grow on me."

Closing her mouth and willfully commanding her lips to smile, she only remarked, "I'm glad, I do tend to use them a lot when I cook."

God, they were being so polite to one another. She felt more strained and uncomfortable than she had when he was letting her have it. She suspected he had only eaten the damn mushroom to make up for having put her on the spot for the sauce recipe. What she couldn't figure out was why he felt it necessary to make amends at all. She had to keep reminding herself this was all a show for Karen, but it was tough going because the attraction felt more and more real.

They had taken to eating at the table in the living room as a way of unwinding after the pressures of the day. Tonight, the low glow of the burning fat-bodied candles not only was reflected by the blue-black depths of her hair, but also helped mask her unease as she fidgeted with the roughly woven cloth napkin on her lap. Desperately she cast around the recesses of her mind for a way to break the polite impasse and put things back on a normal footing; then she disparaged of her sanity for even wanting to.

After dinner, Karen and Tim disappeared suspiciously, leaving Greg and a decidedly awkward-feeling Andrea sitting on the sofa. She perched on its edge and felt sixteen again. Karen and Tim seemed determined to play the scheming parents out to find a match for their recalcitrant old-maid daughter. They had only forgotten their "We'll leave you young folks alone now, we know you don't want us old fogies around" exit line, and she rather suspected that had only been an oversight.

Greg lounged negligently back into the sofa cushions, looking totally comfortable and at ease. His legs were casually crossed, and his arms stretched back to encompass the long lines of the sofa back. He didn't seem to feel the slightest bit awkward over their being so obviously thrown together, she thought resentfully. In fact he seemed to be actually enjoying the situation. She stifled the urge to smack him.

Her suspicions were confirmed as she watched him taking in her poorly concealed squirming with the superior attitude one would expect of a physician who had identified some teeming colony on his microscope slide and knew the precise antidote to bring it under his control. His foot gently beat the air as he spoke. "What those two don't understand is that all of this obvious maneuvering is unnecessary. I may be slow on the pickup, but I'm not stupid. Living with you the past few days, I've come to realize that you're special. I'd be a fool to let you go simply to prove to Karen that she can't manage my life for me. I dropped empty acts of rebellion when I left my teens.''

Time for a hasty exit, Andrea realized. This was getting to be a little heavy. Even if he was the most handsome man to cross her path that she could recall, he needed a nursemaid, not a wife. That inexplicable something vibrating between them could just inflict itself on some other lovelorn twosome. Long ago she had learned the odds against marriage. Now her acquired distaste for the matrimonial state had her labeling him a hypochondriacal wimp. He wasn't, of course—not really. And she knew it, but she was grasping at straws. Disparaging him was a last-ditch protective effort to shore up the widening breach in her defenses.

Nervously, she rose to her feet. "Yes, well," she began, hating the slight tremor in her voice, "I've spent so much time on the upstairs apartment that I really must devote some time down here. I think I'll try to strip some of the paint off the dining-room French doors. If you'll excuse me…" Her voice trailed off weakly.

Greg groaned and grimaced. "I have spent hours upstairs today painting and hanging kitchen cabinets. I was hoping maybe we could drive down to the lakefront and watch the whale fights.''

Andrea was too late to prevent the escaping laugh. "I haven't heard that line since I was back in high school.''

"Actually, that's about the last time I used it. I've been rather too busy since then to keep up with the latest expressions used to put the move on a good-looking woman.''

"Sorry, but whether or not you've been through a long dry spell, I really do have to accomplish some work around here. I can't stand that bilious green in the dining room much longer.'' That was another problem with doctors. They led such directed, narrow lives. Imagine not even dating seriously for that length of time. Doctors spent so much energy immersed in their specializations that there was no room left for depth in any other aspects of their lives. They were shallow.

On the other hand, Andrea knew she was conveniently forgetting her own lack of depth in forming serious relationships, and she had also overlooked the total competence Greg had displayed in doing the handiwork around the house. He couldn't be *that* narrow and accomplish what he had.

Greg stood with a lithe movement that belied his physical condition. His arms were flung over his head in an unaffected stretching motion, and Andrea was utterly appalled by the sudden dryness in her mouth and the abrupt rise in her pulse rate.

His yawn stopped midstretch as he noticed her fascination. Either she had a very readable face, or else he had taken a rotation through psychiatry that gave him uncanny insight. "You can fight it as much as you want, Andrea. But there is something special between us," he said, "a definite magnetism flowing around us and working on us. We have to decide if it's going to be the undeniable attraction of North-South poles or the unfightable repulsion occurring between like poles. I choose going with the flow and not wasting energy trying to twist it into its opposite. It seems to me that would be an exhausting, and in the end, useless exercise in frustration." He crossed the room and slid an arm around her shoulders, gently walking her from the room. "Now, if you're quite sure you wouldn't care to reconsider my former suggestion, I guess after taking two naps today, I can manage to scrape up enough energy to spackle the cracks in the wall while you strip the woodwork."

Andrea latched on to his last offer as a line to safer topics and feelings. Greg gave her a knowing glance when she ignored the entire first part of his lecture and commented "You know before you can spackle, you'll have to first score the crack into an inverted V so that it's wider in the back than on the surface. That way the spackle won't pop..."

"I know how to plaster, Andrea," Greg interrupted imperturbably. "I grew up in an old farmhouse and my parents were absolute sticklers on renovating the proper way." He patted her shoulder. "You just change your clothes and take care of the stripping. Now there's a job I hate. I'll handle the walls, and I promise you won't regret a thing come the light of day."

Andrea rubbed the tip of her nose and squinted at him. "Sorry. It's the teacher in me. I don't mean to be insulting."

"Don't worry about it," Greg advised. Then he sighed as he picked up a plastering spatula and tested its weight, muttering contemplatively, "I wonder if this is what Karen and Tim had in mind when they deserted us to a romantic evening together."

Andrea laughed. "It seems Karen doesn't know me all that well yet. If she had bothered to consult Tim, I'm sure he would have suspected as much. I guess I'm not the candle-and-moonlight type."

"Romance is an acquired taste. We'll take it slow. Start with a kiss or two in the plaster dust and work our way right up to hugging behind the paint-can stack. You'll love it. Especially with the terrific teacher you've got. I've made the study of women my lifework."

"In and out of school?"

"Hey, I was a devotee of the gentler sex long before I was a devotee of medicine. I broke my buns becoming captain of the high-school football team so I could impress this one little cheerleader."

Andrea paused, intrigued. "Did it work?"

He grimaced. "Yeah, but she turned out to have nothing going for her but a mean cartwheel and the best split I've ever seen. That's when I learned to check a little deeper than the surface for beauty." He looked directly at her.

Andrea sat on the ladder steps, deciding to ignore his last remark and find out what she could. "Where'd you go to high school? Karen's mom is living in Winnetka, a few miles away. That's definitely not farming country."

Greg was surprised. "You thought I grew up someplace like Winnetka? Heck, no. Too rich for our blood. Loretta married money. We didn't have it as kids. We grew up in Pennsylvania, out in the country. Dad had a nice little farm. We were

comfortable, never lacked for anything important, but by no
stretch of the imagination were we rich.''

"So you went to high school there?"

"Yep, followed by Penn State and Johns Hopkins."

"Were you happy?" Andrea was genuinely interested now.

"Oh, yes. You won't believe it, but I never drew a serious
breath until my senior year of high school. I had a ball. I got
good grades mainly because the teachers all liked me, not because of any real effort on my part. And the girls fell all over
themselves to get to the football players. Yes, I had a good
time. Mom and Dad doted on me. I was an only child, for all
practical purposes. Loretta was so much older she was gone
by the time I was six. When my folks died in my senior year
I had to do a lot of growing very fast. I had only myself to
rely on for my future, and I knuckled down."

She hadn't meant to bring up sad memories. She stood and
winked. "Yeah? And what about all those collegiate women
and young nurses at Hopkins?"

"Well…" He made a deprecatory gesture.

Chuckling, she left to put on her grubbies.

The next day, Tuesday, found Greg wandering downstairs
after a frustrating few hours spent trying to help Tim connect
the upstairs kitchen appliances. They had worked in tight,
cramped quarters the whole while and neither was in a very
jolly mood. Tim entered the kitchen first and tried to head off
an explosion by blocking Greg's view, but it was useless. Greg
saw the way Andrea was making scalloped potatoes to go with
dinner's main course of honey-glazed ham. She was using
canned cheddar-cheese soup. Andrea tensed when Greg took
the can in his hand and studied it. She had intended to have
the casserole in the oven and the soup can buried deep in the
garbage when they came down, but hadn't quite made it.

Greg was thunder in a cloud thick with electrical charges
that was rapidly losing control over its occupant bolts. Sooner
or later, the tensions in the house were bound to get to him
and he would let fly, zapping Andrea with his sarcasm about

her dependency on the bounty of canned-soup companies as he had the first two days. Her nerves frayed further as she realized this wasn't the time. He walked by with a noncommittal "Hmm, looks good" as he finished inspecting the proceedings on his way to the bath for a quick shower. "I'm starved."

Andrea dropped the handful of potatoes she had been carefully layering and simply stared after him. No suggestions to look into the savings of buying soup by the case? No queries as to the presence of mushrooms in the sauce? She decided he was just gathering his strength to lower the final boom with as much effect as possible. He was waiting for her to be off her guard. Well, he wouldn't get away with it. She wouldn't be frightened off, and she wouldn't change her cooking style either. There wasn't time after working all day to grate all that cheese and make the dumb stuff from scratch if they wanted to eat at a decent hour. And it tasted the same anyway. She simply would not apologize for her cooking. It was good. Unorthodox perhaps, but good.

At the end of the evening, Andrea was alarmed to discover that when not eye to eye over a can of soup or a mushroom, it was very easy to fall into an effortless camaraderie with Greg. Typically, people involved in distasteful remodeling work found their nerves on edge and their tongues quick to go for the jugular of anyone within sarcasm distance. They had spent the evening with the nauseating odors of sealant and paint remover, forcing them to open windows, which alleviated the smell but left them to freeze while working. Things should have been strained. She should have been consistently biting her tongue to hold back the verbal abuse she normally threw around under such conditions, but she hadn't. Instead, Greg had tuned the radio in on an oldies program. The evening had been spent singing along with the Four Tops and the Four Seasons, occasionally demonstrating a nostalgic dance step from high-school sock hops past.

He really was fun to be with, Andrea realized ruefully as they munched their way through a bowl of hot popcorn but-

tered with real butter and celebrated a final adieu to the awful
green dining-room wall.

She thought she had cleverly evaded his good-night kiss and
whatever other moves he had intended to bring into play. But
she must have been less subtle than she thought because Greg
had laughed and said, "Run if you want to, Andrea. You can't
get far in this little house. Time is on my side. Along with
both of the house's other occupants, I might add. You haven't
got a chance, but the chase will make it more interesting." He
kissed her on the tip of the nose despite her evasive tactics.
"Go to bed," he instructed. "I'll see you in the morning."

Andrea closed the door on his grin and brushed her teeth
with a vengeance born of desperation. It simply wasn't fair.
Here she was, odd man out in her own home. There had been
an uprising and the tenants had taken over the landlord's premises. How had she missed the coup?

She was running scared.

Wednesday evening found everyone grossly overtired. The
men had spent the day lugging furniture up to the efficiency
apartment, retrieving Karen and Tim's boxes of stored household items from the basement and trying to set up a semblance
of a living arrangement. That project would take days to complete, but enough was accomplished to warrant a christening
celebration and the inception of a genuine residency in the
upper apartment.

Andrea was tired as well. She had run her morning aerobics
class. Then the junior high's teachers had complained about
the students' general rambunctiousness, no doubt due to the
cold snap currently sitting over Chicago and the students sudden indoor confinement. She had really put them through their
paces in an effort to bring their energy levels down to a manageable level. The crowning blow had come with a phone call
from the Chandler Leisure Center, whose late-afternoon class
was instructorless due to a flu bug. That last unexpected aerobics class had been sheer torture.

At least Karen had thought to make a salad and start a

gelatin mold to set. But Andrea didn't even think twice about opening a can of not just any soup, but cream of mushroom soup, to throw together an easy tuna casserole. She was too exhausted to even contemplate anything more complicated.

Karen bounced into the kitchen, as much as was humanly possible for a pregnant woman to bounce, and announced, "We need to celebrate the inauguration of the upstairs apartment. I'm going to bake a cake. What kind of exotic recipes have you got floating around?"

Andrea was not so tired that she didn't realize the implication of her next move. If the thunderbolts finally zapped, so be it. She reached into the cabinets to withdraw a can of tomato soup. After handing it to a bemused Karen, she took a great deal of perverse pleasure in looking up her recipe for tomato-soup cake.

Karen almost gagged. "Are you sure about this?" she asked with one hand over her mouth and eyes wide.

"It tastes just like a spice cake, which I don't have the ingredients for. Use the tube pan, and I'll make some penuche frosting. It's really good. I love it. So will you."

"Well...if you're really sure..."

"Trust me. You'll like it." If nothing else could serve to force Greg to show his true colors again, this would. Andrea suspected he would prefer an agonizing death, asphyxiated from sealant vapors, than to eating tomato-soup cake.

But she was wrong. They sat on the floor, surrounding a pile of chunky rainbow-hued burning candles. Karen leaned back, groaning as she patted her burgeoning stomach. "I really must find out from the doctor what kind of exercises I can do while I'm pregnant. Now that I'm feeling well again, I can literally feel my muscles turning into limp spaghetti. If I don't start moving now, I'll never get back into shape when this is all over."

Plainly horrified, Andrea looked up from gathering a fingerful of frosting from where it had dripped onto the cakeplate. "Over my dead body. I've said it before, that kid is only half-baked. You'll put yourself into premature labor and lose it for sure.''

Greg seemed about to speak, but Karen cut him off. ''All I know is that if I've reached the point in this pregnancy where cake made from tomato soup tastes good, then pickles and ice cream at midnight must be next. I'll be a two-ton Tess long before the baby comes if I lie around the way you two seem to require.'' She cast an accusatory glance encompassing both Andrea and Tim.

Greg glanced down at the fluted white paper plate in front of him, empty except for a few crumbs. He seemed to be caught in some internal struggle, but whatever it was passed quickly. Calm again, he reached for the serrated knife they had been using on the cake and sliced himself his third decent-size serving. He looked meaningfully into Andrea's flashing blue eyes while taking a large bite.

He was only eating it to annoy her, she knew. She was irritated that his calm acceptance of her planned dig made her feel small and childish for instigating the plan. ''You're not fooling me for one second, Mr. Hotshot Doctor. Your repressed taste buds are shrieking their revulsion and committing suicide by the dozen while you sit there pretending to be calm. I can hear their cries of agony all the way over here. You're trying to break me, and you won't get away with it, do you hear me? I will not fall in love with a food fussbudget. I will not allow it. I won't!''

Two pairs of eyes swung to catch Greg's reaction to this unwarranted outburst. Tim looked especially interested. He had grown up next door to Andrea. In all those years, she had never displayed the temperamental side of her nature to anywhere near the extent she had shown it since Greg's arrival five days ago.

''Is that what you're doing, Andrea?'' Greg asked in polite, interested tones. ''Falling in love?''

''No!'' she denied, now almost yelling in her horror at her own condemning words. ''I could never fall in love with someone who falls apart over the ingredients in a lousy cake!''

Greg watched Andrea's face redden with the heat of her words. According to Karen, Andrea was always calm, nothing seemed to faze her. She'd even faced Karen and Tim's problems with an optimistic logic, not even acknowledging that everyone else had given up, merely wringing their hands and gnashing their teeth. Now here she was, downright irrational. How long would it be before she realized that it had not been Greg falling apart over the cake's ingredients, but rather Andrea herself?

"We'll come back to this interesting topic another time," he promised, his eyes gleaming. "When we're alone. Right now I think it would be more productive to get back to Karen's concern over exercising." He turned his attention to his niece, infuriating Andrea further with his easy dismissal of her display of temper. She was itching for a fight and it had been denied her, producing a feeling quite foreign to her normal good nature.

"Now there are many exercises that are perfectly all right for a pregnant woman. In fact, if you look around, I'm sure you'll be able to find a prenatal exercise class. That way, you won't have to worry about every little thing you try. Those classes are carefully designed to eliminate any potentially harmful movements. I believe I said it before: if you're physically fit, chances are good you'll have an easier delivery and quicker recovery. I always recommend some type of physical activity to my patients, even if it's only a brisk walk."

One of the candles hissed as it drowned in a puddle of its own wax, and Tim looked doubtful. "Are you sure about this, Greg? She was so sick..."

"Naturally I don't know all the details, and she should check with her own doctor before she does anything. But if it was simple morning sickness, no bleeding or anything, there's no medical reason why she shouldn't do gentle exercises. I'm not suggesting she go in for Olympic training."

Andrea was trying to settle down, having realized at last that she was the only one out of control. It was all to no avail as Greg once more turned to include her in the conversation.

"Now there's a class you might consider offering, Andrea. I could help you in deciding a program of appropriate exercises, and you'd make a lot of expectant mothers happy." He waited patiently for her reaction.

Andrea looked at him as though he had just sprouted a second head. "Are you out of your mind? Pregnant women make me crazy. I want to encase them in Saran wrap and put them on a shelf for nine months, not worry myself sick lest I cause one of them to miscarry."

"You must get over this archaic notion that pregnant women can crack and break like an egg. In many ways a woman's body is functioning at its peak during a pregnancy. What are you going to do when you find yourself having a baby? Go to bed and set a timer for nine months? You may as well get over your fear now, because sooner or later it's going to happen to you, and you won't be able to put your head under a pillow and hide for the duration." Greg's impatient gaze pinned her.

"There is no reason for me to get over my fears, either now or later. I doubt if I'll ever have children."

Greg's gaze sharpened even further. "What do you mean? Is there something I don't know about? Are you unable to have children for some reason?"

The hardness of his tone surprised the other three, and made the question an important one.

"Physically I wouldn't know, as I've never been in the position to find out. But I do know that emotionally I couldn't handle it. I'll never have children."

Tim sat back, sighing and shaking his head.

"I don't understand," Greg probed disbelievingly. "You love children. What the hell—you even have a Brownie troop. Nobody but a bona fide kid-lover would take that on if they didn't have to. Look at the time you spent working on that Pinewood Derby car for the kid next door. Don't try to tell me you don't like children."

"Of course I like children," Andrea interrupted impatiently. "I never said I didn't."

"Then what exactly did you say? What is the problem?"

Andrea's voice rose. "There is no problem! Any problem was taken care of when I decided not to have children! Now if I were to get pregnant, then there'd be a problem!"

Greg leaned forward to emphasize his next statement. One hand supported his tilting posture while the other pointed at his chest. "Andrea, *I* want to have children."

Now Andrea leaned forward. They were virtually nose to nose. "Bully for you. I am not stopping you."

"Evidently, you are." Karen and Tim might as well have been invisible for all the attention they received. Andrea resented the patient forbearance in his tone as Greg explained what he saw as the simple facts of life to her. It smacked of condescendence. "Perhaps I have not made myself adequately clear the past few days. *You* are the one I plan to have carry my children—a fact that will require one or more nine-month pregnancies on your part. Therefore, unless you want to spend a large portion of the next few years in bed, which would be unhealthy for you and my unborn children and which I would never allow anyway, you had better address yourself to overcoming these fears, nameless as they seem to be."

Karen's peripheral debate with Tim over whether the calories in a second piece of cake would be worth it or not had stopped. Now her head whipped back and forth between the two conversants with the speed and agility of a Ping-Pong ball in a championship tournament. Her amazed look said as clearly as any words that when she had set the ball in motion a few days back, she had never anticipated this fast a response.

"There is no way in hell," Andrea began forcefully, less than an inch from Greg's nose, "that I will ever carry your baby or babies. So you can just pack your...whatever back in your old kit bag and find somebody else to dump this on. I'm not interested. Not now, not ever."

"Give me one good reason why not." Greg knew Andrea was not indifferent to him. He knew half of her ill humor was a camouflage, an effort to deny the attraction between them. He saw through it. He had assumed she was equally aware of the reason behind her feistiness. Maybe she hadn't reached that point of awareness yet.

"I have no intention of discussing this any further. We are supposed to be celebrating the completion of Karen and Tim's apartment. I hardly call arguing with you much of a celebration. As a matter of fact, I would consider it rather dampening."

"Fine. We'll discuss it tomorrow."

"No, we will not. It is none of your business. Furthermore, tomorrow is a free day, and I intend to spend it in Lombard at Kohler's Trading Post checking out the secondhand furniture."

"I'll go with you."

"I don't think so. This is one of my favorite leisure-time activities. I don't want it ruined with a lot of badgering."

"Okay, I promise I won't badger you," Greg gruffly pledged. "Just let me come, and I'll behave."

Andrea shot him a disbelieving glance. "Your fingers are probably crossed behind your back," she accused.

"Scout's honor," Greg swore solemnly, displaying three fingers raised in imitation of the Scout pledge sign.

"Oh, all right, but if you start in on me, I'll leave you stranded in Lombard, and that's a promise, not an idle threat." She turned to glare at Karen and complained, "This is all your fault!"

Karen gasped at the unfair recrimination. Her hand went to her chest in a dramatic gesture. "My fault? I had nothing to do with this, other than wanting you to meet my only living relative outside of my parents," she said in wounded tones. "It was a great honor I paid you. Shows how highly I think of you."

"Oh, spare me. Why couldn't you have introduced me to some senile doting aunt or a harmless old uncle with a beer belly?"

"Probably because I don't have either one. It's him or nothing, I'm afraid," Karen pointed out reasonably.

"Aachhh, I give up." She glared at Tim, and it was his

turn to come under fire. "Why'd you have to marry somebody with such weird relatives? Couldn't you have been a little more selective?"

Tim was clearly wounded. "Hey! Don't blame me. Haven't you ever heard that love is blind? It's not my fault I fell for her, hook, line and sinker. I was bedazzled by her seductive charms and roped up to the altar before I even knew what I was doing." He pulled his wife over and began planting wet kisses in all the ticklish spots up and down the side of her neck. "She was so romantic and wily," he protested while Karen giggled helplessly. "Such a woman of the world, I couldn't help myself."

Andrea threw up her hands in disgust and rose to gather up the paper plates. "That does it, now they're getting mushy on me. I'm leaving before I gag. Dr. Greg here can take notes. It's been a long time between women. He told me so himself. Probably needs a refresher course."

"Perhaps you'd like to give me the opportunity to demonstrate my abilities of total recall." Greg had his own temper back under control and was grinning up at her.

"No, thanks," Andrea said. "I've had about all I can handle for one evening. I'm going to see if Lisa can't be more gracious company." She started toward the stairs, suddenly needing to talk to her best friend and Tim's twin.

"Say hi for me," Tim instructed.

"Will do," Andrea absently agreed, intent on not tripping down the stairs.

Tim's attention turned to his wife's only living relative other than her parents. "You don't seem too upset by all this."

"It'll just take longer, that's all." Greg sighed as he stretched his arms high over his head. "She's a tougher nut to crack than I first thought. But she'll crack, never you fear. In the meantime, it would be nice to know a little more about what I'm up against. I couldn't figure out why a woman like her wasn't snatched up long ago, but I'm beginning to see. I'll bet the men around here aren't as blind as I thought, but have simply been shut out by Andrea."

"Possibly so," Tim agreed thoughtfully. "She certainly hasn't dated much since we've been here."

Karen nodded her head in agreement. "Lots of male friends, but strictly friends, if you know what I mean."

"Do you know what it's all about?" Greg questioned Tim directly, since he'd known Andrea the longest.

"I might have some ideas," Tim admitted reluctantly. "But I think the answers should come from Andrea. It's not my place to spill her secrets."

Chapter Six

Andrea paced the short length of Lisa's apartment living room, made an almost military about-face at the far wall and returned to stand in front of the chair where her friend sat. Every word Andrea spoke was punctuated with wide hand gestures and dramatic body language that showed a blatant disregard for the room's furnishings. The subdued light escaping from the pink tiffany lamp shade lent an even ruddier hue to Andrea's flushed complexion as she flung rash comments and rhetorical questions, one terse word after another across the room. "I tell you, Lisa, I'm being driven out of my own home. A stranger in my own land."

"Come now, surely you're overreacting. How can he have such a strong effect on you if you truly feel nothing?" Lisa imperturbably flicked a wide-tooth comb through her wheat-colored bob. "If he really left you cold, you'd be able to ignore him, just like every other man you've bumped into since hitting puberty."

"It's not that easy," Andrea assured her. "This time, the man's a permanent fixture on the premises. Believe me, it's a

lot harder to ignore. Besides, this one would get under anybody's skin.''

The tilt of Lisa's head combined with the expression on her
peach-tinted lips clearly spelled her disbelief.

The look acted as a pinprick to Andrea's self-righteous balloon, and it suddenly deflated, leaving her to fold dejectedly
into a casually upholstered tan corduroy armchair, staring at
her naked fingernails, each one propped against its opposite in
a thoughtful pose. "I ought to buy myself some fingernail
polish," she interposed morosely. "It's time I started taking
care of myself. Mother's right. The clean, well-scrubbed look
is all right for little girls with pigtails, but a woman should
cultivate her looks a little. Even Greg insinuated I could use
a little cosmetic aid."

"Do you hear what you're saying?" Lisa demanded. "Now
I know this is serious. Tell me everything, but this time in
some kind of coherent order."

Under Lisa's direction, Andrea began. "It's been awful.
Since the moment I opened the front door to him a few days
ago, I haven't been myself. Jumping all over everybody at the
least provocation. Perfectly awful," she repeated for lack of a
better adjective.

Lisa moved impatiently and Andrea tried again. "From the
time he first rang the doorbell, we've been at each other's
throats. And it's not that he's a dog and I'm being a snob or
anything. If anything, he's every red-blooded woman's Amer-
ican dream, at least on the surface," she admitted.

"So what's the problem then?"

"He's a jerk." Andrea stated it empirically, albeit with a
regretful sigh. "Not only that, he's a wimp as well."

Lisa sounded as though she were strangling and Andrea
looked concerned until she realized her friend was really struggling against laughter. "A jerk and a wimp, huh? Quite a
damning combination. You won't mind if I ask you to elaborate a tad, will you?"

Andrea had no objections. She had come to talk it out,
hadn't she? "In the first place," she began with dark enthu-

siasm, "he hates mushrooms and I might as well employ Chinese water torture as serve him anything with canned soup as an ingredient. The maturity of his attitude lags a *minimum* of twenty-five years behind the rest of his body." Here she blushed as she thought of the rest of his body and paused in her narrative to see what effect her dire accusations were having. Lisa didn't seem overly affected one way or the other, so she plowed on, determined to recruit at least one person to her own camp.

"He has no stamina or physical reserves whatsoever. Eight weeks ago he caught hepatitis. Eight weeks! And he's still taking naps and can't seem to get his strength back. Karen thinks we ought to get married so he has someone to bond with and that will make him recover faster. Can you believe it? Who am I, Florence Nightingale? Haven't I got enough aches and pains of my own without marrying into a whole fresh supply?" The questions were increasingly rhetorical, as Andrea gave Lisa no time to respond.

"His life has been so closely directed for so long, he's lost sight of anything other than doctoring. And not only is he a doctor, but he's an obstetrician! We'd never have any alone time, although he swears he's going to concentrate on broadening his horizons now. How can he? He'll always be getting called into the hospital. And worst of all—" this last came with a certain touch of relish "—he's fiscally irresponsible, just like my dad." She sat back in the chair, well pleased with her presentation and its irrefutable logic.

"My, you certainly have covered all bases, haven't you?" Lisa responded with a gentle smile. She set the comb down and began to use both hands to tick off Andrea's complaints. "Let's see if I have this right. His taste in food is a little conservative, he's slowly recovering from a debilitating illness, and he's intelligent and hardworking enough that you feel secure he'll be successful in his chosen field. The only thing I'm not clear on is the fiscal irresponsibility part." She raised an expectant eyebrow, evidently waiting for Andrea to elaborate.

Andrea wore a slightly disconcerted expression. She could have coped with the first three, she told herself grimly. But the money, now that was enough all by itself. She raised her head to tell Lisa so. She had her on that one. "Karen says he went through medical school on loans. That means he has to be thousands of dollars in debt. You know how I feel about getting involved with anyone like that."

"If this is the best you can come up with, love, you really are grasping at straws."

Andrea gasped her indignation. "What do you mean?"

"What I'm saying," she said with a kind smile, the type used in explaining the facts of life to an idiot, "is that you and I both know that a lot of people don't like mushrooms. A lot of people put in long hours to establish their careers. Hepatitis is not in the same ballpark as hypochondria, and medical school is wildly expensive. Almost all doctors have to take out loans, *but they pay them back.* They're no more or less irresponsible than the rest of us poor slobs. Now," she continued in false solicitude, "why don't we try to get to the real heart of the matter? I find it odd that you've never bothered to manufacture excuses for avoiding a male before. I think you've never been interested enough to worry about the consequences."

Andrea thanked Lisa for lending an ear to her problems and returned home thoughtfully subdued. With the new boiler heating efficiently and Karen and Tim's back bedroom nicely vacated, there was no reason for Greg to sleep on the sofa. She missed seeing his dark head starkly juxtaposed against the cream sheets of the fold-out couch. The room seemed to lack life. In a reflective gesture, she rubbed her hand the length of a nubby pillow. Her hand clenched involuntarily, its fingernails digging into her palm. Resolutely, she forced it open, even as she forced her mind to accept the truth of much of what Lisa had said.

The roadblocks she had thrown up against Greg were petty, inconsequential half-truths. The crux of the problem lay within herself. His easy laugh and bantering manner as he worked on the dining room with her spoke of a sense of humor that would surely bloom with proper encouragement. His loans were probably within reason. Medical schools were expensive; not many could afford the tuition without floating a loan. In her heart she knew he was not the type to get in over his head. She was sure he had every expectation of paying them back. Yet, would she be able to overcome her fears regarding loans and money in general? She had watched her mother age years too early under the weight of her father's charm and wit. He too had been a doctor. And doctors were always good for a loan from the bank. But when this doctor didn't find doctoring "fulfilling" enough and went off to a low-paying research job after taking on school loans, mortgage payments and clinic equipment debts, then the banks weren't so thrilled. They got downright testy.

She had both loved and hated her father. And her childhood had scarred her. She was only just beginning to realize how deeply the scars ran. She had vowed to be self-sufficient, never relying on anyone else—the way her mother had her father, the way Tim had Karen. Where did it get you? Living on somebody else's charity. Could she relinquish that hard-won control to a second party at this point? The intellectual knowledge that Greg wasn't like her father, that he could balance desires and reality was still only an intellectual realization. It had yet to be internalized.

But Andrea continued to argue with herself. Even if she did internalize all her wonderful insights concerning the homeless M.D., wasn't it just a little *too* coincidental that he was trying to move in on the first female he saw right after emerging from medical school? How very convenient that just when he was ready to get on with his life Andrea suddenly seemed to embody his wifely wish list of attributes. Then again, it was also possible he was simply feeling sorry for her. He had to know by now that her backbone consisted of ninety-nine percent mush. Possibly he had twisted gratitude and sympathy into what he thought was love. Some morning he'd wake up and realize what he'd done, and bingo, he'd be gone. Think

of all the good-looking women an all-female clientele doctor
would see. If—and this was what Andrea really suspected—
Greg was simply ready to settle down and anybody would do,
he would be better advised to wait a bit. Someone better would
surely come along. Meeting some strange schedule Greg had
set up for his life was not a very good basis for marriage. And
Andrea was determined to point that out to him at the earliest
opportunity.

Schedule be darned! She wanted somebody who wanted
her—not the fulfillment of some nebulous daydream of what
married life between a high-school quarterback and an infat-
uated cheerleader would be. Andrea couldn't do a split to save
her soul. She hadn't even made the first round of cuts at cheer-
leading tryouts. Maybe she should point out to him that
unquestioning pom-pom waving was not her style.

Then there was Peggy. If he knew about Peggy, understood
what had happened eleven years ago, he might stop pushing
so hard and give her a little breathing space…time. What she
ought to do was explain her point of view and maybe give
him a chance to convince her of his sincerity.

Giving her head a decisive nod, she left the room to get
ready for bed. Yes. Tomorrow. She'd stop hiding behind manufactured excuses. Mushrooms shouldn't be allowed to stand
in the way of a chance at true love. They were only a fungus,
after all. Nothing might come of it, but at least she wouldn't
look back later, wistfully caught in what-could-have-beens.
Her shoulders straightened resolutely. Armed with her toothbrush, she closeted herself in the bathroom.

Thursday dawned clear and bright. Unusual for Chicago's
grayest month of the year. Andrea watched the faint early-
morning light struggle through the kitchen windows. There
was something about clean windows, she mused. They max-
imized the light. Later in the day, when the sunlight came
streaming in, the antiquated kitchen might appear almost
quaint. But since the change from daylight saving time to standard three weeks ago, there hadn't been a whole lot of light

at six in the morning, and one needed a certain amount of…imagination when viewing the unremodeled kitchen.

She looked up as Greg entered the room, humming a popular tune.

"Why are you dressed in sweats? Are you going running?" she asked.

"Nope," he replied laconically.

Andrea raised an eyebrow in silent question and Greg relented as he turned to light the flame under the teakettle.

"You agreed last night that I could spend the day with you. So I'm going to your exercise class with you."

"Uh, Greg, I don't really think that's a very good idea. Why don't you wait here until I'm done? Go for a quick mile run or something. We'll spend the rest of the day together. I promise."

Greg was evidently feeling stubborn this morning. His single "Nope" spoke volumes. "I won't be that out of place. Surely there must be a few men in your class. Even if they just come to ogle the instructor, I'll bet there are some."

"Three. But that's not the point. What I'm trying to say is that most of these people have been coming for months. I do sixty minutes of intensive stretching and aerobics. They all keep pace pretty well, and I've stopped taking it easy on them."

"I won't hold the class up, Andrea," Greg promised, dismissing her worries from over the top of his teacup and leaning back against the countertop.

"It's just that you shouldn't jump right into this. You've got to work your way back gradually. You've been sick, for crying out loud!"

Greg methodically refilled his teacup, paying strict attention to the task before raising his eyes to hers and responding, "I won't overdo. I'll stay in the back and stop if it gets to be too much. I can always sleep in the car on the way out to Lombard. It's a good hour's trip, isn't it?"

"You'll have a relapse! Why can't you be reasonable about this?" Andrea was beginning to sound distraught.

Greg gave a low roar, "For God's sake, Andrea. I'm a doctor. Stop the overprotective-mother routine and credit me with some intelligence. I know what I can and cannot do! Maybe you ought to stop and question why you're so concerned over me. It just might be a highly productive line of inquiry."

Andrea recoiled a step. Greg was right. She was overprotective and did worry too much. She'd make a lousy mother. She'd always be trying to smooth the kids' path, smothering them with her concern. If Greg wanted to have every muscle ache for the next few days, that was his problem. He was, after all, all grown-up. And he had asked a viable question. She turned the puzzle in her mind for an instant and gave up.

"Fine." She shrugged before gathering her reserves around her like a cloak. She looked at him carefully, noticing the jaundice had all but disappeared, leaving his mahogany orbs clear and bright. "Just tell me one thing: Are you doing this to prove a point?"

"No. I want to see what you do. I figure it'll give me one more key to the elusive Miss Andrea Conrades."

"Because if you are," she persisted, "it's a waste of time. I know you're not a wimp, and I'm sorry I called you one. You've done remarkably well, considering how sick you were. I only said those things about you because I was panicking. I'm attracted to you. You make me feel things I've never felt before. I'm not sure I want to feel them, either." Her eyes searched the room, unable to look directly at him while she made this admission. "Letting myself feel these things instead of fighting them…well, it's not as simple as it sounds. It means facing a lot of emotional issues I'm not sure I'm ready to face." Finally she looked directly at him. "But I'm going to try, Greg. I really am."

"That's all I'm asking. For both of us to make the effort. If it doesn't work out, it won't be from lack of trying." He kissed the top of her shiny hair in a light gesture and wrapped the lean length of a masculine arm around her waist. "Now, we'd better get moving. Those early-morning exercise fanatics await." And he guided her toward the front door.

By nine o'clock they had both showered, eaten a more filling breakfast than just the tea they had managed earlier and were back on the road. Andrea was driving because the exercise class had indeed been hard on Greg. He drifted into sleep, one hand cushioning the side of his head from the cold window. Taking in the long muscular body folded into the cramped seat next to hers, Andrea sent up a short prayer on a wry chuckle.

May he not regain his strength too quickly, she implored the heavens. Operating with only half his normal steam up, he was proving difficult enough to handle. She could only imagine the hardships involved in keeping up with the man beside her when it was full steam ahead.

She parked on the opposite side of Saint Charles Road from Kohler's Trading Post and gently shook Greg's shoulder. "Greg? We're here. Wake up."

It was amazing how easily he made the transition from sound sleep to alert wakefulness. That ability must be a medical-school entrance prerequisite. Without that particular skill, students would never make it through the long grind of internship and residency, she guessed. At any rate, he sat up immediately, passed a quick hand over his eyes and looked around expectantly. With no doubt as to where he was, he opened his door and circled to Andrea's side, courteously escorting her from the car.

Crossing the blacktopped street, they passed through the unlocked gates of the trading post. Greg stopped so suddenly that Andrea knocked up against him, a fact she didn't seem to mind in the least. She had made her decision to try to make things work and was now at peace with herself. After she steadied herself, her laughter rang out. She glanced up and caught the incredulous expression on Greg's face as he viewed the place.

She turned to look with him, trying to recapture the overwhelming sense of awe the trading post had inspired the first time she'd stepped through its gates. "It's really something, isn't it?" she questioned, absently flicking the rope of long hair the light wind had tossed in her face back over her shoulder.

Greg squinted in the bright morning light as he studied the seemingly endless rows of rusting refrigerators, old wringer washers, broken chairs, and shopping carts full of nameless gizmos. Surveying the chaotic scene with its casually parked trailers filled with church pews and school desks and the two low-lying buildings, he agreed. "I had no idea you were such a master in the art of understatement." He took one more look around before looking at her for the first time since entering the odd setting. "I'm surprised this is allowed within the city limits." Andrea laughed as he inquired further, "Have you ever actually bought anything here?"

"Well, I can see you're settling on the right side of town. You're a true North Shore snob already."

He pushed the hair back from her face for her, tunneling his hands under its heavy fall. "No, I'm serious. Have you ever bought anything here?"

"Absolutely," she assured him while rummaging in the depths of her shoulder bag. She placed the cloth-covered rubber band retrieved from its confines between her lips while she pulled her hair back with both hands. Speaking in muffled tones, she poked the air with an available elbow to indicate the surrounding area. "This is mostly for people looking for parts and pieces of things they need to repair something they already have. I did buy some of those for the house, though." She indicated a sorry-looking pile of storm windows and doors farther back on the lot. "Fit perfectly, too." She guided him toward the door of the first building after successfully wrapping the rubber band around her hair at the base of her neck in an off-kilter but effective George Washington ponytail. "But I must admit, most of the nice things I'm interested in are inside."

"I'll just bet," Greg muttered in a disbelieving tone.

"You don't really expect them to dump the good stuff out

here to the mercy of the elements, do you? And let me remind you, you invited yourself along on this particular sojourn, so lighten up. I enjoy this place, so at least pretend to be having a good time, okay? Watch you—''

"Damn it anyway! You let your warning go a little late. Why the hell are those things hanging there?'' Greg glared up at the tangled collections of ice skates hanging from the low rafters by the strength of their laces. The entire assemblage swayed from the force of his collision. "I damn near lost my head at the neckline!''

Andrea sighed. What had she been thinking of? This would never work. So what if he was the most devastatingly handsome man she had ever bumped into? So what if his look, not to mention his one kiss, sent her pulse racing and put her heart under as much strain as a ten-mile run? He'd had his head in his books too long. He was unsalvageable. Once the sexual highs had faded, she'd be stuck with a handsome, high IQ'd, boring stick-in-the-mud. Her foot tapped impatiently as she took in his irritated mien. No flair for fun. No spirit of adventure. She would curl up and die married to a man with no sense of humor. He may as well be a hundred years old.

Greg sensed Andrea's perturbation and pasted a sickly smile on his face, but he quickly gave up the struggle. "Give me a minute, honey," he pleaded. "My head hurts like hell. I'm sure it's an interesting place. Just…give me a minute.''

She had to laugh. Her mood lightened. He was impossible, but he was trying…she'd settle for that. "Okay, but that's all you get, a minute.'' She started determinedly forward. "Now, as I was saying before you walked into those skates, watch your head. There are a lot of things displayed from the ceiling as well as in the aisles. So be careful.''

"Thanks, I'll do that,'' he responded wryly, ducking a collection of outdated iron rug-beaters and other undefinable tools. He turned sideways, having to edge his way through a crowded aisle. "Are you sure this is safe? I've never seen so much stuff in one spot. It's got to be a fire hazard.''

Andrea stopped to throw him a warning look over her shoulder. "Would you prefer to wait in the car while I browse?" she inquired acidly, both hands planted firmly on her hips as she stared at him.

He threw his hands up in a gesture of surrender, quick to placate her. "No, no. I am nothing if not a good sport."

She let an inelegant snort give her opinion of that and momentarily stopped by a table so full of romance novels that some had slid into a heap on the floor. She thought about thumbing through a few, but Greg's despairing "You wouldn't make me spend my day picking out junk books, would you?" made her move on. She could always come back later.

The aisle after the one with the twenty-five-hundred-dollar antiquated three-station barbershop innards displayed two massive pecan-finished corner cabinets jammed behind several other items. She stretched as far as she could and tipped her head sideways to read the scrawled chalk pricing: "Three hundred ninety-five dollars or both for six hundred and ninety-five dollars." Her head remained tilted while she considered it before turning to Greg. "That's probably fair, don't you think?"

Greg's hands were stuffed into his jeans back pockets while he rocked from heel to toe, studying the pieces. "They're certainly good-looking," he allowed. "What did you have in mind for them?"

Andrea folded her arms across her midriff, a position her father had consistently disparaged as "hugging her buggy," and again returned her attention to the corner cabinets. "They'd be perfect in the two corners of the dining room where the windows don't interfere with the wall space they'd need...that is, if I could find a pecan dining set to complement them."

"Are you going to buy them?" Greg inquired, interested to see how Andrea did her shopping.

Andrea seemed startled by the inquiry. "What? Oh, of course not. I haven't got that kind of money. It'll be at least a year before I can afford anything like this."

Taken aback, Greg couldn't help asking, "Then what are we doing here? These will be long gone by then."

She responded pertly, "This is called window-shopping. Getting to know the market before you make any decisions. It's fun, and you never know, they may still be here. Some of these things have been here as long as I've been coming. And that's several years."

"But if the turnover is so low, how do they make any money?"

"I read an article in the paper written about them a while back. Don't lose any sleep over it. They do just fine." Her fingers trailed lovingly over the finely grained wood as she moved on. Halfway down the aisle she stopped again. Gesturing toward a dining-room table perched high on top of another, four small carpet squares under its four legs its only concession to preventing damage to the supporting tabletop, she questioned, "What do you think of that?"

Greg's mind was evidently already wandering, and he responded with a vague "What?" before looking around to see what Andrea was pointing at. Shaking his head negatively, he reminded her, "Only four chairs, and I don't see any leaves for extending the table."

Andrea chewed a fingertip thoughtfully. "Never thought of that. Still, if I bought that table, it might keep me from taking in any more strays for a while." Then she waved the thought away. "No, it would never work. Lack of space doesn't seem to deter me. We'd probably just end up eating in shifts or something." Determinedly she strode on.

"Uh, Andrea." Greg had to speak to her back as the aisles were too swollen with furniture and other odds and ends to allow walking abreast.

"Hmm?"

"Can we talk while we look through this junk?"

"It's not junk." Andrea was quick to correct him. "And we are talking. Or do you mean *talking?*"

"The latter."

"The old meaningful dialogue of college days gone by,

hmm?'' She fingered the intricacy of an ornately carved plaster-and-gilt picture frame before agreeing. "Okay, shoot."

"More specifically," he began in impersonal professional tones that already had Andrea cringing, "I would like to discuss some of what came up last night. You don't seem the narcissistic type who would overly worry about losing your figure or children messing up your place. The exact opposite, in fact." He seemed to grow less sure of himself as he went along. "I thought that if we could at least…talk about it…you know, so that I could try to understand what you were thinking along those lines…" The slightly uncertain wistfulness in his "Please?" took the sting from the formalness of the request, letting her see the vulnerability he sought to hide.

She turned and studied his face thoughtfully for a full thirty seconds, totally forgetting the Waterford Curraghmore pitcher she had spotted tucked away in an étagère off to one side. "Yeah, well, I guess this is as good a time as any. We may as well get it out of the way." She turned and walked a few steps while she gathered her thoughts, oblivious now to the furniture around her.

"Who's Peggy?"

Andrea whirled around. "How did you know she had anything to do with this?"

"It wasn't difficult." He shrugged. "When Karen lost her balance on the stairs, you called her Peggy and were upset way out of proportion to what actually happened. That, coupled with your evident fear of childbirth, leads me to believe something traumatic happened to a pregnant woman named Peggy, in all likelihood in front of you." He stopped, waiting for her to affirm or deny his assumption.

Absently she flicked an offending cobweb from her cheek and took care of the resulting itchy spot with a fingertip. "That's really very good," she commended. "You've managed to jump right into the crux of the matter."

"So tell me about it. Who is she?" he prodded.

Andrea answered slowly, thoughtfully. "She's my sister.

There's Jenny, who's twenty-nine, and then Peggy, who turned thirty-two a month ago.''

"And?" he prompted.

"Are you sure you want to hear this?"

"Yes." His tone was positive. "By the way, there's the table and chairs you want. See? It's in the same pecan tone as the corner cabinets we saw earlier.''

She turned to challenge him. "I thought you wanted to hear about my deep-seated childhood neurosis.''

"Oh, I do. I do. I also don't want to ruin your shopping expedition. Look. It has fantastic gargoyles carved on the legs and two leaves for expansion. It's perfect. I bet those are the table pads that go with it, too. Now, go on. I'm quite capable of entertaining two thoughts at one time, you know.''

"Are you being flip?" she demanded.

"No, I am not being flip," he said, growing exasperated. "I am merely trying to get into the spirit of the day. I thought that was what you wanted." He was becoming indignant now.

Mulling it over for a moment, Andrea decided to give him the benefit of the doubt. "Well, okay. It's just that I've never told anybody about this before. Here I am trying to be open, and then it seemed as if you weren't really interested." She examined the cause of their rift. "You're right," she admitted. "It would be a perfect match.''

Curtly he steered her forward by the elbow. "I know. Now let's get back to Peggy.''

It was probably silly to take these things so seriously. She forced herself to relax and tell the tale. Possibly it was all a question of putting things into perspective. It had been years ago, after all. "As I said, Peggy's thirty-two. That makes her eight years older than I. When she was nineteen, she had to get married. It broke my mother's heart, but Peggy was convinced it was true love and was ecstatic over the baby. How do you like that highboy?" Greg was right. There was no reason why they couldn't enjoy the outing and talk at the same time.

He gave it his full attention before commenting, "No. Too big for the room size."

Andrea looked at him with renewed respect. Again he was right. It was too big. "Maybe you're in the wrong field. Interior design might be right up your alley."

His impatient gesture made his opinion clear.

"Anyway, I thought it was all terribly romantic. Eleven-year-olds do, you know."

Greg nodded in agreement. It was practically a fact that girls of such an age sopped up anything smacking of romance.

"He was awfully good-looking." She sighed. "Just proves how deceiving looks can be, I guess."

"Meaning?"

"Meaning that when she was four months pregnant, she lost the baby. They'd only been married a month and were living with my parents until they could find an apartment they could afford." Andrea's voice dropped to a whisper as the painful memories came back. "Well, suffice it to say, she lost the baby. Ted, the stinker, was delighted. Seems Peggy and the pregnancy had interfered with his plans for his higher education. Night school wasn't fast enough for him. Since he had only married her because of the baby, he saw no reason to stick around after it was lost. He walked out the door and never looked back. Peggy was devastated, and believe me, so was I."

"I can imagine," Greg muttered sympathetically. "Eleven. Even little problems are monumental at eleven, but something like that..." His voice trailed off as he became lost in thought.

Chapter Seven

Andrea rubbed an irritated brimming eyelid while perusing
the room in a distracted manner. "Yes, well, unless you want
to go through those shelves of *National Geographic* back copies, why don't we head on back to the other building?"

Greg's vision momentarily settled on the magazines in question before he dismissed them. "No, I don't think so. Frankly,
those things give me an inferiority complex. I keep wondering
what I'm doing slogging away here when there are so many
other exciting things to be done. Some of the spreads they do
on the various explorers and remote corners of the earth only
serve as full-living-color reminders of the humdrumness of my
life." Purposefully he twined his fingers with hers and led her
from the building and into the crisp fall air.

Breathing deeply, Andrea noted, "You don't realize how
musty the air is in there until you come back out." Together,
they began weaving their way through a stand of rusting refrigerators blocking the path to the outbuilding. "You can't
seriously be upset about not being an explorer, can you? My
goodness, it's a struggle for you to face up to a mushroom; I

can just imagine you with fried grasshoppers or bird's-nest soup."

"It's not very nice of you to continually harp on a man's few failings. Haven't you ever heard you can get much further building on a person's positive aspects?"

"First, I'm not sure how far I want to get, and second, I wasn't harping on your failings, I was merely pointing out that you are what you are, which is quite a lot, and there's no point bemoaning what you'll never be. From all accounts you're an excellent physician and there are many, many people out there who would kill to have any area at all of real competence. Some of them would settle for being best at jacks, if that's all that was available to them. You just remember about the grass being greener and all of that. You're a doctor; enjoy being a good doctor. My Uncle Jim, Dad's brother, wasted most of his working life hating his career choices. And the funny thing is, his discontent followed him to each new career. He has yet to figure out that it's a mental outlook that will never change unless he changes it himself, internally. The job has little or nothing to do with it."

She stopped to remove her elastic band from her hair and gather some errant strays into the shining mass trailing down her back before redoing the ponytail. "Sorry," she muttered, "I didn't mean to lecture, but you touched a sore point."

"Don't apologize," he ordered with a peculiar glint in his eyes as he watched her. "You've given me some fascinating insights. I'll have to think about what you've said. Food for thought, as it were." Once again, he gave her a strange glance. "You're quite deep. Not your stereotypical physical-education instructor interested only in muscles, are you?"

Watching him kick a soda can out of their path before holding the door to the second building open for her, Andrea sighed. "I'd like to belt you one for that prejudicial remark. We are not all brainless jocks. There's a lot of theory and philosophy behind what we do. I could quote parts of Socrates' dialectics, places where he said 'What a disgrace it is for man to grow old without ever seeing the beauty and strength of which his body is capable,' but I won't. I could quote Plato's *Republic*, 'Anyone who can produce the best blend of the physical and the intellectual sides of education and apply them to the training of character is producing harmony,' but I won't do that either. It wouldn't be fair since I have admittedly spent the better part of the past week attributing all kinds of unsavory characteristics to the stereotypical doctor and lumping you in with the worst of them, I might add.''

"So kind of you to let me off the hook like that," Greg muttered ironically. He surveyed the cramped, crowded building and started determinedly down an aisle, viewing furniture stacked haphazardly, as much as three pieces high.

"Now that you've told me off again, let's get back to your sister's story." While turning sideways to squeeze past a bumper pool set jutting out into the aisle, he investigated the frame of a plaid-cushioned toboggan sled that wasn't in bad condition. "That happened when you were eleven, and you saw it as an eleven-year-old. It's time you went back now and viewed it through the eyes of an adult since it's obviously still coloring the way you view all male-female relationships. By the way, how did she lose the baby?"

"I don't really know. That's not really the type of thing that would be discussed in front of an eleven-year-old, you know."

"Hmm, you're right about that." Andrea watched the muscles of his thighs strain against his faded jeans while he crouched to check the count on the number of balls in the pocket of the bumper pool table. The rippling pull of his shirt as it clung to his shoulders and arms was fascinating.

"It's not really that important, I was just interested," he explained, rising from his squatting position and stretching to relieve a cramp. Andrea's heart immediately threw in three extra beats, maybe four. But who was counting? He eyed her levelly, making her feel like the quintessential emotional female, incapable of a logical thought. "But that's all moot anyhow. Just for conversation's sake, let's discuss the husband for a minute."

Now they were in front of a massive ornately carved slab of wood. Positioned in its middle was an oval, slightly distorted antique mirror. It was elegant, but seemingly useless. The whole piece was also in dire need of refinishing. What did one do with a box approximately seven or eight feet tall, five feet wide and a foot-and-a-half deep? Andrea's brow furrowed thoughtfully as she studied it.

Noting her puzzlement, Greg helpfully noted, "It's a bed."

"What?" Andrea turned a blank look up at him. "What does Peggy's husband have to do with beds?"

"Not her husband—this, right here. It's a Murphy bed."

Quickly, Andrea's amazed countenance turned back to the object in question. "You're kidding. Really? How does it work?"

Peggy's husband was relegated to the back burner while Greg showed her the mechanics of the bed. "Seriously. This side here with the mirror adds to the room's decor during the day when the bed is up against the wall. Then at night, you pull it down and inside, waiting for the lights to go out, is a double mattress just right for two. Perfect for some cramped area where you need the sleeping space but can't afford to lose the room during the day."

More intrigued by the erotic idea of a bed impatiently waiting behind the scenes for the two of them to put out the lights than the space-saving factor, Andrea only admitted, "I do have to kneel on the bed to open some of my dresser drawers. It would be nice to get the bed up out of the way when it's not in use, but three hundred and ninety-five dollars? And that doesn't include the mattress."

Greg shrugged. "I'm telling you, these things won't be here when you come back. The pieces I can tell you're interested in are one-of-a-kind things. They'll be gone if you don't snap them up." He said nothing further, only followed Andrea when she glared and stubbornly walked away.

Not willing to spoil the day by getting into a discussion of their divergent views on managing money, she prompted leadingly, "About Peggy's husband…"

Greg's look told her more clearly than words that he knew precisely what she was doing. Knowingly he took the bait. "Yes, about him." He gave her a considering look. "Has it ever occurred to you that you're still looking at him through an eleven-year-old's eyes? I wonder what you'd think of him if you met him today and saw him through the eyes of an adult." His hand raised to ward off her impending interruption. "No, now just think about it. You said it was terribly romantic and he was wildly handsome. But you also indicated that your sister was barely nineteen. Stop and logically think of the boys available to a girl just out of high school. By definition, he had to be pretty immature." Once again, his hand staved off her instantaneous rebuttal. "Before you say anything, let's try to get a hold of your sister's yearbook and see some pictures of the guy. I'm sure you're viewing him through rose-tinted glasses and that's why you were so disappointed when he walked. If you'd bother to ask your sister, she'd probably tell you it was the best thing that ever happened to her. Who'd want to spend the rest of her life married to a man who didn't love her?" He raised a questioning eyebrow at her. "Unless your sister suffers from some arrested form of adolescent unrequited hero worship."

Andrea bristled at the accusation, considering it unwarranted as he had never even met her sister. "Don't be ridiculous!"

His smile melted her anger as his arm slipped around her. "I thought not. Now let's get out of here. We can explore more outside if you want, but I need some fresh air again."

They left the stuffy confines of the building and began poking through an unexplored area. "Look at this!" Greg bellowed, startling Andrea with the intensity of his yell. "I've always wanted to own the Brooklyn Bridge, and the Golden Gate Bridge is the next best thing," he said enthusiastically. "Damnation, they've got the Arc de Triomphe, Big Ben and the leaning tower of Pisa, too! How am I going to make up my mind?"

Convinced she had just witnessed the simultaneous collapse

of every brain cell in his head, Andrea edged closer to see what had precipitated the aberration. "What in the world are you ranting about?" she questioned, even as she realized what it must be. There, in lilliputian splendor before her, was an entire selection of obstacles, all that remained of some now defunct miniature golf course. Europe's and America's major landmarks were there, complete with holes for golf balls and signs warning of water hazards, and the rules for play.

"Greg?" she inquired dubiously. "You're not seriously thinking about buying that, are you?" In horrified fascination she watched the smirk on his handsome face grow. So much for her no-sense-of-humor accusation.

Greg was so engrossed in his study of the find that he didn't even hear her query. Instead, the cool November sun sent flashes of fire through his thick mahogany hair and he rocked on his heels, hands stuffed into his jeans pockets while he grinned a silly little grin. "How many times in a man's life," he asked rhetorically, "does an opportunity like this arise? The Golden Gate Bridge!"

"Snap out of it, Greg. You look like you're going into a trance!" Andrea burst out, trying to get through the smug bubble he had spun around himself upon spotting this treasure. "You can't possibly buy it."

That got through as nothing else could have. He frowned, and turned his attention to her. "Why not?" he demanded.

She took a deep breath. Why not? "Well, for one thing, it's totally impractical. What would you do with it? Use it for a car-hood ornament? It's six feet long! You have no place to put it," she pointed out triumphantly.

"Don't be such a stick-in-the-mud," he shot back before returning his attention to San Francisco's famous landmark. "We'll set up a miniature golf hole in the backyard. The kid next door, what's his name, Jimmy? would love it." That self-satisfied smirk was growing again. He rubbed his hands together in delight before abruptly turning about and starting off toward the main building, leaving Andrea to stumble and stutter after him. "Come on. I'm going to buy it. Nobody in their right mind would pass by the chance to own San Francisco's Golden Gate Bridge."

"But you can't. What if you get an apartment with no yard available? What will you do with it then? After all, you're only staying until Karen has had the baby, remember?" Andrea's voice was acquiring a certain desperate quality. She simply couldn't believe anybody would throw away a hundred dollars on a miniature golf hazard.

Greg didn't even break stride. "Has anyone ever told you that you have a basically negative personality? All your can'ts and shouldn'ts are causing you to miss out on an awful lot of the spontaneous fun of living."

"What? Look who's talking!" Andrea blurted out. It was unbelievable that the original straight man was accusing *her* of being no fun. Of all the nerve.

"Okay, so I have some catching up to do. But who's doing the complaining now that I'm making a stab at it, hmm? You can't have it both ways, my dear. Now close your mouth," he directed after a look over his shoulder informed him that her generous lower lip was hanging down in stupefaction. "And let's search out whoever we have to pay so we can locate a hamburger place. Lunch should have been two hours ago. I'm starved."

"I never finished telling you about Peggy's Ted," Andrea called after his retreating back.

"So tell me in the car," he told her in a disinterested tone. Clearly his main interest now lay in claiming his bridge, as if someone else would snatch up the dumb thing before he could get to it, she thought furiously.

"It's now or never," she threatened, thoroughly irritated with him.

He turned to her with a facade of patient forbearance. "Okay, what about him? The guy was a jerk. There's little that can be added to that."

"You know how you said because he married a nineteen-year-old he had to be, by definition, immature?"

"Yeah?"

"That I was only looking at him through an eleven-year-old's rose-tinted glasses?"

"Yeah?"

"He was junior at the University of Chicago. In premed."

Greg looked back at her with a glint of humor in the depths of his eyes. "I really must look the man up someday," he promised. "Not only has he made you afraid of childbirth and its tandem effect on marriage, but he's also managed to make you afraid of marriage in general and doctors in particular. I have a lot to take up with the man, should we ever meet. Right now, however, I have a bridge to buy, so if you'll excuse me…"

He laughed outright as Andrea refused to accompany him, stomping off instead toward the car. "Damn, pompous *M.D.*," she muttered under her breath as she strode off, the appellation M.D. coming off as a particularly vile invective.

Greg found her there quite a bit later, the entire contents of her purse now dumped over the car's bright yellow hood. He sighed as he took in her bent form foraging through the morass of coupons, pens and loose change that had escaped from her wallet, listened to her mumbled soliloquy on the ancestry and disgusting personal habits of car keys. Clearly, she was in need of a caretaker—someone who would at the least keep track of her shoes and have a spare set of car keys available at all times. "They're in your pocket," he informed her in a kind tone, which she took immediate exception to.

"They're not," she snarled back. "I already checked." And she turned her jacket pocket inside out to show him. "And stop looking so darn smart. If we don't find them, we could be stranded here forever."

"It only took us a little over an hour to get here. Surely it would only take Tim an equal amount of time to rescue us," he pointed out with calm logic. "Now check your pants pocket, which is what I had in mind in the first place."

"They're not there. I never put my— Don't say a word," she instructed as her slender fingers withdrew the offending key from her jeans back pocket.

"Had you sat down, I'm sure you would have found them

without any help,'' he offered solicitously, but she only sniffed
haughtily in response.

It was fortunate that Friday was a busy day for Andrea. She
tried to stay away from mirrors, afraid of seeing steam rising
from her ears. It was hard to ignore her reflection in the aerobics class, though. "To the left, two, three, four. And
right...." She ignored the wall of mirrors and tried to dance
the edge off her frustrations, exhorting her class to follow.

Had she actually considered anything deeper than a surface
relationship with that lunatic? He had kept up an innocent
facade while repeating the trading-post owner's directions to
a truck rental place. He had totally ignored her protestations
that the bridge was only about six feet long. It was a small-
scale replica of the real thing, not the real thing itself. Surely
they could manage to get it into the car somehow. And the
trailer he had rented was definitely a gross case of overkill...

"Now twist. Keep those backs straight."

Her fury had taken root and grown as she watched the men
struggle with first the two massive corner cabinets she had
admired, the dining-room set Greg had discovered, the old-
fashioned Murphy bed that would take weeks to refinish, the
bumper pool table, the toboggan and then finally, San Francisco's Golden Gate Bridge.

"What do you think you're doing?" she had hissed in his
ear while he was tucking in the table pads and using them to
keep the pieces from knocking together during the long ride
home.

He had shrugged. "Well, I'll need furniture when I get an
apartment. You can store it for me until I need it...."

*"Two circles now. Fast runners in the front of the gym,
slow runners in the back..."*

"Greg," she had implored on a note of panic. "Think about
this. How are you going to pay for all this? You've just spent
at least two thousand dollars. You've already got loans from
your schooling."

Greg had spoken firmly. "Don't insult me by casting me in
your father's role. I know exactly how much I've charged to

my credit-card bill and what my monthly loan payments are. I'm not getting in over my head."

"But—" Andrea had begun desperately.

"There are no buts about it," he had affirmed implacably. "And you may as well know right now that those kitchen cabinets you were foolishly going to let go are arriving tomorrow. Tim and I will install them over the weekend. He's taking out the old ones while we're out today."

"What?" she'd gasped.

"You heard me. I went over Monday while you were at work. You were right. They'd adapt perfectly to your kitchen dimensions. It's ridiculous to pass up a bargain like that. For heaven's sake, they're practically giving that display away."

"I suppose you're lending me those too?" she had questioned sarcastically. "Going to take them with you to your new apartment as well...?"

"Back to your places now for thirty jumping jacks," she directed her class. Slowly, some of the worst of her anger was working its way out as she returned to her memory....

"I'll rent them to you for the next few months with option to buy. How's that?" he'd said.

He had looked disgusted with the entire direction of the conversation. Well, too bad for him.

The women in the early-morning class were looking at her strangely, and she realized she had lost count and must be past the usual thirty jumping jacks limit. "Sorry," she muttered, changing into a two-count forward kick. "Now back, one, two, and side, one, two. Opposite side. Again, forward..."

By the time four o'clock rolled around, Andrea felt that she would at least be able to speak to the occupants of her home in a civil manner. Her feelings of anger were unwarranted and short-lived.

"Hi." Greg kissed her on the forehead as she tossed her purse and books on the old Formica table, all that remained of the kitchen she had worked in only the day before.

"Hi, yourself," she grunted ungraciously, all her former ire returning at the sight of her gutted kitchen.

Greg was intent on ignoring her surly behavior and indicated the books on the table with a stab of his thumb. "I didn't think PE instructors did homework. What are the books for?"

Andrea chose not to rise to the slur, instead answering his question straight out. "Two of my seventh graders have been diagnosed with early curvature of the spine," she related. "I want to make sure none of the things we do in class would be detrimental. I also want to find out if there's anything I could add—stretching exercises or something that would help them out."

He was obviously impressed. "Where were the teachers like you when I was in school?" he inquired.

Andrea was not in the mood to be impressed by his compliments, however, and made a disparaging noise in the back of her throat. Looking around in the sure knowledge that she had utterly lost any control of her life, she asked, "How are things going?"

"Not bad, not bad. Tim's home from class. He'll be down as soon as he's changed his clothes. We'll work for the next hour and a half or so bringing in the new cabinets. I've got them all uncrated and the floor marked off as to where they go. I thought we'd go to a burger place for dinner and then to the Pinewood Derby. Jimmy says it starts at seven. I know our car is going to win," he predicted in happy anticipation. "My car always got a ribbon when I was a Scout. After that, I noticed in the Park District brochure that there's a free lecture on birding tonight at eight o'clock and a walk tomorrow morning at the Keay Nature Center."

Andrea looked blankly at Karen who had just entered the room with the level Greg had sent her to find. "Birding? Is that like hunting? I hate hunting of any type. I'm not going to trap innocent little birds. You know who'd get stuck cleaning the feathers off. You can forget it. The whole idea makes me gag."

Laughingly Karen explained, "Birding only requires a pair of binoculars. It has nothing to do with killing the little dears, merely identifying them. Greg's to the point where he can stay awake all day now." Greg grimaced at the way his niece made him sound like a five-year-old finally able to give up his afternoon nap. "Today he actually couldn't fall asleep when he lay down and ended up reading me bits and pieces of a birding manual. Fascinating stuff."

Karen yawned meaningfully. "It seems there are over six hundred species of birds indigenous to the continental United States. Birders keep track of how many they can spot."

"Sounds real boring." Andrea looked at Greg in wide-eyed wonder. Was he actually going to insist they do this?

"He's trying to show you what a fun person he is, I think," Karen answered her while rolling her eyes expressively.

Knowing full well what his response would be, Andrea shut her eyes in resignation and plaintively questioned, "It's such a cold, ugly night, couldn't we stay home and read the encyclopedia instead? It would have to be more entertaining than a birding lecture, for heaven's sake."

"And who spent yesterday lecturing me about my attitude? Hmm?" Greg held the level to the cabinet he had wrestled into place and leaned to make an adjustment in its position. "Buck up, it won't be so bad."

"Geez, Louise. I know I owe you one. But birding? I ask you...."

"Tsk, tsk, my dear. Watch that mental attitude of yours."

In the end, Andrea capitulated. After all, he had been a good sport the day before, even if she had been madder than hell at him over the high-handed tactics he had employed and his inability to grasp anything but the loosest idea of financial stability. She did insist on fried chicken instead of burgers, though, as the thought of the latter reminded her of yesterday's lunch, which in turn reminded her of yesterday in general, and that memory made her blood boil. *The Golden Gate Bridge, indeed!*

Jimmy proudly introduced his parents to Greg while ushering them all into the grammar school's gymnasium. In barely controlled excitement he pointed out the extended length of assembled track sitting in splendor in the middle of the gym's wooden floor. The air hummed in hushed anticipation, the level rising each time a blue-shirted Scout entered the room and stood in line to register his car. The tension was almost palpable by the time Jimmy's den was called for their race. Greg squeezed his hand, instructing him not to worry as the cars were set behind the gate at the high end of the track. Several Scouts averted their faces, unable to watch as three fathers drafted to act as judges leaned over the finish line, waiting to pick out the first three cars while the official starter dropped the gate, allowing the cars to start down the track.

The pressure Greg's hand exerted on Andrea's waist increased noticeably as he and Jimmy intently watched their car finish first by one-sixteenth of a length. A first place in either the second or third heat would put them up for the races deciding best of pack and entry into the divisional championship derby against other troops in the area.

"The whole trick," Greg confided to Andrea as Jimmy's car clinched best of den, "is the wheels. You have to be sure to sand any burrs off the nails holding the wheels to the car and nail them in perfectly straight, but not too tightly. Then be sure to keep the paint when you decorate the car away from the wheels, and no glue near them, either. Finally, a little powdered graphite to help them spin freely." Andrea filed the information away in her useless-trivia fund while Greg took his graphite tube from his shirt pocket and blew a little more into the car's critical areas.

Greg was as proud as any parent when it finally came time to determine best of pack. Andrea knew he would make a good father. His ego was obviously strong enough to allow him to come down to a kid's own level without feeling silly about it, as evidenced by the real enjoyment he was having this evening. The car ran beautifully the first time down, finishing first easily. Jimmy clenched his father's hand on one side and squeezed Greg's on the other as the gate lifted for the second run. Andrea watched in disbelief as their six-inch streak of silver spit off a wheel halfway down the track, skidding to a distant sixth finish. Frantically, Jimmy and his father worked to tap the recalcitrant nail and wheel back in for the third heat, Greg diplomatically remaining in the background. Andrea could see his fingers spasmodically moving, echoing each adjustment made by John McKnight.

Greg's exhorted "Come on, you stinker!" was barely discernible as the cars were set up for the third heat. It was a disaster. As if the manufacturer's warranty had just expired, three of the midget cars simultaneously lost wheels immediately. They careened down the runway in a race all their own, jumping their grooves and jamming adjacent cars. Jimmy's pride and joy had developed a vindictive show-them spirit of its own, spewing one wheel after another, finally sliding on its bottom to a third-place finish in spite of itself.

"See?" Greg grinned. "My cars always show."

All concern over the lost wheels were forgotten as Jimmy threw himself into his mother's arms, screaming, "We made the finals! We did it!"

When he was finally calm, his manners were remembered and Greg and Andrea were soberly thanked for all their efforts with a mature handshake. Andrea looked wryly at her hand. A handshake instead of a kiss? Jim confided, "The cookies were the best part, Miss Conrades," before stipulating, "especially since Mrs. Nyland wasn't hurt." She guessed he didn't want to appear totally callous, even at his young age. Watching him shake hands with Greg in as adult a fashion as he could muster, Andrea couldn't help but realize that if Jimmy had been Greg's own son, he wouldn't have had to remember his manners. The boisterous finale would have automatically included him. He would have done the last-minute repairs and shared in the victory celebration from its inception and not just as a tacked-on "you too" remembrance. Come to think of it, had it been her son as well as Greg's, the heartfelt hug and excited kisses would have gone to her, too—and for no other reason than that she was his mother. Who else would a child turn to in the thrill of victory? Sharing totally in *your own* child's every emotional peak and valley…it was an exceedingly heavy thought.

Chapter Eight

Andrea hadn't said much during the short car ride to the Park District's building where the birding lecture was to be given. Pondering the wonder of her own progeny hadn't left her much in the mood for conversation. Not only was she worried about childbirth per se, but how would she ever figure out if Greg was in love with love or with her? What a mess.

In the lecture hall itself, her thoughts slowly churned. Whole new concepts were taking root and growing in inverse proportion to the strength of the gradually dimming lights.

"Welcome to tonight's introduction to birding. Our talk tonight will be followed by a birding walk tomorrow morning. For those of you able to participate, we will meet in the Keay Nature Center parking lot at eight in the morning."

What would it be like to have her own child? To share a child, she revised, as the feat was impossible on her own. Any sophomore biology student could tell her that. She'd need help to accomplish anything along those lines. Her child. And Greg's. A child conceived with Greg. She turned to study him with a new perspective.

"Aristotle was one of the first birdwatchers of record, cataloging approximately one hundred and seventy species. Of course, he was not the first to watch birds. They play prominently in early man's cave drawings in Spain and France, Egyptian hieroglyphics and ancient Chinese potteries. Science then was liberally mixed with fancy. Birds' flight and feeding patterns were carefully watched for the omens the Greeks and Romans sought. Our word auspicious comes to us from the Latin *avis*—bird—and *specere*—to look at.''

Andrea had made it a habit to refrain from coyness. Her instinctive honesty acknowledged that she was attractive. Up to now, it had been very much her own choice to remain uninvolved. But Greg wasn't allowing her to brush him off as easily as she had the others. More and more, she was questioning whether she really wanted to. He had his faults, true, but didn't she? In the anonymity of the darkened room, she detachedly measured the man beside her. Starting with the thick thatch of deep brown curls he despaired of ever taming, and continuing down the silhouette of his brow and lineal patrician nose, her vision descended feature by feature, finding nothing to criticize until she at last reached the white athletic shoes with their three green stripes. Ah, no one could ignore the size of the feet sprawled out in front of that chair. Size thirteen, at least. Her triumph was short-lived, however, as she sorrowfully admitted to herself how truly picayune that one flaw was.

Clinically there was every possibility that she and Greg could produce a brood of rather spectacular children. That was the honest truth. But getting there from where she was now was something else entirely.

''Why study birds? We could get into the explorer's cliché, 'because they are there.' It's valid enough, but there can be so much more to it...''

Could she bring herself to go to bed with the man? She knew the facts of life; she taught adolescent girls. It was her job to know. Many of them felt far more at ease talking to the female physical-education instructor than to their parents or the male science teacher. She took another covert look at Greg.

He seemed oblivious to her internal turmoil, having eyes only for the speaker.

"Birds can be an early index of trouble in the food pyramid. Many environmental effects of chemicals first appeared in the bird populations...."

The problem was that children weren't had clinically. Greg would never allow any test-tube babies while he was warm and breathing. And well on the road to recovery now, there was no question of his being anything but warm and breathing. His body radiated its warmth in heated waves, pulling and tugging at her, beckoning her toward his glowing center. Could he possibly be as oblivious to the magnetic pull he emanated as he seemed? His total concentration seemed to be on Darwin's theory of evolution having roots in studies of a certain Pacific island's ground-finch population.

What would it be like to sleep with Greg? Not merely the slumber implied in the rigid definition of their act on his second night in her home, but sleeping with him in the fullest sense of the word, with all the opulent and fertile connotations it gained when applied to a man and woman together.... To sleep with Greg. Previously, when thinking in terms of sleeping with a man, she had always thought of it in more or less a generic sense—with man, in the abstract.

Now suddenly, with the thought of a flesh-and-blood man beside her—with Greg beside her, she decided that it might be sort of fun. In fact it might be downright pleasurable, erotically speaking. Erotic...now there was a word by definition rich in its sensual implications.

"In the words of Henry Beston, 'We need another wiser and perhaps more mystical concept of animals. We patronize them for their incompleteness, for their tragic fate of having taken form so far below ourselves. And therein we err, and greatly err. For the animal should not be measured by man. In a world older and more complete than ours they move finished and complete, gifted with extensions of the senses we have lost or never attained, living by voices we shall never hear. They are not brethren, they are not underlings. They are other nations caught with ourselves in the net of life and time, fellow prisoners of the splendor and travail of the earth.'''

My gosh. She was all set to tiptoe naked through the tulips and the speaker was waxing philosophical. Anyone who found a lecture on birds sensually stimulating was in dire need of mental aid. A psychiatrist. One with a great deal of experience in lost causes would be best.

"Uh, Greg?" Andrea whispered in his ear, "I'll be right back, okay?" He nodded absently and Andrea was off her chair, heading for the door, her shadow temporarily blotting out the projector's thrown image of a red-winged blackbird. It was some sort of native to the area.

She went to the ladies' room and washed her face with cold water. The irony of the situation was almost too much. She, who was always so cold during the winter months, was over-heated now in late November. That alone was enough to convince her that she needed help....

Back in her seat she found that concentrating on each slide made the rest of the bird lecture manageable, if not exactly inspiring. Still, Andrea breathed a sigh of relief when it was all over. Greg's arm rested naturally across her shoulders as he lightly guided her to the car.

"Did you enjoy yourself?" he inquired politely as he leaned forward to start the engine.

"Oh, yes. I particularly liked the Shakespearean freak wreaking havoc on our native birds by importing and releasing the starlings into New York's Central Park because Will mentioned them in his plays."

"That was interesting, wasn't it?" he asked, obviously delighted in his assumption that she had found the talk intriguing.

"Oh, yes," she repeated. "Listen, do you think we could stop for some ice cream and root beer to bring home? I'm awfully hot."

Greg looked at her in surprise. It was anything but warm outside. While the car heater was good, it wasn't *that* efficient. But he didn't question her, rather he turned into a midnight market's parking lot. "Do we need anything else? Bread? Milk?"

"Mmm, no, I don't think so. Well, maybe you'd better get some painkillers, too."

Concerned with her request coupled with the seeming hot flashes, Greg placed a professional hand on her forehead. "You don't feel warm. Are you sick?"

"Uh, no. It's just that, um, we're out of them, and…they're good to have around…just in case…you know." She didn't know if she was sick or not. Anything was possible at this point. She certainly felt weird, and it would certainly be easier to blame her problems on a bug rather than the effect Greg had on her. Darn it, she wasn't even married yet, and she still had no privacy. She needed time alone, just to think. Maybe she could send them all out tomorrow. The Cubs and Sox had made a run for the baseball pennant, but the season had run out before they'd made good their threat. That left the Bears, but football was played on Sunday and Monday nights. She'd have to think of something else.

While waiting for Greg to emerge from behind the *Chicken Whole Fryers Only 49¢/lb* sign that was plastered across one of the brightly lit storefront windows, Andrea put her head back against the seat's headrest and meditated on her life's recent turns. Now that Tim and Karen had moved upstairs, she mused, it was going to be increasingly difficult to maintain any type of distance, emotional or otherwise, as far as Greg was concerned. The sixty-four-thousand-dollar question was, Did she really want to? Lately, her body seemed to have a mind of its own, openly rebelling against the restrictions it had lived under for so long. She had been slow in her development all her life. Maybe this was some type of delayed adolescence hitting her.

She doubted it. She suspected it had more to do with Greg himself and the kind of man he was, rather than the status of some unbalanced hormone coursing through her bloodstream. Watching Greg appear, it seemed only right that the automated doors should swing open without his touching them. After all, her heart raced and her pulse slammed inside her veins without his touching her. Perhaps he was some heretofore unknown god recently descended from Olympus. Perhaps they could bottle him and sell his essence…Eau de Greg toilet water. It would beat musk hands down. She smiled at her own whimsy. Greg gave a bemused grin of his own in response as he slid through the open car door.

"Did you miss me?" he questioned, leaning over for a quick kiss.

Andrea found herself answering honestly, "As a matter of fact, I did. In the span of one short week, you have managed to thoroughly worm your way into my life. The car did seem empty without you." She sounded a little surprised.

Greg seemed pleased and gave her another kiss—one that wasn't so quick.

The house was dark upon their return. Apparently, Karen and Tim had decided to make an early night of it. Andrea and Greg quietly drank their black cows, sipping up the root beer as it foamed in response to the ice cream. She noticed the way Greg kept trying to set up meaningful eye contact, but her own slid uneasily away. She just wasn't quite ready. Finally, she withdrew and closed herself in the bathroom to get ready for bed.

The navy and beige shower curtain had just swished over the rod behind her, enclosing her in the privacy of the tub, when she heard the bathroom door gently crack open. She was going to have to install a lock on the damn door if she was going to make it through the next few months.

"Can I come in?" Greg's head poked around the door.

"Would it matter if I said no?" She sighed in resignation.

Cheerfully, his response came as he entered the room. "Not really. I need a shower too. I thought we'd conserve water. The government's environmental agency would approve."

"That's probably why our taxes are so high—too much regulation."

"Come on," he urged. "It'll be fun."

"Can't you wait ten minutes?"

"Brother, what a party pooper. Oh, all right. I'll wait outside the door. But I'm going to leave the door open a few inches so we can talk. Okay? I think it's time." She felt the draft of the door once again being opened and took a quick peek around the edge of the shower curtain. She could just catch a glimpse of a jeans-clad leg. He must have settled on the hall floor just outside the door.

"Now it's occurred to me from some remarks that Karen and Tim have made and my own observations that you're not used to a lot of hugging and touching. You keep shying away from me. Here's how I see it. I shower; I use deodorant. You shower; you use deodorant. I'm attractive. You're attractive."

Andrea wondered if he'd ever been on the debating team in that high school in Pennsylvania. He would have been a killer. He could carry on both sides of the debate all by himself.

"I like you, you like me. There's no real reason for you to back away all the time. That mess your sister was involved in just doesn't cut it as reason enough. You want to know what I think?"

She could hardly wait. "What?" she answered obligingly and began to rinse her hair. She had used too much shampoo and her head refused to stop foaming.

She was right to have been leery because Greg continued, "It's just that most women, men too for that matter, even if they remain virgins, have at least experienced a little petting as teenagers. That way, the path is paved for further intimacy when they're ready. But I suspect you're starting from scratch. What you need, and what I intend to provide, is a little remedial fondling to sort of get you used to my touch gradually. Before you know it," he cheerfully informed her, "I'll have you totally addicted. You won't be able to live without it. So what do you think of my analysis?"

Andrea sputtered under her cascading bubbles. The man was too much. "I've had some boyfriends, you conceited clod," she replied defensively. She hadn't allowed them much freedom with their hands, but she'd had a few. Reaching from

behind the curtain, she snagged a towel and wrapped herself
better than a mummy before stepping from behind the curtain.

"I love you, you know," Greg said after seeing her and
laughing. "Here I thought that when I finally got around to
deciding to settle down, it would take me several years of
research to find the kind of woman I needed. I'm very picky,
you know. Not too easy to get along with, either."

There was no need to state the obvious. She felt bad enough
about falling for him without his rubbing her face in it.

"And instead," he continued conversationally, "here you
fall out of the sky and into my lap. The perfect woman. Manna
from heaven, as it were." She could see him unbuttoning his
shirt out in the hallway through the partially opened door.

"That's ridiculous," Andrea contradicted him. "The whole
thing is very earthbound. I did not fall from the sky. You
tumbled in *my* front door. And without being terribly pleasant
about it, I might add." She might as well get the story straight,
she thought.

Greg ignored her. "As I was saying, who would have
thought? Just as I'm ready to actively campaign for a wife,
the perfect candidate shows up. Terrific sense of humor; good,
if unorthodox cook..."

He would have to qualify any compliment, she thought.

"Good-looking, sexy as hell, loves children. Perfect," he
concluded, as he reentered the bathroom and stepped around
Andrea to toss his shirt on the radiator.

Andrea watched as he began removing his undershirt and
her mouth went dry at the magnificent torso being bared in
front of her. She quickly left the room. Greg should stop and
listen to himself talk, she thought as she rubbed herself dry in
her bedroom. She had been too angry over his buying the
Golden Gate Bridge the other day to finish the talk she had
planned. And it still sounded to her as though once the burden
of medical training was over and he was ready to make a
family commitment, he were grabbing the first person of the
female variety to pass by, rationalizing as he did so that she
was the woman of his dreams. She was starting to suspect

buckteeth, four eyes and cooties would have been passed off as inconsequential. He was ready to settle down, in capital letters.

Toweling her hair, she thought about the man left behind in the shower and was stabbed with a fierce longing, somewhat akin, she suspected, to Eve's consideration of a certain apple in a certain garden. There wasn't another woman within a ten-mile radius of that soap-slicked tub, Andrea postulated, that wouldn't grab with both hands the opportunity standing literally at her fingertips and head for the nearest clergyman. She sighed. She wasn't most women. It was doubtful she could give him the things he craved—home and hearth...children...the unfailing love and devotion every marital participant deserved.

Greg reappeared in an amazingly short period of time wrapped in one of her new burgundy-red towels. Speaking from her doorway, he continued the conversation as though there had been no interruption, assuring her, "Not to worry. I won't rush you while you're feeling harassed. I know what I want, and I intend to get it, but I'll give you the time you need, too."

"How much time?" she questioned suspiciously. He was being entirely too accommodating, considering what she'd already seen of his personality.

"Ohh, at least another day or two." Her lips were pinched as she watched him turn away to hum jauntily on his way down the hall to his own room.

Andrea took advantage of his absence to blow her hair dry in the steamy bathroom, aiming the dryer first at the mirror to clear it of its moisture-laden fog, and next at her own thick locks. Then she went back to her bedroom and flicked her electric blanket to five as she passed the bed en route to the dresser. It was chilly in the house and going to get worse. The new thermostat automatically set the heat back to fifty-five in the evening. With that in mind, she knelt on the end of the bed, giving herself enough room to open the dresser drawer and remove a floor-length red and black plaid flannel night-gown, its collar and cuffs trimmed with delicate white lace.

Just as she was about to unwind the large towel and unfold the gown to change, Greg waltzed into the room, sporting nothing but a ratty pair of old pajama bottoms that clung to his hipbones and seemed to stay there by force of habit.

Clutching the towel tightly to her slight bosom, she gasped in affronted dignity, almost as though they hadn't just shared the bathroom. "What are you doing in here?"

Greg frowned in an offended, displeased manner at the blanket control box where a glowing red light mutely testified to its bed-heating capabilities. "Nasty things, electric blankets," he commented as he followed the cord to its outlet. He reached down and gave a self-satisfying yank, effectively cutting off its power source. Rechecking the control box, he seemed pleased by its blank face. "I'm quite sure anyone interested in doing a bit of research would discover a direct relationship between the rise in the divorce rate and the advent of artificial bed-warming devices."

"To a certain portion of the population, artificial means are all that's available," Andrea responded in a saccharine tone.

"Here's where I intend to demonstrate another of the benefits of having a husband. Get into the bed," he directed, pulling down the blankets and spread with one hand while pointing to her flannel nightie with the other. "And get rid of that. I'll chuck these," he indicated his worn bottoms with a flick of his hand, "And we'll keep each other warm."

Andrea ignored him, snapped the nightgown free of its neat folds and prepared to slip it over her head. "Greg, every night at ten-thirty the temperature drops to fifty-five degrees in here. I'm freezing. Now kindly get out of my room so I can go to bed. I'm not in the mood for any more games."

"Andrea, Andrea," Greg admonished sorrowfully. "When will you ever learn? I am not playing games with you. You told me yourself I didn't know how." He plucked the gown from her grasp and pushed her toward the bed. "Now get rid of the towel and get into bed."

He held up a placating hand as he saw the promise of rebellion flash in her blue eyes. "I just want to hold you and cuddle a little during the night. Come on, humor me, I'm a sick man."

If only he *were* still sick. Now, well on the road to recovery, he was becoming more and more difficult to handle. If she thought events were slipping out of her control a week ago, they were child's play in comparison to this. Here was a scene she couldn't have dreamed in her wildest imaginings. "I don't care how much body heat you radiate. During the winter I sleep in a flannel gown, knee socks, the electric blanket on medium and sometimes even a robe. You're going to tell me you can replace all that?"

Greg sat on the edge of the bed contemplating her blue-tinged lips. "Knee socks, too, hmm? I had no idea things were that bad. Let's feel your feet." Obligingly, Andrea placed her right foot high on his thigh while she waited expectantly for him to pass judgment. She bit her lower lip to keep from laughing out loud as he paled in the face of the icy-cold invasion of a rather intimate area. Quickly he grabbed it away and held her foot between two warm hands. "Yes, well—" he cleared his throat and started again generously offering "—tell you what. You go ahead and put some socks on. But no nightie. Think of it as a scientific evaluation of the principles of the Indians of Tierra del Fuego. Didn't they all sleep with their feet toward the fire with the idea that if their feet were warm, their bodies soon would be as well?"

Trust Greg to put her first night nude in his arms into *National Geographic* terms. Andrea sighed and reached into the drawer for a pair of thick, bright red knee-highs, the action signifying her capitulation. It just wasn't worth the trouble to keep fighting. She, who had managed to keep men at a distance all these years, was about to share a bed with a man who made her crazy. She inserted both thumbs into the top of the sock, rolling it up between thumbs and fingers, and bent over to insert her toe. The tuck in the top of her towel responsible for holding the togalike arrangement together began to loosen, and she didn't bother to make a stab at refastening it. It wasn't worth the effort. He was going to win by simply wearing her down.

His dark eyes flared with cooper sparks in anticipation of the towel's ultimate capitulation. "This could get good. We may have just come across the up-and-coming replacement for black stockings and garter belts."

"Shut up," she advised, thinking to herself, like heck he was going to win. She called upon that one percent of her backbone that didn't consist of mush, grabbed the flannel granny gown and slipped it over her head. She removed the towel from under the safety of its bulky folds and slid between the sheets, shivering as the cool percale made contact with her few uncovered areas. "Couldn't we have the blanket on for just a few minutes? Sort of preheat the sheets?" she queried plaintively.

Not even bothering to remove his pajamas, Greg climbed in beside her with a frown and nestled up to her back, spoon fashion, pulling her against him to improve the fit. "No. We'll be warm in no time. Think of all the energy we're saving."

The truth of the matter was, he did seem to be emitting an awful lot of heat. She was starting to feel incredibly warm, and that warmth seemed to focus around the hand that draped around her to cup a small but firm breast in its gently callused palm. She snuggled back farther against him. This was better than old-fashioned Victorian warming bricks by a long shot. "What are you doing?" she murmured sleepily.

His head lifted from its desultory shoulder-nibbling activities. "I'm kissing what should be your lovely alabaster shoulders. It's supposed to be sexy. It's just hard to properly pull off through all this fabric."

She stifled a giggle at his hurt tone and hastened to assure him, "Oh, it's very erotic, truly it is." She squirmed a little farther backward. He really was as good as an electric blanket any night of the week. Greg gasped as she snuggled more deeply. His hands began to roam a bit and he moaned under his breath. Andrea was sure it was just this type of situation her mother had warned her against when she'd shown her first interest in boys years before. "Uh, Greg?" she gasped. "Maybe this wasn't such a great idea." Anything that felt this good must be wrong, and she was sure her mother would agree with that sentiment.

Greg pulled her around, denying her claim. The imprisoning ropes of his arms held her to his lanky length, aggressively burning her with the undeniable proof of his arousal. "Oh, no, sweetheart. We've just immeasurably improved on the original concept." A shudder ran through him as his mouth closed over her own trembling lips. One hand eased under her nightie before holding her more tightly against the cradle of his hips, impressing the strength of his desire upon her in no uncertain terms.

"Oh, Andrea," he muttered against the softness of her mouth. "I thought I could hold you, lead you gradually into wanting what I want, but I can't." He leaned back to try to read her face in the dark. One hand cradled her head by her ear, its thumb stroking from the bridge of her nose along the line of her high cheekbone. He kept their hips in tight contact while he implored her, "Make up your mind now. Tell me if you don't want me to touch you. Now, while there's still a remote possibility of stopping."

It was Andrea's turn to search the darkened planes of his face for answers. She couldn't read his face in the room's velvet darkness. What did he want from her? "Greg?" she asked uncertainly. She could feel his body tense, awaiting her rejection.

"I want to be the one to show you, Andrea. Let me be the only one to know your sweetness... Please. Let it be now."

Suddenly, none of it mattered anymore. She would probably spend the rest of her life coaxing his smiles and avoiding bankruptcy court, but to spend even one night wrapped in his arms like this would somehow be worth it. What she felt for the dark man holding her so closely transcended mere liking, leaving it behind as inconsequential.

"Yes, Greg," she breathed, hardly able to take in the import of what she was saying. "I want you to be the one. Show me. Show me now."

"Thank you," Greg offered humbly, slipping her flannel covering up and off, and immediately lowering his generous full lips to the creamy skin of her neck. "You won't regret this. I promise I'll take care of you. Always."

Andrea didn't argue the ridiculousness of his vow because his marauding mouth was wreaking havoc on her sanity as it worked its way down her body fastening itself finally upon the peak of one quivering, swollen breast. "Do you like this, Andrea?" His sensitive fingers joined in, adeptly tormenting the other nipple, and Andrea gasped at the strength of the sensations he was able to produce. No one had ever touched her so intimately. No one but Greg had successfully breached the barricades.

Slowly her own hands began moving, seeming to have an innate knowledge of what to do to bring him pleasure. They skimmed the surface of his broad back, barely touching the warm skin, making him shiver in response. Taking heart, she moved on, allowing her sensitive fingertips to smoothly glide down the distance of his muscled arms and then onto the firmly delineated planes of his chest, provoking each new-found territory with teasing little circles.

Momentarily stopping his feasting, Greg paused, giving all his attentions to cataloguing the intense feelings her touch caused to surface. Andrea welcomed the respite as her senses threatened to overload. She closed her eyes, waiting for him to continue. A moment later, she regretfully opened them, a sense of foreboding telling her that she was not to know the fruits of her momentous decision. "Greg?" she questioned uncertainly.

Greg looked torn in half, pain furrowing his brow as he collapsed on his back next to her. "It's not enough," he said.

"What are you talking about?" she responded, but she already knew.

"It's too soon. You're thinking of tonight, and I'm thinking of tomorrow. It'll probably kill me to stop at this point, but this is only a part of the whole picture I'm looking for. It's not the whole picture itself. I want you to clearly see the distinction. Anyway, this was to be a slow wooing, and I apologize.''

"For what?" she asked, bewildered and wondering if she'd just been insulted or complimented.

"For rushing you."

"But Greg, I could have stopped you if I'd wanted."

"Nope," he declared empirically, jackknifing off the bed. "You were a goner. I'm going into the other bedroom. I can't handle all this temptation." He leaned over and kissed a soft breast and Andrea shivered. "I'll see you in the morning, love" was all he said as he closed the door behind him.

Andrea flopped back down on her pillow, crossing her arms in exasperation. How about that? He considered her putty in his hands. It was disgusting. It was true. She turned to punch her pillow into submission, then eyed it speculatively. Carefully she turned on her side and pulled the pillow tentatively into her arms. Hmm, the piece of fluff was definitely a second best, she thought, but at this point it was better than nothing. Her final rebellion was to lean way out over the edge of the bed and plug her blanket back in. Then she flicked the control box to high with a flourish of her hand and didn't bother to replace her nightie. It only took her an hour and a half to fall asleep.

She slept a short time, awakening a few hours later, in a sweat. This was a real first, she thought ruefully. Andrea was a blue blood, not by virtue of any impressive ancestry, but rather her own lamentable tendency to shiver during all months but two weeks in mid-July. She was definitely overheated. Again. She threw on her nightgown and left the bedroom. She was startled to find Greg making hot chocolate in the kitchen.

"Couldn't sleep," he mumbled with a shrug. His color rose, and he hoped that Andrea wasn't aware that old medical students could sleep anywhere, even upright, at the slightest excuse. But, he reminded himself, her dad had been a doctor and she might figure out how much peace she had cost him.

"I need a shower," she announced baldly. "Late November, and I'm sweaty. I *never* sweat, no matter how hard I work. Not from the beginning of November until early May. It's strictly a summertime activity for me."

"Women don't sweat anyway."

"You don't spend as much time in a girls' locker room as I do. They not only sweat, they smell when they sweat."

"They don't," he contradicted.

"How do you know? They teach you that in medical school?"

"My mother told me," he answered smugly. "Men sweat, women perspire and ladies glow."

Andrea groaned, "Oh, good heavens above." She hit him with the pillow she was for some reason still clutching. "That's ridiculous."

"Hey!" Greg's muffled protest was all but lost in his efforts to resurface. He knocked the pillow free, grabbed her and found himself staring down the open neckline she had never buttoned. Andrea watched his eyes glaze over as he studied the lightly swathed globes that rose and fell just below the open slash in the yoke. She held her breath, watching the gradual transition and loving the feminine knowledge of her responsibility for it.

He freed one hand to trace a lazy line beginning just beneath one ear, traversing the slim length of her responsive neck, resting temporarily to check a kindling pulse point. His touch then continued down, exploring the shallow valley between her breasts, his finger sliding through the revealing beads of moisture still to be found there.

"Uh, you wouldn't care to retest your mother's theory, would you?" she questioned breathlessly. "See if you can push me past the lady's glow? Sort of like the princess and the pea. Separate the ladies from the women." Her suddenly free hand began a two-fingered walk from his waist and proceeded up his chest. "We could consider earlier a warm-up. Practice."

Greg snapped out of his reverie. "Practice, my rear end. Stop that!" He slapped her hand. "I've created a monster. I'm going back to bed...by myself, mind you, so I can maintain my virtue. I've never accepted second best yet, and I'm not about to start now. I want it all, lady. And I'm going to have it. Now we'll hear no more about practicing tonight, because if you don't can the come-on, you're going to have difficulties waking up tomorrow. I know how you're looking forward to that bird walk."

Chapter Nine

Dawn came annoyingly early Saturday morning. It brought an equally annoying shoulder-shaking with it.

"Come on, Mary Sunshine. Up and at 'em. Birds are at their most visible first thing in the morning. Rise and shine."

My, but he was disgustingly happy and energetic this morning, she thought. That could easily be chalked up as a point against him.

She mumbled into her pillow and tried to cling to the blankets that Greg was ruthlessly ripping away. "It's too early. The walk doesn't even start until eight..." One of her eyes opened and tried to focus on the bedside clock radio.

"It's only five o'clock. It will not take us three hours to get ready."

"Eight o'clock, pah! They're going to miss everything interesting. Now at six, anything worthwhile will be up scratching around for breakfast. The early bird and all of that."

Andrea crawled out of bed, shaking her head to clear it. One look told her he was serious. She shook her head again, this time in disparagement. "Greg, we can't go without the group. We won't know what we're looking at." She shrugged into her floor-length blue velour robe and lifted the bed skirt to check for her slippers. She needed them. The heat hadn't even kicked on yet, it was so early.

Greg sat on the edge of the bed and began working into a set of thermal-weave long johns, pulling them up under his short robe. He intended to dress in her room, she gathered, because a pile of neatly folded fresh clothes sat on the bed beside him.

"Not to worry. I bought a bird guide the other day at that bookstore on Central Street. Seven ninety-five for the paperback edition. Incredible." He shook his head to show his disbelief.

"I'll start breakfast," she muttered in resignation.

But Greg caught her hand, pulling her between his now jean-clad thighs. "How are you this morning, honey?"

Andrea's eyes wandered, measuring the cracks needing to be plastered on the wall behind him before meeting his gaze in a more straightforward fashion. Her hand awkwardly raked his hair back off his forehead in a nervous gesture. "You were right. We should wait until I'm surer." Her eyes went back to taking inventory of the cracks. "But it would have been an experience."

His arms encircled her hips and he lay his head on her breasts before commenting, "You're sweet and I want you desperately. But I'm afraid it's all or nothing for you and me." He tapped her forehead significantly. "Now tell me what's going on up here. Do I have to protect my flanks from ambush while we're at the nature center? Check over my shoulder all day?"

Andrea laughed. "None of the above. I'm frustrated, but I'll survive."

"I'm glad," he crooned, lifting his head to study her face. "I want you to make that awful health-food milk shake for breakfast that you're so crazy about. When we do start working on our little project, I want you in top form. Little Emmett should get off to the best possible start."

Andrea looked confused. "'Emmett'? Emmett who?"

Greg stood to walk her out to the kitchen. "Emmett is going to be my firstborn son," he informed her seriously. "Heir to one-half of my sterling genetic code. I do not want said code damaged or impaired by poor nutrition on his mother's part." He reached into the box holding everything that had been removed from the dismantled upper cabinets and located the blender. Gravely he handed it to her.

She clutched the blender to her bosom while glaring at him. This was laughable! "How could you possibly be so cruel as to stick a defenseless baby with such a terrible name?"

"There is nothing wrong with that name," he insisted, growing indignant. "I have carried it for thirty years."

"Greg is the diminutive for Gregory, not Emmett. Your name is Gregory. Karen said so."

"My name is Emmett Gregory Rennolds, Jr. My son will be Emmett Gregory Rennolds the third."

Andrea tipped her head and knocked an ear with her palm to clear it. What was she doing at five-fifteen in the morning freezing in a fifty-five degree kitchen, arguing over a fictitious baby's name? "What is it with you? Every time I start thinking we might have a good thing going, you do something like this. If you actually expect some poor woman to spend twenty-odd years cringing every time she has to call her own flesh and blood by name, let me suggest you marry her, get her pregnant and fill in the birth certificate on the sly. *If* I were ever to have a son—" and she stressed the if for his benefit; there was no point in letting him think she had totally buckled under to the spell of his charisma "—he would be christened Emil, after the one-quarter genetic code passed on from his maternal grandfather. I *might* have my arm twisted as far as Gregory Emil, but that's it. You'll have to find some other poor besotted female to sweet-talk into that one. Emmett. What a horrible name."

Greg cracked an egg into the blender and handed her a six-ounce can of frozen concentrated orange juice after pulling the opening strip for her. He almost knew the recipe by heart.

"Some other besotted female? Are you admitting to being besotted?"

Andrea peeled a banana, broke it into chunks and tossed them into the blender. The peel was unceremoniously dumped on the top of an overflowing brown grocery bag converted to garbage use. "All I'm saying," she said, avoiding his question, "is that I'm not so far gone that I'd let any son of mine be called Emmett. I'm sorry you got stuck with a rotten name, but I see no reason to perpetuate the crime on future generations. You're going to have to compromise a little, at least on this one issue."

"Emil would be a hundred times worse," Greg returned pugnaciously.

"This is an entirely ludicrous discussion. I am not now, nor will I be in the foreseeable future, pregnant. So why are we standing here arguing over this? The sun's not even up yet, for goodness' sake!" She ended yelling, as if arguments were only allowable during daylight hours.

Greg hushed her and looked meaningfully toward the ceiling. "You'll wake them, and Karen needs her rest."

Andrea merely stared at him for a significantly lengthy period of time. Finally she shoved a glass of the finished breakfast concoction into his hand and advised, "Here, drink this. And by the way, you'll have to take the garbage out before we go. I'd do it, but my shoes have disappeared again."

Greg tossed the drink down in one long, shuddering motion. It was the only way he could stomach the stuff. "They're by the back door. Remember, you stepped on that piece of ice, only it wasn't totally frozen and your shoes sank in the water? You didn't want to track through the house."

"Oh, that's right. I forgot. I don't suppose you know where my keys are?" She arched a hopeful eyebrow in his direction.

"Try your purse. I seem to remember being amazed to see you actually putting them where they belonged."

Andrea brightened. "Thanks. I never would have thought of looking there."

"I've said it before, you need a keeper," Greg grunted in

mock despair as he deftly hefted the heavy garbage bag into the crook of his left arm. "I'll meet you at the car. Bring the green plastic bag off my dresser, would you? I bought two pairs of 7 × 35 mm binoculars the other day."

"Am I supposed to be impressed?"

He shrugged his shoulders. "Beats me. It's what the bird book suggested."

"Where is this infamous bird book? You may as well bring it along since we're actually going to go through with this."

The two hours before the guided tour of the nature center began served only to impress upon Andrea how basically incompatible she and Greg were. True, Greg had been correct in that there were a lot of birds up and about. Unfortunately, to the uninitiated, they all looked alike.

"What's that?" she inquired while shading her eyes from the early-morning glare with a hand. She pointed to a preening bird strutting on a low branch fifteen feet over their heads.

Greg looked in the general direction of her wavering forefinger. "Where? I don't see anything."

Andrea pointed more emphatically. "Right there. Just follow my finger and look." She wondered if bird dogs had as much difficulty pointing out their prey to their hunting partners.

"I still don't...oh. That? Let's see..." Greg began industriously flipping through his book. "First thing to do is determine its size. Robins are the measuring stick you go by. So, is it bigger or smaller than a robin?"

"I don't know. I don't see one around to compare it with." Her eyes turned in a slow, searching arc. "I think they all went south already."

Greg exhaled an exasperated sigh. "Lots of robins stay all winter. You only notice them in the spring because you're looking for them. It's a fallacy that they're the first sign of spring. But that's all beside the point. I'm sure they don't mean exact micrometer comparisons. Generally speaking, is that bird roughly the same size as, smaller than, or larger than a robin?"

"Oh, well, if that's the case...my guess is, maybe a little smaller. What do you think?"

He ignored her query and turned back to his guide. "Fine. Smaller. Now what are its distinguishing characteristics, starting with the markings around the eyes?"

This was starting to resemble the Grand Inquisition. How the devil was she supposed to see its eyes from this distance? "I can't see that far."

"That's what the field glasses are for," Greg pointed out in false equanimity.

"Right," she mumbled while raising the forgotten glasses to her eyes for a closer look. She lowered them to take a new fix on the bird before elevating them again. Then she tried a third time to no avail. She simply could not find the stupid thing when looking through the binoculars.

"Oh, hell. Give me the damn glasses," Greg rumbled in disgust, strangling her with the neck strap as he tugged the glasses away.

"Hey!" she gasped indignantly. "Use your own!"

Dropping hers with a snort and picking up the pair hanging forlornly around his own neck, he instructed in short tones, "Look, you keep your eyes on the bird while you raise the binoculars to your face. The glasses have a much narrower field of vision than your eyes, and you'll never find it otherwise. Hell, where is the thing?"

"I think it just flew away."

He turned to her, an annoyed furrow deepening in his creased brow. "Did you notice anything at all about it?"

Helpfully, she offered, "It was kind of brown. Yes, a mottled brown, with some white."

Greg crouched, not wanting to sit in the nature center's six-inch layering of composting damp brown leaves and pine needles. He showed her several silhouettes and full-color pictures of various birds with a quick thrusting jab of an index finger. "Was his profile like this? Did he hold his tail up or let it drop like here? What about this one? It's kind of mottled brown."

She tried not to get nauseated from the rapidly flipping pages of color wavering in front of her eyes. How was she to differentiate between so many brown birds? There must be twenty or thirty, all sporting variegated tones of brown. "Greg, I really didn't see it all that well. Maybe we'd better just forget that one and hope for better luck next time. Surely they won't all fly away so fast...."

Greg rose from his crouch and impatiently remonstrated, "You're going to have to get the characteristic markings more quickly, that's all. No bird is going to sit still for twenty to thirty minutes while you catalog its each and every feature."

Andrea was cut to the quick. She placed both hands on her hips and glared. "You've got binoculars. Why don't you see how quickly *you* can identify them?"

"I can't do it all," he snapped back in aggrieved tones. "One of the keys to success is delegating and cooperating. In this case, that translates to you spot 'em and I'll find 'em in the book."

"You make it sound so easy," Andrea snorted as she stomped off. Stopping again, she pointed to a fence some fifty feet in the distance. "There's one."

Squinting in the proper direction, Greg made a disgusted sound. "That's a pigeon, for heaven's sake."

"So what's wrong with pigeons?" Andrea demanded.

"Nothing's wrong with pigeons. They're a dime a dozen, that's all. I was hoping for something a little more unusual."

By the time the professional guide arrived, they had spotted a crow, a mallard duck and two more mottled-brown, smaller-than-a-robin birds that wouldn't sit still long enough to be identified. And Greg and Andrea were barely speaking to each other.

Greg drove home with a white-knuckled grip on the steering wheel. He was the first one away from any intersection where a red light dared stop them, no contest. Andrea breathed a sigh of relief when he finally pulled to a stop in front of her own little bungalow. They found Karen and Tim in the kitchen.

"So how'd it go?" Karen queried from her position on the

floor where she sat trying to organize the boxes of foods removed from the cabinets into some semblance of usable order.

Greg rolled his eyes. "Don't ask." He left for his room
telling Tim to wait a minute and he'd help him mount the new
cabinet he was working with onto the wall.

"What's with Prince Charming?" Tim wagged his head at
Greg's departing back. "Birding wasn't quite the fun-filled
outing he had in mind?"

"Once we had someone who knew what they were doing
with us, it was fine. She helped us identify two cardinals, male
and female, a yellow-shafted flicker, the biggest blue jay I've
ever seen and nine sparrows—seven house and two white-
throated. Those are kind of brown mottled birds, a little
smaller than robins with some white on them. It was fun.
Much to my surprise, I actually enjoyed myself." Her index
finger paused reflectively against her lower lip. "I don't think
Greg had a very good time, though. I think he was expecting
something a little more exotic. The lady explained that we
were fortunate to live on one of America's four great migratory paths, the Mississippi flyway. Evidently, during the fall
and spring migrations, there are a lot of unusual specimens
coming through. Unfortunately, Greg's taken up the hobby a
month too late and most of the unusual ones have already
come and gone." Andrea shrugged. "Now he has to wait until
May."

Karen chuckled, "That must be driving him crazy. He never
was too good at goal postponement."

"I've noticed," Andrea returned dryly, thinking of their
own relationship, but the remark went over Karen's head.

Tim interceded. "Listen, Andrea, if he's going to sulk in
his room much longer, maybe you'd better help me. I need
someone to hold the level while I position this cabinet and tell
me when I've got it right."

"Sorry, *mon cher*." Andrea carelessly waltzed her way to
the doorway connecting the dining room and kitchen. "I'm
working in here today. Let the Credit Prince help you, they

belong to him anyway. I didn't want the darn cabinets in the first place."

"Andrea," Tim retorted, "you're being a trifle small about all of this. He was thinking of you."

She had intended to go blithely on her way, but that stung. "Just as I'm sure my father's buy-now, pay-later purchases were all intended to benefit my mother. No, thank you. I don't need that kind of devotion."

Tim wasn't finished with her, though. Not yet. It was time for her to put another aspect of her childhood into perspective, ready or not.

"Listen here, young lady," he said, sounding paternal. "Have you ever stopped to think about how much rental apartments go for these days? You looked for him. You should know. Then put food, utilities and laundry on top of that. Now think of the small sum he pays you for the room and all those services. You've made it possible for him to well afford a hefty monthly payment on the furniture he bought the other day and these cabinets and *still* come out smelling like a rose. It's time you stopped trying to push him into your father's mold. Greg's a far cry from going down the tubes yet. Now get the level, would you?"

Andrea looked at him a little uncertainly. He had a knack for making her seem petty when he discussed her differences with Greg. Sighing, she capitulated. "All right, all right. Where is it?"

"It's on top of the refrigerator, and stop looking like Saint Joan at the stake. I'm sorry to have to yell at you, but someone has to make you see reason. He loves you. You love him. It's elemental. Stop building complications into it."

"I said 'all right,' didn't I?" She retrieved the tool and plopped it on the cabinet Tim was propping into place. Leaning over, she squinted. "The bubble's off to the right...oops, too much, back a little the other way...almost, just a hair... There."

"Great," Tim grunted. "Draw a line on the wall across the

top so I can put it down and start some screw holes into the studs.''

"Well, hurry it up," Andrea grumbled as she followed his instructions. "I want to make some hot chocolate. I can't seem to get warm after being outside all morning."

Tim quirked an inquisitive eyebrow in her direction. "For as long as I've known you, you've frozen all winter, every winter. Why don't you break down and turn up the heat?"

Andrea gave an inelegant snort and turned away. Always cold, hah! Not anymore. He should have seen her last night!

Greg came back into the room seemingly in an improved frame of mind. He and Tim began to battle with the new cabinets while Andrea hovered over the hot pot where she warmed her hands as well as the water for hot chocolate.

Work progressed quickly until an hour or two after a slap-dash cold-cuts lunch. Karen sorted the spices, throwing out anything more than a year out of code and munching on a cache of Oreos she'd found. Andrea went back and forth between Greg and Tim, proclaiming cabinets level, fetching assorted drill bits and screws, and providing slivers of wood with which cabinets were shimmied. Her head buzzed, but just being in Greg's presence had a way of doing that to her. However, gradually it began to ache with an intensity that threatened to virtually incapacitate her. She gave in to the inevitable when Tim, who stood three steps up on the ladder, kept missing the screwdriver she was holding up to his back and finally turned to see where she was.

"My God, Andrea, you're as pale as can be. Why didn't you say something? You're sick, aren't you? Go to bed. We'll manage without you."

Karen looked up from her rolls of unwound shelf paper and set her scissors down. "You look awful," she concurred. "I'll plug in the hot pot again and bring you in a cup of tea. Go tuck yourself in and put the blanket on high. I'll try to find a thermometer for you once I get the water going."

"It really isn't necessary, Karen. Don't go to all that bother. I'll be fine. Really." *Oh, my.* She shouldn't have shaken her head no like that, she realized, because the room was definitely spinning. And she wasn't going to talk anymore, either. Her voice was reverberating around the inside of her head like a drumroll in an echo chamber.

Greg had been consumed with wrestling another cabinet in through the back door when Karen led Andrea from the room. At first he'd noticed nothing suspicious, as Karen had come back and put on more water for tea; she and Andrea often had tea in the afternoon. But when he observed her putting the small pot on a tray along with a mug and disappearing into Andrea's room, it clicked: Something was wrong.

Karen almost dumped the boiling pot into Andrea's lap when Greg came bursting through the door demanding, "What's going on? What's wrong with Andrea?"

"Nothing is wrong with Andrea," Andrea mumbled through pain-stiffened lips. "Other than the fact that I'm dying, everything is just fine. Now go away. I'm not up to entertaining at the moment." She closed her rapidly glazing eyes and concentrated on not hyperventilating.

Greg took her at her word and began a one-man crusade to stave off her dire fate. "Karen, go get my bag out of my room. And hurry up about it, will you? She looks awful." He raked an exasperated hand through his sawdust-powdered hair, stopping when he only succeeded in inflicting pain as his fingers caught in the tight curls. "I don't understand it. You seemed fine earlier on our walk. What is it, your stomach? Your head? Do you still have your appendix? Maybe I ought to take you to the emergency room. Is your hospitalization any good?" Turning to Karen in irritation as he noticed her still gawking at the end of the bed, he spoke harshly. "Where is my bag? What are you waiting for, Christmas?"

"Greg," Karen said in amazement. "If this is an example of your bedside manner, I think you ought to reconsider your vocation in life. A doctor can't afford to fall apart every time somebody gets a little ache or pain."

"Can we go into your analysis of my career choice later on? Just get the bag." He studied Andrea's pale countenance

"'Little ache,' my foot. It's probably double pneumonia. Maybe strep throat." He picked up her hand and patted it solicitously. "I wonder where we could get a culture done without having to wait at the hospital."

Andrea shook her head in despair and was again immediately sorry as the room went into a tailspin. He was talking about hospitals, infected lungs and throat cultures. But he had yet to even ask what part of her body actually hurt. "Greg," she informed him, "I just have a headache. I'm probably catching a cold or the flu. There's no need to get so excited. I'm just going to lie down for a while, and I'll be fine. Scout's honor."

"I take it all back, Andrea," Karen advised as she came back into the room. "You were right, but for the wrong reasons. If you marry him, he'll drive you crazy every time you sneeze. This must be why doctors don't treat their own families. They fall apart at the seams when it's one of their own."

That got Andrea's attention. *Is that why he was so upset? Was she really one of his own?*

Greg paid Karen no heed, his attention totally on Andrea's suffering visage. He popped open his bag and stared in disgust at its limited contents. He could listen to her heart and lungs. That was about it. "Sit up a little, honey. I want to listen at your back."

Honey. He had called her honey. Wasn't that the sweetest thing? Even though Greg was bellowing around the room like a wounded buffalo, making her head clang like the largest bell in the church belfry, it suddenly all struck her as rather... sweet. Boy, she must really be sicker than she thought.

Greg took her temperature and found it slightly raised. "Do you have any aspirin substitute?"

She held her head to still the echoing his booming voice had caused and whispered through gritted teeth, "You bought some last night, remember? But I'm not going to take it unless this gets a whole lot worse. All that stuff nauseates me."

Greg stared at her in open astonishment. It was clear he

thought she had more than one loose screw in her brain. "This is ridiculous," Greg spoke indignantly. "You're virtually incapacitated, and we should try to get your temperature down."

"It's not all that high, Greg. And it seems to me a clear-cut case of the cure being worse than the disease. I told you. The pills make me throw up and my temperature's not that bad. If you would just let me sleep it off, I'm sure I'd be okay in no time."

He felt her head one more time, possibly for luck, she suspected. His calm, more collected medical demeanor was rapidly slipping into place now that his sense of emergency was fading.

"Well, I suppose you know your own body."

She should hope she did. But he still looked doubtful as he pulled the covers up to her chin and kissed her pain-puckered forehead.

"Stay in bed and try to sleep. When I'm done with Tim, I'll make a can of bean-and-bacon soup and some popcorn for dinner. It's not gourmet, but it'll be filling. Call if you want Karen to make a fresh pot of tea."

Andrea's appalled voice stopped his exit. "Popcorn and beans for dinner?" How could anyone face such a prospect? Her weakened condition certainly precluded even the mere thought.

Gently he chided her. "Surely you know popcorn and baked beans are incomplete proteins that complement each other perfectly. Like red beans and rice. Buck up. It won't be so bad." There seemed to be a slightly sadistic gleam in his eye as he continued. "Besides, I thought you'd be ecstatic to see me using soup in the menu."

With amazing agility for a man his size, he was through the door and had it closed before she could manufacture an effective retort.

Andrea's headache proved to be not much more than that. Work on the house progressed nicely as winter slowly lost its grip on Chicago. December, January and February passed in breath-fogging tones of gray. The kitchen was finished and gorgeous. The old Formica table had been replaced with a work island/breakfast bar complete with an indoor grill. Karen's stomach had assumed astonishing proportions. The dining room sported lush paper on its walls and magnificent pecan-tone cabinets in its corners. Tim was only a few weeks short of his law degree and had three job offers with good, reliable—although not LaSalle Street—firms. Tim informed them that all those fancy downtown firms weren't ready for his brilliance anyhow, and he'd give them a few more years to prepare his office suite before tackling that bastion of high-powered partnerships.

Greg was the only fly in the ointment. He had spent December and January working on Andrea along with the house. He had taken up unofficial residency in Karen and Tim's vacated first-floor bedroom. And for those two months he had seemed firmly entrenched. Even his sister Loretta had stopped calling and Andrea was sure she was suspected of sorcery.

Things had begun to fall apart in February. Greg's personality dictated action on knotty problems. That trait of his was in direct conflict with Andrea's cautious approach to life. He saw no progress in their stand-off. She felt like a penniless orphan in front of a candy-store window display. My, how she wanted it, but she was afraid she didn't have or even truly know the price.

Greg's practice blossomed. Andrea was eaten up with jealousy each time the phone rang. How could so many honey-voiced women's bodies all malfunction at the same time? Sometimes at night she dreamed of them crawling out of the bungalow's woodwork and sliding into the bed just down the hall, comforting Greg while she shivered in her solitary bed with nothing but knee socks, flannel gown and robe, and an electric blanket. Andrea just knew it was only a matter of time before Greg forgot whatever it had been that had attracted him to her in the first place and took up with one of the mellow-sounding sweethearts on the other end of the phone wire. She was cynical enough to suspect they weren't all flocking to his office just for his medical skills. *Heck no!* They had eyes, just as she did.

Greg spent early February harassing her unmercifully. He had an uncanny ability to zero in on her weakest spot and worry at it like a dog with a bone. First there were her middle-class mores and the old double standard. What if the school found out she was living with a man? What would the parents say? What would *her* parents say? Definitely hitting below the belt.

It was the last week in February before Greg, tenacious to the end, finally admitted defeat. The confrontation took place in the kitchen, where so many of their confrontations had. Pots were tossed about and scrubbed with enough vigor to remove their aluminum coating along with the grease. Andrea suspected he would have gladly substituted her neck, given the opportunity.

Was she or was she not going to marry him in the foreseeable future?

She just wasn't ready to make that commitment quite yet.

Had he or had he not given her over three months to think about things since he had gotten serious?

He had indeed.

Did she or did she not love him?

She suspected she did.

Did she believe he loved her?

She wanted to...

He threw up his hands in disgust, soapsuds flying in all directions. They spattered on the floor, on the clean drying kettles and on Andrea herself. That had done it. He gave up. Nothing he did convinced her of his love. Not his lack of dates—and he'd had plenty of opportunities—not all the work he had put in on her house when he should have been concentrating on building up his practice, nor his patience in waiting for her to come around, nothing.

Greg fixed her with a narrow-eyed stare. ''I've found a nice apartment between Northwestern University and the hospital. I'm going to sign the lease tomorrow and move this weekend.

It's available the first, which is Thursday, but I'm too busy to shop for a bed and such until Saturday.''

Andrea literally wrung her hands. Just when she'd finally gotten used to him being around, he was going to take his marbles and go home. Well, she'd always known he would. That was why she hadn't wanted to make a commitment, wasn't it? But Saturday was only five days away! And good grief, the bungalow was almost as much his as hers at this point.

"What about the cabinets?" she asked. "And the dining-room furniture you bought? The Murphy bed we're refinishing down in the basement?" She looked at everything around her, bewildered. Without Greg, the place would be almost person-ality-less. Heavens, she still had the Golden Gate Bridge in her garage, just waiting for a warm spring day to be set up in the backyard. Even though she'd known this was coming, it was still catching her by surprise somehow.

"Keep 'em," he said disgustedly. "They're only things, Andrea. They can't keep you warm at night the way I could have."

"But...but they were so expensive..."

Again he snorted in derision. "When are you going to get over your money hang-ups? Money buys *things*. That's all it's good for. Big deal. And money certainly can't buy me what I really want...your love...now can it? So what good does it do me?"

When she just stared at him, he threw the dish towel he had been drying his hands with down on the cabinets and left the room with what sounded an awful lot like a snarl....

Tuesday, Wednesday and Thursday evenings he had watched her, following her every move until she felt ready to break apart. What was he looking for? She actually felt like porcelain. One good bump, and she would shatter. And late that night, in the bed heated only by electricity, she worked to bring herself back under control. If tomorrow night was to be their last together, she wanted to remember it with pleasure. The end of a cherishing time. Sleep came with the determination to have as normal a day as possible followed by as warm an evening as possible. She would not crack.

And then it was morning. Andrea sat on one of her new breakfast stools and bemusedly gazed across the breakfast bar. She looked past Greg's dark head, which was bent over the *Tribune*'s sports section, and stared out the recently installed triple-glazed window. Absently she cradled her breakfast milk shake and wondered if it would actually reach the predicted seventy-one degrees. It was only March 2 and Chicago winters never gave up that easily. It had to be a trick of some sort.

Andrea rose and rinsed her glass in the sink. Turning back to Greg's engrossed face, she inquired, ''Do you want a cup of coffee before I go?'' The thought of leaving didn't seem to be breaking him apart, she thought a little resentfully. He seemed as relaxed and calm as could be.

The sound of her voice broke the early-morning quiet and Greg glanced up with a start. ''What? Oh, no, I guess not. This is fine, thanks.'' He indicated his own glass containing the dregs of his breakfast drink with a wave of his hand and frowned. ''It says here they may not be able to have Wrigley Field ready for the Cubs opener. All the snow we've had has kept them from working on the field. It's been too muddy since the snow's melted and now there's more snow expected when the cool front comes through later on today.''

''That's too bad,'' Andrea responded, sounding almost sincere. *Who the heck cared?* How could he discuss baseball at a time like this? Well, if he could forget the morning's real significance, so could she.

She forced her thoughts into returning to more practical matters. Maybe if the warm weather was only due to last a day, she'd better figure out something to do with the girls outside. Early spring fever would be a foregone conclusion on a day like today. The parking lot should be dry enough to use if the field wasn't.

Again she glanced at Greg's closely cropped mahogany curls as she kissed him and readied herself to leave. She loved him, she acknowledged. But she hadn't been able to bring herself to the point of commitment and babies yet. She wanted to, at least on an intellectual plane, and she hoped Greg understood that. A while back, he had said he would wait for her to come to him, to tell him when she had successfully cleared all the hurdles. But she suspected that tomorrow's move signified the end of his patience.

Andrea felt petty and small as she absently patted a hand along the kitchen windowsill, searching for her car keys. What was wrong with her that she couldn't trust in his love enough to take that final step? She was managing to open up enough on other fronts. There had been a serious money discussion late one night in front of a fireplace so hot, the flames burned with a blue light. Of course, that had been when Greg had talked in terms of "us" and "ours." Now she guessed that it was back to "me" and "you."

He had been ill at ease that night, and she had known why as soon as he blurted out, "Andrea, I'd like to see you mortgage the house."

She had forced herself to remain pliant in his arms, but internally her stomach had twisted into knots. Her mind had raced in two conflicting directions at once. This was the man she purported to love. Love without trust was nothing. But a mortgage on her hard-won clear title? Oh, no.

"If you'll study the tax laws, you'll see that it makes a great deal of sense for a person in our tax bracket to have a mortgage. Not only can you deduct the interest off the income tax, but you could use the capital freed to invest in tax-free investments, like a retirement savings plan or something. Especially once we're married and filing jointly, we'll end up saving a lot in the long run. I'd like to show you some facts and figures if you'll let me." He'd treated their marriage as a foregone conclusion back then.

Rationally, Andrea had known that what he was saying made sense, but emotionally...oh, no. Her house. His wary posture exuded defensiveness and she'd wondered if her own anxieties were as easily read. It was hard, but she had forced herself to follow her new line of trust. "No, I don't want to see any facts or figures, Greg." Then she hurried to allay his clear disappointment. "No, it's not that. It's just, well...I trust you in this. If you feel that's the proper way to handle the available funds, then I'll do it." Poking fun at her own cold feet, she wryly added, "Don't take it wrong if I keep a little that's easily liquidated, okay? Just in case I revert to my usual chicken behavior and decide to run."

Collapsing on top of her, Greg had ruffled his hands through her hair and leered menacingly, "It's too late now, baby. You couldn't run fast enough. You'll never get away from me."

The soft pile of the area rug had tickled the nape of her neck as he had proceeded to demonstrate the extent of her captivity. Holding her hands over her head in one of his own, he had let the other roam the slender length of her neck and down over the gentle curves of her breasts. Her shirt had been easily pulled up and out of the way, and he had bent to kiss the trembling tips of the small uncovered mounds.

"Oh, Andrea," he had breathed as she arched helplessly underneath him. "You've come so far. There's such a little distance left. Hurry, love. I'm a glutton. I want everything. I'm waiting for the day you come to me freely, trusting in me and my love. Give me the gift of all of you, and not just the inconsequential things. On that day you won't be able to keep me out of your bed and we'll start a loving worth something and a marriage worth sharing." His head had dipped, allowing his tongue to torment the shallow well of her navel. "It's so hard to be patient. Don't make me wait forever. Come to me soon."

Her stomach had trembled against the slight force of his breathy plea. "I'm trying, Greg," she'd whispered in return, craving his touch and no longer surprised by that knowledge.

"It would be good between us, Andrea. I know it."

"Would it, Greg? I've taught all the facts...but I never...this is...different than I expected."

"And this is just the tip of the iceberg, sweetheart. You and I, we could have it all, if only you'll let us." She was never really sure if she heard him, since they'd drifted off in front of the fire soon after, but he'd never mentioned it again in such a serious vein. Instead, he had teased her and watched with hot, hungry eyes that spoke of his impatience. But his waiting was over now. He was calling the game. Her side had defaulted, and he'd be out looking for a more willing partner after tomorrow.

Andrea's thoughts were cut off as she frowned at the empty windowsill. "Greg, do you know..."

Reaching around to the countertop behind him, Greg's hand disappeared between two of her new harvest-gold Tupperware canisters, reappearing a moment later, the missing keys dangling from a crooked finger. His eyes never leaving the paper, he informed her in preoccupied tones, "Your shoes are under the radiator in the bathroom."

"They are? How'd they get there? Never mind. Thanks." He was obviously too engrossed in the continuing saga of the mayor versus the city council to be paying much attention to the migratory patterns of her running shoes. She retrieved them and left. The promise of a beautiful day was somehow spoiled by her self-acknowledged failure to take that final step in trust.

Chapter Ten

The cold front arrived halfway through seventh period. Thankfully, that was Andrea's last teaching class of the day. She herded the girls in to shower in preparation for their biology class and wondered why she bothered. The addition of a little honest sweat could not possibly worsen the odor of the formaldehyde-soaked fetal pigs being dissected in that wing of the school.

She watched as the mercury plummeted. Forty-two degrees in forty-five minutes, until it hovered just below freezing. Lead-gray clouds blanketed the sky in foreboding until they finally severed earth from the last persistent ray escaping the sun's ball of orange.

Andrea left the school building just about then and edged her yellow car out from between a colleague's battered station wagon and a visiting parent's shiny sedan. Anxiously she glanced skyward as the first fat flakes drifted down in aimless abandon. She'd better stop at the grocery. These were typical Chicago blizzard conditions. The clash of a retreating warm front and militant cool front mixed with the possibility of lake-effect snow and barely freezing temperatures could easily combine to spell big trouble. She watched a flake settle on the windshield, not fooled by the wiper's momentary success in dealing with it. These were fat, lacy flakes. Anyone knew big fat ones mounted up much faster than the little pellet kind. What's more, Chicago was ripe for a blizzard. There hadn't been more than five or six inches of snow on the ground at any one time in the past two winters.

Just to be safe, five days' worth of groceries were loaded into the rear of the car. She had bought two gallons of milk. There was something about having milk in the house when you were snowed in and cut off from the world that lent a sense of security, even if you never drank the stuff. But they would drink it, she assured herself self-righteously. There was Karen to think of. Pregnant women needed lots of milk. Otherwise the baby would take the calcium from the mother and Karen's teeth would rot. She went back and got a third gallon.

There were two inches of snow on the ground by the time she slid down the alley and parked the car safely in the ramshackle garage. She eyed it critically as she went around to the back of the car to retrieve the groceries. The garage would have to be next on the list. With her luck, she'd find the weight of some new snow collapsing the roof of the thing on her meticulously polished car if she didn't remodel it by next winter.

Dropping her keys and purse into the top of the nearest bag, she grabbed that one and its neighbor and began lugging them up to the house. "Hi," she said brightly to Karen, who had seen her struggling and was holding the back door open. "Have you listened to the weather at all? What are they predicting?"

Karen eyed the groceries suspiciously. "What'd you do? Buy out the store?"

Andrea ignored her condescending tone. She hadn't bought anything they wouldn't eventually use. She just wouldn't have to go to the store for a while, that was all. She set sacks on the countertop and paused to catch her breath before going back for the rest. "Better to be safe," she puffed dismissively.

"What're they saying? I missed it on the car radio while I was in the store."

Karen looked at her in pitying superiority. "The way you overreact to a few snowflakes, one would think you must have been snowed in for a month with no food or supplies at an early, impressionable age." Shaking her head in mock disparagement, she enlightened her. "We're only due for four to six inches, a little more by the lake. Since it's Friday and they're expecting temperatures around thirty-five to forty all weekend, there'll be no problems by rush hour Monday morning. You see?" she questioned rhetorically to Andrea's retreating back as she left to carry in the rest of her purchases. "You've done it again. It's March, for crying out loud. What did you expect? Oh, my Lord. Three gallons of milk?"

By six o'clock at least four inches of snow had fallen, the beauty of its whiteness lost in the increasingly hazardous swirls of thick flakes. Andrea hummed around the stove, checking the simmering stew and adding a can of cream of mushroom to thicken its gravy. She covered her bread dough and set it out to rise. There was something about the weather that brought out the pioneer spirit in her and demanded a bit of bread-baking.

Greg came out of the bathroom freshly attired in clean though threadbare jeans, loose sweatshirt and no shoes. If only those swooning women patients of his could see him now. She looked at him critically. They'd still swoon. He looked darn good, even in faded blue jeans and worn socks with holes in the heels.

He noticed the four place settings as he passed the open dining-room French doors. "Karen and Tim coming down tonight?" The closely knit group still ate supper together several times a week.

Andrea nodded in affirmation. "I don't think they're going to stay very long, though. Karen cleaned their apartment from one end to the other for some reason, and she's pretty tired. She wants to go to bed early."

Greg chuckled in appreciation. "I know how she feels. I've

been up since that phone call at one this morning. I'm dead on my feet." He stretched and yawned in a visual demonstration of the extent of his fatigue. "But if she does that again closer to the end of the month, make her stop. She should start conserving her energy. A lot of women get that last burst of energy and use it up housecleaning instead of recognizing it as a sign of impending delivery and saving it up for the long haul of labor. Keep your eye on her," he instructed, before finally stopping the fascinating display of stretching his muscles.

"Roger. Will do." Andrea saluted in acknowledgement of his order. Then, because she didn't want to dwell on the time coming when he wouldn't be there to stop her himself, she asked, "How was the delivery last night? I didn't think to ask this morning."

"Not bad, just long. They only called me in so early in the labor because the husband was falling apart and had his poor wife half crazy. She couldn't keep herself under control and take care of him, too. It happens some times." He shrugged dismissively. "Especially when the man refuses to properly prepare himself and go to childbirth classes. I finally had to ask him to leave the room. He had absolutely no idea what to expect and certainly wasn't expecting what he got."

Andrea looked at him in wide-eyed astonishment. "Wasn't the wife angry with you?"

"Actually, she was relieved. Without his fussing and fuming we got her back to proper breathing techniques, and she was fine. She said it served him right. It'll be a good long time before he's back in her good graces, I suspect. He missed one of the peak emotional highs of his marriage through his own damn fault." He wagged his head in disbelief at the man's evident stupidity.

Thoughtfully Andrea stirred the stew, this time adding a cup of sour cream and a healthy slug of red wine to the broth before turning off the flame and reaching for a hot pad to rescue the browning biscuits from the oven. She didn't hear Greg's approach until his arms encircled her. His hands caressed her flat belly while his lips moistly nibbled her neck, burrowing provocatively beneath the silky lengths of black hair.

"I helped that baby into the world, and all I could think of was how much I wished you could have trusted in my love."

Andrea found it grating the way he was speaking in the past tense now.

"I'd have had a tough time keeping my hands to myself if you were swollen with our child," he advised. "And if you were laboring to give birth, no force on this earth would have been strong enough to pull me from your side." His hands came gliding up to cup her rapidly swelling breasts in their strong, capable grasp. As he applied an aching, wonderfully firm pressure to them, he whispered in her ear, and his warm breath made her shiver as it gently gusted against her soft cheek. "After the baby's born, the father—that would have been me—cuts the cord, making the child his own person, his own entity. They hand him to the mother—that would have been you—and I'd have helped you put him to your breast. God, Andrea, you have no idea what a special moment that is—the intense emotional bonding I have seen between a husband and wife in the delivery room. Grown men weeping, supercilious little smiles plastered ear to ear, they're so moved by the miracle of life before them."

Surreptitiously, he wiped a glistening eye before reclaiming her breast and gently pressing her to lean back against him. "I fully intend to do my share of eye wiping when my time comes," he said. "I'll admit I've come damn close just watching other couples."

Andrea turned in his arms, locking her own arms around the back of his neck. She was filled with the wonder of Greg's harshly whispered words and his total ease with his own manliness that he could confess to an ability to not only cry, but to anticipate with pleasure a time when he would do it in public, his emotions raw and open for all to see. With each new insight he gave into himself, he made her love for him deepen further, as it did at that moment. Inside her, the fear of losing her chance of sharing a life with him was beginning to balance with the worry of jumping into a marriage without being certain.

There was an unspoken agreement that dinner was to be a lighthearted affair. Frequent trips to the window confirmed the radio's observation that the storm center had stalled over the city, the heavily laden lead clouds intent on dumping their entire contents before moving on. Twelve inches of snow lay on the ground by ten o'clock and it was falling so thickly that anything standing more than two feet outside the windowpane was lost in the intense whiteout. Andrea's spirits rose as the drifts grew. There was no way Greg was going to be able to move this weekend, and he was too busy at work to do so during the week. She might get another whole week of Greg in her life as a result of this ridiculous March blizzard.

After dinner the room's four occupants lounged in front of a determined fire that crackled and spit in an effort to rid itself of the moisture and snow clinging to its newly fetched log offerings. There was no need to panic; Andrea had bought enough groceries for several days. It being March, streets would be plowed or the snow melted to an easily accessible level within a day or two. Greg had no imminent deliveries of his own and he was not on call for the other doctors this weekend. He must realize that his move would have to be delayed, but he didn't seem unduly upset. And there was no other reason not to enjoy the novelty of being snowed in so late in the year.

Karen lay on the floor doing exercises designed to ease the pressure in the small of her back. It seemed to help. "Good thing the baby's not due for close to three weeks," she huffed. "Be just my luck to deliver in a blizzard."

Greg carelessly agreed. "Yep. I'm glad I'm not on call. Anyone due anytime soon is probably in labor right about now. Severe changes in the barometric pressure like we've had today tend to get things moving. Full moon, too, according to some people, and we've got both tonight."

"You're kidding."

"God's truth." Greg drew a pious cross over his heart.
"Cross my heart and hope to die." He sat up, supporting
himself on his forearms, and Andrea knew they were in for a
lecture pulled from his fund of trivia. "We tend to forget
man's affinity with the elements as civilization gets more and
more sophisticated, taking us further and further from nature
by creating these unnatural climates...warmth from central
heating in the winter, air-conditioned cool in summer." He
seemed to realize he was starting to lose track of his topic and
gathered himself into an upright, seated posture to make a
better presentation. "As I said, we've lost sight of the close
affinity man and nature originally operated under. All kinds
of things affected man. Tides, full moons, whatever..." He
waved his hand in a distracted gesture. "They all affected us,
even down to regulating our sex drive. Still do to some extent,
in fact."

Karen and Andrea both gasped a simultaneous *"What?"*

Greg was not to be swayed. "No, really. For example,
Karen, didn't you tell me your baby was due toward the end
of the month?"

Karen eyed him suspiciously and answered slowly, "I'm
due the twenty-first."

"Ah, the twenty-first of March. Couldn't be better. How
terribly primitive of you two."

Tim looked intrigued. Curiously, he asked, "Why's that?"

"I just know you shouldn't have asked," Karen groaned.

Greg was thoroughly warmed to his topic now and ignored
Karen in favor of answering Tim. "Primitive man, naturally
enough, spent a lot of his time outdoors. Now," he quizzed
Karen, "when is the longest day of the year? The day man
would be exposed to the most sunshine?"

"Anybody knows that," Karen groused. "The summer solstice. When is it, the twentieth or twenty-first of June?"

Greg congratulated her with a brilliant smile, quite taking
Andrea's breath away. That smile could belong to her.

"Right. Now a woman getting pregnant around then would
carry through the summer, fall and winter. She'd deliver nine

months later, right around the spring equinox, sometime during the last half of March or so.''

Tim looked puzzled. "So?"

"So," Greg explained. "A baby born at that time of the year would have six full months of decent weather, possibly more, to grow and mature before the hard winter months set in, giving him a much better chance of survival."

In spite of herself, Andrea broke in, "You're going to tell us that the tides are high in the middle of June, right? And they drove early man into a sexual frenzy, causing him to impregnate any female within his range."

Greg frowned in her direction. "Not very likely."

"Okay, I give up. What got to him around the solstice that provided for all those springtime births?" Karen ungraciously questioned, finally giving in to her curiosity.

"Pay attention, now," Greg instructed. "This is good. There's a gland at the base of your throat. It's very light sensitive and," he paused dramatically, "one of the hormones it manufactures is a sexual stimulant. Being light sensitive, it works overtime during the month of June when the days are the longest, putting primitive man's libido into overdrive and thereby ensuring lots of early-spring babies." He sat back, looking highly pleased with himself.

Tim only looked puzzled. "But if this gland is on the inside, how does the light get to it to sensitize it?"

"Skin is translucent, not opaque. Filtered light does get through, especially in a narrow area such as the throat."

Andrea was rather intrigued by the entire discussion. "And here I thought baby booms were caused by electrical blackouts."

Greg and Karen laughed and Tim observed. "Huh. I happen to know they're caused by...ouch!" He rubbed the rib Karen had reached with her kick and gave her a wounded look. She didn't look the least penitent, having given up her back presses to deliver the blow.

"They don't want to hear your theories, Tim, dear," she

advised sweetly. "Let them use their imagination, why don't you?"

For such a sweet little thing, she had a way of getting her point across. "Uh, sure. Well, anyway, here we are now, about to become proud parents." He placed his hand on his wife's stomach, watching his hand jump as his child moved underneath it. "I'm really looking forward to it. I don't regret a thing. Even if I've infringed a little on a friendship in the process, it's all worked out perfectly. We'll figure out some way of paying you two back later." He thought a moment. "How about free legal services for the rest of your life?" He looked expectantly to the spot where Greg's head lay resting on Andrea's tummy, noticing the absentminded, loving finger play Greg was being treated to as Andrea's hands roved the thicket of curls, gently massaging the lines of fatigue from the corners of his eyes and teasingly tugging the lobes of his ears.

Karen, too, noticed and musingly commented, "Maybe we've already paid you back, eh Andrea? After all, had we not been living with you, you'd never have met Prince Charming, here."

"Yes, Greg's a very special friend," Andrea responded awkwardly, not exactly sure what else she could say. It certainly wasn't what Greg wanted to hear because she could feel him fall back emotionally—there was a tensing in the mood of the room just before he withdrew physically.

"I'm tired," he announced, stretching and yawning to add veracity to the claim. "Feel free to stay and fire-gaze, guys, but I was up most of the night and need to catch a few winks." He looked at Andrea intently. "I'd hoped you'd be coming with me by this point, light of my life. But I guess we're both relegated to another night of thinking about might-have-beens."

He left the room, but the easy mood was gone. Tim and Karen excused themselves and Andrea went to bed shortly thereafter, but Greg's words continued to buzz through her head—just as he had intended, she was sure.

She lay there a long time. Her foot dangled restlessly out

from under the covers. She couldn't sleep. All she could do was think of Greg. The thought of the nights he had mentioned sharing brought a warm flush, and she kicked her foot farther out from under the blankets in a useless attempt to regulate her body temperature.

They'd been in bed a little over an hour. Was that enough of a nap that she could go wake him up for a last little necking session? Sort of a last hurrah, as it were. It just might be possible to work him out of her system once and for all.

She gave the idea serious thought. Maybe if she gave him twenty more minutes. Surely that would be enough sleep to revitalize him.

She listened as a door shut somewhere overhead, followed by the sound of running water. What was wrong up there, for heaven's sake? That was the third trip to the bathroom tonight. She wondered if Greg thought four and five trips to the bathroom every night during a nine-month pregnancy produced a bonding effect in a marriage, or was it just the actual delivery? How did he feel about bonding during the 2:00 a.m. feeding?

Wait a minute, the footsteps were heading in the wrong direction. They were going into the kitchenette, not back to bed. And the lightness of the steps sounded like Karen's. More running water. Andrea could almost visualize the filled tea-kettle being thumped down on the burner and the flame being flicked on. No other footsteps. Tim must be sleeping.

Andrea wriggled out of the tangle she had created of her blankets. A cup of tea with Karen might be just the thing. Maybe she'd find some herbal so they wouldn't be drinking caffeine at this time of night.

"Hi," she whispered, coming through the door. "You need some company?"

"Hi, yourself," Karen answered back listlessly. "You can't come in. Tim might wake up and come out. He's taken to sleeping in the buff lately. He thinks it's going to save time getting dressed when we have to go to the hospital." Karen shrugged in defeat. "What a joke. I'm going to be pregnant forever."

Andrea pushed the door a little farther open and sidled past Karen's boldly extended stomach. "Don't you worry," she whispered confidentially. "Did I ever tell you about the time Lisa and I decided to get even with Tim after he cut her doll's hair off at the roots and gave it to his hamster to nest with?" She ushered a glum Karen in the direction of the kitchenette. "Let me assure you, what with growing up next door to each other and one thing or another, I've seen pretty much of what that boy has to offer. It would be difficult to offend my tender sensibilities at this point."

Karen laughed in spite of herself. "You guys must have driven your parents wild."

"Oh, we did, we did," Andrea assured her. "Now tell me what your problem is. How come you're still awake?"

"God, I don't know. My back hurts no matter how many back presses I do, the baby's never coming, and I feel so weepy and shaky. I think I'm getting the flu. Even my stomach is all cramped."

Andrea settled back in a kitchen chair and studied the dejected features of her friend's face while they waited for the tea to brew. "Look at it this way: If you catch the flu now, you're sure to be over it by the time you deliver. You've got two and a half weeks left, after all. And I guarantee you, you won't be pregnant forever. The laws of nature preclude the possibility."

Karen gave an unladylike snort, expressing her opinion of the laws of nature. "It'll be just my luck to be the first ten-year pregnancy in the medical books."

"You want me to go downstairs and ask Greg if there's anything you can take to help you sleep?" It was a better reason for waking him up than anything else she had thought of so far.

Her plans were bound for failure, however, as Karen brushed away the offer. "No, don't do that. I'll be fine. Sometimes you just need a good cry, you know?"

Sometimes you needed other things as well. And it was rapidly becoming obvious that Andrea's needs were bound to remain unappeased. Under the circumstances it would be better to be a good scout and try to help Karen since she was the only option available at the moment. "Go get the cards." Andrea sighed in resignation. "We'll play Old Maid and I'll tell you about the time Tim, Lisa and I got assigned the leads in the second-grade production of *Beauty and the Beast.* Lisa was the beauty, Tim was the prince after the beast got kissed, and I was the beast."

Karen was already giggling and Andrea stopped in her narrative to admonish her, "Well, go get the cards. That's not even the funny part. Now that I think about it, breaking the zipper and getting stuck sweating inside a hairy-beast outfit twice my size wasn't particularly funny either."

Peering into the pot sometime later, Karen stopped giggling long enough to inform her cohort, "We're out of tea again. That was the second pot."

"We couldn't be." Andrea leaned forward to inspect the pot and frowned. "I can't believe it. I suppose we'll both float away if we make a third. I was all set to tell you about the sterling blind date that sadist you're married to fixed me up with for the freshman cotillion, too."

Checking the digital clock on the oven, Karen grimaced and announced, "It's three o'clock. We really ought to try to get some sleep. I'm not feeling sorry for myself any more, but my stomach feels worse than ever." She stood up and groaned, "All that tea sloshing around down there. Yuck."

Andrea was drawn toward the living-area window and absently looked out. "No sign of any letup," she advised. "There's darn close to two feet of snow out there." She turned, thinking to tell Karen good-night, and was shocked to find her bent over, gripping a chair back with tightly clenched fists.

"My God, what's wrong? You really are sick, aren't you?"

"It's this damn back. As soon as I think it's letting up, it comes back again. It's going to be one hell of a home stretch if this keeps up."

"I'm going to get Greg," Andrea informed her. "There

must be some crazy exercise that could help alleviate that. God knows he had a long enough list of them he wants me to teach.'' She strode determinedly toward the door leading to the steps. ''Don't move. We'll be right back.''

Ruthlessly Andrea ripped the pillow Greg clutched from his grasp and shook his shoulder.

''Hmm? What is it?'' he groggily responded.

''Wake up, Greg. Karen needs you.''

''I'm awake. I'm awake. What does she need?''

''She's been awake all night. Her back's killing her.''

''How do you know? Have you been awake too? What's wrong with you?''

Andrea eyed him impatiently. She wasn't going to be drawn into a discussion on that right now. ''Never mind why I'm awake. I just am. We've been drinking tea and playing cards but now she's in pain. Listen, would some of those weird things you were describing for that prenatal exercise class you wanted me to teach help her? She needs some sleep.''

''Don't we all,'' Greg observed drolly. He groaned as Andrea ruthlessly pulled the sheet and blanket away. Rolling to the edge of the bed and pulling himself to a sitting position, he sat there for a moment adjusting his eyes to the light before reaching for a robe and gray sweat socks to protect his feet from the chill of the floor. ''All right, I'm ready. Lead on. But she had better be in extreme pain.''

Evidently Tim had awakened during the interim. His face was twisted into a mask of concern as the two trooped back up the stairs. ''Maybe I should call the doctor,'' he greeted them. ''She says she hasn't been to sleep at all yet.''

''Oh, for heaven's sake,'' Greg groaned in despair. ''How easily they forget. I am a doctor, an obstetrician even. Remember?''

Andrea laughed at Tim's expression.

''Oh. That's right. You are, aren't you?'' Tim stepped back to allow their entrance with a nervous hand raking through his tumbled blond hair and a slightly puzzled look still visible around his eyes. He seemed to be having trouble assimilating the early-morning events. His hand trembled slightly as he gestured them in and there was a slight imploring quality to his tone as he uneasily queried, "Can you see what's wrong, Greg? I'm afraid I'm not much good when someone's sick."

Great, Greg thought, this was just what he needed after last night's delivery. His niece's husband was going to fall apart over a probable muscle spasm. He'd be terrific when delivery time rolled around. But Karen's questioning "Uncle Greg?" caught him up short. Something really was wrong. She hadn't called him Uncle Greg since she had turned fourteen and considered herself all grown up, certainly too mature for uncles only a few years older than herself.

"What's up, sweet pea?" he lightly queried while he studied the white brackets of pain around her mouth and the set, slightly flared nostrils. She stood where Andrea had left her, still gripping the back of the chair with bloodless knuckles. This was more than a back spasm. He'd stake his framed copy of the Hippocratic oath on that.

"First I thought my back was just out of whack. Wouldn't be the first time in the past few months. But now... Oh, Uncle Greg..." She burst into tears. "I'm losing the baby, I just know it. My whole insides are being wrenched out!"

Andrea watched him open his arms to his niece. She noticed Karen's use of Greg's toweling robe to sop up her tears of anguish. She didn't need a doctor to tell her this was serious business. Tim distractedly paced the breadth of the living room, detouring through the small kitchenette area, finally stopping to place both palms on the Formica breakfast table in front of Karen. "You are not losing the baby, Karen. Tell her Greg," he directed. "I'm sure it could be any number of other things."

Oh God. It was all happening again, Andrea thought. Karen was going to lose the baby. Any chance of survival would be ruled out by the freak March blizzard ruthlessly piling and drifting snow outside the tight little bungalow. There was no way to get to a hospital. Even the best doctors needed proper equipment, and the blood-pressure cuff and stethoscope Greg kept at home would only go so far.

How could people open themselves up to this kind of vulnerability? The old it'll-never-happen-to-us syndrome, she supposed. Had there been enough time to build a strong enough relationship between Karen and Tim to weather this kind of strain, or would their marriage fall apart like Peggy and Ted's? Andrea watched from a distance, a detached spectator viewing the unfolding melodrama from the safety of the audience. Her emotions would allow nothing else.

"Come on, baby girl," Greg urged, he too slipping back into childhood terms of endearment. "We're not giving up that easily. It's too late for you to lose the baby. Even if we deliver it within the next ten minutes, chances are it'll be fine. It's only a few weeks early, not months and months, and your calculations could have been off by that much, you know. Not to worry. Here, put your arms up around my neck and stick your backside out a bit."

As she followed his directions, Greg put his palms low on her back, just above the swell of her buttocks. Andrea could see the sinewy muscles in his arms contract and harden as he used his weight to apply pressure to the area. "Feel better, honey?"

"No," Karen whimpered. "That makes my back feel better, but now I'm nauseated and trembly. There's something wrong, I know it."

Greg looked to Andrea over Karen's head. "Pull out the kitchen chair," he directed her. "Come on, honey. Sit here." He backed her up until the backs of her knees were against the chair. "Put your arms on the table and rest your head on them. That's it." He glanced up. "Tim, you lean over the back of the chair, put your hands here and press. Got it?"

Tim nodded in a distracted manner, clearly still worried, although Greg's professional manner had gone a long way to reducing the panicky tension in the room.

"Now it's my professional judgment that while you two insomniacs were up here sloshing in the tea, Karen was in preliminary labor. By all the signs, she's well into transition now."

Tim looked up. His befuddled mind homed in on the only pertinent point he had been able to grasp. "You mean she's in labor? The baby's coming? Oh, my God," he groaned as Greg nodded in affirmation. "What are we going to do?"

"We are going to remain calm," Greg directed with a meaningful glare over Karen's head. "There's no way of knowing how long this stage of labor will last. If the snow lets up anytime soon and the plows get out, she may very well still deliver in the safety of a hospital bed. If not, remember that lots of women choose a home delivery. It's not the end of the world."

Two hours flew by under Greg's determined orchestration. "Andrea, see if you can make it next door to borrow some disposable diapers. I hope Jimmy's kid brother isn't toilet trained yet. We'll need them later."

He paused to thoughtfully consider a few more necessities. "Tim, find the heating pad. We can use it to keep the cradle warm until we're sure the baby's temperature has stabilized. Oh, and while you're downstairs, get one of my stretchiest sweat socks, preferably one with a hole so we don't waste a good one. We'll cut off the foot, tie off the stretchy top and use it for a hat on the baby to conserve body heat. All the newborns at Evanston Hospital get little stretch caps. We can do just as well. I'm going to do a quick examination while you're gone. Come on, sweet pea, I'll help you over to the bed."

"Oh, Andrea, you back already?"

Breathlessly, Andrea thrust a handful of toddler-size diapers at him. "She's got more if we need 'em," she gasped. "Oh...and she sent this bulb thing. Some kind of nasal syringe they gave her at the hospital. She said they used it during Rex's birth, but she's never needed it since and Karen's welcome to it."

Greg looked at the small blue plastic aspirator as though someone had just handed him the Hope diamond. There was a touch of awe in his voice as he breathed, "That's wonderful. A real help. This baby will be born with all the amenities."

"Also, here's four receiving blankets. They've been washed in baby detergent."

His spirit clearly renewed, Greg rubbed his hands together and declared, "Now we're cooking. We need your sewing shears and a way to sterilize a few things. Have we got any rubbing alcohol? Where'd you put that brush you use for scrubbing under fingernails? I want to be sure my hands are as clean as we can get them..."

Minutes later, Greg was back. He and Tim had Karen propped up in the bed in a semiupright position. "Okay, baby girl, prop your legs up and let them fall apart. I think we're closing in on the end of this little ordeal, you'll be glad to hear. Let's just check."

The only sound during his brief examination was from a snowplow on the main street a few blocks away. It was too late to do them much good.

Before Greg even said anything, Andrea knew from his expression that this was it. His words only confirmed it. "Okay, kids, it's time to go to work. The main event is all set to go." Andrea only wished she was. She watched in speechless fascination as Greg calmly directed the scenario. "Sit all the way up, Karen, and hold your knees. That's it. Tim, get on the bed behind her and help support her. Great."

Greg laid his large hand on Karen's stomach to feel the start of her next contraction. "Here we go. Deep cleansing breath, Karen, and release it. Deep breath again, hold and push as long as you can." Karen's breath wooshed out and Greg looked up. "Don't waste the contraction, honey, grab another breath and keep pushing. You can make up for it between pains...."

Twenty minutes later, everyone in the room was covered with a fine sheen of perspiration. Especially Karen. The delivery was going to be tough.

Greg had made Karen move to the end of the bed, and he leaned over her there, trying to widen the birth canal. He spoke without even looking up. "I'll tell you one thing, this is no preemie. This little stinker's bigger than some of my full-term babies."

Within a few minutes the baby's head had emerged completely and Andrea was surprised when Greg stopped there. She looked anxiously from Greg to the soon-to-be newborn's head and back to Greg. The baby wasn't crying. Didn't they all cry right away? What was normal? Greg reached for the blue plastic aspirator and directed, "Pant, Karen. Don't push. I know it's hard. The urge is overwhelming, but try hard. Tim, pant with her. Short and shallow. That's it." He wielded the aspirator with efficient, economical moves and managed to clear the infant's air passages; there was a collective sigh when the baby gave a short, faint whimper.

"Now," Greg breathed in relief, "let's get the little devil out into the light and see what we've got here...go ahead, honey, push for all you're worth."

As Greg eased his grand-nephew into the world, and Karen's labors were coming to an end there was the sound of the snowplow turning down their block. By the time Karen had the baby on her tummy Andrea had called the paramedics.

Minutes dragged by but the ambulance finally arrived. After struggling with their litter up the unshoveled walk the paramedics carried Karen and the baby down the two flights of stairs. Thank goodness the blizzard had lessened to a few stubborn flakes. Greg squeezed into the back of the ambulance with Tim as he continued to monitor Karen's condition. There was no room for Andrea. She had to stay behind by herself, unable to follow as her car was thoroughly blocked in the garage by the snow-clogged alley. She watched with wide eyes set in a white face as the paramedics prepared to close the rear ambulance doors.

Greg happened to glance up and see her shaken mien. "Don't worry," he called as one door was locked into place. "We'll take care of her. Once I get her to the hospital, I guarantee she'll be okay." He smiled that special endearing grin of his, but the paramedic closed the other door on it, severing her from its warmth.

Andrea watched the ambulance pull away. Through its rear window she could see Tim clutching the swaddled baby. Then the ambulance turned onto Central Street and out of her sight. For a long time she just stood there, thinking. There was a missing piece here. She could feel it, just out of conscious reach. She gave up as she realized she was shivering. She went inside and put the teakettle on again. At this rate she was going to run out of teabags before she could get to the store for replacements.

Busy. She needed to keep busy. She absently beat the floor with a sock-clad foot. Working at stripping the Murphy bed was totally unappealing. So was cleaning out her linen closet. There was no book or magazine that looked interesting in the entire two flats. Finally she got down a one-thousand-piece jigsaw puzzle of a huge plate of spaghetti and spent three hours separating edge pieces from middles and trying to fit them together.

Then, when she thought she could stand it no longer, Greg was back. He'd taken a taxi from the hospital, and he looked bushed as he shucked his down coat and curved cold hands around the mug of hot tea Andrea held out to him. It was only natural to discuss the early morning's events.

"So that's the awe-inspiring, bonding process of giving birth," Andrea said.

"It wasn't a very good example."

"It certainly isn't a neat process, is it?"

"You have to remember that this was *not* a normal delivery. You're never going to want to get married and have a baby after seeing that, are you? I guess I don't blame you," Greg disclaimed disgustedly. "It was pretty bad." He left the counter he had been leaning against and started walking to his bedroom, believing for the first time he really was going to lose their little war.

Surprisingly, Andrea returned, "You were wonderful. So

calm and in control." She barely heard his response as she was stopped in her tracks by a blinding realization.

Calm and in control. *Calm and in control!* And there it was, as clear and definite as the March wind off Lake Michigan. It was the missing piece. This had not been an easy birth. He'd said so himself. Things had gone wrong. The baby had been too big for Karen and even had breathing problems. There had been real danger. Yet Greg had been the epitome of cool, doing what needed doing and never losing his professionalism. And that had been with his own niece, someone she knew he loved. She thought of her own light bout with the flu and contrasted his behavior then. Greg had absolutely fallen apart. She hadn't realized the significance of that then, but…he had to love her! He had to love Andrea herself, not merely the image of a wife and generic home life a wife would provide. She held on to his bedroom doorframe, looking at him through new eyes. Suddenly, she knew—she was as certain of his love as she could ever be.

"You say it's not always like that?"

"I said it, but I can't guarantee it. Rough deliveries do happen." Greg threw himself backward on his bed and laid the back of his arm over his eyes and forehead. Andrea sat cross-legged at the bottom of the bed, studying his drawn, tired features with compassion.

"I can see how that kind of thing can really take it out of you. You must have been terrified of losing Karen. What would you do if it had been me? Would you have been so calm?"

"I doubt we'll ever find out after this disaster," Greg grunted in disgust.

Andrea pulled at the blanket as she said, "Oh, I don't know about that."

Quickly Greg raised his head up off the mattress, his narrowed eyes almost pinning her to the bed. "What are you saying?"

Andrea shrugged. "Maybe all the pain and fuss is a way of ensuring we stop and note the specialness of the event."

"You mean that?" he questioned uncertainly, hope beginning to flare in his mahogany eyes.

Andrea looked him directly in the eye for the first time in several weeks. "Greg, have you completely given up on me? Is it possible for you to still love me after the hard time I've given you?"

He answered impatiently. "I told you over and over again that I loved you. For some reason you have refused to accept it."

Her eyes didn't waver from his. "I'm asking you here and now. Do you love me, now…today?"

"Yes," he answered unequivocally. "I do."

She sat back on her heels. "I love you, too."

Cautiously, he continued. "And you'll marry me?"

"Absolutely."

"When?"

She put her finger to her mouth, thinking. "Mmm, if you weren't so exhausted, I would suggest we look for someplace within walking distance that could do a blood test. That's how sure I am. I accept that you love me. Do you accept my love in return?"

He collapsed back on the bed in sheer relief. "I've known all along you loved me. The problem has been getting you to admit it." He let out a stream of air. "Thank God. I thought for a while there I'd have to actually find an apartment by this weekend. I was never so glad to see a late-winter blizzard in my life."

"What?" she shrieked, not believing her ears.

"I was trying to push you into a decision, my love. I never thought you'd let me leave when I gave my ultimatum. But you were going to let me go, weren't you? Lord, I was scared." He raised his head to look at her. "What made you change your mind?"

She looked discomfited. "Actually, it was the difference in the way you handled my little headache and Karen's major problems. The light dawned about ten minutes ago."

"Well, I'll be." He thought about that for a minute and

cleared his throat, collecting himself. "Well, I hope nearly losing one relative was enough to convince you for a good long time because I'm not sure I could go through another ordeal like that one to prove myself again." He was quiet for a moment before gathering himself again. "But be that as it may, let's discuss my fatigue for a moment. Maybe if you made a little lunch while I took a shower, I could revive myself enough for a hike to the clinic. It's only a mile or so. What do you say?"

"The quickest would be creamed tuna on toast," Andrea warned.

"You going to make it with cream of mushroom soup?"

"I could check if they have any cream of celery next door, but it'll take longer."

"Never mind. I'll close my eyes and offer it up in the interests of getting this little project under way before you have time to change your mind. Uh... Now, about christening our firstborn, Emmett—"

"Oh, good heavens! Don't press your luck. I said that I loved you, not that I'd gone over the brink into insanity. I'll make a deal: I'll make the lunch, we'll eat it, get the tests and license, and you can work on converting me."

And he did, directly afterward.

*   *   *   *   *

Dear Reader,

A Knight in Tarnished Armor is a very special book for me.
It was inspired by a very special woman, my best friend,
Diana Gafford. She will never be written about in history
books, but like millions of women she is a true heroine. At
that time she was running a business by day, teaching college
by night and being a loving single mom to two children
twenty-four hours a day. I know she was frequently tired, but
she faced every day with a smile on her face and a song in
her heart.

So I wrote this love story for her and for all the other unsung
heroines like her, the ordinary-extraordinary women who are
accomplishing small daily things that are the truly great
things.

My fantasy hero, Christopher Stone, is a gift to all these
women. He is the kind of man so many women are looking
for. Yes, he is rich, handsome and famous, but more
importantly, he is loving and compassionate, too. Not only
does he commit to the woman he loves, but he willingly
enters her world and commits to her children, as well.

I always write about loneliness, vulnerability and the need to
connect to others. I believe that no matter how great the risk,
it is better to love than to do almost anything else.

So, *A Knight in Tarnished Armor* is a gift from my heart to
yours.

With love to all my readers,

Ann Major

A KNIGHT IN
TARNISHED ARMOR

Ann Major

This story is for the young people who inspired it—
Lauren Major, Helen Brakebill, Kate Donaho,
Colin Guinn and Trey Guinn.

One

Christopher Stone jammed his foot on the brake pedal. Tires screamed and spun gravel as his Jaguar careened to a stop on the narrow private road of his ranch. Curls of dry summer dust swirled around the black car and obliterated his view of the desolate path that led up the hill to his beloved child's grave beneath a grove of trees—obliterated, as well, his view of the barren mountains and of his white ranch house perched atop a nearby hill that overlooked the dazzling Pacific.

From his notorious father, Christopher had inherited his golden, rebel-without-a-cause good looks. From his legendary mother, he'd received a restless, smoldering sensuality. His hair was reddish gold and rakishly long; his famous blue eyes were dark and stormy. He was well over six feet tall, with bronzed skin and the lean muscular physique of a man who spent much of his time out-of-doors.

The critics said he couldn't act his way out of a paper bag, but Christopher had an overwhelming screen presence. He was the highest paid actor in America. In his five *Tiger Force* movies, he had played the part of *The Tiger,* the ultrahero of the comic books and video games, who wore a mask and had a hidden identity. *The Tiger* was the adored idol of millions of little boys, but since Christopher never posed unmasked for publicity shots, he could go almost anywhere without being recognized.

Christopher ran his hand across the stubble of beard that he hadn't bothered to shave. He opened the car door and sank back against the seat when the dry desert heat engulfed him. The hills were wild and bare except for a few of his horses that grazed on the top of the hill. A pair of white horses stood apart from the others and turned their magnificent heads toward him.

He gazed at them without interest. Once, the ranch had been his favorite refuge from Hollywood and unwanted publicity, from his ex-wife, Marguerite, from all the demands of his film career and the hectic, fast-paced frenzy of his personal life. Now he hated the place. Maybe if he'd never moved out of L.A., Sally would still be alive.

Dear God. Today would have been her fourth birthday.

In his mind's eye, he saw her in happier days, toddling beside Marguerite's swimming pool in Malibu that was filled with huge brightly colored floats. Sally's favorites had been a green turtle and a purple dinosaur. The next vision was of her small body floating in the dark pool.

Christopher folded his arms across the steering wheel. He closed his eyes and he sagged forward as he rested his forehead upon his forearms. Pain spread through him like an innervating illness. His arms and legs were leaden weights. The tie at his throat was choking him. His suit was a straitjacket that made him feel sticky and hot.

He couldn't bear to walk up that lonely hill to her grave and read the letters of her name etched deeply in stone.

Why had everything he was, everything he owned, alway

meant so little? Why the hell couldn't he get on with his life and film *Tiger Force Six* like Cal wanted him to? Why did he continue to torture himself like this?

Because it was his fault. He should have known how to save her. Hadn't he, too, suffered the misfortune of having been born to Hollywood royalty? His parents had given him everything—fame, wealth, the best schools—everything except the things he most craved—their attention, love, care. Had he done any better as a parent?

From the passenger seat he picked up four red roses wrapped in cellophane and a battered stuffed horse that Sally had loved and had called White Horse, and he got out of the car. Slowly he climbed through the rocks and brown grasses until he came to her tombstone. He knelt in the shade before her grave. The four roses slipped through his fingers. He wanted to say something, but there was nothing to say. No one to hear.

Sally was gone. Lost to him forever.

He gazed up at the wide blue sky, at the blue ocean stretching endlessly. He was on top of the world, but all he could feel was the emptiness.

A twig snapped behind him and he jumped.

He could see no one in the trees, and yet he knew he was being watched by unfriendly eyes. He scanned the hills and saw only a faint breeze ruffling the brown grasses.

Then Marguerite's voice came from behind the largest tree, an ominous, disembodied whisper. "Very touching. Red roses and White Horse. *The Tiger* in a sentimental mood."

Hatred and loathing filled him. "What the hell are you doing here?"

"She was my child, too."

"When were you ever a proper mother?"

"You've got to be the most awful man God ever created!"

He laughed softly. "That should have made us perfect for each other."

Marguerite stepped from the shadows into the sunlight. She wore black with white pearls. Her wildly passionate, feline face with its high cheekbones and slanting eyes was carefully made up, her raven hair tied back in a black bow.

Her eyes burned into him with the hot dark force of a devil's eyes. He saw the sun glinting off the barrel of the gun she pointed straight at his heart. She had always been unstable, unpredictable. She could pull that trigger as easily as she might smoke her next cigarette.

The roses seemed vivid stains of blood on the brown earth. The bleak emptiness of the landscape was in his heart, in his soul. He was more dead than alive.

He stared at the gun and got up slowly.

If only she would.

He walked toward her, his bold blue eyes and insolent smirk daring her to do it.

"You're crazy!"

"Another virtue we share," he goaded.

"S-stop," she screamed.

When he didn't, her hands began to shake.

"Go ahead." His voice was hard and violent. "Put me out of my misery. You sure as hell put me in it. Finish me off the way you did our daughter."

Tears sprang into Marguerite's eyes. The gun wavered. Her fingertip trembled on the trigger. She hesitated, backed away from him, staggering clumsily, and then dropped the gun.

She sank to her knees. "You knew I couldn't."

"No, I didn't." The taunt in his low voice was like a spark set to dynamite. "Go ahead. Pick it up. Blow me away."

When she just stayed there, her face a turmoil of rage and despair, he leaned down to pick it up himself.

"You're always so smug, so ready to blame me for everything," she began. "It wasn't all my fault!"

"If it makes you happy to believe that—"

With an incoherent scream, she sprang at him. "You ruine

my life, too!'' She began pounding his chest, her long red nails clawing his face. "I loved her, too. I—I..."

She bent and twisted against him, but his arms were like iron. He crushed her hands behind her back and held them tightly until she broke off her struggles and burst into sobs.

He stared down at the wreck of her crumpled, tear-streaked face and saw through the blur of his own tumultuous emotions, a pathetic grief as profound as his own. They'd come as close as two people could to destroying each other.

He hated her.

How could he hate this poor broken creature?

He was amazed that he felt nothing, absolutely nothing. All his bitterness over their awful marriage and her part in the death of their child was gone. For the first time Marguerite's misery touched something deeper in him.

He had used her as a scapegoat so he could hide from his own guilt.

"I thought she was in bed that night," Marguerite said pleadingly.

He caught her in his arms and began to shake her so hard the black ribbon in her hair came loose and fell to the ground beside the roses. He didn't want to hear any of it. Her words brought back the horror of it all, and he drew a harsh breath. He wanted to lash out at her, to blame her as he always had in the past.

That was too easy.

"It was an accident," he managed roughly at last, letting her go. "There was nothing you could have done."

"You don't really believe that."

"Yes, I do. I know I've said and done things—terrible things—to you." He hesitated. "I'm sorry. Not that either of us can go back and undo any of it. Sally's gone. We won't ever have a second chance."

Inexplicably his words seemed to fill her with some new emotion. She started to say something, but no sound emerged from her trembling lips. Still, something in her desperation communicated itself to him.

"What's the matter?"

Her eyes widened, and she drew a deep breath.

Tears had made her rouge run. Gently he touched her cheek. Her hand came up and grabbed his, and for a long moment she clung to him.

"It wasn't your fault, Marguerite. I should have been there that night. I'm to blame for everything."

There was a look in her eyes he had never seen before.

"You don't understand," she whispered, her face twisting in an agony he couldn't fathom. "How could you?"

Then she turned and ran from him, stumbling down the hill.

Yanking the knot of his tie loose with one hand, Christopher sped along the freeway toward Malibu. What the hell could Marguerite want now? Hadn't they said it all last week at the ranch? The only thing he could think of was money. That's what everyone always wanted from him.

He drove fast, and with such impatient anger that he passed everything that moved. His air conditioning was blasting. His tape deck was blasting, too—hard rock music that pounded through him. Christopher picked up his car phone and restlessly punched in his agent's number.

"I'm sorry, but Mr. Fayazano is in a conference," Cal's secretary answered smoothly.

Nobody who was anybody in showbiz answered his own phone.

"Who may I say is calling, sir?"

"Christopher," he replied mechanically.

"Oh, Mr. Stone." The feminine voice became honeyed. "I can put you through immediately."

As usual, Cal came on the line with a roar. "Where the hell have you been? When the hell are you going to get back to me about *Tiger Six?*"

"I haven't read it." With one hand Christopher guided the Jaguar past a speeding Cadillac. The driver honked furiously.

"Work is the best way to forget your little girl."

Christopher heard Cal cover the mouthpiece and say to his secretary. "Tell him I'll call him right back."

Christopher stomped his foot down hard on the accelerator. A Volkswagen full of teenagers and surfboards pulled in front of the Jaguar just as the Jag leapt forward. Christopher had to brake suddenly. "Damn."

"What?"

Christopher's voice was brittle. "I don't want to forget Sally. You got that?"

"A year is a helluva long time for an actor..." Cal's gravelly tone died ominously. "Even a star like you, to stay out of the business. Younger guys pour into this town every day—leading-men types. Stars are short-lived commodities. You're not looking so hot, pal."

In spite of himself, Christopher shot a swift glance into the rearview mirror. He didn't much like what he saw. "So I had a bad night," he muttered.

"A year and a half of bad nights. Your fast life is showing, pal."

The three garage doors of Marguerite's sprawling pink palace came into view, and Christopher quickly pulled over two lanes, swerving in front of the Cadillac. He stopped in front of her triple-car garage. The Cadillac raced past him, horn blaring, a fist and finger elevated over the roof, but Christopher didn't notice. He was too caught up in the dark feelings of misery that the pink walls aroused in him.

Behind those walls he had lived with Sally and Marguerite until he had walked out.

"Bye, Cal."

"Wait a fungus minute."

Christopher slammed the phone down, got out and strode

toward the wrought-iron gate. Rust dripped from the iron onto pink stucco. Dead bougainvillea vines clung to the trellises.

Marguerite damn sure wasn't keeping the house up, and it was his house, not hers. Marguerite had opted for cash in the divorce settlement. Then she'd become emotional and had refused to move. Christopher hadn't been able to boot her out when Sally was alive. Since Sally's death, he'd been too numb to care.

The intercom was still broken, so he jammed his fist hard on the doorbell and leaned against the wall.

No one came.

Damn. He rang it again and then kicked the wall; he picked a rock up and pitched it across the driveway. Then he went back to the wall, heaved himself upward, grabbing onto the top of it and yelling before he remembered the housekeeper spoke no English. He began again in fumbling Spanish just as the maid headed out the door to unlock the gate.

She didn't bother to look at him. *"Calmaté. Ahorita vengo."* Constancia was as short, fat and as sullen as ever.

He nodded and said sulkily, *"Buenos días,"* and dropped lightly to the ground.

She had never liked him. On the phone she always pretended she couldn't understand him. Today she corrected him. *"Tardes,"* she murmured under her breath.

"Whatever. Morning. Afternoon. What the hell difference does it make?"

She glared at him, pretending not to understand for a long moment. *"Nada,* to a man like you, señor." She turned and shuffled toward the house, and as he stared at the gate, he realized he was going to have to open it himself.

As he raced across unswept Saltillo tiles to catch her, pink stucco closed around him like prison walls. He saw weeds in the flower beds, filth in the fountains. Constancia led him across the patio into the house and shut the huge, hand-carved, wooden doors that Marguerite had scavenged in San Miguel de Allende from the ruins of a monastery.

Inside, Christopher felt close to panic. His throat was dry and choked. He yanked at the knot of his tie.

No lights were on. There was only the blinding glare from the ocean splashing across the large empty rooms. Only a perpetual gloom lingering in every corner.

Marguerite had sold the best pictures and the furniture. There were bare spots on the walls and indentations in the pink carpet. All that was left was the cheap stuff—a plush pink satin couch with armrests of tacky gold. And the mirrors. She hadn't gotten rid of those massive gilt-edged monstrosities she'd always loved preening in front of.

The worst thing about the house was the silence.

It had been a mistake coming here again. He went to a window, and that was a mistake, too.

Beyond the terraces and the swimming pool, the Pacific was blinding-white dazzle. All he saw was the empty heart-shaped pool. One night while Marguerite entertained a lover, his little girl had walked in her sleep out to that pool and drowned.

Today there were no floats. Only dead leaves drifted on that placid surface.

Dear God. He should never have agreed to leave Sally to film *Tiger Force Five* in Australia. The weekend she'd died would have been his weekend to have her, had he remained in L.A.

His throat burned as if a giant hand had squeezed his windpipe. He looked away.

Her voice caught him off guard.

"I didn't think you'd come."

He started.

Marguerite smiled. "You may go, Constancia." This in melodious Spanish.

Marguerite leaned against the golden arms of her hideous pink couch and made a false theatrical gesture for him to sit beside her. She called herself an actress, but like so many of the unemployed beauties in Hollywood who called themselves that, she almost never worked.

She wore a flowing purple dress that looked like a gypsy costume. Her black hair was bound by a purple turban. Immense gold earrings dangled to her neck. In one hand she held something that looked like a legal document.

Uneasily, he sat down beside her. "Why did you ask me to come by?"

Her rings flashed as she wrung her long slim fingers.

"Is it money—again?"

She flushed and then gave him one of her too-bright, theatrical smiles. "No...and yes."

He sensed a major problem. There was a long silence. He waited—restlessly crossing a leg over his knee and then uncrossing it.

"Christopher, I've done you the most terrible wrong."

He sprang to the edge of the couch. Like when had that ever bothered either of them before? She was very pale. Their truce since the ranch had them both off balance. If he couldn't insult her, what could he say?

She was staring uncertainly at the document. Carefully, she set it on a low, glass-topped table and smoothed it flat. "At the ranch you said we didn't have a second chance."

"Look, I don't hold you responsible." He couldn't stand being in the house with her another second. Poised to bolt, he stood up.

"No..." She touched his jacket sleeve. "You're always so impatient, Christopher. This is hard for me."

He sat down, took a deep controlled breath, and stared at the pink stucco ceiling.

"I should have done a lot of things differently," she said. "I—I cared about all the wrong things. I cared about you for the wrong reasons. I was even jealous of my own daughter because you loved her. Christopher, I've done you the most terrible wrong."

That again. He couldn't stand this.

"We both made mistakes," he said grimly. "There's no need to go into a maudlin recital of each and every one of them. It's not as if we can change anything."

"We can."

"What the hell are you driving at?"

She lifted the document from the table and handed it to him.

He snapped the crisp paper open and scanned it quickly. It was a birth certificate dated a year before their marriage. Even though the names of the mother and child were those of strangers, his heart began to hammer in quick, dull thuds.

He looked up again, puzzled, wary. "What does this have to do with me?"

Marguerite leaned toward him, her dark nervous eyes looking anywhere but at him. She brought a cigarette to her lips with trembling fingers and handed him her lighter. Dutifully he flicked the lighter open. Flame licked the tip of her cigarette. She sank into the pink cushions and inhaled deeply. "We had another child...another daughter...before Sally. Six years ago when I was living in Texas."

The dull thuds in his dry throat became a violent tempo. "You damn— Tell me you're lying."

She closed her eyes.

As he watched the smoke curl around her still-pale face, he knew she wasn't.

We had another child. In the tense silence of that shadow-filled room, the phrase repeated itself like a savage refrain in perfect time with the wild, palpitating rhythm of his heart. He clenched the paper, nearly ripping it until she gently pried it from his paralyzed fingers.

"Is she dead, too?" he managed at last, his whisper hoarse.

"No. She's alive."

Relief flooded through him. "Thank God."

"I used an assumed name at the hospital where she was born and made up a father's name. I told the lawyer and the adoptive parents that the birth father was dead."

"Wishful thinking, I'm sure."

"I couldn't have given her away if I hadn't. I thought you and I had broken up for good. You had gone to South America to shoot *Tiger Force Two*. I didn't know I was pregnant when you left."

The entire conversation seemed unreal. He wasn't really here in this nightmare house listening to this tale told by a madwoman.

"Why the hell didn't you tell me this before?" His voice sounded far away, like a stranger's.

"I tried to call you in South America, but you wouldn't take my calls. I truly believed you were gone for good. I grew desperate. I didn't want to raise a baby alone. When you finally came back, I'd already signed the final adoption papers. I was so ashamed I couldn't bring myself to tell you when everything was all right between us."

All right between us. His mouth thinned to a cynical line.

"I was so afraid I'd lose you again. I thought we would have other children, that I could forget that first baby. So I got pregnant with Sally quickly. But having Sally just brought the pain of my lost child back. I was jealous of you for being able to love Sally. I felt so guilty. I blamed you for everything."

In a daze he watched her squash out her cigarette and light another. So much came clear—her seeming indifference to Sally. Her depressions. Her irrational resentments and jealousy.

He buried his head in his hands.

Nothing they had done to each other mattered any more.

Only this child.

A clawing surge of fresh paternal anguish threatened to tear his insides apart. Another child. Was she lost to him, too?

At last he looked up. Into the vacuous, slanting dark eyes of his ex-wife.

"Christopher, you have no idea what it was like to keep such a secret."

With an effort he managed to keep his voice level. "Why the hell are you telling me now?"

"Because it's haunted me." She smiled nervously in that bright artificial way of hers as she tapped her cigarette against the ashtray. "I should have told you a long time ago."

Watching that tapping cigarette, Christopher didn't trust himself to speak. She went on, easily. "I'm moving out of the house. I'm going on with my life."

"It's as simple as that then," he said.

"I can't help it if I'm not as complicated as you." She seemed to hesitate. "There will be certain expenses."

"So, it's back to money as usual?" A suave brutality laced his hard voice. "You've only been saving this juicy tidbit for the moment it would be worth the most."

She recoiled. "Why do you always have to be so nasty about everything?"

Dark animal emotion raced hotly through him. His eyes narrowed. He clenched his hands into fists. But when he spoke he kept his voice mild. "How much?"

She smiled. Studying him, she lifted her cigarette to her lips.

He stared at the slim beautiful face of the shallow, neurotic woman who had once held such captivating power over him, of the woman who had made him so unhappy for so many years. He was amazed to find that despite this new bombshell, he felt nothing for her. Even the hatred was gone.

Their passion had raged like a mutually destructive inferno until even the final hellish embers had burned themselves into extinction. In the cold void, it seemed incredible for him to imagine that he had ever been so deeply involved with her.

He was free at last.

Once he had longed for this moment—to be over her completely. But the price he had paid had been dear.

He pulled out his checkbook, and she named an appalling figure, which under any other circumstances, he would have told her was absurd.

He didn't flinch a muscle as he wrote the check.

It was nothing compared to all that he had paid before.

"Who has my daughter?" was his only question.

Two

What was Dallas, a highbrow scholar of metaphysical poets, doing in a run-down marina restaurant in South Texas, praying with more religious fervor than she'd ever imagined she possessed that her cook wasn't drunk again?

What bizarre twist of fate had left Dallas childless and manless for most of her thirty-two years and then made her the legal guardian of four, energetic hellions—*children* being a euphemism for this orphaned tribe of wild Indians? Guardian, too, of the failing restaurant and down-at-the-heels marina the kids had inherited, not to mention their pets—one dog, two molting parakeets, a blue heron, a much-abused gerbil, two aquariums and three cats?

It was Saturday night, and beach-weary customers poured into the marina restaurant. From the cash register Dallas Kirkland looked up expectantly every time the front door banged against the gray wooden wall.

Please, God, let it be Oscar. Please...

And every time it wasn't, her smile wavered. She kept hoping to see Oscar's craggy, weather-beaten face. She kept hoping to hear his surly growl of welcome as he swaggered past her in low-slung jeans carrying his jam box to the kitchen.

How gentle, cerebral Dallas would have longed for her old serene life at Rice University spent studying poetry, gathering research in hushed libraries and writing her dissertation—if she ever had a spare second for such longings. But there had been no spare seconds since her sister's death a year ago.

There was only constant chaos.

And disaster.

Unfortunately, tonight was a typical Saturday night. The restaurant was a tumbledown shack on pilings with big wooden decks sprawling over the Intercoastal Canal. The setting sun painted the warm waters of the canal livid red. The marina was a favorite stop for beach goers on their way back to the city from the barrier islands that fringed the Gulf of Mexico.

At the cash register Dallas played hostess, waitress and cashier. She frantically scribbled orders for shrimp baskets and burgers, took money and showed people to their tables. Through it all, she fought to keep smiling.

High above the register, a blue neon sign in the shape of the state of Texas flashed on and off. A muggy, salt-laden heat drifted through the open windows. Dallas loved Bach, but her customers, who drove trucks with huge tires and four-wheel drives, preferred the raucous Western music that whined from the jukebox.

Her thick glasses slid down the aquiline perfection of her perspiring nose for the hundredth time. She pushed them back, swiping at her wispy, golden bangs as well, and tallied the sum on her order pad.

"That'll be $32.56, please," she whispered, poking her pencil through the blond knot at the top of her head. She picked up a menu and fanned herself. The humid stir of air made her sleeveless cotton T-shirt stick to her damp breasts.

"What! $32.56?" her customer bellowed, slamming his half-finished beer down on the glass countertop.

When she nodded, the sunburned giant pushed his black baseball cap above his burn line and glared. She glanced past him at the line of customers. Slowly, his big red hands began counting out a wad of bills that looked as wet and bedraggled as he and his wife and kids did. He came up short.

"You got any money on you, honey?" he hollered to his wife whose plump cheeks were a perfect, sun-broiled match to his.

Dallas bit her lip as his wife set her beer down and fumbled through her purse. From a tangle of gum wrappers and keys, she plucked three torn dollars and two quarters.

Bravo.

Behind them, an impatient crush of customers curved around the back wall to the dark kitchen. More tires crunched outside on the shell drive. The front door kept banging.

Dear Lord. Dallas's tense gaze darted up to the clock under the blue neon sign. Where was Oscar? What was she going to do? It was madness to keep taking orders without him.

In the dining room and on the decks, the tables without setups outnumbered the tables with them. Instead of working, Rennie and Jennie, her twin teenage nieces, were fighting over the phone. Eleven-year-old Patrick had disappeared. As usual.

Kids!

The last strains of a Western ballad were dying as the customer handed Dallas his sandy clump of bills. As she made change, six-year-old Stephie tiptoed up to her, her dark innocent eyes flashing from beneath her black bangs with the immense self-importance of one who bears dreadful news.

With an anxious heart, Dallas sank to her knees.

"Oscar's laying on his couch, and he won't wake up. Not even after I pinched him. There's lots of bottles all lined up, and his breath stinks again, too."

Stephie's childish voice was faint, but Dallas heard every horrible syllable. Oscar was in his houseboat, drunk again, and

Dallas wanted to cower under the counter for the rest of the night.

But the bill of a black baseball cap peeped over the counter. 'Ma'am, my change?'

"Stephie, go tell Rennie I need her. Run!"

Just as a sullen Rennie appeared, two silver-haired snow-birds barged to the front of the line. "We've been waiting half an hour."

"I'm sorry."

Dallas turned to Rennie. "Dear, you've got to cover the cash register."

"Aunt Dallas, I was talking to Jimmy Sparks!" A teenage moan of total despair. "And Jennie's talking to him now! What if he asks *her* out?"

"Concentrate on the cash register. I'm going to put Jennie in charge of the dining room and the deck."

"You'd better make Patrick do something, too," Jennie wailed as Dallas took the phone and said goodbye to Jimmy for her.

Dallas found Patrick, hiding out next door in the den of their house. He was curled in a suspiciously innocent pose, book in hand, in front of the TV. His favorite two cats, Harper and T.C., conspiratorially napped beside him on top of dozens of baseball cards.

"What were you watching, young man?"

Both cats' ears perked toward the sound of her voice. Patrick didn't bother to look up.

"Nothing." He spoke in a monotone.

She touched the top of the TV. It was warm.

She tapped it. "Patrick!"

His lips tightened; his cheeks reddened. That was his guilty look.

She moved toward him. Without looking at her he handed her the remote. She flicked it on.

The screen instantly filled with *The Tiger*. As always everything except the ultrahero's short blond hair and hard mouth was concealed, but his skin-tight costume revealed a male body that was lean and tough and sinewy.

Christopher Stone!

She was momentarily paralyzed.

From behind his black-and-gold mask, his bold blue eyes stared straight into hers. They seemed to touch her mouth and the swell of her breasts with such insolent contempt that she shivered. His jaw tightened. His dark male spell seemed to mesmerize her, and she gave a little incoherent gasp.

Was she crazy? He was a cartoon character. She despised the man as well as the role he played. With a shudder, she switched off the set. The very last person she wanted to think about was Christopher Stone. As if he hadn't made enough trouble.

He'd been calling her for days, making outrageous demands because, horror of horrors, Stephie was his biological child. He'd offered to pay all expenses that had been involved with her birth plus a lavish settlement toward her child care.

When Dallas had gone to her brother for help, Robert had sided with him, saying, "Mr. Stone is not our problem. He is the solution to our problem. You can have your nice life back at the university. We can send the kids away to the best private schools. And we can unload that dog of a marina."

"But that would mean breaking up the family. Stephie doesn't even know she was adopted."

"Then tell her. Sooner or later we all have to face reality, baby sister."

"Don't call me that."

"You're living in the real world now, not your ivory tower. And not on some fellowship or grant. The kids' insurance is almost gone. Soon, keeping you all will cost me a fortune."

"Not if I can make the restaurant and the marine pay."

"The miracle word is *if*."

"You wondered why Carrie and Nick entrusted the kids to me and not to you. This is why, *big* brother."

Dallas hadn't spoken to her brother again.

The lamplight shone on Patrick's golden hair, and Dallas focused her attention on the boy once more. If only he wouldn't lie quite so often. "Your book's upside down," Dallas murmured quietly.

His flush deepened, and he flipped it over so quickly both cats jumped.

"Why don't you quit 'reading' for now, dear?" She picked up his book. "I need you out front."

"Things were different when Mother and Daddy were alive."

Dallas pushed her glasses up her perspiring nose and looked at him. "Don't I know it."

"They never made me work in the restaurant," Patrick continued resentfully. "You're not very good at running help or kids. Why don't you just give up like Uncle Robert wants?"

"Patrick."

"I bet you really want to take that money for Stephie so you can send the twins to boarding school and me to military school."

"Why, you've been eavesdropping."

"At least I know what's going on." With tearful eyes, he jumped up, jammed his hands into his jeans and stalked rebelliously past her toward the kitchen.

She longed to go to him, to pull him into her arms. But he wouldn't allow that except at bedtime. She set the remote on top of the television. "Patrick?" He turned. "I'm not giving up."

"Yes, you will." He opened the door, and she couldn't see his face. All she saw was the stiff, proud pose of his small body.

"I didn't quit the university and move in to take care of all of you because I wanted to send you to military school."

For a second he remained frozen at the door in his macho-guy stance. Then he was a little boy again, flying across the room into her arms. His cheeks were damp, but he made no sound. He always tried to act tough.

She knelt and clutched him fiercely. Until he finally insisted on pulling away.

"No one. Not even Mr. Stone is going to tear this family apart. I don't care if he does play *The Tiger*."

Patrick's voice was muffled. "*The Tiger* always wins."

"This is real life, honey."

"Maybe that's why I'm so scared."

Fires blazed beneath sauce pots. Oysters and shrimp sizzled in deep fat. Exhaust fans roared.

The marina kitchen was a madhouse, and Dallas in her white, grease-spattered apron was the madwoman at its center. At least, Pepper Canales, the marina's waitress, had finally come.

Dallas leaned over her cookbook and read. "Three minutes." Her glasses slid down her nose as she eyed a bubbly basket of pale, thickly battered shrimp that didn't look done.

Rennie came up to her and handed her the cordless phone. "It's Mr. Stone."

Not *again!* "I told you to tell him I was busy!"

"He won't take no for an answer."

Dallas grabbed the phone. "Mr. Stone, I won't sell Stephie to you and that's final."

"Did I ever once mention the words sell or buy where Stephie was concerned?" he murmured in a silken, holier-than-thou tone.

The muscles of her stomach constricted at the low, velvet-smooth sensuality in that maddeningly superior voice.

"Why do you always twist everything around to make me look like the bad guy?"

"Maybe because you are the bad guy, sweetheart."

"Good night, Mr. Stone." With a greasy finger she pressed a button and disconnected him. "There…"

Before she could hand the phone to Rennie, it rang again.

"You obviously want more money," the beautiful male voice whispered sweetly the second Dallas answered.

"You really are a loathsome man. I don't want your money."

"Those who have protested the loudest have always gotten the most," he replied cynically.

"Maybe you run with the wrong crowd."

He was silent. Then he took a new tack. "It's a pity you're not one of my fans."

"Mr. Stone, I despise the brutal, immature movies you make. You glamorize violence. You probably think you can take anything you want by force."

"If only I could," he purred. "So you *have* watched my movies?"

"Why don't you just hang up and leave me alone?"

"Because you have something I want."

Dallas was conscious of an implied intimacy in his words. His voice played with them, played with her. Blood pounded against her temples. She felt vulnerable, wary.

"I'm not one of your Hollywood starlets. Your fame, your money, your sex appeal will get you nowhere with me."

"I'm flattered that you think...I'm sexy."

Great clouds of steam rose from the pots on the stove. Dallas was so mad that she imagined invisible clouds spurting from her brain, as well.

"I can't deal with this—with you—at the moment," she whispered through gritted teeth.

"Maybe that's because you're not very good when it comes to dealing with realities."

She stared at the boiling pots, the sizzling fryers, the stacks of orders. "You don't know anything about me or the realities I have to deal with."

"Oh, but I do. Your brother has been a fount of the most fascinating information." Again, Christopher spoke with deadly softness.

"I can't believe that Robert dared to discuss me with you."

"He dared."

On a deep breath, she held the phone away from her face

and glared at it. She felt furious and betrayed. And hurt. The tiny kitchen with its boiling pots and fryers was suffocatingly hot. She could see Pepper frantically darting about in the dining room, managing the kids and customers.

For a long moment the odious individual on the other end was silent, too. But in Dallas's imagination she could feel his fathomless blue eyes boring into her. She wanted to hang up, but she knew he would just call back.

What had Robert told him? Surely not... No, not even Robert would be that treacherous....

Still not speaking, she propped the phone against her ear and held it there with her shoulder. She began chipping a tomato onto four plates with quick savage strokes. When she was done, the vegetable looked like a madwoman had shredded it. A timer went off and she rushed to the oven and pulled out a tray of rolls.

Mr. Stone remained ominously silent.

Desperately, she checked her stack of orders and bent over the deep fat fryers. The shrimp wasn't ready yet.

At last Christopher spoke again. "Are you still there?"

"If I hung up, you'd just call back," she snapped.

"So we're beginning to understand each other."

"I wouldn't say that."

"But I would. Just what are you trying to prove with this Pretend-Mom-Cinderella routine? You didn't even adopt Stephie. Your sister did, and she and her husband died. Your brother told me you're the bookworm type."

"I'm Stephie's legal guardian."

"I'm her real father."

"I don't think there's anything *real* about you, Mr. Stone."

"Maybe you don't know me as well as you think you do." He started talking again in that deep sexy voice of his, only this time it was laced with bitter sarcasm.

Jennie dashed frantically into the kitchen.

"Just a minute, Mr. Stone." Dallas covered the phone.

"Aunt Dallas, Rennie and Patrick are making me do all the

work again. Patrick took the garbage outside, and he hasn't come back. Rennie is talking to Jimmy.''

"Why can't you kids ever cooperate?"

Rennie rushed in. "Aunt Dallas, table ten is getting mad."

"Tell them two minutes—max," Dallas whispered.

"Are you there?" Christopher demanded.

"Sorry. I'm afraid you're just one of the many crises I'm trying to deal with around here," she apologized in a sweetly false tone.

He uttered a low expletive.

"I find such language offensive, Mr. Stone."

"What exactly are you trying to prove, Miss Kirkland?"

Jennie grabbed two glasses of ice water and headed into the dining room.

A bit of grease splattered onto Dallas's arm.

"Ouch. Damn it."

"What happened?"

"As if you care." Instead of answering him, she drew a breath and sucked the wound until it stopped stinging.

"What the hell happened?"

"I burned myself. Okay? What am I trying to prove? Look, I'm just trying to hold a family together, a goal a man with your background couldn't possibly understand."

"Maybe I'm not some two-headed monster. I'm Stephie's father."

"Look, Mr. Stone, there's nothing fatherly about you. I've read all about you—about your famous parents with their ten marriages, about the custody battles they fought over you, about your little girl drowning in the swimming pool when you were a million miles away, about all your escapades since her death."

"I'm surprised a stuffy highbrow like yourself reads junk like that." His voice was cold and concise.

"It's hard to miss two-inch-high headlines when I'm in the grocery checkout lines. You don't know the first thing about being a responsible parent. The smartest thing your ex-wife ever did was give Stephie up for adoption so she could have a normal life. If I gave you Stephie, you'd destroy her."

There was a long silence. "How would you know?" he asked, his voice so hard and cold she shivered. "You never even had a kid of your own, Miss Kirkland."

The blood drained from her face. She clutched the phone more tightly. She closed her eyes and fought to ignore the pain. But that only gave him time to plunge the dagger deeper.

"Maybe you don't know much about raising kids yourself. Who made you God when it comes to deciding who should be a parent and who shouldn't?"

"The law," she said, frantic to be rid of this awful man. "I'm Stephie's legal guardian."

She scooped up a basket of shrimp and another of fries and tossed them blindly onto a platter.

"You'd still be the legal guardian to your blood nieces and nephew."

"Stephie is just as much a part of this family as they are."

"It's useless to argue with you," he said at last.

"I hope that means you're going to give up."

"Not on your life, lady." His last word was a careful insult.

"Look, I've got a dining room full of customers, shrimp to fry, mountains of potatoes to peel. My cook is drunk and didn't show."

"Sounds like the ideal environment for my daughter. Are you sure you can manage all that and care for a six-year-old, too?"

"Mr. Stone, goodbye."

"If we settle out of court, we'll all be better off. Stephie. Your brother—"

"Stay away from Robert."

"He's a lawyer, and he's on my side. He thinks it's in the best interests of all the children for you to give Stephie to me."

"My sister adopted Stephie. She entrusted her to me. I'd die before I'd let you have her."

"The last thing I want to do is hurt you, Miss Kirkland," he murmured in that velvet, tightly controlled voice. "I just want my child."

At just that moment a frightened-looking Stephie peered around the door.

How much had she heard?

Dallas sagged against the counter. "Dear Lord."

"What's the matter now?" Christopher demanded.

"It's Stephie," Dallas whispered. "She was listening."

Stephie raced into the kitchen and threw her arms around her aunt.

"Who are you talking to, Aunt Dallas?"

"Oh, nobody important, darling."

Christopher snarled some inaudible sound into Dallas's ear.

"What's adopted, Aunt Dallas?"

Dear Lord... Dallas was so upset, the phone slipped through her trembling fingers and splashed into the deep fat fryer. With a scream, Dallas grabbed Stephie and pulled her away from the stove and splattering grease.

Admidst curls of golden shrimp tails, one end of the phone bobbed out of the fryer like the stern of a submerged ship.

"Oh, dear..." Dallas murmured. "I guess that really is goodbye, Mr. Stone. The shrimp look done, too."

Stephie pulled at her apron. "What's adopted?"

Dallas forgot the phone and clasped the child more tightly. She looked into Stephie's huge, dark eyes.

"Oh, honey... It means... Your mommy and your daddy wanted you very badly. More than anything."

"But they're in heaven. Do you want me?"

Dallas felt a faint tremor go through Stephie's tiny hands.

"You know I do."

"Does it mean I'm different than Rennie, Jennie and Patrick?"

"In a way. We'll have to talk about it tonight."

"Are you going to send me away?"

"Never. I'd sell my soul first."

Three

South Texas was bigger and flatter and hotter than Christopher remembered. It was uglier, too.

The only thing he liked about it was the endless blue sky with its dramatic thunderheads billowing against the horizon.

The sail across the bay from the city had been longer and choppier than he had planned. All he had on was a thin black cotton shirt and a pair of ragged white cutoffs. Even though his clothes were damp from salt spray, he was sweltering. His hat had blown off, so he'd gotten burned. He hadn't brought enough water, so he'd drunk way too many beers. As a result he felt slightly queasy—ill equipped to deal with the Kirkland witch, who had had the audacity to quit taking his calls after her lawyer had advised her not to talk to him.

His hand tightly gripped the tiller of his thirty-five-foot sloop. He was oversteering, but he couldn't seem to stop himself. He was used to board sailing, which was quite different from handling a yacht. From the canal he could see the marina. Heat waves made the restaurant, the decks, the house, the

swimming pool and the docks shimmer. As he came closer he
saw two kids on the dilapidated dock he was heading for. A
dark-headed girl and a taller, blond boy who had a skateboard
tucked under his thin brown arm were watching Christopher
with the avid curiosity of experienced spectators who recognized impending disaster when they saw it.

Damn.

This was the first time Christopher had ever docked a yacht
by himself. The last thing he wanted was an audience.

The film critics always said he couldn't act. He hoped to
hell they were wrong because here he was in Texas about to
play the most important role in his life. He usually wore his
golden hair longer than he did in the movies. It was longer
still, and he had dyed it a rich tobacco brown. He was wearing
wire-rimmed glasses, too. Down below he had a duffel bag
full of jeans, Western shirts and oversize belt buckles to give
him the look of a Texas rancher.

As the white boat raced across the smooth water, he realized
he was coming in way too fast. Only yesterday his sailing
instructor had tried to warn him that he wasn't ready to sail
alone. Nevertheless, here he was at the helm, recklessly giving
it a try.

In his three sailing lessons. Christopher had always stopped
by running into something. He ripped his glasses off so he
could see. But the brown contact lenses he was wearing to
disguise his famous blue eyes, muddied everything. He knelt
to cut the power and jammed the engine into neutral.

Damn it. He was determined not to ram the dock this time.
Still, as a precaution, he yelled, "Kids, you'd better get the
hell out of my way!"

He might have done okay if he hadn't seen *her*.

The black-haired little girl was a six-year-old version of
Sally.

His daughter.

She was barefoot and in shorts and standing a bit pigeon-
toed just like Sally used to. She was holding a hermit crab.

There was a blue heron beside her. Her long black hair was tangled as it blew about her face.

She was everything he'd imagined—soft, beautiful, adorable—and more. So much more.

And then she looked at him.

Until that moment he'd never believed in love at first sight. *His child. He had a living child.*

He knew a wild elation that was intensified because of the long months of grief, bitter guilt and despair. His gaze brushed the shining darkness of hers, and like a blind man who has regained his sight, suddenly his future held the promise of something very bright. He knew that no matter what it cost him, he would fight to win her.

He forgot the boat, the engine—everything save his child.

The white hull of his yacht charged toward her. The heron's great wings began to flap awkwardly. He saw Stephie's dark eyes fill with fear as she watched the huge bow wave. Her mouth gaped open, and she screamed. Then the older, blond boy yanked her hand, and they both raced for the safety of the shore.

Stephie's scream brought Christopher to his senses. He cut the power, shoved the tiller to starboard, jammed the gear into reverse, but he was too late. Although he missed the dock, the sleek white bow slammed into the concrete bulkhead, rode up it and then slid back into the slip on a shudder.

When a group of tourists drinking on the deck of the restaurant pointed at him and laughed, his cheeks grew even redder and hotter beneath his sunburn—if that was possible. He sheepishly ran his hand through his brown hair.

Not the inconspicuous landing he had hoped for.

But he'd sure as hell stopped.

The wind blew the yacht against the wooden dock.

His brain was still in a state of panic. What was he supposed to do next?

The boat started drifting out of the slip when he remembered—he had to tie her up. He lunged aft and grabbed a piling. He opened the lockers and pulled out a tangle of dock-lines.

The slim boy with his skateboard still tucked under his arm ventured back onto the wobbly dock. Stephie had run away.

It was just as well she had. Christopher was still so shaken from seeing her, he wouldn't have known what to say.

"Need any help, mister?"

"Nope." Christopher drawled the word like a native-born Texan. He was holding on to the piling with one hand and trying to untangle the line with the other.

The boy wouldn't leave. His young piping voice broke into Christopher's thoughts again. "Hey, you look sort of famil-iar."

Christopher started, but he didn't look up from the dockline. Hell, he didn't even recognize himself when he looked in the mirror. Then he remembered—his glasses. He'd taken them off. Quickly he put them back on and nonchalantly combed his forelock over his forehead. He looked up then and peered at the boy through his glasses, pretending they improved his vision. "Well, you don't look familiar," he drawled in his best Texas accent.

Now that the boat was no longer moving, the humid heat felt like one hundred and ten degrees. Christopher's black T-shirt soaked up the sun's rays and clung to his perspiring skin. He needed a cold drink, but when he opened his cooler there was nothing but empty beer cans floating in lukewarm water. He pulled out a can and crushed it with his bare hand before tossing it in disgust to the floor of the cockpit.

The kid watched him and then looked into the cooler. "Did you drink all of those—all by yourself?"

Christopher ignored Patrick and kicked the cooler over so that water and empty cans rushed out into the cockpit.

Patrick's eyes popped open. "No wonder you hit the dock."

"Damn it, kid."

"Patrick," the boy said in a level tone.

Christopher stared at him.

"Hey. Are you sure you couldn't use some help with those docklines, mister?"

Grumpily, Christopher tossed one onto the dock. Patrick threw his skateboard down and picked up the snarled line.

"You're pretty rough on your equipment, kid."

Patrick glanced from his skateboard to the black marks on the bow of the yacht. "Look who's talking."

Christopher's gaze narrowed, but so did Patrick's.

"You play hardball, kid."

They kept staring at one another for another long silent moment, two males challenging each other.

"I bet your mother's looking for you."

Patrick's stare wavered, and his hands fumbled with the knot, yanking at it harder. "I live with my aunt 'cause..."

For a second the boy looked like he might cry. But he didn't stop what he was doing, and the knot came loose. Deftly, he made a loop, slid it over a piling and tossed the end to Christopher.

Christopher remembered that the kid's parents were dead. Suddenly he was struck by something brave in this small, thin-faced boy. This kid tackled grief head-on and asked for no quarter.

"Hey, I'm sorry...Patrick." Christopher's drawl was deeper, gentler. Vaguely he was aware of a new respect as well as the flickering birth of some powerful emotion he'd never felt for any child other than his own.

Their eyes met again. Christopher's gaze was uneasy.

"It's okay," the boy said. A smile flashed fleetingly across his thin young face. "Really." He began to untangle another line. "Where're you from?"

Christopher shifted from one foot to the other. "I got a ranch, west of here." Which wasn't exactly a lie.

"You don't look like any rancher I ever saw."

Christopher grimaced.

Together they tied up the boat. Christopher was aware of

Patrick going around after him and silently checking the cleats and retying most of what he had done.

After the boy had finished, and the boat was secure, Patrick lingered on the dock as if he didn't want to leave. "I could throw those cans away for you."

Christopher felt reluctant for him to go, too. "Okay."

Patrick bounded on board and began picking them up with the enthusiasm of a friendly puppy.

"Thanks," Christopher said.

"How long are you staying?" Patrick asked.

"Do you always go around sticking your nose in other people's business?" Christopher demanded. Only this time there was a trace of affection in Christopher's hard drawl.

Patrick assumed a tough stance and crossed his arms upon his skinny chest. "My aunt runs this place. I'm supposed to collect money from newcomers. I came down here to tell you not to take this slip 'cause it belongs to her boyfriend. And he's sailing over tonight. Only you took it before I could tell you."

"Then I'd better move."

"No!" Patrick glanced anxiously toward the damaged bow and the bulkhead. "I mean…I think you'd better stay right where you are."

Christopher remembered the way both kids had run for their lives, the way the heron had flapped for his, the way the yacht had plowed into concrete, and the memory triggered something he thought he'd buried along with Sally—his sense of humor. Sheepishly he said, "No telling what I'd tear up getting out."

Patrick grinned from ear to ear. "No telling…"

Christopher smiled and reached across the cockpit and ruffled Patrick's blond hair.

For once, Patrick didn't pull away.

"Kid, you mind telling me something?" Christopher made his drawl sound very casual. He squinted hard at a billowing thunderhead. "How come you don't think I look like a rancher?"

"'Cause ranchers as old as you have faces and arms that are always real brown and leathery, and their foreheads and legs are real white—and they always wear jeans and hats."

"Well, er, that's how my men look. I stay inside mostly. I run things."

"Oh. Then you're not really a rancher?"

The kid couldn't have come much closer to hitting the nail square on its fibbing head.

Later, Patrick came back with papers for Christopher to fill out, a six-pack of canned drinks and two bags of ice. As Christopher watched the little boy swagger from the marina to the slip under the weight of the ice, he realized the kid reminded him of himself at that age. He hadn't been shy, either, and he'd always tried to act tough.

Christopher paid for a week. Patrick took his money and watched him write the phony name, Chance McCall, in a flourish of black swirling letters at the top of the page.

When the boy left, Christopher checked the nick in the bow. Then he got the hose and began to wash the decks.

Half an hour later, Christopher was still stowing his gear when he heard the purr of a diesel auxiliary. A beautiful yacht almost exactly like Christopher's was heading straight toward Christopher's slip.

Patrick ran out to the end of the dock beside the slip next to Christopher's and began waving his arms and shouting. "Over here. Take this one, Gordon."

Gordon glanced toward Christopher's yacht. A grim, pained expression marred Gordon's lean, tensely handsome face.

So this was Gordon. *Her* boyfriend. He was tall and thin with curly black hair. Christopher sipped his beer and broodingly watched Gordon land his yacht with perfect precision into the smaller slip.

There was an orderly way about everything Gordon did. He

was wearing a floppy hat that tied under his chin, big dark glasses, a long-sleeved white shirt and long khaki slacks. Thus, Gordon was neither wet nor burned. He shifted into reverse, touched the tiller deftly, and the yacht came to a gentle stop dead center in the slip. Gordon picked up the correct lines with his boat hook and secured them quickly and efficiently with no help from Patrick.

Christopher watched as Gordon exchanged his sunglasses for regular glasses. He took out a leather case, cleaned both pairs of lenses, before putting one away and the other on. Then from an ice chest packed with ice that hadn't dared to melt, he took out an icy can of beer bearing a pricey foreign label.

Christopher got up and went over to introduce himself. "Sorry I took your slip."

"It was my fault he took it, Gordon," Patrick said.

"No, it was mine," Christopher cut in.

From the house a beautiful blond woman emerged and called to Patrick.

"I have to go," Patrick muttered, picking up his board and racing toward the house.

The two men were left alone.

"Gordon Powers." The stranger gave Christopher a long look before inviting him aboard.

"Chance McCall," Christopher drawled.

Where Christopher was tall and powerfully built, Gordon was even taller, although thinner, and more elegant. Gregorian chants were being played on the compact disc player down below.

"You're not from around here, are you?" Gordon said immediately.

"What makes you say that?"

"The accent. It's different."

Christopher flushed darkly. "I've got a ranch—west of here."

"Do you now?" Gordon gave him an odd look. "I'm an

attorney." He held out a beer, but Christopher, who had had his fill of beer for the day, took a diet cola instead.

Gordon knew everything about every part of his yacht. Christopher wanted to question him about Dallas and Stephie, but once the guy got on the subject of his yacht's electronics, there was no diverting him. Gordon was smart, but listening to him was like hearing someone read an engine manual aloud in a monotone.

Christopher lay sprawled against a stack of blue boat cushions, watching Gordon twist black dials as he droned on about the technical marvels of each piece of equipment. The yacht had self-steering devices. Gordon could punch in numbers, and his boat would sail a perfect course for whatever mark he selected. It would tell him the speed and how long the trip would take.

"Hell, this yacht's a genius. No wonder you made a perfect landing," Christopher muttered at one point.

Gordon's eyes turned to ice. "The equipment was off."

That figured.

"Patrick tells me you date his aunt," Christopher prompted.

"Yeah, we've been dating for quite a while. Everything was great until she assumed custody of her nephews and nieces."

"You don't like kids?"

"I've got three of my own—and a matching set of ex-wives to go with them. I never see my own kids. All I do is pay. I was going to marry Dallas, but now—"

"Does she know how you feel?"

"She doesn't listen to me anymore. Dallas lets those kids run roughshod over her. She used to be a brilliant, sophisticated woman. But after only a year of living out here and dealing with four undisciplined kids, illiterate customers and drunk help, she's become totally irrational."

Christopher didn't find that hard to believe. "What makes you say that?"

"Well, one of the kids is adopted. The real father will pay through the nose for her. All Dallas has to do is give him his kid. We could farm the others out, and she could concentrate on me again. But do you think she'll listen—''

Christopher's hand tightened around his cola can.

Gordon was an ally. Why did Christopher have this insane urge to punch out the perfectionistic jerk's lights?

"Hell, no." Gordon's dark face grew grim. "She wants me to defend her case. Do you think she realizes that I can be choosy when it comes to women? They line up to date a lawyer."

They did more than that to get a movie star.

Later, Christopher wouldn't allow himself to dwell on what Powers had said because he found himself thinking of Dallas in a more sympathetic light—something he didn't want to do. What kind of woman turned down an easy life, sacrificed both her cherished intellectual interests and her own love life for the sake of four children who weren't even hers?

A bloodred sun was sinking into fiery waters when Patrick wandered, barefoot and shirtless with a fishing rod and a bait bucket onto the dock. Christopher went below. Without enthusiasm, he eyed the only food he had brought—a loaf of bread and jars of peanut butter and grape jelly.

He switched on a light and began reading *Tiger Force Six.* While his stomach growled, he scribbled notes in the margins.

The heat in the cabin grew stifling. His mind drifted from the script to Dallas Kirkland. Finally he poked his head out of the hatch. While Patrick fished, a great blue heron warily inspected the boy's bucket.

"Hey, Patrick, what's your aunt like?" Christopher asked.

Patrick's face softened. "She's neat! Nice! And as pretty as one of the angels in Stephie's book of Bible stories."

Sweet and pretty.

Damn. Christopher knew how to fight witches; he didn't have any experience with angels.

He needed to rethink this challenge. He decided to shower.

He went back below, tossed his script into a drawer, switched the lights off in the cabin and went into the bathroom.

The shower was icy, but it felt good against his hot skin as it blasted away the salt and grit. Because of the running water, he didn't hear the melodious lilt of a woman's voice calling down to him. He dried off and then wrapped the damp towel around his waist and strode into the main cabin only to stop abruptly when he found a woman there.

She was framed in the hatchway, a vision of soft, female loveliness with the red fire of the setting sun backlighted in her golden hair and upon her golden skin.

She was peering into the darkness of the cabin. He was a shadowy presence she couldn't see all that well.

He recognized her instantly.

The highbrow. Stephie's guardian.

Only this woman didn't look much like a highbrow. Her thickly lashed blue eyes were luminous. There seemed to be tiny flecks of gold in them. Her fragile face was as perfectly sculpted as a porcelain figurine's.

She took his breath away, and he couldn't stop staring.

"Why, hello there," he whispered.

She was beautiful, but not in the way he was used to. He knew she was no young virgin, but she looked like one. Her education—obviously mainly from books—had not touched her in the way that his real-life experiences had hardened him.

"Surprise, darling," she said softly, welcoming him with a sweet warmth he had longed for all his life.

Gordon Powers was a lucky bastard.

Christopher's heart pounded. The teak flooring seemed to rock gently beneath his bare feet. He sensed some new, never-known-before danger. Against his will, he was drawn to her.

"I cooked you some shrimp—your favorite."

Then it came to him; she couldn't see him in the darkness. *She thought he was Gordon because he had taken Gordon's slip.*

Christopher knew he should tell her who he was at once, but he didn't want her to go. Not yet.

She was the enemy.

The unusual gold flecks in her irises caught the light of the sun and sparkled.

But a beautiful enemy.

He had always had a weakness for beauty.

"Shrimp. How nice of you," he murmured.

"Sorry I was late," she said. "I wanted to cook the kids a balanced meal and get them settled for the night so that we…" Her voice died on a suggestive note.

"That sounds too good to be true," he whispered hoarsely. "Wonderful."

"I've been neglecting you," came that velvet, heart-stirring voice.

"Is that a fact?" he asked enthusiastically.

"But all that's going to change—tonight."

"I can't wait."

She began descending the stairs. His hungry male gaze followed her thin, elegant, bare feet and ankles, her long golden legs, the swell of creamy thighs. She was wearing skin-tight white shorts and a thin T-shirt that molded her body. His throat felt hot, dry.

So this was the witch who had his child.

Patrick was right. She had the face of an angel.

And the body of a seductress.

Which was a lethal combination for a man like him.

She was slim, and she moved with astonishing grace. Sunlight splashed over the vee of her neckline, and his gaze followed its path. Christopher felt so warm, he was burning.

He moved toward her and joined her in the dazzling fire of the sunlight. His hair fell across his brow, and he shook it out of his eyes.

She stepped back, aghast. "Why, you're not Gordon!"

"No." Christopher smiled. "You're not what I expected, either."

"You should have told me who you were at once," she said.

"Indeed?" His lips parted into one of his quick, bold smiles. His eyes went over her and flashed just as boldly. "I've never been able to resist...anything so delectable looking..." His gaze lingered over her breasts, her narrow waist, her flaring hips. "So absolutely delicious in appearance..." His ravenous gaze finally settled on the shrimp. "As home-cooked...crustaceans."

She blushed charmingly from her sun-kissed nose to her neckline, and he moved closer to pluck a shrimp from her trembling hands.

Their fingers touched, and a swift hot current raced through them both.

She jumped back, startled.

He told himself it was just his sunburn that made his skin tingle. He took a shrimp from the platter. It was still sizzling, and it burned his fingers. He popped it into his mouth. His white teeth crunched into it. Then he swallowed it. His hot gaze roamed her lush soft curves. "Delicious." He grinned broadly. "You're a very talented...lady."

"Who are you?" she demanded in a low amazed voice.

"Your guest," he murmured. He bit into his second shrimp and quickly ate it. There was something very sensual about eating shrimp and watching her. He licked his lips. "I didn't realize I was so...hungry."

Her frightened eyes met his, and it was as if she touched him. He felt on fire. He saw the wildly fluttering pulse at the base of her throat, and he felt an answering excitement of his own.

He was used to women wanting him—because of who he was. But this was different.

She was the enemy, he reminded himself.

He liked her anyway.

"Don't be afraid," he said. "Not of me."

"Oh, I'm not."

He heard the husky quiver in her voice.

"Oh, yes, you are."

Shakily she moved a tendril of golden hair out of her eyes.

He kept staring at her. She was more beautiful in person than she had been in the pictures his private detective had furnished him with. He was used to photogenic women, to being disappointed when he actually met famous film beauties.

She clutched the railing by the stairs.

Vaguely, he remembered his glasses—who he was, who he was supposed to be—and the danger to his plan if she recognized him. Fumbling, he grabbed his glasses from a nearby shelf.

"I wish I was wearing mine," she said weakly as she watched him put them on. She was making the kind of inane conversation strangers make to avoid an awkward silence.

"What?"

"My glasses. Gordon prefers me in my contacts."

"Gordon?"

"I thought this was his boat." She kept playing with that golden tendril, winding it and unwinding it around a fingertip.

"Oh, yeah. Powers. I...forgot all about him. I met him. I sort of accidentally took his slip."

"Your boat is almost exactly like his. I'm sorry to have bothered..."

Christopher moved nearer. "Sooner or later we were bound to meet."

She sank against the stairs, but she was so close he felt her breath, light and warm, flutter against his throat. Her sweet fragrance enveloped him. He felt hotter than ever.

"Maybe it's divine intervention," he said smoothly.

Her fascinated gaze ran fearfully over his muscular arms and chest, stopping where his hard brown abdomen met the stark whiteness of terry cloth. Her flushed look made every cell in his body conscious of his male nakedness beneath the towel.

"I—I don't think so," she whispered. "I made a mistake. Not that I blame you for getting the wrong impression."

"Are you sure it is a *wrong* impression?" he queried softly.

"I'm not that kind of girl."

"What kind?"

"The kind you think I am."

"So you can read my mind?" His eyes gleamed.

Her senses seemed to catapult in alarm. "I'd better go."

He laughed, a husky throaty laugh. "You just got here."

"But I don't know you."

His sensual mouth curved. "Then I'd better introduce myself."

"No!"

Again he laughed.

"Please…"

His gaze lingered on her golden throat. He watched the wild beating of her frantic pulse at its base. He saw the faint beading of delicate perspiration drops there. More than anything he wanted to reach out and touch her. Would her skin feel like satin? Would her mouth be delicious?

He *had* to know.

He thought she read his every thought. The pupils of her eyes grew so enormous that only a ring of blue encircled them.

"I'm not going to hurt you," he heard himself say.

Slowly his hand touched the curve of her shoulder, moved up her throat to her earlobe. Gently he stroked her.

She was soft, warm, living satin. She didn't move away from him. Instead, she sighed deeply on a long shudder.

He felt the heat of her engulf him, and his own breathing grew harsh. His lips longed to follow the path traced by his exploring fingertips. He lowered his dark head toward hers, and she began to tremble.

The world grew very still.

"No," she whispered, frantic.

She was quivering like a frightened animal, wanting him to kiss her and yet terrified. There was some mysterious duality in her nature. She was hot, eager. At the same time she was as cold as ice. He sensed that to kiss her now was to lose her forever.

So he stopped.

For a long tremulous moment she stayed there, powerless to move her body or her eyes away from his.

He stepped back to give her breathing room, and that was a mistake. She flew up the stairs. Christopher forgot he was wearing only a towel and raced after her, stopping short when he saw Gordon standing on the dock.

Gordon's expression darkened as his gaze swept from his girlfriend to the beaming, towel-clad Christopher.

"What the hell were you doing down there with him?"

Dallas was too upset to answer.

"Don't ask," Christopher murmured on a suggestive note.

Gordon grew even angrier. "You stay out of this!"

"Just trying to be helpful," Christopher said cheerily.

"Oh, dear...." Dallas wailed as she clambered off the boat.

"The last thing I want to intrude upon is a lover's quarrel," Christopher said, his manner meek and overly solicitous.

"We are not lovers!" Dallas screamed down at him.

Christopher felt sharp joy at that declaration, but he made his face carefully grave. "Sorry. Wrong impressions...again."

As he descended the stairs that led to his cabin, he didn't look the least bit sorry.

"You started this!" Dallas shouted down to him.

He paused on the stairs. "Thanks for the shrimp."

"You gave him my shrimp?" Gordon's voice thundered. To Christopher he yelled, "Give them back, you fiend."

Christopher looked at Dallas. "Fiend? Maybe if he had asked me nicely—"

"I said fiend and I meant fiend!"

Christopher snapped his hatch shut as Gordon howled with rage. Christopher's windows were open, and he heard their muffled voices.

"I thought he was you, Gordon."

"The hell—"

"I really did. I mean... Oh, it's too confusing to try to explain."

Christopher heard Gordon explode. "Get them back!"

"What?"

"My shrimp!"

"You mean, go back down there?" She was aghast. "What if he takes his towel off? Besides, he's probably already eaten them."

She knew him better than she imagined.

As she spoke, Christopher ripped off his towel and plunked another shrimp into his mouth. It was moist, succulent—delicious and a hell of a lot better than peanut butter.

He pulled his script from his drawer and reached for two more shrimp.

Enemy or no, she was damned talented in the kitchen.

He remembered how hot and silken she'd felt in his arms, how she'd jumped back when he'd touched her, and he wondered about her other talents.

What would she be like in the bedroom?

Four

What would she be like in the bedroom?

As Christopher sat alone in his darkening cabin, contemplating this question instead of the script that kept blurring, a dozen male fantasies came and went in his overly active imagination.

In his favorite, Dallas lay naked across his forepeak bunk with her golden hair tumbling about her soft body. The golden flecks in her brilliant eyes were wantonly ablaze as this delectable phantom enticed him to her by crooking a fingertip.

On a groan that was half angry frustration and half jealousy, Christopher threw his script down. He rubbed his eyes with the back of his hands.

Dear God. What was he doing to himself?

The tiny windows didn't let in any breeze, and the cabin was stifling again. He arose and slid open a hatch.

The purple sky was blackening. The humid air smelled as tangy as the marshes. On the distant horizon, the city's lights twinkled like diamonds, but the beauty of the night was lost on Christopher. All he could think of was her.

Banjo music drifted from the restaurant as did sounds of boisterous laughter. Although he was hungry, he wasn't tempted to join the raucous festivities. He was too conscious of the yacht next to his, too conscious that Dallas had gone below with Gordon and stayed there—alone, with him, for hours. He kept seeing her as he'd imagined her in his cabin. Dear God. Christopher kept remembering the way she'd looked so soft and lovely with the fire of the sun in her golden hair. She'd been so anxious to get away from him.

What the hell was she doing down there so long with Gordon?

The Gregorian chants were still playing—the Credo, the Agnus Dei. What kind of guy played weird stuff like that when he made love to a woman? Maybe highbrows who read John Donne and Andrew Marvell liked religious chants. She damn sure hadn't come out of *that* cabin.

Who was running the restaurant? Who the hell was taking care of Stephie? Christopher remembered all the arguments he'd had with Dallas over the phone when she'd thrown up the sensational stories about him as proof he was too irresponsible to care for his child. He stared at Powers's yacht. Who was *she*—to call him irresponsible?

Above the chants, her whisper floated to him. "He's out there—watching us. I can see him."

"Relax. Forget him."

A light flicked on in Gordon's cabin.

"I—I can't," she said. "He's just sitting there. Maybe if he'd go below…"

"What do you want me to do—go ask him?"

"No!" She sounded frantic.

Christopher turned on his own radio to a rock station. The hard beat obliterated the softer psalm tones.

A second light flicked on in their cabin.

Christopher turned up the volume of his music. He felt like

he was involved in a bizarre duel for this woman, his enemy. Through the portholes, he could see the man and the woman clearly. They were seated on opposite bunks, arguing now.

For the first time he noted how reflections from city lights and the sparkling stars turned the dark water to shimmering satin. He gave a low whistle as he appreciated what a hell of a pretty night it was—even if it was Texas.

It grew later, the night blacker, the stars brighter. Christopher's loud rock music was the only music still playing.

The childish sob that woke him was soft and fragile.

Christopher shot bolt upright.

A little girl was lost and crying somewhere in the night.
Sally.

In a thousand dreams he'd heard her soft cry.
But this wasn't Sally.

The soft frightened cry came again.
He wasn't dreaming.

He heard the metallic clanking of the shrouds against the mast, the lapping of the water against the hull. The thick heat enveloped him. His body was bathed in perspiration.

He was in Texas.

The terrified whimper came again, and a cold caress of fear raced down the back of his neck.

He jumped up and snapped on his jeans. Deftly he turned the music down. When he came out of his cabin, the yacht next to his was dark and silent. So was the restaurant. There was no moon; he couldn't see anything but stars and the distant city lights. The wind had died to a breath.

He heard the broken sobs again, and he sprang lithely onto the dock. A white nightgown fluttered at the far end of the dock. A little girl with long black braids was walking across the rough wooden planks.

Stephie!
His daughter!

He started to call to her and stopped himself.

As a child he'd walked in his sleep. So had Sally. He remembered how terrifying it had been to be awakened suddenly and to find himself in a strange place with a strange person.

"Stop," he whispered. "Please. Stop."

As soundlessly as a ghost, she glided toward the deep black water at the end of the dock.

"Stephie…"

Black braids twirled. The lacy hem of her nightgown tangled around her legs. Her glazed eyes stared through him unseeingly. "Mother—"

"No, honey. I'm your—" he choked on the word "—father."

She gave a terrified little cry and ran.

This was worse than his recurring nightmare. In his dreams, Sally was crying, and he was an impotent statue, unable to do anything other than stand by helplessly and watch in horror as she sank into the pool.

Not this time. This wasn't a dream. This was Stephie. He was going to save her.

When he sprinted across the rough slippery boards, a protruding nail tore his heel open. She took a faltering step; her tiny foot found empty air. She cried out, but he was there behind her. As she fell, he caught her.

His child.

He knew an intense paternal thrill as he lifted her firm little body to safety. What he wanted more than anything was to take her away with him, but the minute he seized her, she came awake wildly. She opened her eyes and read the deep emotion in his. Her wiry body began to writhe. She was little, but she kicked like a mule.

"Easy," he whispered gently.

She pressed her hands against his chest and screamed. "Aunt Dallas!"

"Honey…honey…." In vain he tried to soothe her as he carried her onto his boat. In his cabin he found Sally's stuffed White Horse.

Stephie threw it overboard and screamed more loudly.

His torn heel left a slippery trail of blood across the white decks of his boat as he lifted her back onto the dock.

Out of the darkness Dallas came flying. With the starlight in her hair, she seemed an ethereal girl running lightly toward him. She was still wearing the same T-shirt and white shorts she'd worn earlier, but her pale face was stricken with fear when she saw him with the child.

"Let her go," Dallas commanded.

"I wasn't going to hurt her."

Dallas's eyes flashed coldly. "Let her go." Like Stephie, Dallas saw him as a threat instead of as a savior.

"I swear I wasn't—" He broke off. It was useless to argue when he was already tried and condemned. Very gently, he knelt to the dock and released Stephie.

"Stephie, darling." Dallas's voice was velvet soft.

Stephie ran eagerly into her aunt's arms. Dallas cradled the child against her breast. At first he felt awkward and rejected as he watched them. Then despite Dallas's coldness toward him, he felt drawn to her. She knew just what to say and do to soothe, just how to answer each of the child's frantic questions. Marguerite had always been too impatient to comfort Sally. His own glamorous mother had never comforted him.

Then he remembered the long hours Dallas had spent with Gordon. Had she been with him still when Stephie had walked in her sleep? Marguerite had been with a man the night Sally had drowned. The horror of Sally's death came back to him and with it, all the old hatred. He zeroed in on Dallas.

His deep voice sliced through the darkness. "Where were you tonight? Why weren't you looking after her?"

Dallas looked up, startled. He towered over her. Still holding the child, Dallas stood up. "I was looking after her, but she walks in her sleep sometimes."

"Tell me about it. If I hadn't heard her, she would have drowned." His face was grim. "You were with Powers."

"That was hours ago."

Christopher glowered accusingly down at her.

Dallas's thickly fringed lashed lowered. "Just who do you think you are?"

Stephie quit crying and attacked him, too. "He grabbed me!" The little girl studied him with huge suspicious eyes. "He was going to kidnap me!"

Stunned, Christopher looked down at his daughter. So, that was why she'd been so scared. She'd intuitively sensed his true feelings. Not that he would admit anything.

"The hell I was! I grabbed you because you were about to walk off the pier!"

"You were too taking me away!" Stephie began to weep dramatically again.

Before he could defend himself, Dallas leaned down and touched his foot and then the smear of blood on the dock. Her gentle touch warmed him through.

"No, darling." She rose slowly. "I—I believe him. He did save your life. And he hurt himself."

Stephie eyed his sharply etched face, his foot, and the bright blood on her aunt's fingertip with grave doubt.

"You should say thank you to the nice man."

"He isn't nice, and I won't say it."

"Then I'll have to say it for both of us." Dallas lifted her lovely face framed with trailing golden hair and stared directly into his eyes. "Thank you," she said softly.

His gaze devoured the delicate curve of her lips. Why couldn't he forget that her skin had felt like molten satin that once? Why did he crave to touch her?

"You're welcome," he replied curtly.

They stood there staring at each other.

"Well—" she broke off nervously.

He laughed just as nervously. She turned to go. But when she carried Stephie toward the house, he followed them.

There was another awkward moment when Dallas discovered him behind her on the porch. She sighed deeply, not knowing how to deal with him. "Thank you…again."

She meant goodbye. But when she pushed open the screen door, he held it for her and then boldly followed them inside to the kitchen.

She looked surprised at that and stared again, but before she could react, a blond teenager with the name Rennie painted across her T-shirt bounded down the stairs. On the third step she tripped on a skateboard and fell.

Unfazed, she pulled herself up. "You found Stephie!"

Dallas tugged a loose red ribbon from Stephie's braid and set it down. "She walked out to the dock. If it hadn't been for—" Dallas turned uncertainly toward Christopher, caught an eyeful of gleaming male torso and blushed.

Suddenly he felt tense and hot and embarrassed without his shirt. His brilliant gaze touched her mouth, the rounded curves of her breasts before he forced himself to look away. When his glance settled on the chrome toaster, damn it if his face wasn't as red as hers.

After that look, neither adult heard a word Rennie said. They were both fighting a losing battle to ignore each other.

"You little rascal!" Rennie said, breaking the tension. "All the way out to the dock! That water's so deep."

"Yes," Dallas said. "But the danger's passed now. Rennie, dear, would you please take her up to bed?"

Stephie defiantly buried her face against her aunt's neck and clung.

Dallas pleaded gently. "Darling, I'll be right up."

Stephie held on.

"Please, dear, so I can tell the nice man who saved you goodbye."

Stephie turned big wet eyes on him. "He isn't nice."

"Stephie, you're being rude."

"What if he's my birth daddy—come to take me away?"

Dallas went as white as paper.

Christopher felt as if he'd been punched in the gut. *Was it all over—so soon?* He stiffened.

Dallas was the first to recover. "So, that's why you were

so scared.'' In her gentlest tone she began, "Darling, he isn't, and even if he was, didn't I tell you I wouldn't let anyone ever take you away?''

Christopher sucked in a long tight breath.

"Now, run along upstairs with your sister," Dallas said.

From the stairs Stephie cast one last dubious glance toward Christopher before racing up them. Then Dallas and Christopher were alone in that homey kitchen littered with kids' sneakers, dishes, bait buckets and cans of pet food.

Their glances met. Never had he been more aware of a woman.

Hastily she averted her gaze and picked up a pair of dirty socks and shakily stuffed them into some tennis shoes. "Have you eaten?''

Christopher cleared his throat. He shook his head.

"There's a bathroom right through that hall where you'll find Band-Aids and medicine for your foot.''

While he was tending to his foot, Dallas prepared something to eat. When he returned, she set a plate of warmed-over fried chicken and beans before him and sat across from him. "We can talk while you eat.''

But they didn't talk, and Stephie's comment about him being her birth father stayed in Christopher's mind. The kid was smart, and she was on to him.

"Your chicken was even better than your shrimp," he drawled in a low tone, on guard.

She set her coffee cup down. "Chicken used to be my specialty.''

He'd felt awkward eating, but he felt more awkward now that he was through, because he couldn't be honest. He tried not to look at her, but every time he did, he felt himself react. Her golden hair circled her face like a halo. Every part of her seemed delicately made and enticingly feminine. For some reason he couldn't think of a thing to say—which was odd. He was used to beautiful women. They had always been easy for him. Why wasn't this one?

"The food was great, really great." He caught himself. "I already said that, didn't I?"

She sat across from him twisting her fingers.

"You didn't need to feed me," he went on.

"It was the one thing I could do—to thank you." Her voice was soft.

"Hey, there was no need."

She was so sincere. He felt like a heel.

Dallas touched his hand, and her velvet warmth flowed into him. Then she looked at her fingers there and she blushed. As quickly as she had touched him, the hand fluttered back to her lap.

He gazed into her frightened eyes. There were mysteries attached to this woman. She didn't trust him. Was it just him? Or all men? He needed to go slowly, very slowly. That wasn't his style.

"Maybe I shouldn't have eaten Gordon's shrimp this afternoon," Christopher conceded in a halfhearted apology.

"Gordon was pretty upset." Her smile was dazzling. "He's possessive. What's his is his. You may not understand that sort of thing."

Christopher picked up Stephie's red ribbon. His roughened brown fingers tensed around the soft satin. Deliberately, he set the ribbon back down. "Oh, I understand." A pause. "I know I haven't any right to ask this." His hard eyes met hers. "Do you belong to Gordon?"

"I—I don't belong to anyone." She was very pale.

"What a shame. You're a beautiful woman."

Paler still, she drew back. "It's the way I want it."

"You're sure?"

"Of course." Her uncertain gaze darted everywhere, but to him. Her voice was very faint. Now she was the one fidgeting with Stephie's red ribbon. "Why did you come here anyway? You're not like anybody I ever met before."

"You make it sound like a sin."

"Maybe that's because it feels like one."

"Is that good?" he murmured. "Or bad."

Her eyes filled with wild emotion. "Just dangerous." Her words died away and left a tension-filled void in the quiet of the kitchen.

"That spells good in my book," he replied, his voice like silk as he watched her lick her dry lips.

She was the one woman he shouldn't even think of, yet he was fiercely conscious of her. He felt excited, restless, wanting something from her that was utterly different from what he usually wanted from a woman.

He leaned closer. For an instant, a charged silence seemed to hang between them. Then she got up so fast that her chair crashed against the linoleum. The screen door banged as she ran outside onto the porch, away from him.

She was scared now. What would she be like when she found out who he really was? Thoughtfully he picked her chair up and set it against the table. Then he pushed the door open. She was leaning against the house, hiding in the shadows, hugging herself. The faint breeze made the bronze wind chimes tinkle. His pulse quickened as he drank in the sight of her.

"What are you trying to do?" she whispered across the darkness.

He stepped outside. "I don't know myself half the time."

"I belong to myself," she murmured in a ragged voice.

"If that's the way you want it."

"That's the way it has to be."

The moonlight turned her hair to silver.

"Really?" He moved nearer. "Why?"

Her breath caught in her throat. "You've got to go now." She shrank against the house. "Back to your boat. I want you to sail away from here and never come back."

"Do you now?" He was standing so close to her, he felt the enveloping warmth of her body. He inhaled the delicate scent of her. "Honey, it's not going to be that easy—for either of us."

Reaching out, he seized her shoulders. A thrill coursed through him even as he pulled her, trembling to him.

"Easy, honey, I'm not going to hurt you."

"Maybe you won't be able to help yourself."

He swallowed. His callused hand caressed her cheek and moved down to her throat. Her skin was as smooth as Stephie's ribbon, only sleeker, warmer. He felt her quiver even at this slight touching from him, and his faint smile mocked her.

For one frozen instant she was still. He leaned over and gently grazed her mouth with his. She was delicious. Warm. Electric. A wildness raced in his blood. She made him ache hotly for everything he had always wanted from a woman and never had. His tongue slid across the edge of her lower lip.

She gasped, and for a second she yielded to the exquisite need he aroused in her, clinging to him hungrily. She ran her hands across the warmth of his muscular chest, twisting her slender fingers into the mat of crisp, golden-brown curls there. Her fingertips hovered in tremulous wonder above the mad excitement of his thudding heart. Nestling closer, she seemed on the verge of giving him all of herself. Then she tensed.

The minute she did, he tightened his arms, forcing her nearer. She bent her head back and sucked in her breath. Very slowly she lifted her hand to his face and traced the shape of his jawline with hot faltering fingertips. Next they explored the curve of his lips.

Again he thrilled to the sensual exploration of her silken touch. Then that mysterious fear came again into her eyes, and she cried softly, struggling to get away from him.

Every male cell felt swollen with arousal.

He let her go. Bewildered, he stared after her as she ran into the house.

What the hell was it with her? She didn't even know who he was, and she was terrified of him. There was no way he could tell her the truth.

And he wanted to.

Five

Christopher was sitting on the porch steps with his forehead buried in his hands, with his frustrated desire burning through him like a brand, when Dallas tiptoed back outside.

"I'm sorry," she whispered on a raw desperate note.

He whirled.

She stood barefoot in the lighted doorway, the masses of gleaming hair flowing over her shoulders like rivers of gold. She faced him rigidly, like a doe at bay, her blue eyes wary, her frightened face without color.

Time stood motionless as those immense velvet eyes caught his.

"I'm sorry." Her voice was softer now.

He knew a real apology when he heard one. He felt flattered, aroused—that, although she was afraid, she cared enough to come back.

"You saved Stephie," she said. "I was unforgivably rude."

"Because I was unforgivably pushy."

Dallas's lashes fluttered against her bloodless cheeks. "There are reasons—"

"So you're haunted by ghosts, too?"

She swallowed hard and nodded.

His mouth thinned.

"Maybe you thought I led you on—by coming aboard your boat," she whispered.

"I thought a lot of things...but not that."

"Maybe..."

He could see the movement of her breasts through her knit T-shirt. Didn't she know that the taste of her lingered on his lips, that the scent of her still filled his nostrils, that he was still on fire for her? "Let's drop it."

"You seem upset."

Christopher clenched his teeth. "I'm fine."

They lapsed into another of their awkward silences, only after a while, it grew less awkward. She came over and sat on the step below his. The warm silvery darkness and the magic of her nearness seemed to erase all memory of who he really was, of why he had come. Nothing existed outside of this tiny porch and the shimmering night that smelled of damp salt air and the sea. Nothing except this woman. Nothing except the hot, tense excitement she aroused in him. She was a tantalizing mixture of sensuality and innocence. He wanted to know who she was, why she was so determined to run from her ghosts and raise four children who weren't even her own.

Dallas was the first to speak. "Stephie said you rammed the dock this afternoon."

"I just started sailing," he muttered defensively.

"Most people start with little boats. They stay in their own ports."

"I'm not...most people. When I have dangerous inclinations, I follow them."

"Such as?"

He stared at her thick, lush, silvery hair, at her slender back, at her narrow waist and perfectly curved bottom. He remembered the hot dark thrill of holding her, and his body tightened. "Like coming here," he murmured quietly.

"You mean setting out on a cruise before you'd mastered sailing?"

He smiled enigmatically. "That. And this, too. Being out here with you."

"I'm not dangerous. You're the one—"

"Oh, but you are—to me."

"Why am I the one who keeps running away?"

"I told you—when I have dangerous inclinations, unlike you, I follow them." His spirits were rocketing sky-high.

"You must lead an exciting life."

"There are those who think so."

"But what do *you* think about your life?"

Nobody had ever asked him that before.

"It's hellishly lonely." He'd been a Hollywood prince, but his low tone was grim as he remembered all the big, perfectly furnished, lonely palaces he'd lived in, all the governesses and servants who'd played Mother and Father, roles his parents had never played. "And I've made a lot of mistakes."

"Because you followed those dangerous inclinations?"

"Partly."

He began to talk about himself. Why had he thought it was hard to talk to her when it was so easy? He found himself telling her about the emptiness of his childhood, telling her hurts he had never confided before. Although he pretended he'd been born into a wealthy ranching family, he stuck to the generalities of his real life, so that he was emotionally truthful. He spoke of his self-absorbed parents, of their neglect. He had been like their pet, not their child. He'd been raised by servants, sent to military schools. He told her how, when he was mad or hurt, he'd done wild stupid things.

She listened, gravely sympathetic, but even as he savored this tenderness, he knew it would vanish the moment she found out who he really was.

When she grew less wary, he asked about her life. She told

him about graduate school, about her sister and brother-in-law dying, about giving up her studies to run the marina and raise their children, about missing her intellectual life.

"Surely there was another solution," he said softly, realizing in amazement that they were talking like friends—instead of enemies.

"No. My brother wanted to send them to boarding schools."

Christopher's gaze narrowed. It was going to be one hell of a fight, taking Stephie from her.

Dallas went on talking. "I couldn't let that happen. So, maybe you and I aren't so different. I do these crazy impulsive things that feel right, only sometimes they turn out wrong. But I had to try this." She paused. "My sister helped me once." A look that was pure pain and all grief came into Dallas's eyes. "S-suddenly what I was doing with my own life didn't seem all that important. Not that it's been easy."

"This would be a big job for anybody."

"Just when I think things are under control something awful happens. Like Stephie—tonight." Dallas turned away, upset.

"But I was here," he said gently. *Whose side was he on?*

"Stephie doesn't usually walk in her sleep, but every time Gordon comes, the kids act crazy. Once, Patrick ran away in a dinghy and spent a night on the far shore. Another time, Rennie and Jennie snuck off on motorcycles with the worst boys in their high school. And now Stephie."

His position on the step above Dallas gave Christopher an unrestricted view of her long legs and thighs. He ached to touch her. With a frown he tightened his grip on the railing.

"Sounds like you need a new boyfriend."

"Gordon says that a woman with four kids can't be choosy."

Christopher's heart was pounding again. He forced himself to calm down. "A woman with four kids had better be."

Dallas began to dust her hands on her shorts as if to go. "Look. It's been nice chatting with you Mr.—?"

"Sto—" He caught himself. "Chance." He tried to smile casually.

"Mr. Chance." Her voice was a velvet caress, saying his name.

"The last name's McCall," Christopher drawled.

She got up slowly. "Well, good night, Chance McCall."

He stood up, too. "Don't. Not yet."

She paused, uncertain.

It was difficult making his drawl light and easy as he framed the question that had been on his mind the whole time they'd been talking. "So why did Stephie say that about her birth daddy...coming to take her away?"

Dallas blinked hard and tried to act casual, too. She dusted her hands on her hips again. "I'm sorry you had to hear that. Stephie is a highly emotional child. We don't know where she gets that trait."

Christopher knew.

Dallas hesitated. "Oh, what does it hurt?" She bit her lip. "Stephie just found out she was adopted. It's been very traumatic for all of us."

"She should have been told a long time ago."

"My sister never got around to it. I think she was afraid it might have made a difference since the other children weren't adopted. Then after Carrie died, I thought it best to put off telling Stephie until she got over her grief. I'm afraid she found out the worst way possible."

"How?"

"I was quarreling with..."

He eyed Dallas intently.

"With her biological father. You can't possibly imagine how horrible it was."

Christopher's hard mouth was pressed tightly together. "Try me."

"I didn't know Stephie was listening. She heard just enough so that I had to tell her the truth." Dallas paused. "I shouldn't be burdening you with my problems."

He swallowed. "Somehow they seem like my own."

"You're very kind."

His strong features were absolutely expressionless. "Kindness has nothing to do with it."

"Stephie's always been insecure. It's been pretty upsetting for her to find out she's different than her brothers and sisters. The worst of it is she knows now that her birth father's alive and that he wants her."

"Why is that so bad?" His voice was strangely hoarse.

"He's absolutely dreadful."

"You know him well?" His mouth twisted sardonically.

"I know about him, and I made the mistake of telling her about him. She's been terrified ever since."

Christopher's drawl was low and tense. "Did you deliberately try to make her scared of him?"

"No, of course not. But we've all been through a lot this past year—more than any of us can handle. And now this. She's only six. It's no wonder she can't handle it. I can't, either. Look, I'm sorry. I shouldn't have told you all this. But sometimes…it all gets to be too much."

"I understand."

"I want to protect her. But this isn't your problem. It's mine. You probably don't even have kids. Right?"

He felt swift, white-hot fury at this assumption. "Right," he muttered, jamming his fists into his jean pockets.

"But you've been a good listener. Wonderful in fact."

He felt like punching out a windowpane. He might have done something stupid, but he was saved when a piece of furniture crashed upstairs in the children's bedroom and the porch ceiling quivered.

They both glanced up and then at each other. She smiled. "Sounds like I'd better go upstairs now and make sure Stephie really goes to bed."

"I'm coming with you."

"You don't need to."

"I have a vested interest."

She looked genuinely puzzled. The ceiling thudded again as if there were stampeding elephants up there.

He grinned. "Let's just say it's been a helluva long day. I sailed across the bay, rammed the sea wall, tore a chunk out of my foot, saved Stephie, met you. I need my beauty sleep. I want to make sure the little monster really stays put."

Together they went upstairs. Dallas opened her bedroom door just as Patrick screamed, "Gottcha!" and pounded two pillows over Rennie's head. Jennie and Stephie jumped into the frenzy. Patrick's pillow broke and zillions of feathers flew in the icy draft wafting from a window unit.

"Kids, please!" Dallas began helplessly.

The kids kept battling amidst snowing feathers.

"Kids!" Christopher's single word cracked like thunder.

Raised pillows froze in midair, and there was instant silence. Through the falling feathers, four young, worried faces studied the stranger towering in their midst.

"It's bedtime, darlings," Dallas said.

At the sound of their aunt's familiar voice, the kids began chattering madly again.

"Bedtime means silence," Christopher said firmly.

"Not usually," Patrick countered.

"Tonight it does," said Christopher in a tone that brooked no further discussion.

Five minutes later the three older children were in blue bedrolls on the floor. Stephie was curled up in the big double bed by Dallas with a gilt-edged storybook.

"Don't they have their own beds?" Christopher asked, settling himself at the foot of the bed.

"Yes. Their own rooms, too," Dallas said. "But they all sleep with me. I know you must think I spoil them."

"No." He was remembering the loneliness of the big bedrooms he'd slept in as a child. He'd had very little love.

Dallas picked up a couple of storybooks. "It all started when I first came here. We spent the first nights in our own rooms. Then Stephie moved into my bed. Then the others."

Christopher glanced at Dallas. "Stephie sleeps with you—every night?"

"She's been afraid...ever since Carrie and Nick died."

"She's a lucky little girl." He had spoken before he thought. There was a warmth in his eyes and his voice. He was beginning to wonder how he could ever take Stephie away.

"Stephie probably got up...because I went downstairs to wash dishes."

"Would you read me the story about the white horses again, Aunt Dallas?" Stephie asked, handing her aunt the book.

Dallas smoothed the child's hair and began a tale about a white knight with white horses and a white castle who saved a princess from a dragon. There were pictures of the knight splashing about in the surf battling the dragon, of the victorious knight carrying the princess to his castle high on a hill. Stephie was soon so absorbed in the story that she forgot Christopher sprawled across the foot of her bed.

Golden lamplight gleamed in Dallas's fair curls. The twins were sitting on top of their bedrolls French-braiding each other's hair as they listened. A shaggy gray dog's tags jingled as he scratched a flea. Two cats lazed in a corner.

With shining eyes, Patrick crawled up beside Christopher and let Christopher ruffle his soft yellow hair. A cozy familial warmth seeped inside Christopher. He felt better then he had in years—since before Sally died.

When Dallas finished the story, Stephie was asleep. Patrick handed Dallas a comic book that featured *The Tiger*, but she shook her head.

"We always read Stephie's story." The boy stared straight at Christopher. "*The Tiger*'s my favorite!"

Christopher swallowed guiltily.

"Tomorrow night," Dallas promised. "Turn off the light." Patrick was about to object, but Christopher silenced him with a look.

Dallas drew Christopher into the hall. When she shut the

door, they were in total darkness. Christopher felt relieved. The cover of Patrick's book had been a publicity still of himself in his mask. Nevertheless, he had felt alarm.

"Stephie loves that story about the horses," Dallas said. "I do, too."

"I thought you weren't the romantic type," he murmured.

"Not in real life. I haven't had much luck with men."

In the darkness she sounded as disillusioned with men as he was with women. Again he wondered why.

"What kind of man do you want?"

"I guess I'm like Stephie. I want the knight with the white horses. Only I'm old enough to know life isn't a fairy tale. There aren't any white knights."

"Maybe because there aren't any princesses worth fighting for anymore." He spoke in a cynical, male, goaded undertone.

"Take my hand," she commanded in a cool voice as if such a comment wasn't what she wanted to hear.

His huge warm hand closed around her delicate fingers. They fit perfectly. As always, her touch was electric. He imagined their bodies fitting together with equal perfection. He longed to draw her into his arms, to lose himself to the sweetness of her warm body in the all-enveloping darkness of the hall. With that thought he brought her fingers to his lips and kissed them. He pulled her to him.

"Don't get the wrong idea," she said, tugging him toward the stairs. "I'm only leading you because I don't want you to break your neck in the dark on a skateboard or something."

"Thanks for bringing me back to my senses," he murmured dryly.

Despite her rejection, a strange, relaxing warmth spread through him as she led him safely past all the obstacles in their path. It seemed to him that he belonged with her in this house, with these children. When they reached the lighted kitchen, he didn't let go of her.

He could see the startled fear in her blue eyes when she glanced down at their entwined fingers. No matter what she might say about her white knight, there was fire in her, desire, warmth—for him. She bit her lips nervously.

"Relax," he whispered.

She yanked her hand free, quickly, too quickly. "How can I with you around?"

"You were good with the kids," he said, attempting to regain his own self-control.

"So were you."

"You sound surprised," he said.

"You don't much look like the fatherly type."

"Why do you keep saying that?"

Her eyes went over his sunburned muscles. At the perfection of his shirtless physique, she drew a deep breath. "You've got that unattached look—no wife, no kids. You've got a boat, your freedom. I've met men like that...who don't want anything else."

"The perfect life." His drawl was very deep, very Texas, and very cynical. "I wish." He was silent. "I'd better go."

But before he could, the screen door was yanked open from the outside. Gordon stormed through it and scowled the instant he saw Christopher. "What are you doing here?"

"Chance was helping me put Stephie to bed," Dallas explained quickly.

"You let *him* go up to your bedroom?"

"She let me do more than that."

Gordon's face went purple.

"Why, she even let me listen to her read a bedtime story."

Gordon whirled on Dallas. "Are you so desperate that an man will do?"

"'A woman with four kids can't be choosy,'" Christophe reminded him ever so softly. "I like kids."

But Gordon didn't hear him because he was already stalkin out the door.

"Gordon..." Dallas pushed the door open.

Christopher's large brown hand closed over hers. "Don

chase him, Dallas. That's the worst thing you can do—if you want his respect.''

"I was going to apologize."

"You weren't doing anything wrong. He owes you an apology.''

Christopher barred the door. He was so close, she had to tip her head back to look into his eyes. Mere inches separated them as he stared down at her with unwavering intensity. They stood for a long moment.

Carefully, oh, so careful not to touch him, she closed the door. "You made him mad on purpose," she accused softly.

"Sometimes I can't help myself."

"Why?"

"I guess I didn't like the way he was treating you. He takes you for granted." Christopher pushed the door back open.

"I thought...maybe you were jealous," she said.

Christopher laughed softly. "Did you want me to be?"

"No! Don't be ridiculous! Of course not!"

"No, of course not," he agreed, but at his quick, mocking smile, she blushed.

"Thanks for what you did and for the advice...about Gordon," she said weakly. "I've made a lot of mistakes with men."

"I've made my share with women," he admitted. "If you're smart, you'll stay away from me."

"So far, you've been kind of hard to avoid."

He smiled sheepishly.

She smiled back. "If you're such a bad news guy, why the warning?"

His white grin broadened. "'Cause I'm not only bad, I'm crazy."

"I don't believe you."

"Really?" He almost laughed out loud. Maybe he was making some progress after all. "Does that mean I'm looking more like a white knight?"

Her gaze touched his broad, sunburned shoulders, the solid

wall of his chest, his snug jeans. "I wouldn't go that far."
But she blushed again—as if she liked what she saw.

"You were telling me about your mistakes with men."

All her color drained from her face. "I'm divorced."

He considered this and shrugged. "Is that really such a big
deal?"

"To me and my family it was."

"Relax. In my case, divorce was the smartest move I ever
made," he said grimly. "Everybody gets at least one these
days."

Her throat worked convulsively. "Maybe where you come
from."

He saw painful memories—her ghosts, he thought—flash
briefly in her eyes. "Where I come from, it's the smallest sin."
His low voice was gentle. "Not the cheapest, but the smallest."

"Well, it wasn't even my smallest. So how long are you
staying?"

"Now that depends," he murmured.

"On what?"

His raspy voice was tensed with emotion. "On you."

She bit her lip and carved a design with her fingernail into
the door frame. One minute she was there; the next she wasn't.
But long after she had gone he remembered the sad way her
lips had twisted and the haunted brilliance of her eyes.

He was more mystified than ever. The more she seemed to
like him, the more frightened she became.

Six

Christopher was in a foul mood as he clenched the phone. He wasn't up to dealing with his volatile agent's ranting. Dallas had ignored him ever since he'd saved Stephie.

The noon sun was white-hot dazzle. Rivulets of perspiration trickled down Christopher's spine. He leaned back against the cushions beneath the shade of his blue bimini. Cal's voice buzzed hysterically. Christopher set the phone down and poured himself a cup of ice water, draining it slowly. What he really needed was a swim in the pool.

When he picked the phone up again, Cal was screaming even louder than before. "Have you even heard a word I've said?"

"As few as possible. Look, Cal, I can't come back. Wrap things up for me there, and I'll show up in Spain when they're ready to start filming."

"How in the fungus hell can production start without your insurance physical?"

"These guys'll bend if they have to. Fix it, Cal."

"There's a lot at stake."

Stephie was tiptoeing daintily across wet grass toward the boat with Patrick. She looked very pretty in blue shorts with her black hair blowing loosely in the wind. She leaned down and very carefully picked two pink buttercups.

"Yeah, there's a hell of a lot at stake," Christopher muttered.

"You said you'd be gone no more than a week."

"Has anyone in Hollywood ever lied to you before, Cal?"

Cal groaned. "Fungus! What am I supposed to tell them?"

"Tell them I'm working on my tan."

"How long—"

Dallas came out onto the back porch of her house. At the sight of her in tight jeans and a polka-dot halter top, Christopher felt a hot rush of desire.

"This is complicated, Cal."

"Just tell her who you are and grab your kid and scram."

Dallas looked up and saw Christopher. He waved. Her hands tightened into small fists at her sides. Then she knocked over a planter and became totally flustered rearranging ivy leaves and dirt into her pot before she dashed back inside.

"Like I said, it's complicated."

"I bet if I flew out, I could take care of it in a day."

"No!"

Christopher stared at the screen door that Dallas closed behind her. "This is something I want to handle myself. She doesn't trust me. Any time I act interested in her or her life or her kids, she gets very threatened."

"Smart girl."

"Yeah, she's smart..." his uneasy smile was deeply sensual "...when it comes to books. This may take awhile. I've paid a month's rent in advance."

"A month! Are you crazy?"

"Read the tabloids." Christopher held the phone away from his ear until Cal stopped yelling. "I've got to win her trust so she won't be afraid to give Stephie to me. The best thing I can figure to do is to work at winning the kids first.''

Patrick and Stephie had nearly reached the dock.

"And here they are, Cal.''

"Don't hang—''

"Sorry, Cal.''

Christopher was securing the phone below when Patrick and Stephie came up to the yacht.

"Y'all come on aboard,'' Christopher drawled, Texas-style.

Patrick shot him an odd look before he jumped aboard. Stephie squatted down and watched them warily from the dock.

"So what's your Aunt Dallas up to this morning?'' Christopher asked casually.

"She cooked us pancakes,'' Patrick said.

"I had cold cereal,'' Christopher said.

"Great big fluffy ones!'' Stephie hollered from the dock, rubbing salt into his wound. "She made homemade syrup, too.''

Christopher scowled at them both.

"I guess Aunt Dallas wanted to show off for Gordon,'' Patrick said.

More salt into an already burning wound. Christopher's grim expression grew darker.

"Only, Gordon sulked and wouldn't eat or speak to Aunt Dallas.''

Well, at least there was some good news.

"Hey, guys, how would you like to help me dive for White Horse?'' Christopher suggested, to get off the topic of Gordon.

"Who?'' Patrick asked.

"It's a stuffed horse Stephie pitched into the drink.'' Christopher stripped his shirt off.

His sunburn had darkened, and his powerful sinewy muscles were now a deep shade of glistening bronze.

"Wow! You've sure got a lot of muscles,'' Patrick said. "Like *The Tiger*.''

Christopher's mouth tightened into a forbidding line. Patrick shifted uncomfortably. A look passed between the boy and man. Then without a word Christopher dove into the water. Patrick peeled his shirt off eagerly and jumped in after him. Stephie leaned over the dock and watched their splashes and kicks and bubbles with huge dark eyes. They both dove repeatedly into the muddy brown water. Finally Christopher gave up and hung onto the dock exhausted. Patrick swam over, pulled himself up, too, hanging in a pose that exactly matched Christopher's.

"I—I think I threw him over there," Stephie said pointing toward the stern.

Patrick made two final dives and came up with a dripping lump. He lifted a stringy tail. "Is this him?"

"That's White Horse," Christopher confirmed.

"Poor White Horse," Patrick said laying the pitiful lump on the dock before Stephie. "Just look what you did."

Stephie grew very sad as she studied the sodden animal. Gingerly she touched him on the nose and water squished out of him. "I could hose him off," she offered.

"Would you?" Christopher's voice was very gentle.

She didn't seem to mind when Christopher heaved himself onto the dock and knelt beside her. Nor did she mind when she brushed against his arm as she tenderly hosed White Horse.

She looked up trustingly at Christopher. "Did you like him a whole lot?"

In the past two days, she had become less afraid. "Yes," he murmured, his smile again softening the harsh lines of his face.

"Was he as white as the horses in my storybook?"

Christopher nodded.

"Will he ever be white like that again?"

"Probably not, but we'll have to do our best to take care of him."

"Maybe if we dried him in the oven?" Stephie offered.

"What about your Aunt Dallas?"

"Aunt Dallas wouldn't mind."

But Aunt Dallas *did* mind.

When Christopher strolled into the kitchen as the children's welcome guest, Dallas was in the middle of a tense conversation with Gordon.

Christopher grinned at them boldly. All conversation stopped. Dallas seemed unable to look anywhere but at him, and he, too, grew hotly aware of her. "Do you have a pan we could use to dry our horse?" he asked innocently.

She got up, snatched a pan from a cabinet and banged it down in front of him. "There!"

"Thank you," he purred mockingly.

Dallas was so flustered, she was speechless, but her eyes wouldn't leave Christopher. Without a word, Gordon got up and stalked out. Only when the door slammed behind him, did she flush with embarrassment at the realization that she'd completely forgotten Gordon.

As Dallas rushed belatedly after him, Christopher's lips twitched sardonically. "Not more boyfriend trouble?"

Tense and silent, Dallas stormed back inside. "As if you care."

"You bet I do." With a slow appreciative lift of his brows, his eyes flashed over her with wolfish delight.

Seething, hating the new easiness between the big interloper and her children, she watched Christopher help them adjust the oven.

To retaliate, she sent the children upstairs to change. Christopher was about to go when she attacked. "Do you mind telling me what's so special about that horse?"

She looked mad enough to strangle him. What the hell had he done? Why the hell should he walk around her?

"I'll tell you sometime when you're in a more receptive mood." His low tone was a deliberate insult.

"Tell me now. There's nothing wrong with my mood."

He drew a sharp breath. "Right. You could probably charm the fangs off any rattlesnake." He set his hot insolent gaze on her until she flushed. "Honey, did it ever occur to you that you're not the only one with a temper?" He opened the screen door with a violent gesture and walked out.

Hours later, Stephie came down to the boat with White Horse tucked under her arm.

"Is he dry?" Christopher asked, glancing up from the nautical knot he was practicing tying.

"Almost. I was afraid he might burn."

"That was nice of you to take such good care of him."

"Aunt Dallas says he needs to sit in the sun 'cause he stinks. She told me to bring him down here to you."

At the mention of Dallas, his fingers snapped the line taut. He forced himself to focus on his little girl. "Did she now?" he asked gently.

His stomach was as tight as his knot, but not even the mention of Dallas could spoil this moment for him. This was the first time his child had willingly approached him alone.

"He stinks because you threw him into the saltwater," Christopher said.

"I was scared of you."

"And are you still scared of me?"

Her big dark eyes shone. "No." Then she turned her toes inward just like Sally used to when she was very pleased with herself. "Why's his name White Horse?"

"Another little girl named him that."

"Doesn't she love him anymore?"

"She loved him very much, but she went away and couldn't take him with her."

"Like my mama."

Her face was very still.

His expression was equally grave. "Yes...like that. I've been keeping him for her. I think he misses having a little girl to play with."

"I'd play with him," she said wistfully.

"Will you tell him you're sorry you threw him in the water?"

She nestled her forehead against White Horse's damply pungent fur. "I'm sorry, White Horse."

"If you promise to take good care of him, I'll let him stay with you—if I can come up every night and tell him good night."

Again, the big dark eyes met his as she considered his request. Finally she said, "You can come up...if you'll read me the story about the white horses."

He wanted to take her in his arms, to kiss her. To tell her he knew what it was to lose someone you loved. Most of all he wanted to tell her who he was, but he didn't want to scare her. So, he held out his hand. She placed her tiny one in his, and they shook on it.

Clutching White Horse to her breast, Stephie withdrew from him and exhaled softly in amazement. Then she skipped all the way back to the house.

That night, when Christopher went to the house to tell Stephie good-night, he secretly hoped to find Dallas reading to the children. He wanted again to feel the warmth of her love for them. But she wasn't there. He read Stephie's story twice, but the whole time he was with Stephie, he grew angry wondering if Dallas was with Gordon. When Christopher went downstairs, he looked for her everywhere.

He was walking by the pool toward the dock when a slim figure moved out of the shadows. "Chance—" Dallas stepped out of the darkness to decorate the night.

A bolt of excitement shot through him. Moonlight turned her hair to silver and made her eyes sparkle. His anger dissolved.

At last she had come to him, and she had deliberately chosen a place where they would have privacy from the children.

Light and shadow emphasized her delicate features, her smooth forehead, her high cheekbones and her slender nose.

Her soft, pink mouth was slightly opened. She bit her lips. Then her tongue licked the bitten spot. He ripped his fake glasses off so that he could see her better.

Why did she have to be so incredibly beautiful?

She hesitated. That should have warned him, but instead of being warned, he reached for her and pulled her to him. Their lips met. At first, he thought merely to taste her once. But she was sweet like warm sugar melting against his mouth. One taste, and he was like a starving man ravenous for more.

He was about to kiss her again.

"No!" she cried, beginning to struggle.

He ran his hand under her thin T-shirt, and she trembled, caught between desire, terror and the will to resist. "Honey, this time you came to me." He shaped his hand to her rounded breasts, and her nipples became instantly erect. His own similar response was equally swift and total.

He forgot everything but her. His whole being pulsed with desire. His fingers roamed lower, over her belly, her thighs. The soft texture of her bare skin beneath his calloused fingertips rocked his senses.

Gradually she stilled. Then she arched her body to fit his. Her leg wound around his leg. She was smooth and warm. He felt hot and tightly alive. Skin to skin. Body to body. Male to female. She shaped herself to him. She was sweet wild magic. His arms tightened, and he silently pulled her into the shadows.

Then his mouth covered hers, and fire raced through him. His hands were in her hair, smoothing it against the column of her neck. For weeks she had tormented him. First, by insulting him and refusing to give Stephie to him. Then by driving him crazy with unwanted desire...

His mouth grew hot as he forced her lips apart. His tongue slid into her mouth. "You are beautiful," he breathed. "And sweet. I never expected this."

"Neither did I."

"I wouldn't have come."

"If only you hadn't." A soft tormented sigh escaped her lips.

"How different life would be if humans were granted all their if onlies," he muttered grimly even as his hands mussed her golden hair. "All the shrinks would starve. I had to come."

Suddenly he was a pleasure so intense she couldn't stop her body from melting into his, her arms from stealing convulsively around his neck while her mouth burned against his with equal fire.

He had known passion, but never like this. Her hunger and fevered madness were a perfect match to his. She unleashed all his power, all his wildness. There had been other women in his life; she made him know none of them had ever mattered.

It was a painful shock to them both when she wrenched free.

Her voice trembled. "Stop it. Please... You must—"

He forced his hands to his sides, knotting them in frustration. His breathing was deep.

"This is all wrong," she whispered. "Why am I doing this when I despise you?"

His dark laughter filled the grim blackness of the night. He smoothed his hair that she had tangled with her hands.

"Did you really think you could fool me?" she cried. "That I wouldn't know what a man like you was after?"

He stared at her in shock. *Had she had found him out?*

"I was just playing along with you tonight," she said. "To see how far you'd go with your dirty little game."

"You should have known I'd go all the way."

"You are a scoundrel!"

"The world has already established that fact," he agreed. But his hands were clenched again at his sides.

"To play on children's affections—just to bed me."

When she did not go on, he stared at her in openmouthed amazement. "Is that all? You mean, you don't really know—"

She was white-faced with anger. He felt faint with relief. She had not found him out after all. "You've got it all wrong, honey," he finished softly.

"Then what was that kiss all about?"

"Come to me any night, and I'll give you a lesson in biology. It's very simple. You want me, and I want you."

"You are a rogue."

"It's more fun to sleep with a rogue than a saint."

"That will never happen."

"Yes, it will, and sooner than you think."

"No!"

His lips curved into a bitter, knowing smile.

"Stay away from me and stay away from my children!"

His eyes blazed into hers with unrelenting determination, but he said nothing.

Only when she backed away and ran stumbling toward the house, did he make a vow in a low inaudible tone.

"No way, lady."

Dallas dashed all the way to her bathroom and locked herself in. She splashed hot water into the tub so the children couldn't hear her sobs and so the steam would cloud the mirror and she couldn't see her face. Then she wept shattering tears of self-loathing.

After years of struggling to redeem herself, of going to church every—no, almost every—Sunday, of burying herself alive on college campuses, of dating safe men, she was still a wanton with dangerous, self-destructive impulses. Why *couldn't* she change?

From the moment she had stumbled onto Chance's boat by mistake, she had known she was lost. Oh, how terribly beautiful he'd been. Right from the first he'd sensed her hunger for his dark powerful body, a longing made fiercer by her years of self-punishing, self-inflicted celibacy. Half-naked in that towel with the planes of chest and his muscular shoulders exposed, he'd been a rampantly virile giant. His brown hair

had been overlong and untidy. His brown eyes beneath dark
brows, his straight, almost aquiline nose, his high cheekbones
and the hard lines of jaw and chin were all set in perfect
symmetry.

Even in those ridiculous intellectual-looking glasses that
didn't suit him at all, he'd been beautiful. And he knew it.
He'd probably never read a book in his life—he hadn't had
to. He was physical and direct. She'd been valedictorian of
her high school.

He brought it all back—all the pain and the heartache and
ruination of so many lives. Why had he come? Why didn't he
go? She felt like he was stalking her. She needed to worry
about the children and the marina. Instead, thoughts of Chance
consumed her.

Hours later, she crawled into bed and fell instantly asleep
only to dream her recurring nightmare. As always, she was in
that surreal, white, hospital corridor. A baby was crying, as it
was being carried away. She was running after it, but its cries
grew fainter and fainter. The silence after that was like death.
She sprang awake in her bed, her heart pounding with terror.

The air conditioner blasted her with icy air. For a long moment she stared at her bare arms gleaming in the moonlight.
Bitter memory replaced the terrible dream. Wearily, she ran
her hands through her hair, got up, pulled on her robe and
carefully stepped over the hushed children.

Why couldn't she forget? *They had promised her she would
forget.* Downstairs she turned on the light, but the familiar
clutter of the kitchen seemed like a prison. She snapped the
light off again and rushed out into the night.

The moon was low against the water as she headed away
from the marina to the beach, and the water glimmered like a
flat black mirror. The warm night air was close and humid.
Her feet sank into the soft wet sand.

She brushed her hair out of her eyes and stared across the
water. Then she sat down on a log that had washed up and
hugged her knees to her chest.

A disembodied male voice came out of the darkness and electrified her. "So the ghosts have chased you from your bed, too," Christopher said very softly.

She glanced toward him and sensed that he understood. "I didn't come down here looking for you, if that's what you're thinking."

"It isn't."

"Don't come any nearer," she whispered. "Don't touch me."

"Okay." He held his hands up to show that he was harmless. "Do you mind if the big bad wolf sits down?" His manner was elaborate with gravity.

She considered. His expression was kind. She pointed to the far end of the log. "Not if you sit there."

"That's very kind." He sat down. The still dark silence enveloped them. "Bad dreams?"

She shuddered. "Awful."

"Mine, too." He paused. "Do you want to talk about it?"

"No."

Again he seemed to understand. His low tone was gentle. "Some things are hard to get over."

"Impossible," she said.

"All we can do is try to do better the next time."

"The next time—" She glanced toward him with glittering eyes. "That's the last thing I want."

"Then you're not just running from your past, Dallas. You're running from life."

"Isn't that just a convenient line because you're on the make?"

"Damn." The single word exploded from him.

He got up, coldly furious. For some crazy reason she grabbed his hand. "Please, don't go. That was unfair of me."

His dark eyes met hers.

"Please," she said.

He sat back down.

"I—I know I would be just another woman to you," she said. "I've had that sort of thing before."

His low tone was tense. "Maybe you're wrong about me."

Was she? Doubt tore through her. She moved closer to him, sliding along the log. She brushed her fingers across the back of his hand. Gradually his arm came around her shoulders: gently he pulled her to him. She let her head fall back against his shoulder.

For a long time they sat like that. Until she said, "Chance, I'm afraid of you because of the past."

He looked into her eyes. "You've been crying." A pause. "Because of me?"

She nodded.

"Don't." His hand stroked her tumbled hair. "I'm not worth it. If you're scared, I'll wait."

"You don't understand. I can't ask that. I don't want you wasting your time waiting for me. A long time ago I made a choice about my life, about the kind of person I'm going to be."

"Everything's different now." A pause. "For both of us."

"I won't make the same mistakes again!"

"Let's pray that neither of us do," he said quietly.

She sensed a pain in him that was as pure and all-consuming as her own.

"Chance," she whispered, trying to hold a light rein on her feelings. "I can't let you mean anything to me."

A wicked gleam came into his dark eyes. "Maybe you can't stop yourself." His voice had become thicker and seductively huskier.

"Just because you're handsome, that doesn't mean I'm going to jump into bed with you!"

"So you admit you're attracted?"

"What?"

He grinned. "Honey, I'm going to be your next time. And you're going to be mine."

She shook her head. But she was afraid.

More afraid than ever.

Seven

The next morning, Dallas stood on the pier while Gordon prepared to go. Impatient, she watched him fuss with his auxiliary and radar, coil his lines as he made everything ready. He ordered her about coldly, and she fumbled, displeasing him. He shouted at her while Chance watched them with keen, cynical interest from his own boat.

When Gordon jumped onto the dock to kiss her goodbye, she twisted her face so that his cool lips barely grazed her cheek. Only when she met the dark insolence of Chance's gaze, did she wrap her arms around Gordon with a show of defiant affection and kiss him passionately.

But it was Chance's hot look, not Gordon's kiss, that made her feel she was burning on the inside. Later, as she watched Gordon sail away, she felt only relief. Then her eye caught Chance's amused gaze, and she knew he saw through her like glass.

A dangerous stranger had sailed into her life, and nothing was the same. After that night on the moonlit beach, Dallas was even more wary of Christopher. She had practically admitted she wanted him. There was now a new closeness between them even though she tried to pretend there wasn't.

Because of Chance, she was more afraid than ever of the latent sensuality in her nature, and she feared any similar tendency in the twins. But while Dallas began smothering her figure with layers of clothing, the girls stripped down to bikinis. Every time she saw their bare brown midriffs, she carried out their cover-ups.

Dallas had more nightmares. Only now when she woke up, she was afraid to go out. Once, however, the terrible feelings so overpowered her that she sneaked out at dawn. When she came to the marina, Chance was there in the darkness, his great body lounging negligently against a piling. His white shirt was open and fluttering, and her eyes were drawn like a magnet to his smooth tanned skin underneath.

They didn't speak, but she felt funny little dartings of sensation in her stomach as she hung there with an insane, suicidal desire to run her fingertips up and down his brown skin, knowing that he would welcome her into his arms. Maybe when she knew the rapture of his lovemaking, she could forget the pain that had haunted her for years. But when he started boldly toward her, her knees began to shake. She stared at him for a frozen second. Then she cried out and raced past him.

It didn't help that the kids adored him. Patrick and he were great friends. The boy had taught Chance to skateboard while Chance had taught him to board sail. Rennie and Jennie were crazy about him, too, and were constantly on his boat in their bikinis, which Dallas imagined Chance enjoyed immensely.

Dallas pleaded with them to stay away from him, but they wouldn't listen. Then one afternoon the girls picked the wrong time to saunter through the kitchen in their bikinis on their way to his boat. Dallas had just burned her pie crusts when she heard the twins' giggles on the stairs.

They flounced through the kitchen carrying towels and their boom box. "Hi, Aunt Dallas—"

Through the haze of smoke Dallas saw long slim legs, wiggling breasts and bottoms. Her smoking crusts tumbled into the trash.

"Girls!"

They stopped, their expressions instantly sulky.

"Where are you two going...dressed, or should I say undressed, like that?" Dallas asked.

"What's wrong with the way we're dressed?" Rennie taunted.

Dallas went over and tugged Rennie's bra strap higher, but that just left more nubile flesh hanging out below. "You seem to have outgrown your costumes."

"You never cared before Mr. McCall came," Rennie said, yanking her suit back down.

"I want you both to change."

"You have a dirty mind," Rennie said.

"And Mr. McCall's is as pure as the driven snow?" Dallas said.

Both girls nodded hopefully.

"Give me a break! If you believe that, you have a lot to learn about men."

Their faces were eager for such knowledge.

"Not that I want you learning any of it any time soon. Either you change, or you help me in the kitchen."

"Why are you so old-fashioned?"

"Believe it or not, we had sex back in the olden days."

"I bet you never did," Rennie accused.

Dallas went pale.

"She's just jealous," Jennie said slyly.

"Yeah," Rennie cut in. "You sneak out at dawn when you know he'll be out there."

"He knows you like him," Jennie said. "He's always asking us about you."

"Girls!" Dallas's stern tone stopped them. "I won't listen to any more of this."

"Well, we're not going to listen to you about him, either."

On that belligerent note they bounded upstairs. When they came back down, they were more sullen than ever, but at least they were covered by voluminous T-shirts.

Dallas's victory was short-lived. An hour later she saw them sprawled across Chance's foredeck on their stomachs wearing nothing except their bikinis—with the tops undone!

The only good thing was that Chance was in the water rigging the sailboard for Patrick. Even after Patrick sailed away and the girls called to him, Chance did not go to them. He waited until Patrick fell and then swam out to him.

Dallas couldn't let the twins get by with such behavior. She had to talk to Chance. So, when the girls left that afternoon to visit friends, Dallas marched down to his boat. Naturally, he was so conceited, he misinterpreted everything.

The instant he saw her, his gaze roamed her shapely length. "I'd almost given up waiting for you to come," he said softly, as he sprang lithely to the dock and grabbed a line with a tanned arm to pull the boat nearer so that she could climb aboard more easily.

His every movement brought the play of his darkly tanned muscles. Wary, she shrank from him. "Don't you dare think I came because I wanted to."

He took her hand, and even this casual touching caused a tingle of excitement to sweep through her.

"Okay. I won't dare." His eyes twinkled with amusement as he turned her hand over in his palm. "Nevertheless, I'm glad you're here," he purred warmly.

"I told you, it's not like that."

"Right." He helped her aboard. "You've been on my mind a lot lately. No woman has ever driven me crazier."

"And I suppose a lot of women chase you." The thought was so unpleasant that she frowned.

"I've had my share, but you don't have to worry." His alert brown eyes touched her mouth and her breasts with a suggestive look that sent hot color rushing to her cheeks. "I like to do my own chasing." He grinned wickedly. "You're more my type."

"You're saying you're the kind of predator who likes to stalk his own prey. That's hardly reassuring."

"I don't think those were my exact words," he murmured dryly. "Would you like a drink?"

She sank onto a cushion as he leaned over the ice chest. "This isn't a social call," she said primly.

"Does that have to mean we can't enjoy ourselves?"

"I came because of the twins. Please, leave them alone."

He straightened abruptly. "Don't you have things backward?" The faintest edge had come into his voice. "They're the ones who come down here and bother me."

Throwing caution away, she persisted, "You seem to enjoy them."

His tone was grimmer. "I like kids."

"There's more to it than that."

"Like what?"

"They're not exactly kids. They're young women." Dallas drew a sharp little breath. "I want you to stop encouraging them."

Christopher's hand clamped around her arm and hauled her to her feet. "Just what are you accusing me of?"

"They're too interested in you."

His hard hand tightened, and, as always, when she came into physical contact with him, she lost the ability to think. It had been a dangerous stunt to come down here and confront him.

He drew her closer. His handsome face was a chiseled mask, but she sensed he was deeply angry. His body was like living muscular bronze. Suddenly, everything was reduced to some primitive level that made her feel dominated by him.

"Is that my fault?" he muttered roughly. "Their father's dead. They're at a boy-crazy age."

"You're taking advantage of their innocence."

"How?"

"You're deliberately attracting them."

"Elaborate," he snapped.

"You've been too clever. You know I can't."

"Because I'm not doing a damn thing."

In silence he regarded her for a long charged moment. Finally he said, "There's only one woman around here I want to attract. Only one woman I'm tempted to take advantage of." Dark furious fires blazed in his eyes. "The twins know it. I know it. And you know it. Maybe that's the real reason you came down here—to tempt me."

Dallas's heart went to her throat. She'd aroused a beast she was now helpless to control. "You know it isn't."

"I don't know any such thing, but why don't you show me—now—exactly what your feelings for me are."

She struggled to free his hand from her arm, but that only made him angrier. His hands tightened into a bruising vise. He dragged her against the lean hardness of his body, and his mouth covered hers in a long, punishing kiss. Her trembling hands reached up to push him away. But when they encountered solid muscle, they gave up and wound limply around his neck.

He pulled her closer and held her tighter until their bodies fused. "Don't fight me, honey. There's no way you'll win."

Desire sizzled through her like a jolt of electricity. If he was hot, he made her hotter. This was what she longed for when she lay awake. Her tongue dipped inside his mouth and ran hungrily along the edge of his teeth. He groaned aloud, and she grew aware of the passionate tremors wracking his body. There was suction on her tongue, and he pulled it deeper into his mouth until she was without breath, without life, without even the will to fight.

At last he ended the drugging kiss. His lips lifted a fraction of an inch. His moist warm breath flowed against her mouth. Her long-lashed eyes fluttered open.

Tenderly his hand brushed tangled gold wisps away from her cheek. "Why do you always think the worst of me?"

"Anybody can see us out here...like this," she whispered. Then she looked past him and found her worst fears realized. Both twins were sitting on the porch railing staring out at the marina. "Oh, dear, the twins—"

"I thought you wanted me to let them know I'm not interested in them," he murmured.

"This wasn't exactly the way I had in mind."

"All we did was kiss."

"Why did it feel like so much more?"

His enigmatic smile was tender. "You know why."

"They'll think I'm a hypocrite," she said weakly.

"You're a woman."

That was the problem.

She started to move away, but Christopher captured her chin to hold her still. Then with languorous slowness, his mouth touched hers. Like a hotly burning flame, his lips moved fleetingly across the satiny softness of her mouth once more before he let her go.

"You're an incredibly beautiful woman. We haven't done anything wrong," he said.

"Will my life ever be like it was? Are you ever going to sail away?"

He stepped in front of the sinking sun, and his long shadow fell darkly across her face. His eyes devoured her. "Only after I've gotten what I came for. And, Dallas, I'm running out of time. We need to talk."

"No—I can't. The restaurant will open in an hour."

"Then when?"

"I don't know."

"You can't put me off forever."

But she could try.

With a shaking hand Dallas was outlining her lips with lipstick. She nearly dropped the tube when she heard a man's heavy stride on the front porch.

Gordon was never early. He was always precisely on time.

She dashed to the upstairs window and peeked through the miniblinds expecting Gordon. Instead, the porch light was gleaming on Chance's brown hair. When he glanced up, she jumped back from the window. Then she turned on the twins who began suddenly brushing their hair innocently.

"What's he doing here?" Dallas demanded, putting the cap on her lipstick and thrusting it into her purse.

"You called Gordon. We called Chance."

Dallas snapped her purse shut. "I thought you agreed not to chase him."

"When we told him you were going out, he offered to baby-sit. I thought it was very sweet of him."

"Sweet?" Dallas almost shrieked the word. "You girls are teenagers. You're perfectly capable of baby-sitting."

"But Chance said he was concerned—that you were leaving us all alone."

"I'll just bet he was."

The calculating nerve of that clever, handsome devil.

Still, Dallas felt a quick twinge of guilt. She had begged Gordon to let her bring the children with her so that they could get to know him better, but he had refused.

"Chance said this place is pretty remote," Jennie explained, defending him.

Dallas picked up her brush. "For heaven's sake, we run a public restaurant."

"He told us that makes it even more dangerous," Rennie said. "Anybody could drive up."

Dallas was yanking the brush through her hair. "Why can't you see Chance is just taking advantage of this situation?"

"How?" both girls wanted to know.

"Why did you call Gordon, when it's Chance you really like?" Jennie asked before Dallas could answer.

"Because...I mean..." Dallas flushed guiltily.

"Ever since we saw you kiss him, you keep trying to pretend you don't like him," Jennie insisted.

"Why, that's pure poppycock," Dallas said. But her voice was unsteady.

"Poppy what?" Stephie demanded brightly from the doorway.

Dallas turned beet red. She set her brush firmly back down on the bureau and drew a deep calming breath. "Forget it," she said calmly. "Look, girls...I've known Gordon for years. He *is* my boyfriend."

"But he's so boring," Rennie said.

Stephie had came into the room. "And he doesn't like us."

"Of course he does."

"Then why doesn't he talk to us and play with us the way Chance does?"

Because he doesn't stoop to playing on children's emotions to get what he wants!

Instead of answering, Dallas pressed her lips tightly together and took another deep breath.

"And he never kisses you the way Chance kissed you." Rennie sighed romantically. "Chance is *so* cute."

"There's more to relationships than...than...that sort of thing," Dallas said sharply.

All three girls looked deeply puzzled. Then Stephie said with an air of immense wisdom, "When the prince kissed the princess like that in my storybook, it was the best part. They got married and lived happily ever after."

"That was a fairy tale. This is real life."

"I like the fairy tale better," Stephie said.

Dallas was at a loss to reply. Fortunately Chance's firm knock resounded against the wooden door. All three girls rushed downstairs to welcome him. Dallas reluctantly followed them. When she stepped into the living room, Chance was already surrounded by all four children. He was dressed in jeans, boots and a Western shirt made of pale blue cotton. His immense silver belt buckle caught the light and flashed at her. Stephie was telling him excitedly that Gerry, their gerbil, had gotten loose from his cage.

"We'd better find him before Harper and T.C. pounce on him and eat him for dinner," Chance said.

"I like your boots," Patrick said.

Chance awkwardly lifted one foot, and Patrick knelt down to study the boot's elaborate stitching. "They feel kind of narrow in the instep," Chance said.

"We cooked chocolate-chip cookies," Rennie and Jennie said.

"My favorite," said Chance.

He certainly had a way with kids.

Over the three golden heads and Stephie's dark one, Chance's brown eyes met Dallas's. He tucked his thumbs in his belt loops and leaned against the couch. Her nerves vibrated in response to his easy warmth.

He had a way with women, too, whispered a treacherous secret voice that Dallas was determined to ignore.

"You didn't have to come," Dallas said.

A slow smile spread across his strong sensual mouth. "I wanted to."

His virile charm was working its magic on her. The pale blue of his crisp collar emphasized his tan. Denim molded his thighs like a second skin. His ridiculous spectacles only made him more adorable. He shook his head slightly so that his silken hair would fall away from his eyes.

Nervously Dallas turned and saw the casual clutter of skateboards, half-filled glasses, dirty plates, discarded clothes and paperback books. "Kids, you know how much Gordon hates messes." She stopped when she met Chance's hard, mocking gaze. She stooped to pick up a pair of Patrick's dirty socks.

"Patrick, get your sneakers," Chance ordered quietly. "The rest of you pitch in. We want to help your aunt make a good impression on her boyfriend." Despite the smoothness of his response, there was the faintest challenge in his taunting drawl.

"We do?" This was a new concept to all the kids.

Dallas flushed. Thank goodness Chance didn't allow them

to debate the point. With his help the room was soon immaculate.

When they finished, Dallas felt awkward being alone with Chance and the kids. Chance kept looking at her, not saying anything and yet communicating a fierce tension that made her feel guilty. At last when the children went into the kitchen, he said, "The kids told me you called Gordon."

"What if I did?"

"If you were lonely, you should have come to me."

"Who said you can give me what I want?"

His glance was dark and unsmiling. "What exactly are you looking for?"

"That's my business."

"I'm making it mine." He spoke between his teeth.

Her voice grew saccharine sweet. "I thought you came over to baby-sit."

His mouth thinned. "That was only one of my reasons."

When the kids came back into the room, the atmosphere was almost volcanic. In the tense confusion, she escaped to the restaurant to check on Pepper and Oscar. Since it was Tuesday, there weren't many customers. Oscar was listening to Mexican polkas while he sliced potatoes, and Pepper was flirting with a rancher. Because she knew Chance was back at the house, Dallas lingered, folding napkins, filling water glasses as she talked to Oscar. Only when she saw Gordon's car pull up in front of the house, did she rush back. She opened the door, and both men leaped from the couch to their feet.

"Doesn't she look beautiful?" Chance's voice was rich and low.

She knew he was furious that she was going out with Gordon, but he concealed his anger with a skillful facade of easy charm. For a rancher, he was a superb actor. Her cheeks grew redder the longer Chance studied her with that possessive hot look that somehow implied she was his.

Why did he have to be so impossible—so arrogantly possessive, so difficult and somehow so dangerous? She had a right to call whomever she wanted, didn't she?

Why did she have to be so drawn to him?

"She does look beautiful," Gordon agreed unenthusiastically.

"Thank you." It was hard to be civil when she was furious at both of them. Anxious to go, she stepped toward the door.

There was a clumsy scuffle of boots on hard wooden flooring as Chance tripped over his pointed toes in his rush to open the door for her. When he lurched into her, he grinned foolishly, charmingly. Then his dark gaze raked over her with lingering intensity.

"You two have fun," he murmured.

Despite the hint of cynicism in his twisting mouth, she sensed some deeper emotion just beneath the surface.

"We will," she snapped. "Watch yourself in those boots. For a rancher, you seem a little unsure in them."

A dark flush stole across his face. He didn't even attempt a smile. "I haven't broken them in yet."

Defiantly, she thrust her hand into Gordon's.

Gordon took her to The Blue Diamond, her favorite seafood restaurant, but she couldn't concentrate on the food or Gordon. Instead, she kept wondering what Chance and the kids were doing. It was almost pleasant to imagine the kids wrecking the house and driving him as crazy as they drove her.

Hours later when Gordon pulled up to the house, the first thing she saw were four motorcycles gleaming darkly in the moonlight.

Dear Lord. Not Rodge and Stew again, and the rest of their worthless pack. Dallas had forbidden the girls to associate with them after that night when they'd ridden off with them.

The minute Gordon braked, she jumped from the car and flew past the bikes to confront Chance and the twins. Chance must have heard her because he pushed the door open from the inside. His face instantly hardened as he saw the wild panic in her eyes.

"What's wrong?" he demanded. He looked past her and saw Gordon's grim look. "Did that bastard try…"

"It's not Gordon, you idiot," she whispered. "It's you. I should have known I couldn't trust you with my children."

"What the hell have I done now?"

She burst into the living room expecting to discover bedlam only to find the four teenage boys grouped around the television eating popcorn and watching a golf tournament. The twins were in the kitchen cleaning up. That was a first. And they were modestly dressed in baggy jeans and huge T-shirts. Patrick and Stephie were watching a recaptured Gerry race on top of the wheel in his cage. The house was even cleaner than when she'd left. She could never have managed eight kids so well.

"It's a good thing I was here," Chance spoke softly from behind her. "Rodge and Stew came over right after you left. I'm not sure the twins could have handled them."

Dallas knew from experience that they couldn't. Not that she would admit that to Chance.

"It's good for boys to know there's a man in the house," Chance said.

He said it as if he felt he belonged.

"I'm glad you were here," Dallas admitted reluctantly. Then Gordon walked in.

The lamplight shone in her hair, on her face. Her gaze grew radiant as she looked at Chance. She didn't even see Gordon.

"Hey, hi there—" This, from her date.

Chance and Dallas turned.

Dallas forced a polite smile. "Oh?"

"Dallas, why don't you come outside and tell me good-bye?" Gordon said stiffly.

"Okay." But her eyes flicked briefly back to Chance before she left.

Outside, at his car, Gordon took her hand. "So, it's over."

"Over?"

"Us. It's you and this muscle-bound, McCall, nut case now."

"No—"

Gordon turned her hand over. "Maybe you can't admit it yet. But I know it. And McCall damn sure knows it. He already acts like he owns you. I was afraid he might strangle me when I came over to pick you up."

"If he said anything—! If he so much as touched a hair on your—"

"No! Look, you deserve to be happy, Dallas. Don't fight him too long. He doesn't know beans about sailing, or ranching, or boats, but he's got money from somewhere or he wouldn't have a yacht like that and time off. Not many men would look at a woman with four kids. And a motorcycle gang, too! The guy's crazy."

"By his own admission."

Gordon smiled, and she reached up and kissed his cheek. He got into his car, and she watched until his red taillights blurred with the other lights on the causeway bridge.

Chance came out onto the porch and stepped under the light. "Where's your date?"

"As if you didn't know."

Chance stuck his thumbs in his belt loops and waited for her to explain. "Well? Is it too much to hope that he's gone for good?"

She stepped onto the porch. "Thanks to you!"

His mouth curved sardonically. "Oh, so it's my fault?"

Dallas nodded.

"And you're furious?" Chance studied her expression. "I can see you're set on keeping me guessing. Does this mean we can see more of each other?"

"I don't think that's wise."

"Why?"

"Gordon was safe. You're not."

"Some women are attracted to danger."

"I was—once. A long time ago I knew someone like you."

"Your ex?"

She was very still. "No. Before him." She broke off.

"Who?"

Her throat thickened. She looked away to the silken ripple of the water and the silver gleam of the masts. "I don't want to talk about him."

The silence grew awkward until his deep voice filled it. "Neither do I. Let's talk about us. I want you to stop being scared. I'm not that guy who hurt you. I want to be your friend."

"No."

"Hell, you're right." Thumbs came out of his belt loops. He reached over his head and unscrewed the light bulb. The porch melted into darkness as he pulled her closer. She struggled, but his arms were tight. He locked their bodies together as perfectly as the last two matching pieces of a puzzle. His legs were long and muscled, his thighs like iron. His husky tone made her shiver. "I've never been the kind of man who can settle for less when I want more."

"Chance—"

He brought his warm fingertip to her lips. "If I keep letting you run the show, I'll never get anywhere." He lowered his head and nuzzled her hair with his lips. "Honey, I don't just want to be friends. I want you. And not just for sex. I think I could care about you in a way I've never cared about anyone."

His mouth crushed down on hers, and he kissed her until she could hardly breathe. His big flexible hands shaped her to him. He was hot, so hot, and he made her hot for him, too. It no longer mattered that they were strangers. They seemed to belong together. He had only to look at her, to touch her, and she was instantly on fire. The powerful heat of his body and the slight roughness of his hands on her skin tantalized her.

"Come to my boat," he whispered in a hoarse low tone.

She reached up and put her fingers across his lips.

He pushed her fingers away. "Dallas, come to me after the

boys go home and the kids are in bed. We don't have to make love. I just want to be with you. I can't wait much longer.'' The sky was a haze of stars, silvered by moonlight. ''Promise me,'' he demanded.

He held her a long time, his body pressing into hers, not letting her go, the torrid warmth of him seeping deep inside her. Why was she silent when she knew she had to say no?

His lips were in her hair again. ''Maybe if I had more character, I'd sail away and leave you alone.''

She brushed his brown hair away from his forehead. ''I'm beginning to think that you're not such a bad guy.''

''Hey, where did that strap of sweetness come from?''

She touched his cheek, mutely pleading for him not to ask what she wasn't ready to give. In the darkness his features seemed harsher and bleaker than ever. She sensed a loneliness in him, a need for her that transcended the physical.

''Come to me,'' he murmured.

She remembered another man, and another night, and the tragedy that had followed. ''No.''

''Right.''

Chance's hot wild lips touched her mouth angrily again and enflamed her; her response was a quick, needy fever that enthralled him. With skilled lips and hands, he took a long time over their wanton embrace. When he let her go, she sagged limply against the darkened wall of her house, her skin so flushed and hot she felt she'd die if she didn't have him.

She was infinitely sad.

''You could at least smile.'' Chance's voice broke the silence that seemed to engulf them.

''No. I can't even give you that.''

Eight

A lonely gull soared against a flame-colored sky. When the wake of a passing tug slapped the hull of Christopher's yacht, he sprang awake instantly.

He was alone, his every muscle taut after a restless night on his bunk. He poked his head out of the hatch. There wasn't a breath of a breeze. He dragged his fingers through his hair and stared at the untouched pillow beside his.

She hadn't come.

He slammed his fist into fiberglass. Pain shot from his knuckles all the way to his elbow.

Damn it, he could have his pick of women. She didn't even know who he was, yet she had that edge as if she intuitively sensed the danger of him.

If he'd been in L.A, he could have raced his Jaguar up and down along the Pacific headlands. He would have watched the raging surf dash itself against the rocks. Here, he felt caged in, trapped. He wanted to step out of the role he was playing and be himself. No more brown contacts, no more brown hair, no more glasses.

No more lies.

He wanted to be Christopher Stone, Stephie's father, Dallas's lover.

He picked up his phone and dialed Cal.

"What do you mean, no progress?" Cal roared, awake instantly, despite the early hour. "This woman who can keep the Tiger at bay, I've got to meet. Why don't you just tell her who you are?"

No more lies.

"I've got to win her first."

"Tell her."

"Three-time losers shouldn't give advice to the lovelorn."

"Then why'd you call?"

"I had to talk to someone. I had to quit pretending—if only for five minutes. Everybody's asleep here."

"It's 4:00 a.m. What the hell do you think I was doing—saying my prayers?"

"You're my agent."

"Not at this fungus hour."

Cal hung up.

It was a first.

Still restless, Christopher picked up his script and began to go over it.

Later when he went to the house, he was told that Dallas had driven into the city and wasn't expected back until late.

She had run away.

He was furious, but he'd go mad if he thought about her. He decided to work. Then Oscar turned his television on so loud in his houseboat that Christopher couldn't think. He stuffed the script into a bag and stalked with it down the beach.

It was almost dark when he returned, but Oscar's television was still blaring. Dallas's Jeep was parked in front of her house. Other cars were lined up at the restaurant. It looked like a busy Wednesday. Why the hell was Oscar's television still on if he was over there cooking?

Christopher decided to check. Oscar's "houseboat" was a rusting trailer on top of a wooden barge with old tires nailed to the sides. Carefully, Christopher picked his way across the littered deck—ice coolers, crab nets, old air conditioners and fishing paraphernalia.

He cracked open the door. The first thing he saw were the opening credits for *Tiger Three* blazing across the television screen.

Christopher's stomach tightened. If Dallas recognized him, he was dead.

Oscar was sprawled across his tattered couch. His stained T-shirt had ridden up his hairy belly. Four dozen beer bottles were lined up along the edge of his coffee table. The houseboat reeked of cheap booze and cigarette smoke.

Christopher slammed the door. Nothing. He strode inside and switched off the set. With a groan, Oscar rolled over. Christopher picked up a beer bottle and flipped it into the trash can. He pitched in more bottles, so that they broke noisily on top of the other. More groans and snores from the couch.

"Oscar—" Dallas's voice was silken.

At the sound of it, Christopher's hand jerked, and the next bottle shattered against the wall.

Dallas's bright head peered inside. "You missed."

He turned. "Right." His gaze drifted down the delicate line of her jaw, the slim column of her neck. Why did just looking at her make him feel so warm he was burning? "Funny, till I met you, I usually got what I aimed for."

Her indrawn breath was followed by an electric silence.

Christopher's hot gaze licked over her shape like lightning. Her hair hung down along one side of her face like a shimmering veil of gold. She wore an apricot jersey dress that clung to every curve. "So you're back?"

Her breath seemed to catch in her throat again. Her fragile poise seemed eggshell thin. But, then, so was his.

"I like your dress," he murmured in a voice that was as dry as dust. "Is it new?"

Warm color came and went just under the surface of her golden skin. "I—I bought it today."

"So you went shopping?"

She flushed again.

"Funny, I thought you were just avoiding me."

Her shaky hand pushed her hair behind one ear. "That's because you're so conceited you think the world revolves around you."

That stung. "Right. You've got me completely figured."

"You don't own me," she said.

"Not yet—anyway."

She went white. "Where's Oscar?"

"See for yourself."

As Christopher swaggered insolently toward her, she unconsciously clenched the door frame for support. Pushing the door wider, he stepped aside so that she could see past him.

Oscar snorted loudly. His filthy T-shirt rode higher, revealing more of his black-haired belly.

Dallas went numb. "What am I going to do?" she asked in a low, forlorn tone.

She moved into the light, and Christopher saw the shadowy smudges of exhaustion beneath her eyes. She was trying to run this place and raise four kids. Her shoulders drooped.

He forgot his own frustration. Before he thought, he said, "I'll cook."

"No!" She drew herself up primly. "I couldn't dream of bothering you—"

"Lady, all you do is bother me."

"I've managed alone before."

He stared at her for a long moment. "I bet it was hell."

"No—"

His gaze darkened. "Some things are hard to do alone."

She backed away from him until she stumbled into the wall. "Why are you such a hard man to say no to?"

When he grinned with new hope, she stiffened.

"Relax, sweetheart. You're not selling your soul to the devil."

"I—I suppose I could hire you—for one night only."

"Oh, I don't want money." His wicked grin flared again. "And I'll never be satisfied with one night only."

"Then what are you doing it for?"

He laughed softly. "The white knight to the rescue."

She was instantly unnerved. "You're no white knight, and if you refuse money, I won't owe you...anything else."

He felt a violent rush of physical desire. "I don't ever work for nothing. White knights carry off their princess."

"You are insufferable."

"Chalk it up to knightly charm."

She stared at him one second longer. Then she bolted through the door.

Christopher followed after her at a leisurely pace. When he discovered the twins fighting in the dining room, he set them to sweeping and arranging tables and chairs. He found Patrick hiding in the house watching *Tiger Three*.

Christopher's stomach tightened as he switched off the set. "We need you in the restaurant."

"Aw! The best part was coming next!"

"Yeah, I know."

Patrick's sharp eyes flicked over Christopher's features and narrowed assessingly. Uncomfortable, Christopher pushed his glasses higher up his nose.

Patrick started to say something and stopped. A telling look passed between the boy and man. Without another word they went to the restaurant.

Despite Dallas acting nervous every time Christopher came near, he enjoyed working with her immensely. He cooked while she took orders, and the night went well. It was as if he was part of a team, part of a family. The kids were enthusiastic to please him. If only Dallas hadn't been so jumpy, everything would have been perfect. But when he came into a room, she left it.

When the last customer had gone, the kids were cleaning up the kitchen, and Dallas was standing behind the cash register, tallying receipts. It was a hot night. A damp sheen of perspiration made her skin glow.

Christopher went over and leaned heavily across the counter. "You're too pretty to be a scholar of metaphysical poetry. Too pretty for a dump like this, too. I could take you away from all this."

She drew back, startled.

"Let me help you with those."

She set down the bills and placed her hand on top of them. "You've already done too much." When he didn't budge she said, "Look, it's late. I'm tired. You're tired."

"Right. We've both got going to bed on our minds."

"Don't start that! Please…"

"You're wrong about me," he murmured in a more serious tone.

"I don't think so."

"We could have a beer on my boat. You might say thank you."

"No—to a beer on your boat." She flipped through the receipts. "Yes—to thank you." Softly. "Thank you…."

"I'd like a *private* thank-you," he said, leaning closer.

"I know what you'd like."

"We could just talk."

"You want more."

His hand slid beneath her chin. "Right. So do you."

She shook her head, moving away from him.

"Damn it, Dallas. Why are you so dead set against me?"

Her blue eyes were unsmiling. "I told you. I've been burned in the past. I'm not quite as naive as I was back then." She paused. "All right, if you really want to know. You don't add up, Mr. McCall. You're a rancher, but you never talk about ranching. You can't even walk in cowboy boots."

"I told you they were new."

"Your accent's funny."

"What the hell's wrong with it?"

"It's just different."

"So—I wasn't born in Texas."

"There are other things. You sailed over here, but Gordon says you don't know how to sail."

"How the hell does he know? He's never seen me."

"That's just it. You never take your boat out."

"Maybe I like it here."

"You have a big boat, but Gordon says you don't know anything about it."

"Just because I'm not a talking engine manual like that nitpicky big-mouth—"

"Look, forget Gordon."

"With pleasure!"

"You're a handsome guy. You could have anyone. Yet you take an interest in me, in my kids."

Christopher shrugged. "So, I like you and your kids."

"That's unusual. You're not a relaxed kind of guy who just sails off into the sunset and leaves everything behind. I keep asking myself. Why here? Why my kids? Gordon said no man—"

Suddenly Christopher was very angry. Angry that she was using his lies to paint him into a corner; angrier, though, that no matter what he did, he got nowhere with her. "I thought we agreed to forget that jerk!" He paused. "You know what your problem is—you've stuck your head inside books so long, you don't know the first thing about life."

"I know that you scare me, and I'm not sure why."

He felt explosive. "Maybe if you came down to my boat and got to know me a little better, you could figure it all out. Would it be such a crime to give us a chance?"

Before she could answer, he stalked out. He was aware of the kids watching him. One of them knocked a glass over, and he heard it shatter behind him. The twins ran over to Dallas.

"Chance—" Dallas called after him desperately.

He stopped, hesitating when he saw her stricken expression. But she said nothing more. If she'd come halfway—

When she didn't, his expression hardened. "You know where to find me, honey." He let the door bang behind him.

Christopher stood on the pier, his body stiffly erect as he fished. Wary, Dallas studied the way his white shirt stretched across his shoulders, the way his jeans molded his thighs. The only thing loose about him was the lock of wavy dark hair that fell over his forehead. Every time he cast, his line was like a whiplash flicking the glassy water.

Nervousness tightened her throat, making her wonder how she'd ever find the courage to speak. She licked her lips. "You'll scare them away—casting like that."

He turned. "The way I scare you?" But now there was no anger in his low tone.

She came to him and took his fishing rod. Their hands touched briefly, and so did their eyes with that same acute awareness they always had for each other.

"Do you really think I give a damn about fishing?"

She swallowed and watched him as he unconsciously shook his hair out of his eyes.

"You've got to do it gently." She flicked the line with a delicate motion.

He jammed his fists into his jeans. "It's hard to be gentle when you're impatient as hell."

"If you really want something, you've got to be patient."

"Believe me, I'm trying."

She felt his eyes burning into her as he watched her fish. A few seconds later she reeled in a silvery fish that jumped and flashed on the pier. Smug with triumph, she started to cut it loose, but Christopher knelt down and did it for her.

"You think you're smart," he murmured, amused.

"I live at a marina. I ought to know how to fish. I do know some things besides stuff in books."

When his direct gaze lingered on her hair and lips before meeting her eyes, a sudden tightness gripped her throat.

He said nothing. She shifted uncomfortably.

"And I do thank you for helping me tonight," she added softly.

"It was fun."

"It was," she admitted shyly. "I—I know so little about you."

He was baiting her hook, and she was watching him and thinking he was good with his hands.

"You haven't told me much about yourself, either," he said.

"Because I can't tell anyone."

"Maybe if you tried, the telling would get easier."

"Maybe I don't want it to."

"No, you'd rather writhe in some never-ending purgatory like that shrimp on your hook. You want to feel sorry for yourself forever."

"No! That's not the way it is!" Pleadingly, she looked at him.

"Hey, I've been there, too," he whispered.

She let him take the fishing rod and set it down. Then she was in his arms, burying her face against his chest.

"I can't touch you like I want to," he said. "My hands are all shrimpy."

He was so tough and strong, but his manner with her was infinitely gentle.

"You feel so good, I don't care."

"Honey, I know what it's like to feel so guilty you want to punish yourself forever."

She clung to him for so long that she grew embarrassed. She pulled away, confused. But when he invited her aboard his boat and offered her a beer, she accepted. Together they washed their hands in his sink.

She wasn't used to beer, and soon she felt as if she were

floating in a dream. She heard his voice as if from a long way away. "Tell me about the poetry you read."

"You don't really want to talk about Donne and Marvell."

"Right." A pause. "I asked, didn't I?"

The single beer filled her with such a mellow warmth that she forgot the danger of him and began to recite poetry. He liked her poems, and though he hadn't read much poetry, he reinterpreted them for her with masculine irreverence.

"You would never make an English major," she said.

"And that's not all bad."

They laughed together in the hushed silvery darkness. Soon they were talking of their lonelinesses, of their little private hurts. Hours passed in the space of minutes, and neither grew bored. She told him of her family, of loving them and grieving for them. He told her how he'd always longed to feel part of a family and never had. His parents hadn't wanted him. They'd divorced and had rarely bothered to see him after that.

"They should never have had a child," she said.

"There are a lot of people who shouldn't."

She paled.

"You told me you were married," he said. "Were there children?"

She hesitated. Again she was in that white hospital corridor. A single ray of warm sunlight was shining on her baby's golden curls as the baby began to cry. "One. I—I lost her. She had blue eyes and blond hair."

"Like you."

"I only held her once." Her voice trembled.

"It's a terrible thing to lose a child," he murmured, his voice and eyes intense. "Someday you'll marry again."

"No."

He kissed her brow. "There'll be other children."

"No. Please..." She put her fingertips to his lips. "Something went wrong with the pregnancy. I can't have more children. That's one reason why my sister's mean so much."

"I'm sorry."

This time she didn't push him away when he drew her close. His hands stroked her hair again; his whispery voice was reassuring. She nestled against him. She wanted this nearness with him; she had ached for it. *But it was wrong.* She squeezed her eyes tightly shut.

"It was a long time ago," he murmured.

"You carry some things with you all of your life."

"Yes, and you and this night are going to be one of them," he said softly.

The heat in his eyes sent flames through her. At his first tentative touch she grew still.

"What's so special about tonight?" she whispered.

"Until tonight, you've done nothing but run. Tonight you came to me."

His lips touched her hair and moved to her throat, and Dallas trembled at their burning intensity. If only...

She shook her head and cringed away. "I can't."

His grip tightened on her arm. "Why?"

"I can't tell you, either."

"Damn it," he muttered thickly. "Do you have any idea what you're doing to me? Do you even care?"

Passion and jealousy and anger were scrawled across his face. His mouth was set in a bitter line. His fists were clenched. "If I could find the bastard who did this to you, I'd strangle him with my bare hands."

For an instant she couldn't breathe. "It's my fault and no one else's."

He ripped off his glasses. "Tell me! Damn it. Trust me."

Slowly her mute gaze traveled over him. His brown hair was blowing across his brow, and she smoothed it with her fingertips. He grabbed her hand, crushing her fingers inside his. She felt his tension, his power, his strength. His white shirt fluttered against the hard muscles of his dark arms and chest. He exuded raw animal courage, bravery. In so many ways he was her opposite. He was completely wrong for her. But when she looked into his eyes, she knew a terrible truth.

She had begun to love him

"You have your own life. You'll go away," she said.

His eyes narrowed. "I'll take you with me."

She was silent, looking past him. "My life is here," she said at last.

"Life is where your heart is." Lightly his fingers touched her face, tracing the curves of her brows and lashes as if she were very precious to him. "Love me."

Miserable, she shook her head. "The risk just isn't worth it."

His brown eyes surveyed her comprehensively. "It is to me." He grasped her shoulders in his hands. "Let me love you, Dallas. Let me show you that you risk losing more by running." He began to caress her.

But at the touch of his lips and hands, she sprang up wildly. "Excuse me. I feel…a little tired."

"Right." Grim understanding glinted in his eyes. Obligingly he let his arms fall to his sides. "I'll see you tomorrow, then?"

She glanced at him in alarm. "No!" Then she shook her head wordlessly.

"Right," he muttered. "We're back where we started— square one. Nowhere."

He didn't try to stop her when she leaped to the dock and raced lightly away.

Nine

Strategy.

It always took strategy to win a war.

Today was Stephie's birthday.

From his yacht, Christopher kept a sharp eye on the kids, especially on Patrick, as the boy stuffed the Jeep with picnic things. Dallas was going to be furious, but, hell, when she'd run away last night, she'd left him no choice.

Why was it that the closer Christopher came to winning her, the harder she fought him? When she had confided in him about the child she had lost, he had felt a new bond. Then she had run again. All day she had avoided him.

The door of her house swung open, and Dallas marched out. Patrick leaned out of the loaded Jeep, stuck two fingers in his mouth and whistled.

At last! Their prearranged signal. Christopher sprang off his boat with his duffel bag and jogged so fast he beat Dallas to the Jeep and opened the door for her.

Stubbornly, she threw her bag on the ground. "Just what do you think you're doing?"

"Excuse me." He pitched his own bag into the Jeep.

"Chance wanted to see Padre Island, so we invited him on my birthday picnic, Aunt Dallas!" Stephie shouted.

"Please, Aunt Dallas!" the older three yelled.

Dallas's gaze went from the kids to him.

"Looks like you're outnumbered, honey," Christopher said.

Dallas bit her lips. "Betrayed."

Christopher's gaze drifted over her. "Sorry you feel that way."

She was wearing a severe black swimsuit that skimmed her body closely, black sandals and a gauzy cover-up. He could see her nipples, the indentation of her navel and much more. Too much more. One glimpse and he was too hot to take another.

"Quit pushing me, Chance."

He smiled at her lazily. "I'm a pushy guy."

"Look, we've got to go."

"Right." He hopped in behind the wheel.

"I'll drive," she said tightly.

"Wrong." He opened the passenger door for her. When she stood by her bag, he started the Jeep.

She stared up at him with blazing eyes. "If you're going, I'm not." She crossed her arms over those delectable nipples and shot him a poisonous look.

"Oh, yes, you are. The kids planned this."

"You're using them."

"Yes." His dark gaze was studying her although she avoided meeting it. He liked what he saw. He would have used the devil himself, to have her. At first he had only wanted Stephie. Now he wanted them all—the whole family. But it was Dallas who was in his blood. Dallas, whose warmth he craved every night when he slept alone in his hard bunk.

"For God's sake," he muttered. "It's Stephie's birthday."

Stephie leaned over from the back seat and threw her arms

around Christopher's brown neck. "Chance is the only present I want, Aunt Dallas. If you don't let Chance come, you'll ruin my birthday. And you *have* to come, too. Or we won't be a family."

Great silver rollers of the Gulf of Mexico dashed themselves upon the beach. Patrick and the twins were throwing a Frisbee. Dallas sat stiffly in her lawn chair and pretended to read, but every so often she peeped over the fluttering pages of her paperback and watched Chance and Stephie.

He was marvelous with her. They were building a magnificent sand castle together. "A castle like the princess's," Stephie glowingly had explained to Dallas.

White Horse was propped on a towel near the castle. Stephie dashed about excitedly, scooping up sand, running into the surf and filling buckets with water and then emptying them into their moat. When a bucketful caused a wall to collapse, Chance threw up his hands in mock dismay. Near tears, Stephie grew very still until he beckoned her into his arms.

Dallas smiled as she watched his brown head attentively bend over the little girl's, his fine silky hair blowing about his forehead and hers. He was as lean and bronzed as a pagan prince. Stephie was talking to him so earnestly. He said something, and Stephie's face was transformed by a sweet, shy smile. Soon Stephie's dark eyes were flashing with joy and she was rebuilding the castle.

Chance was so gentle with her. All of the sadness that had haunted Stephie vanished every time she was around him. Funny, she had been terrified of him at first. *Like me*, Dallas thought.

Everyone was having a better time because of him. During the drive when she and Chance had sat stiffly silent, the kids had chattered excitedly because he was there. When Chance had found a deserted place near the dunes for their picnic, the kids would have left her to unpack, if Chance hadn't insisted they help. He had made a game of it, and they hadn't minded.

The castle built, Chance and Stephie joined the Frisbee game. Now, Dallas was the only one left out. She felt odd, watching her family play without her. Suddenly Chance caught the Frisbee. Instead of throwing it to Rennie, he held it until Dallas looked up. When she did, he tipped his head challengingly. She shook her head, hoping that her refusal was very poised, very adult, infinitely superior. His dark eyes danced with defiant mischief, and he threw the disk at her anyway.

She saw everything in slow motion—his wicked grin, the flick of his wrist, the whir of the yellow disk right at her. She screamed. Her paperback sailed into a puddle as she leapt to catch the Frisbee.

She landed on her nose in the sand with her chair on top of her. Everyone laughed as she picked the Frisbee up and slowly stood, dusting herself off.

"Throw it back to him," Stephie screamed excitedly, jumping up and down. "Throw it back."

Dallas ran a shaky hand across her damp forehead. He was watching her. They all were. But she was only aware of him.

He was like a god with the sea breeze blowing his hair, with the sun gleaming on his dark skin. His gaze narrowed on her face and figure, his eyes seeming to physically touch each part of her. He drew his head back, the angle faintly mocking.

She was aware of the pulse beating wildly along her neck, and she knew she was every bit as excited as Stephie.

Then he smiled at her—sheepishly, charmingly, daring her to admit she, too, was glad he'd come. But that she ever would, even though she felt such a sudden rush of sheer joy, her own lips twitched traitorously.

"Catch this if you can," she shouted. Defiantly, she threw the Frisbee just out of his reach. Quicker than lightning, he jumped and caught it, his cocky glance filled with male triumph. Then he tossed it to Rennie, but Dallas had joined the game.

Once, Dallas and Chance both ran after the Frisbee. When

she was about to catch it, he caught her and lifted her and spun her around and around until she forgot herself and she shrieked giddily. Her hair whirled loose like a golden cloud. She was flying. She was free and young like a child.

Slowly he let her down so that her soft body slid the muscled length of his. She felt hot and trembly.

She wasn't a child. Neither was he.

His eyes touched her mouth with a suggestive look that sent feverish color flooding up her neck. She gasped. Quickly she stepped back, sucking in air, smoothing her hair, straightening the thin black strap of her swimsuit that had fallen, not daring to look at him, although she was conscious of his hot dark eyes watching her.

The kids grew quiet. There were raised eyebrows, knowing glances between the girls. A red-cheeked Patrick averted his eyes and dug a hole in the sand with his naked toe.

"Hey, you guys," Chance cried, picking up the Frisbee. "Whoever catches this gets a dollar." He sent it flying down the beach, and all four kids went racing after it.

The tension was broken; everyone resumed playing until they were breathless and exhausted and begging Chance to stop.

"I'm hungry," Patrick said, throwing the Frisbee toward the card table set up near the Jeep.

The children dashed toward the table.

Chance turned to Dallas. "I'm hungry, too."

The kids were hidden by the dunes. When Dallas realized she was alone with him on that windswept beach, her heart beat faster. "Why don't we eat, then?" she whispered.

He swaggered nearer. "You tell me."

The laughing glint had left his brown eyes. Something elemental seemed to hover in the air. When he reached for her hand, she let his warm fingers entwine with hers. He led her over to the table.

Patrick swallowed a bite of his hamburger, looked up at them and beamed. Out of the blue he announced, "We used to do this with Mom and Dad. It's almost like we're a real family again.''

Chance lifted his head. The warmth in his eyes made Dallas feel slightly dazed. Having Chance with them did make it feel like being in a family, and she was more attracted to him than she had been to anyone.

When they finished eating, Chance said, "Kids, would you mind cleaning up and packing the Jeep?"

"Aw!" Patrick looked disgusted. "We just got here. Do we have to go?"

"Not till your aunt and I get back from our walk."

The kids became instantly quiet, their bright eyes darting speculatively from Chance to Dallas. A significant, grown-up look passed between them. Stephie clutched White Horse shyly.

Jennie was about to object that it wasn't her turn to clear the table, but Rennie silenced her with a sisterly kick.

"Ouch!"

A hush fell upon the table. Rennie rolled her eyes innocently. "Sure, Chance, we'd all just love to clear up."

"Walk as long as you like," Patrick said, encouragingly.

"Till it gets dark," Rennie said, winking at her scowling twin.

Stephie rushed up to Dallas and whispered into her ear. "Please don't say any more mean things to Chance."

When Dallas glanced up at Chance, his inscrutable brown eyes met her wavering look. There was such an aura of male sensuality about him. Her nerves leapt erratically. "You've certainly won over the kids."

His hand closed over her wrist, and she felt her heartbeat flutter. He twisted her around to face him. "Good. That only leaves you."

Every bone in her body seemed to melt. The seascape became a wonderland filled with magic as hand in hand, he led her into the darkening twilight. When they were out of sight of the Jeep, she let him fold her into his arms.

"You've won me, too," she admitted breathlessly as he arched her roughly against his hard body and kissed her.

He ended the kiss. Their lips parted slowly, reluctantly. Then he picked her up and whirled her as he had done when they'd chased the Frisbee. Only this time there was moonlight in her hair, and there were no children watching.

They fell down laughing together in the wet sand. A velvet black canopy sprinkled with sparkling stars enveloped them. A dark wave glimmering with white light dashed over them.

Their laughter died.

The whisper of the waves and wind held erotic promise.

He bent his head to nuzzle her damp hair, and his breath sent shivers of excitement through her.

"I've lain awake every night—wanting this." His hand caressed her breast, his callused fingers molding themselves to the shape of it, kneading her nipple until it crested and her blood flowed in her arteries like hot lava. His fingertips grazed her mouth, tracing its voluptuous fullness until she opened her lips and suckled his fingertips provocatively like a wanton, wanting all of him.

His breathing grew ragged. The moonlight streamed across his face. His gaze was intense and smoldering, his full lower lip half parted with desire. He seemed different tonight, fiercer...hungrier.

She moaned sensuously. He gripped her arms so tightly he hurt her, his body pressing into hers. There was only darkness as more warm waves slid over them, only darkness as his lips burned across her skin, burned through the thin layer of her suit, touching her everywhere. He was muttering things she could not understand, his mouth and hands evoking feelings she'd never felt, and she was lost in that sea of swirling sensations and unaware of time or her surroundings. With her eyes tightly shut, she surrendered shudderingly to the abandoned desires of her body. Then salty foam crashed over them, and he pulled her up so they wouldn't both drown in the tidal surge. Another wave followed the first, and they began to laugh. He started to kiss her again.

She touched his lips with her fingertip. "We can't," she whispered. "The children are waiting."

He stopped kissing her and smiled. "Later...then..."

She clung to him, her body still burning where his hands and lips had touched her. "After we put them to bed."

He lifted her from the soft sand and carried her into the surf. Then they dived beneath the waves.

He held her once more as passionately as before, their wet bodies touching and growing hot again. Her arms wound around his neck and her lips trembled beneath his. She pulled him to her tightly.

"Later," he whispered, teasing her.

Laughing, she chased him all the way back to the Jeep.

Sand crabs skittered in front of the Jeep's bobbing headlights, and occasionally there was a fatal pop under the tires. Christopher was oblivious to the scurrying crabs, oblivious to the white dazzling moonlight on the sand and waves. Oblivious, too, to the damp cool sea breeze whirling into the Jeep. All he felt was the warmth of Dallas's slight fingertips he held pressed against his molten thigh.

He could smell her. He could still taste her.

Later.

Rock music throbbed on the radio, and his heart pounded as violently as the wild music. He bit his lips so that he would taste his blood instead of her. But it didn't work. He kept remembering the way she'd felt beneath him in the waves—warm and yielding, shuddering every time he touched her. Every jolt of the Jeep was a fresh stab of fire in his loins.

The white beach stretched before him, as endless as the roaring waves, as endless as the night. He drew a harsh, ragged breath.

He gripped the wheel and bit his lips again, but not even

the sharp metallic flavor of his own blood could make him forget the fierce, hot longing.

He wanted her too much. She'd made him wait too long.

Christopher's heart sank when Dallas alighted from the Jeep and teased, "Would you hose the Jeep off, please?" When he scowled, she handed him the hose and sent the children inside to take showers.

He took her wrist and kissed the ardent heartbeat pulsing there. "This is torture. I can't wait," he muttered.

"You'll have to," she whispered gaily. "The Jeep will rust if we don't wash it."

"We?"

"I like you this way—mad for me," she said, touching his lips with the tips of her fingers.

When he tried to press her to him, she jumped away.

"Minx!"

Her teasing eyes flashed playfully, but she had her way. Christopher and the kids unloaded and washed the Jeep while Dallas put things away in the kitchen. Each kid had to shower and dress for bed. They ran out of hot water and a fight erupted between the kids. Christopher attacked his own chores ferociously to dull the edge of his need.

It didn't work.

The minute he saw Dallas's golden hair gleaming in the lamplight while she read huskily to the children, he felt driven to the brink of madness. He had to coil his hands into fists to keep from reaching out and touching her. Finally he went to his boat and took a cold shower. As always, his radio played rock music.

When he stepped into his main cabin wrapped only in a towel, she was there. Like before, she lowered herself down the companionway. Her yellow hair that was damp from her shower flashed with scintillating lights. So did the golden flecks in her blue eyes. His gaze swiftly went over her body. She was sexier than hell in tight jeans and a clingy pink shirt.

Her long-lashed eyes lifted uncertainly to his. At his hungry look, her skin glowed a rose color.

Dear God, she was afraid again. Not again. Not when passion throbbed in every cell of his body.

He had to go slow and easy; he felt wilder than the music—out of control. He went and switched off the radio.

"No, leave it on," she whispered.

He turned it back on, and the jungle beat of the music throbbed with the same wildness pulsing in his blood.

He went to her and brushed his hot lips against her forehead. His fingertips trailed from her shoulders down her bare arms. She began to tremble, but she did not kiss him back. A look of infinite sorrow passed fleetingly over her lovely face.

Something was wrong.

He didn't want to stop, but some shred of willpower enabled him to. With an unsteady hand he tipped her chin back gently and looked into her eyes. He was so wild for her that he felt he was on the verge of splintering into a thousand pieces. He wanted to strip her and pull her, naked, against him.

"What's the matter?" he murmured hoarsely.

That desperate look he hated came into her eyes. For an instant she froze. Then she tried to run.

"No. Not tonight, honey," he rasped. He flung himself in front of her and closed the hatch. Then he placed a muscular brown arm on either side of her and pinned her to the wall.

"Let me go! You don't understand!"

He crushed her against his chest, imprisoning her. "Kiss me," he whispered, his body on fire.

"No." She began to fight, kicking him, trying to slap him.

He caught her flying wrists behind her back. "You've got to trust me," he murmured. "I can't stand this anymore. I lie awake wanting you, aching for you."

"You wouldn't if you knew—"

"I still would."

She closed her eyes. Her lashes were damp with unshed tears. "You don't understand!"

"Give me a chance to try."

She began to fight him again, bending and twisting against him, but he held her fast. He felt her panicked heart hammering madly. When she screamed, he let her go.

"Honey, do you really want to always run from everyone who tries to get close to you?"

"Yes!" Her hands were like claws; one of her nails nicked his cheek. A bright line of blood beaded against his dark skin. She drew back, still at last, and gasped in horror, touching it gently.

"Don't!" He winced. "It stings like hell!"

"Oh, dear." She was heartbroken. "I never meant—"

"It's a scratch," he muttered savagely. "Nothing." A pause. "You've got to tell me what's wrong."

She collapsed against him, gazing up at him with dull, lost eyes. "I'm so sorry."

"I said forget it. Just tell me—"

She went to the bathroom, brought back a damp washcloth and placed it against his cheek. "I can't believe I—"

He touched her hair. "Hey, it's okay."

"Maybe you're right. I'll lose you if I tell you, but I'll lose you if I don't." The distant forlorn quality in her voice filled him with fear.

She turned away as if she were too ashamed for him to even look at her. "I didn't tell this to my husband until after we were married. When I finally did, he left."

"What could be so awful?"

"I gave my baby away!"

"What?"

Her face was as white as frost. "The child I lost wasn't my husband's. I had her when I was seventeen. You see, my parents had died, and, oh, I was miserably lonely. This boy came. Suddenly I felt alive again. I was so mixed-up. I didn't know much about boys or love. I went with him once. It was awful, and I knew that night I'd made a terrible mistake. But I got pregnant. Carrie took care of me until the baby was born, and

Robert urged me to give up the baby and I did. But the shame, the tragedy of never being able to have another baby... You see, I was supposed to forget and go on with my life, but I couldn't. You want to know something crazy? I celebrate every one of her birthdays.''

"When was she born?"

"September the tenth."

"Oh, honey...." His low tone was infinitely gentle.

"I still dream about her, only she's always a little baby. I'm in the hospital. The nurse is carrying her away."

A single tear had beaded on Dallas's lash. It fell and slid down her cheek. Christopher caught it on his fingertip where it glistened like the saddest jewel.

"This September she'll be thirteen. I wake up sometimes and wonder what she's like, if she's really all right, if her adoptive parents love her as I would have. Chance, it's like a part of me is missing."

He knew too well. "Why don't you try to find her?"

"I wish she would look for me someday, but I could never look for her."

"Why not?"

"Because I made all the choices. She has the right to make hers. I don't want to disrupt her life, to risk harming her in any way. She has another family now."

"Why not a letter then—to the adoption agency?"

"I did write, but I never heard anything."

"Don't give up. It's only natural for adoptive parents to be threatened by the biological parent." His grim voice dropped to a whisper. "Maybe someday."

"You see why I gave up everything to take care of my sister's children. When I lost my own parents, I made terrible mistakes. I couldn't let that happen to them."

He held her for a long time. He knew what it was like to lose a child, to death and to adoption, but he had mixed feelings about a woman giving up her baby. Marguerite had given

Stephie away. His own mother had all but abandoned him for her career and a succession of husbands and boyfriends.

But the longer he held Dallas, the more he came to realize that what Dallas had done wasn't the same. She'd been a child herself, completely unable to care for a baby. The father had been a boy. She'd acted in the best interests of her child.

"So this guy went away and left you pregnant," Christopher said.

"No. I left him. He would have married me, but my child came first—her life was everything. He didn't love me, and I was too mixed-up to love anybody. We would have had to live with his parents. I would have had security for a while and my child, but we couldn't have had a real marriage. We were both too immature to make it work. I wanted my child to be part of a real family. He finally agreed."

Christopher thought of all the mistakes he had made in his own life—his rebelliousness, Marguerite, Sally and his self-destructive craziness after her death. How could he judge Dallas?

Softly he began to kiss her. "I'm glad you told me. I've done worse," he confessed in a bleak vague tone.

"Maybe someday you'll tell me."

"Not tonight," she whispered, wrapping his arms around her and scooping her onto the bunk.

"Then we'll have no more secrets," she said.

No more lies.

He wanted that even as he wondered if they could survive it. He clung to her, his arms tight and hard around her, determined to have her this once even if it cost him everything. He began to kiss her, his mind spinning deeper and deeper into the eye of a wild passionate whirlwind.

She was as breathless as he when she reached up and took off his wire-rimmed glassed.

He felt naked and exposed as she studied his face. He tried to look away, but she held him still and traced the male beauty of his chiseled features with her fingertips. "You're so hand-some—just like a movie star."

He recoiled.

She withdrew her hand and pecked him gently on the tip of nose. "Not that I want you to be a movie star. I want you to be ordinary—just like me. A rancher...who can't sail."

"Honey..."

Her mouth closed hungrily over his, and his world began to spin again. Her tongue touched his wantonly, and whatever foolish confession he might have uttered was carried away in the flaming whirlwind of his passion.

He wanted her. Tonight. He had to explore the mysteries of her satiny skin, of her long limbs, of her golden hair. His mouth drifted from her lips, down the delicate line of her jaw, her warm neck, to the hollow between her breasts and then to her navel. As sensuously as a cat, she arched herself up, wel-coming his lips.

He tore off his towel and straddled her. She gasped with delight and ran her fingers over his shoulders and his chest and down to his waist, lingering over sinewy muscles, and threading her fingertips in the springy hair that covered his chest. Her touching was filled with a breathless urgency that drove him so crazy he would have shredded the pink shirt, if she hadn't ripped it off herself along with her jeans.

At the sight of her body, so pale, so sweetly voluptuous, the wild hunger to have her grew more acute. He pulled her beneath him with a tigerish ferocity and bathed her with his tongue. Then he moved, sinking deeply into her velvet warmth and made her his.

She was perfect. Astonishingly so. Sensations and emotions beyond anything he had ever known consumed him. She made him whole. In the final fiery explosion of ecstasy, he knew that he wanted her forever.

Afterward, he opened the hatch, so that the sea breeze would drift across their perspiring bodies. Beneath the stars they lay in a languorous tangle of coiled limbs, savoring this gentle satiated touching as much as they'd revelled in the wildness. He liked the way her foot lay trustingly on the top of his, the way her head furrowed against his wide chest, and he felt a sweetness, a closeness to her he'd never known before.

They rested in that state of wanton bliss until dawn. Then she got up and kissed him endlessly—until he was so aroused he couldn't bear to let her go.

The sky was aflame when she tiptoed through the dewy grasses back to her house.

Never had he felt so alone. What had happened to him? It was as if he were incomplete without her and couldn't bear to be parted from her—even for a few hours.

No more lies.

He had to tell her.

His eyes felt scratchy and red from wearing his contact lenses so long. He took them off and lay back down alone.

How in the hell could he ever explain?

Ten

Dallas slept until golden sunlight streamed into her bedroom. Bathed in that warm glorious flood, she lay in her bed after she awoke, smiling radiantly as she remembered dreams of wonderlands and paradises shared with Chance. In one he had worn dazzling white-and-silver buckles. He had ridden a white horse like Stephie's knight. How he would laugh if she told him she had dreamed he was her white knight.

She stirred. Just thinking of him made her skin flame. She threw off her sheets and let the light caress her. The bedrolls were empty. The children had gotten up hours ago. Thank goodness. She couldn't have faced them. Not when she felt so soft, so vulnerable. Not with the warm pleasant scent of him clinging to her skin. Stretching, she remembered the delicious passion of the night before, and then the sweet aftermath when Chance had held her for hours.

It seemed to her that ever since her parents had died, she had craved love. At last she had found it.

Not that Chance had actually spoken the words, but he

hadn't had to for her to know what he felt. Chance accepted that she had given up her daughter. Dallas laughed at her former doubts. It was all too wonderful to be true.

She got up and showered, moving with a languorous, remote, unfocusing air as she dressed and readied herself to face the children. Once she wrote the name, *Mrs. Chance McCall*, on her steamy mirror, and then quickly rubbed it out, thinking herself silly and young.

This morning she wore shorts that showed her legs, and a blue shirt that clung to her breasts. Into her hair she wound a matching blue ribbon that brought out the color of her sparkling eyes.

When she found Patrick watching *Tiger Four* downstairs, she sank dreamily beside him on the couch. He wasn't supposed to be watching an R-rated movie, but she was too happy to reprimand him. Not even the sight of Christopher Stone masked as *The Tiger* bothered her as much as usual. Vaguely, she wondered why he had stopped pestering her.

She scarcely watched him on a conscious level, but on some other level she did. A lock of his short golden hair stirred across his brow like silk in the wind, and he shook his head the way Chance did sometimes.

The way Chance did sometimes...

She leaned forward to the very edge of her chair. Did she only imagine a resemblance? Her gaze narrowed. *The Tiger*'s mask concealed his features except for his mouth that was exactly like...

Exactly.

Every muscle in her body tensed. She remembered Chance recoiling when she had removed his glasses and said he looked like a movie star.

The mouth, the smile, the jaw—were the same.

But *The Tiger*'s eyes were blue.

Contact lenses! Glasses! No wonder Chance was always taking off his glasses. He could see better without them.

The Tiger's hair was sort and blond.

Chance had let it grow and had dyed it.

She began to tremble. Her heart that had been soft with love hardened with hate. Just as quickly, the hate was washed away by a tide of soul-numbing sorrow. The man she had come to love had used her.

The Tiger spoke, and her heart fluttered at that familiar raspy tone. Whatever lingering doubt she had, dissolved. From the first she had sensed there was something wrong with his accent. He had said he hadn't been born in Texas.

Fool. With a cry she flung herself from the couch.

Patrick looked up as she fled. "Hey, don't worry, the *Tiger* always wins. Watch how he outsmarts Rhydor. This is my favorite part."

She stood at the door, paralyzed, until the movie ended, and letters that spelled *Christopher Stone*, blazed across the screen.

She went into the kitchen and brewed a pot of coffee. If she was a fool, he was a monster. He had let his own child die, and now he wanted Stephie.

Dear Lord.

Patrick came into the kitchen and grabbed a cola from the refrigerator.

"Put that back. You can have orange juice or milk," she said flatly.

His lip curled. But one look at her, and he minded. He splashed orange juice into a glass. "Isn't the *Tiger* the best?"

"The very best," she whispered. *The best lying bastard there ever was.*

She took Patrick into her arms. "Why don't you skateboard or something? I—I don't feel too well."

When he nodded and let her hold him, she was deeply touched. He never used to let anyone hug him. Not until Chance had come. Chance had brought the boy out of his shell.

When Patrick left, she covered her face with her hands. What was happening to them? Because of Chance, Patrick had learned to reach out to people; he had quit lying. Stephie was less afraid, the twins less defiant. By not realizing who he was, Dallas had allowed him to cleverly thread himself into all their lives. She had awakened this morning feeling loved and cherished. Now she felt shattered. Christopher had used her; he had cruelly deceived all of them—to get Stephie.

Dallas's disillusionment was profound. There was no way she could believe that a movie star could possibly be interested in her. Once again she had made a terrible mistake with a relationship. Only this time she had involved four children. She couldn't believe he cared for them at all.

Dallas went to the window and lifted the curtain. Christopher was moving about on his boat. For a dizzy moment she remembered the blazing thrill of his expert lovemaking. How he must be laughing at her. She thought of how she'd clung to him for the whole night. She was ashamed of the way she had revelled in what his hands and mouth had done to her. Now she felt herself brought low by every kiss, every torrid moan. He hadn't had to force her. She had wanted him too desperately. No doubt he'd considered her no more than a delightful diversion to be enjoyed while he claimed his daughter. He probably even despised her a little. He had a reputation for treating women callously. Was he planning to accuse her of being unfit to be Stephie's mother because she had slept with him? The coffee on her empty stomach made Dallas feel nauseous, and she pitched a cupful into the sink.

Last night she had nearly wept at the sight of blood on Chance's cheek. She looked down at her nails and longed to claw him like a cat.

No. She doubled her hands so that the nails were concealed. The curtain fell back into place. She began to wash dishes. Her hands trembled, and she broke a glass. She cut her finger on a gleaming shard and watched her blood flow onto the white porcelain.

No, she wouldn't go to him. She would stay in the house and compose herself. She would wait until he came for her.

Then she would be as clever as he and show him that he was not the only one who could be deceitful.

Dallas had been careful never to be alone that morning. When she heard Christopher on the porch, she clutched Stephie tightly, shrinking behind her as if she were a shield.

When Dallas saw his tall figure through the screen, a mixture of confused emotions coursed through her. He hesitated a moment as if he, too, found it difficult to face her. Then restlessly he pulled the door open.

His face was dark with telltale guilt. He tried to smile, and she sensed the uneasy tension in him that he was fighting to conceal.

She was just as nervous. Her cheeks flamed. Her brow was damply perspiring. She clasped her hands together so he wouldn't notice she was shaking.

He saw.

Unaware of the terrible adult tensions in the room, Stephie flipped the page of her storybook and commanded, "Read."

The deep timbre of Christopher's anxious voice filled the kitchen. "What are you girls reading—the white knight story?"

"No, Chance!" Stephie cried. "It's about a wolf that comes to the house of some goats and they let him in when they're not 'sposed to. And he eats 'em all."

That about summed it up. Dallas stared straight at an illustration of the unlucky goats.

For an instant Christopher didn't speak. "Honey, are you sure you should be reading her such grisly stuff?"

"I think it's a good preparation for life."

His mouth tightened with disapproval.

"I like it," Stephie chimed.

"Well, I don't." He leaned down and snapped the book shut. "You run out and play," he commanded briskly. At Stephie's startled look, his manner became gentle. "I want to talk to your aunt."

As soon as the child was gone, he took Dallas into his arms.
"What's wrong now?" He was staring at her white face and
frowning as if he was genuinely concerned. "Honey..."

The endearment was so tender, so anxious, so perfect. A
muscle in her stomach pulled. Oh, he was good. So good. And
he felt good, too. *He was a monster.* But her heart began to
race absurdly. Why couldn't she be immune to being crushed
against the hardness of his virile chest?

She felt on the edge of hysteria. Her mouth was too dry for
her to speak; her eyes misted. She turned away so he wouldn't
see.

But he saw. He took a quick breath. "Don't cry, Dallas."
A pause. His fingers stroked her neck with expert gentleness.
"I can't stand it when you cry." He kissed her brow.

When she felt her own treacherous response to the comfort
of those lips, she jumped away. "Don't. Not now. The children might come in." She bit her lips and wondered how he
found it so easy to lie when it was killing her.

"All right." His voice held a faint note of exasperation. "If
you're sure it's just the kids."

"I'm sure." She drew a deep breath and sighed.

"We've got to tell them about us sometime."

"No!" she snapped, terrified.

The question in his fake brown eyes seared her.

Careful.

In a calmer voice, she continued, "Of course, we will, but
not today. There won't be enough time to explain. I—I have
to take the kids into town."

"I'll come with you."

She rushed to the window. "No—"

His dark watchful gaze followed her. "I've never seen you
like this before."

She whirled. "Like what?"

"So nervous. If it's guilt about last night—"

Oh, you should be an expert on guilt. For an instant her
eyes blazed. "Oh, it's not guilt!"

"Then what is it?"

She lowered her gaze. "Maybe I wasn't sure what you'd think of me."

"I'm crazy about you," he said ardently, going to her and drawing her into his arms.

His face was very still. His hot dark eyes lit a fire inside her, and her heart began to beat wildly. He was lying. He was manipulating her with soft looks and sweet words, and she was so starved for love, she almost believed him.

"You can't come because I'm taking them to my brother's," she said softly, shakily.

"I see," he said in a level voice.

"No, you don't." She forced herself to touch his hand, to smile at him, and her heart twisted at how these tendernesses from her softened his hard features.

He lifted aside the molten gold of her long hair, pushing it away from the base of her throat so his lips could brush the vulnerable heartbeat there. She gasped when he kissed her in such a charming, loverlike way. Then she told herself not to be a fool. He was an actor.

In a rush she began again. "I'm going to leave them there all night, so that you and I can be alone."

His arms tightened around her waist, and he molded her closer. The hunger in his fathomless eyes made the muscles of her stomach contract sharply.

"We'll have the whole night, Chance. Just us."

"I can't wait." He bent his head and kissed her ear. Desire licked through her at the darting probes of his wet tongue. "Have you ever made love in the morning?"

"Chance, no! I—I mean we can't this morning." A pause. More softly. "But tonight I'll show you just how much last night meant to me."

His low voice was husky. "I'm looking forward to it." He forced himself to let her go.

She turned away. "Oh, so am I."

But she wasn't.
Not at all.

The heat of the day was dying, and the violet sky was streaked with mauve when Dallas came back from the city. She stopped at home, packed the Jeep with wine, food, the twins' boom box, towels and a blanket before continuing on to pick up Chance.

"Where are we going?" he murmured, kissing her after he climbed into the vehicle.

One kiss and she was melting and clinging to him, surrender quivering through every female cell. "The beach again," she managed shakily, pulling away reluctantly.

"I'd better go back for my suit," he said.

"Oh, you won't need it." With no effort she made her voice light and breathless as if in husky anticipation. She ran her fingertips along his muscular arm, and a mixture of dread and excitement tingled through her.

At his sudden groan she yanked her hand away. His dark smoldering gaze focused on her, and she felt the magnetic power of his charm. Her cheeks burned. He started to say something, but she couldn't bear to listen to more of his lies. Quickly she turned on the radio so she wouldn't have to.

But his silence was almost worse than his talking would have been. He watched everything she did with an intensity that made her nervous. He was so keenly intuitive, she wondered if he suspected something.

She was too aware of his virile silent presence beside her. Nor could she stop the tantalizing memories of the night before. Every time she looked at him she remembered the way they'd lain in the sand with the surf curling over them, the way they'd driven for miles afterward with the wanting fierce between them. And all the rest came back, as well.

When she came to the turnoff to the beach, he placed his hand on her thigh and ignited a heat that shamed her. She stepped on the gas so that the Jeep made the turn on two tires.

"Sorry," she said curtly when he was thrown against his door.

A white grin flashed across his tanned features. "Easy. We have the whole night."

She forced a smile even as her heart filled with dread. She drove even faster than before.

A big yellow moon rose over the gulf. The rhythm of the music was a savage beat pulsing through her blood.

"Can't we stop?" he murmured after they'd sped past several likely looking spots.

The Jeep whirled past still another spot in a rush of throbbing rock music and flying sand. "No!"

His dark gaze scanned her features, his own expression inscrutable. Her nervous fingers curled around his hand. "I—I want to go farther than we went last night," she murmured on a boldly breathless note.

"I'm up to whatever you are."

The miles whirred past them in a blur of sparkling waves until they had gone so far there were no other cars. The beach road grew rougher. The gulf had washed it out in places, and she had to drive through shallow water.

"Aren't you afraid of getting rust under your Jeep?" he asked.

"It'll be worth it."

The cool damp sea breeze caressed her. The wild music aroused her. The longer she drove, the more she craved him. But she drove thirty miles down the beach before she took a deep breath for courage and braked. Her fingers flew to her car keys and then froze. *She'd better leave them there.*

It was a beautiful night. The moon washed water and sand with gold. Endless beach and glimmering waves surrounded them. It seemed to her that they were the only two people in the world. Her heartbeats echoed in a wild, deafening roar that blanked out the surge of the surf. She glanced toward him. He seemed relaxed, seemed to suspect nothing. His hand moved to her shoulder and eased her spaghetti strap lower. She laid her head back so that his mouth could explore her shoulder, and he pressed a kiss against the curve of her neck.

As his expert mouth moved across her bare skin she was filled with that strange combination of fear and exhilaration. His large warm hands began to roam and skillfully mold. Everything he did aroused a warm flood of exquisite sensations that terrified her.

At last his lips covered her mouth in a long, drugging kiss. The kiss was like a narcotic, weakening her will and relaxing her rigid muscles. She could feel her heart thumping against her ribs. Her arms slid limply around his neck. She didn't want to desire him, but some strong primeval instinct overpowered all her will to resist.

If she didn't act quickly, she wouldn't be able to. She slid free of his embrace. "Let's swim."

"I'd rather spread the blanket on the sand," he murmured.

Her heart fluttered wildly. "Not yet." She touched his hot cheek with her palm. "Why don't we work up an appetite first?"

"Honey, I'm already starving."

Dallas looked up at him from beneath sweeping eyelashes. "I want to hold you in the water," she whispered. "To feel the waves curl around our hot bodies. It's a fantasy of mine."

As she began to pull off her shirt, he took a deep controlling breath and hesitated for a second only. Then gently, carefully, he helped her. She tossed her shirt into the back seat. Her fingertips hesitated at the clasp of her bra. He tore off his own shirt and threw it carelessly on top of hers.

His dark naked torso gleamed. Dallas's pulse fluctuated in alarm at so much rippling muscle. He looked strong and powerful, like some primitive noble savage. She thought of what she was about to do to him, and some inner vice warned that there might be danger in pushing a man like him too far.

His hungry dark eyes watched her unfasten her bra. That, too, she removed. Quickly he unlaced his boat shoes while she untied her sandals. These were quickly tossed to the back.

Then she undid the waistband of her shorts. He watched her peel yellow cotton and silky panties down over her thighs. Nervously she pulled them lower. His possessive gaze blazed a fiery path over her nude body. With a stifled groan, he finished undressing.

She was just as affected by the sight of him. He was beautiful. Lean sinewy muscle gleamed. He was virile, all-male—dangerous. But his expression was tender.

She loved him. More than anything she wanted to know again the ecstasy of his lovemaking. She continued to look at him, her emotions and thoughts tearing at her. Maybe...she was wrong about him.

No. He had made a fool of her.

"Honey, what is it?"

Her mouth went dry. She drew a deep breath. "Oh, nothing." Self-consciously, guiltily, she averted her eyes.

"Don't be afraid," he whispered gently.

"I'm not," she managed in a softer voice, but when he tried to touch her reassuringly, she bolted.

He ran after her, catching her at the water's edge and pulling her down into the foaming waves. The water was cool, but his mouth was warm, and she was as dangerously vulnerable to his lovemaking as ever. Every kiss sent passionate shivers racing down her spine. She was on the brink of total surrender, when he murmured, "How about that blanket now?"

Numbly she nodded.

His mouth crooked, utterly charming her. Once more he kissed her. Then he left her and swam out into the surf to wash himself off.

For a second longer, she watched him, no longer wanting to trick him, even as she despised herself for hesitating. It was now or never. This was not the time for second thoughts. When he turned around, she was already racing toward the Jeep. He called out, but she only ran faster.

Shells cut into her bare feet, and she cried out in pain. But his footsteps thudding behind her kept her running.

Breathless, she threw herself into the Jeep. She turned the keys in the ignition. Jammed her foot on the accelerator.

Nothing happened!

He loomed nearer. The surf roared. All she heard was his harsh panting. She twisted the key again. All she felt were the thuds of his running feet hitting the sand.

Frantically she twisted the key a final time.

He grabbed the door handle. "What the hell do you think you're doing?"

The engine sputtered to life.

He banged on the window as the Jeep inched away. "Dallas!"

She looked into the wild fury of his eyes and stepped on the gas. He fell back as the Jeep shot forward.

She heard his furious shouts and stopped a safe distance from him, rolling her window down and leaning out. "Nice night. As they say in California—enjoy...*Mr. Stone.*"

"Dallas! Wait! I can explain!"

"No!"

"You can't leave me like this—without money or clothes."

"Right!" She threw out a towel. "That's more than you deserve."

"Dallas!"

She stomped on the accelerator. Tires spun sand all over the towel.

A mile or so down the road she stopped—to put on her clothes.

Eleven

Through the salt spray on the windshield Dallas saw the blur of her house and the restaurant beside it.

Go back and get him.

Her teeth sank viciously into her bottom lip. She jerked the wheel, accelerated and swerved onto the shell drive. Then she leapt out without bothering to unpack and went straight to the restaurant to work. If Oscar and Pepper knew something was wrong, they asked no questions.

It was late when Dallas unplugged the jukebox and locked up after the last customer. In her bedroom she collapsed without bothering to turn out the lights. In a state of sleepless exhaustion, she lay fully clothed, staring up at those burning lights.

A thousand times she was tempted to drive back for Chance. A thousand times she stopped herself. What she had done was nothing compared to what he had done to her.

But at first light, she went to his boat almost hoping he was there.

He wasn't.

The yacht strained gently against her dock lines when Dallas pulled on them. She had so many questions. Perhaps she could find answers here. Warily she slid his hatch open and eased herself into the darkened cabin.

Inside one drawer she found the script for *Tiger Six*. She pitched it back on top of several others. Inside another drawer she discovered his clothes, or rather his costumes—Western shirts, jeans, enormous belt buckles. Angrily she slammed that drawer shut on a tangle of jeans and belts. In the last she found a large envelope stuffed with photographs of herself and her family plus type-written reports about her. There were letters from his lawyer that made Christopher's intentions damningly clear. A chill went through her as she read the documents.

Her eyes burned. With shaking hands she threw everything back into the drawer. There was no doubt that what he had planned all along was to take Stephie. As always, Dallas had been so eager to find love that she had blindly slept with the one man who wanted to use her. She had seen only what she wanted to see, believed what she'd wanted to believe.

With a leaden heart she returned to the house and called Robert, saying only that she'd be late picking up the children. He argued even after she told him it was an emergency. Then he started asking her about Chance.

"Not now."

"The kids can't quit talking about him. He sounds great."

"Maybe to you."

"The kids are anxious to go home. I could drive—"

"No! I—I mean not just yet."

"I want to meet this guy."

"No!"

"Dallas—"

She hung up on him.

No way did she want the children and Robert around when she had it out with Christopher.

The morning dragged on and on, and despite her anger and

her fear of Christopher, she began to worry that something terrible had happened to him. So it was with a curious mixture of dread and relief that she watched a battered blue pickup unload him at the marina.

Christopher climbed out, exhaustion in every stiff muscle of his body. He cringed with every bleeding step he took across the rough drive, clutching his towel about him.

Not that she believed he was beaten. She braced herself for him to come to the house at once.

But he didn't.

The longest hour of her life passed. She chewed her lips until they were raw.

Finally she couldn't stand the suspense and went down to him. From a distance he appeared to be dozing nonchalantly on his cushions in the shade of his bimini. At her footsteps, his eyelids flickered alertly open. His hair was still long and brown, but his famous eyes were a piercing blue.

The Tiger's eyes.

He went as still as death when he saw her. Although her heart began to pound, she was determined not to show her fear. He got up and leaned over to pull the dock line tight so she could step on board.

Christopher said nothing. Finally she burst out, "Quit looking at me like that!"

"Like what?"

"Like I should feel guilty."

"And do you feel guilty?" His cold blue gaze was intense.

"That sounds like something a crazy actor who's spent too much time on an analyst's couch would ask."

"I've never been to a shrink."

She flushed. "You know you had it coming."

His mouth tightened. "Right. You would think that."

"I'm not the guilty one here."

His face took on a cold seductive expression that attracted her even as it repelled her. "Right. I'm the bastard. You're the angel. Black and white. Maybe your life's that simple, *angel*."

She raked her fingers through her blowing hair and looked away. There were smudges of blood on the floor of the cockpit—from his feet. She imagined the long walk over shells and sand and the occasional bits of broken glass. She saw the dark shadows under his eyes.

"Angel!" He said the word viciously. "The last thing I expect from you is kindness."

"Don't worry! I—I don't feel any. You're worse even than all those newspapers said you were!"

Christopher kept looking at her with those icy blue eyes. "Then I won't bother defending myself. Narrow-minded people always believe what they want, no matter what the truth is."

"Quit trying to make me into the bad guy."

"You're the one who refused to let me even see my child. You left me thirty miles down the beach without shoes or a stitch of clothes while you went home and slept like a baby. You went through my things."

"You used me," she accused.

He slumped back against the cushions. "Because you were so set against me you wouldn't even listen to me."

"I knew you'd lie."

"I had no choice." His face was as bloodless as a statue's. "I had no choice."

"Why did you make love to me?" Tears began to stream down her cheeks. "Maybe I could have forgiven you the rest, if only it weren't for that." She buried her head in her hands because she couldn't bear for him to see her cry.

"I'm not proud of what I did."

Dallas flushed miserably. "That makes two of us."

"If I could undo it, I would."

"Ditto."

"But I couldn't get anywhere with Robert. He kept demanding more money for Stephie. Every time I agreed, he wanted more. When I tried dealing with you, I got nowhere. I came here to see what was going on.''

"You did a little more than that. You won the children's trust and mine. With lies. You pretended you cared.''

"I do care.''

The passion in his voice sent fresh longing surging through her which made her more ashamed then ever. How could she—*want to believe him?* "It was all a game, an act, a role to you.''

"No.''

She looked up, her tears gone. "I want you gone.''

His icy gaze studied her. "It's not that simple.''

She got to her feet. "It is to me. I hate you now.''

Just for a second she thought she saw some terrible vulnerability in his eyes that was equal to her own. She had a crazy, odd feeling that she had cut him deeply.

"Be careful that you don't push me too far,'' he warned, "I didn't lie to you about my feelings. There was nothing false in my kisses.''

"No…''

"Nothing false in my lovemaking. I burned for you then…as I burn for you now.''

Her fingers twisted the bottom edge of her shirt; her nervous palms were moist. "I—I can't believe you,'' she whispered even as his tender words made her blood race like liquid fire. "I can't—''

"Then believe this, you little fool.''

She lunged wildly away, but he was quicker. He seized her, his arms encircling her. Her legs tangled with his rock-hard thighs. His mouth ravaged hers, his tongue roaming possessively inside her mouth.

Every barrier between them vanished in the heat of that destroying kiss. With his hands and mouth, he made her his. One minute she was spinning in that dark whirlwind of his fiery passion, craving him as undeniably as she craved breath, air, life itself. In the next she clawed him frantically to escape.

He let her go.

She fell back limply against the lifelines. He saw the blood on her lips and, thinking he'd hurt her, touched them gently with his fingertip. She jerked her head away.

"That may work in the movies, but not in real life," she said bitterly. "I wonder if you know the difference."

His dark face paled. "I'm sorry I deceived you."

"Oh, so that makes everything all right."

He clenched his hands into fists. "No. Damn it."

"For once you're right about something!"

In the distance a car door slammed. Neither of them heard the soft eager approach of a little girl's running footsteps. Neither of them saw her stop and crouch low behind a nautical gear box on the deck when she heard their angry voices.

"Dallas, listen to me. Don't be like all the others. You don't know the hell it has been—living a fishbowl existence. Don't judge me on what a sensational press has written. Writers who don't know me make up stuff about what I do, about what I feel. I'm not that person.

"The last few weeks have been the only good, the only real thing in my life for a long, long time. I wasn't pretending that I cared for you and the kids. I was born into this crazy movie-star existence. I can't even begin to tell you how awful it was. My parents lived soap-opera lives and thrived on the publicity. They fought over me in endless custody battles, and when one of them won me, he or she ignored me."

He stopped for a second before continuing.

"Honey, my life has always been like a circus, like some nightmare carnival ride. My marriage to Marguerite was no different. She never wanted me—she wanted Hollywood—the glamour, the money, not that any of it ever made her happy. None of it has ever made me happy, either. It wasn't real. Only you. You were real, Dallas. The kids were real—not just Stephie, but all of them. Patrick, Rennie, Jennie. For the first time I felt I was part of a real family."

Dallas had looked away, into dark water when he began

speaking, not wanting to hear because she was too afraid she might believe. Tears glimmered in her eyes as every sweet word and every sad one tore into her heart. *Did he have any idea how she longed to believe him and ached because she couldn't?*

"You deserve an Academy Award for that speech," she managed at last, her choked voice like ice.

"Damn it. Dallas, I'm telling you the truth. What would you have done? You had my child!"

Something fell on the dock, and he looked up abruptly. "What was that?"

Dallas glanced toward the dock. "Probably just something the wind knocked over."

"Hell, I lost my train of thought." He ran his hands through his hair.

"I had your child," Dallas reminded him dully.

"Right." A pause. "I couldn't just go away and leave her here. If you'd known who I was, you would have thrown me out the first day. I would never have gotten to know any of you."

"At least I would have known what I was dealing with. A snake." She paused. "I loathe you. You are the vilest human being I've ever known. I don't care if you are Stephie's father. I want you gone."

His face twisted. "If only it were that easy."

"You walked out on her mother seven years ago. Why don't you just do the same thing now?"

"You don't even begin to understand about Marguerite. I was crazy about her, but our relationship was a destructive force in both our lives. I didn't know about the baby when I left her. I damn sure didn't know about it when I came back to her. She was too scared she'd lose me again to tell me the truth. She thought she could forget and go on with her life, but the lie ate at her and destroyed any hope we ever had of an honest relationship. The minute I found out about Stephie I came here."

Dallas's temples pounded sickeningly. "We were doing just fine before you came."

"Oh, right. What about Stephie nearly walking off the dock that first night? What about her being all mixed-up and afraid of everything? I think she's grown attached to me."

"Because she doesn't really know you. You're not who you pretended to be," Dallas said. "I've read awful things about you."

"I wish I could say they were all lies."

"All those women."

"I regret them. I went crazy...after Sally died. Those women didn't mean anything to me."

"I doubt they felt as casually about it as you do."

"It was different with you."

She was looking at him closely, some part of her believing him. He seemed so sincere. Why was it so hard to keep telling herself he was a monster? Why, despite his glamour, did he seem a real human being after all, too real? She remembered the baby she'd given up, the agony of the years wondering about that unborn child. How could she blame him for wanting to find his daughter?

But when he moved toward her to draw her closer, she sprang away, shaking her head. "Don't you dare come near me."

"Okay," he said. "We'll take it slow, if that's the way you want it."

"I don't want anything from you, Mr. Stone."

"I'm not leaving here without what I came for."

There was a small frightened cry from the dock. Then there was nothing.

"What was that?" Christopher demanded.

"It sounded like Stephie."

In a single leap he was off the boat. Behind the gear box they found White Horse thrown down and abandoned.

Robert had brought the kids back anyway.

"Stephie..." Christopher's voice was a whisper.

"She must have heard us."

"Dear God. If anything has happened to her, I'll never forgive myself. I thought you said the kids were at your brother's."

"I—I thought they were."

Christopher knelt down and picked up the grubby white horse. "White Horse was sitting by the pool the day Sally died. He's all I have left of her."

The unbearable anguish in his bleak, frightened voice struck Dallas to the heart. Her anger vanished. Without thinking, she touched his arm and said gently, "Stephie's okay. She's upset. She does this sometimes. We'll find her."

His hand closed over hers tightly. "Right, we'll find her."

"It's not your fault," she murmured.

No matter how she might hate him for what he'd done, he loved Stephie as much as she did. Maybe he had lied to her and used her because of that love. Maybe he was wild and terrible. Maybe she even hated him.

But it was funny how none of that seemed to matter. How the only thing that mattered now was the love they both shared for their lost little girl.

Twelve

Stephie was gone!

Christopher was exhausted—physically, mentally and emotionally. He'd walked nearly all night; it had been dawn before the battered pickup had stopped for him.

Nevertheless, after Dallas and he searched the marina, calling to Stephie and she didn't answer, he ran up to the house and barked out orders to Robert and the children, sending everyone in opposite directions to look for Stephie.

Christopher was the one who found her, though.

Because the first place he looked for her was at the pool. She was lazily floating in the deep end, clinging to a black inner tube.

He strode up to the water's edge. "Stephie, why didn't you answer me when I called you awhile ago?"

She turned her head away.

"You have everyone worried. They've all looking for you."

No answer. Only the tiny movement of her small hand, only the silver wavelet rippling away from her clenched fingertips.

He sucked in a heavy breath. The glassy water was a turquoise dazzle. Stephie's black hair was loosely flowing across the surface as she lay on her back staring up at the sky. When he jumped in, she continued to hold her face away from him.

"Clouds go by so fast," she whispered, closing her eyes when he swam up to her. "Where do you think they're going?"

"Don't you know you shouldn't ever swim alone?"

"I'd like to ride on a cloud."

"I said you shouldn't swim..."

"I've got my tube."

"That doesn't matter, Stephie."

"You're my birth daddy, aren't you?" For the first time she opened her eyes, and her dark eyes seemed to pierce all the way to his soul.

A pause.

"Yes."

"You came here because you want to take me away."

"I wanted to see you. Is that so wrong?"

She looked back to the clouds. "I don't know. Aunt Dallas seems to think so."

"That's because I tricked her. Have you ever done something to a friend you wished you hadn't?" He began to gently pull Stephie and the tube toward the shallow end. "You knew who I was right from the first."

"But I thought you were bad."

They had reached the steps. "What do you think now?"

"Your real little girl died, didn't she?"

"Yes. But you're my real little girl, too."

"Am I the only little girl you have now?"

"The only one."

She let go of the tube and wrapped her arms around his neck. "You're my only daddy, too, and I don't think you're bad. You'll have to tell Aunt Dallas you're sorry."

His forehead touched Stephie's. "I already did. She won't listen."

"She does that to me, too. Sometimes Patrick hits me first, and when I hit him back she just sends us both to our rooms." She frowned. "I like your eyes better now."

"Thank you."

"How did you make them brown?" Before he could answer, her grip around his neck tightened. "Please don't take me away from Aunt Dallas and the kids, okay? 'Cause I love 'em."

"I love them, too."

"Even Aunt Dallas?"

"Especially Aunt Dallas."

"Like the knight loved the princess?"

"Right... Well, not exactly. Honey, I'm afraid there's no such thing as fairy-tale love."

"That's what Aunt Dallas said."

"And I'm not much of a knight, either."

"You are to me."

"Then I'm a tarnished one."

"Guess who Chance really is, everybody," Stephie announced in a happy piping voice as he carried her through the screen door on his shoulders. "He's my birth daddy!"

For one paralyzed second there was a profound silence in the crowded kitchen. Everyone seemed to hold his breath. Only the faint rush of the sea breeze rustling the bushes outside could be heard. All eyes focused on Christopher and Dallas.

Dallas turned beet red.

Everyone started talking at once.

"Christopher Stone," the twins gasped in an awed breathless duet. "Wow! We know a real movie star."

"The Tiger!" Patrick gave an excited war whoop. "I knew it all the time!"

"Liar!" the twins yelled.

"I did!"

Christopher was aware only of Dallas. Every drop of hot

color had swiftly drained from her face. She swayed back into Robert's supporting arms a grim, confirming look passing from younger sister to older brother.

Robert was tall and blond, a masterful male version of Dallas. He had the same golden flecks in his blue eyes. He held out his hand to Christopher and introduced himself. His handshake was firm and welcoming. Christopher sensed an ally.

"Last night, when the kids couldn't stop talking about this Chance McCall, I couldn't figure it out," Robert said. "Now it's all beginning to make sense."

"Where was Stephie?" Dallas asked quietly when her brother had finished, concern for the child in her every breath.

"In the swimming pool."

"Dear Lord. Stephie, darling, why didn't you answer when we called?"

"I got scared when you said those mean things to Chance."

Dallas went even whiter at this censure. She turned to the twins. "Rennie...Jennie...bring some towels."

Not wanting to miss a second in the kitchen, the twins obeyed instantly, streaking like lightning to the bathroom and back with a bundle of fleecy towels.

Dallas reached for a towel at the same moment Christopher did. Their eyes met. Her fingers tightened just for an instant on her end of towel and then relaxed, letting him pull the soft cotton from her.

Dallas slumped weakly into a chair. Robert began to make coffee. On the surface everyone tried to act calm, and yet Christopher felt tension running through them all.

He leaned over Stephie as he wrapped her in a towel and then took a second one and dried her hair. When he was done, he sat down, and Stephie crawled up into his lap and put her arms around him.

Dallas went still paler at the sight of the little girl clinging lovingly to her father. When the coffee was brewed, Robert poured his sister a steaming black cup. "You look like a ghost. Maybe this'll help."

She gulped it down gratefully, trying not to look at Christopher and Stephie.

Robert was the first to recover. "I think this is for the best," he said in his most lawyerlike voice.

"Robert, please." Dallas set her cup on the counter with a clatter.

"I was only trying to help."

"I wish you wouldn't."

"This doesn't have to be a tug of war," Robert persisted.

"Then what is it?" she demanded through gritted teeth.

"Why don't you face the facts, Dallas? He's her father."

"We've been through this before," she said tightly.

"You're her mother. I told you that last night the kids couldn't stop talking about him. In the few weeks he's been here, they've formed an extraordinary attachment to him. Whether you like it or not, he's earned a place in this family. Besides that, it costs an arm and a leg to raise four kids..."

She jumped up. "Well, I don't like it! It always comes down to money with you, doesn't it? And I can't stand you taking his side in this, either! You're my brother."

"Did it ever occur to you that you might both be on the same side?"

"No!"

"Then maybe it should. I think if you tried, you could work out a compromise that would be fair to everyone. You need his help. The kids need him."

Dallas whirled on Christopher. "You must be very happy."

Gently, Christopher set Stephie down and stood up. "No...."

"You knew exactly what you were doing, and you think you've won. *The Tiger* always wins. They all love you—Robert, the children—all of them, except me. You've torn this family apart with your lies, with your deceit."

"Dallas, stop it." Robert was aghast.

Christopher seemed to steel himself to her cold voice, even to the fury in her eyes. "No. Let her say it. She has to get it out. I did trick her, and what I did was wrong. Even though I did it because I cared about...everybody in this room.''

"Liar! Don't listen to him," she whispered. "He's as cold and as inhuman as that...muscle-bound idiot he plays."

"I like *The Tiger*, Aunt Dallas," Patrick dared to say hesitantly.

"We do, too," said the twins, moving closer to Christopher.

"Dear Lord! I can't stand any more. Mr. Stone, tell the children goodbye. Then I want you gone. They'll forget you."

"No, we won't," Patrick said.

"You don't have the right to make this decision for us," Rennie muttered.

"Kids, don't make it harder for her than it already is," Christopher said quietly.

For a second Dallas hesitated and stared at them all with desperate haunted eyes. Then she raced upstairs, stumbling over Patrick's skateboard.

The skateboard rolled down the stairs, crashed into the table and turned over on its side. Patrick's eyes grew huge with guilt when she nearly fell, but no one said a word. The only sound in the kitchen was the soft, dying whir of the skateboard's spinning wheels.

"Wow!" Jennie gasped.

Rennie kicked her, and Jennie looked embarrassed.

Patrick was the next to speak. "I wish you really were *The Tiger*, Chance. 'Cause he always wins.''

Christopher swallowed hard as he gravely considered the boy's words. "Hell, I wish I was him, too."

"Go after her anyway, Chance," Patrick urged. "Maybe she just needs a hug."

Christopher sank to his haunches and picked up the skateboard. "That makes two of us."

Patrick came flying across the kitchen into his arms.

Not to be left out, Stephie threw her arms around both of them. Rennie and Jennie giggled nervously, and then joined their brother and sister on the floor.

Christopher hugged them all for a long time, drawing a kind of strength from their love and faith in him that he'd never known before.

Finally he got up, knowing he had to face Dallas.

Robert came over and picked up the skateboard. "This house is a mine field." He handed the skateboard to Patrick. "Why don't you put this away for once? We've got broken hearts already. We don't need a broken neck." To Christopher, he said, "There's only one way to win Dallas— I know because I'm her brother. Don't give up."

Christopher pounded on Dallas's bedroom door for an eternity before she finally answered.

He heard her muted voice, still and small, float across her room. "Oh, if you won't go, come in."

He entered and closed the door.

She was lying on her bed in the shadows, shaking. "When are you leaving?"

"I'm not—without you."

She sat up on her elbows. "You can't stay!"

"No," he agreed. "I've stayed way too long. I've neglected my work, my business associates. My agent even hung up on me the other morning, and that's a dangerous sign in Hollywood. You're coming with me. You and the children. As I see it, there's only one solution."

"That you go!"

"No."

She stared up at him blankly.

"I'm asking you to marry me." With a knightly flourish, he sank onto a bended knee.

She sprang up, her blue eyes burning brightly in a face that was white with horror. "Are you out of your mind? Get up!"

"If you believe everything you read—"

"Be serious. What kind of marriage could we possibly have?"

"It couldn't be worse than any of my parents' marriages or than my first one," he replied bitterly, rising.

"What sort of person says something like that?"

His mouth quirked. "Can I help it if I have only my own experience to speak from? Our marriage would be as good as most of the ones I've known."

"That sounds so cynical."

"As you've pointed out, my life hasn't been ideal."

"Don't you even care about love?"

"I don't know much about love other than what I've read about or seen in the movies. It's a word people slap on to everything to excuse the most stupid, self-destructive behavior."

"I gave up my own child because her father didn't love me. How could you possibly even think I'd consider marrying you without it?"

"This is different. You were a child yourself then." He stopped. "We're already a family."

"No."

"We're two responsible adults."

"That's debatable."

"Damn it, Dallas. Six lives hang in the balance. If you marry me, we all win."

"Wrong. We all lose."

"We'd be together."

"For how long? You only want this because you want your daughter. These kids have already lost their mother and father once. I won't risk a divorce that would shatter their lives all over again. You'd try to take Stephie then. If I marry you, that will strengthen your claim to her."

"I don't give a damn about that. Do you think you can be both father and mother? You're working yourself to the bone, neglecting the kids and you're not making a dime with the marina or the restaurant. I've got money. You can go back to school, finish your degree, go into your own field."

"You are as cold and inhuman as that muscled freak you

play. I'm not something you can buy and sell or bribe. You don't give a damn about the kids or me going into my field.''

"I don't blame you for feeling that way right now. I tricked you. Maybe I was wrong to do it, but the other night when you were in my arms, I know you felt something for me."

"That was before I knew who you really were."

"I am still the same man. Your response to me was real. We'll find that again, and it will grow—if you'll let it."

Dallas was trembling with fury and with pure raw pain. "I don't want you—ever again."

Without warning, he moved toward her. When she tried to make a run for the door, he barred her way. "There's no escape," he said with a gentleness that belied the terrible power of his will. He caught her chin with the edge of his large hand and forced her to look at him. When she did, she froze. He knew his eyes were blazing with the full, unleashed force of his determination to have her. "Either you marry me, or I'll fight you every step of the way. The press won't leave you alone as soon as they find out you've got my child."

She sucked in her breath and stepped away from him. "Why do they have to find out?"

"Believe me, they will."

"Because you'll tell them?"

"Maybe this once the jackals will be useful to me."

"You are a devil."

He shrugged. "No. but I'd make a bargain with him to get you and the children. Desperate men do desperate things, Dallas. Maybe I don't deserve your trust right now, but the truth is that I want to marry you because I care about you."

"No. This is the easiest way you can think of to get Stephie."

"I want you, too." His voice softened for a moment as he caught her face again in his rough hands. "How can you doubt that? How can you forget how it was when we made love?" As he brushed his knuckles lightly across her cheek, she shivered at the wanton memories, and the sudden heat in her eyes sent flames through him. "Do you really want to live without what we can have together?"

"No!" She bit her lip. "I—I mean yes! I won't think about that night. And I can't stand it when you touch me."

"Can't you?" Christopher's unwavering gaze held hers. Just for an instant he thought he saw love and longing there before her guilt and fury obliterated them.

"The fight will tear Stephie apart," he promised grimly. "Custody fights always hurt the children. I've got money and power and the natural rights of a biological father on my side. What do you have on yours other than the most stubborn nature God ever gave a woamn?"

Dallas tightened her hands into small fists at her sides. "Only the fierce desire to protect Stephie."

"Why can't you see that we want the same thing?"

Dallas turned to flee.

"You have to marry me, Dallas. There's no other way."

Thirteen

The Tiger had won. Today was their wedding day.

In hushed whispers, Stephie and the twins were admiring the beaded silk gown and veil on the bed.

"It looks like the princess's dress!"

It looked like a shroud. Dallas felt numb, unreal, displaced. Nothing in this exquisite bedroom seemed to belong to her. She lifted the cold silk from the bed; downstairs she heard the wedding guests' laughter and gaiety.

She was Christopher's prize. He had terrorized her into this. Today he was triumphant. His beautiful white ranch house was packed with his glamorous friends, his flowers, his champagne and his wedding gifts. Succulent odors from his kitchen where caterers worked drifted up the stairs. Outside on his lawns, blue-and-white tents and picnic tables had been set up. Canopies fluttered over walkways and drives. And beyond were the hills and the Pacific. This was *his* world.

Christopher had given Dallas an upstairs bedroom to change in, and as she slipped into the lavish white gown, she glanced into the mirror and saw that her skin was as white as snow. Stephie and the twins wore matching pink organza dresses, and they were flushed with happiness. When Dallas finished dressing, they began to jump up and down. They had been overjoyed ever since she'd agreed to marry Christopher.

Stephie had said, "I'll have a real family again."

Dallas felt close to tears. What would happen when Stephie's little-girl dream did not come true? What would happen when the marriage inevitably ended, and Stephie lost her brother and sisters and Dallas forever? Dallas knew that if that happened, she would never forgive herself for not fighting Christopher harder.

Still, did she have a choice? As Christopher had predicted, reporters had stormed to the marina and pestered them with endless questions. Suggestive stories that speculated about Dallas's relationship with Christopher had appeared in all the national scandal sheets. When Patrick read one of these stories entitled "*The Tiger*'s Secret Baby" and asked her about it, she had telephoned Christopher begging him to call off his jackals.

"Only you can stop them," he had replied coldly.

"How?"

"By marrying me."

When she had met with her lawyer, who told her that Christopher had very legitimate paternal claims to Stephie, and a legal battle could prove long and expensive, Dallas had grown more terrified. Without money how could she fight him? Then she received a threatening letter from his lawyer. She read it over and over until its message had burned itself into her brain. Another article appeared saying that she had no right to Stephie, that she could offer Stephie none of the advantages Christopher could, that any judge would see that.

Patrick and the twins kept asking why she didn't marry Christopher. They were as afraid of losing Stephie as she was. At last she decided that she couldn't fight them all.

Dallas had called Christopher and agreed to his terms. He'd

sent a jet the next morning to pick them up. When she got off the plane, Christopher was at the airport, more handsome than ever now that his hair was its natural reddish gold. His dazzling blue eyes had filled her with warmth. Then she'd seen the press behind him, snapping pictures, screaming questions, and she turned away from him coldly.

His face had grown as closed and distant as hers. Of course, he'd charmed the children because that suited his purpose. But to her, he'd remained cool.

Although they lived together at his ranch house, their relationship hadn't improved. They spoke only when necessary. Often when she was alone she wanted to cry because it all seemed so hopeless, but she was frozen inside. She tried to stall him, but because of Christopher's imminent departure for Spain, he'd insisted they marry at once.

She might have fought longer had not another article appeared: *"The Tiger* Living With Woman Who Has His Secret Baby."

Cal made all the wedding arrangements.

So it was with a troubled heart that Dallas pinned on her wedding veil. She wasn't a real bride. This wasn't her wedding day; this was her funeral.

Robert, who had come to California to give her away, rushed into her bedroom and smiled ecstatically. "Who would have thought you'd do something this sensible?"

Her fingers itched to strangle him. Instead, she threw her bouquet at him, but the flowers bounced off his chest.

"Why can't you act like a normal brother and console me?"

"That's normal?" He looked at his watch. He stooped to pick up the tangle of blossoms and streamers. "Girls, y'all run along downstairs."

When they were alone, Dallas said, "I—I can't go through with it."

"Nonsense." He replaced her bouquet into her shaking hands. "All you have is bridal jitters."

"You only want this because you're such a social climber!"

"Hell. Who else would marry you? You've got four kids, a money-losing marina, a couple of worthless English degrees, no money, impractical expectations…"

"While you're listing my assets, don't forget to mention a supportive big brother."

"This is the real world."

"You're telling me."

"He loves you."

"No. He's had all those other women. Starlets…"

"So what? You have a past."

She turned as white as her dress. "It's not the same."

"Oh, because you're a woman, you get to play by different rules?"

"Of all the low-down, sexist—"

"Look, he was a bachelor, in grief over his little girl. He was rich, famous. Most of those women threw themselves at him. One of them broke into his house. He found her naked in his bed when he came home one night. He was drunk. She was beautiful. He was lonely. He wanted her. But he threw her out. She went to the press and said he'd brought her there and tried to seduce her. She even sued him for palimony."

"How do you know that?"

"He told me."

"Did he tell you he loves me?"

"He's marrying you, isn't he?"

"That doesn't mean anything!" she cried softly.

"I've seen the way he looks at you. The kids adore him."

"He's only doing this to strengthen his claim to Stephie."

"You're wrong, Dallas."

"Oh, why is it that you've never once listened to me?"

Robert patted her hand. "Can we work on that one later? The wedding march is beginning."

Dallas was so heartsick that she wanted to throw herself down on the bed. Robert was pulling her toward the door. She drew a deep, resigned breath, and she let him lead her down the stairs. But with every trancelike step, her heart knocked madly with unbearable dread.

When they reached the threshold in the immense living room crammed with guests, the air grew thick with the cloying fragrances of a thousand flowers—roses, carnations, orchids, irises. Dallas's hand went to her throat. She was suffocating, dying. Then she saw Christopher standing in a pool of sunlight beside the minister and the children. His cool blue gaze slid to her as if to impel her forward.

She stood frozen where she was.

An expectant hush fell upon the crowd as she pushed Robert away, but she saw only Christopher. His dark features seemed chiseled of stone. If she'd hoped to see some softness in him, she found none.

Never had he seemed grimmer. He didn't want her. He was using her to get his child as he had used other women—to forget his grief. He was a movie star, and she knew nothing about him except what she'd read. He wasn't real. She was an ordinary woman who couldn't mean anything to him. Dallas closed her eyes because she couldn't look at him without loving him.

No. She couldn't still love him. She had loved a dream. This man was an indomitable stranger, and the thought of marrying him chilled her.

"No—"

Her soft cry rang out above the dying strains of the wedding march. All eyes were upon her—some politely curious, some covertly hostile. She felt only Christopher's.

For an instant she didn't realize she'd spoken.

Then she knew that no matter what he did to her, she couldn't marry him. Not if he didn't love her. Maybe she would lose Stephie anyway, but she had to fight for her. And even as she knew this, she was sorry she couldn't marry him. He would never know how sorry.

Alone, she faced Christopher across that throng. In his black tux, he looked menacingly huge. He had the power, the legal rights and the money to crush her for this humiliation.

She turned her back on him and walked out of the house to the waiting limousine that was there to whisk them away to their honeymoon. She heard Christopher's racing footsteps behind her.

She was opening the white car door when he caught her. His hand closed over her wrist, and she winced as he pinned her against the car.

"I can't, Christopher," she whispered. "I tried, but I can't."

She expected violence.

He drew a ragged breath and stepped back. "You've always been afraid of me," he said quietly.

"I was right to be." She searched the grim darkness of his bleak face and felt fresh despair because she could read no softness for her there. The blue eyes were hard. His mouth was set. She couldn't tell him that she had been afraid of loving him, that she was still afraid of it any more than she could tell him that she loved him anyway.

"You can go," he said at last, bringing her hand to his warm lips and kissing her fingers.

"What?"

"I won't have you afraid of me."

The children were huddled together on the veranda, and she called to them.

They stayed where they were, not wanting to come.

"It's okay, guys," Christopher said. "The fight's over. You've got to go home with your aunt."

When they came slowly forward, Christopher knelt down and looked into Stephie's eyes. "I won't fight you for Stephie," he said to Dallas. "You're right. She belongs with all of you."

Stephie's big dark eyes grew luminous as she studied her father. Then she threw her arms around him and clung. So did

Patrick. Both children began to sniffle quietly. The twins stared at Dallas, their pretty identical faces tragic.

"Some day you'll all understand," Dallas said.

"You'll probably marry someone dumb like Gordon," the twins said.

"Girls, it's over." Christopher's voice was clipped and final. "You have to go home with your aunt."

"We want to stay."

"I'll be on location in Spain."

"Will we ever see you again?" Patrick asked.

"Hell." Christopher ruffled Patrick's yellow hair that was so like his own. "That's hard to say."

"Maybe...someday?"

"Right. Someday."

Had Christopher looked at Dallas he would have seen the single glistening tear that traced down her white cheek. But he was looking at the children.

Dallas brushed the tear away and got into the limousine. She sank back against plush white leather, thankful for the sound of the air conditioner drowning out the children's goodbyes. In the short time they had known him, all of them had come to love him.

At last they were in the car. Christopher leaned down to the window and said to Patrick, "Don't go out on that sailboard alone, and don't leave your skateboard on those stairs anymore, either." To Dallas he said, "I'll have your things sent."

"There's no hurry."

Although Christopher looked away at the Pacific, as if he couldn't bear to look at her, she couldn't tear her gaze away from him. His eyes were the same dazzling blue as the ocean's. Pain constricted in her chest. She would never see him again.

"The offer's open," he muttered in that strange indifferent voice he'd used ever since she'd come to California. "If you change your mind, call Cal. He'll put you in touch."

Look at me! All you have to do is tell me you love me!

He straightened his long lean body and backed away.

She felt desolate.

The limousine was driving away; everyone but Dallas turned around to wave goodbye. Clouds of dust swirled behind the limousine.

Patrick said in a low dismal voice, "I can't see him anymore."

Everyone turned around and grew still and silent. Dallas could feel them blaming her.

When the limo jolted over the cattle guard and out the gate, Stephie tugged at Dallas's sleeve. "Why wouldn't you marry my daddy?"

"I—I..."

Stephie's eyes were so dark and imploring that Dallas couldn't answer her. Instead she looked out the window.

Magnificent headlands jutted out into a beautiful blue ocean. This beautiful, warmly sparkling day was to have been her wedding day. Tonight would have been her wedding night.

She had fought to escape that fate and had won.

Why, then, did her victory feel so hollow?

Why was the pain in her heart so intense that she wanted to die?

Fourteen

Life went on at the marina, but not as before. Dallas and the children seemed to have regressed back to that awful time after Carrie and Nick had died. Only this period was darker, blacker—more profound. This was new grief piled onto old.

Stephie cried at night and had to be constantly watched because she walked in her sleep. Dallas's nightmares were more frequent. She would wake up and long for Christopher's comforting arms about her before she reminded herself of his treachery. The twins took up with their wild crowd again, and every day they became more difficult to handle. Oscar felt the tension and drank more. So Dallas worked harder, and accomplished less. Robert told her that the kids' insurance money was almost gone.

Christopher had left his yacht at the marine; Oscar was supposed to take care of it. But when he drank, he forgot to check the bilge pump and the lines. So Dallas found herself doing these things. Every time that she stepped into Christopher's cabin to pump the bilge, she remembered the happy times and the sad times she'd spent with him there. Funny, as the days passed, how hard it became to recall the bad times. Funny, how it got harder to hate him and easier to love him.

At first she had been too ashamed to allow herself to dwell on their night of passion. But gradually her anger dissolved, and her softer, truer feelings emerged. She remembered the lean glory of his naked body writhing on top of hers. She remembered the hot force of his mouth burning gently across her skin. But most of all she remembered his tendernesses, his kindnesses. If he were so bad, why had he helped her with the kids, with the restaurant, with her acceptance of herself?

She lay awake in her bed and tortured herself by imagining him there, his calloused hands exploring her until she quivered, imagining his hot lips tracing over her body. She drove herself mad, remembering him.

He never called or wrote.

And every day that he didn't, the ache to have him near, to hear his voice, to feel his touch grew inside her.

Was he forgetting her?

The days dragged by, suffocatingly hot, scorching days.

Rennie found a picture of Christopher's beautiful costar in a magazine that Dallas took and shredded into a hundred pieces. But she couldn't forget the girl's bewitching green eyes, or the seductive promise of her pouting lips.

One night at supper, during a lull in the conversation, Patrick said, "I wonder if he misses us, too?"

No one had to ask who he was.

"Of course," Stephie said wisely, piercing a pea with her fork and bringing it to the tip of her nose so she could inspect it with her crossed eyes.

"He hasn't written or called," Patrick said, echoing Dallas's silent worries. "It's been a month."

"I know how long it's been," Dallas snapped. "Of course he's forgotten us."

The twins rushed to his defense. "Maybe he's just hurt."

"His name is Stone isn't it?" Dallas said. "That's what he's made of."

The look that passed between all four kids infuriated Dallas. "You're going to ruin your eyes if you don't quit staring at that pea, Stephie. Either put it down or eat it!"

"I don't like peas." Stephie set her fork down defiantly.

"It's rude to say insulting things about food, young lady."

"It's rude of you to say mean things about my daddy. Why do you hate him?"

Dallas was stung to the quick. "I—I don't hate him."

No one was pretending to eat anymore. They were all looking accusingly at Dallas until she felt very uncomfortable.

"Look, surely you don't still think I'm the bad guy, do you?"

"Oh, no, Aunt Dallas." They shook their heads.

"Then why don't we all get back to eating our dinners?"

Not a single fork lifted.

The next day, Christopher's telephone calls began. He always asked for the children, never for Dallas. They would talk to him by the hour, and she would feel absurdly left out. And every night when he called, the ache for him inside her grew.

She loved her children, but she needed another adult to share her thoughts and little every-day crises. She had grown used to leaning on Christopher, to counting on his help and advice and comfort. Who was she kidding? She wanted him. She loved him. She couldn't forget him.

And never did she want him more than the morning that the letter from the adoption agency came. When she read the name on the envelope of the agency she'd given her baby to, she didn't dare open it until Christopher called that night.

Only when she heard the phone ring and Patrick shout his name did she slit the envelope. Inside, was a letter from the adoptive parents of her baby. It told of their gratitude to her for the gift of their beautiful daughter; it told how they loved her more than anything.

Blue ink blurred through Dallas's tears of joy as she read of her daughter's successes. Like her mother, her daughter was number one in her school class.

Dallas clasped the letter to her heart. Her little girl wrote poetry and was going to major in English. She was a highbrow. *Like her mother.*

A picture and a poem that Dallas hadn't noticed fell from the envelope. She picked them up and studied the photograph. Her little girl was a beautiful young woman. The poem was a letter of love to her birth mother.

Dallas's hand began to shake as she looked at the phone on the bedside table. Christopher was talking to the children. More than anything she wanted to share her wonderful news with him. But her fingers froze when she touched the receiver.

He didn't love her. All he had ever wanted from her was his child.

When Patrick stepped into the bedroom a few minutes later, he found his aunt in tears. When she saw him, she yanked her hand from the phone so he wouldn't see.

But he saw. "You want to talk to him, don't you?"

She shook her head.

"Pick it up," he said gently.

"I—I can't."

Patrick strode slowly into the room like a little man. Very methodically he lifted the phone. "Aunt Dallas is in bed crying because she misses you and wants you to come back!"

Dallas grabbed the phone. "That's not true! I was crying because I got a letter from the adoption agency about my baby."

"Kids, hang up!"

The downstairs extension clicked.

"Was it good news or bad?" Christopher asked quietly.

She could feel the tension in him, his genuine concern. She was only talking to him on the telephone, but she felt connected to him—body and soul.

She held her breath. Now. She should hang up on him.

Why did she cling to the receiver as if it were a lifeline? "Good..." she whispered at last.

Across thousands of miles of ocean, she felt his joy at her happiness in the warm timbre of his voice. "Honey, that's wonderful."

She was filled with a golden happiness.

For a second longer she held on to the receiver.

"Dallas, I—"

More than anything she wanted to hear what he was going to say. But she hung up.

Only to be instantly sorry.

The next day was a nightmare. Dallas had heard from her child, and she had spoken to the man she loved. In a single hour she had made contact with two of the people she had loved and lost. She had felt Christopher's joy for her, his intense caring. Then she had willfully, stupidly ruined everything.

If he had deceived her, she had been equally cruel. She began to think that she had been blind to him, that she had judged him unfairly before she had even known him.

If only he would call again, she would tell him how sorry she was for everything.

But he didn't call.

If the children were very disappointed, she was crushed, and she knew it was her fault.

She had lost him—again.

All day she tormented herself by thoughts of him turning to his costar for solace. As the day ended, her longing for him grew.

It was a beautiful warm summer night, and the moon was nearly full. After she put the children to bed, she was too miserable to sleep. So she stepped out for a solitary walk along the beach. As she wandered toward the causeway bridge she saw a strange apparition.

The knight from Stephie's fairy tale was riding toward Dallas on a white horse and leading another behind him. The moonlight gilded the knight's bright hair. The breeze blew it across his brow. He shook his head faintly.

She knew that gesture.

Christopher.

But he was in Spain. She had lost him forever.

The ghostly knight came nearer. Her heart seemed to stop beating.

It was Christopher in a suit of dull tarnished mail.

She froze. Then she was running toward him, her gauzy skirt flying, her golden hair loose and spreading about her shoulders. She stopped breathlessly just before she reached him.

They devoured one another with their eyes.

"I'm sorry," she said on a low whisper.

The horses whinnied softly.

"So am I."

"I love you," she said. "I love you."

"I know."

"You do? How could—"

He leaned over and tried to lift her onto his horse, but his armor made it hard for him to move. "Put your foot in the stirrup," he commanded.

She did, and he pulled her up.

"Your armor's all black."

"It was the best Wardrobe could manage-on such short notice. I imagined you'd think it suited me better than the shining stuff."

"It's cold, too."

"Stop complaining. You should be wearing it."

"Why did you come back?"

He took a quick breath. "Don't you know?"

She felt his golden hair brush against her forehead as he pulled her against his armor and kissed her. His lips were hot and wild, and she felt the pent-up agony of all the fierce hunger in him that had brought him back to her. The hand at her neck held her close while his other arm crushed her against his armored chest. Dallas clung to him; she was as shaken as he. His mouth moved roughly across her face to her throat.

"Honey, I couldn't stay away. God help me, I tried. I tried to forget you, to blot out all the memories."

"So did I."

"But the harder I tried, the stronger they got."

"You're a movie star."

"Until you came into my life, that fate was a sentence in hell."

"You really want me? And not just because of Stephie?"

"Oh, Dallas…" He broke off in a sigh. "There has never been any woman I've wanted more." He caught her face in his hands, holding it still. "Aren't you going to make me say it?"

"What?"

He grinned. "You know."

"What?"

"That I love you, you little idiot. I love you. Only you."

"You said you didn't know much about love."

"I didn't—until I met a good teacher. You taught me everything I ever needed to know."

"Where did you get the horses?"

"Cal had them flown in from my ranch. The second one is for Stephie."

"She's in bed now. Do you want to see her?"

"Later. Much later," he whispered. "Now, the only thing I want is you."

She looked into his eyes and saw his love as well as the pain she had caused him. For an instant, she was filled with guilt.

She would spend the rest of her life making it up to him. And she would start tonight.

She arched her body to fit his and her gauzy skirt rode up her thighs.

Christopher closed his eyes and took a deep breath. Then she reached up and began to kiss him.

They were on his boat, their pulses throbbing as they tore off their clothes. He came to her, and he was so breathtakingly magnificent that she touched him first, her impatient hands moving over him boldly, stirring the hot flames of his passion until he could stand it no longer and clasped her tightly against the hard contours of his body. Her heartbeats accelerated as his mouth claimed hers.

He had come back for her.

Not just for Stephie.

Most of all for her, too.

His large hands closed over her breasts.

He had come back for her—and this glorious knowledge made everything he did for her in bed more wonderful. He began to kiss her—everywhere—until her throat was hot and her skin was ice.

His golden head lowered and his tongue licked sensitive flesh, sending a livid tingling current of desire tracing warmly through her. She moaned softly.

Fire and ice; she had felt them before. But only for him.

"I have to have you," she whispered desperately.

"At last you admit it," he said quietly.

At last.

He drew her down onto the bunk beneath him. Her golden hair spread out beneath his brown arms. His lips burned hers, and then he kissed her eyelids, her cheek, her earlobe, passionately, murmuring love words.

It seemed to her that every inch of her body was covered by the heat of his, and the ice was dissolving in the fire of his passion. For an instant he was very still. His eyes met hers, and she saw all his love as well as fierce need. He brushed her cheek tenderly with a fingertip. A familiar welcoming warmth seemed to flow in the depths of her body. It seemed to her that all her life she had waited for this moment.

"I love you," he whispered. "Only you. There will never be anyone but you."

"I love you, too."

Then he was inside her. And what happened after that was too wonderful for words.

Epilogue

Dallas was a bride in misting white. Again she hesitated on the threshold of Christopher's immense living room crammed with wedding guests. Only because this time, the sight of Christopher standing beside the minister with the children filled her with happiness.

Again the house was filled with flowers and friends. Only this time Dallas's golden-haired birth child and her adoptive parents were there. Marguerite had come, as well.

Outside, the sun was shining and the Pacific was sparkling. Tents and canopies had been set up. The white horses were wearing garlands of flowers. It all seemed like a wonderful dream. Dallas felt that she was a princess, and that Christopher's white house was as dazzling as the white castle in Stephie's story. And Christopher had turned out to be her knight after all.

Dallas caught the rhythm of the wedding march, and a white satin toe peeped out from beneath her skirt. Hesitating no longer, she took the first step. Surely this was the happiest moment of her life.

When she reached the alter, Christopher held out his hand, and as she reached for it and let him pull her close, she knew that at last she had found love.

Here by his side was where she had belonged, where she would always belong.

They were a couple. Part of a family.

They would love each other forever.

*   *   *   *   *

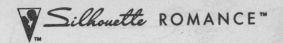

Silhouette ROMANCE™

What's a single dad to do when he needs a wife by next Thursday?

Who's a confirmed bachelor to call when he finds a baby on his doorstep?

How does a plain Jane in love with her gorgeous boss get him to notice her?

From classic love stories to romantic comedies to emotional heart tuggers, **Silhouette Romance** offers six irresistible novels every month by some of your favorite authors! Such as…beloved bestsellers **Diana Palmer, Annette Broadrick, Suzanne Carey, Elizabeth August** and **Marie Ferrarella,** to name just a few—and some sure to become favorites!

Fabulous Fathers…Bundles of Joy…Miniseries… Months of blushing brides and convenient weddings… Holiday celebrations… You'll find all this and much more in **Silhouette Romance**—always emotional, always enjoyable, always about love!

SR-GEN

WAYS TO *UNEXPECTEDLY* MEET MR. RIGHT:

♡ *Go out with the sexy-sounding stranger your daughter secretly set you up with through a personal ad.*

♡ *RSVP yes to a wedding invitation—soon it might be your turn to say "I do!"*

♡ *Receive a marriage proposal by mail— from a man you've never met....*

These are just a few of the unexpected ways that written communication leads to love in Silhouette Yours Truly.

Each month, look for two fast-paced, fun and flirtatious Yours Truly novels (with entertaining treats and sneak previews in the back pages) by some of your favorite authors—and some who are sure to become favorites.

YOURS TRULY™:
Love—when you least expect it!

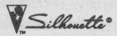

SILHOUETTE® Desire®

Do you want...

Dangerously handsome heroes

Evocative, everlasting love stories

Sizzling and tantalizing sensuality

Incredibly sexy miniseries like **MAN OF THE MONTH**

Red-hot romance

Enticing entertainment that can't be beat!

You'll find all of this, and much *more* each and every month in **SILHOUETTE DESIRE**. Don't miss these unforgettable love stories by some of romance's hottest authors. Silhouette Desire—where your fantasies will always come true....